POD

TONY WARDLE

POD – first published in Great Britain 2014 by Tony Wardle.

A CIP catalogue record for this title is available from the British Library

ISBN 978-0-9571874-2-9

Cover design and layout: The Ethical Graphic Design Company Ltd.

Printed and bound in the UK by Stephens & George, Goat Mill Road, Dowlais,
Merthyr Tydfil CF48 3TD. Registered in England, Company number 411176.

To my gorgeous children, Niki, Jazz and Finn.
(I told you I was writing a novel)

Author's Note

The idea for *POD* first came to me decades ago when I lived in Brighton within sight of the sea. Having been brought up by the sea in Cleethorpes and sailed across its surface in the merchant navy, it has always been a source of wonder. What I lacked back then was the ability to quantify the devastating scale of humankind's influence on the globe, which is central to this book. It seems that all the wondrous influences that have coalesced to produce myriad life forms are irrelevant and can be trashed at will in a pointless race to produce ever more things ever more quickly.

And then I met Juliet Gellatley, we loved, we married, we had children and, sadly, we then divorced but continue working together. I stood cheering when she founded the vegan campaigning charity, Viva!, and inevitably became drawn into its work. I saw first-hand the sickening reality of factory farming, the brutality and fear of slaughter and I researched the reasons behind our collapsing environment. I then had a surfeit of knowledge with which to complete *POD*.

Although a fictional novel, every assertion made in this book, every claim presented as fact, every reference to research, every comment on the state of our nations is scientifically accurate. Yes, the book is fictional but its essential driving force is factual. It is a sobering thought that the human race has become something of an evolutionary aberration – and nature does not tolerate aberrations indefinitely.

Chapter One

Charlie Mottram hated chickens. It wasn't a passing dislike – he actually loathed them, which was a little unfortunate considering he owned something like a hundred and eighty thousand and they surrounded him every day of his life. Of course, he wasn't aware of it but the feeling was probably reciprocated.

Charlie stuck his hands deep into the pockets of his green boiler suit and shuffled across the yard in his wellington boots. 'Yard' wasn't really an adequate description for over the years it had expanded remorselessly and concrete had flowed over the old meadow in stages until it had obliterated every blade of grass, weed, sapling and flower. As each of the six huge, system-built, windowless broiler sheds had sprouted, every one a monument to his growing affluence, so the concrete had increased accordingly and now linked all the sheds together in one huge apron of ridged aggregate covering several acres.

After his wife left him, Charlie even dispensed with the flower garden that had once surrounded his house on all sides, providing the only visual relief in a remorselessly stark landscape. When that had disappeared, the house stood like a piece of masonry jetsam cast up on some paved foreshore. It was neater that way, required less work, he told himself. The truth was, he hated flowers almost as much as he hated chickens. Or rather he hated the memories their prettiness invoked, the sudden, stabbing reminder of loss their perfume wrenched from him when he least expected it. He hated that hollow feeling in his stomach that could strike without notice, triggered simply by a place name, a piece of music, the aroma

7

of a particular flower or almost anything for that matter and which had the power to suck the air from his lungs and leave him momentarily breathless. The feeling of helpless despair, of hopelessness and of mind-numbing emptiness that followed lasted far longer than it should.

There were trees and fields off in the distance, beyond the twelve foot-tall chain link fencing with its razor wire topping but Charlie had rented these out long ago. He saw no irony in the name of his concrete and pre-fabricated surroundings – Willow Bank Farm.

He was a chicken grower – not a breeder but a grower. And he never referred to his chickens as a flock; not as animals or even birds, they were a crop. And like a crop they were sown and harvested, not according to the seasons but to a strict timetable laid down by Golden Promise International. The US multinational corporation processed and sold prime whole table chickens, chicken portions and a huge range of processed chicken products from pies and pasties to gourmet ready-made meals. More importantly, they bought every one of the chickens Charlie cared to produce.

Day old chicks were put into the sheds on the precise date decreed by Golden Promise. Exactly forty-two days later – not forty-one and not forty-three – the crop was harvested. Local lads from the Barley Mow pub earned a few extra quid as catchers, grabbing the terrified birds by their legs or wings and stuffing them into crates. The crates were loaded onto lorries and transported some forty miles to the nearest of eight Golden Promise processing plants.

Once the birds were hung on the overhead conveyor by their feet, they were virtually untouched again by human hand until they were slipped down a metal cone into their plastic bags ready for sale. Throat cutting, scalding, de-feathering, gutting, beheading and feet severing were all carried out by machines that someone, somewhere had got out of bed one morning specifically to design. They had, at some time, sat down and faced the intellectual challenge of how to sever a chicken's head from its body safely while the corpse trundled remorselessly along its overhead track – never stopping, never slowing and never deviating.

The solution was an Archimedes screw which gradually stretched the head and neck until – POP – the head was simply torn off.

As a simple farmer – which was how he always described himself – Charlie was impressed by the innovative mind of the designer. He wondered what he would have come up with had he been given the brief but felt sure it would not have been an Archimedes screw, of that he was certain. Ingenious!

The production line ran almost non-stop, which was why the timing for growing birds and delivering them was so crucial. Lorries needed to arrive at pre-determined times with birds which all weighed exactly the same 2.4 kilograms. The only way the system could function, churning out chicken flesh at less than the price of tomatoes, was through uniformity and economies of scale. Golden Promise had to dictate the exact date and time that every lorry load of chickens arrived in the unloading bay – which meant they had to control the timing of the growing schedule, also. Birds were merely commodities in a meticulously planned flow chart.

It was an irony that only after their lives had been taken was anything remotely nice said about the chickens and then it was emblazoned all over their plastic wrappers – 'Farm Fresh', 'Prime Quality', 'Premium Grade'.

Charlie negotiated his way around a huge pile of fresh litter comprised of chopped straw and wood shavings, dumped on the concrete outside number four shed, adjusting his flat cap to shield his face from the bright sunlight as he did so. The birds inside the shed had only two days to go before slaughter, when the flooring would be cleared out, the shed sterilised and new litter laid down prior to receiving another batch of thirty thousand tweeting little balls of fluff. They were fine at a day or two old but their crime was, they grew into chickens, reckoned Charlie.

It was these next two days that would determine his profitability. He opened the door into the shed and waited unil his eyes grew accustomed to the dim interior light, especially designed to reduce aggression amongst the birds. He no longer noticed the extraordinary babble of thirty-thousand chickens' voices nor the stench of ammonia from their excreta, nor did he register the warm and fetid atmosphere that seemed to fill his mouth and lungs like soup. Charlie's task was to scan the shed for dead and dying birds and that was all that preoccupied him. Pinned to a board on the wall beside the entrance was a list which Charlie scanned before turning and walking in amongst the chickens. It was his death list.

The floor was half the size of a football pitch and was covered entirely by a sea of white-feathered birds. Charlie Mottram ploughed through them and the animals separated before him like a feathered bow wave, clambering one on top of the other in their panic to escape. After almost every pace Charlie stopped, bent down and picked up a dead bird, dangling it from his hands by its scaly feet. Before long, both hands were full of corpses and he dumped them in a pile. Things did not look good and he felt the usual anger bubbling up inside, a reaction to the precarious nature of his life.

Golden Promise had made him wealthy but at a price. It was like the relationship between a junky and his supplier. Charlie had been lured in, seduced with money and a sense of importance. The quid pro quo was that he had been stripped of initiative, deprived of the need to make decisions – they had deskilled him.

The old days may have included endless hours of boredom in a tractor cab, traversing fields back and forth but he had had to make decisions which were based on weather, temperature, wind and rain and gut feeling. They were all decanted from a reservoir of experience which had begun to slowly fill when he was probably no more than four or five years old.

He thought back on the old days with longing. The isolation of a tractor cab, wind shaking and rattling the plastic, a force six westerly, its rain made tangy with the salt whipped from the crests of tumbling rollers of the Irish Sea and dashed against the water-tight housing of his grumbling machine. Inside – a flask of tea, sandwiches and Radio Two. And, of course, a wife to come home to, a wife to share inconsequential conversation with, a wife to relate experiences to no matter how unimportant they might be. It was as though recounting the days happenings was what gave them form and made them tangible and feeling the warmth of someone else next to you beneath the privacy of a thick duvet was what gave life its purpose and made the repetition of tomorrow and the day after seem worthwhile .

Without that process of sharing Charlie felt as though nothing had any importance and he was denied a real life.

Of course, it probably had never quite been like this but distance and defective memory had smoothed away the rougher edges.

And now? He was instructed on what birds to rear, exactly the right temperature at which to keep the shed, what level the lighting had to be for each stage of the birds' growth – and it had to be kept on for exactly twenty-three and a half hours in every twenty four.

Again, the ingenuity of big business left him almost awe struck. Someone had worked out that keeping the lights on almost constantly encouraged non-stop eating and rapid growth, given a little supercharge with the daily administration of growth promoting antibiotics in their feed. Actually, growth-promoting antibiotics had been banned by Europe but with the compliance of his vet he had simply substituted them for 'therapeutic' antibiotics and their ability to produce growth was identical.

Why were the lights switched off for just half-an-hour? Charlie had shaken his head in disbelief when he had been told – if the lights glowed constantly and a power cut plunged the sheds into darkness, the chickens would panic because to them it was an entirely alien experience. The panic would result in frenzied crowding near the doors and suffocation, which could wipe out thousands of birds. Just one half hour of darkness a day, however, allowed them to become accustomed to it should the unexpected ever happen.

Charlie was also told what to feed them, what therapeutic and prophylactic antibiotics to use and in what quantities and what supplements to administer. Golden Promise had seduced him with cash and in return they required much the same from him as they did from the birds – conformity, uniformity, obedience and subservience. It wasn't the birds he hated so much, he realised, as what they had done to his self-esteem, his pride.

The only element of chance remaining in the operation was how many birds might die before they could be sent to slaughter. That was the only imponderable in an equation dictated by world-wide supply and demand and it was in the last few days of their forty-two day life span that the answer came.

Despite still being chicks – albeit muscle-bound travesties of a real chick – none of the birds would be physically capable of living much beyond their allotted time thanks to the skills of the selective breeders, geneticists, feed manufacturers and climate controllers whose skills had all been used to bring the birds to their most profitable peak at precisely forty two days and get them to slaughter before they died. What happened after forty two days was of no concern to anyone.

Rapid growth produced cheap chicken meat but it also resulted in dropsy – a potentially fatal disease triggered because their tiny hearts could not pump sufficient blood around their ballooning bodies and it pooled in the lower parts of their torso. It also produced jelly-like bones, rendering some birds incapable of walking to the feeding and watering points so they sat where they collapsed and quietly died from thirst and starvation. These were the 'starve outs'.

Charlie could sustain a death rate of around one thousand five hundred birds – about five per cent of his production; a percentage that was anticipated and expected and therefore built into the margins. His chart told him that the death rate had already passed the two thousand mark and was heading up towards seven per cent. If and when it hit ten per cent, with three thousand birds dead, he would barely cover his costs. Twelve per cent and he would be out of pocket. Things weren't looking good.

Charlie noticed that one of the feed conveyors, which ran the length of the shed some six inches from the ground, was juddering and jolting from a displaced roller or worn bearing. He knelt down to examine it and immediately felt the wetness of the faeces-sodden litter dampening his knees. The problem was underneath the conveyor and much as he hated doing it, he had no option but to lie down on his back and crane his neck to see beneath the belt. A roller had become dislodged and he would probably need tools to replace it.

It was then, as he was about to stand up and go in search of his toolbox, that he noticed a chicken standing alongside his head, intently watching his movements, like a plumber's mate awaiting instructions. Normally the birds came nowhere near him when he was in the shed but this one stood close to his face, cocking its head first to one side and then the other as though helping him to evaluate the situation.

"Fuck off," Charlie said without anger as he made one last attempt to free the roller, grabbing it firmly and twisting it away from its spindle.

The bird took a step closer and remained looking at Charlie only inches from his face, its head moving towards him in short, jerky movements. When it pecked it did so with such extraordinary speed and force – so fast, so powerfully that Charlie had no hope of warding it off. Its beak struck him in his left eye and he involuntarily jerked his head to one side, banging it sharply on the unyielding metal of the conveyor and pain shot through him like an electric current.

Strangely, it was his head which hurt, not his eye but when he felt liquid running down his cheek he instinctively knew it wasn't blood but aqueous humour, the fluid which filled the eyeball and that he would be now permanently blind in that eye. He touched it with his hand and squinted through his one seeing eye to observe the liquid and, as he thought, no trace of blood.

It was as he staggered to his feet that the pain hit – like a red hot poker had been forced into his eye socket and he cried out as he staggered across the sodden floor of the broiler shed.

Unusually, the chickens rushed towards him and he felt the soft resistance of packed, feathered bodies around his legs, pliable but nevertheless resistant like balls of cotton wool entwining his feet, obstructing his legs. Through his one eye, Charlie glimpsed the daylight which outlined the access door and lurched towards it, his upper body inclined forwards, his arms stretched out before him like someone impersonating a Halloween ghost. He tried to run and as he did so he shouted meaningless, disconnected words at no one and nothing in particular as anger and fear swept over him.

Charlie felt himself on the point of losing balance and so thrust his feet and legs forwards desperately, trying to make them work to catch up with his falling body, kicking out at the chickens as he did so, desperately trying to clear a path through the living bodies.

It was a fruitless effort and almost in slow motion, he lost his equilibrium and crashed to the floor full length. As his head hit the sodden litter, the stench of ammonia from forty days of accumulated chicken shit stung and blinded his other eye, filled his nostrils and made him gag.

It was that which prevented him from seeing the chicken which struck his right eye. Its aim was unerringly accurate, picking a space between the fingers which covered his face. Now completely blind, he could feel the weight of the birds as they clambered over him and sensed the insulating warmth of their feathers which began to clog his mouth and nostrils, suffocating him. His eyes burned with pain and he felt none of the other pecks which rained all over his body. Death was extremely slow in arriving but it was inexorable.

Chapter Two

Josephine Aldous hated her husband. When the realisation came it allowed no room for doubt or change of heart. It was as sudden and conclusive as if her prize crockery dresser had collapsed amidst the designer splendour of her kitchen – a few seconds of terrible fear and apprehension as it wobbled, a metaphorical crash and clatter and then the unavoidable survey of the damage. She had looked at the broken pieces of her life which were strewn around her – the shattered certainties, the death of expectations, the metamorphosis of love into something much more destructive – and had no idea what would replace them.

Jo wandered slowly across her garden, smiling involuntarily at the trill of bird song, holding her face up to the warmth of the early evening sun. Had there ever been real love? She wasn't sure. The unequal nature of their relationship in the early years had made it impossible to judge. He had led and she had followed, trailing behind like a puppy. It was a union of unequals and the certainty of his emotional supremacy had made him arrogant. He had taken her for granted.

But, god, he had been handsome. Tall, big, with a hug that could engulf you, that promised safety from everything and anything threatening. Hair dark, almost black and shiny, huge brown eyes – and teeth, a bit uneven but oh so white. He was the catch of all catches in her teenage years – the leader of the pack.

He was the reckless one – but always reckless with control, with the brakes lightly applied. He was always the outrageous one – but an outrageousness that never really outraged anyone.

POD

He was so devil-may-care – but in reality cared just enough to avoid opprobrium. He was, Josephine realised, already a consummate politician before he had even left school.

Now they role played – she the dependable (although becoming increasingly less so) wife and mother, he the generous provider. Perhaps she should be grateful. Her lifestyle was privileged and comfortable – a beautiful house, a wonderful garden, all the money, travel and self-indulgence anyone could ever use and, most seductive of all (to some), a position of importance within a privileged and cloistered community. She was someone who, albeit second hand, wielded power. She was a politician's wife – a politician headed for the top. She found Stephen's political ambitions difficult to embrace and when she thought of him as a future prime minister the only emotion she felt was contempt.

She knew she had started down the final straight of their marriage when she began to view herself as a whore. After that, she ended their sex life and moved into a separate bedroom. Stephen had tried everything but tolerance, tenderness and love to re-ignite the passion – flattery, booze, lingerie, ridiculously expensive dinners – and often all at the same time but it usually ended in too much to drink and a demand for sex. Once she had given in and the smell of his body, the feel of his increasing weight and the same old, hoarsely-whispered fantasies made her want to puke and push him from her.

Jo pressed some dislodged turf back with her foot, happy to have the symmetry of her lawn disturbed by badgers digging for worms and cockchafer grubs. She saw them most evenings as the last vestiges of light disappeared and the great bank of Scots pines, birch and oak, which flanked one side of the garden, turned into a black and seemingly impenetrable mass.

Ironically, it was the fox that had been the final straw. There had been foxes in the remoter part of the garden since they had first lived there but only when the incredibly pretentious and camp choreographer from the next house complained about them did Stephen pay any attention. They had eaten his peacocks, the man claimed, and Stephen immediately went in search of a shot gun. Poor bloody peacocks in Surrey!

Jo had watched the vixen all Spring, first as she stretched out on the edge of the lawn, suckling her cubs in the early sunshine and later as they played like kittens, tumbling over each other in mock fight – possibly pretending to catch peacocks! And Stephen wanted to shoot them to appease his neighbour. It probably had more to do with his hopes of getting a donation from the man towards his leadership election expenses.

Jo had not shouted nor threatened, in fact she had not even raised her voice:

"If you shoot just one of the foxes – if you even try to shoot them – I'll leave you. Do you understand?"

Stephen tried to laugh it off but Jo said nothing more and when he had chuckled himself to a standstill he said:

"You don't mean it! Do you?"

Jo looked deeply into his eyes and replied quietly: "Oh yes!" She saw the incomprehension turn to hurt then disbelief before changing to fear. For the first time in their life together she was conscious of a reversal of the power structure – she was in charge.

"Are you telling me that a bloody smelly fox, a scavenging piece of vermin is more important to you than I am?"

In the split second before she answered Jo was conscious of evidence tumbling through her mind, pros and cons cartwheeling in from deep recesses, memories of times forgotten, memories of times she had chosen to forget:

"Yes, Stephen, that's what I'm saying!" And they both knew she meant it.

"Bloody charming!"

He did what he always did when confronted with things emotionally demanding – walked out and never referred to it again. He left the foxes unmolested but it was the end of pretence for Jo. So what was she going to do about it? Seemingly nothing because that was a year ago and she was still here.

Now, every time she stepped out into the wild and beautiful acres she looked at every flower, every tree and every shrub as though it was the last time she would see them, trying to store away the memories for a time when they would be gone.

As the year progressed, she first celebrated the arrival of snow drops as they hung their heads in the January chill. They were followed by clumps of yellow primroses, demanding to be looked at – pretty, old fashioned and never changing. Then came the bluebells, first smearing the shade beneath the trees with just a hint of colour before swirling the most beautiful blue wash into every corner of the copse.

Bright white blackthorn blossom was the first to bring the shrubs back to life and by autumn it would have turned into little black fruits with which she made sloe gin. It was followed by the heady scent of hawthorn blossom, smothering the bushes in cream before tingeing to pink as it aged. And in the height of summer, foxgloves and gloriously flamboyant hollyhocks speared the air, displaying their beauty unselfconsciously. She had grown the hollyhocks from seed gathered from a little restaurant in a Turkish village and she could never look at them without remembering it and happier times.

Perhaps things would get better! No, nothing would change by chance – she would have to make them better but she felt no inclination to do so. This was, she knew, the hiatus, the pause, the calm between one life and another. She knew she was about to enter the unknown but did not know when she would make the jump. It would presumably be when she could find the courage to leave that which she loved best – the beauty around her.

Jo placed the misted bottle of wine on the white, wrought iron table and poured herself a glass. She bent her head and spoke to it as she did so:

"Okay, I know I said I wouldn't today but – well, it's such a nice day and it is after six."

"It's the first sign of madness, mum!" Danny's voice interrupted as he walked towards her from the French windows dressed in his cub's uniform. "Have you seen my neckerchief?"

"Where's it normally kept?" Jo asked.

"In the chest of drawers but it's not there."

"Did you look in all the drawers?"

"Well… it wasn't in the usual one."

"Look in the others."

He turned with a show of exasperation and headed back to the house: "I don't suppose Dad's around, is he?" he called over his shoulder.

"No, he's gone to Horsham or Hove or Halifax or somewhere bloody boring to address the faithful. If you're going down on your bike you're to come straight home. Eight thirty at the latest. Okay?" Danny raised an arm in response.

She sat back on her chair and sipped her wine. From the elevated position of the garden, between gaps in the trees, she looked out over Weybridge. Apart from an occasional glimpse of a gable end in the far distance or the top of a chimney stack, all she could see was trees. But they were like markers and from them she could map the town in her mind – almost every road, every friend's house and a jumble of memories. She was thirty six years old and had never lived more than two miles from where she now sat.

She reckoned she was still pretty and was quite happy with her figure – neat, compact, curvy and men still at times looked at her lasciviously. She was lazy about her hair and left far too long between renewing her streaks and having the roots touched up and could rarely be bothered to do anything but hold it back with a large clip but again, it usually looked good.

Her major fault was her foul mouth. She loved the expressiveness of swearing, loved the shock it could produce but mostly enjoyed the fact that it annoyed Stephen.

There was a formula for local moneyed girls, at least those devoid of any particular talent, and she had followed it exactly: St Bride's Catholic girl's convent – not just because her family was Catholic but because it was prestigious; courtship and eventually marriage to a boy from St Theobald's Catholic College – also local, also prestigious. A teenage spent circuiting a select few pubs – the Flint Gate, the Greyhound until it was closed, the Hand and Spear and the Queens Head, loyalties altering as fashion or landlord changed.

Only the tennis club and rugby club provided variety but it

was always the same circle of friends, half of whom were related through blood and the other half through sexual liaisons or marriage and increasingly, as time went by, divorce.

Then came settling down, secure in the substance and wealth of an achiever and the ultimate prize – a house on St George's Hill. From where she was sitting she could point exactly to where John Lennon had once lived – and Dick Emery. Over there was Eric Syke's house, over to the right was Cliff, Sir Cliff, Richard's old place and the house just there had once been Tom Jones's.

This was probably the most exclusive estate in the country, walled and gated from the rest of the world, a rich and rambling oasis of huge mature trees, lakes, small woods, private roads and sweeping gravel driveways. What an irony that these privileged, spacious acres had been the birth place of socialism.

Edmund Winstanley had brought his band of Diggers here after the Napoleonic wars to build the very first commune, before being hounded out by the establishment. Now the establishment had made it its own, none more so than her husband who intended to be leader of the Conservative party and introduce policies that would erase the last vestiges of socialism from the statute book. Stephen's philosophy was simple, although not for public consumption – if you're poor you deserve to be.

Jo knew she had been betrayed, not by Stephen but by her parents, her school, her friends. They had all channelled her down the route that privileged little middle-class girls took – helped to lever her like a pea into a very predictable pod. And that's how she now saw herself – a pea in a pod devoid of individuality. If she were to so much as hint that she might leave Stephen, her family would think she was mad. They thought she had done extremely well for herself and she blamed them all for their blinkered, suburban complacency – but most of all she blamed herself. Whatever the pod was, she was there by choice.

It had taken Jo a few years to realise it but she knew she had undersold herself. She lived with a man who aimed to be the leader of the country and the thought terrified her. He hoped to chart a nation's destiny, something so enormous in its implications that she could never even contemplate aspiring to it yet knew she was more intelligent, more capable and had greater vision than Stephen – and it was that which frightened her. Not that she was particularly gifted but that he was not.

"Bye mum!" Danny waved as he rode down the drive on his bike and she watched him disappear behind a rhododendron bush on his way to the scout hut.

"Bye, Dan! No later than eight-thirty!"

Jo was overwhelmed with feelings of love and a desire to protect Danny. She rested her head in her hands and could feel her eyes filling with tears, partly because of her love for Danny, partly for what she knew lay in store but mostly for her lamentable cowardice.

Chapter Three

Stephen Aldous hated party workers. He was utterly contemptuous of the way they questioned him – the way they would tonight – their voices heavy with concern as though they really understood their questions and cared about his answers when he knew that most of their concerns had been gleaned from the Daily Mail's editorials.

He would stand in front of them as a member of the shadow cabinet, ostensibly with no specific purpose other than to inform and encourage their constituency party. Rubbish! They knew why he was doing the rubber chicken circuit up and down the country and he knew it too but no one would be honest enough to admit it. He was buying votes for his eventual campaign to be elected party leader and their support would be crucial if he was forced into challenging the present incumbent.

He turned the car off the M23 and followed the Haroldean signs. He was exactly on time and as always, it would start with drinks and polite chat and if he was lucky there might be someone under seventy who didn't cup his ear and say 'pardon' every time Stephen spoke. Then would come an uninspiring dinner followed by his speech and a question and answer session.

Hardly one of the people present would have the intelligence to formulate a genuinely provoking question and they would already know the answers to those they did ask but would still pose them with pomp and gravitas. And he would have to answer as though he cared. It was a charade he hated but which he did at least once a week – the necessary price of creating popularity.

It wouldn't matter that Josephine wasn't with him as she

wasn't expected to participate at this stage of his campaign. But later, when the meetings became bigger, more formal, then she would need to be there, smiling, reassuring, normal, loving and benign – all the things she wasn't. Pushy, provocative, confrontational and above all else, honest, was how he would now describe her. They were exactly the qualities that would guarantee he would never be elected.

Maybe it was a phase she was going through, perhaps she had too much time on her hands. The answer was probably to have another child but fat bloody chance of that! One thing he knew for certain, he would not dare let her loose on a constituency party in her present frame of mind. But she would change – when the vision was truly within his grasp, she would change. She had to; she could not deny him or herself the ultimate goal.

Stephen found the Haroldean Conservative party offices without difficulty and recognised the grey-haired old man with a white rose in his buttonhole standing outside to welcome him. His face switched into smile mode as the old man gestured him into the empty car parking space as though bringing a jet aircraft up to the terminal steps.

"John, how are you. How nice to see you!" Stephen beamed as he climbed out of the Jag and extended his hand towards the man.

"Stephen, lovely to see you, old boy. Are you well? And your delightful lady wife, Josephine?"

The evening followed the exact pattern of a hundred others and by the time brandy arrived Stephen was finding it hard to concentrate. He was relieved when John called for attention, tinkling his fork on an empty glass. As the noise died down, Stephen consciously changed his expression to one of serious contemplation but the introduction seemed to go on forever.

Stephen knew he was imposing – six feet two and good looking. Okay, so he was getting a little thick in the middle but a bit of gym work would get rid of that. And all right, there were the first glimmerings of a double chin but the women still loved him. He knew if he wanted to, if he didn't care about his career, he could screw himself silly on these jaunts. There was always one who was attractive enough, comparatively young enough and who eagerly put out to him.

And there she was, directly opposite him at the table right now, fortyish, blonded, signs of booze in her face but extremely pretty. Every time their eyes had met they had lingered, long and promisingly and now her smile contained far more promise than humour. Her husband sat next to her, his hand on her thigh beneath the cover of the table cloth, staking his claim, aware of a distant threat but so inconclusive as to make him doubt his instincts. In fact, his wife was offering her body to Stephen as blatantly as if she had gift wrapped it and adorned it with a huge bow. The exchanges between her and the honoured guest were so loaded that the air almost crackled.

Stephen had been trying to steal a glimpse of her legs and the width of her hips all evening and hadn't yet managed it but instinct told him he wouldn't be disappointed – if he had intended to take her up on her offer, that is.

Before he was a leadership contender he had resisted few of these opportunities, often going to great lengths to consummate the liaison. But rarely did he return for second helpings. That would be injudicious, would risk discovery, encourage emotions to blossom but mostly – once was enough. The name of the game was excitement and, if he was honest, power.

There was something deeply satisfying about having done something so intimate, so outrageous with someone else's wife, he thought smugly. Secretly lapping at her secretions, filling her with your own, transformed the relationship – not just between you and the woman but also her husband. Always you made discoveries about them of which they were oblivious, always it stripped away whatever veneer they had chosen to camouflage their real selves. The fact that you had committed such an outrageous act of betrayal – violated the inner-most core of a man's life – was somehow deeply satisfying. Any feelings you had for that man – be it respect, liking or even fear – they were all suffused by contempt with just one ejaculation. But probably the most satisfying aspect was that you had done something which could devastate another's life, perhaps even destroy them if they found out, and yet you didn't give a damn about it, their precious wife or them.

But that was all in the past – now it was just a game, a 'wouldn't it be nice if' little fantasy but the temptation was growing stronger with every constituency he visited.

"And so I give you our hope for the future, Stephen Aldous!"

Stephen drained the remainder of his red wine, his eyes never leaving those of the woman opposite him. It was a dangerous game but he loved it. He stood and waited for the applause to die down. The room fell silent and still he waited. It became almost funereal and just before it spilt over into embarrassment, he spoke, his booming voice echoing from the walls:

"They say that you are the party workers… " Someone had once told him he had the oratorical style of then pre-war fascist rabble-rouser, Sir Oswald Mosley, and he had worked on perfecting it ever since. He thrust his right arm forward, index finger extended and allowed it to roam over his audience.

"They say you are the party faithful…" He needed no notes as it was one speech with fifty variations and he had delivered it a hundred times or more.

"They say you are the backbone of the party…! They are wrong!" He punched the words out one at a time and waited for a tiny element of uncertainty to register in the eyes of his audience. "You ARE the party!" The applause was overwhelming and Stephen's eyes sought out the blonde woman, now with a rapturous look on her face and he felt the familiar old surge of excitement.

Chapter Four

Al Dwight hated almost everyone in his world but now that he no longer wanted to punch them, he felt sure he was getting to grips with his new life.

He took a long shot from just below the baulk cushion, attempting to pot a red which hovered over the bottom left pocket. The cue connected with a satisfying 'thunk' and the cue ball hissed over the green baize, a winner from the moment it began its run. It clacked against the red which plopped into the pocket, rebounded from the bottom cushion and headed back up the table, slowing as it did so. It nudged the baulk cushion and came to a halt barely an inch from it.

It was a superb safety shot and had he missed the red it would have caused his opponent real problems. As it was, he had a perfect angle to pot the yellow and get the cue ball back down the table and amongst the reds. Of course, he didn't have an opponent but he was used to that.

As Al sighted along the cue, Trevor the Hat, a tall, skinny man in his thirties with lank dark hair and baseball cap covered in badges appeared in the periphery of his vision. He struck a pose alongside the table – left hand on left hip, right knee slightly raised, head lowered and forehead placed on the clenched knuckles of his right arm in a parody of Rodin's The Thinker.

"Piss off, Trev, you're in my line of sight."

Trevor took two paces, twirled and went into another pose. Again it was Rodin but this time The Embrace, minus the female element of the sculpture. A babble of quietly spoken but incomprehensible art-speak tumbled from his lips, like a contributor to a Radio Four arts programme, thought Al.

Trevor moved across the floor of the recreation room, stopping every couple of paces to strike a new pose. Al moved alongside him, placed his hand in the small of his back and quietly impelled him towards the door.

"There you go Trev, go and be a sculpture somewhere else."

Trevor began to sob artificially but suddenly his words became comprehensible: "You don't understand! You Americans are all the same – Philistines, materialists, cultural imperialists…"

"Trevor go and have a hamburger or something, for Christ's sake…!"

"Please don't speak to Trevor in that way and it would help if you curbed your aggressive attitude, Alexander."

Nurse Protz seemed to have materialised, as always, from nowhere. The tiny, slight, young woman held Al with her pale blue, enormously round eyes. She was superbly attractive, shapely and pocket sized. She could be coquettish when she wanted, tossing her blonde pony-tail from side to side and, it seemed to Al, there was always a hidden promise of something very basic, very dangerous lurking deep down inside – as threatening as the sexual lure of the female spider for the male. He hated her but more disturbingly, he was afraid of her and that was an emotion he had rarely felt before in his life. Everyone was afraid of her.

When she entered the room she dragged with her an aura which washed over everyone, reducing them to silence without her speaking a word. On the rare occasions when she became jolly and tried to initiate silly games and other forms of therapy, she created an atmosphere as tense as piano wire. Patients laughed when it was expected of them but it was unreal, unnatural and often touched with hysteria. It was like children being tickled against their will, never sure when the pleasure would turn to pain, never sure whether they would be able to stop it.

Nurse Protz appraised Al with a smile which was entirely devoid of warmth and he put his face close to hers, looking into the emotionless blue pools.

27

"Al, my friends call me Al – but you can call me Mr Dwight."

"You've been doing so well, Alexander, it would be a shame to have to go back on medication…"

Al lowered his voice so no one else could hear: "Don't threaten me, lady!"

Nurse Protz held his stare, her eyes unblinking, blank, giving nothing away. When she did speak her tone was as confidential as Al's but what made her words infinitely more chilling than his was the fact that she had absolute power and he had none: "And don't throw your weight around, don't treat the other patients as though they are inferior to you…" She paused and when she spoke again it was like glass splintering: "And don't oppose me."

The sideways glance was barely discernible; perhaps it hadn't happened but he was sure it had flashed towards a chair in the corner where Rose McCaullay sat in a PVC covered chair, urine trickling down on to the floor from beneath her sodden clothing. She looked old, infinitely older than when she had arrived a month ago. She had been psychotic, screaming at the top of her voice: "I'm a virgin, I'm a pure virgin," and needed to be sedated – anyone would need sedation after trying to castrate their husband with a carving knife, Al thought. But this? It was the price of dissent, of being mouthy.

Rose's chin rested on her chest, her jaw hanging open, slack, motionless. A river of frothy saliva cascaded down her chin onto her knitted cardigan, spreading out in a big, dark stain. Her hands were clutched together in front of her and shook uncontrollably, her eyes dead, unseeing, unblinking.

"Do I make myself clear, Alexander?" Nurse Protz' voice had lightened but was no less threatening for that.

"Perfectly, Brunhilde." He knew it was a weak response but it was the best he could manage. How could someone so young – certainly no more than mid-twenties – weighing little more than seven stone wield such power? He knew for certain that of all the supposedly dangerous nut cases in this locked ward, nurse Protz was the most dangerous, the one most in need of help.

All his instincts were to confront the woman, put a brake on her, try to stop her from oppressing the inhabitants of this dejected little empire, populated by life's casualties – 'failures' was what he really thought. He had never hit a woman in his life but had come perilously close on several occasions with nurse Protz. One whack, just one and he knew he would not see the outside world again for a very long time. It would be Broadmoor if she had her way – she had already threatened it. Al broke off, tossed his cue clattering onto the snooker table and walked out of the recreation room. It was no good, he had to get out, put distance between him and Protz, avoid any potential conflict.

He had no resources, no contacts or friends on the outside and, most worrying of all, no passport – that was locked away somewhere with the rest of his possessions. He walked slowly out into the central corridor area which was the stem of a T structure – the left branch of the T was the female dormitory, the male dormitory was the right branch and the public areas which served them both made up the stem of the T. What Al Dwight did have, however, was the glimmering of a plan which he had already begun to initiate.

Almost as though to remind himself that there was a little hope, he went into the lavatories and chose the stall furthest from the door and opened the small window in the wall ahead of him, checking if anything had changed. It had not and so he walked back up the corridor to progress another part of his plan and on reaching the office marked Charge Nurse, knocked and entered.

"Do you mind waiting until you're asked to enter," Peter Dealey snapped from his seat in front of a desk on which his feet were resting, a newspaper in one hand, a cup of tea in the other. He looked exasperated.

"Oh I'm so sorry, I can see how busy you are, Pete. It's okay if I call you Pete, is it, Pete? Or would sir be preferable?"

"You're not doing yourself any favours, Al. This isn't a game."

Al appraised the man in front of him – thirties, greying stubble which was a bit too long to be designer and a bit too short to be a pukka beard. He had a broad, good looking face, wide mouth and had graduated from the social work school of 'be calm, reasonable and endlessly patient whatever the provocation'. He was professionally ever-understanding and Al wanted to grab him by the collar and shake him until he rattled.

He disliked Protz but he had contempt for Dealey. He was an identikit composite of weakness and was probably more in awe of Protz than anyone else on the ward and desperate for her approval. As a consequence, she was allowed complete latitude and effectively ran the place. Al was certain she was dispensing sex for Dealey like a consciousness-altering drug – just a little now and then, infrequently but regularly, enough to keep him panting, wanting more, enough so that the tingling urge in his groin never fully abated. Protz controlled him just as she controlled everyone else.

As he stood there, Al realised that what Dealey was saying was right – it wasn't a game and he made an instant promise to himself that from this point on he was going to become a model patient. "Sorry, Pete, you know how it is with us New Yorkers, got to get our retaliation in first".

Dealey smiled a wearied smile. "What do you want Al?"

"How do I get stuff out of my possessions, the ones that were taken off me – you know, if I need something?"

"Like what?"

"Well, like a watch. This one's starting to play up and there's a spare with my gear."

"You make a request to me in writing. I'll investigate the circumstances and if I approve it I'll write out a requisition. You then give that to an orderly who will take it to the store for this block and someone will release it to them. You'll sign for it and hand over your old watch."

"Oh good," Al smiled, "and I thought at first there might be a whole pile of bureaucratic shit involved." Being a model patient was not going to be easy. "Oh by the way, Pete, Protz wants to see you. She's in the Rec room."

Before Al had finished the words, Dealey's feet were off the desk, he was on his feet and brushing a hand through his hair. Al stood to one side and let him past as he went in search of nurse Protz, listening to his feet squeak down the vinyl-clad corridor. When he heard the door to the recreation room swing open, he began to rummage through the paperwork on Dealey's desk and quickly found what he was looking for, folded it and slipped it into his back pocket.

Al Dwight moved with purpose, a spring in his step, and headed back to the lavatory block and the same cubicle. The block was empty and he stood on the lavatory pan, opened the little window inwards and took hold of the one of the two bars which covered the opening, testing it for resistance, pulling and pushing to see how loose it was. There was no movement and from a trouser pocket he took out a table knife, prized free a chunk of chewing gum from the base of the bar – chewing gum that had been coated with loose mortar so that it looked almost indistinguishable from the real stuff – and began digging at the hole that had already been started, prizing away yet more of the mortar which held the bar in place, dropping it into the lavatory pan.

It flaked away reasonably easily but his main concern was whether the bars were welded into a metal framework for if they were, they would be almost impossible to remove without demolishing a large part of the window reveal and that would certainly be detected. He was hoping they had simply been individually cemented in when the building had been converted from a residential school into a psychiatric hospital.

He thought of the claustrophobic, stultifying oppression that formed the boundaries of his and everyone else's existence and was certain of one thing – if you came into this place sane, you would be crazy after a month – and he'd been here for four. He continued hacking at the mortar: "The bastards won't destroy me…" he whispered but wasn't convinced.

Chapter Five

"There! And I hope it bloody chokes you." The plate banged on to the table with such force that the gammon rasher bounced into the air and skittered across its pine top, followed by pieces of sautéed potato.

"Charming!" said Stephen Aldous without passion, as he scooped his brunch back onto the plate, trying to avoid breaking the yolk of his egg. He then stirred his coffee methodically as though nothing unusual had happened. It was one of his most enraging traits, to remain utterly calm in the face of someone else's anger. Eventually he spoke, his voice friendly, low pitched and intimate.

"It's not worth it, Jo. It's not important enough to warrant tantrums."

It didn't have the placating effect he'd intended – and he knew he had chosen the wrong word the moment he had said it.

Jo placed her hands on her hips and spoke with an affected whine.

"Oh, the little woman's having tantrums, is she? Well she isn't, she's bloody angry – angry because you always have to be right, don't you, Mister bloody infallible."

Again, Stephen spoke with studied calm as he began to cut at the bacon in front of him.

"All I'm saying is that he can't always have it all his own way. Sometimes kids have to do things they think they don't want to do – or claim they don't like…"

"He doesn't like it," Jo interrupted.

"It's just laziness. Good god, if parents didn't force their sprogs to go to music lessons we'd have no musicians. All kids complain about having to do things but believe me, they're grateful later in life. He enjoys it when he gets there".

"This isn't piano lessons it's bloody horse riding and it makes him sneeze, it makes him itch and it gives him asthma. Those are damned good reasons for not doing it, you pompous arse."

Even as she was speaking, Jo was marshalling other barbs – little derogatory phrases designed to puncture his pride. She stored them ready for use in ascending order of spitefulness. Like a general, she would deploy them carefully for maximum impact as the conflict escalated.

There was one, however, which she had never used, which she knew constituted her nuclear arsenal. Once it was despatched there was no retracting it and its aftermath would be messy. It had been filed away deep in her subconscious until recently but now every time they shouted at each other it leaped to the fore begging to be used – it was right there on the tip of her tongue, urging for her lips to form the words. But it was mutually assured disintegration and no situation had yet been bad enough for her to despatch it.

"It's got bugger all to do with what's good for him, it's what you want. A nice ruling-class pastime that will go down well with your supporters. Oh, and if he ever goes hunting, that would be the ultimate badge of honour for you, wouldn't it? That would ensure devotion from the green wellie set, wouldn't it...?"

Jo was escalating the argument, forcing it towards a major confrontation over an issue which, if she was honest with herself, amounted only to irritation and was far from being life or death. She knew that she was witnessing the last throes of a failed marriage.

"Stop arguing, you two – I can hear you out by the garage."

Danny stomped into the kitchen wearing jodhpurs and riding boots, dangling a silk-covered skull cap from one hand. Behind him came a tall, elegant, auburn-haired woman who looked as though she had just stepped down from the front cover of Vogue.

"Hillie," shouted Stephen, jumping up from the table and striding over towards Jo's sister. He engulfed her in a bear hug and she responded by clasping her arms around his waist. "You look as gorgeous as ever. Been indulging in a bit of retail therapy again, have you?"

Hillary freed herself and spun around, displaying a light-weight, crocheted coat which looked as fragile as gossamer and was stunningly beautiful. It was made with Knightsbridge in mind, not the leafy suburbs of Weybridge. "Like it?" The question was aimed at Stephen, not Jo.

"Absolutely gorgeous," he said, beaming at his sister-in-law. He turned to Jo: "You could knock the socks off the faithful if you wanted to – a bit of outrageous indulgence now and then is no bad thing." But there was a sting in the tail: "You're still an extremely good looking woman for your age." The implication being that at her age she should think herself lucky to be attractive but it may not remain that way for much longer. Had it been said by anyone else it would have been completely unremarkable – but it wasn't anyone else and Jo felt a tiny, physical jolt of annoyance somewhere beneath her solar plexus.

At thirty-four, Hillary was two years Jo's junior and was unquestionably beautiful. She had her own circle of friends but they were mostly nonentities by her own reckoning and she made no secret of her intrigue in the whole political circus which surrounded Jo and was utterly bemused that Jo was bored by it. Hillie loved to be admired and flattered, fawned over and feted but Jo had watched from the side-lines for so many years – from teenage – and had seen the results. Anyone who fell into Hillie's trap, who responded in the gormless way that men do when they think they are in with a chance, was quickly treated with contempt – with the exception of Stephen, it seemed, but then he was benign and didn't count being a brother-in-law.

It was like a never ending battle in which Hillie had to prove how desirable she was. Only those who resisted her were given the intimate treatment – the rapt attention, the touch of hand on arm, the admiring gaze, instant laughter and body movements that flowed – lithe and sinuous, carrying overt sexual promise. It was as though any and every man had to fancy her.

Those who fell into the trap and showed their interest were mostly peremptorily shunned. The unspoken promise of future carnal delights was promptly erased. Hillie had a wonderful way of dismissing fawning suitors – an imperious glance down her aquiline nose as though they smelt. Trouble was, it seemed to make them keener so Jo felt there had to be some sub context at work which only men could divine in Hillie. Certainly she couldn't. Of course, she reasoned, it could just be that men are extraordinarily stupid once they let their cocks start doing the thinking.

It was, thought Jo, utterly demeaning but even without her having said anything she knew that to Hillie it was the game that gave her life its frisson. Jo was convinced that Hillary was a lousy lover. No one with that much front could have a great deal left in reserve. In any case, it would be far too messy for her. It was for the same reason that Jo felt sure Hillie had never had children – that and the anticipated destruction of her figure.

She was stunningly beautiful and everything about her seemed flawless, from the translucent skin to the pearly white teeth, the unblemished eyes to the model-like figure. It came as a shock to Jo when she realised that if Hillie wasn't her sister, she wouldn't like her. But their shared history and the fact that she still had the ability to make Jo laugh out loud kept them together. Hillie's wit was perceptive and as sharp as a razor in some restricted areas – usually with men as the brunt.

Jo knew that Hillie would adore the attention she could expect as a senior politician's wife and would cultivate it assiduously to the point where she was never off the front pages. She would fete journalists, pout and pose and give them everything they wanted. Wonderful – so long as nobody asked her an intelligent question! That was catty, thought Jo.

But Hillie wasn't in politics – she was married to Stuart, an extremely boring but very successful solicitor whose corporate work would never gain him so much as a local newspaper report. She was a frustrated media junkie and would never understand why Jo avoided the spotlight.

As and when the opportunity arose, Hillie was ever-ready to remind Stephen that she would be the asset to his career that Jo now refused to be. Or at least, that's the way it seemed to Jo. Maybe it was all in jest, a gentle wind up – but still the sharp little knife of annoyance slid quickly home whenever Hillie took on that role.

"So what was the marital tiff about?" Hillary said. "Or shouldn't I ask."

Stephen and Jo's responses came out together. Jo said "No" and Stephen said "Just the person." He went over to Danny, took him by the shoulders and spun him round to face his mother and aunt.

"Apparently, Danny says he's not too keen on going riding any more. Do you think we should give in to him or do you think he'll thank us eventually if we insist he keeps it up?" Stephen beamed as though he had solved the situation simply by posing the question.

Hillary turned her nose up: "Personally I hated it. So disgusting and smelly – all those great, gaping, plopping bottom holes and steaming piles of doobry." She shuddered theatrically and Jo could feel the anger welling up inside her. "But then you're not me, are you Dan. You're a regular little soldier aren't you. You like riding, don't you?"

Danny looked at the floor and spoke hesitantly. "S'ppose so. But I don't like the asthma."

"See, I told you so," said Stephen, beaming even more broadly. "He's all right!"

Jo's annoyance overflowed. She had been side-lined by her husband and sister and a fundamental decision which concerned her child had been usurped: "It's got fuck all to do with you, Hillie so keep out of it." She turned to Stephen: "Dan's only saying that because he doesn't want to fall out with you, you buffoon." Again, a little word carefully chosen to undermine his arrogance. Of course it didn't have even passing impact.

She threw a tea cloth on to the table as if to underline her contempt but with Danny present, she did not want it to escalate into an all-out row.

Stephen saw the chink of silver amidst the boiling storm clouds and deftly deployed his political skills – without surrendering his position.

"Look, he's having a day out today, a hack along the beach

and it might make all the difference – give him a taste for what riding's all about. Let him go, see how he gets on and we'll talk about it tomorrow. Okay?" Stephen's tone was conciliatory and even though Jo knew she was being out-negotiated she had lost her appetite for battle.

"I'll take him today because the stable's made special arrangements and we haven't told them he's not coming – but it's the last time." She busied herself looking for car keys, dark glasses and handbag and felt guilty that she had purposely chosen confrontation when simple, stubborn refusal would have been far more effective. Essentially, she had lost the battle for today.

"Ready Dan?"

He smiled at her without enthusiasm.

Jo loved being around horses but it was years ago that she had lost her nerve for riding. There was no particular incident, it just happened.

She breathed deeply on the cocktail of stable smells – hay and straw, hoof oil, saddle soap and the powerful aroma of horses themselves. If she breathed too deeply the pungency of it all could make her sneeze. She didn't even mind the smell of fresh dung as horses, she thought, must produce the sweetest-smelling shit in the world.

Little girls were attracted to horses like bees to honey and there was always a gang of them around. In between dunging out, watering, feeding and tacking up, they chased each other, screamed and concocted alliances which were just as quickly broken. It was only a matter of time before someone sulked, bitterly spitting out the words, "It's not fair!" And it was all so they could end the day with a free ride and possibly a lesson. She couldn't see Dan doing that, which probably summed up his lack of enthusiasm. Jo smiled to herself as she acknowledged that what interest Danny had in horse riding had little to do with either horses or riding but a lot to do with the bevy of girls. He probably wasn't even aware of it himself.

The girls ranged in age from six to sixteen and gave up most weekends simply because they were potty about the animals. It seemed to Jo like only yesterday that she had been one of them.

There was the usual collection of comic, stunted little Shetland ponies with their huge personalities as well as larger ponies of every conceivable description, breed and cross breed. A file of them, surmounted by mostly girl riders, were headed towards the outdoor manege looking for all the world like a Thelwell cartoon.

Danny was not riding his usual pony today for his first major hack but a white West Highland called Angus. Angus stood in the day stable waiting to be loaded into the horse box for the journey to Worthing, his head hanging motionless over the half door with an expression that looked like thunder. But then, he always looked like that. He was a grumpy old boy but supposedly with impeccable manners when carrying an inexperienced rider.

Jo wandered aimlessly around the stables, peering over half doors, patting horses' necks, rubbing mucus from the corner of an eye, letting the palm of her hand be licked and trying gently to enfold the soft, wet tongue in her fingers. In one stable, she watched quietly as a family of mice played tag over the generous mound of clean straw, finally disappearing beneath it when she made a sudden, inadvertent movement.

For the first time in months, perhaps years, she felt no sense of urgency, no diary date that had to be kept, no sense of guilt that she should be somewhere else, doing something else, preparing for something else. She was happy – perhaps content was a more accurate description – and a sense of enjoying the here and now enveloped her.

This was a world she had grown up with, taken for granted, and had never thought back on it in any depth until now. Over there, in the indoor manege, was where she had first cantered and to this day remembered the instruction that had started it and how it had made her feel – fearful, apprehensive, thrilled:

"Okay, whip in the inside hand and when you reach the letter M, I want you to shorten your reins, go into sitting trot and kick him on. Keep your left leg on and make him keep on the track round the corners. If you feel him falling in, put your leg on even harder and give him a tap with the whip in front of it to reinforce the instruction."

She did it all and the pony lurched into a headlong canter, getting faster and faster around the school as she tightened up with fear, gripping with her knees as if her life depended on it – did depend upon it, in her mind. The harder she gripped, the more he took it as an instruction to go faster and the sheer exhilaration, the sense of not being fully in control, the danger, made her pulse race and her heart throb with the joy of discovery. What the hell had happened to that feeling?

To anyone observing, it was a little girl having a riding lesson but to her it was one of life's most magical moments. Jo realised her childhood was not something she had passed through like a tunnel, now gone and left behind, its experiences obscured by the demands of passing time. It was interwoven into her daily life like the intertwined cords of a rope. One cord was the politician's wife, one cord was a mother and one cord was her childhood, alive and fresh in her memory, an integral part of her being and of understanding her son.

When Danny had finished opening the last of his presents one Christmas morning and had dropped paper, string and present with an exclaimed: "Is that all?" Stephen had reacted with horror, telling him not to be so selfish and ungrateful. Jo said nothing, remembering that same feeling so exactly, as clearly as if it had been her sitting there on the carpet. She knew it wasn't a complaint about lack of presents but an expression of sadness that the excitement was over for another year – a lifetime!

Stephen had never had that empathy with Danny, or with anyone else for that matter because there was only one strand in the fabric of his life and it was him, Stephen Aldous the ambitious. She pushed the thought of Stephen from her mind.

And there, somewhere deep down inside that stable block, hidden in the corner of an empty day stable, was where she had first allowed someone to feel her breasts – a greedy, thrusting hand that had pushed insistently up beneath her sweater and fumbled interminably with her bra clasp. When in frustration she had finally put her own hands up behind her back and freed them, she had felt wanton. Her mother's favourite expression to describe sexually obvious young women popped up in her mind. Jezebel! She was a Jezebel and the naughtiness of it sent a little thrill shooting through her breasts. The eagerness with which Dominic Sykes had grasped at first one and then the other had slightly shocked her; that's not how it had been in her fantasies. The disappointment was acute when after only seconds he deserted her breasts and tried to thrust a hand down her jodhpurs – she had not even had chance to start enjoying the sensations and she never forgave him for that. It was the one and only fumble he was ever to be allowed.

"Mum." Danny's voice made her start. The horse box had been driven into the yard and girls were running an assortment of horses up the tail gate with determined efficiency. She had been oblivious to it all.

"We'll be off in a minute."

"I think I'll come with you." Jo hadn't even consciously made the decision – it had seemingly been made for her.

She saw the flicker of disappointment in Danny's eyes and knew instinctively what it was.

"There's no room in the box," he pleaded.

"I'm going to drive." The disappointment was still there. "But don't worry, I don't expect you to come with me, you can go in the box with your mates." His face lit up.

"Cool, mum! I'll see you down there." He turned and ran towards the lorry with the enthusiasm of youth. Jo knew that, heightened by the danger and excitement of what was to come, a crowd of girls and a boy or two in the accommodation between the horses and the driving cab – from which adults were banished – was exactly the kind of place that would generate their memories. Friendships would be built in the enforced closeness and enmities would be exaggerated – and there would be little sexual frissons that Danny probably wouldn't even understand but they would provide some of the contours of his growing up that would give it shape and meaning.

She would never want to deny him those inexplicable flashes of excitement which were the most memorable elements of discovery. No, she wouldn't do that to him – destroying the magic by swamping him with adult demands and certainties.

She suddenly felt sad and resentful as she realised that Stephen had precisely the same effect on her. She knew that she wanted a little sexual frisson – well, perhaps not that little, come to think of it.

She remained behind the lorry as it slowly ground its way through first the Surrey and then the Sussex countryside towards the coast, very rarely even touching 50 mph. But she was content with that. The country roads were blinkered with stands of old oaks, ash and sycamore tinged with autumn and occasionally they gave way to panoramic views across open countryside, the green of grazing meadows and the tired straw colours of newly harvested cereals.

She consciously tried to hold on to this unusual feeling of peace and calm which had appeared without warning. She was not aware of thinking about the future, nor of the past for that matter, and when her thoughts strayed there, she ruthlessly brought them back to the present, wrenching them away from the wells of self-pity, blame, recrimination and fear where she had so frequently drawn water in the past.

The realisation came logically and without surprising her. What she was feeling was confidence – a sense of strength, perhaps even belief in herself – not as a mother or a wife or a public figure or as the partner of a future prime minister but simply as herself. It had been a hell of a long time coming but now that it had arrived she knew it was impossible to return to this morning.

There could be no more manufactured battles with someone she no longer even liked. The decision was clarifying in her mind and as it did the sense of wellbeing intensified. Fear of the conclusions which would flow from this decision – a fear which had kept her impotent for a year or more – was evaporating. She would get another garden, a different garden, a garden which was hers alone. She would ensure that whoever bought her house would love animals and she would pass on the custody and care of her foxes, badgers and squirrels. That was not a problem. And she would tell Danny closer to the time when she knew what their new lives would consist of and he would understand.

But the grey suits – the unprincipled, smug, privileged, dangerous king makers of the Conservative establishment, who were planning on selecting Stephen as their man, to represent their interests and obey their instructions, would not want to confront the possibility of him being fatally wounded by a separation, or even worse a divorce. They would come to call on her but she would deal with them. They would be persuasive and if denied, their entreaties would turn into pressure which would rapidly become threats. And the threats would be fulfilled because that was their way – but she would also deal with that.

The thought made her apprehensive and she was aware that her breathing had become shallow – but it was not enough to make her doubt her decision.

Jo was only partly conscious that she had driven past two or three very beautiful country pubs and yet had felt no need to reward her positive frame of mind with a glass of wine.

When she arrived at the beach there was already a gathering of four-tracks and individual trailers belonging to people who had brought their horses separately. Thin little waves marked the low tide mark, leaving a wide expanse of puddled and ridged sand between it and the banks of shingle on the shore. It stretched uninterrupted for miles in both directions, providing a wonderfully free terrain for uninhibited cantering and galloping.

The air was crisp and clean, tinged with that unmistakable sea weed smell and the visibility was perfect – clear and sharp and the seagulls, disturbed by the clatter of horses hooves on wooden ramps, wheeled effortlessly on the breeze. The kids chatted, shouted and joked as they tacked up their mounts, their excitement barely contained. And the horses fizzed and jittered in unison with them, moving this way and that, equally as excited by this change in their routine and the knowledge of what was to come.

Danny paid little attention to Jo as one of the older girls helped him to fit Angus's bridle. The scene transformed quite suddenly and all the young riders were mounted, the adults on their high-stepping horses trying to keep them calm and at the same time shouting instructions. Danny turned to look back over his shoulder and throw Jo a smile – mainly to ensure she was watching.

They moved off in a rising trot but it lasted for no more than few yards before one of the trailing horses decided to challenge for the lead. As if by agreement, the whole herd broke into a canter which, within a stride or two, became a full-blooded gallop towards the distant sea. Calls to rein back were drowned by the excited shouts and whoops of the kids who had no intention of obeying. Wedges of wet sand and sea spray flew into the air from the horses' hooves and those who were not amongst the front runners were showered with them. But it was all part of the fun.

Standing waiting with Jo were the least experienced riders, for whom there had not been enough mounts. They watched in awe and envy as the posse of horses thundered across the beach, hoping they would still have energy left when it came to their turn.

It didn't take long before the pace eased into more contained canters as the horses and ponies broke into separate groups, the choice dictated more by individual friendships of the riders than proficiency or size of horse. Their images appeared almost in silhouette against the glare of autumn sunshine reflected from the surface of the gently rolling sea. Jo could still pick out Danny but only because of Angus's squat stature.

As she watched she became conscious that she was smiling – a smile which must have been there for minutes. There was going to be more of this, more of Danny and her enjoying life together. She intended to actively seek out experiences for him, stacking and stashing the memories away for later recall just as she had done with her garden. She had the sudden, bizarre thought that all she was constructed from – all anyone was constructed from – was a collection of memories. Strip away the memories and who were you?

The smell of fresh coffee would no longer evoke the morning after a night of passion, with a man whose name she could barely remember. The reasons why she would always hate anyone with the name Roger would no longer exist and she might even like eating peas without the memory of them having stuck in her throat as a three-year-old. If memories were the currency that paid for the complexities of character, she was going to save them like a miser.

Horses and riders had hacked backwards and forwards along the edge of the incoming tide until the ballooning bubble of energy with which they had started began slowly to dissipate. The group in which Danny was riding began heading back towards them and there was a purpose about the horses which filled their trotting with urgency. Someone had begun to tie hay nets to the side of the lorry for when the horses had finished their day's exertions.

"Who the hell put those up?" demanded one of the instructors, cantering towards the lorry with a face filled with thunder. "Get them down and out of sight now – don't just stand there gawping, get the nets down and don't put them up again until we've finished!"

Little girls leaped into action, one of them shouting over her shoulder: "It wasn't me! It's not fair! I told her not to!"

The group of riders began to mill around the horsebox, their faces glowing with the satisfaction and thrill of the ride, the fronts of their bodies, from boot tips to the top of their hats, dripping with sand and sea water, excitement driving their shouted conversations as they related tales of what had happened, what nearly happened and what might have happened.

Danny started to dismount but as he did, Angus shied as though irritated and Danny tumbled to the sand where he scrambled on to his hands and knees looking up to his pony as though he could not quite believe what had happened. Angus spun around with extraordinary speed and kicked out with his hind legs in a full-blooded assault on Danny. One hoof caught him on the shoulder, the other made a sickening thud as it crashed against the side of his head. The little boy fell to the ground as though pole axed and lay there motionless.

Jo's scream of, "No-o-o-o-o-o" echoed across the beach and a thousand seagulls took to the air, adding their own chorus of screams as though in empathy.

Chapter Six

Pride swelled his chest whenever Peter Willis walked his two-hundred plus acres, which he did from time to time to check fencing, hedgerows, gates and the other essentials that went to make up a dairy farm. He sometimes played a silly game and tried to count how many trees he owned, each stretching skywards from amongst the hedgerows, standards that marked the boundaries of his fields. Trees somehow felt more permanent than dairy cows, a more tangible measure of his success.

His father had not been a land-owning farmer or even a tenant, just a farm worker and so Peter had not been privileged in any way and there was no land to inherit, no farmhouse, no barns and outbuildings, no herd and not a single acre that came his way on his father's death. But that had never disconcerted him and even as a young farmhand he had promised himself that one day he would own two-hundred acres and it would be grazed by a pedigree Friesian herd that other farmers envied.

He was now thirty-six and that was precisely what he had achieved with just one slight amendment – the herd was of pedigree Holstein's, which looked very like the black and white Friesians but were larger, higher-yielding animals. They were now commonplace throughout the entire industry, supposedly increasing its profitability but the fact that most of that profit had been snaffled by supermarkets with their enormous purchasing power and ruthless cost cutting was another story.

He forced himself to think of other things as the injustice of it began to sour his day. The fact remained that whatever he had, he had achieved by himself and he owed no debt of gratitude to anyone.

Peter clambered over the style into what everyone knew as the quarry field and which still bore signs of its history – a twenty foot high sand bank ran the right-hand length of the long narrow field, gradually reducing in height until it petered out by a gate at the far end. This gate led into the field which ran along the top of the bank. The bank itself, with its soft structure of sand, made it ideal for rabbits and as he entered the field they scattered before him, seeking refuge in their burrows.

Making up the left-hand boundary of the quarry field was the river Mander. It entered the field as a slow, sluggish, deep river but crashed over a ten-foot weir in a thunder of spray and rainbows and immediately transformed into an entirely different waterway. It ran and sparkled over gravel, twisting and turning between tall willows, the main stream sweeping from one bank to another leaving gravel shallows on one side of each bend.

There was one right-angled bend with a high bank that Peter loved to stand on as it granted an uninterrupted view of some hundred and fifty yards upstream towards the weir. He always approached it warily, his feet treading lightly and quietly as invariably a kingfisher would hurtle silently out of its burrow in the bank just below his feet and disappear upstream in a flash of iridescent blue and red-orange plumage. The quieter he was, the closer he could get before it launched into its arrow-like flight.

Upstream, he could see little dace taking midges from the surface of the stream in sparkling flashes of quicksilver and occasionally a larger rise or swirl would break the surface, which he knew to be the tell-tale signs of brown trout.

He could have rented out this beat to a few rods for several hundred a year but it had never crossed his mind to do so, just as it never occurred to him to fish for them himself. Their very presence contributed to the beauty of a scene from which he gained so much satisfaction.

In fact, he allowed no one to fish on his land with the exception of local children. He had been one of them once and the river had been an indispensable part of his growing up and had nurtured his love of nature. To deny other kids that pleasure would be mean and churlish, he felt, particularly when they caught very little and invariably put back what they did catch. They certainly did not appear to have the guile to catch a trout.

Peter saw himself as a new breed of farmer; one who genuinely respected and loved the wildlife that his farm was home to and one who had eagerly accepted the Government's move away from direct subsidies and supposedly towards environmental rewards. He knew that most of his farming neighbours paid lip service to environmentalism and gave not a toss what form the subsidies took so long as they kept coming. Many appeared to regard wildlife as a nuisance or at best quarries for a bit of Sunday rough shooting.

He had never understood other farmers' attitude to the creatures which lived on their land, passed through it or visited it in their migrations, just as their forebears had done for probably thousands of years. He marvelled at the excuses farmers created to shoot and trap, to snare and poison. The harsh cawing of a group of crows as they took off from a nearby tree reminded him of one particular practice that revolted him.

Crows, rooks and their young were blasted from the sky as though they carried a deadly threat in their black wings, as reviled as Nazi Stuka dive bombers set on destroying all that was civilised. The birds were killed when they were at their most vulnerable – living communally in rookeries that might hold fifty, a hundred or even more nests concentrated together in the highest trees.

When the young had just fledged and were capable of flight but had not yet departed to embark on a life alone, the guns would gather beneath the trees. The hollow report of 12-bore shotguns, clouds of gun smoke and the acrid smell of cordite filled the air as little black bodies tumbled from the sky like bags of soot.

The young, newly-fledged birds knew only the rookery and were afraid to leave their home and so circled around and around. Their parents, like all parents, could not abandon their young and circled with them, calling and cawing in fear and confusion. As the number of birds diminished under the hail of shot, some would realise the hopelessness of their situation and wing noiselessly away to escape the carnage.

For the men below, it could not even be considered sport; it was little more than target practice using living bodies. And all because of an old myth that these birds would peck out the eyes of new-born lambs.

Peter doubted it had been true in the old days when ewes gave birth to just one lamb and would be more than a match for any predatory crow in defence of her baby. Now that sheep were manipulated and artificially inseminated into bearing twins or even triplets in mid-winter, when there was a dearth of food, it was conceivable. But as on most lowland farms, ewes gave birth in lambing sheds so even that explanation was threadbare.

A similar excuse was used to snare and shoot foxes – that they took new-born lambs. Peter had never in his life seen a young, healthy, viable lamb that had fallen victim to foxes. They were invariably dead or dying when they were taken. There was no hunting or trapping on his farm and no shooting, not even rabbits.

Few of his neighbours shared his views and were bewildered by his refusal to allow the hunt on to his land. It particularly incensed those local dignitaries who rode to hounds and felt it their right to traverse any land they chose in pursuit of their quarry – but it bothered Peter not one jot.

Most farmers, on the other hand, allowed the hunt free access to their land, even those who, like him, had only dairy or beef cattle. When he had asked his immediate neighbour why he allowed the horses and hounds to rampage across his fields his answer was telling: "Some very powerful people in the hunt, Peter, very powerful!"

Peter had built his farm field by field, cow by cow, and perhaps once, way back, a little mutual back scratching might have been helpful but it was now too late. He wanted no favours from anyone and was not prepared to grant any.

He continued along the river bank into the pipe field where a large-diameter water main appeared from out of the bushes and crossed the river at right-angles, about eight feet above the water, disappearing underground on the far side. A coronet of metal spikes encircled the pipe at both ends, their purpose being to deter people from using it as a bridge. The concept had failed spectacularly as two or three of the upright spikes at each end had been bent flat along the length of the pipe and it had been like that for as long as Peter could remember.

On hot summer days, local kids would clamber along the pipe before hurling themselves off into one of the deeper gullies below, to be engulfed by the river's extraordinarily chilly water, even in summer. He had once been one of them and it was another game he had no intention of curtailing simply because he was now a grown up.

Again Peter stepped gently and cautiously towards the river bank making no sound with his feet. He reached the trunk of a large willow and holding on to it, slowly bent forward until he could look directly down into the water below, trying to see through the skittering reflections of sunlight on the dappled surface.

And then he spotted what he had hoped to see – two pale, whitish crescents close to each other and each about an inch across, a foot or two below the surface. They hung there like little motionless half-moons in a firmament of dark water. He knew they were the protruding bottom lips of a pair of chubb and from the lips he was able to trace their dark, thick bodies down as far as their tails, which moved languidly in the stream, helping them to hold their position. None of their beautiful colour showed from above the water – not their olive green backs which faded into bright silver flanks and bellies nor their bright red fins. He estimated their weight at around six pounds each – good-sized fish.

Chubb would also sometimes rise to a surface fly but much more gently than trout, barely giving away their position with the tiniest of swirls or a sudden sucking action that merely dimpled the surface as the fly was drawn into their mouths.

Peter strolled across the pasture of the pipe field, disturbing a hare which startled him with its speed as it bolted from a clump of docks almost underfoot, its distinctive long ears laid back, its powerful back legs driving it forward at a pace which made him feel virtually disabled. Within seconds it had traversed the field and disappeared into the five acres of barley where no doubt a variety of other wildlife concealed itself.

He followed the course of the long-disappeared hare, up along the margin of the barley and onto the track which led back to the road. Peter took his time, looking around him at trees and distant houses, a spire, the gable end of a fine Georgian stable block – all the markers that had proscribed his life.

So what if he had been to London only once and wasn't that impressed with the experience? It was here where his life had begun and, he hoped, where it would end. He had been christened beneath the steeple to his right; he had been married there, his children had been christened there and he hoped fervently that when he died he would be buried there, amongst old friends and many others whose personalities had helped to sculpt his life. Perhaps not all of them were friends but death and decomposition would probably produce some kind of accommodation.

He felt no need to go anywhere else or be anywhere else. He knew precisely who he was, where he belonged and his place in this microcosmic community, which was a whole world unto itself.

He knew the seasons and the winds, the rain and the frost and how they constituted the most important tools of his trade and dictated his working life. Farming might look boringly repetitive on the surface but timing was everything and it was these shifting and uncontrollable elements that determined the timing and therefore the pattern of his working life.

Spring and autumn muck spreading with its stench that everyone complained about but which he barely noticed. The annual application of selective weed killer for perennials, just the right amount of spring fertiliser so the crops did not overreach themselves, the first cut of silage which would hopefully be early enough in the year to allow the grass to grow sufficiently to provide two further cuts before autumnal fading light and falling temperatures stifled its growth. Then there was the decision whether to grow a few acres of barley for selling or maize for silaging.

These same actions were repeated year after year and the

skill came in knowing precisely when to perform each one. He could only be sure he had it right when totting up the annual balance sheet.

Peter exited on to the quiet country road which did little more than join two villages together. The branches of its high and mighty trees soared upwards from its hedgerows and met overhead forming a vaulted arch as beautiful as any cathedral and through whose leaves shafts of golden sunlight speared downwards, painting and patterning the dusty tarmac.

A couple of hundred metres down the gentle hill he turned into a short lane with a cottage on one side. It was where he had grown up and he could never pass it without a glance at the vegetable garden, where he had learnt so much at his father's side. It delighted him that it was still there as were the huge blackcurrant bushes that he had planted as mere twigs. There was the same rhubarb, gooseberries and redcurrants even though the rest of the garden had been gentrified with chimnea, statuary, barbecue and sun loungers.

He entered the five-acre field of permanent pasture that ran alongside the upper reaches of the river. Although separated from the rest of his acreage, and therefore not entirely convenient, he had bought it when it came up for sale because it carried him across that magic finishing line – five acres added to his then one-hundred-and-ninety eight! He had hit his boyhood target!

He used this field for cows which were in the last stages of pregnancy. Normally, he would remove them to a barn a few days before their due date but in the centre of the field was a cow suckling a calf which she had recently delivered and which he had decided to leave where it was for a couple of days. He must have got his dates wrong or, more likely, the cow had delivered early.

A midwife cow intervened between him and the mother, staring at him with a mixture of concern and threat, hoping to frighten him away. He ignored her menace, walking straight towards her until she turned and trotted out of the way.

He examined the little calf – a bull and of pure dairy breed. Worthless! It wasn't something Peter agonised over, it was just one of the facts of life that some calves had a value and some did not. Male calves sired by dairy bulls were valueless, those sired by beef bulls he could sell on. In the past he had made perhaps fifty pounds from dairy bull calves by selling them into the intensive veal trade but that market had disappeared with mad cow diseases and had never re-established itself.

It was not a trade he approved of but so long as consumers created a market, who was he to argue with them? Peter hefted the little bull calf in his arms and headed back towards the road and up to the farm. He had no need to tether the mother as she was preoccupied with the fate of her calf and trotted behind him without any bidding, concern etched into her huge bovine eyes. Peter calculated that the calf had now been with his mother long enough to have drawn all the colostrum from her udder and the milk flow would have started.

He checked the ear tag number and for some reason remembered the history of this particular cow without need to refer to his very precise notes – a catalogue of repetitive mastitis, recurring lameness and laminitis and a drop-off in yield during her last lactation, which was her third. He had almost decided to cull her last year but had given her a reprieve and this would now be her last calving.

Man, calf and cow turned into the farmyard with barely a space between them. He carried the calf through into the long milking parlour with it endless clusters of metal sheaths that fitted over the cows' teats. The mother was still close behind him and he placed the little animal down whilst manoeuvring the mother into a milking stall and clipping the chain behind her to keep her there.

He picked up the calf again and walked out of the parlour and as he did so the bellowing of the mother began – high pitched, desperate and demanding. Peter barely heard it as after years of separating thousands of cows and calves, he had become inured to what was an essential part of dairy farming.

He placed the calf in an empty stall while he went across to the house, returning with a rifle in the crook of his arm. Again he lifted the calf, slinging it under one arm, the rifle occupying the other, and walked behind a shed where a shallow scrape had already been dug in the earth. Through a thin covering of soil, other small, black and white corpses in various stages of decomposition could just be seen at the bottom of the shallow pit.

He placed the calf on the ground at the side of the pit where it stood motionless, bleating, looking up at him, responding with its own feeble call to each bellow from his mother. Peter slipped a round into the breach, sliding the bolt shut with a satisfying, well-engineered, well-oiled thunk.

He raised the rifle and aimed at the calf's forehead, not difficult as it remained motionless, its head thrust forward still bleating as though demanding something of him. He had carried out this task hundreds, perhaps thousands of times without agonising but suddenly, as his eyes took in the outlines of little corpses in the scrape below and the living creature in front of him, he froze. An extraordinary sensation washed over him which almost evoked a scream. It was horror, despair, self-loathing. Was this to go on for the remainder of his life – taking new borns away from their mothers and killing them? Was it all as unimportant as he had always believed, this production line of death?

He looked down at his hands, which were shaking uncontrollably and he screamed into the afternoon sunlight; "Get a grip, you stupid bastard, get a grip!" Peter then shook himself as though the grief that had possessed him was in droplet form and could be shed. It was now a battle – to give in to despair or do his job. With gritted teeth he took aim once more but became conscious of movement ahead of him and it distracted him from his task. Raising his eyes, he saw the head of the mother cow peering around the end of the shed some fifteen yards or so away, snorting fiercely from her nostrils as though hyperventilating, looking directly at him. Her distinctive face – almost entirely white and devoid of all black markings apart from her ears – was unmistakable.

Peter momentarily lowered the rifle as he decided how best to handle the situation. It was the wrong thing to do. With extraordinary agility, the cow rushed around the corner of the shed and straight at Peter and he remained motionless, even when she lowered her head and her intention became clear. She butted him with such force that his feet left the ground, the rifle spun away and as he landed, she was on top of him, spinning around to kick and stamp viciously with her hind legs. And she kept on kicking as Peter tried desperately to stand but failed. She did not stop kicking until Peter was a bloodied and lifeless mass. She turned and with her head, pushed his body until it rolled down the side of the shallow scrape to join the other motionless corpses at the bottom and then turned her attention to her still-bleating calf.

Chapter Seven

When the nightmares came, Jo Aldous was not surprised. What did surprise her was the fact that they had waited so long to appear. Without warning and without reason, it seemed, they suddenly slithered beneath her consciousness to drag her writhing and sweating from her sleep almost every night. She wondered why they had delayed their spiteful little games until the crisis was over – surely the four weeks during which Danny lay unconscious would have provided the perfect opportunity and had a far more rewarding outcome.

They could have taunted and terrified her with imaginary horrors only for her to awake to find the reality even worse than her nightmares. Now, when the shakes and sweats had subsided, a grateful calm was all that ensued because Danny was perfectly okay with only a distant fear that he might develop epilepsy.

During that interminable period of watching and waiting, Jo slept little and was almost permanently in a dream-like state from a combination of exhaustion and near paralysis spawned by dread. It would have required little effort from her subconscious to have whisked its bleak imaginings from their unknown hiding places and used them to play games with her frightened mind. Perhaps it knew that whatever transitory tortures it devised they would pale into insignificance alongside the torment, fear and guilt that dogged her waking hours. Nothing could be worse than watching her unconscious son with the ever-present dread of losing her beautiful little boy.

Despite what the doctors said in those dark days, no matter how frequently they reassured her, Jo was terrified that Danny would slip away from her. All that could keep him clinging on and eventually drag him back to consciousness, she felt, was her presence, her voice, her songs, her conversation, her thoughts, her love, her caresses and kisses but, strangely, never her prayers.

If there was a god, he or she had run out of credibility as far as Jo was concerned. Any being or power who could allow this awful thing to happen was hardly likely to respond to her pleadings to make it all better. And if it did – what a sick little game it was playing. After years of never having the conviction or courage to deny god, she now found herself bitterly atheistic and completely unafraid that her rejection of a deity would threaten either her or Danny. She had torn up the insurance policy.

Perhaps it was the thought that there is only one life and no cosy, celestial ultimate destination that fuelled her panic. Once he was gone he was gone forever, she knew that, and there would be no sweet and glowing reunion when her time came and she was raptured up to heaven. Perhaps it was this that stoked her fear but she doubted it and guessed that even the most devout mother would be just as terrified at the prospect of losing her child.

And so she barely left his bedside, sitting and talking endlessly to him, just like she had always talked to him as she tucked him into bed, even before he could comprehend her words. She would run through the day's activities, reminding him of the highlights, the things which had made them laugh or the treats they had had and as he grew older, he would remind her of anything she had forgotten. It was an essential preparation for sleep, a gliding into that calmer world of imagination suffused with the reassurance of shared experiences and love.

The hospital had provided a bed alongside Danny's in a room in the private wing and Jo barely left it. She played music there, occasionally watched TV, read but mostly talked, quietly and intimately, frequently caressing Danny's brow or holding his hand and watching the livid bruise on the side of his face turn from blackberry colour to a sallow yellow.

She watched one particular spot intently as it started to fade and convinced herself that when it finally disappeared Danny would emerge from his coma.

The only thought to occupy her mind other than Danny was the horse that had lashed out at him. She had been around horses most of her life and there was something strangely unnatural about the way this one had kicked him. It wasn't straining at the reins, not on its toes, agitated and angry, there were no rolling eyes or staring whites and its ears weren't back but pricked. She was convinced that its actions were not fuelled by anger or fear but by something else – something she couldn't identify. It was almost as though the animal was preoccupied with something, somewhere else and had responded without premeditation in much the same way a person reading a newspaper would brush away a fly that came too close – barely conscious of the action.

The hospital reassured Jo that all Danny's vital signs were good, that his brain activity was normal, that he was in the shallowest level of coma and that he would emerge from unconsciousness sooner or later, probably sooner. They could not guarantee there would be no brain damage but thought it unlikely. She wasn't sure she believed any of their reassurances.

Stephen's visits were regular but fleeting. He would pop in, ask a question or two – "How's he been?" "Any change?" "Can I get you anything?" And then he would proffer an excuse for having to go – "A meeting of the shadow cabinet." "An interview for The World at One", and leave with a peck on both her cheek and Danny's.

Jo was surprised by her reaction to him. She did not hold Stephen any more responsible for Danny's condition than she did herself, or Hillie or the riding school or the kid who had put the hay nets out. It was an accident and nothing more and she had no intention of pillorying Stephen for it. So why did she hate him so much?

She had no need to dig deep for the reasons – they came tumbling out of their own accord. She wanted someone alongside her whose love for their son was equal in strength to her own because only they could understand the intensity of her pain. It would have even eased that pain a little because there would have been some bizarre assurance that their strength combined would have provided the rock to which Danny's damaged mind could cling. It would have even allowed her an occasional moment or two of respite knowing that the vigil for their son was being maintained by someone who was as emotionally dependent as her; someone whose love and concern she could trust without doubt; someone who would never waiver and who would keep the beacon burning that Danny could navigate by and come safely back.

Stephen provided none of these things and worse, there was the awful realisation that he didn't really love their son – not deeply, not passionately. He couldn't love him or he would not have allowed every other aspect of his life to take precedence, even 'popping out' to buy Hillie's birthday present shortly after arriving one day.

"Leave the fucking thing, it doesn't matter," she snapped.

"We have to keep life as normal as possible," he responded and Jo wanted to kick him. As Stephen pulled the door gently shut behind him Jo caught his whispered 'bye' and hoped he would never come back.

In moments of calm she tried looking at their situation from a different perspective – his. He had a public as well as a private persona and was, by most people's reckoning, an important person – perhaps even a very important person. He was a potential prime minister and the demands on his time from the party and media were constant, she knew all this.

There was an endless round of policy forums, strategy meetings, lobbying opportunities and there would be select committees and prime minister's questions to add to the list and he would have to prepare for them. As a shadow minister he also had to expose the weaknesses and failures in his opposite number's policies and performance, to make him look inadequate and incompetent because largely through that man's destruction could he construct his own edifice. A failure to do so and the prize he so coveted may well be handed to someone else. Perhaps he felt it was important to show the electorate that he could still function even when under such demanding personal pressure.

Jo added to the list even more demands that she knew Stephen faced and was unconvinced by any of them. She knew that had she been in Stephen's position she would have still acted as she was doing now because there was nothing more important in the entire world. Stephen's reasons for his absence were not reasons at all but excuses.

She knew that had he withdrawn from public life until their son's fate was determined, people would have forgiven him – even loved him for it. The reason he didn't was that politics had become his life and it was this that defined him, not his family. They were simply one of the required accoutrements.

Jo had unique access to the private Stephen and knew that the impression he created in public was a sham and that he was shallow, insensitive, crass, uncaring and thick skinned. He was a man with a sensitivity by-pass. She found herself spitting out a word that she had never before used in her life and would have recoiled in shock had she heard anyone else use it:

"The man's a cunt!"

The saying of it was extremely satisfying and she felt her bitterness beginning to drain away the moment it was said. In a quiet, small voice, almost with a purr of satisfaction, she repeated: "The man's a complete cunt," and then smiled to herself at her audacity.

Jo then tried to look at herself from Stephen's perspective and found a string of misogynistic stereotypes leaping into her mind – hysterical, over-wrought, depressive, intense, over protective... She accepted that all of them might have a little currency but rejected them as a valid assessment of who she really was. That was not the real her, merely the person a small part of her had become as she battled to maintain a life and a position that she no longer wanted. She was convinced that once she walked away from them – stepped back into the shadows as she saw it – these less attractive additions to her character would simply melt away.

One evening, just when she was beginning to feel that she had perhaps been too hard on Stephen, she watched him in a Newsnight interview and listened intently as the presenter rounded it off by asking about Danny. Stephen's whole persona changed from the confident, bombastic politician into someone entirely different. His shoulders seemed to crumple slightly, his eyes cast down towards the floor and his voice became small and intimate. He looked fragile. It was a Stephen Jo had never seen before.

He talked intimately of fear and dread, of panic and despair – feelings he had never expressed to Jo. He then warmed to his subject with a touching exploration of the father and son relationship, days out by the lake sailing a boat and a sad little smile tweaked at the corner of his mouth. For the first time since Danny's injury Jo felt the glimmerings of warmth towards her husband that had been long absent. And then she watched as the wistful, introspective smile stayed in place just a little too long.

Jo screamed at the TV: "You bastard, how dare you use our son like that – you bloody bastard."

She paused in disbelief and a small, tired voice interrupted the silence: "I'm thirsty, mum."

Chapter Eight

Within a week of Dannys regaining consciousness they returned home and life assumed something resembling normality but Jo knew that, for her, it could never be the same as it once was. The trauma she had lived through with Danny had shone a searching light into all the little recesses of her life and she now knew what was vitally important to her, what was routine and what was dross. There was, it seemed, an awful lot of dross and very little that was truly important.

Having had what felt like an epiphany, the dreams began. They were surreptitious at first – indistinct and impossible to understand as they had no subject, no comprehensible words, no people and certainly no monsters. There was no running through treacle or vertiginous falling and no transformation of friends into foes in that ultimate betrayal that is worse than monsters. They were little more than a feeling created by sounds.

The sounds were distant but indecipherable and Jo was certain they were voices but no matter how hard she strained to hear them, they never took on the form of words and remained like a night breeze sighing through unseen grass. They were quiet and censorial, like an old crone whispering behind her hand to others in harsh and unforgiving judgement of something she had done or said or thought. It was like walking into a room when conversation dies suddenly and you know it is you who was the subject under discussion.

They did not come every night but would last for a few days before disappearing only to return a few days later. When they did, there seemed to be a heightening in their intensity – an indistinct new sound in the background that was chillingly cruel but had no definition, a more insistent, harder, louder pitch to the tone that was much, much more threatening but which would then die away to the same background level of unrelenting admonishment.

She would detect something that might have been a laugh but colder than any laugh she had ever heard; a scream perhaps, a plea for mercy, a sense of hopelessness in audible form, the impotent dread that a torture victim might feel before the interrogation or the terrifying disbelief of stepping on to the gallows. She felt the inconsolable grief of a mother newly bereaved of her beloved child.

Invariably Jo awoke at some point and lay in bed more afraid than she had ever been from any childhood nightmare. There was an overpowering feeling that she was at fault and had brought this censure on herself by being guilty of something profoundly unsavoury and shameful. This was a jury sitting in judgement on her but she was not allowed to see the charge sheet or hear the evidence.

The disturbing truth was that she knew she was both victim and perpetrator, witness and jury, prosecutor and defender and judge. Jo never doubted that she was entirely responsible for what was happening and the awful question was whether she had done anything, any things, that were deserving of it. At night that thought terrified her; during daylight hours she was able to dismiss it as catholic guilt.

Of course she tried to rationalise the dreams, putting them down to the trauma of thinking she might lose her son but that was only partially successful. The fact remained that her mind appeared to be disturbed and was exhibiting it through the medium of dreams.

That was as far as her analysis went because there was nothing in her life that she was aware of that had the power to produce such disproportionate distress. When one morning, after she had just woken, during the first few minutes of the day as she lay in her bed with the sun rising outside, the dreams returned. There was no mistaking that she was awake – not drowsing but fully awake and it was then she knew she had every reason to be concerned.

Jo tried to occupy herself with the daily routine of being a mother but increasingly she neglected her role as wife almost as though she was preparing the groundwork for being single. When that preparation would be complete and she could walk away from her marriage she still did not know. She was, however, aware that she was not ready yet, not strong enough, not mentally equipped and that admission added further to her troubles and stung her deeply – she was weak.

The confidence and certainty she had felt before Danny's accident had transformed into fear and dread. There was just too much uncertainty in her life for her to take such a dramatic step at this moment even though there was no doubt in her mind that she would still do it. She felt certain that the two situations were linked – her decision to leave Stephen and her dreams – and there was some slight satisfaction in that because there was a cause and effect she could comprehend. The effect might be utterly disproportionate to the cause but there was nevertheless some kind of clarity lurking within her confusion. If that's all it was, it could have been a lot worse.

Often without fully realising it she found herself making her way to the riding school where Angus, the horse that had kicked Danny, was stabled. She would make her way over to his stable where his head peered out from over the half door, eyes hooded as though drowsing, head still except for the occasional flick of an ear and exuding an overwhelming impression of boredom.

She found herself talking to him as if he was a small child: "You been a naughty boy, Angus?" "It's not polite to kick people you know!" Jo felt no anger towards the pony and apportioned no blame but never invited Danny on these visits because there was a fear that together, he and the pony together, would reawaken the fear she had endured for four long weeks and which she was still trying hard to expunge.

After a couple of visits there was no longer any admonishment and she would often stand there in silence, scratching behind his ears, occasionally murmuring meaningless little phrases: "Who's a good boy, then?" "Oooh, you like that, don't you?" She had begun to bring him digestive biscuits and the moment she arrived at the stable he would push her forcibly with his muzzle, demanding his treat.

Eventually she found herself looking him in the eye, staring deeply as though by so doing she would see through into some inner being; an inner being that would provide her with answers as to why he had done what he had. She knew it was ludicrous and that he was just a horse who had done what innumerable horses have done but nevertheless there was an indistinct feeling that somewhere, somehow, there was something to be learned.

She spoke to a stable girl: "Is he all right?"

"Oh yeah, as good as gold."

"Is he being ridden?"

"No, not since…" Her voice tailed away.

Jo gave her arm a squeeze and went back to her car.

It was a couple of weeks before she returned to the stables and was looking forward to seeing grumpy old Angus. As she crossed the yard Jo could see that the half door was shut as usual but there was no head protruding through the open top half until she got close and then, with a sudden movement, a little wild-eyed head shot out. It wasn't Angus but a tiny Palomino who had to stretch to get her neck to rest on the top of the door.

Jo turned to a stable girl who was sweeping the yard: "Where's Angus?" There was a momentary hesitation before the girl replied: "I'm afraid he's been put down."

"What?" yelled Jo, almost in a scream. "He can't have been!"

The girl looked terrified: "We started working him to see how he was and get him fit and listening again and he seemed fine but the first customer who rode him got kicked – she used the whip once and he did it again." The last phrase was shouted as though this final justification was beyond argument. "They just couldn't risk keeping him or even selling him…"

Jo paused and tried to understand her own feelings but did not even enquire about the rider. As if scolding her, the stable hand continued.

"It was a girl – but she's okay. Had two big blackberry bruises on her backside. Lucky he caught her there."

Jo's attitude changed and she small-talked with the stable hand: "Thank goodness she was okay." "There must have been something wrong with him." "When was it?" But she was aware of feeling an irrational sense of loss far over and above the normal feelings for a dead horse or pony, particularly one with which she had had no great contact and which had caused her such fear and anguish.

The remainder of the conversation passed in a blur and Jo left the stables as quickly as she could, leaving her car behind and walking rapidly down the lane towards the rear entrance to St George's Hill. She felt an overpowering need to be active, moving and by so doing, perhaps feeling back in control of a situation which had run away from her.

The long, winding road through the wooded, privileged acres, passed the lake before skirting alongside a golf course. As she passed the lake Jo saw the little ducks who were always in residence – a mixture of Mallards and white ducks which, she presumed, must at one time have once been pets in a nearby garden. The ducks certainly drew no distinctions and flocked together, harried and chased each other and attempted to mate with no concern as to colour or background.

It had been a while but Jo once frequently brought Danny here to feed the ducks and there had been white birds amongst the glorious, glistening, green-headed males and dowdy brown female Mallards as long as she could remember.

Whether through recognition or simply because many people who passed this way fed them, the ducks made a bee-line for her, heads angled forward, feet working frantically beneath the almost mirror-like surface, each leaving the 'V' of an ever-expanding wake behind them.

They squawked and quacked in anticipation as they arrived at the shore, the more adventurous amongst them waddling up the bank to be first in line.

"Sorry, chaps," Jo said with real regret, "I haven't got anything for you!"

And then she remembered the packet of digestives that had

been destined for Angus, delved into her bag and retrieved them with glee. Then came the responsibility of seeing that no duck was left out of the offering, even hurling little pieces far beyond the furthest in an attempt to reach the little black moor hens who were skirting around the fringes in hope of a titbit but not prepared to confront their more aggressive cousins.

Jo found huge delight in the beauty of all these little creatures: their gleaming feathers bejewelled with the sparkle of water droplets, their sharp, black eyes and orange beaks and feet and their absolute affinity with the water that was their home.

All biscuits dispensed, Jo continued through the wooded estate but now calm and at ease with herself and life. It had been the simplest therapy imaginable but it had worked wonderfully.

She exited through the imposing wrought iron gates into a residential part of the town and made her way to the High Street. She was sad that Angus had gone but her feelings towards his loss were now what she would describe as normal.

Being Saturday, the pavements were crowded with unhurried people and Jo found herself perusing a butcher's window, decided to buy a chicken and went in. A busy little Italian woman was inspecting a piece of meat:

"How much you want for this?" she said, pointing to a piece of beef topside in the front of the cabinet.

"It's £8.40," replied the young butcher in a way that Jo saw as offhand, dismissive.

"No, no, that much too much. I give you £4!"

"Sorry, madam, it's £8.40."

"Robbery. It only worth £5. I give you £5."

"It's a fixed price, madam. £8.40 and I couldn't discount it even if I wanted to, I'm not the manager."

The little woman's voice was becoming more and more insistent: "I make you my last offer – £6. That it – not a penny more!"

The butcher turned away to serve Jo and the woman shouted at him: "Okay, okay, I pay but it not worth it!" She paid her money bad temperedly, grabbed the now wrapped meat and hurried out of the shop.

The young butcher looked at Jo and raised his eyebrows: "I wouldn't mind but she does it every Saturday!"

Jo laughed and the world suddenly felt normal.

She strolled down the High Street with no particular purpose in mind, feeling light and airy – and free. She passed a pavement stall made from pasting tables and covered in posters and leaflets but barely registered it. From behind her she faintly heard a word muttered just loud enough to reach her ears and which sounded like "scum". Jo thought nothing of it but the same female voice came again and this time it was clear, distinct and spat out with venom. "SCUM!!"

Against all her instincts, Jo turned to see who was the target of the spite and found herself looking into the eyes of a terrifyingly aggressive young woman of probably no more than twenty with piercings and tattoos, matted dreadlocks, baggy trousers and boots. The word that immediately came into her mind was 'unsavoury' and, confusingly, she knew the insults were aimed at her but had no idea why.

For a politician's wife, the golden rules to avoid confrontation were simple and she had been well drilled in them – keep moving, don't make eye contact, do not respond, remain silent and if possible place someone between you and the 'nutter'. She had already broken two of the rules and then immediately broke the third when, from nowhere, words formed by outrage and injustice demanded a reply: "Why me? What have I done?"

It was never going to be an intellectual debate. "Horse murderer!" screamed the woman. "Bloody horse murderer!"

Jo felt as though she had been punched in the stomach and for a moment her mouth opened and closed but no words came out – until the anger interceded and she felt herself colouring with indignation.

"You stupid bloody woman." She almost inwardly groaned as she heard the words echoing down the High Street but continued anyway: "I would never have put that pony down, he was incredibly important to me. I loved that pony!"

Her final statement almost shocked Jo and she wasn't sure whether she was revealing a previously unacknowledged truth or whether she was simply iron-cladding her riposte.

Her heart sank at the realisation that dozens of shoppers were staring at her and knew she had to get away. As she was about to turn and continue up the High Street, her heart pounding and her head in turmoil, another woman appeared from behind the stall and approached her but with a demeanour that oozed conciliation.

If the crusty woman was from Mars, this woman was from Jupiter. Her shoulder-length hair was a cascade of shiny, blonded, clean waves and curls; her face was beautiful with wide-set blue eyes and full lips and discreetly applied makeup; her long skirt and top were classy but at this moment the most important thing about her was her concern. She took Jo by the arm and ushered her into a shop doorway.

"I'm really sorry about that…"

Jo wasn't ready to capitulate just yet:

"I had absolutely nothing to do with that pony's death. Good god, I spent a month with my child unconscious, thinking he might die, the last thing I wanted was more death."

"I don't doubt you for a minute," replied the woman in a soft, intimate voice, "and I apologise for that onslaught, it was spiteful after what you've been through." The woman shot her a brief smile and Jo realised that whoever this woman was, she knew precisely who Jo was and therefore her connections and as a result she could feel her guard rising.

"Apparently that's mild for her," added the woman, gesturing with a backwards toss of her head towards the tattooed accuser who was still eyeing them like a vengeful pit bull terrier straining at the leash. Three or four other people of mixed ages who were tending the stall were also staring in their direction. "The story has got round that you wanted the pony…" Her voice tailed off. "You know, because of what happened to your son. I only heard about it today."

"So what the hell's it got to do with her?" Again Jo realised she was being drawn in and regretted it. She knew she should have just shrugged, said okay and gone on her way.

"All these people care deeply about animal cruelty, how we use and abuse animals, treat them as objects, kill them and eat them without a second thought..."

Jo became suddenly conscious of the carrier bags she was holding emblazoned with the words 'Weatherall's – Quality Butchers', and even more conscious of the dead chicken within, felt her hand tightening on the handles and the slight and surreptitious movement that moved the bag partially out of sight behind her right leg.

"We want to end cruelty to animals – that's why we're here talking to people..."

Jo interrupted her: "You too – that's what you do?"

"Yeah, that's my life, that's what I do."

Again Jo cut across her: "But what on Earth has that got to do with someone putting down a pony that couldn't be trusted with children? And I repeat, it had nothing to do with me. In fact, I was so upset when I found out earlier that I've just been wandering around trying to come to terms with it."

"I'm not blaming you but the pony didn't have to be put down, did he?"

"No – no it didn't," Jo answered thoughtfully, considering the question and registering that the woman referred to Angus as 'him' and not as 'it'. The woman continued.

"His life was just as important to him as my life is to me or yours to you, wouldn't you say?"

Again Jo considered the question, really considered it and conceded that it probably was. More than that, she largely believed it. The woman's approach was warm, open and friendly and either naturally or cleverly enfolding and Jo instantly warmed to her.

A group of young people pushed past them in the doorway as they exited from the coffee shop within.

"Please, can I buy you a cup of coffee," asked the woman. Jo hesitated. "Come on, it sounds as though you could do with one." She spoke to Jo as though she was a friend.

Jo declined with a shake of her head and the woman continued to chat away to her almost as if they were old friends. Her voice was low and intimate, her eyes holding Jo's steadily and quite naturally, not like someone who knows they are meant to make eye contact but finds it difficult so fixates on the bridge of your nose. At one point her hand reached out and touched Jo on the arm in an act of intimacy that could have been interpreted as pushy but felt entirely natural. Jo noticed the slight Northern accent and judged, by the hard final 'g' in words ending with 'ing', that she was probably from Manchester or thereabouts.

The woman explained that because of the work they do and their constant exposure to human's inhumanity to other creatures, it was impossible not to become extremely passionate about the appalling cruelty that animals suffer and its ubiquitous nature, often resulting from ignorance and indifference or sheer, commercial exploitation. To some animal lovers, she explained, it was raw and painful and difficult to cope with, their emotions spilling over into frustrated anger. Others learned how to channel the pain and anger into something more positive and rather than pillory, they were determined to bring about change through information and education.

It required no explanation that the female Rottweiler a few feet away was from the former school while she was from the latter. And it was clear that the homily which Jo had just listened to had been polished and practiced over time. It was, nonetheless, utterly rational but left more questions hanging than it answered. What cruelty? Why? By whom? Why wasn't it stopped? What about the police or RSPCA?

The woman finished by saying, "…by the way, my name's Wendy – Wendy Carter."

"Jo Aldous," Jo replied automatically. "Strange bedfellows, you two," said Jo motioning towards the aggressive woman.

"Can't choose your comrades," answered Wendy Carter with a smile. "There's only one qualification for this work – are you prepared to act to save animals?"

They moved out onto the main pavement as another group of people exited from the coffee shop in whose doorway they stood, which took them closer to the stall and its array of literature.

"Want to have a quick look – see what it is I'm prattling on about?"

The way it was phrased, as a self-deprecating invitation, made it almost impossible for Jo to refuse and so she took the remaining few steps to the stall.

"Our main concerns are over farmed animals, the way they're reared and slaughtered and the awful impact this has on the environment and human health," Wendy explained but Jo was only partially listening.

As she cast her eyes over the different leaflets she was surprised to see numerous well-known faces looking back at her – of actors, singers, a model, a politician. Some were even A listers but clearly, they had been convinced enough by the arguments to allow their names to be associated with the organisation. There were a couple who were well known for their involvement with animal welfare but so many others...

There was one printed image to which Jo's eyes kept returning and it was of ducks. It was difficult to work out quite where it was taken but there was a sea of dirty white birds filling the foreground and stretching away into the darkness which framed them on three sides, a darkness from which it was only possible to deduce that this was a building of some description but it was impossible to judge the scale of it, where the boundaries began and ended.

There was little space between the animals, one bird touching another so they appeared to meld into one and it was only in the foreground that the detail of individual birds was clear. They were all dirty and dishevelled across most of their bodies – their heads, necks and backs – while their feathers were frayed and tatty at the extremities. Their undersides were almost black.

In a few cases, raw wounds were clearly visible which bloodied the birds' wings, the bright crimson standing out starkly like neon against the grubby white of their plumage and the enveloping darkness of their surroundings. In the immediate foreground were two corpses which appeared to be in an advanced state of decomposition. Almost featherless and discoloured with patches of bile-coloured green, the only indication that they had once been living creatures was their beaks.

The whole composition disturbed Jo but there was one aspect of it that reached deep inside her and touched a nerve and that was the look on the faces of the ducks. Their eyes appeared blank, unseeing, dazed – as though they were simply going through the motions of living, moving endlessly in choreographed unison around and around their prison in a pointless search for something they knew they would never find.

Jo chided herself, dismissing her feelings as sentimental anthropomorphism and then she realised what it was that had shaken her. It was an image of the ducks she had fed earlier in the day on the lake beneath the trees in the sunshine. The eagerness with which they dashed towards her with their flapping wings and perfect feathers, their glistening, pristine and almost dazzling whiteness, pierced by little black and beady eyes full of anticipation and expectation. The contrast was stark and depressing.

"Where was that taken?" asked Jo. "Abroad?"

"Norfolk," replied Wendy. "It was taken inside a shed of one of the biggest duck producers in Europe. There's another ten sheds on that site, each holding about fifteen-thousand birds."

"Is it genuine?"

Wendy laughed. "I can assure you it's genuine. I took the footage myself undercover – had to smuggle the tape out in my knickers."

Jo looked closely at Wendy and didn't even try to hide her disbelief. The whole thing seemed so incongruous. She looked back at the picture and was confused by the contradiction between this shocking image and Wendy's laughter – laughing at something she obviously hated.

"Why are they kept like that? What's the difference between them and ordinary ducks – the ducks we eat?" "They are the ordinary ducks that people eat and they're kept like that because it's cheap. Pile 'em high, sell 'em cheap. That's factory farming." Wendy put an emphasis on 'ordinary' and it registered with Jo that her own use of the word 'we' wasn't repeated by Wendy, instead it was substituted by 'people'. People ate ducks but that number clearly did not include Wendy Carter.

Taking Jo by the arm, Wendy pointed across the road.

"See that supermarket? Every single duck on sale in there comes from sheds like this one – just about every duck in every supermarket, Chinese restaurant and butchers in the country – in most of the world – is reared like that. Aquatic animals that have evolved to live, play, feed and even have sex on water, never see a drop except the stuff they drink from little metal tubes. That's how they produce ducks these days."

Had almost anyone else claimed this, Jo would not have believed them but again there was something about Wendy's directness – her sincerity – that demolished objections before they were even articulated.

It was a skill that some had and others didn't and it reminded Jo of how inexplicable it was that with some people she would debate and never argue whilst with others, after just a sentence or two, she would feel the anger rising inside her and hear a hard edge creep into her voice whilst her words became more confrontational. Wendy Carter did not elicit that kind of response.

"Really?" was all Jo could think to reply.

Wendy gathered together some leaflets and booklets, put them into a paper carrier and handed them to Jo.

"It can be a lot to take in so have a read through some of these if you're interested. Even better…" Wendy picked up a small piece of paper and handed it to Jo. It was an invitation. "I'm giving a talk tonight at Weybridge Hall and you're invited! That's one reason why I'm here today – drumming up business." The smile was again winning.

"Please come if you can. And if you have a chance to look at any of that stuff and you've got any questions, feel free to ask me tonight or give me a ring whenever you like." The invitation was followed by a card – Wendy Carter, Founder & Director, Action for Animals.

Jo thanked her in an uncommitted way, turned and walked away, butcher's bag in one hand, anti-butcher's bag in the other. The irony of it did not escape her.

"By the way…" she heard Wendy's voice behind her and turned. "It's just as bad for chickens!"

Wendy's face broke into a huge smile and Jo could not prevent herself from responding similarly despite the fact that a ludicrous sense of guilt washed over her and she could feel herself blushing.

She quickly turned away from Wendy and found her pace increasing, the sooner to put distance between them.

At home, Jo tossed the bag of literature on to the kitchen worktop and placed the chicken, still in its plastic carrier bag, in the fridge and then spent the next few minutes wondering why she had done that and not unpacked the bird and placed it on a plate as she would normally have done.

As Jo busied herself making tea and cutting a sandwich she switched the radio on to hear the familiar sound of The Archers theme tune – La de dah de dah de dah – la de dah de dah dah and smiled unconsciously. She had sung along to it so many times and could never hear it without thinking of Danny as a toddler. At the first bar he would break into a dance – the first music he had ever properly responded to. He would sometimes specifically ask for it by saying 'lah de dah' and couldn't understand why Jo was unable to produce it on demand at the touch of a button.

Barwick Green it was called and Jo had no idea why she knew that. She suspected she was probably one of only a handful of people in the entire UK who did know it. Now, if it was the final question on Who Wants to be a Millionaire...

Neil was currently worried about something to do with his daughter and his pigs although they were not the same worries. David and Ruth Archer sounded as though they were about to enter into a suicide pact as Andrew the vet informed them that one of their dairy cows was a TB reactor. Despite being the epicentre of the Midlands, few of the characters had accents apart, of course, for Ruth. Her misplaced, sanitised Geordie tones had made Jo want to scream a decade ago and yet here they were, as strong and unrelenting as ever. She would have better been able to bear it if it had been a proper, powerful Geordie accent – 'Wy aye' and all that.

But there was something wonderfully reassuring about this more than fifty-year-old, twice-repeated, daily story of country folk which was a world removed from the images she had seen earlier in the day. The Archers was the real Britain and she was not to have her comfort zone invaded by a zealous animal rights nut case, no matter how charming she appeared to be.

Jo's eyes flicked towards the paper carrier bag of literature and then ignored it. Or at least tried to.

Jo Aldous heard the phone ring, half lowered herself off the kitchen stool and then stopped. As the answer machine clicked on and Stephen's distorted voice filled the kitchen, she slipped back on to the stool and listened with apparent disinterest. He sounded jubilant and the words were fired out like victory rockets.

"I did it, Jo. I did it! Charlie's going next week and their backing me for leader. We did it, darling."

Jo thought to herself that the correction from 'I' to 'we' was a gesture only but then, she didn't deserve to be included in the celebrations as she had played little part in the strategy that had produced the success.

Stephen made his apologies for not being able to come home but at no point did Jo feel inclined to pick up the receiver and share the news with him.

As soon as the phone went dead, Jo felt spiteful, mean and churlish for not having at least congratulated Stephen on what was without doubt momentous news. He was almost certainly going to be the next prime minister. It was no less momentous for having been anticipated for so long.

Just as it is almost impossible not to smile when someone else smiles, or yawn when a total stranger yawns, Jo did feel a momentary sense of elation in response to Stephen's joy but it was flitting and short lived. The most powerful emotion was one of near despair. It wasn't Stephen's jollity she had heard but barred metal gates slamming and echoing on her plans, shutters clattering as they descended, obliterating the light which had so recently begun to shine into her life, illuminating the way forward. No matter how difficult the decision to leave Stephen had been before that phone call, she knew it had now been multiplied several fold.

Her first impulse was to reach for a glass of wine in the hope that life and the decisions she had to take would all appear much simpler. She thought to herself that she was going to need to be strong and she had better start exercising that strength right now. It was a decision that lasted half an hour – long enough to pick up the phone and cancel dinner and to glance through some of the literature that Wendy Carter had given her. It did little to improve her mood but at least it excited her curiosity and gave her something else to think about.

Chapter Nine

Stephen Aldous tried once more to reach Jo on his mobile but failed and in frustration left a message. He had wanted to talk to her in person because he could hardly contain the excitement which surged through him and was desperate to share his news. Anyone observing Stephen would have had no idea that he was even the slightest bit excited as he had learned over the years that it was politically expedient not to reveal inner feelings because someone always registered it and this gave them a little knowledge about you and knowledge is power. Each unguarded exhibition of emotion gave them a little more power and eventually, in the right hands, it had the ability to rebound and possibly be used against you.

Being a politician was akin to being a poker player – you could smile and laugh or scowl and glower as much as you chose but not genuinely so. You could look worried or perplexed, confused or disturbed so long as none of these exhibitions of emotion was real. Each had to be a conscious product of control so that in the end, almost every emotion was equally carefully stage managed with a constant, conscious eye on how you appeared to the outside world.

Stephen remembered one old cynic once telling him that if he ever wrote an adulterous love letter he should always reread it out loud before posting it, imagining he was a prosecuting lawyer and was reading the letter to a jury in a crowded courtroom. He guaranteed a rewrite would follow. Stephen had essentially been rewriting even as he spoke for years now.

If challenged, he would have acknowledged that it was an extraordinary way to live life, where nothing was as it seemed.

He had even found himself stage managing grief when he was almost crippled by the genuine article.

He had attended the funeral of his first political benefactor – an old and courteous gentle man of the shires who had held three of the four great offices of state – home secretary, chancellor of the exchequer and foreign secretary. The top prize – prime minister – had eluded him however, probably because he was too nice. Stephen genuinely loved the man and as he walked along behind the cortege all he wanted to do was cry. Instead, he was conscious of how he held himself, the angle of his head, the expression on his face, what he did with his arms and just how much he allowed his shoulders to slump.

It was not good enough simply to feel grief, it had to be communicated so that no one could be in doubt as to its depth and effects and no matter how profound, there had to be a visual reassurance that you were, after all, in control. As with all things in political life, it was essential to stay in command.

Public speaking had similar constraints. Even when fired and angry or concerned and caring – particularly when there was genuine feeling involved – you never spoke from the heart. Each sentence was slowly-delivered with careful construction, where the pace of delivery allowed each word to be selected with precision before it was slotted into place. The whole sentence was a fabrication in its truest sense, an interweaving of warp and weft to create a veil that allowed a glimpse of the emotion beneath but offered no battle colours around which anyone could rally and provided no hostages to fortune. It was a delicate tip toeing through different interest groups, any one of which it might one day be necessary to call upon for favours. It was a careful balance – providing them with enough meat on which to temporarily feast but without sating themselves and without littering your future with embarrassing promises and without contradicting past statements or claims.

'Oh what a tangled web we weave, When first we practice to deceive!' Stephen would have eagerly agreed with Sir Walter Scott, if he had ever read any of his works.

It was a game and all the players were aware of the rules and mostly abided by them, if only for their own survival. Stephen reckoned he could tell a practicing politician simply by his or her speaking voice, even when ordering turf for the garden or discussing a golfing fixture.

He was fully conscious of the fact that after two decades in professional politics he had become a chimera of an ordinary man but had no regrets about that and held no envy for anyone outside his immediate political sphere and never questioned the choices he had made. There was no introspection over his chosen path and no concerns about the man he had become. Truth was, he was inordinately proud of his achievement – of hailing from a minor public school yet rising through the ranks of hundreds of politicians to stand on the brink of the ultimate goal.

He had started with a good hand, of course – charm, looks and likeability and had worked hard at the rest. He didn't anguish over policy too much, firmly believing that it was often more important to be decisive than right. Weakness, vacillation and failing to make decisions could be far more destabilising than making the wrong decision instantly.

There were, of course, those who marked out their career by being exceptions to the political rule. Some were passionate and driven politicians who believed they had a purpose in life or a specific constituency which they must faithfully represent. They all knew the price they would have to pay for this rebellion – sacrificing all hope of preferment, no promotion, no power, no chairmanship of select committees, no access to the top table and not a great deal of hope of being selected by the Speaker at question time. It was a lonely furrow these people ploughed and in the end they got nowhere, nor did their constituents.

They even marred their chances of lucrative directorships and consultancies as no company wanted a Don Quixote on the board. The handsome retainers paid had little to do with an MP's integrity and intelligence and far more to do with an ability to open parliamentary doors, tap into influential networks, knowing the right ears into which to whisper and having favours to call in. They were all about influence.

Of course conformity was not accidental, it was how the Palace of Westminster operated and how it got things done. There were, of course, a few working-class bullies and their hatred of those who represented centuries of tradition. But they were simply and effectively ostracised. Even some members with the correct background could be similarly shunned – the mentally challenged and flailing aristocrats, myopically pursuing their own bizarre agendas.

The rules of parliament were no different to those of the military, top rugby clubs or the public school system from which this consciousness emanated. Play up, play up and play the game, know your place and, just as importantly, know when to strike and do so without sentimentality or emotion.

This unity of purpose was essential for success and it was quite extraordinary how even the rebels, who entered parliament spitting nails and scornfully demanding root and branch change, mostly deflated like punctured balloons after a few years. It was quite remarkable how seductive the Establishment was but it was this that had made Britain great and Stephen had always been eager to sign up to it. Despite the proliferation of regional accents in parliament and changed values elsewhere in society, the power structure was pretty much as it had always been and would remain that way for just a little longer.

All these old values, Stephen knew, did not appear to sit comfortably alongside Facebook and Twitter. And yet… Let the peasantry, so to speak, amuse itself with time-consuming toys because despite total suffrage there were now more Old Etonians in the shadow cabinet that at any time since the war.

The Labour party had impaled itself on its own blunt and rusty sword by jettisoning its socialist values and pretending to be diluted conservatives. If the polls and recent by-election results were to be believed, the country had decided it preferred the real thing to a bunch of turncoats.

The decision to emulate the Tories had emasculated Labour to such a degree that the party's image represented a limp and tattered flag drooping from a shattered flag staff, the holes and tears a result of friendly fire and not that of the opposition. It was now incapable of rallying even its own kind and the future belonged to the Conservatives and, although he could barely breathe the words, to him, Stephen Aldous.

*

For the last two days he had been cloistered in a policy forum with the Shadow Cabinet at a country house hotel in the Midlands and it was due to end today – Saturday. He would then return home and he and Jo would go to dinner with an old friend and useful political ally. As breakfast finished, however, all that had changed. Stephen was conspiratorially called to one side on the terrace and was told by the party chairman, Charlie Whiston, almost in hushed tones, of new developments.

"I'm afraid Archie's not well."

"Nothing serious I hope," replied Stephen with mock concern for Archie McKinnon, the party leader.

"It's the big C – prostate cancer. Of course he says that it's been caught early and there's every chance that surgery will remove it entirely and he'll be fighting fit in time for any election. He might be right, of course and having someone challenging for the Premiership who can't get a stiffy is probably a damn' good thing for our party considering some of the sexual peccadillos that've bedevilled us in the past. Not sure about the incontinence, though!"

Stephen tutted and clucked in all the right places.

"However, he's been persuaded that even if he does beat it, concern over a recurrence is like handing a weapon to the other side which they will use remorselessly. Not easy to tell him that it's also a reminder to the whole country that he isn't a young man. Known as the old man's disease, you know."

Stephen could feel his breath becoming shallower and shallower because he knew what was coming next – or at least he hoped he did. Many in the parliamentary party did not want Archie to lead them into the next election and this lack of confidence had developed a head of steam which could no longer be ignored. Almost everyone was beginning to feel that a challenge to his leadership was inevitable – and sooner rather than later. It was certainly the view of the Grandees – the king makers – and they had not been slow in taking Stephen into their confidence, not just to keep him in the loop but because they had earmarked him as the putative challenger.

They would, of course, put up a stalking horse against Archie; someone with no prospect of being elected so that the blood was on his sword. Others would then join the fray and Stephen would bide his time before declaring himself a candidate – the loyal candidate who had no option but to stand in order to unite the party. It was a cover and everyone knew that but importantly, it was within the accepted rules. Of course, they had never said it as such but the signals had twinkled as brightly as the flashing lights at a seaside funfair.

Now here he was, poor old, unwitting Archie, rendering the subterfuge superfluous and handing them his career in a kidney dish along with his eviscerated prostate. Stephen would be saved from the potentially poisoned chalice of participating in the challenge of a sitting leader.

Was he still the chosen one? If he wasn't, he did not know what his reaction would be but felt sure he would lose all interest in continuing in politics. The City would beckon but it was the last thing he wanted, despite the not inconsiderable rewards he could expect. He wanted to be king!

"Anyway, the outcome is that Archie will announce next week that he is standing down and the battle will be on, Stephen, the battle will be on…"

Spit it out, you stupid old dodderer, Stephen thought to himself. Are you backing me or not? He looked intently at Charlie and saw those gimlet-like eyes and immediately erased the word 'dodderer'. He knew the man better than that. He was a ruthless operator who disguised it beneath a cloak of diffidence.

"…and, of course, you know what that means Stephen?"

This time Charlie stared intently at Stephen, an almost sombre look on his face, a negative look of rejection it seemed.

The old so-and-so's playing games, thought Stephen. Say it, say it, say it. His breathing was now almost entirely suspended.

Charlie's face broke into a broad grin and he shot out his hand to shake Stephen's: "Congratulations, old boy, I know you will do us proud and be the next Conservative prime minister."

"Thank you Charlie, thank you very much indeed," said Stephen, pumping Charlie's hand as though bringing up water from a hundred feet below. He had rehearsed his response over and over again for just this moment but it failed him. "I won't let you down," he heard himself saying but was happy enough with that.

"There's a long way to go yet, though," continued Charlie, "and there will be at least three other challengers, perhaps more. But you've got the best people behind you and I know you've already done some sterling work around the constituencies to get them on board. We're all confident that we've made the right choice and that you're the man for the job. Josephine's going to have a big role to play – but of course you know that. Wives are so important. But she's up to the task, isn't she?"

It was a rhetorical question but Stephen heard himself muttering something about, "Of course, all the way." But Charlie's words drove a thin sliver of fear into his guts which he quickly tried to dismiss. He was on the brink of the greatest prize in British politics and of course Jo would support him, of course she would. Wouldn't she?

"Cancel your arrangements for the rest of the weekend, Stephen, this has now become a strategy meeting and there's a lot of work to do."

Chapter Ten

Jo called a taxi and had it take her back to the stables where she had left her car. From the car park she could just see the stable that Angus had once inhabited and her heart sank on seeing it and a void opened up in the pit of her stomach which momentarily seemed to suck all her breath into it. She was almost resentful of the little Palomino, stretching its neck above the door in curiosity, as it seemed all wrong for it to be there, like a piece of a jigsaw in the wrong slot.

The indescribable yet unmistakeable warning that preceded her waking dreams tingled inside her, distant but nevertheless present – and it was gone as quickly as it came. Her dreams still came and went and were mostly sleeping dreams, sometimes running their course after she had awoken like a recording that had a beginning and an end and could not be interrupted. Sometimes, they worked the other way round, coming to her as she lay in bed preparing to sleep, always preceded by the same sensation, a signal as clear and unmistakable as the dimming of lights before the curtain goes up on a stage play.

She could not sleep until they had ended but always on these occasions they would revisit her in the night. Their frequency, though, had reduced and this gave Jo some reassurance that the whole experience was a passing phenomenon.

Jo had become entirely pragmatic and was no longer disturbed by the fact that she had these dreams. She could rationalise them easily enough but she could not insulate herself from their content. Why was her mind subjecting her to what felt like someone else's concentrated misery and pain and why did it appear to be admonishing her for that suffering?

When she looked beyond her failed marriage, there was nothing else lurking in the recesses of her life that could possibly have caused such misery to others and on such a scale. About the worst thing she could recall was picking on Amanda Donohue and calling her a four-eyed fatty. And for that she had later been mortified and apologised a couple of days later, even giving her a jam doughnut by way of recompense. Not complete absolution, no doubt, but it was contrition of a kind.

A shrink would have a field day, starting with catholic guilt, followed by her sense of betrayal where Stephen was concerned and no doubt ending on her own sexual frustration – they would all find a part in the predictable diagnosis. She had no idea what a shrink would advise but she knew what the priest would say: 'Reassert your faith, Jospehine, support Stephen wholeheartedly and take him back into your bed.' She could hear it now, delivered in intimately hushed tones as though he actually knew what he was talking about. She almost chuckled at the simplicity of life as seen through the eyes of a chaste Irish peasant.

She drove back towards the High Street, intending to pick up an Indian takeaway from the restaurant overlooking the cricket green, and her route naturally took her past Weybridge Hall. She could see briefly from the car window that the doors were open and people in bright red Action for Animals T-shirts were handing out flyers to passers-by. Her interest was aroused but she knew it was pointless looking for a parking place and so cruised on, rounded the bend into the High Street and headed towards Monument Hill. At the triangle opposite the Ship Hotel she saw a parking space and without thinking pulled over.

She strolled back along the High Street, telling herself that she was simply going to have a look and on reaching the hall strolled uncommittedly towards the entrance, in much the same way as she entered a shop when she did not want to be bothered by the sales assistant.

Jo passed through the outer vestibule, where a variety of stalls had been set up around the walls, and entered into the hall itself, wanting to see how many people were inside, as though that fact had any bearing on her eventual decision. She was surprised to see the hall almost entirely full – perhaps 200 people – with others still entering. She found one of the last remaining seats on the back row and sat down trying not to draw attention to herself. She felt certain that no one had recognised her and was grateful for that.

A tall, greying middle-aged man welcomed people, who not only filled all available seats but were now standing around the walls. Jo was surprised to see that most of them looked perfectly normal, mostly middle class, middle aged and mostly women.

He was clearly the opening act and spoke in a measured yet impassioned way about a campaign the organisation was running from their Polish office to prevent the live export of horses by road from Poland to Italy for meat. Horse meat, it seemed was a passion for some Italians but for preference it had to be fresh, not frozen or even chilled. Poland's huge rural economy was largely undeveloped and on many farms it was still horses that pulled the carts and ploughs. By breeding an extra horse here and there and retiring others too old to work, the country had a surplus of animals which farmers were keen to sell to the Italians at highly inflated prices – although still cheap by Italian standards.

He claimed that overcrowded transporters could be on the road for three days without stopping to rest the horses, feed them or water them. It all sounded fairly shocking but didn't impassion Jo until he showed a short DVD.

Apparently it was a Polish lorry filmed in the Czech Republic en route to Italy and the caption indicated that it was two-thirty in the morning and dark. The camera appeared to be positioned on a low structure somewhat akin to a railway platform, illuminated by a few dingy lights on poles, their shades reflecting the feeble light downwards. Headlights could be seen approaching out of the darkness and materialised into a long, slat-sided lorry which swung around in an arc in front of the platform before reversing up to it. As it reversed it jerked and bumped and a clatter of what could only be hooves could be heard from inside.

The tailgate was dropped down on to the platform to form a ramp and inside the transporter three horses were down, one completely on its side the other two on their knees. They stood with little urging but made no attempt to leave the vehicle until head collars of a fashion, roughly-made from rope, were slipped over their heads and they were led away into the dark, disappearing from view.

Jo had never seen horses quite like this. They appeared utterly defeated, not a trace of resistance left in them, entirely at the bidding of the men who came for them. Their whole demeanour was beyond her experience – horses who had come from hell, or so she thought, and knew that where they were going was even worse and that there was no return. Their fate was sealed and no compassion, pity or empathy could be expected and none would be offered. Jo counted about fourteen of different sizes and types being led away to what she hoped were stables, rest, recuperation if that was possible, and feed and water.

Eventually the lorry was empty yet three of the men still seemed preoccupied with it. The camera moved forward and its little floodlight partially illuminated the space which had just been vacated. It was inches deep in excreta and urine could clearly be seen running down the gap between the floor of the lorry and the tailgate.

In the furthest right hand corner was a particularly big pile of excreta and it was on this that the men concentrated their attention. Bizarrely, one of them began kicking at it viciously as though it had done something specifically to upset him. A second left the interior of the lorry, jumped off the platform and went around to the side where he began thrusting a long stick with great force into the pile through one of the slats adjacent to it. It appeared to be offering resistance as the stick stopped dead with each thrust rather than sliding effortlessly into the soft mush.

Jo heard her loud, involuntary inhalation as the pile of excreta suddenly moved and a horse's head wearily raised itself from amongst the filth. The vicious kicking and prodding continued whilst a third man slipped a rope around the creature's head and hauled on it with all his might as though competing in a tug of war competition. Eventually the horse raised itself, its hooves slipping and scrabbling on the sodden, slippery floor. As it did so a cascade of liquid excreta flowed from its body and Jo could see that beneath the shit and piss was a little grey mare.

As she was forced to move towards the tailgate it became clear that she was trembling all over and all the signs of suffering that the other animals had exhibited were accentuated in her. She had clearly been down for a very long time and in the swaying and bucking vehicle she had undoubtedly been trampled, possibly for hours and streaks of blood began to show through the brown mess that was continuing to drip from her, revealing more of her colouring and trampled flesh.

She made her trembling legs move with great difficulty but Jo was transfixed by her face. It was that of a creature who is close to death and the only sensation was pain, the only emotion resignation. She reached the platform and then began down a ramp to ground level and it was there that the inevitable happened and she collapsed, sliding down the ramp and out of camera range.

The voiceover explained that she remained where she fell until 8.30 the next morning, six hours later, when a vet euthanised her. No one was going to foot the expense of calling him out in the middle of the night.

Jo was aware that she had been biting on her knuckles throughout the sickening drama of one little horse's fate filmed months ago. That she was dead and gone lessened the impact not one jot and Jo found that tears were running down her cheeks. As she reached for a tissue from her bag the men in the film reappeared, leading the same horses they had just unloaded back into the transporter, one after another and Jo heard herself whispering: "No, no, no!"

They had not been fed, rested or watered despite their appalling condition and the voiceover claimed that the lorry was trailed and their ordeal continued for another 48 hours. When they eventually reached their destination of Cagliari in Sicily, most had to be dragged from the transporter by chains and a tractor. But they were still alive and therefore suitable for slaughter for human consumption. Very soon after, pieces of their flesh would have been on sale throughout Italy as fresh carne de cavallo.

It was with huge relief to Jo that the imagery ended and the final appeal to support Action for Animals was made so that the trade in Polish horses could be reduced even further. Jo registered that the man making the appeal was himself clearly upset and she wondered how many times he must have seen the footage and understanding perfectly why it still had such a powerful impact on him.

She could see Wendy Carter preparing to take the stage and compared to the horror that had preceded her, the contrast was stark. She stood up in front of the audience, a smile on her face as she introduced herself and within her first few sentences took charge of the hall; her openness, warmth and absolute confidence reaching out and almost caressing those in front of her.

She moved around as she spoke but her eyes never lost contact with her audience, roaming across their faces so that eye contact, no matter how briefly, was made with almost everyone, including them in her talk, making them feel that she was talking directly to them. It was a consummate exercise in public speaking.

In her hand she held a glass of milk and her whole demeanour was that of someone who was in their element and unphased. Jo thought the glass of milk was a bit odd, a bit too cool and waited for her to drink from it but she didn't.

"I'm going to talk to you about the white stuff – milk!" Wendy Carter said, as she held the glass up to the light as a wine connoisseur might and peered up through it before lowering it again and placing it down.

"We all know its natural, pure, that it is healthy, comes from contented animals grazing green pastures and is essential for strong bones, don't we? And, of course, it's a must-have for our children. Well, if we do, we're all wrong!"

Jo felt an immediate surge of resentment at what sounded like an accusation that she had somehow failed Danny by giving him milk to drink – insisting that he drank it. And she could feel similar resentment emanating from some people around her through incoherent mumbles. Her conviction when she came in that she would almost certainly be subjected to some kind of animal rights diatribe was not disappointed and the thought occurred to her that she didn't need to listen. Before it could translate into action by getting up to leave, Wendy Carter continued, heading off any putative rebellion:

"Please believe me when I say that I'm not accusing you of being negligent or bad mothers, not at all. For goodness sake, it's government policy – all governments – to encourage milk drinking and they even provide generous subsidies to farmers to produce the stuff. We have been encouraged for decades to feed our children milk, starting back between the two world wars when people's health was appalling. It did provide nutrients for people whose diets were severely lacking just as recommending them to eat their grannies would have also provided nutrients. But with the benefit of science we now know a great deal more about nutrition and what constitutes healthy and unhealthy food. What I'm saying is that you have been misled – we have all been misled for a variety of reasons but primarily commercial ones.

"Don't get me wrong, I'm not saying that cow's milk is intrinsically unhealthy, it isn't. It's a perfectly healthy food for babies – baby calves! It is brilliantly designed to help a teetering little calf grow into a great hulking animal in twelve months or so. Compare that with the rate of growth of a human infant – very different isn't it? A calf needs fast physical development in order to survive predation and the milk that will provide it is his mother's milk. To a human baby, brain development is the most important factor hence its comparatively slow physical growth. The food which perfectly provides that is her mother's milk. Cow's milk is designed for calves, human milk is designed for human babies and each has evolved to have a different combination of nutrients to achieve these priorities.

"Here's another bizarre little fact. Do you know how many different species of mammals there are?" She didn't wait for a response as she strode backwards and forwards on the dais in front of her audience, a sheaf of paper in one hand but not referring to it. "It's about five-thousand! And do you know how many of them drink milk after weaning? Us – that's all – just us – human beings. We're all big babies really." The chuckles Wendy Carter's words produced from her audience were tinged with embarrassment, it seemed to Jo.

"I say 'we,'" continued Wendy, "but that's a very qualified we as, believe it or not, over seventy per cent of the global population doesn't drink milk at all. Good god, how do they survive? In fact they survive extremely well and in many instances are far healthier than we are. The reason they don't drink cow's milk is partly cultural but also because they have lactose intolerance. Lactose is one of the sugars in milk and babies are born with the ability to produce an enzyme called lactase whose sole purpose is to digest lactose. At weaning, just as nature intended, most people's bodies cease to produce lactase because that's when, throughout evolution, we stopped drinking milk. It's a biological indicator that we're not supposed to drink milk after weaning.

"Lactose intolerance isn't restricted to foreign cultures I can assure you and it affects a significant percentage of people in the UK, too."

Jo couldn't contain herself and shouted out a question, which was delivered more aggressively and louder than she had intended.

"So if it's unnatural for adults to drink milk, why are only some lactose intolerant; why isn't everyone?"

Wendy Carter's eyes immediately fixed on Jo's and her demeanour remained warm and inviting, making Jo regret the tone of her question.

"I will be taking questions at the end," Wendy began, "and so could I ask you all to hold them until then but this question is very pertinent. With continued exposure to cow's milk some people have developed a mutated gene but it is not our natural state and although we may avoid the worst excesses we don't necessarily avoid them all. The classic symptoms are bloating, indigestion and flatulence. Good god, the tele seems to be packed with ads offering a cure for one or the other. Millions of people suffer these symptoms and it's almost certain that many of them are partially lactose intolerant but never show in the official figures and are not even aware of it themselves. Giving up milk would be a lot healthier than constantly taking indigestion tablets or eating bacteria-laced yoghurt – which, of course, also contains milk.

"But there are other problems with dairy milk. We hear a great deal about food allergies and top of the list of foods that cause it is cow's milk. Some of the symptoms are obvious, such as acne, wheezing and reddening of the skin but some are hidden. There is strong evidence to show that the main cause of childhood anaemia is cow's milk allergy. It irritates the intestines to such a degree that they start to bleed – not profusely but very, very small amounts of blood which are excreted from the body and never noticed. It's called occult intestinal bleeding."

Jo listened to this demolition of a national institution with growing incredulity. It was as though someone had told her that the late Queen Mother used to moonlight as a dominatrix in a Victorian brothel. Her overwhelming reaction was why, if all this was true, had she never heard a word about it. Okay, she'd given up full-fat milk long ago but that was logical and had official backing – it made sense. But all these other allegations…?

"Okay, I now want to turn to purity." Wendy again picked up the glass of milk and held it aloft. "This is a half-litre glass and in it are some somatic cells, pus cells to give them their common name – yes pus, the yellow stuff that oozes from sores. How much do you think is in there – how many cells? A few hundred, perhaps a few thousand?" She looked around the audience as though inviting someone to guess but there was no response. "In this glass are up to two hundred million pus cells." There were audible sounds of revulsion from the audience. "Drink a pint-a-pus a day doesn't have quite the same marketing ring, does it? But it's all quite legal – that is the limit allowed by EU regulations.

"So pure it isn't but it's not only the presence of pus that shatters the claim that milk is healthy, it's also the saturated fat, cholesterol and animal protein it contains, all of which are linked to the degenerative diseases such as heart disease, strokes, diabetes, obesity, osteoporosis and so on that kill most people in the West!"

Wendy Carter then embarked on an explanation of just how cow's milk was linked to this wide range of human diseases, occasionally referring to her papers to read directly from one or other of the reports she referred to. It was a potentially complex scientific and medical resume but Jo found that she could follow it easily enough. She wasn't sure if she would remember any of it but the path charted through what could have been an impenetrable morass of science speak was precise and understandable. Wendy Carter ploughed on, taking her audience with her.

"There is one particular study which should have changed pubic policy towards farming and our diet, giving all governments the information on which to recommend a move away from meat and dairy. In practice, it was almost completely ignored. It's called the China study and was an extraordinary collaboration between Oxford University, the Chinese Institute of Preventive Medicine and Cornell University in the US. It amounted to the biggest epidemiological study ever undertaken – the study of real people leading their real, everyday lives.

"I think most people are now aware that saturated animal fat isn't healthy but this study discovered something else, something that is still little talked about. Animal protein is even more damaging to health than saturated fat!"

There was a barely audible reaction of disbelief and Wendy paused for a moment to allow the woman's claim to fully register.

"This is truly a profound discovery because it turns on its head years of accepted nutritional advice. The big problem is that it's not reflected in most other studies for the simple reason that researchers haven't bothered to examine protein, assuming like you that it is vital to our diet."

Jo listened to Wendy's free-flowing delivery, her command of the science, her control of the audience and admired the conviction she so clearly had. There was a lurking envy of someone who had filled their life with such a compelling subject – a cause – that at least provided meaning and form, contours that were comprehensible and a perspective from which so many other aspects of life could be viewed – and would be viewed very differently through this prism of knowledge if it was accurate. Jo began to wonder what she'd done with her time over the last decade or so.

But was it knowledge? Was what Wendy Carter saying true? Was some of it true, was any of it true? She had no idea but clearly the woman believed it to be true. Or was she just a consummate performer, a smiling, polished, beautiful, fragrant con artist who was playing them all like a virtuoso violinist. Was there any difference between this appeal to people's self-interest and the old EST weekends or Scientology, where damaged people were reeled in with psychobabble and signed up before being relieved of their money. Jo's natural reluctance to ride other people's hobbyhorses or to believe simple answers to complex problems sank its claws deep into her consciousness and refused to let go.

But the fact that she was considering closely the claims being made by a woman she had only just met and was making comparisons from her own experience, disturbed her a little and she put it down to the polished professionalism of the delivery rather than the content, which made it all seem so plausible.

The only claim she accepted without hesitation was when Wendy Carter accused politicians of refusing to act on the science even when it was sound. She knew from experience that knowledge and truth were not the lode stones by which politicians navigated. If it was inconvenient, science would be trashed by other, tame, scientists. If it threatened the interests of powerful lobby groups then counter claims would be produced masquerading as science but in reality possessing just a scientific veneer with little depth beneath. It didn't need to be sound for journalists to run splash headlines, reporting it as fact and spreading sufficient doubt to confuse the public.

Jo's own arguments with Stephen over tobacco and smoking confirmed the claim – almost fifty years of prevarication and obfuscation, often driven by bribery, had delayed any meaningful action against tobacco. When she tackled Stephen and asked why it wasn't at the forefront of his party's policies;

why didn't they have a programme to slash the number of people who smoked, he'd simply laughed at her:

"If we persuade all the workers to stop smoking they'll live forever and we'll never be able to afford the pensions." Jo understood Stephen well enough to know that beneath the laughter lay truth. "And besides," he continued, "do you have any idea what the tax take is on tobacco?" Jo also knew that party funds were much healthier as a result of donations from the industry, once made openly but now covertly through a whole bevy of organisations and individuals.

Wendy Carter continued in the same vein: "There are some cancers, and specifically some types of breast cancer, that are directly linked to oestrogen and there is now a growing volume of science linking milk and dairy products to breast cancer. Do you know what the cancer rate is of traditional Chinese women who eat an almost animal-free diet? It's one in ten thousand! For western women it is one in eight! Just play with those figures for a moment. And no, it's not all in the genes because when Chinese women move to the West and adopt our diet, their risk quickly increases to become the same as ours."

Wendy Carter's delivery brooked no doubt, quoting the authorship of various doctors, and Jo found herself listening intently even though she knew that some doctors, or professors for that matter, could be bought as easily as anyone else.

Jo sensed a change in the audience as Wendy Carter captured their interest. Rather than write the woman off, Jo now wanted to corner her, grill her, push her for chapter and verse on her claims. She determined to arrange a meeting with Wendy away from the hall as she wanted her full attention and took Wendy's agreement to that as a given. When you were a politician's wife everyone had time to give you.

Wendy Carter now changed tack: "But at least we know we can rely on milk to produce strong bones for us and our kids. So here's an interesting thought: what happens to the more than two-thirds of the world's people who don't have dairy products? Are their bones all floppy and bendy, are they perpetually being rushed off to hospital with fractures? The truth is that the countries with no culture of dairy consumption, such as Japan and China, have far stronger bones than we do. They get most of their calcium from plant foods.

"Osteoporosis is the classic indicator of bone disease and the countries which drink the most milk and eat the most dairy products have the highest rates of osteoporosis, those who eat the least have the lowest. Doesn't make sense, does it? In fact, the science is divided but much of it shows that animal protein causes our blood to become acidic and the body can't survive like that so it neutralises the acid with the only calcium available to it – our bones. Thank you."

"There's a real irony in all this. We obtain vast amounts of milk from captive animals, make it a central plank in our national diet by selling it as an essential health food and in truth it's the opposite, it destroys our health. The modern dairy industry is so unbelievably cruel that there is almost a poetic justice in it – pay back for what we do to the animals."

At last we've got there, thought Jo. We've had the softening up and now comes the real purpose of the evening, to show us how cruel we are to animals and make us feel guilty about it. Nothing better for winning converts than self-interest aligned with guilt. Jo felt the flicker of a smile – manipulation had that had been worked to perfection by the Roman Catholic Church for centuries.

Suddenly it was over and Jo did not wait for questions but felt the need to get up and move about. She went quickly into the outer vestibule and perused the various stalls before the crowd emerged from the main hall. There were 'cruelty free' cosmetics, 'dairy-free' chocolates and sweets, vegan recipe books and more literature in the form of leaflets, pamphlets, reports and magazines, than you could read in a year.

One of the stalls was playing a video in which very little seemed to be happening. Two men were digging away at the ground on the edge of a forest and the pile of earth beside them seemed to indicate that they had been digging for some time. A voiceover suddenly drowned out the sound of clinking spades and muffled conversation between the two men: "A fox has taken refuge in this disused fox earth to try and escape from the fox hounds. These terrier men placed a terrier down the hole almost two hours ago and he has been attacking the fox underground for most of this time."

With a sudden movement, one of the diggers dropped his spade and with a shout close to jubilation, reached inside the hole and began pulling with all his might at what might have been a piece of rope. It took a while for Jo to realise it was a tail – the bushy tail of a fox. The tug-of-war continued whilst the other man continued to hack away at the entrance to the hole with his spade. Again the voiceover cut in: "They can't remove the fox because the terrier is holding on to her and has wedged itself into the tunnel to prevent her from escaping."

With a scrabble and shouts the fox began to appear from the hole as the man continued to haul on its tail. It was followed by a terrier whose teeth were sunk into the fox's face. The digger grabbed the terrier and tried to prize his jaws apart with shouts of "Leave, leave", but the animal refused to release his hold so the man reached for a heavy stick and hit the dog hard across the muzzle with it and it immediately let go with a yelp of pain.

Like a victor displaying his trophy, the terrier man held the fox aloft by the scruff of her neck with one hand, a huge grin dissecting his ruddy, round, farm-worker's face. With his other hand he pointed to her distended nipples from which milk was dripping and he did so over and over again, laughing each time. There appeared to be great humour in the fact that he was about to kill a nursing vixen.

Jo was barely aware of what was happening because she was frozen, her senses overwhelmed by something which was powerful enough to obliterate time and place and day and identity and obscure all other sounds, all other people. It reached inside her and dragged out her terror and displayed it like the terrier man displayed his fox. As the vixen was held aloft she screamed – a non-stop, endless, unbroken, high-pitched, ear-shattering scream of terror and it was her terror that fuelled Jo's. She felt an arm around her shoulders and was just conscious that whose ever arm it was it had stopped her jerky, uncontrolled, backwards, sightless staggering away from the video, away from the screaming fear of a little animal.

Jo looked at the person who had stopped her retreat and who was signalling to the stall holder with a finger across her throat to cut the sound. It was Wendy.

"It's my dream, it's my dream, that's my dream..." Jo mumbled imploring into Wendy's face just inches from her own. "It's not exactly... it's not just like that because there's more but it's the same thing... it's one of the things." Jo was barely coherent and clutched at Wendy's free arm and suddenly became lucid. "I have terrible dreams and I hear that screaming or something that sounds just like it – I hear the sounds of terrible suffering but I never thought..."

Wendy gently moved her away from the people who were now streaming out of the hall: "I think we could do with a drink. Know a nice pub?"

Chapter Eleven

Al Dwight felt a little surge of excitement as he reviewed the requisition form in front of him on the table in the ward recreation area – a nondescript scrap of paper bearing the name of the hospital at the top and the all-important signature of Peter Dealey at the bottom and written in between were Al's details and the sentence: 'Please release one Longine's watch.' And below it was a second line in the same handwriting: 'One US passport'. Except that it wasn't the same handwriting but looked passably like it.

Al had guarded the handwritten report he had stolen from Dealey's desk as though it was a certificate of his sanity. He had sat with it in front of him in a quiet corner in the recreation area, hour after hour, attempting methodically to copy as closely as he could the small, backwards-sloping script. He wasn't helped by the fact that his own handwriting was forward sloping, large and enthusiastically impatient while Dealey's was mean, controlled and cowed – the writing of someone who would almost certainly keep a woman's passion on hold whilst he carefully folded his trousers and methodically flossed his teeth and would be impatient to wash her dried-on aromas from his hands. A man he felt was so afraid of dying that he was terrified of living – at least that was Al's interpretation of the pinched and ungenerous writing of a person about whom he felt almost nothing positive.

Despite the contempt in which he held Peter Dealey, the man had bested him because no matter how diligently Al practiced he could not produce a single word that looked anything like the original. And then, from some distant conversation with someone unremembered, he recalled the claim that if you wanted to reproduce a signature it was best to turn the original upside down and copy it that way. All the characters then transformed into something other than handwriting and became simply an irregular design which could be reproduced without the inbuilt patterning and programming of your own handwriting exerting itself. Al assumed that if it worked for a signature then it must also work for handwriting. The problem was, he did not have a complete pattern to copy. He had the 'one' but not 'passport' or 'US' in capitals.

With scissors and Pritstick he began to snip away at Dealey's original letter until he had assembled the word 'passport' from individual characters, along with a complete 'one' which he found there. He wasn't concerned about the capitals as there were no others on the simple little form for comparison. Having completed his forgery collage, Al turned it upside down and tried copying the words on to scrap paper but it looked like the creative attempt of an educated spider. Al felt his frustration welling up inside and spat out the words, "Fuck, fuck, fuck!," with venom.

The outburst seemed to trigger something and Al placed the words 'one passport' on the scrap paper and traced over it with a ball point pen, pressing firmly to ensure a strong impression. He then removed the words and filled in the impression beneath them with a pen. It worked perfectly.

With the practice run over, Al knew he was now committed and he could feel his fingers tremble slightly as he placed the words on the requisition form below the line 'One Longine's watch' and began carefully to trace their outline. He then filled in the impression with matching ballpoint. When finished, Al pushed his chair back from the table, balanced on its back legs and reviewed his work. "Yes," he shouted to no one in particular. Passable, he thought. Not brilliant but passable – certainly passable to a ward orderly who had absolutely no interest in the paper at all and to a bored store keeper who had probably never seen a forgery and had certainly never contemplated that anyone would try to deceive him with one.

Should there be any query as to why he needed his passport,

Al could think of several convincing answers but it was a question that was never likely to be asked by disinterested people methodically chugging through the routinism of just another day. The only danger was if a referral was made back to Dealey with some query or other but on balance Al felt that was unlikely. Once he had the passport he could activate the rest of his plan, be away from this stultifying, depressing place, obtain some money from somewhere – although where he wasn't quite sure but there must be someone who still liked him enough to proffer a loan or who owed him a favour – and then up, up and away back to the Big Apple.

Al found an orderly and handed him the requisition slip and a tingle of excitement flickered through his body – something he had not experienced since he had given up shoplifting. Returning to clear up his creative efforts from the table, he smiled ruefully and shook his head almost in embarrassment as he remembered the last time he had 'hoisted' or, as those who were hoisters pronounced it, 'oisted' with their strong London accents.

For Al it had never had anything to do with need and it was not a culture he had been born into nor one whose cloak he had slipped on for kudos or acceptance. In fact he hated the hardened, predatory eyes of those thieves he knew, who constantly watched and calculated, awaiting their opportunity. They traded on other people's joys and sorrows when their attention was elsewhere, waiting until they were at their most distracted and then dispossessing them. They gave not a damn for sentiment, attachment or need and never allowed even a shard of conscience to deter them. It was as though anyone who was thieved from deserved it; that the onus was on them to defend their possessions. They were, Al thought, as vultures gorging themselves on still-living bodies – and acquaintances were as fair game as strangers.

The thought occurred to Al that acquaintances were all that any of them had, with not a genuine friend between them. Even in the supposed neutral territory of the pub, thieving was still in the forefront of their minds. He had seen one hoister pick a fight with an acknowledged hard man, knowing he would take a beating until he called it off. "Okay, okay, I've had enough, you win!" To the victor, the satisfaction of witnessing public humiliation, to the vanquished nothing but a bloodied and bowed loss of face. And yet...!

Clutched out of sight in the loser's hand was an ostentatious, solid gold bracelet which he had grabbed from his opponent's wrist and which was the real purpose of the scuffle. The man assumed, rightly, that the loss would be put down to the bracelet having been sent flying during the fracas.

Al did not rank himself amongst these kinds of people and never boasted of what he had stolen as they did nor did he ever steal from individuals. His thieving was driven solely by excitement, an occasionally-repeated reaffirmation that he was alive and that that most infrequently experienced of all human emotions could be conjured up whenever he felt the need. It was his equivalent of sky diving or motor racing but much more readily accessed. The fact that it was also profitable was not a factor.

Al could not remember the path that had led him from accountancy to second hand car dealing, property speculation and thieving but it had been incremental and with no one conscious decision behind it.

Above all, it had been a game which exerted its siren call as deadly, it transpired, as any mythological ladies perched on rocks. The call to break free, to metaphorically throw his arms back and expand his chest and bellow an alpha male roar overwhelmed his tenuous desire to have a safe profession and a secure income, particularly such a joyless profession as his – and one which he hated.

He had arrived in Surrey with a wife, a company house, a senior position with Pneumatic Products and a two year secondment from the US. He was a company man through and through and was encased in a cocoon of company expectations and acceptable behaviour and had a career which contained no anticipated deviations, its path snaking out in front of him like painted footsteps, disappearing into infinity on some endless dusty pavement. He had hoped that coming to the UK would enable him to break free and become a butterfly, spreading his colourful wings to soar across this strangely small country.

What he discovered was that everything was indeed small – small houses and small roads, small cars and small food portions, all of which he loved. But his job was exactly the same as it was in the US, including the accents around him which were mostly American. The realisation that this was all there was so long as he remained an accountant stultified and frightened him and yet he had never discussed these fears with his wife, Diana. Even when he made the first tentative moves to become a different man, still he said nothing.

Those moves were triggered by his local pub, or at least by the people who inhabited it. They were well-educated if not intelligent, although a few were that as well. On one side of the equation were two High Street accountants who appeared every day within minutes of their offices closing and they sat together, drank Famous Grouse and were as permanent as the painted sign which hung outside declaring that this was the Barley Mow. Eventually they would take their florid faces and slurred speech home to bed only to repeat the performance the next day. Whether there were any Mrs Accountants Al had no idea but if there were, their attraction was eclipsed by the amber glow of a blended Scotch.

On the other side of the equation were the well-spoken wheeler dealers who flitted from one short-term occupation to another. Most could talk assuredly, most had the confidence of a middle class upbringing and there was a club-like atmosphere amongst people who seemed to have known each other for most of their lives. Few of the women in the pub were independent but accompanied one or other of the men, whose partnerships changed with the same regularity as their chosen work.

One week they were small-scale manufacturers of paving slabs, another they were gardeners. A few months later they had seamlessly transformed into painters and decorators before becoming jobbing builders. There was the incredibly deceptive, fast-talking, endlessly-restless, slightly-built man who provided security for rock stars. Known as the bionic man, he was the only genuine, hall-marked, five star psychopath that Al had ever met, a man you crossed at your peril. Despite having a son, he was also gay, although everyone was terrified to acknowledge it, including him. Any reference to it would have ensured a lengthy hospital stay.

There was the public schoolboy who lived in his old Ford Granada; the ex-chemical engineer who was slowly spending his redundancy money on sky diving; the guy who drove what looked like a circus lorry delivering antiques to the Continent; and there was the pornographic photographer who had once been a reportage photographer until the barbarity of some war or other fucked his brain and turned his nose into a dripping cocaine repository. And there was the second-hand car dealing to which most of them turned their hand at some time or other. Only a couple were what Al would call 'professional' dealers.

What amazed Al was that all these people prospered to some degree. They all had cars, ate out at the only expensive local restaurant, never seemed short of enough to gamble on the weekend horse races but most of all they never seemed to worry. When one business or employment collapsed they and whoever they were working with helped out others with their tenuous projects and so new partnerships were forged. It seemed that both women and jobs encircled these idiosyncratic people like contra-rotating merry-go-rounds.

Al looked at the accountants and thought they were joyless, sad and dispiriting and even more disturbingly, he saw the barstool alongside them beckoning to him. He looked at the others, the drop outs and chancers, the feckless and the unqualified and realised they always seemed to be laughing. They didn't anguish over professional qualifications or pensions, or even tax for that matter, and were endlessly relating amusing stories of things which had happened to them.

Nothing happened to Al that raised even a smile or was worth relating to anyone. And that's when temptation began to tug at his well–tailored collar. It did not have to pull very hard as Al had already decided that emptying dustbins was preferable to his current employment.

It had started with buying a couple of cars and selling them at a profit. A few more dubious purchases followed and these too showed a profit. Eventually Al joined the ranks of the dealers he termed professional by buying his own car lot in a prime location. He then reasoned that he could apply the same logic to buying and selling houses.

When he was earning enough no longer to need Pneumatic Products he resigned and laughed when, as he knew they would, they raised the spectre of dispossessing him of his house. He laughed again when he took from his inside pocket three pictures of different houses, all of which were his and all were bigger, grander and more expensive than his company semi.

Throughout it all he sailed on, blithely seeking a dream rather than following one and ignoring the increasingly desperate calls of distress from Diana.

It seemed that with his resignation it was not only his employment that ended but many of the boundaries that defined him and his life. He was like a sailor on shore leave, free at last of the monotony of daily routine; he was his own man and could do and say whatever he pleased; he could set new and more liberal boundaries and eventually almost none at all. It was then that he started occasionally to shop lift, although it was a fairly short-lived period as the contradictions of his new life eventually began to collapse on top of him and he knew it was time to start trying to reassert control.

The last time he had stolen, the time he had decided that it was not a suitable pastime for a grown man, was after he had sold to a local car dealership the small plot of land which was his car lot. He had walked out of their offices with a cheque for £500,000 in his briefcase and felt on such a high that he just had to steal something. He found the only decent shoe shop in town and after a prolonged and purposely confusing pretence of not finding exactly what he wanted, walked out with a pair of Charles Jourdan co-respondents in his shoulder bag nestled snuggly alongside his cheque.

Al was still smiling as he glanced around the dehumanising institutional environment that was now his home but was not really looking at it, his mind exploring happier times elsewhere when such places occupied no part of his consciousness.

He knew the local police reasonably well and when, on one occasion, they attended a shout next door to his sales site, they parked their car alongside his sale models – they also left the keys in it. When they returned, the red and white striped Ford Focus was rotating serenely on a turntable six feet above the ground with its blue lights flashing and a multi-coloured banner across its windscreen declaring, Car of the Week.

Al chuckled when he thought of the rather strange, middle-aged man who visited the site regularly on an old, sit-up-and-beg bike, attired in flat cap, rain coat (whatever the weather), bicycle clips and pop-bottle glasses. Al was convinced he still lived with his mother.

He would stroll up and down the cars, make some asinine enquiries as though he intended to purchase and then always ask to use the toilet. On emerging he would operate a Le Man's start, running alongside his bike until it had reached a respectable speed and then throw his leg over it and pedal away to whence he came. On the occasion Al was thinking of, the man emerged from the toilet, executed his running start and then wobbled around uncontrollably, his feet rotating like windmills as they desperately sought the pedals which were no longer there. Al had removed them.

He did feel just a little guilt when he remembered the old Rolls Royce he had sold to a pompous banker from the City of London. Al had bought it cheaply as, unusually for a Rolls, the paintwork had deteriorated to such a degree that there was no longer a single gleam or glimmer from anywhere on the vehicle, simply a dull and lifeless matt finish. Respraying was an expensive proposition and so Al kept it out of sight until it rained and then, as the raindrops caused it to shimmer and shine – if not quite like new then at least sufficiently to make it appear something like normal – it was placed in a prime place at the front of the lot. As soon as the rain ceased, the Roller was spirited back under cover.

The intention was not entirely to deceive but simply to present the car at its diminished best, gain interest and then agree a deal on the paintwork.

It was on a particularly rainy day that the banker bit and bought. Had it been almost anyone else, Al would have been honest but he disliked the man's arrogance to such a degree that he remained silent. Having bought the car the banker did not drive it away but wanted it delivered to London, paid half the price in cash and agreed to pay the other half on delivery, which presented Al with something of a problem. If he was to escape instant detection he could deliver only on a rainy day but unfortunately, after the sale, Britain entered into a long dry spell, with Al proffering increasingly imaginative excuses as to why he was unable to bring the car to London. He watched the heavens like a sailor and on the first forecast of rain he was up in London waiting for it to start. He returned with the cash in his pocket and a smile on his face.

It was only in retrospect that Al became aware that as his prosperity increased, his personality began to deteriorate. Wealth had never before been his motivation but suddenly it became the measure by which he judged himself and misguidedly, he started to believe that it was also the measure by which others judged him. He became crass, boorish, boastful and intolerant of those who were financially struggling but most importantly failed to notice that the friends he had made since arriving in the UK began to drop by the wayside until he also was left with only acquaintances.

That condition was completed when Diana left him. Her increasingly desperate calls for Al to take a grip on both himself and his life failed to register, simply drifting away like water through sand.

She moved out the same day she told him her decision, blaming him entirely for having sacrificed their love on the altar of macho self-gratification. He well remembered feeling as outraged as he was shocked. He could not understand why, claiming that he had never so much as kissed another woman, which was true. Diana's response was simple: "You just don't understand, do you?" And with that she loaded her already packed bags into her car, turned and said:

"I loved you Al, I loved you totally and you've trampled over it like it was nothing." He thought back now and realised what a crassly stupid, self-obsessed idiot he had been and that she had been right.

"Where are you going," he asked.

"I'm moving in with Matt Williams and no I don't love him but I like him, I find him attractive and he cares about me and after what I've been through with you Al, I'm prepared to settle for that for a while."

"How long has it been going on, for Christ's sake?"

"Long enough. I'll be back to get the rest of my things next week." And with that she was gone.

If Al's life had lacked restraint prior to Diana's departure, the accelerator was pressed to the floor after it. The next day, as dark descended, he took a four-wheel drive off the rank and drove at high speed to Matt Williams' impressive, detached, mock-Tudor house, set back from the road in the best residential quarter of Walton-on-Thames, close to the river. A large and beautifully manicured lawn spread out in front of it like a multi-striped table cloth, a fountain of cherubs spurting water heavenwards made it look like a suburban imitation of a stately home.

Al pulled into the drive before executing a sharp right hand turn on to the lawn where he revved the engine like a formula-one racing car driver, slammed down the accelerator and shot forward, executing an endless series of hand-brake turns, wheelies and vicious braking maneouvres that piled soft earth in front of the tyres in unsightly mounds. As his fury subsided and he finally left what had once been a lawn, Al performed a delicate little side-swipe with his Shogun that sent the cherubs cartwheeling across what looked like a battle field, leaving a spout of water shooting at an acute angle across the devastation to mark where they had once wetly cuddled each other.

Neither the darkness nor Al's rapid departure were ever going to deceive Matt Williams as to who was responsible. While Diana might like the man and thought him attractive, Al knew him to be a tough, even ruthless operator and had no doubts what the bill would be for his angry outburst. It came the next day – a beating by two of Matt's men which left Al just short of needing hospitalisation.

When he was mobile again, Al continued frenetically to buy and sell as though constant work would somehow dull the hurt that Diana's departure had caused; that if he kept busy and didn't think about it then it may not exist. He tried desperately not to think about it because the pain was like slivers of glass sliding into his guts. He loved her, he had always loved her but he knew that he had treated her like she was of no consequence.

On the few occasions when he allowed quiet reflection, usually after a couple of drinks, he knew he had nothing to blame her for, that she had laboured on with him far longer than most women would have done and that he had destroyed her love. He so fervently wished that he had destroyed his love for her at the same time because his future now felt bleak and soulless, as empty as her heart. She no longer cared for him and the realisation was like a physical hurt as was the thought that there was now no one who cared for him.

The couple of drinks inevitably turned into many and he would grab hold of some perceived injustice that he could blame on Diana, relish it, amplify it and make it the centrepiece of his despair. Only that way could he thrust the responsibility back on to her, recasting himself as victim. The more importance he could place on that one perceived act of disloyalty or spite or betrayal, the easier he could transform his love into artificial hatred and recast Diana as a bitch or a harlot or a hard-hearted cow.

It was one such night that he drank almost to oblivion and staggering back to what had been their home, passed the one remaining call box in the area and decided to use it. Even as he now thought about it Al wanted the earth to open up and swallow him as he could not believe what he had done, in fact was so ashamed that he would have given everything he possessed to have had the memory surgically removed if that was even remotely possible. Sadly, what he currently possessed was almost nothing.

He had called Diana from the phone box and threatened to kill her. He was so drunk that he failed to hang up and collapsed in a heap on the floor of the smelly little box amongst old urine, cigarette butts and trodden-in traces of dog shit. Matt had insisted on having the call traced and when the police arrived, Al was unconscious, his back propped against the glass and metal side with a pool of vomit in his lap, adding to the noxious atmosphere of that last remaining public telephone box.

No charges were pressed but the first psychiatric question mark appeared on his official records. The second was when he took an axe to his erstwhile assistant Nigel Burns. Having discovered that Nigel, a man he liked and trusted, had been thieving from him by syphoning off money from cash deals, Al was not only angry but hurt. It was like a betrayal at a time when he needed no more betrayals. In the new world he now inhabited, justice was swift and violent and did not involve the police or courts, fines or prisons and was dispensed quickly with no appeals or mitigating circumstances. It was almost biblical in its simplicity.

Nigel had thieved from him – he had sticky fingers, as the saying went. It was therefore from his fingers that Al had intended to extract compensation or at least retribution, not by severing them as was stated in court but by hurting them, possibly breaking them. The blade of the axe was pointing upwards and it was the heavy back that Al intended to bring down.

It was the first time in his life that he had ever resorted to violence and he was clearly useless at it. He had not even thought at any length about the manner in which Nigel might react. Perhaps he might be holding a phone with one hand while the other was displayed on the desk in front of him, fingers neatly extended awaiting two kilos of forged steel to descend upon them, effecting a redesign. Or perhaps Nigel might say, "Fair enough," and offer his digits for Al's attention. In the event, Nigel sat at his desk, saw the axe descending, leaped out of the office window and hurled down the High street like an Olympic sprinter, screaming over his shoulder: "You crazy fucking bastard."

Despite the role this bizarre little tragi-comedy had played in getting Al where he now was, he still found it difficult not to laugh; at Nigel's reaction, at his own incompetence and at the fact that he had even considered such a violent response. It was far more pantomime than mad axe man. The court, however, did not see it that way. During the interminable wait for justice, house prices collapsed and with them Al's empire. He was declared bankrupt.

Compared to the other tragedy of his broken marriage it seemed like small beer and he thought he was taking it all in his stride until the Receiver asked him about the gold signet ring on his little finger.

"It was a present from my wife, my girlfriend as she was then, the first Christmas we spent together." Al found himself reminiscing. "It was upstate New York in a little inn in the middle of the forest – hot punch, log fire…" The receiver interrupted him.

"I'm sorry but I'm going to have to ask you to remove it and hand it over."

"What?" Al was incredulous and looked at the man imploring. "But it was from my ex-wife, it's all I've got to remember her by…"

The receiver looked at him in a strangely benign way. "Sorry! Now if it was a wedding ring that would be different."

Al responded immediately: "It was a wedding ring. An early wedding ring but my fingers got so fat that I had to move it to my little finger." As he continued looking with pathetic anticipation at the man who, he decided, could only be an accountant, the man smiled: "Well, perhaps that's all right then, let's say no more about it." Maybe he wasn't an accountant after all!

Al twisted the ring on his finger as he thought back on that dark day and the panic, almost despair, that the simple request to hand over this ring had produced in him. Despite offers there had been nobody since Diana for he now saw loyalty to her almost as compensation for his previous failings.

Al got up, disturbed by the detail in which he had reviewed that part of his life – the first time he had done so. He went into the lavatory block without looking at the excavated barred window, chose his usual stall, closed and locked the door, lowered the lid of the WC and sat on it. His thoughts were still rampant and he considered his position. So what if the orderly returned with his watch and passport, so fucking what. Removing the bars, stringing some torn sheets together and

111

POD

swarming down them was simplicity itself but what then?

He had no comfortable bed to go to, no warm body to lie beside, no one to put an arm around him, to caress him to say: "Oh Al, I have missed you. I'm so glad you're back." If he went to the pub the best he knew he could expect was: "Fucking hell, look who's here," or, "You've turned up again, have you, like a bad penny."

Al leant forward on the lavatory seat, placed his head in his hands and wept silently, the warm tears salting his mouth and running between his fingers. It was the lowest trough of his life and for the first time he thought that perhaps he deserved to be where he was.

Chapter Twelve

Michael Widdows gunned the accelerator of the big, ancient New Holland so it could maintain its speed up the inclined Hurstpierpoint road, leaving Pyecombe away to his left, the plough clanking and clattering behind him, its shares folded in so that it was no wider than the tractor.

There was something not quite right about the day but Michael had no real idea why. It was just that everything seemed in sharper focus; brighter, more colourful, more distinct than normal. There was a clarity in everything he saw and his thoughts pushed and pulled at him in a manner which was disturbing, as though someone else had taken control of his consciousness.

In his right rear view mirror he could see the queue of traffic building up behind him and he could distinctly sense the drivers' frustration, hear their muttered obscenities and he found it oppressive. For the first time in nearly fifty years he had concerns for those he was delaying, wanted them gone, to be on his own. He found the bonnets of their cars threatening as they dodged their noses out and back again, hoping for a chance to overtake.

Michael knew it was illogical – unreasonable even – but as he passed Little Rock farm down below him to his left, he felt an irritation far greater than was merited. Farmers they were not, having long ago given up 'proper' farming for horses, both livery for other people and their own for taking punters out on hacks. Irrationally, it felt like some kind of farming community betrayal.

For the first time in his life, his eyes looked beyond the farm set in the shadow of the treeless, crouching lump of

113

Wolstenbury Hill, guarding the route between coast and London, as it always had and in whose shadow much of the farm's land languished.

What must it have been like up on that hill, three, four thousand years ago when iron age and bronze age farmers had found it necessary to secure themselves behind defensive ramparts, yet ventured out to wrest a living from the land. He felt a powerful connection with people who had never before warranted a thought as they, like him, had urged reluctant lands to yield a living. He felt the connection like an unbroken thread reaching down through the millennia, a kinship with people about whom he knew nothing and for whom he had never spared a thought until now but who had faced the same battering of winds and down-pourings of rain.

They, too, may have cursed the deer for trying to live by consuming some of their crops, the badgers for digging in search of their supper of worms and the birds for opportunistically trying to snaffle the seeds, broadcast by hand. And had they upbraided the summer droughts and winter freezes just as he now did.

Michael Widdows felt suddenly very small and insignificant and the sense of immortality that had comforted him throughout his life fell silently away leaving him feeling inconsequential and very, very vulnerable. He was a bit-part actor in a drama that was ancient before he was born and would continue remorselessly after he had gone. His whole life felt suddenly trivial – pointless.

He cast his eyes back to Little Rock Farm and its strange array of horses, with their stocky frames and feathered legs revealing their draft or cob origins. Safe, predictable and well mannered, he guessed, and at the rate of twenty five quid a pop, good business. The sole use of this land was now to service horses – for grazing and for growing hay and haylage for winter feeding.

Michael shook his head in disbelief as he caught sight of two new, top-of-the range green and yellow John Deere tractors sitting idly in the yard a hundred or so metres away, unblemished by so much as a fleck of working mud. Why on earth did they need two unless, of course, business was so good that it was better the money went on American imports than being gifted to the tax man. He was suddenly conscious of the clunkings and rattlings of his ancient old machine and realised that what he was feeling was envy – unbridled envy. They had adapted to the worsening situation and he had not – found other uses for land that was remorselessly losing its fertility and ability to grow crops profitably.

It had become almost impossible to stem the downward spiral of soil degradation with increased applications of oil-based fertilizer, to temporarily coax a little more productivity from soil whose vital nitrogen and trace elements were disappearing through the necessity of repeating the same crops year after year.

Even the application of ever more gallons of expensive herbicides to spray weeds into submission; increased dousings of pesticides and fungicides to weaken the hold of insects and moulds were failing because, increasingly, the insects managed to prosper despite what was now all out warfare. They had an innate ability to mutate and change almost overnight, it seemed, to quickly develop resistance to whatever was thrown at them whilst at the same time forming alliances (Michael avoided preceding it with the word 'military' but that's what it felt like) with other, unrelated organisms by passing that resistance on to them.

He, it seemed, had no choice but to rely on Monsanto, Syngeta and Wellcome whilst his miniscule enemy relied upon billions of years of evolution. He could almost hear them laughing at his feeble efforts, knowing that time was entirely on their side.

Each new weapon he was supplied, heralded with superlatives and sold at premium prices, quickly wilted and waned on the front line when faced with the overpowering superiority of his microscopic enemies. Hybrid, supposedly high-yielding, strains had become low yielding on a downward spiral of seeming inevitability. Again his thoughts went involuntarily but apologetically to the long-departed ancient men, women and children who had inhabited the huge hill to his left and he felt that he was betraying them.

"I don't bloody believe it," Michael shouted at no one in

particular, as regular splotches of mustard yellow leaped out at him, standing proudly brilliant across most of the land to his left, where grazing horses moved slowly and methodically, heads down, avoiding them. They screamed for attention, just as they had three weeks ago and he shook his head in disbelief. Ragwort was a killer to all grazing animals and while they were presently avoiding it, if forage or grazing became short and they became hungry, or as the plants died, they might well be eaten. What would follow would be the slow and painful but inevitable destruction of the horses liver and with no antidote.

It was not a problem right now as while the leaves and stalks were still green and rich in their natural taste deterrent the horses would not touch them – nature's extraordinarily brilliant way of ensuring their reproduction went unmolested and they could spread their genes across the countryside. But once they had fulfilled their purpose, they would shrivel and brown and as the colour diminished so would their foul taste but the toxin would remain and be devoured along with the last of the autumn grass. Horses died in agony every year because of indolent ragwort management practices.

Okay, it wasn't easy to deal with but it had to be done. Michael's preferred way was to cut it as soon as it had grown tall enough, when the flowers were just opening but long before they had been fertilised and started to produce their minuscule white parachutes, and then bale it all up. He would take the bales to some isolated spot away from any animals and leave them to rot. God almighty, it wasn't difficult, the plants remained in flower for weeks, providing plenty of opportunity. And what's more there was a legal requirement to control the stuff.

What angered Michael even more was that these plants were days away from fruiting, some probably already were, and with the next strong westerly wind, clouds of seed would blow directly across his land. He determined to have a word with Harry on his return – tell him to find some bloody use for his pristine, idle tractors.

He crested the hill and just as he began the descent towards Clayton on the Weald below, indicated right and hauled the big tractor and its rig off the road and up the chalk path towards the Downs, passing the two landmark Clayton windmills which had been there his entire life – and much longer. Fortunately, this was a weekday and so tourists were few. There would be no irritated motorists having to reverse back up the track to look for a point where both vehicles could pass.

The two windmills had garnered no more than a handful of visitors. There was Jill, the smaller, pretty, square windmill made from white timber and supported on four splayed legs. For her to work, the whole body of the mill had to be cranked around until her sails were facing windward. Jack was much bigger, round and black and the sails protruded from a dome which sat atop him. It was the dome that was rotated in his case.

Everyone in Sussex and probably far beyond knew of Jack and Jill in their dominant position on the Downs, ideally placed to catch the wind. And Michael had been driving past them all his life to reach the fields which lay just beyond. The mills themselves remained in excellent condition, tended by a band of dedicated if eccentric volunteers who spent their Saturdays and Sundays explaining their workings to families filling time. Occasionally, they would even be treated to a display of grain being milled into flour to show practically how it was done.

He was surprised at how often he allowed himself a little reverie about the mills, or more precisely the house which lay just uphill of them, hiding behind a straggly hedge. It seemed to happen most when the day was bright and cheerful as it was today, whisps of cloud scudding in front of the sun, driven by a warm westerly. As always, it spurred pleasant memories from some forty years back, thoughts of how things might have been – memories that came a little more frequently than Michael was prepared to admit. Perhaps it had been a very similar day to this day and it was the beauty of it that caused those distant events to return in extraordinary clarity. Today they were particularly strong, startlingly clear and Michael allowed himself to slip back in time more completely than he had ever done before. He knew he was indulging himself, willing the past to enfold him and he didn't care.

The house and garden now looked sad and ignored – neglected – whereas once there had been a beautiful vegetable garden and flowers timed to fill each season with dazzling colour and constant perfume that varied from week to week and from day to night. The house seemed permanently to be enlivened by the comings and goings of friends and colleagues, Londoners mostly, some with faces which looked familiar but to whom he could rarely attach a name. That of course was when the house was owned by Henry Longhurst, the golfer, golfing writer and broadcaster.

Michael knew him well but not as an equal. No matter how kind, polite and inclusive Henry had been, there was always the distance generated between employer and employed, between famous and unknown. He called on Michael regularly to flail a hedge or dig a plot, to cut grass or mow a field.

He was very much a man of the time with his neat sports jackets and flannels and even neater hair but incongruously, a huge, gaudy American motorcar sat in the drive alongside his study. It was part of his pay deal with one of the big broadsheet newspapers – the Sunday Times, Michael seemed to recall. It was a Ford Thunderbird and he desperately wanted to remember the colour but couldn't – was it pink or yellow, or perhaps it was powder blue? Whatever it was, it stood out like a merry-go-round at a time when cars were mostly somberly hued and small.

It would have suited Terry Thomas perfectly or Liberace but not Henry. Despite this, and despite the odd self-deprecating remark he made about his flashy motor, Henry seemed enormously proud of it.

It was immaterial, really, for these were not the details that Michael wanted to remember. It was just that the more completely he could recall the day in question, the more details he could drag out of their hiding places, the more completely he could will himself back in time. Why he wanted to had always been a mystery.

Again he looked across the mills and towards the house and felt that one little touch of one-upmanship that he had over the mill tourists. He knew all about the third windmill, which escaped their attention entirely, hidden as it was away behind the house and obscured by the hedge. And he had been privileged to see it put to its use way back then – a little bit of history although, perhaps, of no great importance to most people.

From the outside it was a sad little mill, emasculated, truncated, sail-less – just a stumpy round remnant no more than a single storey high, black and unobtrusive with a felted roof. But it had retained its name and it was that identity that allowed it to hold tight on to a sense of its past. It had not been demolished or destroyed but simply truncated and retired and it eschewed all pity because it was, after all, still Duncton. And it was in Duncton's big, dramatic, round, foreshortened windmill room that Henry Longhurst had written his copy.

On the day that Michael remembered so clearly, Henry Longhurst had amused himself by running Michael through his routine for filing his golfing reports, for whichever newspaper it was. He would hide away at his desk in circular Duncton with its book-lined shelves and write his report in longhand. Once finished, he called it through to the newspaper and then opened a half-bottle of chilled Champagne, drank it where he sat and discarded both bottle and sheets of copy into a large wicker wastepaper basket. On this particular day, it contained the detritus of perhaps a dozen weeks – a pile of empty bottles and innumerable sheets of almost illegible writing with a myriad of crossings out.

It was the first time that Michael could ever remember being envious. He would have loved Henry's lifestyle, even though he knew nothing about golf and had no interest in it. But lurking at the back of his mind was a belief that things such as this did not happen to farmer's boys.

Also on this particular day, a stranger came crashing into Duncton: "Have you finished yet, dad?" It was Henry's daughter. She was young and slim and extremely pretty with cascading, glowing brown hair but most of all it was her eyes which grabbed hold of Michael and transfixed him. They were sparkling with life and confidence emanated from her like an aura.

"Michael's just leaving," Henry replied, "but I'm sure he'd like some beans. Show him which ones were picking at the moment – there's some containers in the hall."

With that, Michael and a beautiful young woman whose

name he could no longer remember, wound their way down the garden and disappeared from view into the lush foliage of the runner bean canes. He picked the beans only sporadically as conversation flowed between them, quickly moving away from the general and seamlessly entering the personal, even the intimate.

Again it was her eyes that ensnared him but now their sparkle was not incidental but directed at him, were sparkling because of him. He was not greatly experienced with women, what farmers' boys are, but he knew that her ready laugh, the touch of her hand on his arm and the long looks from beneath her dark lashes which held his gaze were unmistakable signals of interest.

Before the thought that 'things like this don't happen to me' could take root, he tried to remind himself that he was tall, fairly handsome, tanned and was not without success with local girls. But this was the collision of attraction that he had been awaiting for what seemed like an age. As he opened his mouth to ask her out, a crashing sound from close by silenced him and Henry appeared through the bean poles just feet from them.

"Have you finished yet, darling? I need you to give me a lift into Haywards Heath to pick Billy up. Come on quickly, sweetie, we can't leave him any longer – he's been waiting there for twenty minutes already."

And so it was over, each too embarrassed to finalise what they both wanted under Henry's uncomprehending parental eyes. Michael had never seen her again but remnants of the thrill, the promise, the desire, the hope had survived forty years and more and still, from time to time, he looked towards the house with a distant hope that she might have returned for old time's sake, just as he did now, perhaps even to progress what was disturbingly incomplete. And all this despite a wife and a family now grown to maturity.

Like him, she would be ageing – old – but he suspected that age would have been incapable of entirely erasing the magnetic attraction that had ensnared him as surely as a wire noose around the neck of a rabbit. Henry, of course, had died decades ago and the house had passed into other hands.

A disturbing wistfulness stayed with Michael, unsettling him as he accelerated up the track, plough clattering and banging behind him, and through the gate of the fifteen-acre field no more than a hundred yards past the house. Unless he could shake it off it would be a long day as every time he turned the tractor around and headed back down the slope at slow ploughing speed, he would have the house directly in his line of sight.

He concentrated on his work – fifteen acres of flax to plough in, flax that he had planted, which had grown and flowered and smeared the Downs with its delicate inky blue but which he had never harvested. He had been told not to by Agricultural Commissioners of the EU and had picked up his generous subsidy for not doing so.

The first time it had happened was with a ten-acre plot of potatoes in the northerly shadow of Newtimber Hill. He had felt almost corrupt as he looked over his shoulder at the turning earth and saw his wake marked by innumerable white dots – perfectly healthy, top-quality potatoes, a valuable food that would eventually disappear whence it came and which no one would ever eat.

That was long since and he no longer wasted his thoughts or concerns on mechanisms designed to maintain a stable price, decisions about which he could do nothing but which ensured him a regular and not inconsiderable income.

Flax was a strange crop and he could not fathom out why he had been encouraged to plant it at all on low-grade land such as this. It was low yielding and the latitude was far too southerly to produce oil of any therapeutic value. That came from colder climes, mostly Canada. His oil, had it been harvested, would have gone for industrial purposes – boiled as linseed oil to preserve cricket bats or other wooden products. The residue would be used as animal feed. Fibre from the stalks could, of course, have been put through a long, watery process to produce linen, except that there was no longer a linen industry in Europe. The next prized crop that he might soon be encouraged and paid to plant, he believed, would be lupins, but again he had no understanding as to why.

Michael engaged the hydraulics and the eight-share plough

unfolded behind him and rested on the flat scrubby soil with its twisted remnants of last year's crop. He set the hand accelerator and the tractor moved forwards at ploughing speed, the mirror-like shares digging deep into the soil, turning it over in eight neat furrows in the first of many remorseless transits up and down the field.

On his easterly traverses, away from the house, Michael concentrated hard on his job and tried to plough as neatly as if he was in a competition. Occasionally, he would allow his view to range over the rolling hills that were the Downs – barren, windswept but with a beauty of their own, a beauty he had grown to appreciate over the years, a beauty that was perhaps more primeval, more threatening than the cosy, hedge-fringed, tree-lined fields closer to sea level.

He also took pleasure in running his eyes to the South where the Channel's waters glinted beyond Woodingdean and Saltdean, the distance ironing out the surface undulations of waves and swell. With the strength of wind as it was, he knew that the surface would, in fact, be flecked with little white horses.

On the homeward, westerly traverses, try as he might, Michael could not take his eyes off the house. The extraordinary feeling of incompleteness would not leave him and for a normally emotionless man, there was a welling up inside that could only be emotion. He could not shake off the feeling of having been cheated, of passion unfulfilled, of fruitless anticipation without end and its persistence worried him because it was utterly stupid. There must be something wrong with him, he decided.

He forced his mind back to the work in hand, looking behind to check the accuracy and neatness of his ploughing. The turned soil was almost white with fragments and flecks of chalk and it had got whiter over the years, of that he was certain, as the humus had been leached away by rain and wind. Nothing ever replaced it and the crops that did grow were dependent entirely upon massive inputs of nitrogen fertiliser from fossil fuels.

Gulls wheeled behind him, descending to grab leather jackets, centipedes and worms exposed in the soil freshly turned by his plough shares but their pickings were lean as the substance which sustained healthy plants also sustained these creatures, too. He was sure that as the white wash of chalk increased over the years so the number of following gulls reduced as the pursuit of food became increasingly less rewarding.

But still the feeling remained with him, persistent, demanding. In all this time, his reveries, when they had come, had been pleasant reminders of a time past and had never afflicted him like this. It disturbed him and he struggled to understand why.

The answer came suddenly and undramatically and made him question his sanity even more. No matter how unlikely or ludicrous, while there was life there was hope and although objectively he knew he would never see her again, while he was alive so there had to be a tiny remnant of possibility, of somehow, somewhere they would bump into each other. Their eyes would meet once more and he would say: "I've missed you." Her smile would sparkle in response as she looked at him once more from beneath her lowered lashes.

The feeling he had at this moment was that someone had stripped away that last little, distant glimmering of hope; he had run out of time and there was nothing more to come, there was no future remaining for the improbable to happen. It was over, everything was over. He knew with certainty that the memories which had sustained him for so long were his alone and she, whatever her name, had driven her father to the station and had never again thought of him. The hurt was as powerful as any real-life rejection.

A flurry of squawking, cawing crows calling raucously to each other in alarm demanded his attention as they rose in a spiralling flock on the far side of the hedge which marked the northerly boundary of the field, disturbed by the approaching tractor. Michael was back at work now and his heart sank for he was almost certain what the cause would be. He stopped, applied the air brakes and climbed down out of the cab, looking for a gap in the wind-battered hedge. Having found it, he climbed carefully over the barbed-wire fence into the pasture where his sheep were kept.

He could see her immediately, a ewe prone by the side of the hedge, her thickening winter coat splodged with red. As he approached, he could see that the detail of her face had been replaced by a bloody mask where numerous beaks had feasted. Her stomach was open and most of the viscera were missing as was the bulk of the two foetuses she had been carrying.

The cause of her death was clear – two or three long tendrils of bramble had become entwined in her thick fleece and the more she had struggled, the more deeply they would have embedded themselves. There was no escaping their grasp. The sheep had died of thirst and fear and the crows were simply doing the vital cleaning up that was their evolutionary job.

It was not the first time it had happened and Michael immediately cast around to blame someone else. It would not have happened if the local wildlife group hadn't targeted him and nagged until he agreed not to flail the hedges this year so there would at least be some hips and haws, elderberries and ivy berries remaining on the bushes to provide food for birds through the winter. It would not have happened if he hadn't agreed to provide some traction power at the county fair last weekend and had therefore been absent from his duties.

He was not convinced by either. He should have checked his sheep and he should have cut the brambles back because he was well aware of their vicious threat which ensnared one or more of his ewes every year but which he mostly managed to rescue in time.

He was angry with himself because sheep farming was highly unprofitable and this dead ewe represented about three hundred quid down the drain. Even with subsidies, it was essential to maximise profits in every way possible, instigating every new piece of advice the industry could offer. He now took his ewes inside for a short period at the end of the summer and in a controlled environment could trick them into early oestrus and through artificial insemination, almost guarantee they would produce twins, even triplets. They would give birth in January and the lambs would be ahead of the field, demanding a premium price as some of the earliest spring lambs. He had now lost the value of two lambs as well as the ewe.

Of course, against that was the inevitable risk that some lambs would die from exposure or that through lack of nutrition, ewes would produce insufficient milk to sustain twins. It was a balancing act that so far had mostly worked in his favour, the twenty per cent of lambs who died being built into the finances.

What was particularly galling, Michael reminded himself, was that after years of disposing of spent ewes for a pittance, he had even found a highly profitable market for them, too – an eager source that took all he had to offer and was prepared to pay a hundred and fifty quid a piece. This mangled old sheep would have been one of them soon after her lambs were sent to slaughter. Perfect timing!

You could say what you liked about Muslims but he would never knock them. Why they wanted to personally cut the throat of a conscious, breathing, struggling sheep for their festival of Eid, he had no idea but if that's what their god wanted them to do, then so be it – and if he didn't provide the animals someone else would. As it was, a truck arrived in March, he was paid in cash for each animal, which were then loaded up and off they went to France. Simple, sweet and profitable and, as far as he was aware, perfectly legal.

Michael still had the walk and posture of an angry man as he made his way back into the fifteen acre field and towards the rumbling, stationary New Holland.

The blow to his head came with a loud crack and no warning and sent him sprawling headlong into the flax stubble. He had no idea what had happened, or where the blow had come from but he quickly sat up on his haunches, his fists outstretched defensively, his head darting from side to side and spinning to look behind him. He could see nothing. What the hell was it? Had something fallen on him, had he been shot? The one thing he did know was that it bloody hurt.

It was then he spotted the still and lifeless corpse of a common gull just a few metres away, partly hidden by a clump of docks. Could it have been that? Could the stupid bloody thing have been so eager to snaffle a few worms that it hadn't seen him? He guessed that had to be the answer because as he lifted it he could still feel its warmth as it drooped motionlessly in his hand.

Almost as a reflex, he glanced back upwards into the Westerly sky and saw nothing but half a dozen large herring gulls wheeling in formation over the Clayton windmills, like a squadron of spitfires. They turned towards him, swooping down out of a thermal, their wings motionless but with a strong wind behind them, pushing them forward, their speed was accelerating rapidly and he froze as they swooped lower and lower until they flew but feet above the ground, faster and faster and it looked for all the world as though they were heading directly for him, that he was being targeted. They were heading for him, Michael realised at the last moment, and threw himself to one side with the unthinking, instant reaction of self-preservation, his extraordinary speed fuelled by the adrenaline of fear.

He felt a wash of turbulent air and heard the whoosh of their wings as they missed their target by inches – so close that Michael was certain he could smell a sickly, fishy aroma lingering in their wake.

The tractor for safety was the only thought that came to him and the twenty five yards that lay between him and it were covered in seconds that felt like minutes, his legs pounding forwards in slow motion, his feet struggling to find purchase but slipping on the dried and brittle flax stems, his heart seemingly filling his chest as he sucked at the air to fuel it. The only thought in his mind was to reach the safety of the tractor's Perspex cab but his foot slipped off the first step and excruciating pain shot through him as his shin scraped the full length of its sharp edge.

The eternity of his flight ended as he swung into the vehicle's seat and massaged his throbbing leg whilst viewing a threatening world through smeary Perspex. Only then did his pulse begin to slow its frenetic racing and his mind struggle to resume functioning on logic rather than reaction.

The last thing Michael wanted to do was continue with the ploughing but told himself he was being illogical. Something about the thermals, air turbulence, the gusty nature of the wind was clearly causing the birds to misjudge distances. It could be nothing else. But he was shaken and his shin throbbed with extreme pain so, for the first time he could remember, Michael decided to take a break in the middle of his working day.

He was about to set the accelerator and engage the hydraulics to raise the plough when a series of deafening crashes triggered his instinct for self-preservation once more and he ducked blindly, throwing his hands over his head in protection. When he dared look up, he saw that the cab was covered in smears of blood with fine white feathers adhering to it and the ground immediately around the tractor was strewn with the bodies of several gulls, some still moving their broken wings in a desultory way. What chilled him most were the huge cracks and splits in the cab's transparent sheeting, the only security he had was disintegrating.

He rapidly engaged the hand accelerator with panic swelling in his breast, heard and saw nothing as he reached for the hydraulic switch to raise the plough but was partly blinded by blood from the initial strike that was now running down his forehead and into his eyes. He missed the switch and groped around to find its location and so was oblivious to the bird that was heading towards the back of the cab, where there was no door, no curtain and no protection. The sharp crack of its high-speed strike was that of a bird dying and Michael Widdow's neck breaking.

In his last moment of consciousness, he grasped at the steering wheel for support before tumbling backwards out of the cab and on to the earth in front of the plough, which seemed to scoop him up without faltering, where he lay prone on its top and travelled along with it, as though borne by some agricultural gun carriage. His final act of clutching at the steering wheel of the New Holland had resulted in the vehicle changing its direction and instead of running parallel to the land already turned over, kept automatically in line as though on rails by the last ploughed furrow, the smaller front wheels had turned outwards and the tractor headed off elsewhere as though escaping from its duties.

With the hand accelerator set and still dictating its pace, the driverless tractor proceeded at perfect ploughing speed, its shares still turning the earth sweetly and smoothly but at a diagonal across the field, progress across its pristine surface marked by a swathe of freshly turned earth, heading away from the ploughed block of land that Michael had earlier created so proudly. It was as though someone intended purposeful disrespect of his lifetime's work and all the time, gulls hung almost motionless behind the New Holland, looking for something tasty to eat.

Prostrate on the top edge of the plough, Michael's arm hung down to drag along the ground and when it encountered a clump of grass or docks, it bounced upwards, his forearm curling inwards to touch his chest before straightening once more. Like a latter-day Captain Ahab, he appeared to be beckoning for all to follow him as he went to his eternity, not on a white whale but a rusty old New Holland tractor and its plough, both of which, like Moby Dick, clearly bore the scars of time.

Chapter Thirteen

Jo Aldous felt as though embarrassment surrounded her like a neon-lit aura which even those in the farthest reaches of the Ship Hotel bar could not fail to see and decipher the reasons for it, without the slightest effort. She could almost hear their mutterings of contempt – stupid, embarrassing, idiotic, pathetic. That she had made a fool of herself she was not in doubt and she simply wanted the memory to evaporate and with it the combined sense of stupidity and vulnerability that engulfed her. Please could things just return to normal.

"You have absolutely nothing to be embarrassed about, nothing, do you hear? Why shouldn't abject cruelty to an animal shock and horrify you? It's normal Jo, it's absolutely normal. Those who aren't shocked by it are the abnormal ones."

The two women leant towards each other, their elbows on the circular bar table looking to any casual observer like old friends. The use of her first name by Wendy registered with Jo and she was conscious that she was essentially being enveloped by a woman she barely knew and yet that small intimacy made her feel more comfortable.

Years of caution were about to be abandoned as Jo could feel a desperate need to talk pressing from within, encouraged by the fact that she didn't give a bugger what anyone did with her innermost thoughts and fears. The guarded, self-censoring that had become a part of her life had never been about protecting her, not about her needs or her image but about protecting Stephen's position and right now she wanted to talk – needed to talk and any perceived need to protect Stephen wasn't going to inhibit her. If this woman wasn't trustworthy the results would be all over the tabloids the day after tomorrow.

But Jo did trust her and realised she had said nothing to anyone about the awful experiences she'd been through – not Danny's accident, not her collapsing marriage nor her nightmares. Of course there had been some exchanges about Danny with her parents but they were clearly unable to cope with their own emotions let alone support her. Others had made enquiries about how 'things' were, how she was coping, little words of advice such as 'keep yourself busy' or 'it could have been so much worse'. But they were trite and shallow like someone feeling the need to end an over-long pause in a conversation, scrabbling for something to say but which had little depth or feeling.

No one had enfolded her, either physically or metaphorically, and allowed her the opportunity to reach within herself, allowing her to unburden at least some of the load she carried. Jo knew that much of it was the embarrassment of people not knowing quite what to say but feeling that at least some acknowledgement of the situation was necessary. All it did was to reinforce in Jo's mind how many acquaintances she had but how few friends.

She had mentioned the nightmares briefly to Hillie and the waking dreams but she had treated them as a joke.

"You're probably picking up the vibes from those two horse-faced bitches in the shadow cabinet planning to plunge a knife between your shoulder blades so they can have Stephen to themselves," she'd laughed without even pausing in what she was doing.

It wasn't so much what she said but how she said it – delivered like a full stop – that worried Jo because it ended the conversation and allowed no opening for her to continue, no encouragement, not the slightest indication that she might be interested in something that was clearly worrying Jo. It was immediately followed by some trivia about a friend who had gone to a clairvoyant and whose predictions were so accurate that Hillie was herself thinking of having a consultation.

"What were you saying back in the hall – about dreams?" Wendy's words contained the invitation that Hillie hadn't wanted to proffer.

*

"Oh, I've just been having some dreams, nightmares really, but it's nothing."

"Well, for something that's nothing it had a hell of an impact on you. Your face was utterly drained. You didn't even seem to know where you were."

"Thanks for reminding me."

"If you want to talk, it'll remain totally confidential. It seems to me that something very profound happened to you back there and I'm not even sure that you understand what it was. Maybe talking will help clarify your mind."

Jo adopted an entirely false and cynical attitude: "Yeah, I can see it now – 'Future prime minister's wife goes bonkers in Weybridge.'"

"Thanks!"

"Sorry, I didn't really mean it." Jo paused and took a deep breath. "Okay, I've been having horrible nightmares that have frightened me – I mean really frightened me, to such a degree that I did start to think I was going mad. There are no people in them, no monsters, nothing like that, just sounds. The only way I can sum them up is that they seem to contain a world of suffering in sound. The screaming of that fox was straight out of my nightmares – not just that, there are other sounds with it but that little animal's dreadful screaming is a constituent part of the night-time horror I've been experiencing. To be honest, I've never identified that particular sound before perhaps because I wasn't looking for it or didn't know what it was but it's there, in my dreams, I now know.

"It's like an orchestra where the music as a whole washes over you and creates the mood, manipulates your emotions but is comprised of different instruments and you don't necessarily identify each one unless you specifically listen for it. I've no idea what the individual sounds are that combine together to create the awful concerto but I know that tonight I heard one of the instruments – one of its very many component parts.

"The big question for me now is, what makes up the other parts and why. Perhaps the only way I'll recognise them is when

I hear them in real life, they'll then have a name, an identity, a source. I wouldn't know what part a violin played in an orchestra if I didn't already know what it was and could identify the sound. This, of course, presupposes that all these sounds do have a physical source. After what I just heard I somehow instinctively know that they do and in many ways that's more worrying than their being the creation of my overactive mind.

"I'd come to the conclusion that it was just, I dunno, just suffering. A kind of generic thing that I was creating by myself, for myself because of guilt, inadequacy, insecurity, fear – Christ knows what else but it was all about me. I was convinced I was the composer, the orchestra, the conductor and the audience but what I heard tonight shattered that. It wasn't generic, it wasn't amorphous, it wasn't faceless but real, horribly, horribly real and it hadn't originated from within me but from outside me, from the real world. I'm convinced now that all the other component parts of my nightmare are out there somewhere and I'll recognise them instantly when I hear them, when they're in some kind of context.

"I've now got to go back to the drawing board and start to try and reinterpret what my dreams are, where they come from and what they mean. I do sense something of a consolation in the fact that it might not be about me after all. But if they're not generated by me then where the hell do they come from?"

Jo paused and took a long draft from her wine, all the time watching Wendy's face, seeing out signs of boredom or disbelief and, most importantly, disinterest. She saw none of them, just concentration and concern.

Wendy spoke as though she was genuinely trying to unravel Jo's mystery. "The mind's a powerful instrument – an incredibly complicated thing with billions of neurons all linking with each other by electrical impulses and it's quite capable of storing the memory of smells and tastes and sounds that you think are long forgotten and producing them when you least expect it. One little trigger and in a fraction of a second a very specific memory is hauled from its hiding place. It may be what happened this evening."

Jo thought for a moment. "It's possible but I don't think that's the case. I know absolutely nothing about fox hunting, I've never taken part or even been to one, I simply knew that they chased foxes on horseback and the hounds killed them. I had no idea they dug foxes out and I've certainly never seen that torture. No one could ever forget that despicable brutality. It isn't the kind of thing that lurks around in your subconscious waiting to surprise you. In fact, if I'd ever seen anything like that back in my distant past I suspect it might have changed my life. I would have made different choices. I'd probably now be one of your members, maybe even standing with your dreadlocked Pretorian guardswoman abusing people on Weybridge High Street." Jo laughed as a she saw the smile spread across Wendy's face.

Wendy was still smiling when she said: "Well, one thing you can rest assured about – you're not bonkers."

Jo's smile transformed into something more wry, more defensive. "There's more to come, Wendy." Her use of the first name was calculated; a matching of progress towards possible friendship.

"Sometimes, late at night or early in the morning, the dreams aren't exactly dreams any longer – they continue while I'm awake." There was barely a pause before Jo continued at a rush. "I know, I know – voices in my head therefore I must be a schizophrenic. Give her the pills, lock her up poor woman, she's been under too much stress."

Jo's eyes had never left Wendy's face as she looked for reaction but nothing in her countenance had changed – no censure, no concern, no alarm flickered across her eyes. She showed no inclination to interrupt and remained listening intently, knowing there was still more to come.

"I don't hear voices, Wendy, I hear screams, I hear suffering. There's no one talking to me telling me what to do, feeding me with ludicrous ideas, instructing me to kill the local priest because he's the devil's spawn and intends to murder every child he christens. It's not like that. In every respect I'm perfectly okay – apart from sounds I don't understand – and sometimes being an irritable bitch." Her smile returned fleetingly.

Wendy's hand reached across the table and took Jo's arm in a gesture of intimacy. "Anyone who can articulate an experience as vividly and clearly as you have is perfectly sane. Yes you do have a problem and you're doing the only thing that any sane person could do and that is you're struggling to understand it. It's the only intelligent response. And in all honesty, in the grand scheme of things, I don't think it's that big a problem."

Jo looked Wendy directly in the eye and spoke with an inflection that was partly dismissive, partly self-deprecating. "Yeah, maybe. Poor woman drinks a bit too much, thought she might lose her son, her marriage is shit and she lacks the courage to do anything about it – no wonder she's stressed! Just as well it's only sound hallucinations I'm having, Wendy, because if they were visual, St Maws would probably build a shrine by the cricket pitch to their most famous old girl and the faithful would come and pray for me to cure their gout or get them pregnant with a baby boy."

They both laughed and Jo went to the bar and bought two more glasses of white wine. As she sat down, Wendy asked: "Your marriage – not good?"

"Like I said – shit."

"So no support from your husband over the dreams?"

"I haven't even told him. It would be like trying to discuss quantum physics with a five-year old. Stephen doesn't do emotions or mind things. He'd probably think all I need is a good shag or an afternoon at Harrods with his credit card. They're the last things I want at the moment – at least from him."

"Oh dear – that bad?"

"Yep, that bad!"

"But you're not leaving him?"

"Not yet, not right now. I can't face the emotional upheaval and I'm not strong enough to support Danny through it all. Fortunately, I don't see that much of Stephen at the moment because he's much too busy trying to get elected so my lovely garden and house are my anchor, they give me a kind of tranquillity."

"Might it be just a phase?"

"Bloody long one if it is – I've been feeling unhappy for years but I knew it was all over about twelve months ago and it just gets worse and worse."

"But you do intend to leave him?"

"Oh yes – just as soon as I can find the strength or something happens to make me go. But I will go, and soon."

Wendy's eyebrows shot up. "Wow! All the predictions are that he'll be prime minister within six months. That's going to throw a spanner in the works, isn't it?"

"And that's another thing. I might not like Stephen any longer and he might be as thick as a plank and not fit to be prime minister but it's something he's worked for since he entered politics. I don't have any desire to hurt him and if I caused him to lose the crown that's almost within his reach, it would devastate him." Jo could see that Wendy was ill at ease.

"What's wrong?"

"Oh dear, I think we may be at odds here."

"About what? Stephen? Politics?

"I've got to be honest, Jo, the last person I would want to see as prime minister is your husband. I think Stephen Aldous would be a disaster for human rights, animals rights and the environment. I think he would be extremely damaging."

For the first time, Jo gained a glimpse of the steel that lay beneath Wendy Carter's benign exterior. There was no equivocation, no attempt to lace her words with euphemisms. This is what she thought and she had delivered it with a rapier-like thrust.

Jo began to giggle and it quickly turned into raucous laughter as she threw her head back, eventually wiping a tear from beneath her eye.

"Oh Wendy, I've waited for years to hear someone say that to my face. I'm so tired of the sycophancy and arse licking. He's a twat pure and simple."

"But you won't try and stop him from getting the position even though you've admitted he's not fit to be premiere?"

"How political are you, Wendy? How closely do you watch the goings on in the Westminster village?"

"I'm interested in specific pieces of legislation but the circus itself leaves me cold."

"Very wise! I've been forced to observe all the wrinkles and machinations, the plotting and scheming of party politics for almost as long as I can remember. Not because I wanted to but because of who I married. It's a pile of shit, Wendy, beautified with the word 'democracy.' I can only really speak for the Tory party but I suspect it's much the same in the Labour party, too, just a slightly different agenda. And when I say slightly different, I mean very, very slightly different. As for the Tories, it wouldn't make a blind bit of difference who was elected prime minister – it could be a monkey on a stick.

"The real power doesn't lie with the prime minister but the people who avoid the headlines – powerful, shadowy cliques, the interest groups that provide the backbone to the party, newspapers and other media interests, corporations who are the party's paymasters. We're talking global interest here and wealth beyond imagination. It's not just power they want but what that power can do for them and it always comes back to money.

"Of course there are different interests in the party which are hyped up and presented as splits or divisions but they're not really anything of the kind because you can hardly slide a thin sheet of paper between them in terms of their policies – their real policies I mean as opposed to the insultingly-simple one liners that are used to try and dupe the public. And believe me, these people have utter contempt for ordinary voters and are convinced from experience that they're eminently dupable.

"'Get government off your backs' means slash benefits and subsidies to the kind of institutions that ordinary people rely on. 'Defending hard-working families' means destroying the cross-subsidy that's absolutely central to a caring society. 'Put you in charge of your own money' means slashing taxes from which the hoi polloi will gain a few quid a week while the wealthy grab thousands. And any benefit the poorer gain is wiped out by having to pay for things that were previously free.'"

"Excuse me," Wendy smiled, "but an anti-Tory diatribe from the wife of a potential Tory leader seems a little, well, out of place! I presume you don't say these things around the dinner table when you're entertaining?"

"I used to – as questions not as statements – but I got fed up with being kicked under the table. And then I realised that it would never make any difference at all to anyone's thinking and gave up."

"But how? Why? It's a bit like – well, like Batman discovering that Robin is really the Joker."

"I dunno. I was never political – at all – and I never saw myself as particularly bright but I started to question, in my own mind, the beliefs and claims that everyone else around me took as gospel. Silly little things like the assumption that the very rich have to be given incentives to make them work while those at the bottom of the heap have to be financially punished to make them work. But I think the greatest dawning came simply from the people I met.

"The one thing a good public school education does – over and above everything else – is produce confidence and absolute assurance in any setting. It's the manners, the self-belief, the polished performance and the veneer of unquestionable competence that oozes from these people that gives them success. That and the old boy's network. But in many cases that's all it is – a veneer.

"To me, the real test is in what they've achieved. It is the Stephen's of this world who've been in charge of our country for most of our past and yet we've staggered from one crisis to another, from one war to the next and Britain's position in the world has slithered remorselessly downwards. It just seems that the social progress that was made – and mostly not by the Tories or the modern Labour party – is all being dismantled.

"I didn't wake up one morning and believe all this, it's been a gradual process of discovery – of realisation – and much of it very recently."

Wendy shook her head: "No wonder you want to leave your husband." Wendy's voice remained low and intimate, almost seductive, as she quietly threw in the occasional question that kept Jo talking. Jo found the process not only helpful in turning confusion into clarity but reassuring. Nothing felt daunting any longer and despite barely knowing the woman, her presence, her unruffled, unjudgemental attitude metaphorically caused the scales to drop from Jo's eyes.

"I don't normally do advice," said Wendy, "but I will proffer one little morsel borne out of my own experience – be honest. Tell Stephen exactly what you're thinking and what you intend to do. Don't spring anything on him. Don't assume anything."

"But I don't know what I intend to do," answered Jo, almost like a school kid who couldn't answer the teacher's question. The clarity disappeared from her thinking in a flash and she could feel confusion reasserting itself like it had simply been waiting in the wings.

"Well, think about what you want to do and come to a decision – for your sake as much as his. Work out what you're prepared to tolerate and for how long then set out a timescale and stick to it. You've said it's too difficult at the moment for a whole string of reasons but don't let that indecision ride on indefinitely. You say you don't want to damage Stephen so why not tell him your marriage is over – if you really are convinced that it is – but that you'll do nothing to prevent him from achieving his goal. I suppose the big question is which goal? Until he becomes party leader, until he takes the top job or until his stint as prime minister is over?"

"Good god no, not that long!" The words shot out of Jo's mouth like they were hot potatoes.

"Great! Your first bit of clarity. So, until he becomes prime minister, then?"

Jo pondered for a moment before answering and when she did the word was drawn out like chewing gum being stretched: "Yeeees, yees, yes. By the last repetition it had become firm and definite. "Yes, that's exactly what I'm prepared to do. The general election is probably about six months away and I can tolerate him that long and he'll be so busy once he's PM that I'll probably never see him. So if I leave three months after that, he'll be secure and I will have a deadline to aim for. Christ, that makes me feel so much better."

"Indecision is a killer," chuckled Wendy.

Jo went silent as she reviewed her intentions and not only did she feel enormously relieved and enervated, she was almost excited. It was the simplest of solutions and it took a chat with a near stranger for her to see it. She knew that to many people, this simple choice, when it finally became public, would be seen as momentous and would hog the headlines for a day or two but to Jo it was simply a template for deconstructing a failed marriage.

She continued to contemplate the practicalities of how and when to tell Stephen as she sipped from her glass and allowed her eyes to range around the bar of the Ship Hotel and its smart but ubiquitous Victoriana-ish décor.

There was the pretty young woman behind the bar – a girl really – with her painted-on smile and eternal jollity and her repetitive phrases that made Jo want to scream. "Yes madam, what can I get for you," even after the third order when it was screamingly obvious what she could get. "No problem!" Of course it's not a problem, it's your bloody job, thought Jo. And the final one that was like fingernails down a blackboard. "Enjoy!"

There were four men in business suits, all sitting separately and looking bored and who stretched out their time at the bar in the hope of making something other than superficial contact with the smiling and fragrant automaton. Probably resident at the hotel and filling in the time between dinner and calling home and bedtime, thought Jo.

There was the middle-aged couple with their Primark clothes who sat at a little round table not facing each other but with their knees pointing outwards into the bar, their eyes following the same path, the one never looking at the other and not, as far as Jo had seen, talking to each other either. Their lifeless eyes indicated it was not the silence that follows a screaming row but the silence of boredom that grows insidiously after endless repetition, of saying the same things year in, year out. Jo empathised with them.

And there were four young men, pushing down the pints and reliving a shared experience that became more momentous and hilarious as time passed and escalated in direct proportion to that amount of booze they drank. Whatever the event, it was almost certainly far more entertaining in its reliving than it had ever been in reality.

This mundane scenario was probably re-enacted with variations in thousands of pubs and

bars across the country every day of the week. It was its mundanity that brought the sudden realisation to Jo that what they were discussing, deciding, was of considerable import. It would cause endless speculation, give birth to a dozen theories. It would be written into the history books and she would be the subject of a spate of columnist spite and invention and the door-stepping would be intense. It was going to be uncomfortable and Jo felt a little chill of dread flit through her but it was more than counterbalanced by the sense of liberation her new plan of action had delivered.

Jo dragged her thoughts back to the present: "You said your advice was from your own experience – what experience was that?" she asked of Wendy. "You married – got children?"

"I was married, now live with someone, well, some of the time, and have one child – a girl of ten. Maisie."

"Why?"

"Why what?"

"Why divorce?"

"I think we just grew apart."

"No, sorry, don't buy that," Jo cut across her. "Much too trite. You don't just grow apart, something pushes you apart!"

Wendy went silent and for the first time Jo could identify reticence in her. Eventually she spoke but it was a different Wendy, a more introspective Wendy, a reluctant Wendy who replied.

"I don't know. Maybe it was me, maybe it was him but it's all fairly recent and I'm still trying to work it out. It's not easy."

"What's not easy? Being divorced or trying to fathom out how it happened?"

Again Wendy went silent and looked down at her glass. "Perhaps both." The pause lengthened. A flicker across the eyes and an almost imperceptible slump in her posture indicated to Jo that life had not always been kind to Wendy Carter. Her eyes were downcast and the hesitation before she replied dragged on and on but Jo allowed her the space.

There was almost something reassuring in whatever turmoil she was experiencing. From a person who until this point had appeared totally confident, entirely self-contained and in charge of herself and her actions, she had become diffident, uncertain – entirely human.

"It was my decision – the divorce that is. My husband was – is – a good man, a solid reliable man who provided the rock on which I was able to build my campaigning life. I loved him – I probably still love him – but I was…" There was a long pause as Wendy searched for the word that accurately described her feelings, "unfulfilled.

"There was no passion left and I needed passion like I need fresh air to breathe. I knew it was a trade-off – that I was sacrificing something precious and dear to me, a friend who understood me and would always be there for me, for something that would make me feel alive again."

"Did it work?" Jo asked quietly.

"Yes, it did but I wasn't to know that having grabbed what I was so lacking I would then miss so badly those other aspects of my marriage that had created our love."

"Oh dear – a real dilemma. Do you regret your decision?"

Again Wendy thought carefully before answering. "No, I can't regret something that felt right at the time, something over which I had no choice but there are no manuals for this kind of thing, no one or nothing to warn you of what might happen, no one to caution you about the turmoil that can whip your emotions into such a vortex that it can easily suck you down to god knows where. Separating had obsessed my thoughts for a long time but when it came it was bittersweet."

Wendy looked Jo directly in the eyes and Jo could see the passion and pain which clouded them behind the welling tears. When she spoke again it was with absolute authority: "It may not be as simple as you think it's going to be – leaving your husband. Forget the politics and the politicians and the media and all the other stuff. I'm talking about you and your relationship and what it does to you here." Wendy touched below her breast with her right hand.

Jo's response was instant. "I pray to god I'll feel something for him so that there will at least be a sense that my years with him weren't entirely wasted, apart from my lovely Danny, of course. I appreciate your warning, Wendy, but it won't happen. I think our marriages are probably very different. Are you now at ease with your situation?"

Again Wendy went silent and thoughtful. "It's certainly over but we did manage a close friendship – well perhaps not close but a form of friendship of sorts that worked some of the time. The end – the real end when we just became exes – was unexpected. Suddenly it was just there." Wendy's eyes were no longer on Jo but were distant, reliving a point somewhere in the past.

"It was new year's eve in the local pub and the chimes had just rung out and you could barely hear yourself think above the whooping and shouting, the kissing and calls of happy new year. I looked down the bar and at the far end Mark was standing with a woman I had never seen before – a very attractive woman. They each had a hand partly raised holding a glass of champagne or wine as if they were about to toast each other. But they remained motionless, looking into each other's eyes, warm, gentle smiles on their faces. They were in their own little world and there was no one else in that crowded pub but them.

"The look on Mark's face told me all I needed to know – that he had finally moved on. But it was the look on the woman's face that affected me most. I think that deep down, I had always blamed him for the fact that passion had evaporated from our marriage but looking at the unembarrassed way in which she displayed her adoration made me realise that I was equally to blame. I had long since ceased to provide the canvas that would allow Mark to paint his pictures of passion.

"For a little while I was devastated. Illogical, I know, but that's the way it was. It was the end of something very important. It was a sharp reminder that I couldn't mix and match relationships; I couldn't reject the bits of Mark that no longer satisfied me and hold on to those other, rewarding aspects of our relationship that had been such an important part of my life."

Wendy was still not looking at her but Jo could see tears running down her cheeks. She reached across the table and gripped Wendy's arm: "How did it make you feel?"

Her response was almost instant: "Empty... Just empty!... Well, that's enough of that." The forced smile revealed her even, white teeth and with her hand she quickly brushed away the evidence of her painful introspection. "I thought we were discussing you and your life!"

"We're both damaged goods, madam," Jo replied, "but you'd expect nothing else at our age."

Eager to move the subject on, Wendy laughed. "Kind of you Jo, but I've got a few years on you."

Jo was not yet ready to entirely surrender the intimacy that had developed between them. "You're obviously a passionate woman and there are lots of subjects that you could have chosen to be passionate about – abused children, the starving in Africa, oppressed women – why animals?"

"Get off my case, woman," Wendy replied with a laugh but in such a way that Jo suspected she was happy to answer now that she was firmly back on her own territory.

"I'm genuinely interested. Why animals?"

"Another time," Wendy said quietly. "I'd have thought you'd had enough horror for one day."

"Briefly – you don't have to go into too much detail. I just want to know the general reasons." Jo hoped her keenness would encourage Wendy by affirming that her interest was genuine, which it was.

"The problem is that the reasons are in the detail! Sure you're up to it?"

Jo just raised an eyebrow in admonishment.

"Okay, when I was a kid – about fourteen or fifteen – I was handed a leaflet in the street and it showed a fox that had been caught in a snare. It had pulled against the wire so hard in its desperation to escape that it had cut through its flesh to the bone. I looked at it in disbelief – that such a thing was legal in a country that bored the pants off you with the stupid claim that we're a nation of animal lovers.

"That fired the starting gun for me and I felt I just couldn't walk past it – ignore it – or I would be almost as guilty as the person who set the snare. In my stupidity – naivety more like – I thought all I had to do was tell people what was happening and they'd rise up and want to change things. I was shocked when they ignored me. Most of them are still ignoring me which is a bit of a sad statement – either about the world at large or me and I haven't yet made up my mind which."

Wendy had begun quietly, almost monotone, as though wanting to get the inquisition out of the way but no sooner had she started her explanations than passion began to inject pace and variation into her words.

"I then found out about the horror of factory farming and slaughter and had no option but to become vegetarian and was determined to work to try and bring about change. The whole of our society, where animals are concerned, is based on exploitation, cruelty and a suspension of compassion. How can anyone drag an animal who doesn't want to die into a slaughterhouse and kill it? Of course most people can't, which is why they allow others to do it for them. Even worse, they then pretend that it's perfectly normal and acceptable and adopt the ludicrous stance that those of us who are revolted by it are somehow weak, intellectually challenged or even overly sensitive?"

Jo grimaced: "Oh dear, I'm starting to feel uncomfortable."

Wendy laughed: "Good!" She paused and sipped her drink. "I'll give you just one more example and it's become almost famous because of the horror it encapsulates. In fact it perfectly sums up humankind's ability to intellectualise and defend almost any horror if the perpetrators stick on a white coat and write a paper about it afterwards.

"My first job in animal rights was with an anti-vivisection organisation and I was almost physically sick when the details and pictures of this case came through. It was a baby monkey. She was taken away from her mother shortly after birth and put in isolation. Her eyelids were stitched together with thick twine to blind her and she was given a cuddly toy to cling on to as some kind of reassurance at the distress of her separation.

"But the toy was part of the experiment and just when she

desperately started to seek solace from it in this dark, strange and unknown world of hers, the toy was taken from her and she was left to her solitary despair and fear.

"Do you know the reason for this so called experiment? To determine the effect of maternal deprivation on blind human babies! Have you ever heard such bollocks – as if it had any bearing on anything or anyone. Workers in that field wouldn't take any notice of it at all – in fact that abject cruelty wouldn't improve the human condition one jot. And even if it did, how can anyone justify such torture on one creature with the pretence that it might alleviate suffering in another creature. Thank god animal rights people broke into that place and rescued that little monkey, found her a home with others of her own kind and rehabilitated her. If they hadn't we would never have known about that revolting experiment – just as we don't know about thousands of other revolting experiments.

"Of course, the real purpose wasn't about helping blind children it was about writing scientific papers and getting them peer reviewed and published. It was about promoting careers because boasting of papers you've had published is a central plank in that. If it was allowed and practicable, some of them would use human babies and what happened in Hitler's Germany is a good reminder of that and what has recently come to light about experiments in the US on prisoners, soldiers and psychiatric patients back in the 50s and 60s.

"They were purposefully given LSD without knowing it and in many cases it has screwed their lives up permanently. And in another prison experiment, men were injected with multiple viruses simply to see what would happen, whether they would combine to produce an entirely new virus."

Jo was about to interject but Wendy cut across her.

"Who could put a chimpanzee in a vat of cold water and slowly bring it to the boil, recording the different levels of agony as the temperature increased until the animal was boiled to death? That also happened a few years ago."

The words were spat out, accusingly, as though Jo were somehow complicit in the atrocity. She didn't respond and Wendy again reached for her glass, sipped from it, throwing Jo a humourless smile. "Does that answer your question?"

"That'll teach me to keep my mouth shut." Jo replied and they both lapsed into a silence that was eventually broken by Jo. When she spoke it was with considerable trepidation.

"Is it fair simply to quote extremes, distressing as they obviously are, when there must be a huge body of work going on that benefits all of us?"

"Does it benefit all of us? Or do we simply never hear of the failures unless they're so profound – like Thalidomide – that they grab the headlines? There are a huge number of failures. Only one in ten of all the drugs passed fit for humans as a result of animal testing ever go into production. They fail when it comes to human studies, that's how different we all are. Aspirin cures our headaches but kills cats. The supposedly safe drugs that do go into general use kill thousands of people every year in this country alone. It's the fourth biggest cause of death and all these drugs have supposedly been tested on animals and declared safe. How's that for demolishing that old cliché – 'my baby's life or a rat's?' That isn't the choice. Testing on animals has driven medical research in entirely the wrong direction, approving drugs that are highly dangerous and rejecting drugs that could be highly advantageous because they have negative effects on some unrelated animal or other."

Wendy suddenly became dismissive, slamming shut the window she'd opened into her world. "That's it, Jo, I've had enough for one day."

"Ok, sure! But just one last thing." Jo's mood had changed but there was one idea that was formulating in her mind and wouldn't go away. It needed an answer.

"You said you shot the footage of the ducks on that leaflet inside a duck farm – do you still do that kind of thing – go into farms and so on?"

Wendy sounded weary: "Not so much anymore because the media's become more demanding and wants blood and brutality not just neglect. We now tend to get people employed in the places we want to expose so that we've got chapter and verse on what happens. But we still sometimes go in at night, from time to time, if we get a tip off about a place and need to act quickly."

Jo again went silent and when she spoke the words were delivered not as a request but a demand: "I want to come with you next time!"

Wendy threw her hands in the air and produced a laugh as false as it was sudden: "Whoa, whoa – you're not serious. 'Prime minister's wife done for breaking and entering'. I can see the headlines now!"

"How often do you get caught?"

"It's only happened a couple of times in god knows how many years – and we don't break and enter, we just walk in. But you get my point."

"So there you are! Not a problem, I'll come with you because I'm on a mission don't forget."

Wendy suddenly became interested: "If we find anything – any abuse – would you be prepared to lend your name to it when we go public?"

Jo went silent as though pondering the question but when the answer came it was said with reluctance: "Any other time and... yeah, I would. But now – I'm really not sure."

"I detect hesitation..." Wendy replied, laughing and pushing her friend's shoulder across the table. "You open to persuasion?"

"No, I really don't think so." Jo hardened up her response and added: "You only want me for my name!" It was said jokingly but beneath the humour was just a trace of cynicism.

She really did not like the idea that she was being used.

"True," replied Wendy and it wasn't what Jo had expected. "You're open support would be brilliant and I never miss an opportunity to publicise the plight of animals – that's my job. But I also like you for you, regardless of who you're married to."

Jo felt a little surge of relief as she was enjoying Wendy's company and hoped it was reciprocated.

"Okay then, can I still come with you even though you can't use me?"

Jo could see she was considering the possibility.

"I'll think about it..." was Wendy's conclusion and Jo's eyes bored into her from beneath knotted eyebrows demanding something more positive. "Okay, I'll seriously think about it but right now I'd better get going – I've got to get back to Clapham."

"Your daughter?" Jo enquired.

"No, she's with her dad this weekend and Mike's at his mum's but it's getting late."

"So you don't have to get back?"

"No, not for anything specific."

"Do you like Indian food?" Jo asked with enthusiasm.

"Yeaaah…"

"Okay, we're going up to the Indian on the cricket green for a meal and then you can spend the night at my place. There's lots I want to ask you… and I'm going to get a wholehearted agreement from you by tomorrow."

Chapter Fourteen

"Brilliant," Stephen, "absolutely buddy brilliant."

Charlie Whiston's rheumy eyes gleamed beneath the smooth helmet of glued down grey hair – gleamed with absolute pleasure, gleamed like a young man's whose declaration of love had been accepted by his adoring sweetheart, gleamed with an intensity that comes solely with victory. But even in the midst of his ecstasy, he still couldn't bring himself to swear and emasculated the word 'bloody' to make it palatable. He never swore – ever, as far as Stephen knew.

Perhaps it was for the same reasons that Stephen himself very rarely swore – nothing moral about it simply a precaution that would avoid a habit developing, and once a habit was in place it was all too easy for a little 'bollocks' or 'shit' to inadvertently sneak out into a world where they would make headlines. Stephen wasn't sure if it was this that fuelled Charlie's restraint but suspected it was simply an ingrained remnant of some far distant Edwardian code of chivalry. Charlie lived and would probably die by this code, serenely unaware that it had atrophied at about the same time as the wearing of spats had ended.

"I can't believe how well we've done, Stephen. We were bally lucky that Andrew read the situation and shoved off to kick start his own campaign but we are up and running, old boy, up and running and I reckon almost unstoppable. We're going to do it hands down, Stephen."

Stephen Aldous looked at the ancient old king maker and realised that this is what the man lived for. Not the acquiring of power, not the wielding of power – at least not directly. He was the power broker, the creator of power, the dispenser, the gate keeper, the guardian. And those upon whom he bestowed this extraordinary beneficence were essentially created from one of his own ribs in that they had to reflect Charlie's beliefs and his vision of how the world should be. They were born in his own image.

Those beliefs, of course, coincided with the policies that enriched him and were calculated to clear as many obstacles as possible from the path of free trade. Those obstacles included organised labour, unproved environmental scare stories and even those that had been proved, political correctness, women's rights, human rights, animal rights or any other diversion which might hinder economic growth. His thinking was simple – allow the wealth creators to flourish and all the rest would follow in due time. Stephen agreed with him.

Responding to the urgency of the situation, emergency calls had been put in to some of the other grandees who occupied the secretive corridors of power and who wielded influence as skilfully and single-mindedly as Charlie. Most had answered the call – Harry (Sir Harold) Cunningham, the Rt Hon George (Georgie) Fiennes, Peter Macintosh and Edward Smith – in fact his real name was Churchill-Smith but Edward had dropped the Churchill some decades ago when he stood for and lost a marginal seat – wanted to sound more man of the people. It was his one and only attempt to get elected but the unofficial name change had stayed with him and the power he had subsequently accreted to himself was far, far greater than most MPs could dream of.

Those who could possibly make it had done so because this leadership election and the general election which was to follow allowed them to wield power once again – something which had been denied them for too many years.

Harry Cunningham was tall and rangy with a stoop that gave the impression that he was permanently inspecting something or other. His head was topped with a mop of salt and pepper where each hair seemed determined to make its own way in life. Georgie was rotund to the point of bursting, with clumps of mousy air on either side of his head, the intervening pate gleaming as though it had been freshly polished. Peter

Macintosh was neat and dapper and would pass as a GP with the perfect bedside manner. Stephen half believed that his thinning hair may have been painted on as it never seemed to grow or shorten. No matter how expensive his clothes nor how well co-ordinated, Edward Smith always looked like an unmade bed and you just knew that if he raised a spoonful of soup to his generous mouth, some would inevitably find its way onto his waistcoat.

Tall and short, bald and hirsute, portly and slim and yet they were all essentially the same. With one exception, each looked as shiny and neat and polished as a newly valeted car. Impeccable with starched white shirts and striped ties from school or club or regiment. The careful stitching of hand-made clothes and gleaming shoes but the mantle they all wore and bound them tightly together was one of confidence – absolute confidence. They were right, they were always right and not one of them had ever displayed – at least publicly – even a semblance of doubt, that debilitating but very human emotion that bedevilled most people.

Unlike those who had preceded them in these same positions, their right to anoint a leader privately, without consultation and without fuss had been snatched away by the party's determined leap onto the bandwagon of supposed democracy. It had led to members mouthing phrases which were secretly anathema to them, such as – one person one vote. The problem with democracy, they all thought, was that it was wasted on the ignorant.

They had fought tenaciously to try and subvert this display of people power, to cling on to their influence and the task of guiding their party in the right direction by selecting its leader, but had failed. The result was democratic elections for party leader and the subsequent disasters that had followed and an almost free-ride for Labour.

This time there would be no mistake – their man would make it, democracy or no democracy. What emboldened them and cheered them was that they believed they were pushing at an open door and there was no truly serious contender to steal the crown away from Stephen Aldous – or at least they believed so.

But when momentous decisions of State and economics conflated as now, no risks could be taken. As a consequence, they had been hitting the phones hard for the best part of two days.

Stephen was fully aware that no matter how tightly they had once held onto the strings within the party, their grip was loosening as a new kind of politician was usurping their power. By the election after this, those of them who were still alive would be mere bystanders. This election was, in effect, their last hurrah and they intended to make the most of it.

There were sitting MPs to contact, prospective MPs, whips, committee chairmen, the 1922 committee, local party chairmen and influential friends and acquaintances. They wanted to take the pulse of the party but mostly they wanted pledges of support that would nullify the only other two challengers who stood even half a chance – Andrew Whittington and Anthony Burbage.

"I have personally spoken to thirty-five local party chairmen, Stephen, and twenty-two of them are solidly behind you, plus there are a few who I think are waverers and can be persuaded. They're keeping their cards close to their chest but that's to be expected and doesn't mean they're against you. I can also offer you the backing of the 1922 committee and judging from the number of MPs I and the others have spoken to, you're in the lead by about fifty per cent to Whittington's thirty-five per cent. Burbage is sweeping up the crumbs. At this stage, that's brilliant, buddy brilliant. And what's more, the other contenders will be getting similar messages so they know they have an uphill battle on their hands."

Stephen had himself phoned no one but had stood waiting to be pulled out of the hat like a conjurer's rabbit so that those making the calls could call upon their putative king as and when necessary to add weight to their arguments, to answer specific questions on policy or to listen to individual bids for a quid pro quo in return for their support. The most common request was for Stephen to make a personal appearance at one of their constituency meetings.

He knew that the next few weeks were going to be utterly exhausting and the only way in which he could even begin to meet the demands upon him – and secure support in the process

– would be to double up, fit two constituencies into one evening, make the speeches shorter and spend less time at each stop. He could almost certainly manage some daytime meetings, too, as most of the constituency members were retired.

Charlie turned to the others in the bustling room and shouted: "Whose spoken to the Press? What's the situation?"

Georgie Fiennes answered. "Yes, I have but not NI, that's Harry's area. The others are as you might expect. They haven't confirmed it but their lack of enthusiasm gives it away – the Telegraph are almost certainly going for Whittington, in a big way I suspect. I'm pretty sure it's payback for something or other but if he fails to win the nomination we can take it as read that they will throw their weight behind us at the general election. Well, they have no other option, do they? The Express is pretending to be independent and doesn't want to show its hand but I'm pretty sure they'll stick their snouts in our trough if we can offer them something they can brandish as a coup. Perhaps an exclusive interview with Stephen and Josephine.

"The Mail are every bit as enthusiastic as we are so we can rely on them absolutely but I don't think we should take them for granted. They've earned our support and we should give it. We need to feed them tidbits all along the way and some major stuff as well – family portrait, Josephine talking to female readers, that sort of thing. I obviously haven't bothered with the Guardian. The Indie has made it clear that the only person they think worth supporting is Burbage because of his environmental concerns. They even describe him as the best of a pretty nondescript bunch. The Star has no interest in the leadership fight but tends towards Andrew when it goes to the general election."

Stephen was aware that the comments were all being directed at Charlie, Harry, Georgie, Edward and Peter Mackintosh – particularly Charlie who was cracking a verbal whip like a metaphorical ringmaster.

"Peter," snapped Charlie, "what's the position with the Ozzies?"

"We know they're ideologically closer to Stephen than the other two but that doesn't mean we can take them for granted.

Okay, first, this is what they're prepared to give us! The Sun and Sun on Sunday will go for us in a big way during the leadership election and will continue as cheer leader in the run up to the general election. The Times will stay aloof for the leadership contest but will come on board for the general election. We have them all – wholeheartedly and without reservation."

"And what's he demanding in return?" asked Charlie impatiently.

Harry Cunningham checked his notes "You've probably guessed it already. Their first demand is that we clear the way for them to retake control of Sky News. They only sold it off to ease their path for the take-over of BskyB but Leveson intervened. They hate being forced into anything so I think it's as much a matter of principle as finance. But for most people that's history now and they feel there will be no unmanageable public outcry to their acquisition of it.

"They're fed up with what they term 'pussyfooting around' and, reading between the lines, I think they mean that the UK is overburdened with so-called independent and balanced news reporting." Harry wagged his two index fingers in the air as he said the word balanced. "They want to turn Sky news into something akin to Fox News – an unbridled supporter of right-wing politics. It would ensure solid, partisan reporting of our policies on one of our leading news channels almost in perpetuity. It really would be something special."

Charlie turned to the room as a whole. "What do we think? Would it be politically possible to do this?"

There was no common feeling amongst those present until Peter Macintosh spoke again: "It would be fairly dirty and I think we could do it but it would cost him. He will essentially have to stuff the Sky News directors mouths with gold to regain control of it but I'm sure we can pave the way to allow it to happen. We'll have to time it right, though. You know, the usual thing, slip the enabling order through in the middle of a crisis. I think we can assure them there will be no opposition from us."

"You said 'first demand', Peter, are there others?"

"Oh yes! That was merely the preamble. They hate defeat

and that's what they're faced with in their pay-to-view Times online news service. They have so few subscribers that they're in danger of losing their Teflon image. And of course, we all know the reason. Why would anyone subscribe and pay out good money for his version of the news when they can click on to the BBC and get all they want free of charge? Their operation is dead in the water here while in the States and elsewhere it's more than compensating for the slump in newspaper sales. This is the future for big media organisations and they know it better than anyone yet they're simply not in the game here in the UK. They're extremely pissed off – to put it indelicately."

"So what do they want, as if we didn't know?"

"Quite! It's their old bete noire again, the BBC," Peter continued. "They want its wings clipped, cut off more like. They are furious that the UK has this ludicrous position where the public have no option but to pay for one TV broadcaster through a compulsory licence fee. It doesn't exist anywhere else in the world and they believe it's an unfair restriction of trade. They want them side-lined to a subscription-only medium and end their dominance over terrestrial broadcasting. They didn't spell it out but it's pretty clear that all the support that's being offered is dependent upon us wielding the clippers on their behalf. Even worse, if we do agree but fail to deliver when we're in office, they've hinted they'll turn their whole news empire against us, attack us and belittle us at every toss and turn so we need to think carefully before we respond."

Charlie did not pause for thought. "I suspect that few of us here are great supporters of the BBC so I don't think it's so much a question of if we want to curb them but whether it's politically acceptable and if it isn't, how can we turn public opinion around? Obviously, we can rely on his news empire to churn out a non-stop diatribe against the Beeb to soften people up…"

Harry butted in: "They're doing that already to some degree but they still haven't managed to kill off its popularity in the public eye."

Stephen was acutely aware that the entire policy debate was being conducted without reference to him and the only opinions being solicited were from the grandees. It was not what he had expected. He had had just a little taste of being the chosen one during the hectic period of telephone canvassing when he was constantly being asked to speak to party members: he had been offered to potential voters with gravity, like a chief of the clan, as though his words, thoughts and observations were infinitely more important than those making the contact. He was pulled from the pudding like a big and juicy plum to impress the impressionable. "Just a minute, I have Stephen here with me and I know he'd love to speak to you." "Would you like to speak to Stephen?" "I know that Stephen is dying to speak to you. Hold on, he's here with me now." "Stephen truly values your opinion and would be delighted if you'll support him."

But the deference had now stopped and he was, he felt, just a bystander at the feast. He was the boy on whose behalf the men were making decisions. Perhaps it was partly his fault and a product of the cultivated deference he had shown to Charlie and the others. In truth, he had no great admiration for them other than the fact that they could make his transition to power glide so much more easily. He knew that the boy had to step forward and show he was a man.

It was vital, now, at the very start of the process to imprint himself on his party elders or it would become increasingly difficult to do so.

"We have to be extremely vigilant," he said quietly, couching his words as though they had been carefully thought about and his delivery attempted to give them gravity. "To have the support of such a powerful media empire would be extremely useful, conclusively persuasive, even. But... the moment we want to introduce a policy which their Ozzships don't like, they can just as easily turn the publicity against us. As we've seen in the past, they have the ability to utterly undermine a government if they choose."

Stephen was pleased, not just with his delivery but the content also. He felt it was an extremely valid point, delivered well. Before he could continue, Charlie intervened.

"Nonsense," he barked. "Newspapers are very good at building people's images, of persuading the proletariat that someone or something is preferable to someone or something else but that's when there's very little else to compare them with. We haven't introduced any policies yet that people can judge us by so building up a picture of a future premier is comparatively easy – keep saying he's good, he's great, he's dynamic, he's what the country needs long enough and people will half believe it. Trying rubbishing that same person when there's a whole raft of policies behind him, policies that have improved people's lives and made them feel better, happier, and they will ignore it.

"Voters are quite capable of calling on their own experiences and if it differs from the one on offer from a newspaper, they will go with their own judgement. I feel we have no option to offer him what he wants and then worry about if we can deliver it – and I personally won't shed any tears over it if we can."

Stephen paused before replying. He could feel the heat of his blood colouring his cheeks and his neckband prickling. This was not what he had been expecting and he knew he must curb his irritation before replying. Actually, it was much closer to anger. He was angry that the whole discussion had referred to 'our' policies, that strategy was being formed without reference to him, that his opinion had been sought on not a single issue and no one had even mentioned his name.

But he was most angry that his view had been dismissed out of hand – swatted away like an irritating fly, even though he knew this was Charlie's technique – to dismiss and diminish opposing views scathingly in order to impress himself on any argument and shoulder his way to victory – it still hurt. Stephen thought he deserved more consideration than this. 'When I have the power…' – he found the thought flitting through his mind and was almost shocked by the realisation of it. 'When I have the power…' he thought the thought again, and this time a tingle of excitement shot down his legs and arms to his toes and fingers.

It was exactly what he needed to flush out his irritation and reclaim the territory that had been grabbed from him.

"So all I have to do, Charlie, is get the unions to roll on to their backs to be tickled, get the lame to walk and the blind to see! No pressure, then." The laughter that ran around the room emboldened Stephen but he could see that Charlie was not amused.

"Don't let's be strong-armed into anything," Stephen continued. "I will get the party's nomination without the support of the press if necessary, that's obvious. As for the general election, my lead in the polls is pretty impressive – not unassailable but strong…"

"You can't rely on them…" Charlie intervened and Stephen cut across him.

"I know I can't rely on them at this stage but our canvassing returns are also extremely encouraging. I have the lead and the one thing about News International is that they always like to back a winner. As things stand at the moment, there is no way that they will risk backing any of the other parties for fear of losing, and that would shatter their pretence that they determine the result of elections."

Stephen could feel his confidence growing as he jettisoned 'our' and 'we' in favour of 'I' and 'me'. This was politicking, this is what he was good at, this is what had got him to the threshold of power.

"Basically, I have no problem with the changes he wants but I won't have them delivered as demands but as requests. I can't commit to policies I may not be able to push through the House, that would weaken me. Politics is the art of the possible and they have to realise that. I need to meet with them if necessary – not somewhere on the other side of the world but in London where it can be done surreptitiously. They're the ones who're asking so they can come to me and I will explain what I'm prepared to do and what I'm prepared to try and do.

"And there has to be no publicity surrounding this meeting, is that understood? Can you fix it please, Harry?"

"Tread very carefully, Stephen, this organisation is a law unto itself." Again Charlie tried to take charge of the agenda.

"There's no point continuing with this until we've met and know precisely what's on the table," Stephen replied, trying not to be too dismissive. Then, as a full stop to underline his termination of the debate, he spoke loudly:

"Now! What's the position with Whittington and Burbage?"

He didn't wait for a reply. "What has to be pre-eminent in our thinking is how to get this whole process over with on the first vote. I have to win it outright at the first attempt because as we all know, if I fail and it goes to a run off which will almost certainly take us perilously close to the general election I simply may not have sufficient time to impress myself on the public. It could be fatal. So all our thinking has to bear this in mind."

He waited for contributions and again it was Charlie who tried to take control.

"Andrew Whittington is the only one we need concern ourselves with and I think Harry, Georgie, Peter and I should pay him a visit – ask him to put the party first and stand down for the greater good. Perhaps offer him the Defra brief. At the end of the day he knows he won't win and he's simply putting down a marker for the future, confirming he's the second most electable man in the party."

"That's one way, I suppose," Stephen replied, again hiding his anger – that Charlie had dared to propose offering a post without consulting him. But he didn't need to bridle as he felt in control now. "But Andrew is a bit of a maverick and I'm not sure he's totally open to appeals for solidarity or the offer of a brief that doesn't interest him, not when a good showing in the poll will help to mould his future career.

"I'll wipe the floor with Burbage so I'm not going to worry about him, he can do as he pleases. But Andrew Whittington is a different person entirely. He doesn't have a lot of charisma and that's the only thing that's held him back. He has intelligence and support, which I think will grow as he campaigns – not enough to win but enough to damage me. I know the man fairly well and I am pretty certain what he's after – he's dropped enough hints."

Stephen paused and looked around the room from face to face and saw he had achieved precisely what he intended – silence and the attention of everyone present. "He wants the foreign affairs brief!" Again Stephen paused for effect. "And I intend to offer it to him!"

There was a roar of protest from the grandees and Archie Smith, who had hardly spoken so far, almost exploded as he voiced his objections, his face crimson and the buttons on his shirt straining against the material:

"Good god, Stephen, you can't do that... With the current turmoil in the world, it's far and away the second most important role in government – a pivotal position. It has to go to one of our men and there's no one better fitted for it than William Mansfield."

Stephen was suddenly aware of his naivety. He should have realised that, of course, he wasn't the only selected one. These men had not only plucked him out as the next leader but many of the key cabinet members, too. They wanted complete control. He wondered how many of these ministers elect had been spoken to just as he had been, and told they were in line for top jobs. If he didn't go along with the grandee's wishes, there would be some very discontented people in all levels of the party who could make life extremely uncomfortable for him once he was elected. He would also be left with a cabinet not of his choosing.

He wasn't going to allow it to happen but outright confrontation at this still tender time might cost him the nomination – unlikely but not impossible. If he were to show signs of being uncontrollable, they wouldn't hesitate to pull Andrew Whittington to one side and offer him their conditional support – conditional upon his deference to their opinions. And by god he would accept it because he knew that they had the ability to swing a large number of the party behind them and he would achieve the prize that he had never seriously thought was within his grasp.

Stephen realised he was tiptoeing through dangerous territory and not yet having the nomination in his grasp, it was time to quieten the horses.

"I understand your concerns entirely, Archie, but we're confronting two issues here. Getting elected and moulding the party in the way we wish to see it. Which one takes priority? It's a no brainer – we have to get elected first and then everything else follows after."

Andrew Whittington was precisely who Stephen wanted in the foreign office but now was not the time to go to the barricades over it, particularly as he did not yet have the top job. So in effect, it was all words and he was good at those. He had to persuade them that he mirrored their beliefs, was entirely on their side and the only conflict between them was over style not substance.

"Don't worry about Andrew, he'll go at the first reshuffle and William will replace him, that isn't a problem. What we have to do to is ensure I not only gain the nomination but that I do it in style and the timing has to be right. From that will stem my authority for the entire parliament and there is only one way I can achieve this and maximise our position."

There wasn't only one way but Stephen, like Charlie and the other big guns, had long since learned to beef up his own demands and diminish alternative views. That was how you got what you wanted. He had quietly reintroduced the 'we' into the conversation where appropriate to reinforce his inclusiveness – albeit temporarily.

"Andrew would sell his grandmother to become foreign secretary. Not only will I offer it to him but I will get him to agree to drop his leadership bid just the day before the vote. That will give it the maximum possible impact and me the greatest possible exposure. If it's a shoe in, the media won't be interested in covering the election in any depth and I will have missed a trick, namely the ability to reach out beyond the party. Knowing that Andrew is going to stand down at the very last minute, I can largely ignore internal infighting and concentrate on the bigger policy issues – the issues that voters need to know about and which will determine which way they vote. We will have effectively stolen a march on the other parties and kicked off our general election campaign early."

Simply by observing their faces and before a word was spoken, Stephen knew he had won the argument. Of course, he had no idea if Andrew would accept his proposition but logic dictated he would. He could stand down and get the second most important job in government or he could fight and get nothing. Five years in the wilderness would not appeal to someone with the ambition of Andrew Whittington.

This was the final straight and Stephen was determined that

nothing would force him to stumble. He knew that the greatest threat came from 'events, dear boy, events' as Macmillan had put it, but he intended to control or at least anticipate those events wherever possible. There were just two more hurdles to go and then he could relax. He would allow nothing – but nothing – to stand in his way now that he was so close that he could almost stretch out his arm and touch the premiership. He was going to make his way into history and the thought almost overwhelmed him with excitement. He wanted to leap in the air and click his heels together but instead said with a smile: "Right, a drink everyone!"

Chapter Fifteen

Life was just one long, bloody compromise, thought Fergal Duff as he tramped through the endless soft rain and watched drops of water move slowly down his fluorescent orange waterproofs before melding into other drops to form tiny rivulets that raced downwards to drip onto his leggings. Boredom showed in every step of his unenthusiastic walk as he ambled along the jetty towards the young salmon pens, with just a momentary straightening of the shoulders as he touched his right hand pocket and felt the reassuring weight of a half-bottle of single malt whisky. Or at least what was left of it.

As he reached the wooden walkway that stretched outwards into the deep water of the loch, bisecting two of the pens, he sheltered momentarily inside the little hut that housed feed, medication, insecticides and all the other paraphernalia of big pharma that kept the salmon alive – some of the time – enabled them to grow and provided profits for his Norwegian masters.

There was nothing racist in his thoughts for he knew only too well that there was absolutely no difference in the methodology, pay or conditions of any salmon producer along the entire west coast of Scotland. They all worked from the same script, word perfect, in the same way that a McDonald's hamburger was identical whether served in Glasgow or Gdansk. Some clever chappies somewhere had worked out precisely how to pare a penny off here and a penny there until inputs, including wages, were at the lowest possible level and outputs, per unit cost of input, were at their maximum.

The fact that the industry was almost exclusively run by Norwegians was neither here nor there, in Fergal's thinking.

Why wouldn't they avail themselves of the lenient regime offered by the London government, the employment subsidies they offered, the glowing endorsements they used to describe aquaculture and their hands-off approach. No, it was not the Norwegians who were the problem but the system.

He was crystal clear in his thinking that he had far more in common with the Larss and Jans and Oles – who were probably at this very moment, in some fjord or other near Stavanger or Alesund, about to do precisely what he was about to do because that is what the schedule dictated – than with any of the corporate owners whether their accents were Norwegian, Scottish or even Mongolian.

Fergal peered out of the hut doorway, looking first left and then right across the rain-soaked terrain, like some guilty shoplifter, before retreating back inside, removing the bottle from his pocket, uncorking it and raising it to his lips. The smoky, peaty liquid tracked a fiery path across his tongue, down his throat and into his stomach where it made its presence known by igniting the contents.

Fergal gritted his teeth and let out a long 'aaaaah'. It was pure theatre as the effects of Scotch had long since ceased to challenge his senses – and particularly one as aged, rounded and mellow as this one. He took great delight in its origins, which were no more than four miles from where he stood. It was almost his patriotic duty to support a local distillery, he thought with a smile, and fervently wished that he had the resources to patronise it regularly. Tomorrow it would be back to the cheaper, blended stuff but at least it was Scottish.

He still thrilled at that word – Scottish! Yes, he was a Scot and more than that he was a Highlander – a Scottish Highlander – and it was difficult to imagine any two words that could engender a greater feeling of pride, of self, of national identity than these two.

Like so many of his friends and school chums, he had served in the Scottish army – the Argyll and Sutherland Highlanders – Princess Louise's. But even that proud nomenclature, that honourable badge of distinction, had been watered down and emasculated as it became the Fifth Battalion, the Royal

Regiment of Scotland. He had marched behind a piper with his chequered bonnet almost touching his eyebrows and his kilt swinging in time to his steps. It engendered a rush of pride so powerful it ensured that he snapped his shoulders as far back as they would go and allowed his ostentatious swagger to give the kilt a life of its own.

No wonder enemies feared the skirl of the pipes because the men who marched to its historic tones were not entering battle and placing their lives at risk for the sake of an English government, nor a German Queen, but for their comrades and the pride of their regiment and their nation, their little nation that had been emasculated and ignored for centuries. What fear these Highlanders had on entering into battle would be suppressed by the expectations of history and regimental belonging.

Perhaps Alexandre Dumas had stolen their creed for his three musketeers – one for all and all for one, and no quarter given. The sense of being feared in battle because of who you were and what you were was as powerful as any drug.

His nation was one which had, for hundreds of years, been ruled by a Southern government of toffs and egocentric bigots, ennobled mostly by the presence of a few Scottish MPs who, it seemed, were afflicted with amnesia and impotence once they settled on to the green benches of the Palace of Westminster. Most government policies were anathema to Fergal while to the government, Scotland was a small irritation, like a pimple on the arse which they hoped would soon go away.

They had left Scots with few opportunities and those they had once had, such as steel making, mining and ship building, had all be taken away to be replaced by... nothing! That was the reality. But in any case, these were all Lowland occupations and the Highlands were what they had always been since the Clearances, wastelands – beautiful, mournful, foreboding wastelands.

Fergal glanced down at the bottle in his hand almost with reverence and lamented the rather sad little dribble of liquid that swilled across the bottom of its glass. By tilting it until the Scotch congregated in one corner forming a small, lightly-golden triangle, it appeared more than it was. 'What the hell' he thought and drained the remnants of his Scottish comforter.

The Nationalists now had his vote, although Fergal's expectations were hardly unbridled. Real power still lay south of the border and even if it didn't, it would still be a case of trying to make a silk purse out of a sow's ear. What could they bring to the Highlands other than gawping tourists and people who wanted to shoot deer for fun. Fergal had no real objection to deer being shot, he had done it himself, but to turn it into a circus for impotent southerners whose rifles were substitute erections, was degrading. The deer were as Scottish as he was and should be taken out by Scots.

He had thought little about deer until one particular beast had slipped beneath his consciousness to establish a powerful presence. He did not see it regularly but from time to time, always in the evening as the light was beginning to dim, it would appear on the hill on the westerly side of the loch. It would stand on its pedestal like some cast Victorian figure, always facing north, its head back and its huge antlers over its shoulders. And there it would stand motionless for minutes at a time, as obviously proud as any Scot could be, a king in his own domain. Killing that beast would be an honour and he would accord it the respect that its magnificence deserved.

One spectacular occasion had burned itself into Fergal's memory and he was always hoping to see it repeated – and hear its accompanying soundtrack. In fact, he had already glanced towards the hill several times as the hour was right although the hill could barely be seen through the mist of softly falling rain. This one time, just this once, the stag had taken up his position of dominance against a cloudless, backlit sky. The huge orange ball of a setting sun slowly descended behind the creature until he became a cameo silhouetted in the centre of a glowing, burning disc.

Alistair Currie played the pipes like an angel but drove his wife crazy with his constant practicing and time to time she banished him from the house. When this rejection happened he always retreated to the same spot on the banks of the loch. On this one day, this utterly memorable day, in the failing light, the sound of the pipes drifted across the still and silent water and the magnificent stag, against his glowing backdrop, inclined his head not one jot in recognition of the melody – it was as though he anticipated it, expected it, deserved it.

The tune was Flowers of the Forest, a soulful lament played at the graveside of many a Scottish warrior killed in battle – a lament that Alistair, like so many other pipers, would practice only in isolation because, like a Gurkha's kukri, when it was publicly produced it had to be for real. Fergal was transfixed by the stag, barely daring to breathe, and huge tears rolled down his craggy face. It was a lament for what his country might have been. It was a lament for what he might have been.

Had he died in Iraq or Afghanistan, perhaps his family could have thought back on him as a warrior, a hero, their emotions heightened by the crisp, drill-perfect ceremony of solemn comrades, of a volley of shots fired over his grave and by the gentle fingering of a regimental piper, fuelling his wife and his children's emotions with a soulful tribute until grief overwhelmed them. That would have provided memories worthy of a hero.

Unlike him, however, they were probably not aware of what a filthy little imperialistic war it was, a war in which he had no desire to die because it would have inevitably defined him and he did not want to be defined by a conflict that disgusted him. If this is what humankind considered noble and righteous then there was something wrong with humankind, thought Fergal – but he had thought that for a very long time. Whether they wore a turban or a keflar helmet was immaterial; there should be a kinship that inevitably moved the species forward as they learnt from mistakes and were educated by new discoveries. It was all going in the opposite direction, of that he was sure.

He was a soldier who had declined to extend his service, sickened by what he had seen and done. In Iraq, victims were collected each morning from wasteland and open drains where their bodies had been discarded overnight. You knew which side they represented by the manner of their deaths. One lot favoured electric drills, blow torches and electric irons; for the other side it was cut throats and severed heads. And the conflict between them? Two slightly different visions of the same god?

Afghanistan was not a real war but a dirty, fratricidal outpouring of spite and hatred in a country locked into the middle ages that had dismembered and killed women and children far more frequently than it had either set of combatants. He has seen trembling women, their identities concealed by all-obscuring hijabs, forced to kneel so they could be shot through the head by a medieval peasant because of some perceived moral failing.

He was a political man – a socialist he would have once described himself as – and to quit had been a political decision as much as a humanitarian one. There had to be an 'instead'. Every new step along the road of life, each new experience, had confirmed his politics – either humankind learned to live together cooperatively or they would destroy each other.

Fergal looked around the tired little hut and contemplated his 'instead'. He was a near alcoholic labourer on a salmon farm that provided the only employment available but was destroying the environment of this magnificent coastline. Every fish he fed, every sick one he culled, every fish he killed played a part in this devastation.

It seemed that whatever the creed or belief, religion or philosophy, the minutiae of maintaining its existence always overwhelmed its vision. That was routinely sacrificed to maintain power, even if that power remained within the confines of its adherents, the bigger picture sacrificed on the altar of personal aggrandisement. Why was it, Fergal thought, that the turds always floated to the top. As a consequence, there appeared to be no template for a life more equable or satisfying anywhere in the world.

In fact, the world was awash with bullshit – bullshit that told people what they wanted to hear, bullshit that they accepted without enquiry, bullshit that prevented them from having to worry, bullshit that kept them consuming the world to death while others packed the dosh away in secret places believing – if they believed anything – that when the shit did hit the fan their wealth would buy them preference, affording them salvation.

His own industry was entirely supported by so much bullshit that he was surprised its authors did not drown in the stuff.

Assurances flowed from the industry association like water from a tap and with about as much substance. There was nothing wrong with salmon farming – at all. All its problems had been solved through the lessons borne by experience and if any criticism looked like leaving an impression, there was always the killer answer to retreat behind – the Highlands would be decimated without the employment provided by the salmon.

Fergal knew all about salmon. Not these flabby, sad, selectively reared, pathetic specimens that he tended but real salmon. He had been born and brought up with them, knew every pool where they might rest in local rivers. Salmon were once creatures of wonder and extraordinary secrecy who had evolved their magical life force long before humankind had set foot on the planet.

Every Spring and Autumn they appeared in the rivers, from where no one knew. They forced their way upstream with a strength and determination that was humbling until they reached the shallowest little burns where the hens fanned shallow scrapes in the gravel with their tails and shed their eggs into them. The ever-attendant cocks then shed their melt in milky clouds that percolated down through the eggs and fertilized them. Once done, the hens then wafted the gravel over their secret stashes to cover them and keep them secure from predators.

It was a precise art as it was essential to keep oxygenated water constantly flowing over their eggs or they would not hatch. These were the very same burns and gravel banks that had given birth to these exact fish. They had come home seemingly from nowhere to somewhere very small and local and definite and no one knew how or why.

Fergal knew that their task was made so much easier if there was a decent depth of water in the rivers and burns as it lessened many of the obstacles they faced, the biggest of which was waterfalls. On innumerable occasions he had stood beside one particular fall on the Adrochney river as it crashed twenty feet sheer down in to the pool below – a roaring, foaming ferment of inhospitable water. When there was a decent flow he knew he would see not a single salmon unless one happened to rise in the pool below the fall for they would navigate this formidable obstacle in an almost unbelievable manner.

With their powerfully muscular tails and bodies thrashing to and fro, they would propel themselves vertically upwards through the descending torrent to the quiet river above and then, having exhausted themselves, would recuperate in a quiet pool or behind a rock whose eddy would hold them against the current without them expending a further calorie. Once rested, they would continue their journey and face more falls, more rapids, more obstacles, including the flies and spinners of anglers and the nets of poachers.

When water levels were low it was a different story. They would still attempt to swim up the reduced volume of water but if so much as a tip of their tail emerged from the surface they would lose propulsion and crash back into the water below or onto the rocks.

If the rains remained absent and the water thinned even further, they would resort to leaping and for many fish it was an exhausting, relentless, constantly repeated effort to satisfy their driving urge to reproduce. At a time like this, the pool below the fall became crowded with salmon and many a time Fergal had cast a fly or spinner amongst them to take a few for sale, knowing exactly when the ghillies would patrol.

He wheeled the feed bin out of the shed, clattering the handle of a landing net which had been propped against an outside wall but was now flat on the pontoon. He made a mental note to replace it on his return, registered that it had stopped raining and admitted to himself that he had drunk too much. That's what introspection did to you, he thought.

In the two large nets which flanked the pontoon were 70,000 fish, creatures who, through no fault of their own, were an insult to salmon. They were from the same Atlantic stock but selective breeding and genetic manipulation had stripped them of their majesty. With a scoop, he flung food in a wide arc to each side and the water boiled with frantically feeding fish. Here, in these nets, lurked no mysteries no questions which defied answers as there were with wild salmon.

Why, when a salmon left the sea and entered fresh water did

its stomach atrophy? No matter how long it was in the rivers it would not eat. So why also did it still rise to a well-placed fly, or snap at his spinning lure, or even grab at a bunch of worms impaled on a hook?

Surely nature could not be so cruel as to deny them the ability to feed but still leave them with the desire? Or was it simply a reflex action beyond their control? No one knew and Fergal was delighted that no one knew. Why, also, did those fish who stayed too long in fresh water undergo the most extraordinary physical changes. The silver of their bellies would transform into a pinkish hue and eventually a deep crimson if they stayed long enough. Why, with cock fish, did their lower jaw turn upwards at its extremity to form an ugly hook – a kype – while their mouth receded from their teeth, transforming them from creatures of beauty into unattractive oddities? Again, no one knew but no doubt someone or other was subjecting them to experiments to uncover the secret.

The biggest secret of all was where the salmon went once they left the rivers and returned to their real home – the sea – leaving their young to grow big enough and strong enough before following them.

The Danes stripped the magic from that conundrum when they discovered great shoals of salmon lurking in the deep, rich waters off Greenland, a country which came with their purlieu. With line and purse seine net, they dragged them from their feeding grounds and despatched them to market.

Fergal knew that this had been the beginning of the end for salmon and with each throw of the feed scoop he was also aware that he was contributing to their decline. And what could he do? He had ignored his wife's urgings to move south because that would have stripped him of what little pride he had left – his identity. How could he be a Highlander in the lowlands of Glasgow or Edinburgh, Falkirk or Livingstone, harping on endlessly about his origins, becoming more homesick by the glass, boring other lonely or expatriate boozers with tales that exaggerated a little more with each telling? At least here he had the mountains and glens and a sense of identity.

*

He continued dispensing the exact amount of feed as dictated by his feeding manual and the fish continued feeding voraciously. Each scoop, he knew consisted mainly of wild caught fish, the little ones such as sand eels and capelin which had no value, except to other wild fish, of course, as their essential feed. He knew that it took three kilograms of these little 'industrial' fish to put one kilogram of weight onto the bones of the captive creatures which surrounded him. Despite yet more bullshit from the industry, fish farming was not part of the cure for depleted oceans as they claimed, it was a particularly virulent organism that promoted the disease.

Fergal's movements were becoming less fluent, more staccato, as the Scotch worked its numbing effects but his mind was still functioning clearly enough to make him smile, albeit cynically. Whoever could have thought of the 'salmofan'? – a colour chart like that in any hardware store, except that all the shades were pink. You could decide which hue you wanted for the flesh of your fish and then feed them the chemicals to obtain it. Without canthaxanthin and astaxanthin their products would reflect a muddy grey colour from the fishmonger's slab rather than the chemically induced pink that mimicked their wild cousins and kept sales buoyant.

Fergal's involvement in supporting this industry was as nothing compared to the Government, that much he knew. They always gave ten day's notice of inspections, during which time the manager could make a valiant effort to douse the water with even stronger pesticides to reduce the infestations of sea lice and then claim their numbers were reducing. Of course, almost every wild crab, lobster and shell fish downstream of the pens would also die. It also gave him time to repair nets and pretend that farmed salmon never escaped. Wild salmon interbred with farmed fish and were genetically weakened by them. They were also just as susceptible to the clouds of sea lice – but neither of these phenomena were reflected in the unemployment figures – well, not yet.

Having thoroughly depressed himself, Fergal wheeled the feed trolley back along the pontoon towards the shed, stooping to retrieve the fallen landing net. He either stooped too quickly or was more affected by drink than he realised but he lost his balance entirely and went headfirst into the loch and it was only seconds before the cold sea water found its way through his layers of clothing and chilled his flesh.

It wasn't the ducking that concerned Fergal as he was a strong swimmer and never bothered with his life preserver but it was certain that someone would have seen his misadventure and come to investigate. If it was the manager, it risked him smelling the unmistakable aroma of stale Scotch and perhaps hearing a slurred syllable or two. It would mean the sack. Angry as he was with the realisation, Fergal Duff was blithely unaware that this was the least of his problems.

"Bollocks," he shouted out loud – and just to confirm it he shouted again. Spurring his legs into action, he struck out, arms and legs working in unison in a polished crawl to carry him the short distance to the pontoon. When he looked up, shaking sea water from his eyes, he expected to be able to reach out his hand, take hold of the wooden decking and pull himself out of the water. He was utterly bemused to find he was further away, closer to the centre of the pen, than when he had started. He had no explanation so attributed it to tidal flow but was not convinced.

He struck out again, redoubling his efforts, finning his legs and arcing his arms powerfully forward as if in a race. But nothing felt right, there was too much resistance and he could feel objects clogging the path of his arms through the water, a huge resistance against his chest, pushing him backwards and counteracting his efforts to move forwards. The pontoon was still no closer and the realisation dawned suddenly that he was trying to swim through a wall of fish who, not accidentally it seemed, were pushing him in the opposite direction.

"Help," he screamed and again, "help". He could see two workers back on the jetty looking as they dropped their work and ran towards him. Again he tried to cry "help" but this time, as his mouth opened, a shoal of fish working together as one, swirled in front of him causing a wave of water to wash over his head, filling his mouth and starting a process of choking that he could not control. Again as one, the fish swam over his shoulders, their dorsal fins clear of the water, their weight and the driving force from their tails, pushing his head down into the water and once there, they ensured it did not resurface until there was not a wisp of breath left in his body.

As quickly as the ferment began, the water became still and silent and a body clad in fluorescent orange waterproofs drifted to the surface and remained there, face down in the water.

At that moment, the clouds cleared to reveal the golden disc of a setting sun as it began to slip gently behind the hill on the westerly side of the loch. As it descended, it illuminated in silhouette the regal figure of a stag with a huge head of antlers. The sound of pipes playing Flowers of the Forest drifted across the now still and silent waters and the majestic stag threw back his head and bellowed a deep and resonant call.

Chapter Sixteen

"Don't you get fed up with it? The cruelty, I mean. Most people try and avoid it and yet you immerse yourself in it."

Jo Aldous didn't look at Wendy Carter as she spoke but stared straight ahead from the darkened cocoon of the people carrier, out through its windscreen at the moving puddles of light thrown by its dipped beam. They were by-passing Reading on the M4 motorway, heading for the village of Theale on its westerly side. At a little after one in the morning, traffic was light and the speedo needle sat at a steady eighty. Driving was Bob and next to him Phil, both dressed in black. Wendy and Jo were in the middle three seats and behind them was Laura, in charge of the camera. All were Wendy's employees.

"I'm not a masochist, if that's what you mean," Wendy answered flippantly.

"Of course I didn't mean that but everything you deal with is from the darker side of life, delving into man's inhumanity. It must be deeply depressing and yet always predictable – a bit like constantly poking a stick into a wasps nest and wondering why you get stung."

"You're a fine one to talk," Wendy laughed, "I haven't been able to get you out of the office these last few weeks."

It was true. Jo had sat through endless videos, read reports, looked at stills and asked questions – many, many questions. It was mostly fitted around Danny's school hours, sports, after school club, visits to grandparents, sleepovers and the rest as she still did not want to significantly reduce the amount of time she spent with him by farming him out. She still sometimes felt almost breathless with fear when she looked at him and found herself performing involuntary, contextless little gestures such as cupping his face in both her hands and kissing him. His reaction was usually predictable, normal, reassuring: "Get off, mum!" But having Marta around had been useful – Stephen's idea, to keep the house running when she was at Danny's bedside.

"Only if she's ugly, got hairy armpits and is built like a prop forward," Jo had said, only half-jokingly, when Stephen had suggested it. It wasn't that Stephen's fidelity, or lack of it, caused her any great concern but she could not bear the thought of him drooling and simpering over someone half his age and causing everyone cringing embarrassment in the process, except himself, of course. In the event, he had 'borrowed' Marta from the Steens on a part-time basis as she was underemployed and it had worked out well so the arrangement had continued.

As it happened, she was pretty, did have a stunning figure and was ludicrously young looking – a schoolgirl herself it seemed to Jo. But there was something tough and capable about her and although unreservedly friendly to Danny and her, she was merely polite, slightly distant, unapproachable where Stephen was concerned. It was no doubt a defence mechanism developed precisely to deal with people such as him but what intrigued Jo was what experiences had such a young girl been through to equip her so well in dealing with arrogant men. One big advantage of having Marta was that she slept at the Steens, so there was little impingement on the privacy Jo held dear, unless she stayed by arrangement like this night.

Lights from an occasional oncoming vehicle in the opposite carriageway threw some illumination into the interior of their car, moving slowly around the dark space as the relative positions changed. Everyone seemed locked into their own thoughts or simply resting with their eyes closed. Jo could not believe that any of them were sleeping with what lay ahead. Certainly her own mind was overactive despite the hour.

No matter how bizarre, how unrealistic or how crazy it sounded, the incident with the fox video had set out a template that was providing form and shape to the experiences she was enduring. Yes, experiences because they were much more than dreams of that she was certain. Perhaps she had grasped too eagerly at that one example of horror, willing it to be a piece in the jigsaw of understanding because if it wasn't, there were no alternatives other than a mind so deeply troubled that the implications were scary.

In fact Jo was aware that she was again indulging in a bout of emotional masturbation, testing herself, prodding, poking, looking for constant self-reassurance that her understanding was correct and it was not simply desperation – a determination to make things fit. Everything she had seen and read confirmed that the indistinct jumble of emotions that visited her uninvited from time to time were emanating from somewhere outside her and not from within. Her subconscious was not the guilty party, she now knew that for certain – or at least she hoped she did.

But still, it didn't prevent her picking away at the scab of self-doubt – pick, pick, pick, hurting, smarting, stinging but never drawing blood. It always resulted in reassurance and confirmation that she was right. And yet she would return again and again to pick once more, again seeking that reassurance.

If it was a weakness then it was one which broadly reflected her life. She had never been that confident despite outward appearances, constantly seeking approval from her parents: "Look at me, mummy." "See what I can do, daddy." All kids did it but she had perfected it, turned it into an art form. Partly it was to compete with Hillie who seemed to garner most of her mother's attention. It had perhaps even shaped her marriage. Stephen was a consummate performer and maybe he sought the accolades that she was selfishly unable to provide because she wanted them for herself.

Bloody tosh, she decided – it isn't like that at all! Introspection had its limits, she concluded. Almost as if on cue, Wendy cut through her thoughts: "Have you told him?"

Jo felt a pang of embarrassment – or guilt: "No!" and then rushed to excuse herself. "I've barely seen him for a couple of weeks."

"No, and I don't suppose you'll see much of him for the next couple of weeks nor the couple after that!"

Jo turned to face her friend and in the partial light could just detect an ironic little twist to her mouth. "Sorry, Jo, it's got nothing to do with me. I just know you'll feel better for it."

"Weak, aren't I?" Jo replied warmly, even though she didn't believe it, her tone excusing Wendy's mild rebuke. "But I will!"

She spoke the words with a firmness that accurately reflected how she felt. She would tell Stephen and there was no procrastination in not having told him, no waiting for just the right moment. Truth was, she hadn't given him a thought recently as there had been so many other things on her mind, far more important, deeply harrowing things.

Nothing she had seen at Wendy's offices had impacted on her as profoundly as the fox video but then it wouldn't – it couldn't. That had been like diving into a cold, cold swimming pool, the shock of it utterly numbing. Nothing would ever equal that because it was a first.

The one piece of footage that came close and did come back to haunt her, was the slaughter of a steer – a beef animal – being killed to provide kosher meat for the Jewish market. The animal was big and burly, his head wide and beautiful, shorn of horns but with curls across his forehead. He was goaded forwards into a metal cage – a crush – that confined him entirely, where he stood upright, his eyes rolling white in fear. You could hear him snorting and the sharp coldness of the day inside that place of slaughter turned breath from his nostrils into powerful jets of condensate – snort, snort, snort – while in the background people in white coats went about their work seemingly without agonising and without concern.

A pivoted, metal plate built into the cage was mechanically raised beneath the animal's chin – a chin lift – forcing his head upwards so that it was immobilised with his throat extended. Bizarrely, it brought to Jo's mind a vision of the mechanics of a gynaecological examination – being prostrate on your back and out of control, the dehumanising sensation of having feet up in metal stirrups – surely something only a man could have invented – the utter indignity of legs spread apart and being intimately viewed by men and women in white coats, the helplessness, the vulnerability, the disgust whilst they prodded and poked and peered.

The shot was close up on the animal and it was difficult to see what was going on around him, and then into frame stepped a man carrying a knife. It was a long knife, eighteen inches perhaps and about an inch-and-a-half wide for its entire length with no taper, and its end was rounded. For some inexplicable reason he flicked the steer's throat with his forefinger – and at that point Jo clasped her hands over her eyes and hummed out loud – lah de dah de dah de dah – to obliterate both vision and sound, afraid she might faint. When she looked again, all that was on screen was a snow storm that indicated the recording had ended.

She remained looking at it for moments and then chided herself: "Come on woman, you can do it – you need to do it!" She reminded herself that it was already all over for that particular animal and he had been killed and eaten probably months ago, maybe even years ago. There was no further hesitation – she grabbed the remote and rewound the footage. She knew what to expect as she had the explanatory notes in front of her. Again the slaughterer – the shochet – came into frame, again he flicked the captive throat with his forefinger and this time Jo noticed the flesh flicker in response and the animal start. It seemed unnecessary and she was angry at him for doing it. The slaughterer then immediately applied the knife to the animal's extended, vulnerable neck and began cutting.

With the first downwards motion, the steer threw his head back violently but it had little distance to travel and the crush banged and echoed and shook with the force of his reaction. Backwards and forwards the slaughterer's arm went, cutting with a sawing action but without ever leaving the neck, travelling to and fro, to and fro from just below one ear to the other. Seventeen separate movements of the knife, Jo counted, as it cut through carotid arteries, jugular veins, trachea, muscle and tendons. But it was the animal's eyes that transfixed her.

What would be written in a human's eyes, Jo wondered, if they were held captive and had their throat cut similarly. She felt certain that what she could read in his distressed eyes was precisely what would be reflected in anyone's eyes – shock, disbelief, despair, incomprehension and a clouding that dulled their brightness – almost a film – that screamed of pain.

His neck gaped open and a cascade of blood poured from the gash, clouds of steam rising instantly from its body-temperature warmth, so cold was that morning – that one morning in which an animal's life was ended in a gruesome death but where all the other life that surrounded him continued without a tremor of recognition. He was unremarked, unimportant, unremembered, except for this one secretly recorded video. But it wasn't finished yet.

With a clank the chin lift was dropped, the animal's head lowered and the gape of the bloody gash that would soon end his life reduced in size but the blood flowed remorselessly. He continued to stare ahead, unfocused, in a terrifying world of his own but clearly conscious. Death, it was claimed, was always instant and Jo counted as this uncomprehending animal stood there, his head held up his legs firm and unbending, not wanting to concede to death. Ten seconds, fifteen seconds, and still he remained standing. Twenty seconds, twenty five seconds, his lifeblood still pouring out of his severed throat but with him remaining erect. At thirty seconds a hand holding something came quickly into frame, touched the animal's forehead and was gone again and finally, the steer collapsed.

It was impossible to see what had happened but the notes said that at that point, a captive bolt pistol had been used to render the animal unconscious – a stun gun.

Jo tried to marshal the emotions that whirled around inside her while she fought back the bile that threatened to make her throw up. How could anyone be so desensitised as to get up each morning, kiss his wife and kids goodbye, pick up his sandwiches and go off to work to cut animals' throats? And at the end of it, 'Had a good day, dear?' 'Oh yes! Managed one hundred and seventy four today so I'm on a bonus. We can afford that new microwave.'

There were innumerable rules and regulations surrounding this, Shechita, slaughter as demanded by the religion, regulations as pedantic and bureaucratic as any council's rule book, which people administered and defended in pious tones. How could anyone institutionalise the taking of life and then camouflage it with clauses, sub clauses and addenda, pretending that it had deep relevance to their lives. How could such piety and pomp and quasi-religious claptrap surround the taking of a life. Did they really think their god would, with his supposedly different demands to everyone else's god, look down from his firmament and say: "Well done my children, you have honoured my name and I am justly pleased!"

Would changing the method of ending this animal's life, to ensure it felt no pain or panic, incur his wrath; how could anyone's eternal salvation be linked to the slicing of an animal's throat? How could they lie – the antithesis of religious commitment – that the process was painless and instant when the truth was staring at them from every slaughterhouse that invoked god's name? What difference could it make to their piety if an animal was stunned before his throat was cut rather than after. How could anyone eat the products of such base callousness?

With that latter thought, a wave of guilt washed over Jo, as she remembered her particular liking for salt beef sandwiches as sold by the little Jewish café in Windmill Street just across the road from the theatre. It was interrupted by Wendy's voice:

"You're quiet."

"Yeah – just thinking."

"Nervous?"

Jo pondered before replying: "No, not nervous. I think apprehensive would be more accurate. Mind you, I do feel a bit like I'm part of an SAS hit squad."

Wendy laughed: "Jo, we're just going onto a farm, we're not about to assassinate Prince Charles. I'll say it again, you don't have to come. You're welcome to stay in the car with Phil."

"You must be bloody joking. I didn't come this far to wimp out."

"Good girl."

Silence enfolded them again but Jo felt the need to speak, to apologise once again:

"Wendy!"

"Yes."

"I'm sorry."

"What for?"

"That I can't associate myself with this video you're going to make. I know it would help you get a lot more media coverage if my name was attached but the timing is just awful. I really do have to maintain my anonymity. You do understand, don't you?"

"Like I said before, there's nothing to apologise for. This was all arranged before I even knew you. We are just doing what we do. This one is for a specific documentary, filmed in a specific way and if it comes off, it will be great." When Wendy spoke again, Jo could hear the chuckle in her voice. "But you will one day – I promise you!"

The click, click, click of an indicator operating confirmed that they were about to leave the motorway at the Theale turn-off and head westwards on the old A4 towards Padworth and Thatcham. Once they had passed through the tall glass and steel monuments to Theale's silicon industry, some of which were still brightly illuminated, there was again little to see on the even quieter back road.

Jo retuned to her thoughts and hoped she wouldn't spend her life mulling over the disturbing images she'd been shown at Wendy's offices because at the moment they pervaded her thinking constantly when there was nothing else to engage or distract her. Again she thought of the slaughterhouse and without seeking it out, an image leapt in Jo's mind entirely of its own volition and she was transported back through the years to a piece of old grainy black and white footage she had once viewed. It appeared to have been shot on a cheap domestic movie camera and showed a clearing somewhere in a Polish forest during the Second World War. The pine trees wrapped around a huge pit like blinkers and it was almost filled with bodies sprawled out in ungainly poses, the abandonment of death.

German soldiers were marshalling a group of men and women forwards to the edge of the pit but all that was required was an occasional shove with a rifle, a push with the heel of a hand. The bedraggled, dirty, silent, defeated, civilian victims of invasion shuffled forwards in their rags and stood on the edge of the pit where their fate was displayed before them. There was no resistance but what looked like resignation and a fear so overpowering that they had become automata.

Who knew what other horrors they had already witnessed, had experienced before reaching this final execution spot. Their crime was nothing more than being Polish, Slavs, untermensch, subhumans, just like all other East Europeans and Russians and had to die in order that other people could prosper. They had to die to provide space – lebensraum – for those who considered themselves more intelligent, better, more deserving – in fact a master race. A twisted theory had been accepted and transformed into official policy by an intelligent nation and was now being put into practice by those instructed to do so – and with ruthless efficiency. Compassion had become a crime and the pit would beckon to any who tried to exercise it.

Perhaps these poor, petrified people of a proud, proud country knew that to resist would invoke a wrath that would demand prolonged pain as the price of insubordination. Perhaps they were more frightened of that pain than death. Perhaps they hoped that compliance would bring a swift and painless end but whatever was torturing their minds, they stepped forward almost without bidding, they knelt down on the edge of the pit when ordered to do so and it required only one of the soldiers to push a head or two forward until their chins were resting on their chests for the remainder of the condemned group to followed suit.

Once they were all bowed and waiting as if honouring their monarch, an officer – as smart as his victims were wretched – stepped forward, his high-fronted peaked cap perfectly in position, his knee-high boots glinting reflected light, every button fastened, straps and belt in parade ground order. He removed an automatic pistol from its holster on his belt and stepped forward. Every movement was sharp and military, efficient and without anguish. He was pruning the roses, pinning up notices, performing a mundane function, this privileged man from a privileged, well-educated race which had produced great musicians and artists, doctors and engineers, scientists and writers.

He placed the gun at the back of the first man's head and fired without pausing. The force of the bullet threw the body forward into the pit where it joined the other executed. God knows what terrors were coursing through the other victims as they waited their turn but they made no movement and the executioner continued his task, stepping briskly between each waiting person, shooting them in the back of the head, unconcerned by sex or age and not glancing at the dead bodies he had created.

When he had dispatched ten people, he had no rounds left and with the same quick efficiency replaced the clip, cocked the gun and shot the person he stood alongside who had waited for this minor hiccup in the production line of death, her agony extended by several seconds. When the final corpse had collapsed into the pit, the officer holstered his gun, turned and walked away out of frame without a backwards glance.

Throat cut, the cow was hoisted onto a mechanical, overhead conveyor; stomach sliced open, intestines encouraged to tumble out and splash floorwards in an avalanche of body fluids, forelegs sliced off and eventually his head cut off before a mechanically rotating drum stripped the hide from him in a ripping, tearing sound that left a naked, butcher's-shop-neat, almost bloodless, fat-streaked carcase behind and which continued its relentless progression with others along its mechanical, overhead highway.

Once the animal was dead Jo found herself more capable of coping with the scenes of butchery as there was no longer fear involved, no pain, no suffering. Just one final action made her want to shout at the screen in protest. A worker, with his belt of razor-sharp knives and steels, swaggered forward in a picture of testosterone-fuelled machismo, took hold of the steer's heavy head, slid a knife through his septum to make a gash and then inserted a big, steel hook into the gash – in one nostril and out the other. With an effort he then hoisted his head upwards with both hands, aiming the hook towards an overhead rail until it slotted over and he could release his burden.

And there it hung, the head of an animal that had never had

a name only a number, alongside a string of other heads from other unnamed animals, dangling by their once sensitive noses, a phalanx of dead, lifeless, clouded, unseeing eyes staring towards the ceiling, unremarked and un-mourned. It somehow felt disrespectful, callous, undignified, unworthy – medieval.

All this and everything else Jo had witnessed in Wendy's office had a resonance with her dreams. Some she was certain she could identify almost in their entirety, others bore a close resemblance to a sound or a feeling that she had experienced. Nothing was absolutely definite but they were all part of the same continuum of pain and suffering to which she had been unwittingly subjected. She wished it hadn't happened but it had and now she had to deal with it in the best way she could – and that was not by masking it with antidepressants or tranquilisers, which she suspected most people would advise and was why she had not been to see her doctor.

She knew how those cows felt because she had been privileged – perhaps privileged was not the right word – subjected to their emotions; she knew how that fox felt for precisely the same reason. It was confirmation of what she already suspected, that she was a receptacle for others' suffering.

What had originally been amorphous and therefore deeply troubling was now assuming a distinct form and the terrifying shadows of the night were gradually disappearing like wraiths. She found huge comfort in accepting this as the answer because it ended the search for a different explanation, perhaps one in which she might be cast as a nutter.

Jo was still aware, however, that she was caught between a rock and a hard place. Not to accept her explanation for her problem dreams left her with the unsettling conclusion that perhaps, after all, she might be going crazy. Accepting it would, almost certainly, be seen by others as proof of her craziness. They would say, and believe, that it was simply impossible. They would need an explanation as to how and why it could happen this way – and, for that matter, so did she.

When the answer came, it came quickly and Jo simply accepted it, almost with the words, "of course!" She was a radio receiver – simple as that! There was nothing visible in the air to even hint at the multitude of different sound and light waves that were constantly travelling through it, each of them carrying extraordinarily complex information, but twiddle the knob of a radio tuner and sounds came pouring out from all over the world – music, dialogue, effects. Press the clicker on a TV remote and what a world you were privileged to enter, a world of even greater complexity yet which was also invisible without that specific hardware. Perhaps she had different but very specific hardware hard-wired into her brain that could interpret the sounds and feelings of some creatures, all of which were the product of electrical impulses, as were radio and TV signals.

Okay, the electrical impulses which allowed animals to function were infinitesimally small but they existed, had always existed in every creature that had ever lived – and that's what mattered.

Jo was aware that, presented to a shrink, her beliefs might sound disturbingly like they came from one of those poor, confused people who thought that sound waves were emanating from their bedroom walls in order to take control of their minds or steal their bodily fluids.

The problem with doctors, she thought, is that at any given time they believe they understand everything about everything to do with the human body. They didn't and it was not that many years ago they were convinced that infections were carried on night air and that the cure for almost every ailment was to open up someone's veins with a scalpel and bleed them. Jo found those thoughts extremely comforting.

She then immediately felt guilty because Reece Evans was nothing like that. He was a kind, tolerant and unassuming man and he secretly fancied the pants off her, although because of his wife, his professional oath and etiquette, he would never admit it. Actually, he wouldn't have to ask twice, thought Jo, despite being years older than her – and then immediately felt guilty. She dismissed the thought because she would not do that to Bethan, who she liked almost as much as Reece. She felt no such compunctions about betraying Stephen.

It had not occurred to her before but it did now – had she perhaps avoided the logical step of consulting Reece simply because of these underlying little frissons? Perhaps the last thing she wanted was her handsome doctor friend looking at her eyes and thinking, 'Poor cow, she's lost it!'

She wasn't convinced that was the reason she had not consulted him. She was almost certain it had far more to do with her own lack of clarity, her confusion which, when combined with her trust in the man, might make her more vulnerable to suggestions to try a particular medication or a course of treatment, counselling or whatever.

Again she sensed she was pick, pick, picking at the scab of insecurity but now it was with far more confidence than at any time since this whole thing had started. She determined she would speak to Reece, just to see what he had to say, perhaps to share her feelings with someone other than Wendy, who was the only one she had confided in so far. Her support had been fundamental in helping Jo to cope and one more ally would make her feel invulnerable. She did not want a ten minute hurried consultation sandwiched between a case of haemorroids and a prolapsed womb, she would take him out to dinner somewhere nice but public and local.

Jo could feel the car slowing but there was only darkness around them, no lights, no landmarks, nothing to indicate where they were. A lay-by appeared on the left and Phil steered into it, slowed to a halt and immediately switched the lights off.

"Okay folks, we're here. The farmhouse is about two hundred metres back down the road."

Everyone exited from the vehicle and while no one raised their voice, they didn't speak in hushed whispers either. There appeared to be a practiced purpose about their actions. The tail gate was raised and green bio security overalls were handed around and they took it in turn to sit on the back of the car in order to pull the legs over their feet. There was then some minor confusion as to whose Wellingtons were whose.

Jo felt very much an outsider and almost as though sensing it, Wendy found her in the weak lighting emanating from the car's interior: "Okay?"

"Yeah, feel a bit of a supernumerary but actually, I'm fine."

And she was, most of her nerves appearing to have evaporated, reassurance coming from those around her who were focussed and apparently relaxed.

"Don't worry, we'll find you something to do when we get there." Wendy said, briefly extending her open hand and touching Jo's face with it in a gesture of intimacy that brought Jo back into their circle.

"We're a bit mob handed tonight and normally there's less confusion," she added.

"Is that for my benefit – the mob handedness not the confusion," Jo asked.

"Of course – got to look after you. We don't normally have a VIP on these little jollies."

The one thing Jo did not feel like at this moment was a VIP – more like a naughty schoolgirl about to embark on a midnight feast.

"Everyone kitted out?" Wendy demanded. As no one demurred she continued: "Okay Bob, spray please. Laura, start filming."

With a little, shielded light fixed to the camera, Laura recorded the mundane task of every person's boots being sprayed with disinfectant, those waiting to be done or having been treated, standing back a little from the car to act as a barrier between the unseen house and their activities. A thick hedge which scalloped around the lay-by almost certainly provided all the screening necessary but caution was clearly a practiced part of the proceedings.

Wendy's voice again cut through the night: "Right, film the sat nav and make sure it registers on the tape – you don't want to get just reflected light from its glass."

The whole process had been explained to Jo – the filming provided proof that they had taken thorough bio security measures with sterile overalls and the disinfecting of potentially infected boots, which conceivably could have been on some other farm previously. The sat nav reading with its date and coordinates was to prove their position and the date and time. Wendy had described the biosecurity measures as a joke but a necessary one to deflect any criticism that would be thrown at them: "Just you wait until you see the shit in there!"

Phil would stay with the car as it was extremely vulnerable stuck out in the middle of nowhere and they didn't want to return to find it stripped or stolen by passing youths fresh from a lock in at some pub or other.

The farm buildings stretched back from the house, away from the road and Bob was to position himself between the house and the buildings in order to warn the filming party via walkie talkies should anyone decide to head in their direction. Their main concern was the farm owner who lived on the job, as it were – their recce had confirmed that his two pig men lived elsewhere. And dogs, of course, but the belief was that there weren't any, at least not kept outside the house where they could bark an alarm.

Bob pulled a balaclava over his head to mask his white face and walked off into the night, disappearing entirely from view within a few paces. Jo knew his plan was to stay close to the hedge that ran between the road and the field all the way back to the house and then quietly infiltrate himself into a vantage point where he could keep an eye on things.

"Okay, everyone fit?" Wendy asked and there was a murmur of assent. "Right, this is the field we have to cross but it looks like it's been ploughed since the recce and not harrowed yet so it'll be bumpy going."

God knows how she can see that, thought Jo, who found it hard to spot the hand in front of her face now that every last light had been extinguished.

"Follow me but if you lose contact, keep going until about fifty metres from the hedge on the far side then turn and walk towards the farm. You can just make out the buildings against the skyline. That should bring you out directly between the farm units and the slurry pit. Get it wrong and you'll be in the shit, literally," she chuckled. "It's the grower pens and the farrowing crates that are the worst so we'll do those first. Let's go – and Jo, stick by me as though your life depends on it." Jo thought she would have felt slightly happier without that last caution.

The gap in the hedge close to the car had already been identified and one by one they filed through it – Wendy, Laura and her. As Jo made it into the field, headlights swung around the bend just a little way back from the farm and headed up the road towards them.

"Everyone down," hissed Wendy. "Flat down. Hide your faces and don't look up!" Suddenly Jo's nerves jangled and she threw herself flat with such energy that the impetus carried her face into the newly turned sod and gritty soil filled her mouth. The enterprise no longer felt like a game.

Apart from bobbling and stumbling over furrows, the rest of the darkened journey was uneventful and eyes gradually became more used to the night. Strange animal noises screeched and squeaked at her from somewhere distant and Jo became aware that she had hardly ever been in such darkness, away from all lights, and felt convinced she was going to stand on something living that would yelp and dart off into the night, terrifying her. A sickly, cloying stench that Jo had noticed the moment they had exited from the car increased in intensity the closer they got to the farm: "What's that stink?" she asked quietly of Wendy.

"Pig slurry," came the answer. "If you get it on your clothes it's almost impossible to get rid of."

Across a small ditch, over a wire fence and they were outside the first of several industrial units, this one the furthest from the road and house – the safest, Jo thought, her heart pacing and her breath barely sneaking in and out of her lungs. She wasn't sure if the cause was fear or the acrid stench of ammonia and its sickly sweet accompaniment that reeked of corruption. A bit of both she reckoned.

Wendy led them towards the building and with a quick flash from a weak torch established the position of the very tall door and which way it opened, placed her shoulder against it and applied her weight. A screeching, grinding noise pierced through the night as it moved back reluctantly on its metal track to reveal the entrance. Jo found herself gritting her teeth and flapping her hands as if this would somehow reduce the noise level.

Wendy was unperturbed and said quietly: "We never break in," and then as an afterthought, "We never have to!" Jo was pleased Wendy hadn't seen her little outburst of theatricals.

With the door now open, the inside of the shed was not as dark as Jo had anticipated, in fact a series of dull glows down either side made it comparatively easy to see.

"Farrowing crates", said Wendy, inclining her head as they walked into the shed down a central path that ran its entire length and had a series of concrete stalls on either side, each one butted up to the next. Looking over the low, dividing concrete walls, the source of the light became clear – in the corner of each unit was a domed light suspended from the ceiling and hanging just a foot or two from the floor. They glowed dully red and beneath some of them huddled the tiniest piglets Jo had ever seen.

Again Wendy explained: "Heat lamps." She removed her back pack and from it took a big yellow floodlight, the kind that could be bought on almost any garage forecourt, labelled with the promise, 'one million candle power.' The lens was covered with several layers of a woman's tights to diffuse its 'million candles', held in place with a stout elastic band.

She switched it on and that part of the shed came to light. Without any prompting, Laura started filming, focussing on the areas that Wendy illuminated with her modified lamp. Jo had not thought at any length about what would happen once they were inside the farm but somehow expected it to be hurried, rushed, urgent – grabbing a bit of footage here, a bit there and then dashing back into the anonymity and safety of the night. That's not how it was.

The women moved almost leisurely from one pen to the next, recording what they saw, ignoring nothing that provided evidence of the way the animals were kept, the conditions in which they lived. Jo found herself constantly looking toward the end of the shed closest to the house, expecting someone to appear and willing the women to speed up, to hurry, not to be so pedantic with their filming.

She looked into each of the concrete pens and found them utterly dispiriting. Each was precisely the same as its neighbour – a container constructed from metal bars sited in the centre of the barren space. Locked into each pen was a very large pig and most were prostrate on their sides but watching intently. A double line of distended, red and inflamed looking teats ran down their bellies and, roused from their sleep by these human intruders, some of the piglets latched their mouths over them to suckle. Some piglets remained snuggled up to their mothers' sides, some lay prostrate on top of their ample bodies whilst others sought the warmth of heat lamp and cuddled together beneath it, their bodies intertwined.

Disturbed by the light, one of the mothers rose to a standing position but it was a laborious, struggling, effort-laden process full of obvious discomfort and strain for any ability to move naturally was proscribed by the bars which surrounded her, bars so restrictive that they touched either side of her body. Her movements were constrained to standing up or lying down – both with great difficulty – or taking half a step backwards and half a step forwards.

The floor was roughcast concrete with not a strand of straw nor a curl of wood shaving to mitigate its cold hardness nor to cushion the vulnerable-looking pink skin of mother and baby.

The sow looked towards the women with penetrating, bright, intelligent eyes – almost human-looking eyes, Jo thought, and she could see the concern written in them. Who were these people, the pig wondered, here, in the middle of the night. More disturbingly, Jo could sense her deeper feelings. No, she couldn't sense them, she could feel them – as clear and distinct as if it was she who was behind bars. The sow was trying to make a judgement as to whether these people, people she had never seen before, with bright lights and guilty, quiet voices, posed a threat to her babies. Jo could feel the panic growing inside her because if the threat was real, she knew there was nothing she could do to protect them, confined as she was, impotent, imprisoned behind bars.

"It's all right lady, we're not going to harm your babies, we're on your side, I promise." For whatever reason, Jo could feel the animals tension draining away but what remained in its place was every bit as tenacious and depressing – an overpowering sense of desperation.

Anger surged through Jo: "Why's this allowed, can't we do

something? Can't the police do something," she demanded of no one in particular and could feel and hear her voice shaking almost in unison with her trembling legs.

She didn't see or sense it coming but felt a hand gently on her shoulder, the fingers curling lightly in a soft grip of reassurance.

"It's okay Jo, we know exactly how you feel. It's how we feel, it's why we're here, it's why we do what we do." Wendy's hand then impelled Jo to turn around until she was facing her, making eye contact. She spoke slowly:

"Jo, this is officially a high-welfare unit, an 'approved' farm that meat eaters pay a premium for." She paused to allow the fact to sink in. "That's why we're here!"

There was no longer a shard of fear left in Jo only anger and revulsion and finally she understood what motivated the people around her. It transformed her attitude to the job they were doing and she no longer felt like a bystander – an impotent observer. How different the reality was to video imagery, stripped as it was of smell and sensation, devoid of interaction and one's own heightened sensitivity. She was involved. She had a job to do and it began with stacking away every visual image, every impression, every fact for later recall when it could be used against those responsible or to persuade others.

She looked again at the stalls with fresh eyes. The only visual relief in the monotone of grey concrete was an area about two feet square, constructed from wooded slats with spaces between each one, positioned inside the crate where the animal's hindquarters would be, whether standing or lying. As the standing sow urinated, its purpose became obvious and the liquid found its exit through the gaps in the slats but not before splashing upwards from some to wet the inside of the sow's legs and the rear portion of her underbelly. Small deposits of what could only be excreta were smeared across and stuck between the slatting and which the sow could not avoid when lying. As a consequence, large areas of her hind quarters were decorated with brown splodges of her own excreta.

Around the pens were other, less distinct, amorphous, glutinous-looking deposits, the source of which Jo knew had to be unappealing and so avoided speculation. In some of the pens were deposits which were not at all amorphous but clear and distinct – dead piglets.

Wendy removed a coiled lead from her back pack to which was attached a microphone which she plugged into the little DV camera.

"I'm going to do a brief running commentary," she offered by way of explanation. "The sat nav again, Laura. Hold it for her Jo, will you?"

Jo felt pleased to be performing some useful function and tried to do this simplest of little tasks very efficiently as though she had done it a hundred times before.

Wendy repeated the name of the farm and the date and then began a description of the pigs' conditions, aiming the light into one pen after another – revealing a litany of neglect and unconcern.

She was clearly struggling to wield the heavy light with one hand while holding the microphone with the other while at the same time continuing her commentary. Without words, Jo indicated that she would take control of the light and Wendy ceded it, simply raising her eyebrows in appreciation. Jo just hoped to god she would shine it where it was wanted but the need soon became obvious with just an occasional direction from Wendy – an extended arm, a pointed finger, an inclination of the head.

"The sow has large abrasions on both flanks, a product of rubbing against the crate's bars when standing or lying down. They are crusted and weeping and need veterinary attention.

"One piglet is emaciated and not thriving. She cannot reach her mother's teats and should be removed."

"Three dead piglets, two recent, one in an advanced state of decomposition." Jo looked at the rotting piglet, tucked away in the corner of the pen – black, shrivelled and putrid but still coiled in a foetal position.

In one pen, Jo swivelled the light to illuminate a dark, black patch on the concrete and then followed it to its source, which was the rear of a prostrate sow. It was congealed blood and it was only when the animal moved to make herself more comfortable that it became clear what had caused it. A fistful of bright red tissue protruded from the sow's vagina. The commentary continued relentlessly:

"This sow has a prolapsed womb." Nothing more needed to be said and Wendy's voice was devoid of emotion.

"The sows' time in these crates will vary from four to five weeks, entering a week before their due date and being taken back to their holding pens when their piglets are removed at about three weeks to be weaned – weeks before they would naturally wean."

In another pen, a standing sow bit at the bar directly in front her – first to the left, then to the right, to the left again and then back to the right, in metronomic regularity.

"A sow exhibiting stereotypic behaviour as a result of confinement – a form of mental collapse."

"Large, inflamed patches on the belly between the rear legs. Ammonia burns."

"Two badly ulcerated teats in an advanced state of necrosis."

"A fistula rupture almost half the size of a rugby ball."

"Three old placentas, two shrivelled almost beyond recognition." The glutinous mounds of afterbirth were streaked with red and black and grey and some were crusted on their upper surface. Others were flat with age, adhering to the concrete floor as if welded into position, the scurrying of tiny trotters making indentations in their surfaces from time to time.

"Okay, we're done," announced Wendy. "Laura, change the flash drive." Laura removed it from the little camera, inserted it in to her jeans pocket through the side slit in the overalls and took a new flash drive from the camera bag, inserting it in the camera.

"Safety precaution," smiled Wendy. "Right, light off Jo – next shed."

They exited from the opposite end of the shed to the one they had entered and the darkness of night once outside was somehow reassuring. Wendy stretched her arms wide so neither woman could overtake her and there she remained for several seconds. Jo could not see her properly but knew she was listening for sounds threatening. There was nothing but a few night noises to be heard.

Another big industrial shed, another tall door on runners and another squeaking, grinding, nerve-racking entrance as it reluctantly squealed backwards as if letting them in unwillingly. The big difference with this shed was its darkness, both inside as well as out.

They stood in complete blackness until Wendy had closed the door behind her and it was then that Jo fully registered the appalling stench of the place. As she moved her feet around she could hear a slopping sound and feel the resistance of liquid on her Wellingtons.

"Okay, light Jo, please."

She obliged without fumbling and the sudden explosion of light produced a cacophony of squealing, grunting, barking noises and the sound of clattering feet and panicked bodies dashing around in confusion and turmoil.

Jo directed the light along the stalls to obtain an overall view before homing in on specifics. Outwardly, the scene was very similar to the previous shed, with pens defined by low concrete walls, but the light which now illuminated the floor revealed that the central walkway was awash with liquid some two inches deep.

"Jesus Christ," she heard Wendy utter the words, almost whistling them through her teeth. "We're paddling through liquid shit, ladies! Okay, hold your breath, we'll start here and work our way down." Jo now knew what was required and shone the light into the first of many pens.

She illuminated a dozen or so bright little faces, half-grown pigs, who jostled each other for positions at the back of the pen to be as far from danger as possible, their eyes always returning to focus on whatever it was that was disturbing them, trying to see through the unaccustomed light, their snouts twitching and wrinkling to see if they could divine a threat.

These were not pink pigs but dirty, muddy, blotchily-brown pigs with just patches of pink showing through here and there, but even that seemed stained and dirty. The floor beneath them was wet and soiled but still they stood there staring and inquisitive. Of course they did for they had nowhere else to go.

Laura began filming and Wendy continued with her

commentary: "Stage one growers, approximately twelve animals, no trace of bedding and a sleeping area that is awash. Despite the claim that pigs like muck, they don't, they are fastidiously clean animals in nature. They like to wallow in mud because of its cooling properties. This is not mud but excreta, which is anathema to them. Every animal, to a greater or lesser degree, is covered in it and they cannot escape, even in their very limited sleeping area."

Wendy made a motion with her head, indicating she wanted Jo to swing the light down and illuminate the front of the pen. She did and it was awash with inches of excreta, a far greater depth than in the sleeping area. Wendy continued with her remorseless but emotionless commentary.

"Slurry pit below the dunging area is full hence the excreta has built up and is now covering the slatted access. Almost certainly this one slurry pit services every pen on this side of the shed and so we can assume that every pen will be affected similarly."

Jo swung the light to illuminate the adjoining pen and it was identical. And the next and the next. Wendy indicated that she wanted to view the pens on the other side of the walkway and Jo obliged. The whole shed, it seemed, was awash with pig excreta.

The commentary continued but Wendy's choice of words now screamed emotion even though her voice remained largely monotone.

"This is the only home these animals will ever know. They will eat, drink, sleep and wake here, in an atmosphere of cloying ammonia and breath-taking filth. Whilst these images are bad, they are not exceptional and what we are witnessing in the two sheds where we have so far filmed, is the face of modern, British, intensive pig farming. This is what is meant by factory farming. It is a system responsible for more than ninety per cent of all pig meat consumed in the UK. There are no rules or laws governing animal farming only recommendations…"

The 'THWACK' of a circuit breaker being thrown made Jo's heart stop and the bright, white light which followed, blinded her and through the cacophony created by hundreds of startled pigs, there was no mistaking the words, barked out with venom, by someone extremely angry: "Right, stay there you bastards or I'll shoot you."

There was what felt like absolute silence as Jo took in the man from whom the threat emanated – a rotund farmer wearing a dirty green boiler suit and flat cap. Held in both hands and pointing towards them was a double barrelled, twelve-bore shotgun. The man's eyes were almost as disturbing as the gaping barrels of the gun, reflecting his barely-controlled anger. Alongside him was Bob, balaclava in hand, a face three shades paler than when Jo had last seen it. He raised his hand briefly which seemed to offer both apology and acknowledgement of his impotence.

Wendy took a pace forward, making her the closest to the thundering pig breeder, placing herself between him and Laura. She sounded like an irate school marm: "There's absolutely no need for that – we're here on official business," she lied and Jo only just caught the hoarse, whispered command to Laura which followed. "Get the tape out!"

Quietly, unobtrusively, noiselessly, Laura did what she was asked.

The man said nothing and kept the gun pointed at them, visibly trembling with emotion.

How dare he? Jo thought and could feel outrage boiling inside her. How dare the callous bastard threaten them? He's the one responsible for this appalling cruelty. What came out did so without a conscious thought directing it.

"Look at me, you retard," she shouted at him, stepping into clear view. "Look at me! Do you know my face? Do you?"

She could see the first glimmer of recognition dawning in his eyes.

"You bloody well should because I'm Josephine Aldous, wife of the next prime minister. Unless you put that gun down now I'll make sure you spend the rest of your miserable bloody life in Dartmoor."

Having delivered her outburst, Jo felt extremely silly but became conscious of the sound of racing car engines as they revved down through the gears and through the open door could see the unmistakable rotating flash of blue lights reflected from farm buildings. The man remained motionless, his jaw slack but the gun slowly descended to his side.

Jo just managed to detect Wendy's words through her grim, ironic chuckle. "Well, so much for anonymity."

Chapter Seventeen

"What the fuck was your wife doing on a pig farm, in Berkshire in the middle of the fuckin' night?"

The gimlety eyes and sharp features of Sean Murphy seemed to bore into Stephen Aldous. He hated the odious little man, who was the last person on god's planet he would want to hold some kind of advantage over him. The very fact that he could hurl aggressive questions at him, make him look ridiculous, demand answers that he did not have, emasculate him, diminish him, portray him as ridiculous and incompetent in front of the very people upon whom he depended for preferment – and still be in the right – was unbearable. It was the subject of nightmares.

Stephen could feel every pair of eyes in the room staring at him uncomprehendingly, wanting answers that he didn't have. Cool was all he had at his disposal but even that was hiding so when he attempted to deploy it with studied non-concern it appeared in a pathetic, threadbare form.

"I'm still looking into it, Sean!"

"Still looking into it, still fuckin' looking into it. I've got the world's media out there, Stephen, every fuckin' journalist on the planet who can take the top off a ballpoint or hold a microphone. They're clambering over each other like wolves who can smell blood and they want answers, I want answers, we want answers, everyone wants fuckin' answers. And we've gotta come up with some, like now!"

Stephen hated everything about Murphy, always had done. His pinched, veined face, the thinning, lank hair, his bitten, dirty nails and nicotine-stained fingers. With Sean's unblinking eyes only feet away from him, Stephen knew that this was a caricature of the man but his detestation went far, far deeper than just his physical appearance.

His background was standard stuff for modern party press secretary – a lifetime in tabloids; a lifetime of feeding the great unwashed salaciousness and sex and despair and failure; a lifetime of destroying the reputations of people who dared to want something better; a lifetime of trying to pick up the scent of betrayal or corruption whilst deflecting the spotlight from their own and their employers' corruption; a constant emasculation of organisations that might pose a threat to media power; a lifetime of elevating consumerism to a deity; and a lifetime of keeping people in their places by diminishing hope and expectation.

Stephen had no moral objection to any of this but you didn't necessarily want its practitioners here, in the inner sanctum of a noble political institution, taking charge by displaying the manners of a lout. Everyone knew that lavatory paper was essential but kept it out of sight where it was useful and didn't pay obeisance to it.

On top of all his other hatreds it was this that Stephen detested most. Sean Murphy did a job but did not embrace the party, its politics or its accepted standards of behaviour – its norms. He was a foul-mouthed hack who would hire himself out to the highest bidder and do whatever he was required to do without agonising or indulging in self-doubt. He was amoral, apolitical and got away with it because he was extraordinarily good at his job.

Stephen feared he may be fighting for his political life and realised he had to demonstrate leadership of some kind despite wallowing in a mire of anger and incomprehension, with nothing practical to offer. It could only be an intervention of style not substance because he had no idea why his wife had done what she had done and had only one shot in his locker with which to defend himself – and her. It was a weak hope but he had to try and show he had some kind of plan, if only to put a brake on Sean Murphy's rhetoric.

"Sean, this happened early this morning while I was in Cardiff. I have no idea what lies behind it because I haven't been able to speak to Josephine. I have no doubt that there is some less dramatic answer than appears at first sight..." Murphy cut across him: "Oh for fuck's sake, Stephen. Your missus is caught in a pig farm with an animal liberation nutter and does a piece to camera that will have rural voters withdrawing their support in droves. I know where my wife was last night, I know where she is every night because I make it my fuckin' business to know..."

"Sean, cool it, you're going-over the top and it's not helping."

Julie Samuels was more usually noted for her silence but when she did speak, Sean listened.

"Okay, okay but this whole situation is fuckin' ridiculous..."

It was the final flurry of someone whose default position was to rant, who ranted because it diminished everyone around him and concentrated the solution in his hands. It was possible his tirades provided the energy from which solutions coalesced, transforming negatives into positives. It was also possible that he simply had contempt for everyone else because they never came up with a solution as workable as his. He knew he was worth the large amount of money he was paid and the subsequent latitude he was afforded.

His whole demeanour changed as he began pacing, backwards and forwards across the room, now utterly disinterested in Stephen, head down hands behind his back, looking at no one, thinking – seemingly thinking deeply – lost in thought. They had all seen it before – everyone knew the Sean process and there was almost a sense of relief around the room as he finally got down to work.

Stephen looked across at Julie, his sidekick, and tried not to signal his relief that Sean had been pacified. She stared straight ahead impassively, not looking at her boss, not looking at Stephen, not looking at anyone, notebook on her lap, pencil in hand awaiting the starting gun.

She had come with Sean as part of the deal and was what he called his researcher but was far, far more than that. She was, his eyes, his ears, his rooter out of facts, his defender – his enforcer. Stephen saw her as a kind of female Bulls Eye to Sean's Bill Sykes, as Bonnie to Sean's Clyde but perhaps more accurately, as Mrs Lovett to Sean's Sweeney Todd.

She was squat and square, her face rugged and devoid of makeup, her clothing utterly unmemorable apart from the high heels which always adorned her solid legs and which made Stephen think that, somewhere, there was something sexual buried deep in her psyche. He, however, had no interest in being the one to unearth it. Her hair was permanently blonded with an orange hue that spoke of cheap hydrogen peroxide and it was always taken back in a ponytail on the nape of her neck.

Stephen could not shake off one particular image which a young, irreverent MP had planted in his mind: "She could crack walnuts with her eyelids." As Stephen considered her stolid, hewn, implacable face, he would not have been surprised to see her do precisely that. But without question, despite her extraordinary taciturnity, she could control Sean with just a few words and she was worth her salary for that alone.

Sean Murphy continued his pacing and expectation mounted around the committee room. Stephen felt he needed to suggest something, anything, and persuaded himself that his suggestion was as good as anything Sean would be likely to come up with and decided to get in first, to play the only card he had that might at least offer some mitigation from this dispiriting mess.

"You don't need me to tell you that Josephine has been through a particularly tough time in the recent past and although I thought she'd overcome the appalling experience of Danny's accident, perhaps this is an indication that she still has some distance to go before she's entirely back to normal."

Stephen looked to see Sean's reaction but he continued his pacing and showed no sign of having heard let alone understood but Stephen continued anyway.

"I know the media understand perfectly how bad her ordeal has been and I'm sure they would respond positively if we were to indicate that this unusual behaviour is part of the shock of coming to terms with what happened. You know the kind of thing – troubled mother who has seen the darker side and now wants to make the world a better place…" His voice trailed away, awaiting approval.

"Bollocks Stephen, that's the last thing we want to feed to these hard-nosed bastards – they're not fuckin' social workers, you know." Sean had not ceased his pacing but Stephen was almost shaking with rage that he had been so peremptorily dismissed. At this precise moment he wanted to kill Josephine.

"Okay, Sean, you didn't like my suggestion so why not do your job and suggest a way of managing this situation which, I might remind you, I am no more responsible for than you."

Sean stopped pacing, walked over and confronted him, his upper body aggressively inclined forwards, his neck extended and his words directed at Stephen and no one else.

"You what? In a few months, Stephen, you're going to be offering yourself to the electorate as a prime minister, the man in charge of the entire fuckin' country, a man with his finger on the fuckin' button so to speak – and not just metaphorically. I can just hear them now: "Nice guy, but holy shit do we really want some loose cannon of a wife, driven doo-lally by having her kid in a coma, tearing around all over the place, consorting with terrorists, making a complete twat of herself on telly...""

"Sean!" Julie's voice cut across him.

"Yeah, yeah – sorry. With respect Stephen."

His apology carried about as much sincerity as could be expected from him. None! Stephen controlled himself, saying nothing, simply watching, observing. Why the man carried the name Sean Murphy he couldn't fathom because there appeared to be nothing Irish about him. His face was mean and pinched, spiteful and defensive alternately, much more Bethnal Green than Ballymena, a restless, fidgety, constantly moving Cockney sparrow but with all chirpiness stripped completely away. But he did hail from Kilburn or Cricklewood or Willesden or some such place where Paddy families had congregated for generations. Not any more though – Petty France, within walking distance of the House, as he never tired of telling anyone who would listen: "Not bad for messenger boy who left school at fifteen, eh?"

His mood appeared to be changing again and his pacing had resumed.

"Right, we have to come up with something very quickly because they're all sitting on a mountain of stuff. They've got stills from a local journalist..."

"How on earth did he manage to get to the story so quickly?" Charlie Whiston interrupted.

"Charlie!" Sean made no effort to hide his contempt. "Every copper's got the phone number of a stringer or two on his mobile and they get good dosh for the tip offs. It's what pays for their holidays in Tenerife. Doesn't the word Leveson mean anything to you? Haven't you been paying attention?" He returned to the job in hand, ignoring the scarlet that flushed Charlie's face.

"They've got these stills, they've got footage of the inside of the farm, which this Carter woman was savvy enough to get straight to PA, along with footage of your wife, Stephen, talking straight to camera outside the farm, oozing emotion and anger like she'd just come out of fuckin' Belsen.

"Who is this Carter woman, Julie, the Mata Hari of the animal lib movement or what? She got a record?"

Julie didn't need to check her notes: "No, she's clean. A couple of arrests at demos for obstruction but no charges brought. Organisation is a nuisance but there doesn't seem to be anything against it. I haven't had much time so I'll keep looking."

Sean appeared pleased: "Good, very good! Right, all this stuff's gone nationwide through PA, every title in the country is sitting looking at it wondering what slant to put on it. The first will be the Standard in its lunchtime edition, followed by TV lunchtime news then the rest of the evening papers and again TV in its evening bulletins.

"The dailies won't be able to run with it until tomorrow, which gives 'em too much fuckin' time to do their own digging around and come up with something none of the others have had time to unearth, something extra that we might not like. They'll be raking through every back cutting and talking to anyone who can string two words together, whether they know fuck all or not. But make no mistake, by this time tomorrow, every outlet in Britain will have run this story, even the Todmorden fuckin' Bugle."

Every person in the room was listening to and watching Sean as though their political lives depended on it – in Stephen's case, literally. There was no glimmer of a suggestion that someone else might now contribute. Sean was at work, Sean would find a way of diverting the damage from this pile of dross somehow or other and any interruption would simply delay the reveal.

"What are the elements of a good story?" The question was purely rhetorical and he barely paused in his delivery as he resumed his striding up and down. "You need a revelation, a hero and of course a villain – and, if you can manage it, a victim who comes good at the end.

"What have we got? Well, we've sure as fuck got an expose, we've got a politician's wife, Old McDonald with a shotgun, a female terrorist, a bloke with a balaclava who apparently shat his pants, so no great threat there – and the lady terrorist is far from stupid. So where do they all fit in?" Again the question was rhetorical because it was clear that Sean Murphy was still working out the scenario and the play list.

"The first one's easy – Mrs Aldous, the erstwhile wife of Stephen here, let's start with her. She has to be the hero – the heroine – because the other alternatives do us no favours at all. She can't be some poor cow driven by her hormones, by the change of life…"

"She's thirty six," Julie interjected wearily.

"For Christ's sake, Julie, I was just illustrating a point…"

"A sexist point," she added equally as wearily. Stephen gained the impression that she was not simply talking to Sean but the whole room. He slightly adjusted his internal assessment of her.

Sean got back into his stride: "She can't be someone MENTALLY DAMAGED.." there was a flicker of a pause while he addressed his accentuated and revised vocabulary to Julie. She briefly closed her eyes and there was the faintest nod of her head in acknowledgement, "…because that makes her a victim and she can't be a victim. The only way she can come out of this is as someone who took a difficult decision for noble purposes. It wasn't accidental. She wasn't carried along by dark, sinister forces wearing balaclava helmets. She wanted to go on to that farm. She was determined to expose the plight of those poor animals. It was her intention because she can't stand animal cruelty and she's delighted with the outcome. She was driven by overpowering humanitarian concerns. Now her part in all this is over .." there was a sharply accented parenthesis in the middle of Sean's flow "… and Stephen, I sincerely hope that it fuckin' is all over… And all she wants now is something done about it."

He turned to Stephen, eager, his face alight with enthusiasm: "Stephen, I'm going to turn your fuckin' wife into a cross between Saint Francis and Mother fuckin' Theresa – with respect.

"Animal Liberation Front terrorism doesn't fit into this scenario at all so our two animal activists – Carter and the bloke with the shitty knickers – are perfectly nice people, okay? Well, for the time being, anyway. I'll be revisiting her and her organisation at some time in the future. For now, they're the ones who facilitated this, and nothing else. Mrs Aldous didn't tell Stephen because she knew he would be worried for her and try and put a stop to it. She didn't want to cause him concern. Okay? All nice and wifely.

"Unless my judgement has suddenly turned to crap, I don't think Carter will be a problem. She's not a wild-eyed, angry kid, she's a pro – and a fuckin' good one by the look of it. Notice how she's kept in the background. She's made no statements, hasn't offered herself for interview with all the material she's put out. She knows she's not the story and that's the way she wants to keep it. It's the pigs and Stephen's wife who're the story and the way we're going to have to handle it will give her the kind of coverage she could only dream about. She's won this one hands down and she knows it. If there's no shit on her they might just let it go."

Julie raised her forearm with its fingers clutching her pen, asking to be given permission to interrupt.

"What?" Sean snapped.

"Her voice is all over the footage, won't that make her a central part the story, at least for TV?"

"No, I don't think so. They've got very limited time and will concentrate on the principle players. They'll use a bit of ambient sound at the front and back, dip her voice and lay their own commentary over. Either that or they'll cobble together as much ambient as they can, strip her voice off and replace it with that, allowing the images and sound to speak for themselves. It won't be a problem." He quickly moved on.

"My guess is that Jo will be overwhelmed with what she's unleashed and she'll be keeping out of your way somewhere, Stephen, that's why you haven't been able to reach her. You've got to get in touch or this whole thing will fall apart and make us look complete cu... idiots. Text her, call her, email her, send a carrier fuckin' pigeon if necessary. But be nice, no bollocking, no screaming, nice, d'ye hear me, considerate, understanding, loving. I know you don't feel it but act it. Tell her no interviews of any kind and tell her to pass the same message on to her friend. In two or three days when this has all passed you can do what you like to her..."

"Hurrrrem..." Julie Samuel broke off from her note taking and stared at him angrily.

"Oh for Christ's sake, Julie, you know I didn't mean anything like that... I'll also be ringing Ms Carter myself, just to be sure – belt and braces.

"Now, as for poor old farmer fuckin' Giles, the fastest gun in the West, he can't be the villain because he was just doing what farmers do. He's a poor, ignorant bloody farmer doing his best to cope, frightened out of his fuckin' life by what he thought were rustlers..." Sean interrupted his flow again, to impart a considered nugget of information as though giving a lecture. "Do you know that it's becoming a big problem – rustling. Some bastard had a hundred and fifty sheep away the other night without the farmer noticing a thing...

"Anyway, we can't pillory him because he's a prime Tory party voter. As you know, it's him and his ilk that make the electoral map of rural Britain look as blue as the fuckin' sky. He's our victim – he's our poor helpless, bewildered, terrified victim."

Sean waited for effect, his head swivelling around the room from person to person, soaking up their incomprehension: "So who the fuck's the villain, then, hey? Who's the nasty bastard whose caused all this furore? I'll tell you who it is – it's the fuckin' EU, that's who!" Again he paused, head outstretched, eyes gleaming, almost messianic.

"It plays beautifully into your supporters' anti-European agenda and the press will leap on it like manna from heaven, well, except for the Guardian but who gives a fuck about them. Once they've got this one between their teeth they won't want another angle, they won't be interested. You know the scenario better than I do.

"Britain's high animal welfare standards, the best in the world lah de dah de dah, being destroyed by unrestricted imports from people who treat their animals like shit so they can sell meat cheaper than we do – and there's nothing we can do to stop it because the fuckin' EU says we can't. Because of this, Old Farmer Giles can't afford to employ enough workers 'cos he can't pay them properly and he can't tuck his piggy wiggies in at night cos he can't afford the blankets. He's constantly having to reduce his standards simply to stay alive de dah de dah de dah. It uspets him as much a anyone else to see his animals living like that but what can he do, it's that or go broke. Time someone did something about it…"

Again Sean looked around and there was not a single voice raised in dissent.

"Right, I need to speak to the farmer, make sure he's on song and doesn't say anything stupid…"

"I'll talk to him…" Julie Samuel interrupted.

"Why the fuck shouldn't I speak to him…?"

"Because you don't do sympathy!"

"Neither do you. I'll act it."

"Yeah, but I act it a bloody sight better than you!"

"Whatever!" Sean conceded. "Okay folks, let's get on with it." He turned to Stephen: "Could I have a word please, mate?" He moved Stephen over to the side of the room, out of earshot of the others and stood in front of him, uncomfortably close.

"You, my friend, were in the shit so deep that it was about to block your nostrils. I might, I just might, have saved your fuckin' skin, but you're not in the clear yet, nothing like.

"I know you don't like me and the feeling's mutual. And I also know that once you get the head's job – if you get the head's job and there is now an 'if' over it – I'll be out on my ear but I'm too fuckin' good to let that bother me. Despite that, while I'm still here, I'll do my very best to save your bacon whenever necessary – not to do so would affect my reputation. In the meantime, may I suggest that you get a fuckin' grip on your wife before she takes us all down with her. I don't give a shit about you but I'm not going out on a failure."

Chapter Eighteen

"Welcome, welcome Signora Aldous, we are delighted to see you!" Marco Fortuoni greeted Jo literally with open arms, walking towards her as though an all-enfolding embrace was the least he could offer, his smile as wide as a piano key board and his accent overpoweringly Italian.

"Oh Marco, for god's sake, it's me your talking to!" Jo said as she kissed him on both cheeks in the comfortable reception area of Weybridge's oldest Italian restaurant, set atop Monument Hill – the hill that, reputedly, the Grand Old Duke of York marched his men up and down in a pointless display of military obedience. "How are you?"

"I'm doing okay Jo, yeah, not bad at all." The accent had not disappeared entirely but both it and the volume had been minimised. "And you?"

"Actually Marco, I think I'm doing okay too – really okay, thank you."

"Good. But I take it you won't be ordering today's speciality of the house – Braciole do Maiale."

"Why, what is it?"

"Calabrian grilled pork chops with piquant red peppers and fennel..." The piano-wide smile appeared on Marco's face once again.

Jo gave him a playful push. "You saw it then?" She grimaced, as though she had done something terribly naughty.

"Jo, everyone saw it and I take my hat off to you – I like a woman of principle. I think you deserve a drink, let me get you one on the house. A Kir?"

"Yes, why not. Thank you Marco."

"Would you like it here or at your table?"

"At the table, please. I'm waiting for a guest, he's called Reece Evans – show him to my table when he arrives would you please, Marco."

Marco conducted Jo through into the bright and tastefully decorated dining room, its pale green and white décor reflecting the white Italianate exterior of the restaurant with its little green canopies that scooped down over the top of each window like drooping eyelids. White linen table cloths and gleaming glass and cutlery spoke of care and quality while obligatory rustic Italian charm adorned the walls in pictorial scenes of a long-gone rural idyll. Old farming implements and artisan pottery silently air-brushed out of existence any thought of farming subsidies and the Common Agricultural Policy – a designer's concept of gentler times past. It mattered not a jot that it was all as false as Marco's accent because the theatrical ambience it generated was an essential contribution to the good times it hoped to provide for its diners.

It had certainly provided innumerable good times for Jo over the years. She sat and sipped from the chilled, pale pink of her Kir and looked around her. The early hour ensured that, just for a little while, she was the only diner and the silence was gently intruded upon only by a muted conversation from afar between Marco and a waiter and the indistinct and muffled sounds emanating from a kitchen in the act of preparation.

In the more than twenty years that Jo had been using this restaurant she had never before seen it empty and it was odd, not unpleasant but eviscerated, unreal with the feeling of a nicely tailored suit hanging ignored on a rail, waiting for someone to slip it on, to give it motion and life and depth and dimensions.

She cast her eyes around the room and the realisation dawned that she had probably sat at all the different tables at one time or another, but mostly at this particular one, her favourite table by the window looking up the road towards Oatlands Village and across the cricket green, now deserted until the Spring, a quadrangle of posts and rope protecting the wicket.

This one restaurant had witnessed a mix of her very different feelings and emotions and those she dined with – a panoply of emotions from which her life had been constructed, occasionally conflicting emotions at one and the same time. Despair when a boyfriend had tried to let her down gently saying that he didn't think they had any future and it was his problem not hers – despair and sadness and disbelief contrasted with his obvious relief. Anger when a different man had assumed the evening would end with sex – her anger combined with his resentment.

This particular dining room had been a central part of her life, had provided the theatre upon whose stage so many celebrations had been performed and so much pleasure generated. There had been pre-Christmas dinners with her parents and Hillie; big parties of friends, with tables joined together down the centre of the room and a tumult of noise as she and they drank too much and shouted and laughed – and sometimes rowed and argued as the alcohol fuelled their sensitivities.

There had been intimate dinners for two to celebrate the consummation of a relationship or to provide the groundwork that might lead to it being consummated. There had been family gatherings with occasional relatives where all were on their best behaviour, each trying to stick to the required script expected of their particular place in the hierarchy – daughter playing the role of dutiful daughter, mother of caring mother and so on.

It was at this table that Stephen had proposed to her and she had accepted without thought because she had expected it – had been waiting for it. Perhaps it would be a suitable, stage-managed irony if she invited Stephen to have dinner here, at this table, to tell him that it was all over. That would truly bring things full circle.

In her pleasant isolation, street lights shafting through the window illuminating idly-drifting dust specks, Jo wondered if the very fabric of this special room might have absorbed the sounds and visions that had provided the milestones to so many people's lives; whether it had soaked up the sensations and feelings, the raw emotions of its passing and returning clientele and held on to them like some organic, living, breathing sponge and even now, secreted deep in its stone and timber, plaster and glass, those memories silently resided as though captured by some ancient force – a primeval recorder. And perhaps, when circumstances were right and it could sense there was a special need, it could reproduce these distant memories like an old video in hazy vision and sound with just a tantalising taste of the emotions that once accompanied them.

Jo realised she had in mind a scene from the film Titanic where the remnants of the great, sweeping staircase of the sunken vessel echoed to a ghost of the laughter and music of its deceased passengers and their long-gone pleasures, the sounds drifting through the still but clouded water, unheard by lazily finning fish and drifting plankton a thousand feet beneath the Atlantic's turbulent waves.

Perhaps, when she got older and her future was visibly finite; when the importance of retrospect began to grow in direct proportion to the diminishing number of years she had remaining; when she had ceased her interest in accumulating new experiences and wanted nothing more than the reassurance and security of old ones; perhaps then she could return here, reluctantly elderly, and delve quietly into the pleasures of a younger woman and remind herself that she had not always been old.

Jo liked the idea in principle but ever practical, decided the process would need some judicial editing as there were a few memories that were like finger nails down a blackboard and she had no desire to revisit them – ever. Despite the warmth that the idea induced she was even more comforted by the fact that she had no desire to start on that journey just yet, despite the complexities of her life. She raised her glass smiling to herself and found the toast 'here's to the future' forming in her mind.

The smile was still on her face as Marco appeared, ushering in Reece Evans with professional attentiveness, gliding across the wooden floor as though on roller skates, head inclined, one arm extended towards her. She stood and hugged her favourite doctor, kissing him hard on one cheek; not an air kiss but a firm planting of lips on a slightly stubble-strewn cheek, pressing, lips puckered.

Although not especially tall, Reece was commanding with his broad shoulders and athletic build, his short, dark, curly hair greying at the temples and his handsome face – handsome in the way that lived-in faces are handsome, revealing both the strength and tenderness of someone who knows who and what they are and have no need of artifice.

"Lovely to see you Reece." And she meant it.

"And you Jo." They sat and Reece ordered a gin and tonic. "How's Stephen?"

"An arsehole as usual!" Jo smiled again as she saw one of Reece's eyebrows rise and his jaw slacken a touch in just a tiny reaction of genuine shock.

"Oh come on Reece, you know he's an arsehole as well as I do. And how's Beth?"

"Well, she's not an..." He couldn't bring himself to say the word. "She's fine – sends her love. Busy immersing herself in the logistics of a studio debate on crime and punishment." There was almost a weariness in his answer. "So, I bet Stephen's not too happy about your starring role."

Jo laughed infectiously: "You could say that. To be honest, I tried to keep out of his way for as long as possible afterwards. I visited people I haven't seen for years, took Danny to play centres I'd normally avoid like the plague and kept contact to texts and phone calls as long as I could until almost all the steam had fizzed out of his ears. I then played the apologetic and humble wife when we did meet – without actually apologising – and it sort of worked. I even volunteered to join him on the stump as good wifeys do. Good god, Reece, I didn't know I was going to be caught – I'd never have gone if I'd thought that."

"So you regret it?"

Jo's response tripped out before she had time to even consider it: "Do I buggery. This may sound incredibly sad to you but I think it's one of the most important things I've ever done – probably the most important." She watched a slow smile paint itself across Reece's face. "Are you taking the Mickey?" she asked.

"Far from it, Jo. I'd have been really disappointed if you'd said it was all a big mistake. I cheered when I saw you on TV – cheered out loud."

"Why?" Jo asked quizzically.

"Because I'm tired of people talking about this and that. I'm tired of debates and consultations, of enquiries and forums and all the other little devices that kid the middle classes that they're involved in creating change; that they're taking action when in fact all they're doing is trying to show how clever they are. They're usually just filling their days with nonsense so they don't have to confront a reality that might demand something of them – get their hands dirty. You actually got off your backside and did something very, very simple that shocked people. You used your position to better someone else's."

"Does it count that it was pigs?"

"It absolutely does. Pigs, people – doesn't make a great deal of difference. It's all exploitation excused by the same ethos."

Reece raised his glass. "To you, Jo Aldous, I'm proud of you!"

Jo felt a warm flush of pleasure and realised her eyes were filling with tears. Apart from Wendy, no one had supported her so overtly and with such enthusiasm in anything she had ever done and it was exactly the affirmation she needed but had never expected. She loved this man but there was something different about him, something more confrontational; he was more forthright, less non-committal. She had the feeling that he had jettisoned his doctor's impartiality and was reaching inside himself for his own beliefs rather than those that would placate and reassure.

There was even an implicit criticism of Beth, something she had never witnessed before. Some couples depressed her immeasurably, particularly those where one of them had jettisoned all concept of caring and support and seemed to find it essential to boost their own self-esteem, their own ego, by the caustic erosion of their partner's. Mostly it was just below the radar but sometimes it erupted into outright hostility – one demeaning the other, undermining them, ridiculing them. Reece and Bethan had never been like that and it was their obvious affection for each other and mutual pride and respect that made Jo like them so much.

"Thank you Reece, I love you!" Jo leant across the table and kissed him on the cheek. "You okay? I mean really okay?"

He looked at her with his big, soulful brown eyes and she could see they were troubled.

"I'm fine Jo – a lot of stuff going through my mind, that's all. Anyway, it was you who had some concerns you wanted to run past me."

"I'll save that 'till later," Jo said jovially, "but I'll just give you a bit of advance warning so you can give me the once over while we're eating. Am I going bonkers?"

"Nothing serious then," Reece replied with a smile.

"What do you fancy to eat?" Jo enquired. "I've made my choice."

"And that is?"

Jo reached for the menu and read from it: "Asparagus with ground hazelnuts gratinee in olive oil and black pepper followed by porcini ravioli in a spicy red pepper sauce, but without the parmesan shavings, and a wild rocket salad." She looked at Reece as though extremely pleased with herself.

"Ditto," he said, slamming shut the menu which he held in front of him but hadn't read.

"Red or white?" Jo asked.

"Oh red," Reece responded enthusiastically. "I can then pretend I'm doing myself good even while I'm reaching for the Alka Seltzer."

Jo chuckled: "A nice little Sicilian then, I reckon. They've got a lovely eight-year old Corvo and we'll have it straight away don't you think, considering you've demolished your G and T."

Reece raised a hand to indicate it was fine with him. "I'm walking!"

There is always a slight hiatus in the initial conversation between friends when they haven't seen each other for a while, as they ease back to where they were when they last met. Jo and Reece passed through that phase quickly and seamlessly settled into an intimacy nourished over many years. But all the time, as they chatted about this and that, through the two courses of their dinner and into the second bottle of Corvo, as the restaurant filled up and they had to raise their voices to hear each other above the hubub, Jo was convinced that her early feelings were correct and something was troubling Reece. Without preamble she cut through a story he was telling.

"Come on Reece, something's wrong, what is it?"

"Clever girl." He became silent for a few seconds and went somewhere else, somewhere a long way away. When he returned, he offered his explanation without gravitas, unemotionally as a matter-of-fact statement. "Actually Jo, my dad died three weeks ago..." Before Jo could respond, he extended his arm across the table towards her, hand raised: "No, no, no! Don't go all sad and mournful on me and tell me how sorry you are. I'm not crippled with grief or anything like that..."

"Nevertheless, Reece, I am sorry – very, very sorry."

He did not acknowledge her concern. "Of course I'm sad," he continued, "I'm very sad to see the lovely old fella die but I've done my grieving and I should now be able to relax into some kind of contentment about the good times we had, the great memories, the warmth and love he provided, the things that he achieved, all the things he helped me to achieve... But I can't. I just can't, Jo."

He looked into her eyes as if asking for an answer. "I'm too troubled! I have no certainty about who I am any longer or what I believe. It just seems to me that we're all..." He grappled for a word that adequately expressed his feelings but, unable to find one, fell back on one which was trite but perfectly summed up how he felt "...fucked."

Jo reached over the table and took his hand in hers. She was shocked – not by the word he'd used but by the honesty that her friend was revealing so painfully and the sense of futility he obviously felt. This was not a time for cross examination and so she remained silent, holding his hand, gently stroking the back of it with her thumb.

"I'm listening Reece."

"You don't want to hear all the nonsense that's churning around in my head, I promise you."

He had averted his eyes and Jo knew that what he really wanted was the exact opposite. He wanted not only to know that Jo was willing to listen but needed her confirmation, required her authority. It was almost as though confusion and sadness were not meant to be a part of his makeup and that it was somehow emasculating to admit they were, demeaning to indulge in them.

Jo wondered if this was a result of spending a working life listening to other people's fears and concerns to such a point that they had been emulsified with his own and his capacity to absorb any more had expired and, like a sponge, they were beginning to dribble out of their own volition, uncontrollable and unwanted. She tried to make light of it.

"Dinner was on me Reece, payment for me yattering on but as your doing the yattering, you're paying now. Okay?" She laughed and squeezed his hand hard. "Reece, I want to hear what's troubling you – please talk to me. Here you are – some lubrication." And Jo topped up both their glasses.

"God, I'm pissed already," he grimaced.

"Me too but what the hell."

"It's nothing dramatic Jo, more an enforced reassessment of everything I've done with my life. You didn't know my dad, did you?"

"I met him a couple of times. I thought he was lovely."

"Have you ever been to Merthyr Tydfil?" Jo shook her head. "You'd probably think it was – excuse my French – a complete shit hole. Well, you should have seen it when my dad was a young man. It was like something out of Germinal."

Jo had no idea who or what Germinal was but it mattered not. The picture he was trying to paint was clarity itself.

"There was the Dowlais ironworks and mining and not a lot else except for the bra factory and Hoover, but they were mostly for women. My dad worked at Merthyr Vale colliery. You probably don't known it but mining is an almost unique industry in that men not only work together in teams, each one trusting his life to the others, but they also live together and socialise together. The word community is grossly overused but with miners it has a real meaning, it defines their lives. Without that sense of belonging, of mutual support and understanding, do you think they would do that god-awful job?

"The only place they ever went of an evening was the miners' welfare – miners and their wives drinking with other miners and their wives. They clubbed together and started the place, they ran it, they booked the entertainment and they could buy beer at less than half the price charged by the local pubs. It cost them comparatively little to get pissed and wash the taste of coal dust out of their mouths, to help them forget the mind-numbing work they'd been doing all day – the same work they would do the next day and the day after that. Getting pissed was as much therapy for working class Merthyr boys as Valium is for Weybridge's housewives. It numbed the senses."

Reece continued with what seemed to be a reminiscence that almost excluded her: "As a coalface worker, Dad was one of the elite and could sink pints with the best of them and I've seen him come home reeling. But he didn't do it regularly because he wanted much, much more out of life – not for him but for me and my sister. He would have thought his life a complete failure if I'd gone down the pit and Meg had done the usual thing and got herself pregnant by a drunken young collier on a Saturday night and produced a string of kids in a little house on the Gurnos estate. Would you believe it, the life expectancy for a bloke on that estate is fifty nine – fifty bloody nine!

"Education was the way forward, he thought, and when I qualified as a doctor he could hardly do up his jacket his chest was so puffed up with pride. And then Meg became a teacher and he actually said to me, over a pint in the welfare: 'I can die a happy man now, Reece bach'. There was nothing else in his life, Jo. How sad is that?

"Knowing your dad is living his life through you puts a huge amount of pressure on. After my mam died, what, fourteen or fifteen years ago, we became his life. He'd lost his politics, detested the chapel with vehemence and we were his self-satisfaction, his pride, his lifetime's success, the confirmation that he had been a good father. Believe me, Jo, the pride your Stephen will feel when he goes to the Palace and cosies up to the Queen won't even come close to my dad's sense of a job well done."

Jo asked the question gently: "Why is that a problem, Reece?"

"The problem is, I could never talk to him honestly about my job or my feelings, because the two are intertwined. Sure, it was fine in the early years when I was full of enthusiasm and determined to go places but then later, as the reality of what I was actually doing came home to me, I found it increasingly difficult to take any great pride in my work. If I'd told him that it would have devastated him, made him think that all his efforts, all his determination, all his hopes and aspirations had been pissed up against the wall. He'd probably have thought I was an ungrateful little shit. I just felt I had to keep it to myself."

"But you're a great doctor, Reece, a kind, understanding, gentle doctor who cares about his patients. Good god, just your presence makes people feel better. I wouldn't be here now confessing things to you, and you confiding in me if you weren't a great, caring doctor."

Reece suddenly snapped out of his introspection: "You haven't confessed anything to me," he said, with an unspoken question mark hanging in the air.

"No, but I'm going to, you can rely on that. It's a treat in store for you." Jo threw him a disarming smile. "Keep going – I want to hear more."

"I'm not sure you do, Jo. You see I'm disillusioned, totally disillusioned – with being a doctor, with the whole medical profession, with…" Again Reece struggled for an appropriate word but in the end settled for a mundanity. "Everything…"

Jo could not hide her concern: "Oh no, not Beth as well. Please not that?"

Reece smiled at her slowly. "No, not that – definitely not that but I suspect Beth's getting the backlash from my soul searching and has probably had enough of it."

"So you've talked to her about whatever it is that's concerning you?"

"Beth's a valleys'girl and probably had a bigger struggle than me. She never forgets it and never stops thanking her lucky stars that she got out and now has a fulfilling job and lives in a posh Surrey suburb. She tries to be sympathetic but deep down I know she's thinking: 'Be bloody grateful for what you've got, boyyo.' I don't blame her for a second but it doesn't make sharing introspection easy. But it isn't just about my job, Jo, it's about life." He tried to make light of it. "What are we all doing here, where are we all going…?"

Jo laughed and shook her head. "When you find out, Reece,

for god's sake tell me because all my assumptions, all my certainties, all my expectations have been trashed, too. But I hope there's a new me deep down there somewhere and I'm certain that eventually it will exert itself and I'll be a different, better, less smug and self-satisfied person."

"A new person? You're going to be a prime minister's wife and you can't get much newer than that." Jo thought she detected a barb, a slight taint of bitterness and it hurt.

"Never assume anything, Reece." Although she hadn't intended it, there was a corresponding tartness in her reply. "I'm not going to be a prime minister's wife – at least not for long. I'm leaving Stephen." It was said with the same finality that Reece had used to announce the death of his father.

Jo watched Reece's face as his expressions flickered through disbelief, incomprehension, uncertainty but finally focused in on what could only be described as pleasure. "Really?"

"Yes, really. I haven't told him yet but he'd have to be utterly thick skinned not to have guessed."

"So he's got no idea, then," Reece said with a twinkle in his eye.

"Bitch," Jo laughed.

Reece suddenly became serious. "I'm so sorry Jo, you asked me here to talk about your problems and I've blathered on about my midlife crisis."

"No, Reece, that's not why I invited you. Stephen's got nothing to do with it. Forget about me for a minute. Give me specifics, why you're feeling so disenchanted."

Reece hesitated, picked up his glass of wine and raised it to Jo wordlessly, sipped then returned it to his lips and sipped again and then again. It was almost as though he was preparing himself to slip slowly back inside his skin to fish for his shadowy troubles. He finally produced some.

"Bloody hell, Jo, I influence almost nothing. I deal in suppressing symptoms not dispensing cures. It's more than thirty years since I started training as a doctor, trained to deal with heart disease and cancer and the string of diseases that kill most of us. And do you know what's happened in that time? Do you?" The question was entirely rhetorical and Jo remained silent. "Heart disease has doubled and so has cancer. More than one in three of us will get cancer – forty per cent to be accurate – and almost everyone risks getting heart disease. Diabetes is running out of control and so is Alzheimers and obesity and the prognosis for our kids is so appalling that it constitutes an evolutionary disaster."

Jo's natural inclination was always to look for a positive in any situation, to chart a path out of problems and even if it was only half a chance at least it provided a lodestone of some kind, something to follow and avoid the crushing burden of hopelessness.

"You can't make such a sweeping statement without some pretty sound evidence, Reece."

"Okay, then, take kids. Would you believe me if I told you that eighty per cent of all the children in Britain are suffering from malnutrition – that's four out of five! Just take that on board, Jo, malnutrition, even here, in one of the wealthiest countries on the planet. And the reason I know it's true is because the government produces a nutrition survey every few years that looks at what kids eat and what it's doing to them.

"I'm not talking about the swollen bellied, hollow-eyed kind of malnutrition that you see in African children – that comes from not having enough to eat, from starvation. This is different. It's about too much to eat but entirely the wrong kinds of food. The majority of kids don't have regular bowel movements, they're lacking nutrients, vitamins and minerals because they're gorging themselves on sugar and white flour and animal fat. It's bloody burgers and coke and fried chicken and cheese strings and crisps and biscuits.

"Do you know, they're getting diseases that once only affected adults and the chances are they're going to start dying before their parents. That's not how it's meant to be. It's a disaster. And what's being done about it? Absolutely bugger all and I can say that because the latest survey has just come out and things have got worse. We're nibbling around the edges of the problem because to tackle it properly means taking on the big multinational food corporations and that's not allowed – in fact nothing's allowed that gets in the way of the free market.

We're killing our kids as surely as if we let them run loose in the road, it just takes a bit longer."

Jo had no doubt that what Reece was saying was true. He was the kind of man who never made claims or issued statements unless he was certain of his facts. And yes, she was disturbed by what he was saying but was even more disturbed by the sense of futility that was pouring out of her friend. She wanted to be extremely practical and say: 'Okay, we've identified the problem now how do we solve it?' It came out as: "What the hell can be done about it, Reece? There must be something."

"That's the worst part, Jo. Bugger all! Do you know why? Because we're not dealing with ignorance or disbelief or lack of resources or lack of evidence, we're dealing with a system where the power, all the power, lies in the hands of huge commercial corporations and their bottom line is satisfying their investors – nothing else, just that! Nothing matters but declaring a decent dividend.

"How do you take that on, Jo, when some companies are wealthier and more powerful than some countries? Add them all together and you have a cartel of global omnipotence and the really frightening thing is that they have the backing of most governments. Sure they're scared of the power they wield but ideologically they're totally supportive."

"They're has to be something we can do. I dunno, trades unions, mass action – something. It's supposed to be a democracy, perhaps we've got to start making demands; perhaps you're misjudging people and they're as aware as you are but aren't sure yet of the best way to go about it."

She was aware that her words were not a world removed from what had been drummed into her at school and in church – faith, faith, faith, the saviour of everything. The last time anyone had talked about faith to her she had wanted to reply: "Yes, shove it down your face like penicillin and it will cure all – life will be perfect." She'd wanted to say it but didn't. Faith was a platitude, a baby's comforter, a security blanket, a pair of blinkers, a pat on the back, a pint of beer and a Valium. She wanted to retract her words to Reece but it was too late.

"Do you really believe all that tosh, Jo? The unions

emasculated themselves years ago and have got no idea how to function in a global market. As for people searching for answers, you're about – were about – to become the wife of a prime minister. What is there amongst the huge raft of policies that Stephen will no doubt introduce that even begins to address this? What will he do that will even acknowledge the scale of this problem let alone deal with it? And then there are all the other global problems? Does he even recognise them, Jo? Of course he bloody doesn't."

Jo's mouth tightened and her shoulders and eyebrows raised while her hands opened with palms up in a shrug of near resignation but she remained silent.

"Precisely! And the other lot's the same. They all wave this banner that they're the knights errant who will defend the health service against any evil foe and it's all bollocks. It isn't a health service it's a sickness service, dispensing pills and potions to keep symptoms at bay. If it was a health service it would be preventing us from getting ill. Degenerative diseases are at epidemic proportions, Jo. Sure we're living longer but it's largely thanks to pills and treatments, early diagnosis and surgery. Do you know, almost half of us is on permanent medication. How could I say any of this to my poor old dad who thought the health service was one of humankind's greatest achievements?"

"But you've never spoken like this before, Reece, why now? It wasn't just your dad dying, surely?"

"That crystalised it because I didn't have to hide from the truth any longer but if you read the literature – read it properly – it's all there. We're scoffing food that's killing us – we're being encouraged to, it's being subsidized with our own taxes and yet people throw their hands up in horror shouting 'what can we do about it?' like it's a visitation from some vengeful god. It's animals, Jo, poor fucking animals and their fat and protein that's at the heart of it all. But how could I tell my dad all this, subject him to my cynicism, my negativity when he was so, so proud I was a doctor?"

"But you still eat meat, don't you Reece? Why?"

"Because I don't give a shit any longer, not about me nor my health. And anyway, I didn't tonight."

"Yeah, but only because I ordered for you. Anyway, I might have got this wrong but I think if you'd talked to him, your dad might well have been even more proud of you, particularly if he was a political man. The fact that you haven't succumbed to complacency, that you're still sharp, enquiring, critical and you're analysing massive global issues that affect us all is pretty impressive, I would have thought. If you're going to fight against something you have to identify the enemy first and then you can plan your strategy…"

"But the enemies are inviolate, huge corporations that laugh at us, have contempt for us and we can't even dent their façade let alone wrest power back from them. It's gone too far. They're the kings of the castle, Jo, and we're the dirty rascals."

"But they're just people, Reece, no matter how powerful they are. The bosses who run these companies are just people with wives and health problems, they're worried about their weight and their children's futures. They're just like you and me – they're not imbued with supernatural powers. They're just people who surely don't want to screw up their future, their kids' future."

"Of course they're ordinary people but the whole thing has gone way beyond individuals and their cares and concerns. It's like a termite heap where the whole edifice is far more important than any single creature. It has a life of its own and that life has to be preserved – at any cost. It simply doesn't have the ability to respond to anything that doesn't contribute to the success and survival of the heap. Whatever else is destroyed, the heap has to continue."

"Come on Reece, you're sounding… apocalyptic. This isn't you, surely this isn't how it really is."

"It is, Jo, it is, that's exactly what it's like. Listen, if the CEO of Monsanto and his board of directors woke up one morning and decided that their – I dunno, let's say animal antibiotics – their antibiotics had contributed enough to creating dangerous super bugs and it troubled their consciences so they wanted to stop producing them, what do you think would happen? As soon as they announced their decision to get out of the market their stock price would collapse and all the other antibiotic manufacturers would rub their hands with glee and increase production to fill the gap. Nothing would have changed except that Monsanto's market position would be weakened, their share price would fall and someone would probably take them over and it would be business as usual."

Jo thought for a moment of the simplicity of Reece's explanation which seemed hard to argue with. She could not allow his well of defeatism to get any deeper.

"In that case they have to be stopped politically. You've used your intelligence and your hunger for…" Jo struggled to find the appropriate word, "…justice, I suppose, care, compassion, call it what you like but you're not lying down in front of them, you've identified who and what they are and what they're doing and that has to be the start of change. Your dad would be proud of you – I'm proud of you."

Reece shook his head and went silent for a moment, raising a single eyebrow in acknowledgement of Jo's compliment.

"Politics hey? And we're back to Stephen! That'll work, won't it? It's the kids that get me most, Jo. You can watch them waddling down the High Street – see a fat mum and you're almost bound to see a fat kid alongside her, thighs rubbing together, swaying from side to side with the effort of simply walking. Are people so fucking greedy that they've given up trying entirely? Sure I blame government and industry but at the end it comes down to personal choice. Everyone knows there's a problem but they still carry on like the tooth fairy's going to come in the night and magic away all their fat and clogged arteries and grant them the gift of eternal life.

"We've got this huge bloody brain and we seem to be utterly terrified of using it to determine our own lives. Let someone else tell us what to do, how to behave, how to lead our lives because it's all just too much bloody trouble.

"That's how the bloody Pope gets away with it, telling everyone that shagging isn't natural unless you want to have a baby. It's how Muslims control their followers and all the pathetic Christian sects – the Mormons and Jehovah's Witnesses and Plymouth Bretheren – you can go on and on. They feed people manufactured certainties, none of which came from any kind of god, and they accept them, deluding themselves that the closer they stick to the ludicrous demands the greater will be their rewards in heaven. It's laughable, Jo, but it's widespread and so utterly, utterly bloody pathetic. This is the same species that split the atom and put men in space!

"Blokes like Stephen, of course, latch on to this because the whole obedience and leadership thing has been instilled into them at public school and they're always hand in glove with the bloody clerics – always have been throughout history, making you believe that profit is good and public service is shit – it must be right because the church agrees. It's about controlling you, directing you to where they want you to go, manipulating you for their benefit.

"And the other lot – the lot that's supposed to represent people like my dad – are so bloody keen to emulate the rich bastards that they adopt all the same policies and philosophies. You hear them in parliament screaming and shouting and yahooing at each other and you'd think that revolution was just around the corner but it's like kids in a playground. It's juvenile posturing, You can barely squeeze a fag paper between their policies. It's wind and piss elevated to political debate and they all buy into this religious crap because they're cowards – afraid to confront fairy tales because those fairy tales have become an integral part of our society – god almighty, there are even unelected bishops sitting in our legislature. Do you know what, Jo, I'm beginning to despair of the human race."

Jo was about to respond but Reece continued, ignoring her obvious desire to say something.

"People like my dad thought they'd cracked all this religious nonsense way back and suddenly it's here again in full force. We're all supposed to respect people's beliefs as though we're dealing with something noble and enriching. I don't bloody respect them and I think their beliefs and their bloody afterlives are bloody retrograde and dangerous – deeply, deeply dangerous. I don't repect them any more than I respect the Flat Earth Society or creationism. It's fairy stories with a feel good factor; an insurance policy in return for commitment."

There was a pause as Reece again reached for his glass

without looking at Jo and she sensed a change in his demeanour. Gone was the defeatism and in its place, destructive anger was etched into his face. He looked like a battered boxer between rounds, distant, thinking of the next move, hurt but determined to get even, waiting for the bell to sound so he could leap back into action.

This was an entirely different man to the one she had known over the years. There had always been cynicism but laced with humour. He had always been able to cut the legs off an argument with a few pithy words of incisiveness but this was close to despair. This was a man flailing at a world which he could not influence and his impotence was obliterating all hope.

Despite the alcohol that was coursing through her, Jo was disturbed – not by his thoughts and beliefs but by the intensity with which he felt them. When confronted with odds of such overpowering proportions there had to be a glimmer of hope somewhere. There had to be others of a like mind awaiting the call to join together and oppose, to chart a different course. To surrender to impotence as completely as Reece was doing left nowhere to go. The thought of him confronting the rest of his life as an emasculated victim worried her deeply because that would be anathema to him. He would not be able to continue to live like that.

"Christ, Reece, history has shown us how people and beliefs and institutions rise and fall. They accumulate power and then it's stripped away from them for one reason or another and things move on. The world is utterly dynamic and how it stands at the moment isn't how it will be in a year, two years, a decade. Change happens and sometimes quickly because ordinary people make it happen. Hope is always there – it has to be there?"

"Why? Why does it? It's like that old piss-take of the Red Flag, 'The working class can kiss my arse, I've got the foreman's job at last'. Or the rock star who grabs everyone's imagination by writing songs attacking unemployment or homelessness and glorifying struggle. And then, within a decade, they've stopped creating anything because the fire inside them has been extinguished by adulation and over-indulgence and they've entirely forgotten how other people have to live. All they want is to walk on stage at the Royal Variety Performance, all ponced up, to bow and scrape to an unelected, privileged product of heredity and sing their old songs about underprivilege because they've got bugger all new to say. It's obscene."

Jo wanted to cry because she felt she was witnessing the descent of a lovely, caring man into an abyss from which there might not be any escape. She was at a loss to know how to encourage him out of what was clearly despair. This was not the kind of evening she had envisaged. She struggled to think of anything positive to say and so reached for her glass and reverted to humour: "Cheers. Here's to the revolution."

To her surprise, Reece smiled. Not a passing apology of a smile, not a polite dismissal of a throw-away line but a smile which lit up his eyes and crinkled their corners. He seemed to sit more erectly in his chair and for the first time that evening she watched him look around the room and he appeared to absorb the bustle and chatter and the flood of enjoyment that emanated from the busy tables. He looked back at her and he was still smiling.

"Eat drink and be merry for tomorrow we die," he said with a belly laugh and raised his glass to Jo, and she reciprocated, feeling a flood of relief. He was back! Well almost.

"And I promise not to mention the millions of people that Mao and Stalin bumped off in the name of revolution." Again it was delivered with a twinkle of humour. "Sorry, Jo, I must have bored the pants off you."

Jo shook her head gently. "No you didn't, Reece." The truth was, he had evoked a whole range of conflicting emotions but boredom wasn't one of them.

"Good," he replied and leant across the table towards her and she met him half way so he could plant a kiss on her cheek. The wine was almost gone.

"Do you know the best thing about revolutions, Jo? It's the music – the Internationale. No matter that the megalomaniacs always betray revolutions, it's the wonderful hope of the people who start them that I love – their determination to produce a better world, a fairer world where all wrongs will be righted and all iniquities banished. And of course, they have no idea in those exciting days that they'll eventually be shat on. I want it played at my funeral."

A few minutes earlier Jo knew she would have been deeply disturbed by any talk of funerals but Reece was now a different man; scathing, dismissive but happy – and pissed. He suddenly held one fist in the air and began singing with a deep baritone voice:

"Arise ye starvelings from your slumber
Arise ye criminals of want
For reason in revolt now thunders
And at last ends the age of cant."

The further he got into the anthem the louder his voice became but it was beautifully mellow, deep, vibrant and perfectly in tune.

As he reached the chorus Reece picked up his half-full glass and began conducting with it, all pretence at singing quietly now gone and his rich tones could be heard around the entire restaurant.

"So comrades come rally
And the last fight let us face
The Internationale unites the human race."

For the crescendo of the reprise he was in full voice,

"So comrades come raa-lly
And the last fight let us face
The In-ter-na-tion- a-al-e
U-nites – the hu-man race."

Spontaneous, humorous applause and hoorays and bravos rang out from around the restaurant and both Reece and Jo dissolved into laughter, painfully aware of the incongruity of a doctor and prospective Conservative leader's wife singing the communist anthem in a privileged little restaurant in a very privileged little suburb.

"Oh Jo, Jo, Jo – what are we to do," he said, taking both her hands in his across the table. "What a selfish shit I am. I haven't paid the slightest attention to your needs."

Jo had long since lost any sense of needing to talk about her concerns and dismissed the idea with a flourish of her hand. Her thoughts had been entirely occupied with Reece and whatever it was that was poisoning his mind.

Reece was emphatic: "Not on your life. Tell me Jo but first, brandy I think." He summoned attention with a theatrical bellow: "Waiter!"

Jo laughed. They were both so drunk that a brandy could make little difference and when it arrived Reece looked at her like the doctor he was, waiting for his patient to reveal her symptoms. Again she laughed, largely because of the juxtaposition of moods but also because of his apparent difficulty in focusing. Suddenly, however, she did want to talk, as much as to say that she was also a victim of introspection, that they had shared concerns, they were both trying to grind an avenue though life and it wasn't easy.

She briefly outlined her experiences, her waking dreams, the awful sense of suffering she felt she was being forced to absorb and her explanation for them. When she had finished, Reece became very serious and pondered for a long, long time before responding. When he did eventually do so, he appeared entirely sober, concerned and thoughtful. It was like he had changed one hat for another – the despairing revolutionary's for that of the benign doctor.

"Forget about the waking dreams, they're no indication of anything. There's a whole string of studies on them and no suggestion that they're linked to psychoses or any other psychological problem." Again he went silent and when he spoke again it was very quietly, intimately. "Have you ever heard of Aberfan?"

Jo though for a moment. "Ye-e-e-s, I think so. Wasn't there some tragedy there?"

"Yes there was – twenty first of October 1966. A colliery spoil heap – slag heap – became saturated and unstable after days of rain and slipped. An avalanche of black mud and stones roared down the mountainside and obliterated a primary school. It killed one hundred and forty four people, a hundred and sixteen of them children."

Reece was clearly attempting to keep emotion out of his voice but was failing.

"My dad was a fit young man then, a ripper on the coal face. They're the men who use air picks, a bit like small road drills, to hack down the rock and scree that sits above the coal seam. The mechanical cutter moves along the coal face cutting coal, moving as far forward as it can until the overhang of rock stops it. The rippers then move in to remove the rock to provide headroom. Some of that rock stays in the pit but some of it gets brought to the surface and is dumped.

"The tip that descended on Aberfan and destroyed so many lives was made up of waste from the Merthyr Vale colliery where my dad worked, some of which he'd hacked out. For a hundred years the mine owners had been tipping on that site.

"When he heard what had happened, my dad took the responsibility on himself. It was his fault, he was to blame, it was his slag that crushed and choked little children and their teachers to death. I was only a little boy but it's seared into my mind. He spent nearly three days and nights without sleep at that shattered school, desperately digging, trying to rescue the children and all he ever brought out were little dead and mangled bodies. It bloody nearly destroyed him."

Jo had no idea where Reece was going with his story but the emotion oozed out of him and he delivered his words almost in a monotone, almost as though it was vital to fillet it of emotion in case the agony of it ran out of control. The battle to do so made his words even more poignant.

"I think what saved him in the end was the National Coal Board. It didn't support him or provide him with counselling or anything like that, in fact it didn't give a shit about him and the others whose lives had been wrecked by that disaster. No, their first imperative was to wriggle and writhe, deny and delay in order to avoid responsibility. Dad was one inconsequential miner with a huge heart and a conscience but who had had nothing to do with what happened. Yet he tried to carry on his shoulders responsibility for something so appalling that it would have eventually crushed him like an ant underfoot had it continued.

"When the allegations started to flow and it came out just how many reports had been written and ignored about the risks of that spoil heap and its geological instability, the warnings about the three streams that ran under that site making it inherently dangerous, he finally began to realise that it was the same old enemy as always who carried the real blame – the owners. It didn't matter that they operated under the banner of nationalisation, they had behaved just like the old private owners. His despair turned into anger and of course no one's head ever rolled but exposure of their incompetence saved my dad's life.

"When they eventually took a large part of the money a horrified nation had subscribed to help the bereaved and used it to clear the tip instead, you can imagine the response in Aberfan. And you wonder why I hate and distrust big organisations."

"It's a horrible story, Reece, horrible."

"But what's it got to do with you, eh?"

Jo inclined her head and smiled quizzically but she was quite content for him to continue talking about whatever he chose. Her supposed troubles seemed non-existent by comparison.

"I'm getting there, Jo, I'm getting there. Most of the children were buried in the Aberfan cemetery and a few years after it had all happened and most people had forgotten, I went to that cemetery to pay my respects, when I was old enough to fully appreciate the horror of it all.

"The graveyard sits on the hillside above Aberfan and the graves are arranged in two long rows, one above the other, looking down over the slate roofs of the village – the same houses where these slaughtered little children once lived, houses where their devastated parents could walk out of the front door, look up the hill and see the memorial to their lost children. The graves are marked by a series of arches, one arch linked to the other as if uniting the children in death.

"There are also benches where you can sit and reflect on the tragedy and that's what I did, I sat and tried to comprehend the enormity of what had happened and do you know, Jo, it completely overwhelmed me. I sat there and looked along those lines of arches, at the headstones beneath them with their gut-wrenching, heart-rending simple messages of love and loss and grief and loneliness and I couldn't cope.

"I stopped trying to think, I couldn't think, because I was swamped by grief – not my grief but the accumulation of other people's grief and desperation at the loss of their children. I felt it emanating from everywhere around me and from afar and it was absorbed into my body like a vapour. I wanted history to be rewritten and the waves of suffering to stop, to be erased – the suffering of hundreds of people, of thousands of people – the mothers and fathers, sisters and brothers, all the aunties and uncles and grandparents and friends, the teachers and children who survived, the men and women like my father who scrabbled at the debris and hugged to them the little corpses they found as though they could bring them back to life with their tenderness but eventually had no choice but to place them on the ground in those pathetic lines of death."

Jo watched the tears welling up in Reece's eyes until one by one they spilled over and coursed down his cheeks. He ignored them, left them to their individual little journeys without attempting to brush them aside or wipe his eyes. Jo remained silent but she now had some sense of where he was going.

"That tidal wave of grief was crushing and utterly consumed me and I almost prayed to a god I had no belief in that it could be erased, that time could be wound backwards and that those dead little souls could see out the day, like they had every other school day, and come home wondering what was for tea, to the comfort and reassurance of their mams and dads. But of course they couldn't.

"The moving finger writes and having writ, moves on. Not all thy piety nor wit can lure in back to cancel half a line. Nor all thy tears wash out one word of it.

"That experience changed me forever, Jo, and just as I absorbed and was humbled by that outpouring of pain; just like my dad was almost destroyed by it, I can see no reason on this

Earth why you should not also absorb the pain of living creatures if you have sufficient sensitivity, if you are attuned to it."

Jo finally spoke: "Even though they're animals."

"Despite our Porches and our quilted lavatory paper and our arrogance, we're animals. There's nothing special about us much as we like to think there is. Jo, you're not bonkers – in fact I suspect you're saner than most people, certainly saner than me."

"Thank you Reece, thank you, thank you." And she meant it. Although the incidences had reduced and she had rationalised them enough to lessen her concerns, Jo had not realised just how much insecurity still lurked deep down inside. Reece had just dispelled it.

Jo paid the bill and they linked arms as they exited from the restaurant and headed slightly unsteadily across the cricket green, Jo insisting that Reece teach her the chorus to the Internationale. By the time they reached the road leading to St Georges Hill they were in full voice:

"So comrades come rally and the last fight let us face,
The Internationales unites the human race."

The words echoed back from the Surrey tile hanging of beautiful detached houses, bounced off the Volvos and BMWs, infiltrated their way through partly-raised blinds of designer kitchens and swirled round the cherubs atop the fountains of water features.

When they reached the point where their paths digressed, Reece hugged her strongly, kissed her cheek and whispered quietly into her ear.

"There's something wrong, Jo, something really wrong. I'm dealing with more and more people who feel like I do – despairing. And I've had three people in the last couple of weeks who are having similar experiences to you. They haven't articulated them as well as you and they haven't rationalised them as sharply – but you're not on your own."

Jo was too warmly alcoholic for the revelation to have the impact it might have. "Christ Reece, there must be something in the water," she giggled.

When Jo reached her house, she opened the door but then failed to catch the handle as it swung open and it crashed noisily against the hallway wall. Stephen appeared from the kitchen with a sandwich in his hand.

"Where've you been?"

"Out," replied Jo.

"I don't think Marta was very happy."

"Why?"

"Because it's nearly ten o'clock and you said you'd be home by nine. She had to put Danny to bed. And you're pissed!"

"Ten out of ten Sherlock." She could not be bothered to explain that she had told Marta she would be back between nine and ten and that she might have to put Danny to bed. "But tomorrow I'll be sober and you'll still be a pompous arse."

"Have you been out with that bloody Carter woman?"

"Stephen, mind your own fucking business."

"Well, I can tell you that her wings are going to be clipped very soon." With that he turned back into the kitchen and as Jo started up the stairs his head reappeared. "Oh by the way, Archie is standing down, I should be elected leader next week." He was trying to be matter of fact but Jo could see he was delighted.

"Congratulations Stephen, well done." And she meant it.

"The election campaign starts now, Jo, and the first public meeting is here in Weybridge a week on Saturday. I'd like you beside me on the platform – if that's alright." Jo detected an edge in his voice that fell just short of pleading and felt sorry for him. Not sorry enough to banish all sarcasm from her reply, though.

"Of course, sweetie, of course." She continued up to her bedroom, stumbling over the top step, "Whoops," and took her mobile phone from her bag and dialled.

"Wendy?… Get your house in order, babe, they're coming for you." Jo giggled and felt like a Weybridge Matta Hari.

Chapter Nineteen

"You're not your usual self Alexander, is there something wrong? You seem a little depressed."

The words were seemingly spoken with concern but Al Dwight read something entirely different into the enquiry. It felt to him like a prod with the toe to a sleeping animal, a gloating observation that he was losing the game, a merciless challenge to come out and continue the fight when the towel had clearly been thrown into the ring, the white flag hoisted.

Al had changed and he knew it, stemming not from regret at individual past actions or even despair at being where he was but from the blinding realisation that he had, as he put it, 'fucked up' his life.

There were just the two of them in the small quiet room with its cheap thriller paperbacks, magazines in which he had no interest and days old newspapers. He put down the one he was reading:

"The only person who calls me Alexander is my mother. My name is Al!" He didn't add that his mother was long-since dead.

Nurse Protz smiled at him sweetly as if he had just paid her a compliment and sat down in the chair facing him.

"Coming to terms with the things we've done can be part of the healing process, even if they discomfort us and make us feel ashamed. Depression, for the right reasons, isn't necessarily all bad, just a step on the road to coming to terms with our past, the road to something better. It's how we deal with it that matters."

Al looked at her long and hard, unblinking, no expression on his face, no desire to enter into conversation with his keeper:

"Just leave me alone." He turned his face away from her, hoping she would heed his clear desire not to talk.

"If only it was that easy, Alexander. You see, while you're here I'm in charge of your mind, so to speak." The smile almost divided her face and hinted at humour but her eyes were unsmiling, cold, dead and those words chilled Al. "So if your mind is disturbed, it's my duty to register the fact and do what I can to help you remedy it."

"Protz, I've been here for four months on a court order, I'm not receiving any treatment and I've got two months to go so why don't you do what all the other staff do – ignore me and just let the clock run down?"

"Anyone who tries to kill a person with an axe has clearly got a troubled mind and that isn't going to be remedied overnight. In fact it could take quite some time – much more than six months." Again the smile was there, sweet and reassuring, so long as you avoided the eyes, thought Al, but the threat was blatant. Or had he become so obsessed by nurse Protz that, to him, everything she did or said contained a threat? He was in the nut house so paranoia was probably the lingua franca and perhaps the problem was entirely with him and not her.

Al's response was spontaneous and immediate and he cursed himself for replying even as he was speaking, having already decided he would not allow Protz to draw him into conversation – ever. He was convinced that anything he said, now or at any time, would be trawled through and any positive insights into his character and state of mind would be discarded like so much garbage whilst all the negatives would be latched onto gleefully, stored away and retrieved whenever they could do the most damage or be used to reinforce her control.

"I didn't try to kill him..." Al hesitated. "Just break his fingers." Even as he said it, out of context and away from the mores of the shabby world of car dealing and criminality he had once inhabited, it did not provide a totally reassuring response. "That's what happens to tea leaves where I come from... came from."

The correction to past tense was not designed simply to

reassure Protz but himself also. From this distance, it was hard to believe that this had once been his world and he was convinced that whatever state of mind, whatever personality defects had lured him into being a part of it, they were now gone – those days were over. Was it being institutionalised that had wrought the change or something else? Or was he just kidding himself that he had changed at all?

No, Al knew he had changed and its cause was no mystery and was the same reason why he had withdrawn even from the limited contacts he'd had in this place of last resort.

He remembered seeking advice from an ex-alcoholic about a work colleague who was advancing rapidly into acute alcoholism himself and seemed incapable of responding to his obvious decline. He would appear from a drying-out clinic and begin drinking again almost immediately and pretend it was by choice rather than need.

Al was told the man would continue his downward spiral until something affected him so deeply that it would allow him to see himself as he really was and from that might spring a desire to claw back a more normal life. It was what he called the 'rock bottom' moment and no one could predict when it would happen, at what stage of the disease and what might trigger it – or whether it would happen at all. When it failed to materialise, the result was often suicide.

Al knew for certain that his rock bottom moment was being asked by the liquidator to hand over his signet ring, the one reminder of a love he had thrown away. It was the inescapable moment of self realisation – he was a failure.

Nurse Protz chuckled: "Let's see – killing him... chopping his fingers off? A world of difference, Alexander, how stupid of me."

This time Al did not respond and picked his newspaper up again, signalling an end to the conversation but which nurse Protz again ignored.

"Actually, Alexander, I wanted to ask your advice." Al felt a sense of doom enfolding him but he didn't really know why. "I'm looking to buy a new car – well, actually a second hand car but one that's fairly new and I gather that used to be your line of work. What should I be looking for?"

"Perfect. Ask a dodgy nutter about buying a dodgy used car!"

His laughter was spontaneous and infected nurse Protz, who joined with him in what Al thought was the only natural expression he had ever witnessed from the woman. She was momentarily transformed into an ordinary human being with a gorgeous laugh that came from deep inside and hinted at a genuine sense of fun. Her eyes were suddenly alight and Al's laughter petered out as he watched her put her hand to her mouth like a little girl self-consciously trying to hide her brace.

He found himself appraising her as something other than a psychiatric nurse and even as he did so he could hear a voice desperately screaming at him from somewhere deep inside, 'no, no, no'. But he continued anyway.

With her eyes alight, Protz was gorgeous, beautiful, and as life flooded through her it transformed her from a guardian of this wasteland into a young woman – a sexual woman. Her skin was smooth and cream coloured from which all blemishes, blotches and broken veins had been naturally banished – the type of skin that cosmetic adverts produced with lashings of foundation to simulate perfection in order to sell their products. Her eyes were large and ridiculously blue, her lips full, her teeth white and even and the pony-tailed blonde hair did nothing to obscure them.

For the first time he noticed the eyeliner, mascara and a hint of eye shadow, but that was all the cosmetic help she had. She was certainly small, with a tiny waist pulled in tight by an old-fashioned silver filigree, nurse's graduation buckle. It emphasised the not insignificant swell of her breasts and the neat roundness of her bottom.

Al guessed he had probably noticed all these characteristics before but fear of the woman had prevented him from acknowledging them. He had thrust them away as though the chalice which bore them was utterly poisoned.

He became acutely aware that it was many months since he had lain side by side with a woman, face to face in warmth and privacy, allowing his fingers to trace the contours of her back, from neck to ankle, brushing and feeling with his finger tips and gently applying pressure with his nails, up and down, never remaining in one spot too long, up and down, cupping and separating, probing and exploring and listening to her breath intensifying, noting the little moans and groans, feeling her body push more tightly against his and registering his automatic response.

It had never crossed his mind that Protz would be capable of responding in such a way as he had convinced himself that every tiny sound of passion she might utter would be an artificial construct designed to ensnare her mate and excite his passions – not because she wanted him excited, not because she needed to exercise her allure but because that way lay control.

And he was certain that when their mouths locked together hungrily, their tongues softly duelling in the combined wetness, each person inhaling the breath of the other, when he eventually ran his fingers along her inner thigh and with slight pressure urged her to part her legs, she might do so willingly, eagerly but his fingers would not encounter excited engorgement nor slide effortlessly though the silky-smooth wetness of expectation but instead would find dry, closed, tucked away self-containment. God, he needed a woman.

The fact that he had thought such a thought at the behest of nurse Protz scared him.

He dragged his mind back to used cars and his distrust of Protz was so profound that he wondered if she really was buying a car or was simply practicing one of the oldest bits of artifice in the gender game, appealing to someone through their specific and greater knowledge. But that presumed she wanted to appeal to him. The inner voice shouted again and again – 'don't even go there, walk away, just walk away!'

She sat down next to him, close to him, and her scent came gently through the disturbed air her movement created. It was not born of bottles or sprays but of a distinct, warm, female body and the intimacy of it fed directly into Al's desires.

"Well, don't buy one from anywhere that has the name Alexander Motors." Again they laughed together. "Modern cars have so many built-in protections that it's not like the old days, Protz, where cars were clocked with electric drills and gear boxes were stuffed with saw dust – well not entirely. Don't try and get the cheapest deal, avoid back street lots…"

"You mean like the one you had…?" Nurse Protz asked with a smile.

"Absolutely!" Again their laughter was shared. "Go to a reputable garage and always get a guarantee such as the Ford one and check that it includes labour as well as parts. A head gasket costs about twenty quid but it can cost over a grand to fit it. If they say it's a one-lady-owner car, have a look at the registration document, it might be Sally Jenkins, owner of the Easy Drive school of motoring."

Protz giggled and was as skittish as a kitten and suddenly Al could see how easily she must have reeled in Peter Dealey and could probably guess how she kept him panting and as eager as a dog waiting for his walkies. Beauty and power could be overwhelmingly attractive, he decided. 'And utterly destructive when stripped of conscience and caring', the little inner voice shouted loudly at him. 'Don't be led by your cock, Al,' it screamed.

"When you're inspecting it, go down to car level and put your eye right up against the rear wing and look along the length of the car to the front. If there are little undulations then it's probably had a bad, front-end shunt. You can also take a magnet and apply it all over the body work. If there are places where it doesn't stick then you know there's filler there under the paint work. Of course, the best way is to fit me with leg shackles and take me with you on a day release!"

Again Protz treated him to a giggle and a touch of her hand on his arm. It was a tiny display of intimacy that Al knew only too well because he had deployed it too many times himself – a way of edging forward a first meeting to a slightly higher plane, establishing the first physical contact.

"Choose carefully and a good used one is by far the best way of buying a car because depreciation on new cars in the first year is ridiculous." Al was trying to ignore the woman alongside him and concentrate on the cold mechanics of used cars. "Like I say, go to an established garage, preferably one that has a dealership, and for the best value look for a slightly older car, maybe three of four years old, but one that's got low mileage on the clock.

Get inside it and use your eyes, ears and nose."

Al kept talking because he was afraid of where the conversation might go when he stopped. "Does it look like a low-mileage car? It should seem almost new and when you open the door it should be smooth and effortless. When you close it, it should shut with a nice, neat satisfying 'thunk'. Is the upholstery clean and pristine, are the pedals unworn, and does it smell new? It's all pretty straightforward common sense, really."

"It might be to you, but for someone who's only ever had one car in her entire life – and that was given to her – it's pretty daunting."

Again Al felt the little-girl-lost appeal but was not seduced by it this time. He felt her natural attitude to buying a car would be to demand a good one from the garage and then offer the warning that if it wasn't, she'd come back and torch the place.

"The only other bit of advice I'd give is, don't be afraid to haggle hard, get the price right down." He suspected that this particular gem of wisdom was utterly superfluous. Again Al reached for his newspaper, again hoping that nurse Protz would take the signal and move on with her day but she didn't.

"You're an interesting man, Alexander. You're quite unlike most of the damaged people who come through these doors."

"That's because I'm not crazy."

It was said with feeling, almost spat out and as he said it, Al focused on nurse Protz's eyes, looking deeply into them and he knew that what she was seeing were his hard, aggressive eyes waiting for a response. And he got it – a momentary flicker in the pale, baby blue and then it was gone but not before he had read it as clearly as the page of a book. It was only the shock of surprise, of ambush, that had produced it but Al knew there could no longer be pretence between them because she knew he was right. Her response was weak:

"People don't end up here by accident."

"No? They can when they have a bent lawyer who does a deal with the court."

"If believing that makes you happy then carry on but remember, I've read your notes." The flirtation was suspended as nurse Protz tried to recover the territory she had inadvertently ceded and the steel fist in the silken glove she had offered revealed itself. It was a reminder that Al knew he should heed.

"It was nothing that a bit of good counselling couldn't have put right."

"Oh, Alexander, what are we going to do with you?" And immediately the little girl was back, demanding attention, asking to be liked.

"Well, not sending me to Broadmoor would be start, which you once threatened."

The laughter was forced this time.

"For goodness sake Alexander, don't take everything I say literally. This is a demanding job and sometimes you fall back on whatever you think may get results, rightly or wrongly. I'm not perfect, you know."

As she said the words, she moved her body and Al's eyes flitted from her face down to her feet and back again, taking in every contour. She then ostentatiously crossed her legs, revealing the swell of her thighs and the briefest glimpse of white knickers and Al knew it was blatant. Her smile was merely a shadow, the head lowered a fraction and inclined to one side, with one eyebrow fractionally raised. What she wanted to communicate was – 'Like what you see?'

His delayed response was weak: "Are any of us?"

Al was flustered and trying hard not to let it show. The rules he was operating under were entirely different to any he had known in the past. His experience of women was wide, perhaps too wide, as there had been a period in his life when he had sought out encounters with alacrity and considerable success. It was all so simple – no lying, no pretence of offering future prospects, no use of words that might infer permanence, plenty of conversation to keep them entertained, if rebuffed always move on – well, there were rebuffs and rebuffs – offer only the here and now, never, ever present yourself as being needy and make them laugh, always make them laugh. Once a woman was laughing you were almost certainly both heading for the same ultimate goal and from there it was simple to slowly escalate the intimacy that would inevitably lead to bed.

Protz was laughing, she was flirting with him so where did

he go from here? Did he propel it forward in the usual way? He felt like a species of spider where the urge to mate was overwhelming but with it ran the risk of being utterly devoured by the female once the passion was spent. Of course he wanted passion, dreamt of it, needed it, thought of it and at times could feel almost consumed by it. But he did not want passion with Protz, no matter how great the visuals. Nothing would persuade him to venture down that path, he told himself. But somehow, the denial lacked total commitment.

In that drab, smelly place, filled with damaged minds, suffused with the constant aroma of boiled cabbage and urine, with its countless false realities and dangerous and damaged unrealities, where normal interactions were seriously proscribed and where there was the constant feeling that every word and action might be judged negatively, Al wasn't sure how strong his resistance might be.

With all these limitations on a life that was abnormal from the moment he had walked through the doors, he was not confident he would be strong enough to resist the oldest allure of all – desire. In the awful, unnatural world he was forced to inhabit, the desire for something wholly natural and reassuring was overwhelming and wanting to indulge desire was the oldest and most natural feeling of all.

Al felt as though he was a character in an Edgar Allan Poe short story where the source of the allure would also be his nemesis. But he could not entirely back away just yet; there was a curiosity to how far Protz was prepared to go or whether it was just a game and if Al was to extend a metaphorical hand towards her she would chop it off.

"I've never see you have a visitor. Do you have someone waiting for you outside?"

Protz spoke gently and there appeared to be no barb in her words but they reinforced Al's sense of isolation. When he did eventually speak it was as much to himself as Protz.

"No, no one."

"I find that hard to believe. You're a very good looking man."

"Careful, Protz, that's almost a compliment."

"Come on, it's not a battle, you know. You are good looking

– a bit of a hunk really. If circumstances were different I'd give you a second look."

'Whoa', the inner voice cautioned. Protz was putting her foot on the accelerator as Al had suspected she might but he wasn't sure how to respond. He paused before deciding to attempt humour.

"No, it'd never work Protz."

"Why?"

"Alexander! You call me Alexander. It would be like shagging my mom."

Al wanted to swallow his words. Too far, too fast. Without meaning to, he had by-passed all the niceties of flirtation and gone straight to the jugular – sex.

Nurse Protz laughed loudly and feigned shock: "Whatever turns you on."

The humour slowly disappeared from her face and she held Al in a steady, penetrating gaze.

"If the reward was big enough, I could go to night classes and learn to call you Al." There was a marked pause: "Al!"

There was both innuendo and invitation in her response and Al felt panic rising in him. She had staked out her claim. He hadn't thought it through and had inadvertently arrived at a point where either acceptance or rejection was necessary, and both terrified him.

Acceptance might satisfy a burning urge but he felt sure it would unleash something he simply would not be able to cope with. It could be near fatal, like a jester and a queen where once humour and novelty had waned it would be the psychiatric equivalent of 'off with his head.' If he didn't meet her expectations, his life would be turned into an even greater hell than it was at the moment.

Rejection was not an option for this woman, he instinctively knew that. She had compromised herself and her position and was vulnerable, as anyone in her job would be, but it was worse than that. The real problem lay much, much deeper and there was no doubt in his mind that her damaged psyche would not accept rejection of any kind.

And so he was caught between two decisions, either one of

which scared him. The only escape route was to offer the prospect of acceptance but play for time – and to do that without it being obvious would not be easy.

He returned her gaze and hoped the confusion and fear he felt was not communicated: "I don't think Peter Dealey would like that very much."

"Peter Dealey can go screw himself." She flashed a theatrical smile at him.

"Protz, be serious for a minute. Nothing can happen between us in here. Yes, you're gorgeous and yes I fancy you like hell," he hoped he sounded convincing, "but it would be disastrous – for both of us. For a start, you'd be in breach of your ethics or code of conduct or whatever you nurses swear to and if anyone found out, you'd be out of job, drummed out of your profession. I'm sure there must be a caveat in there somewhere that says you can't shag your patients. Christ almighty, you'd even be handing me power over you. Get up my nose one day and I might grass you up. There'd be no come back on me."

A glimpse of steel was back on view: "It would be your word against mine and I think I know who they'd believe."

Even as she said it Al was convinced she was right, in fact he felt certain that she would not leave even the possibility of it to chance. In anticipation of making a move on him she had probably already started entering comments in his file, such as, 'Mr Dwight appears to be harbouring sexual desires towards me. He has not attempted overt physical contact, has not tried to force himself on me but it is a situation which needs careful watching'.

"Of course you're right but that wouldn't happen would it? I'm not that sort of guy. You want to know the real truth, Protz. I don't function too well as the passive person in a relationship and that's what I would be in this god awful place. You're my boss, my jailer, my mind reader, my keeper and I'm – well, I'm fuck all. When I'm someone again, Protz, when I'm someone, just you watch yourself because I'll come calling."

Al watched her eyes intently, fairly pleased with his performance but audience reaction was all. She remained steadily staring at him, unblinking, giving little away but her eyes were warm. She stood up suddenly, saying, "I don't like passive," and walked to the door and turned. "Not bad for starters, Al."

He could hear her feet on the polished vinyl floor as she walked away and the vision of a passport pinned beneath the bottom of the drawer in his bedside cabinet brought him the comfort he desperately needed.

Chapter Twenty

More overtly theatrical than a bunch of strolling players, thought Wendy Carter as the two men from the Charity Commission announced themselves, their faces as sombre as paid mourners at an India funeral. Not a glimmer of a smile, not an inclination of the head in greeting, not a pleasantry between them and there would not have been even a handshake had Wendy not proffered hers and kept it outstretched, hanging in the air like a dead offering. Only then did the first and smaller of the two investigators make peremptory contact with it in order to defuse the growing embarrassment. It was done, thought Wendy, to impress upon her just how seriously they viewed the situation.

"I am Martin Kenwright and this is my colleague, Mister Ashley Wilson," announced the short, slim, neatly-suited, mousey-haired and bespectacled leader of the pack. The prefix of Mister was somewhat superfluous as Wilson was tall and big and wide and could never have been confused with a Miss or Mrs, particularly as two clumps of black hair on either side of his head were divided by an extremely bald pate. Kenwright is the terrier, thought Wendy, and Wilson is the muscle and the thought almost made her laugh for Wilson looked about as threatening as Friar Tuck.

"You received my letter?" enquired Kenwright.

"I did," Wendy replied as she conducted them through to the meeting room where two of the charity's trustees were waiting, seated around an oval table. They rose as the trio entered and introductions were completed without anyone shaking hands.

Matthew Price was tall with a full head of well-maintained

grey hair, his neat suit and striped tie hinting at a profession or 'something in the city'. He was, in fact, a retired broker late of the Baltic Exchange and was a lovely, gentle man who attended every demonstration, his beautifully-modulated, public school tones at odds with his shouted slogans and insults, making them sound almost like compliments.

Janet Tate was a middle-aged fuss pot who ran a small animal sanctuary. Her clothing – long skirt, jumper, cardigan and scarf – had the stamp of an Oxfam charity shop about it. Both trustees held Wendy in high esteem and on one memorable occasion, Janet had compared her to Jesus Christ. Not a bad achievement for an atheist, Wendy thought!

She loved them both for they were reluctant trustees who had no desire to monitor or modulate her actions but were there solely to fulfil the legal requirements and respected her too much to intervene in her campaigns. Wendy knew that both would be feeling uncomfortable in this situation and the best she hoped from them was silence.

"Please take a seat," she invited and they did so, Kenwright and Wilson both removing papers from their briefcases, arranging them on the table with self-importance. Wendy felt contempt for them, not because of who they were but because of what they were – bureaucrats. They produced nothing, invented nothing, inspired no one, had no vision and they thrived not on risk or desire or creativity and had no compulsion to change the inequities of life but merely to administer them, ensuring that all the Ts were crossed and all the Is dotted.

These were the same kind of people who, she thought scathingly, sat in the backrooms of concentration camps ensuring their records of who was shot or garrotted or gassed, and when, were entirely accurate, as was their list of belongings the State could expropriate. Their little figures, their records, their commitment to conformity and uniformity were far more important than what those figures represented.

As Kenwright was about to speak, Wendy cut across him: "In your letter you gave us no indication of what the complaint was about or who'd made it. You simply said that you believed there was a prima facie case that we had acted outside our charitable objects. We haven't been given an opportunity to prepare any defence – or was that intentional?"

She was not too concerned about displaying her resentment because she knew they were hatchet men sent to carry out Stephen Aldous's instructions. The result was a foregone conclusion and the only imponderable was how vicious the sanctions would be.

"We have simply adhered to our procedures. It's a letter similar to those we send to all charities against which complaints have been registered. There is nothing personal in this, Ms Carter."

No, of course not, Wendy thought and like an entomologist he would watch the pin penetrate the bug but be uninfluenced by its squirms and wriggles. She determined she would do neither and would front this out the best she could.

His words sounded reasonable but his body language was entirely confrontational. He did not have to act the hard man as did Wilson because an unyielding, passionless sense of purpose oozed from his every pore.

"You said there is a prima facie case against us but you never asked for an explanation or even a comment from us so how did you reach that decision?"

"We looked at your website and found much there that caused us concern," Kenwright responded. "That's why we considered the complaint had merit and that is all we decided, Ms Carter, that there is some merit in it, and we're here now to listen to your explanation. Whether we find against you or not is largely down to you."

"I'd like to express…"

"If you will allow me Ms Carter…" Kenwright interrupted her with sharp authority. "You will have your say in a moment but first I need to explain the nature of our investigation and its implications."

He launched into an appraisal that had all the spontaneity of a flight attendant's safety announcement, reminding her of all the advantages her charity was accorded – exemption from corporation tax, relief from commercial rates, the

Government's contribution through Gift Aid and an exemption from inheritance tax. It did what it was meant to do and reminded Wendy of what she had to lose.

The situation was serious, as she knew it would be and she thought about what had created it – her involvement with Jo Aldous. Was she resentful, she asked herself, and did she, with her charity teetering on the brink of oblivion, regret their friendship or blame Jo? She felt not a trace of resentment towards her friend because this was a threat she had lived with all her campaigning life – she knew that one day they, or someone like them, would come for her. And it was for this reason that her records were accurate, not wishing to provide them with any obvious cause for censure. If they wanted to nail her they would have to dig deep for evidence but whatever their findings they would not destroy her.

If they shut down her charity she would simply continue her work with the non-charitable arm of Action for Animals but with considerably less funds. The premises were in the name of a separate holding company in preparation for just this eventuality – so let the buggers do their worst!

"…a complaint has been made against you under Clause Four of the Act," Kenwright continued, "and our initial investigations give us reason to believe there is a case to answer. However, if we do find you at fault, I am obliged to explain to you our powers under the Act. We can dismiss you as director of the charity and replace you with someone of our choosing; we can dismiss the trustees and again replace them with people of our choosing. We can in extreme cases, close a charity down, expropriate its funds and give them to a different charity but one with similar objects."

Wendy knew all this and her comment was simply to exercise her cynicism: "You have complete power then," she spat the words out.

Kenwright hesitated before replying: "Yes," and Wendy was certain she could see the trace of an ironic little smile twitching at the corner of his mouth.

"If I may?" he continued. "If we find the trustees have been financially negligent, we can demand reimbursement of any money which the charity has lost because of them, no matter how large that sum might be."

Wendy felt her heart almost stop – it was not just her they were after but her trustees, too. That had never featured in her thinking and the change in dynamics left her momentarily floundering and feeling guilty as equanimity fluttered out of the window. The only resources any of them had were their houses and now they might lose them, thanks to her.

"I have to say, I find your approach little short of bullying, Mr Kenwright, and I object to it most strongly…" It was hard to determine who was most shocked by Matthew Price's interruption, but it was probably Wendy. "We are all decent people here who do what we do to help those who are suffering. We are caring, conscientious people and I doubt any of us have more than a parking fine against our names. To start by telling us of the terrible penalties you have in store is not on – it's just not on! Is it meant to cow us, is it?"

Emboldened by Matthew's outburst, Janet Tate joined in: "Quite, quite, well said Matthew. This woman here (Janet indicated towards Wendy) is a saint and rather than threatening her you should be applauding her, rewarding her. She has given her life to helping animals, to stopping their suffering…"

Having stepped far outside her comfort zone, Janet ran out of confidence and ended her outburst with a quiet admonition that Wendy had to strain to hear. "You should be ashamed of yourself Mister whatever your name is."

Although she had asked them to remain silent, Wendy was pleased with their defence of her. There was nothing quite like honest outrage and their simple outburst was incredibly warming – an injection of humanity and emotion into a stilted inquest. Wendy smiled inwardly, wondering why she had been demoted from Jesus to merely a saint.

The mood was not lost on Kenwright and he responded directly to Janet and Matthew with what sounded like genuine concern.

"I'm sorry if you find what I said disturbing but I am talking about extreme cases and, unfortunately, I am obliged to offer these cautions at the start of every investigation. It's the required procedure."

His words were lost on Janet who snapped back: "Then the procedures should be changed," before withdrawing into herself once more and, through her body posture, signalling that the debate was at an end.

"Can we know who made the complaint?" Wendy asked.

"Complainants have the right to remain anonymous."

"And you have the right to over-ride that anonymity so I ask again, who made the complaint?"

"We have decided to respect their wishes in this case."

"Of course you have, Mister Kenwright!"

Kenwright continued with his preamble and Wendy found herself wondering why it was always men – it seemed she had been pitched against them for most of her life. It had started with her father when she was fifteen and he had given her money to go to the hairdresser. She never got there because of a display mounted in the High Street by a local animal group. They were seeking signatures for a petition against the slaughter of baby seals on the vast, white, frozen, icy wastelands of Nova Scotia.

Wendy looked at a series of pictures of hard-faced men wrapped in thick clothes against the cold, going about their work – work that scarred the pristine white wilderness with great smears of scarlet. One picture showed a man with an ice pick raised above his head with both hands, about to begin its forceful descent. The target was a seal pup, snug in his beautiful, cream-coloured coat on the ice where he had been born, on the ice that held him captive until that same coat developed water resistance, allowing him then to seek refuge in the chill waters of the Atlantic.

The pup looked up at the man with enormous, utterly innocent eyes just feet away from his mother, whose eyes were also transfixed by this alien in her world but hers were clouded with fear. She was not confined by lack of water resistance and could have hauled herself clumsily to the edge of the ice shelf and safety but she did not do so because she was a mother and would not, could not, abandon her pup.

The next picture revealed an almost identical scene except that the pick was halfway through its descent. In the third picture, the sharp point of the pick had penetrated the baby's skull and blood had begun to smear the ice whilst the mother was clearly in motion, lumbering towards her baby.

The pictures that followed were of a sharp knife, of hauling the little carcass into a position for skinning, of cutting, slicing, pulling and tearing until all that was left was a Canadian fisherman walking away with the pelt in his hand of a little creature which had been alive just minutes earlier and was worth just two or three dollars.

What remained in his wake was a skinless, furless, bloodied little corpse; a tiny, insignificant pile of formless red flesh whose blood had stained the ice all around him. And nuzzling what was left of her pup was a mother seal who herself was not wanted because her fur was not of sufficient quality but who had hauled herself through her pup's own blood in her concern.

The final insult was the killer raising his index finger to the camera he had just spotted, his face contorted with contempt.

This may not have been the first time the mother had been forced to watch her pup slaughtered, Wendy was told, because the killers visited every year at this time and would be back again next year and the year after because the Canadian government sanctioned the slaughter as a tiny boost to the incomes of its underemployed fishermen.

Why they were underemployed was no longer debated because it discomfited everyone – politicians, fishermen and scientists alike – and reminded them of their incompetence and greed.

Wendy knew none of the background as she fought to control the bile that burned away at her throat and the near paralysis and incomprehension that flooded over her. Into the collecting tin went her hairdresser's money as Wendy fought back tears, shocked at humankind's inhumanity. She was almost as shocked when her father was furious at her wasting his money.

The images were life changing and she had to know more about the barbaric trade and so she read. The Grand Banks of Nova Scotia had, over the centuries, been mythologised by song and poetry, literature and testimony, its mists and ice, its winds and storms providing the backdrop to countless tales of endurance and risk. What took seafarers there was fish – cod – which, beneath its inhospitable surface, shoaled in their millions just as they had done for millennia.

In the 1960s, Canadian government coffers swelled with the proceeds of fishing revenues as the world was invited to help themselves to the creatures and eight hundred thousand tons were hauled from the deep each year by trawlers of multifarious nations. By 1980 the bounty had diminished to a mere two hundred and fifty thousand tons but still the invitation to come and fish remained as trawlermen reported no difficulty in filling their holds, owners poured scorn on the nay-sayers and scientists proffered assurances of infinite sustainability at this reduced but still generous figure.

Just a year later, in 1981, something unlooked for, unforeseen, unpredicted, unexpected, unscientific, unnerving and utterly undesirable happened. The cod disappeared in their entirety and never returned. They had been disappeared by avarice and unconcern as an entire ecosystem was erased and forty five thousand fishery workers woke up one morning and had nowhere to go and nothing to do. And so they moved their destructive practices from one species to another with the excuse that seals were predating on 'their' fish.

It marked the beginnings of a fight that would define Wendy's life. Through university and onwards, she had fought against animal abuse and her zoology degree was taken to assist that fight. Even for the first few years as a 'professional', working against animal abuse, she found it difficult to control the anger that it induced, the contempt for those responsible and those who encouraged it by purchasing the products of cruelty.

Suffering, she discovered, was ubiquitous but largely ignored. Having viewed endless imagery, armed herself with testimony and fact and reinforced it with scientific research, she felt empowered, felt she could change the world. Looking back on her naivety caused her to smile but then, back then, she felt she could do it single-handedly if necessary.

That aim necessitated forceful argument which often tipped over into displays of anger and contempt and head-on conflict. Stickers with simple judgments such as Meat Is Murder or Warning – Dead Animals, were stuck on fridges and packets of meat, shop windows and restaurant menus.

She was a disciple, a pathfinder, a zealot and a champion – a champion of the animals, she believed. But the realisation dawned slowly that the enemy were not laying down their carnivorous arms and surrendering in large number, only some were seeking information from her, few asked her to expand on her claims and people were not flocking to gather beneath her banner in the numbers she had anticipated.

But something happened to her twenty years ago and had remained with her like an epiphany. Having exhausted all the leaflets she had been handing out in a local shopping centre one lonely Saturday – leaflets exposing the barbarity of snaring foxes on this occasion – Wendy Carter sat on a wooden bench alongside two young lads talking endlessly about this and that as they munched their way through their McDonald's hamburgers.

For once she did not engage them or challenge them, but found herself fighting off a sense of futility which was stealthily wrapping its arms around her. She felt isolated and very, very alone and wanted to cry not confront. At the same time, a black evangelical preacher began his diatribe in near monotone, almost shouting his message of salvation or damnation as he marched backwards and forwards in the open space of the pedestrian square between the shops, sweat glistening on his balding head, his long, ill-fitting raincoat reaching down towards his shoes, a bible held in one hand pressed close to his chest, the emotional equivalent of a stab vest.

Backwards and forwards he paced, forwards and backwards, just the odd biblical phrase intelligible through the ranting of his strong Jamaican accent – the threat of eternal damnation and suffering, the promise of redemption and salvation.

He looked over the heads of those wandering by with their laden carrier bags and those resting on the smart benches, unwrapping sandwiches and never making eye contact with them. He looked over and above their mundane but sinful lives; he looked always to somewhere distant, to some place beyond the 'Everything Must Go' sale signs, to where sunlit uplands issued their siren call of forgiveness and resurrection, peace and tranquility, redemption and eternal salvation.

But he was the only one who saw this vision for not a single soul, sinful or otherwise, listened to his words of admonishment; no one paused in their pursuit of mammon, not one person interrupted their hurrying, scurrying day to discover the secrets to which he held the key and would, if they would only take heed, place them one day on the right hand of God in the hereafter.

Not a single person stopped to listened to him and no one took a leaflet from his wrinkled, shrivelled, widow's-stooped old lady accomplice, who stood immobile, one hand extended bearing a leaflet that would provide free entrance for one to the kingdom of light if only that one would listen; if only someone would grasp the holy grail. How long that leaflet had drooped disconsolately from her old believer's blue-veined, arthritic fingers was anyone's guess but Jo imagined that if it was ever grasped and removed, it would take with it a layer of skin from her thumb and forefinger as the graft was broken.

The consensus of those who hurried past was undoubtedly that he was a nutter. He, on the other hand, knew without a scintilla of doubt that he was a messenger of God Almighty and was doing his work.

Why, wondered Wendy, did he do what he did, day after day, so frequently that he delivered his words by rote? What was his purpose? What was the ultimate aim? If it was to save the souls of sinners then it was a failure. If it was to stem the rapidly advancing tide of secularism then it was equally irrelevant. What satisfaction and motivation could he draw from a lifetime of being ignored? Perhaps the very rare attention from another desicated and wrinkled husk of an old lady, whose life was now lonely and stripped of meaning, might provide the impetus to keep him going.

Perhaps it was the dialectic that inspired him – that beneath the image of disdain and disinterest his words were inflaming passions which would eventually blossom into commitment. Or perhaps he did what he did for no other reason than it was that which defined him. Whilst his words sheltered beneath a cloak of godliness, simply standing there repeating them ad infinitum provided the contours to his life and gave it meaning and it mattered not one jot whether anyone listened or not.

As Wendy sat pitying him, the traces of a disturbing thought began to slide stealthily through her. Is this how people saw her? Did they simply dismiss her confrontation, her accusative rants, her promises of a kind of salvation for humans and animals alike, in the same way that she and all the people around her dismissed this man? Was she an embryonic nutter, so committed to 'the cause' that she had blinded herself to the fact that her aggression and anger drove people away from where she wanted them to go?

Why did almost every media interview she give seem to finish with her talking over the interviewer, raising her voice, drowning them out, determined to get her views across? Like the wandering disciple in front of her, had she mistakenly fallen into the trap of believing it was simply words that mattered, not how they were delivered, how she presented herself. She was trying to bludgeon people into changing their ways. Had she made the same mistake as this man and had blinded herself to the manner in which change came about?

The thought chilled her and she tried to view her approach to campaigning objectively. Unlike the preacher, she was not peddling some story of fairies and hobgoblins for which there was not a scintilla of proof. The suffering of animals was acute and cruel and ubiquitous and it was backed by overwhelming evidence. Animal products were at the root of almost all human degenerative diseases and day by day the evidence was accumulating that livestock production was the single biggest threat to the global environment. But although peoples' reactions to her and the preacher were the same, their reasons were different. They ignored him because he was irrelevant; they ignored her because she discomfited them.

Perhaps she was merely a victim of youth in that waiting for change was not an option, she wanted to make it happen now because in the time span of her life, at this young age, a year was a very long time, a decade an eternity.

The agonising continued against the audio track of a ranting, evangelical black preacher. She was not obsessed and one dimensional. There was another side to her life – of music and theatre and restaurants and friendships and sex. When she enjoyed herself it could be with the same energy as she campaigned and, yes, she could be abandoned. Self-doubt was suddenly submerged beneath a tidal wave of embarrassment as she remembered drunkenly dancing on a table at a charity dinner and of attempting to eat the floral display as a joke.

But that was all twenty years ago and it marked a turning point in Wendy Carter's life. She learned the lessons of communication, the importance of humour, of encouraging not admonishing, of listening as well as talking, of charm and likeability. She had long since developed the art of talking to a camera, of subtly reeling in an audience, of using her sex appeal if necessary, of not allowing herself to be riled by aggressive interviewers and of always being able to support any statement she made.

And running through everything she did and said was the steel of determination to get people to change their diet and shopping habits and that drive came from the first image of abject cruelty she had ever witnessed, which was permanently pinned to the notice boards of her mind. And finally it was beginning to work as a whole nation became increasingly aware of the links between diet and health, as learned bodies were calling for a massive reduction in meat and dairy consumption and to save a collapsing environment.

No matter how one-sided the present confrontation she would use all the techniques that had been so hard learned and not allow herself to be riled by these two-dimensional men who had come to close down her charity. But her contempt was so pervasive that she hoped she would not yield to the temptation to take them on.

…and the nearest exit may be behind you. Oxygen masks will descend from the panel above your head… Kenwright had still not finished his lecture. He had moved on to financial matters and the grants that Wendy made from one part of the organisation to the other but she had no fears on this score as everything was entirely legitimate – at least she hoped it was. Jo's advance warning had given her time to check and recheck and ensure that all the paperwork was up-to-date.

"As you should be aware, your non-charitable side can say whatever it likes and it is up to those who feel offended to seek redress through the courts if they don't like it. However, if those words are paid for by your charitable side, their purpose has to be charitable and they have to act with the same restraints as a charity would – be balanced, fair and not propagandist. In other words it is necessary for them to act as though they were a charity, and that does not appear to have been the case.

"Also, when you are campaigning against things which are entirely legal then particular caution is necessary – it is not entirely disallowed but a one-sided view would be seen as political campaigning and could therefore be considered improper if not carried out with strict adherence to the Commission's guidelines. There needs to be a reasoned assessment of what it is you oppose, incorporating explanations from both perspectives. Reading through these pages, you appear to have had an unrestrained time riding roughshod over all these nostrums." He looked around the table with a quizzical look on his face which approximated a smile, as though awaiting applause.

Oh dear god, thought Wendy, is this the level at which it's to be conducted?

Such was the monotone of his voice that Kenwright had moved on from administrative issues to the actual complaint without Wendy realising it:

"As I said, while political campaigning per se is not disallowed, this type of prosletysing, head-on assault strategy certainly is." There was a long hesitation before he added: "If our assessment of the situation is correct, of course. But down to specifics."

"I'm sorry, what head-on assault?" Wendy asked.

"On your website – the nature of your claims is absolute, leaving no room for argument or debate and it is that which concerns us most." Kenwright handed around printed copies of the web pages and when everyone had glanced through them he spoke:

"The substantive element of this complaint is those pages that deal with the environment – pages which are published by your non-charitable arm with a grant from the charitable side of your operations."

For the first time his colleague Wilson made a contribution: "In all, we have counted almost twenty prima facie transgressions of either the Commission's guidelines or your charitable objects and I think this sets some kind of record." He tried to sound stern but the effect was almost comical as though Wendy had achieved something noteworthy.

"So, down to specifics," Kenwright said with relish. "In the first section, on global warming, you write as if there is absolutely no question that global warming is happening and that it is entirely man's fault. You can't make an absolute statement like that when there is a huge amount of dispute and controversy over whether it is a reality and even if it is, whether humankind is the cause or whether naturally occurring phenomena are to blame."

"There is absolutely no doubt about it... No serious scientists would question our statement. Mr Kenwright, if I solicited opinions from all our supporters and then published their replies as fact, what would be your reaction?"

"I would consider it opinion and not fact."

"Every major scientific organisation in the world not only believes that global warming is real and results from human activity but has published the science to support that belief. The body co-ordinating this huge amount of research is the Intergovernmental Panel on Climate Change, under the auspices of the United Nations – not exactly a hill-billy organisation. Over a thousand peer-reviewed papers have been published to confirm that global warming is happening and that we are responsible and governments across the world agree – they're not doing much about it but they do agree."

"There is always a division in scientific opinion and the fact that one group predominates isn't reason to dismiss the minority view. Often minority views have proved to be correct," Kenwright contributed in a measured tone but sounded pleased with his contribution.

"I agree," Wendy answered, "but minority views only have validity if they're based on sound research. You can't just manufacture an alternative view and call it a hypothesis unless it's underlined by some good science. Those who claim global warming isn't happening have put forward numerous counter arguments, some of them utterly ludicrous – that the Earth is, in fact, cooling and not warming; that far from melting, the ice shelf is expanding; and that polar bear numbers have never been higher; and so on and so on.

"Those who concede that global warming is real but it's not humans who are responsible blame it on naturally occurring phenomenon such as recurring weather cycles, volcanic activity or sun spots. It's all nonsense – and that is my measured scientific opinion. Do you know why I dismiss it out of hand and don't include it in our published materials?" She did not wait for a reply. "Because it is nothing more than opinion, which we have already agreed is not permissible. This disparate group of antis have been unable to publish a single piece of scientific research to prove their points."

"Can you prove what you claim?"

"Mister Kenwright, it really shouldn't be up to me to prove a negative, it's up to those who lodged a complaint about our materials to provide you with the evidence that their complaint is justified, that they're right and we're wrong.

"Just look at the names behind those who make up the antis. It's people like the Costa Rica Free Trade Organisation, the Heritage Foundation, the Homeland Institute – all rabid, ultra-right-wing free market bodies who aren't interested in science but know that if real action is taken to curb global warming it will mean an end to the global policy of constant growth and consumption – and consequently the end of them. And they're mostly funded by the oil industry, have close links to the US neo-conservative Republicans and wouldn't know a scientific paper if you stuffed it up their nostrils.

"Okay, that is a bit of a political diatribe but if you want the references for it, I have them."

"That may all be well and true but it is not up to the objector to provide proof that they are right and you are wrong – you have to be able to substantiate every claim you make. That's how it works."

Wendy's heart sank even further at this bureaucratic nit picking and saw Kenwright watching her with a quizzical look on his face but there was also distinct interest there. Wendy wondered if he had arrived expecting to meet a bunch of people with piercings and dreadlocks who were happy to sacrifice scientific rigour to boundless enthusiasm.

"We will need to see those papers, Ms Carter." He consulted his papers again: "You claim that livestock for meat and dairy production are the second biggest cause of global warming gases and you've used a global figure of eighteen per cent..."

"Yes, as published by the United Nations Food and Agriculture Organisation," Wendy cut in. Kenright held up his hand.

"Not in dispute Ms Carter," he replied, again looking extremely pleased with himself, "but the position with UK livestock agriculture is different. Our higher environmental and animal welfare standards ensure that UK emissions are kept at just 3.8 per cent – according to the Government."

"Yes and it's complete nonsense, if you'll excuse me saying so. And what's even worse, the Government knows it's complete nonsense and the only explanation for it is their determination to underplay the dangers from livestock emissions in order to protect farmers. But it's also so they don't have to introduce potentially unpopular policies such as removing subsidies for meat and dairy which will force the prices up. If they published the true figures they would have no option but to encourage people to eat less meat – and that might cost them votes. Faking the figures removes the need for this."

Kenwright's chuckle was as false as a stick-on beard. "Not one for understatement, are you Ms Carter?"

"I'm not one for bullshit, Mister Kenwright." She didn't wait to see the impact her profanity had on him, mainly because she could see that the battle was probably lost. But she refused to go down meekly. "I hope you'll soon discover that I never make a statement unless I can prove it," she paused, "beyond doubt." It was delivered with a warm and encompassing smile.

"And in this instance?"

"The Government's statistics are what's called 'farm gate' figures. They only consider what happens actually on the farm, ignoring the production and use of nitrogen-based fertilisers, all the imported fodder and high-protein supplements and the foreign trees which are felled to provide the land on which they're grown. They ignore imported meat and dairy and the gases they produce and they exclude all the transport and energy used in moving animals on and off the farm, slaughtering them and chilling and distributing the meat."

"And your proof?"

"I have an email from a senior civil servant in the Department of Agriculture…"

"A mole…," Kenwright offered theatrically.

"If you like," Wendy smiled back at him. "Government figures on this are impossible to penetrate – but not once you know they're false and why, then you can nail them. But there's more than that, in particular a report published by Cranfield University which says exactly the same thing but with scientific chapter and verse."

"But on your website you imply that the Government knows its figures are false, something you can't possibly prove."

"The Cranfield report was commissioned by the Government – Defra – and they quote from it extensively, or rather they quote the bits that are convenient to them, so they're well aware of its existence. You have a choice here, Mr Kenwright, either ministers don't bother to read the reports they commission and ignore briefings from their civil servants, in which case they're utterly incompetent; or they are aware and choose to ignore them, in which case they're duplicitous. Which adjective would you prefer we use?"

Kenwright merely raised his eyebrows. "There could, of course, be political reasons for it."

"Of course," Wendy replied, "but I don't think we should try and second guess people's motivations, do you Mr Kenwright? We are meant to deal solely in facts, aren't we?"

For the first time, Kenwright exhibited just a trace of embarrassment, knowing that Wendy was right. He hid it by consulting his notes carefully and continued to read them as he spoke:

"I am not querying your claims that livestock are – probably – the primary cause of desertification and deforestation in the world and subsequently the main reason for loss of biodiversity

ff– the wording you have used is carefully chosen to accord with the UN's claims. However, you again imply that the Government is lying over its claims about soya for animal fodder." Kenwright moved the inquisition forward but now there was a distinct lessening of the authority with which he posed the question.

"We repeat the UN's claim that all deforested Amazonian land is used for either cattle grazing or growing soya fodder for export," Wendy could see his nod of agreement as she outlined her case, "and eighteen million tons are imported into Europe every year from the Amazon rain forest alone and is mainly used for pigs and poultry but also some goes for cattle production. It follows that almost every piece of meat that's eaten in Britain and the rest of Europe comes from animals that have, to some degree, been fed rainforest soya.

"We believe that's a vital piece of information for people who want to reduce their impact on the globe, not least to lessen the pressure for more tree felling and all that follows from it. Wouldn't you agree?"

Kenwright almost imperceptibly inclined his head as if agreement was not his to bestow.

"The approach of successive ministers of agriculture has been that soya beans are primarily grown for their oil and that the cattle cake or meal that's left after oil extraction is merely a residue – a by-product," Wendy continued, "and that ending imports of soya meal would have no impact on the loss of forests in the Amazon because the same amount of soya would continue to be grown.

"Do you know how long it took me to expose that claim?" She didn't wait for a response. "Five minutes. I simply went online and checked the prices with several animal feed providers and oil extractors and the truth is that a bushel of soya beans produces four dollars-worth of oil and seven dollars-worth of meal – an entirely different picture to that claimed by our Government. The trade is worth over $100 billion annually – some by-product. And before you ask, yes I can prove it as I embarrassed the last minister of ag and wrung a confession from him that I was right and he was wrong – but only because he had no option."

"And he stated it as clearly as that, did he?" Kenwright looked disbelieving.

"Of course not, he's a politician but he reluctantly agreed with my figures – in writing – which is the same thing."

Kenwright didn't respond but leafed through his papers. Wilson interjected with a quiet reminder: "Antibiotic resistance?"

"I want to go back to global warming for a moment," was Kenwright's response, ignoring his colleague in a not very subtle reminder to everyone as to who was in charge. "I'm particularly concerned by your – can I call it shroud waving? – about the long-term effects of global warming, the tipping point, point of no return. I think you refer to it as positive feedback…" he looked to Wendy for confirmation.

"Yes, positive feedback, but it's not my phrase, it's a scientific term." She emphasised 'my' in a minor display of irritability which she could not control.

"Again you have put yourself on a collision course with Government as you directly contradict its chief scientific adviser – and I'm talking about the emissions of methane from the Arctic ocean and the areas of permafrost." Kenwright's attitude had gone back to how it was at his arrival and any sense that there might be a benign soft centre to his impermeable exterior had disappeared. Similarly, Wendy was growing tired of what she saw as a time-wasting charade.

"Yes, and yet again the Government is wrong, Mr Kenwright. Locked into Greenland's permafrost are billions of tons of methane and as global warming increases and the frosts start to melt, methane is released. The more that's released, the more profound global warming becomes and so more methane is released and on and on in an unstoppable, uncontrollable phenomenon, the outcome of which no one can predict other than it will not be to humankind's advantage. And it's a similar story with the bed of the Arctic Ocean…"

"Yes, yes, you say all that on your website and you also say that positive feedback may have already begun and drastic action is needed immediately. The chief scientific adviser does not disagree with you over the process but is clear that it almost certainly will not begin until about 2050, which gives us considerable latitude in finding an answer to the problem."

"So everything is okay then, is it? Does the CSA provide the references for his claim?" Wendy's irritation was winning and she felt outraged that she was having to explain herself to a man who clearly had no understanding of the subject and was relying upon crib sheets provided by Stephen Aldous's advisers and what reading he had done before turning up to try and nail her.

"He doesn't provide any references because his statement is speculation based on science that was available to him at that time. There has probably never been any phenomenon as fast moving and dynamic as global warming in the whole of human history. All the models which have been established to try and predict the outcome are wrong – dramatically wrong. It's all happening three times faster than anyone predicted…" Wendy saw Kenwright's face twist into an unmistakable parody of doubt. "And that's the opinion of the National Academy of Sciences," she added, with the flamboyance of a whist player trumping her opponent.

"Mr Kenwright, I am a scientist myself, why on Earth do you think I would want to exaggerate a situation which is so profound, so threatening that it doesn't need exaggeration?"

"Because your interest is in getting people to stop eating animals and the more drama you can bring to the situation, the easier it will be for you to persuade them to change their diet." He had departed from his script and had entered into the same ill-informed disbelief and prejudice about global warming that almost every media outlet had encouraged and which he had fallen for. Wendy was furious.

"The permafrost has already started to melt and methane is being released from the seabed of the Arctic – not in 2050 but right now – the process that knowledgeable scientists desperately feared is underway, Mr Kenwright. Peer-reviewed science, Mr Kenwright, that has appeared in both Nature and New Scientist."

Kenwright did not respond but lowered his eyes to his papers where he kept them, pretending to search for further enlightenment. Wendy was certain he was aware that he had overstepped the mark, sacrificing his impartiality and was angry with himself for having done so. She was also aware that Wilson had stopped taking notes during the exchange and she was tempted to ask him to minute their statements so that Kenwright's prejudices were on record. But that, she knew, would be an open declaration of war.

Wendy found herself becoming more and more agitated – angered by the man's pretence that he was dealing with the accuracy of claim and counterclaim which required careful explanation and analysis when he was, in fact, the hired fire raiser, sent with one purpose only, to burn them out of their house. Suddenly it felt important that she should let him know that she understood precisely the nature of the charade they were conducting with such po-faced solemnity.

She had not planned it, in fact had tried to avoid it, but Wendy Carter's old instincts to confront aggression with aggression took over: "Okay, Mister Kenwright, let's stop pussyfooting around. You know who made the complaint and we know and everyone knows why. We've been sitting here for days waiting for Stephen Aldous and the Tory party to act and now they have – and the outcome is a foregone conclusion. We don't stand a chance against that kind of muscle and you are here as the hatchetman to demand retribution – to deliver the coup de grace – so why don't you just get on with it?"

Wendy was shocked by Kenwnright's reaction. Gone was the dry and dusty bureaucrat's passionless neutrality and she watched as his face coloured, his eyes widened and his lips retracted into a thin line. He was clearly fighting a battle to maintain self-control and there was a measurable pause between the end of Wendy's diatribe and Kenwright's response, during which the only sound in the room was breath noisily entering and exiting through his nostrils. His face was immobile, his eyes unblinking but focused fiercely on Wendy, holding her gaze but somehow not seeing her.

He eventually looked away but not because she had out-stared him and caused him to back down but because he needed to regroup his thoughts, which he did by pointlessly moving the papers around on the table in front of him, lifting one and looking at it, replacing it and taking hold of another but raising neither long enough to glean any information from them.

"I would like you to withdraw that allegation!" When he finally spoke it was with an intensity that disturbed Wendy and the words were delivered not as a request but a demand, and behind that demand there appeared to be unbending steel. This was no longer a lifelong bureaucrat speaking but a man whose very core had been penetrated and while his words dripped with outrage they were eclipsed by another, different, unexpected emotion – the man was hurt and he wasn't acting, of that Wendy was sure. She had deeply offended him and the whole rationale of his life. He might be a boring bastard who stuffed himself greedily with minutiae but he was proud of what he did, proud of his impartiality, proud of his independence.

Oh shit, Wendy thought, I've got this one completely wrong. She was not concerned at having offended the man, she could live with that, but what worried her was that however sound her defence would he now simply dismiss it as retribution and as both of them knew, there was no appeals procedure?

Before she could respond, Janet coughed nervously and began to speak, uttering only the first syllable before Matthew cut across her: "I'm sure there was nothing personal in Ms Carter's words…"

"Thank you Mister Price but I would like to hear from Ms Carter." It demanded a response.

Wendy did not reply immediately but tried to disentangle the contradictory feelings that were jostling for position – embarrassment at having got it wrong, the humility needed to apologise, respect for this dowdy little man's inner strength but riding high above them all was the thought that she might after all not have blown it. If Kenwright was truly independent then perhaps he would consider her defence impartially despite the insult. If this man had been sent to drive the dagger into her back then he was a superb performer and no one could be that good, she thought. Wendy was aware that it really was now down to her.

She could not help but stare at Wilson who was frozen rigid, his mouth open, eyes wide, papers held motionless in mid-air. He was not shocked but terrified. But she needed to respond. Honesty had extracted her from more situations than she could remember and almost as her default position she reached for it once again.

"I am going to eat so much humble pie, Mister Kenwright, that Uriah Heap would be proud of me. I can see that I've deeply offended you and it wasn't just unprofessional of me to say what I did but wrong. I got it wrong and I apologise for that wholeheartedly." She watched his face intently, trying to read if her words were in any way mollifying him but he had reinstated his implacable façade. "All I can do in my defence is to be honest with you. The circumstances of this complaint, as I'm sure you would agree, are unusual. I do know the source of it and worse than that, I know that one of those responsible, a man in an extremely high position within the Opposition, used the words: 'We are going to clip the wings of that woman.' He obviously has no doubt what your finding will be. Hence my outburst, which was prompted by an overriding sense of injustice. I mistakenly thought that you were the instrument of that threat – the hatchet man." Wendy raised her hands and shrugged her shoulders as if to say mea culpa.

She then stripped all formality from her voice and continued: "Mr Kenwright, please believe me when I say I'm sorry because I am. Will you accept my apology?"

Kenwright hesitated several seconds before responding. So you're not devoid of theatre, thought Wendy. Eventually he spoke:

"I accept your apology, Ms Carter and I understand the reasons for your outburst even if it was unnecessary. It is something of a shame because your responses to my questions have so far not been entirely unimpressive."

Even while Wendy was still trying to translate his convoluted response, Kenwright was on his way once more. He posed questions to her about the role of livestock in creating superbugs and antibiotic resistance, about nitrogen pollution and the creation of oceanic dead spots, of soil degeneration and its loss of fertility but something had changed in the dynamics of the exchange. Kenwright had muted his aggression and appeared to be anticipating logical answers to the questions he posed; and Wendy knew that her replies no longer carried the barb of resentment. They now understood each other.

"Just one final thing," said Kenwright, "I would for a moment like to return to the question of deforestation and its role in producing greenhouse gasses. I feel the UN does not adequately address one aspect of it."

Oh god, thought Wendy, despite their new understanding it was another boring, esoteric question about something so vibrant and extraordinary. She wanted to take the grey man's arm and conduct him to the top of the Dudhusaga falls on the borders of Goa and Karnataka and watch the waters cascade down hundreds of feet in tiers. She wanted him to look out across the rainforest below, running for more than two thousand miles along the Western Gatt mountains – stretching away into the distance like so many heads of broccoli and the only indication of its teeming wildlife, a distant white flock of little egrets winging above the deep green foliage like flakes of snow.

She wanted to take him along the Mandovi river and in its muddy bank find the footprints of a tigress and her cub who had passed that way only the night before. She wanted to sit silently with him beneath the trees and listen to the ting-ting-ting-ting call of a coppersmith bird and the raucous, seemingly scornful laughter of a hornbill. She would get him to bathe in the clear cool waters whilst kingfishers of different hues and sizes flitted to and fro.

She wanted to take Mister Kenwright through the forests of Costa Rica and search for little red-eyed tree frogs, to try and spot an unmoving, moss-covered sloth high in the canopy, to wonder at the magnificently beaked toucan and to glory at the flamboyance of hurtling scarlet macaws as they screeched to each other like teenage boys. And she would like to go out early with him to catch sight of a resplendent quetzal and its cascading tail feathers before it disappeared silently back to its secret hiding place to miss the warmth of the day.

Would he thrill to the echoing evening call of dingoes in the far distance, cast off his grey suit and sit in a crystal pool beneath a gentle fall and watch silver snoof shoal around his feet, look in awe at the towering mahogany and kapok trees, relish the heady scent of the ylang ylang blossoms and spot iguanas scampering through the branches of pochote trees, ignoring the huge thorns that cover every inch of their trunks and branches and which afforded protection to these ancient little dinosaurs. She would take him where he could hear the terrifying roar of the diminutive little Howler monkey and dodge the sticks they threw to deter intruders. She would lick a strand of grass and insert into an unobtrusive hole in the ground and watch his shock as a tarantula appeared from its hiding place.

She would terrify him by kicking over a stone to reveal a worm-like, deadly, banded coral snake and forget to tell him that he was safe because its jaws were was so small it could not possibly bite him. They would listen quietly at first light to hear the rumbling purr of contentment from a jaguar as it tackled its night's kill. And she would tell him to guard his backpack as a troupe of little capuchin monkeys swung through the palms, keen to empty its contents in search of sandwiches or fruit.

She would then take him to Belize and have him look over the barren, flat, devastation that remained once the forests were felled. She would have him sympathise with a huge Jabiru stork as she stood amidst the nothingness waiting, waiting, waiting for her home to be returned – waiting, waiting, waiting for the inevitable bullet that would end her turmoil.

And Jo would take Mr Kenwright into the little town of Belize City and have him look at the hopelessness of black young men – their colour ensuring they remained at the bottom of the social scale. He could not fail to understand their frustration that no matter how many trees were felled their lives remained the same, their unemployment, their poverty unchanging. He would see why they had to survive the best way they could, their predatory hustling fuelled by alcohol.

"No blame seems to be apportioned to the logging trade for its share of the greenhouse gasses that are produced in these regions of the world – and that surely is an omission?" Mr Kenwright's insistent voice brought Jo back into the confines of her office.

"Not really. They fell their trees and take them to make furniture and other products which may last for a hundred years or more before decaying and producing CO_2. Their actions are devastating in many ways but it's what they leave behind – the stuff that's of no interest to them – that's at the root of the CO_2 problem. They burn it for the cattle ranchers who follow behind them because they need clear land to sow grass and graze cattle for hamburgers and so everything is destroyed – the valueless, non-target trees, palms and saplings, vines and epiphytes, shrubs and creepers. And, of course, once they've gone not only do these plants cease producing oxygen but they no longer absorb CO_2.

"The ridiculous thing is, the soil is extremely fragile so within a few years it turns to dessert and so they chop down more trees. Anyway, loggers are often not involved any more as the forests are increasingly being felled simply to create grazing or grow soya."

Kenwright looked at Jo with raised eyebrows. "Yes Mister Kenwright, the Rainforest Alliance, Greenpeace, Old Uncle Tom Cobley and all!"

"I will need all these papers, you do realise that don't you, Ms Carter?"

"I do, Mister Kenwright, and if I supply them and if they're as I've said – what then?"

"I will consider you have mounted a very sturdy defence"

The two horsemen of the apocalypse gathered their papers together and made their departure but this time there were smiles and handshakes, Wilson taking his cue from Kenwright. Wendy saw them to the door and Wilson exited first and before following him, Kenwright turned to Wendy and in a quiet voice said: "You're not the only one who doesn't like being used, Ms Carter!"

Chapter Twenty One

Josephine Aldous sat in her car parked alongside a rather bleak football pitch. A blustery, northerly wind rattled the skeletal fingers of the tall trees which made up the border of the park furthest from her. A gaggle of little boys chased hither and thither in pursuit of the ball over muddy grass whilst instructors barked out directions, advice and encouragement. She watched their skinny, little, mottled legs as they tried to pass, dribble or run with the ball, attempting to emulate their Premiership heroes and beneath their red or yellow tabards lurked the names of those heroes and the colours of the clubs that paid their inflated salaries.

Danny wasn't particularly good at football – most of them weren't, although the screams, directions and frustrations emanating from their fathers standing on the touchline gave a different impression. She watched Danny throwing himself eagerly into the fray and whatever he lacked in skills he made up for in energy, commitment and sheer enjoyment and Jo was happy with that.

She could not keep the engine running indefinitely and the chill began to bite through her winter clothes and puffs of wind snapped at her face and ears as it flurried through the half open window. She kept it open so she could respond to Danny's frequent shouts for her to watch or to tell him that, yes, she had seen that – whatever it was. She could have dropped Danny off and driven the short distance back home to the warmth of her kitchen but this was her boy and someone should be there to witness those things that were important to him. Sharing was the very essence of childhood and everything was diminished if mum or dad were not part of it – an essential element of a secure growing up, she told herself.

Jo was resentful – not that she had to watch Danny because she enjoyed it despite the privations but because Stephen did not ever watch his son. She had reminded, chivvied, chased and nagged him but there was always a reason why he could not. She could have compiled a list of them. She had no particular knowledge of football and did not even like it that much when her boy was not participating but on top of everything, she was the sole mother here and for that reason alone, Danny would have liked Stephen to be present – it was a man thing!

Every time Danny was forcefully tackled she felt just a small, subconscious flutter of concern and when he was sent sprawling, face down in the mud, that flutter became a lurch. Seeing him unconscious, still and utterly vulnerable on a windy beach, fearing he might be dead, was an image that would never leave her.

Part of her wanted to remove Danny from all threats, keep him close by her, never letting him risk so much as a graze but Jo was much too smart to give way to that kind of maternal over-protectiveness. She knew that being a parent involved risk taking; it was a series of constant decisions – when to let your child go out of the house without you, when to allow bike riding other than in the garden, when to let him walk to school on his own, when to leave him on his own, even for a short time. Each decision was accompanied by risk and it was from those risks that responsibility grew and a child made the long, long process of emerging into adulthood self-confident, secure, safe and capable of looking after himself.

What had happened to Danny and the terrifying experiences that flowed from it would not allow Jo to stall that essential process – no matter what cartwheels her heart was forced to perform, no matter how suddenly her stomach lurched with paralysing fear.

Jo continued to watch the horde of little, steaming boys dash first in one direction and then the other. She reached for the Sunday newspapers on the seat beside her and sifted through numerous supplements in which she had no interest, and could hardly imagine that anyone would have, until she found the magazine section.

In between casting an eye at the football match to see how Danny was doing, she flicked lazily though its pages hoping that something would leap out and spark her interest. It rarely did – in fact she thought the Sunday Telegraph was probably one of the most boring newspapers on the market and wondered why on earth she even bought it, deciding that it was either Stephen's influence or a replica of her marriage – a persistence based solely on familiarity.

There was an article about robbers who were emptying Italian tombs and how a Mister Maurizio Fiorilli was going to bring them all to book. There was an interview with crime author Ruth Rendell, entitled a 'A Woman of Mystery' and extracts from the private letters of Dirk Bogarde, purporting to reveal his volatile relationship with his film directors. None of them really interested Jo. She thumbed through it again from the back this time, past TV times, motoring, books, theatre, cinema and then a full-page picture of a black cow caught her eye. It was on a left-hand page and was why she had missed it first run through.

The title was enigmatic, 'Mad Cows (and livid lambs)' but the strap line beneath made her pulse race just a little and a sense of excitement grabbed her: 'Marauding elephants, aggressive sea lions, snap-happy crocodiles... as animal attacks on humans reach frightening levels, scientists are beginning to understand exactly what the beasts are thinking. And it's not good. Will Storr reports.'

A thought occurred to her so abruptly it almost made her start. It was the same kind of gut reaction, the same kind of concern that makes you suddenly miss a breath when you realise you have forgotten to collect your child from school or have gone out and left the front door open. The fear of her own nightmarish experience and the pursuit of its genesis had blinded her completely to the belief that had once preoccupied her, that there was something disturbing, something not quite right about Angus's actions. She had looked into the pony's eyes seeking an answer, had stood for long periods in his company, stroking, rubbing, offering treats in the belief that somehow, he would eventually provide the glimmerings of an answer as to why he had done what he had.

His destruction had brought her search to an end and as the memories of Angus faded so had her concerns. There seemed little point in pursuing that rather bizarre line of thought any longer – and then Jo remembered that it wasn't just a passing concern but an overpowering belief, a certainty, a compulsion that there was something important to discover, something base, fundamental, vital. That urgency had also disappeared but she could feel its resurrection as she read.

She found her eyes devouring the pages, looking for something that had a resonance with the thoughts that had occupied her mind shortly after Danny's accident. It was there immediately, just a couple of paragraphs down from the opening line: 'After centuries of being eaten, evicted, subjected to vivisection, killed for fun, worn as hats and made to ride bicycles in circuses, something is causing them to turn on us. And it is being taken seriously enough by scientists that it has earned its own acronym: HAC – human animal conflict.'

There followed a whole string of examples – from mountain lions to wolves, zebras to chimpanzees, all written in almost apocalyptic style but Jo desperately wanted figures in order to gauge whether this was a real phenomenon or a flight of journalistic fancy from some freelance trying to earn a pound or two.

She scoured the columns and found some statistics. Shark attacks have doubled, it said, but provided no numbers. Jo seemed to remember that the frequency of shark attacks globally was counted in mere tens and so a doubling was hardly worthy of the rhetoric in which it had been wrapped. Injuries from cats and dogs in Beijing had risen thirty four per cent while in Australia it was twenty per cent – again, hardly earth-shattering stuff. Perhaps there was simply an increase in the numbers of cats and dogs in those countries.

In Britain, the figure for dog bites had doubled in four years with four thousand people having been treated in hospital. More interesting but the figures were a few years old. It quoted the stingray attack on Australia's real-life Crocodile Dundee, Steve Irwin – a well-aimed barb into his heart – and quoted two other similar incidents but well separated by time.

Jo glanced up to make sure Danny was not seeking her attention and tried to understand why her surge of excitement on reading the headlines was turning into leaden disappointment as she perused the detail – disappointment that it didn't appear to be the disaster she first believed it to be. Why on earth should she want more people to have died, more families to have been stricken by grief and loss, the world to be faced with a catastrophe? She was quickly aware that this was not what she wanted and what she was seeking was, yet again, proof that her strange beliefs were normal.

Despite reassurances from Wendy and Reece, she wanted to be able to quantify her normality, to be able to present it almost in scientific terms. Yes, she was convinced that Angus had acted bizarrely and, yes, she had some understanding of why she was absorbing the fear and pain of animals but it was all still a bit bloody weird.

Her first thoughts had been that here, in these pages of a weekend newspaper, may lie an answer. The disappointment was that it didn't appear to be and she was slightly cross with herself as she knew better than most how newspapers worked. She should have known bloody better. It was, however, a quick judgement as she had still only skim-read the article and calmed herself, went back to the beginning and tried to read through it methodically.

Once case history followed another, mostly from the areas of the world where humans lived in close proximity to large, wild animals. She read on:

'All over Africa, India and parts of South-East Asia, elephants have started attacking humans in unprecedented numbers. Not just killing – they're rampaging through villages and stomping crops, terrorising local populations in any way they can.

'What's happening today is extraordinary. Where for centuries humans and elephants have lived in relatively peaceful co-existence, there is no hostility and violence. When you see reports of elephants running into crops or attacking people, they're highly stressed and there are multiple stressors – violence, lack of food, lack of water, their families broken up, their society is collapsing. All of these things are human derived.'

The person being quoted was a Dr Gay Bradshaw, a world authority on elephants and director of the Kerulos Centre for Animal Psychology and Trauma Recovery, in Oregon. The author continued:

'Bradshaw describes the elephants as being 'under siege' from the locals. But the violence against humans has increased so suddenly, and reached such levels, that these traditional factors aren't thought to be sufficient to explain it. Bradshaw and her colleagues now think that there's been a massive, pan-species, psychological collapse throughout the world's pachyderms. In essence, we're witnessing the dysfunctional shenanigans of a generation of depraved elephants. These are individuals who have become psychologically fractured after being orphaned at a developmentally delicate age or are suffering from post-traumatic stress disorder after watching their families being slaughtered.'"

While the figures provided had not excited Jo, she could feel her blood beginning to rush again as someone with knowledge, with science behind them, was outlining precisely the thoughts that had been flitting in and out of her mind for weeks now. Whoever Gay Bradshaw might be, she was now a heroine. Jo continued to read more of her thoughts:

'"You could make a parallel between elephants and people who are undergoing genocide and war,' Bradshaw says, 'They've gone through massive killings and many have sustained culls or severe poaching, so they've witnessed the violence and they're traumatised.'

It was then asserted that it wasn't solely elephants who were attacking humans and that a similar phenomenon was being seen in many different species. Suddenly, Jo's Christmas day, birthday and holidays all rolled into one as she said out loud, with huge satisfaction: "That's more like it," and continued reading, hoping to unlock just a little more of the mystery.

Attempting to redress the claims was a Professor Peter Carruthers, of the University of Sheffield, who dismissed the idea that animas had sufficient intelligence to make such a profound decision, in fact he called it misguided sentimentality. Taking it a step further, he insisted that animals don't consciously even feel pain and therefore don't deserve our sympathy. 'When vets and vivisectionists anaesthetise their subjects they are indulging in schmaltzy, greetings-card reasoning.'

"What?" Jo screamed. "What? You arsehole – you deserve all that's coming to you." She had no idea what she meant by that but decided, anyway, she hated the human race and it's self-interested denial of the glaringly obvious.

She continued searching and found another po-faced explanation for the inexplicable. It was all to do with habituation and loss of fear, said a British veterinary scientist, Dr Paul McGreevy. If animals lose their fear of humans then they start hanging around them but are still prepared to defend themselves, which they do when contact becomes inevitable.

Conservationists were, of course, also in the firing line. Their crime was to have reduced the hunting and killing of animals and offered them protection and as a consequence their numbers had increased and we were paying the price for it.

There was then a run through the intelligence of animals from someone who explained that sheep can remember at least fifty faces of other sheep, even when they've been separated for years. John Webster, professor of animal husbandry at Bristol University, had discovered that cows can get extremely anxious, have between two and four best friends but also have enemies and can bear grudges for years.

As she read the next paragraph about the complex mental state of animals she found a lump forming in her throat at the thought of the onslaught humans had unleashed on them.

'"Elephants, for example, stand vigil over the bodies of dead companions for a week, before gently covering the corpse with earth. Then they visit the gravesite for years afterwards, taking turns to handle the bones. 'They lift them with incredible sensitivity.'" The claim was by Doctor Tammie Matson, the WWF's human-animal conflict specialist.

Jo lowered the magazine and watched the boys' football match but without seeing anything. She tried to absorb what she was reading and came to the conclusion that humankind was deeply flawed. Yes it had an extraordinary ability to paint beautiful pictures and to write music that could reduce you to tears, and despite the altruism, kindness and self-sacrifice that the species was capable of, it was never these gifts, these traits, these finer aspects of the human psyche that formed the template by which society functioned. No, that was always the preserve of people like Stephen, to whom truth was frequently an inconvenience that had to be navigated around.

Where were the people of vision who could inspire society with a thirst for knowledge, mould it and encourage it in a way that everyone, no matter who they were, could find excitement in facts and feed on them hungrily, using them as a compass to chart a path through the complexities of life? Her eyes focussed on Danny, still running, still happy and a great sadness swept over her which she literally shook her head to disperse. She raised the magazine again and continued reading.

The text established that it was not just humans who could display altruism and ran through a large number of recorded cases amongst animals – between animals of the same species and those of entirely different species, such as the one involving a crow and some kittens. A nest of kittens, which had been abandoned by their mother, or more likely she had been killed, were clearly starving. The crow went off in search of worms and brought them back for the kittens to eat and succeeded in saving them. Eventually they became friends and played together. There was also the pygmy chimp who watched a bird fly into a glass screen and fall to the floor, unconscious. The chimp picked the bird up, climbed to the top of tree and placed him on a branch and stretched out his wings as if for flight.

The article then moved on to communication . 'Perhaps the evolutionary achievement humans are proudest of – and is thought by some to be the very seat of consciousness – is language,' said Doctor Paul McDonald, of the Centre for Integrative Study of Animal Behaviour, in Sydney, Australia, who claimed that even chickens talked to each other. Other little gems were revealed – that if a hawk flies over a chicken, it gives a particular call whereas if it's a fox, it's a different call.

A wolf's tail has thirteen to fifteen different positions which send different messages and when this is combined with ear position, gait, odour and sound, gives an extraordinary range of communication.

The author added a summing up which almost made Jo cheer: 'As a species we have been at the top of the food chain so long that we've forgotten that 'humans' are mere anthropoid apes. In our hubris, we imagine we are an animal apart. For centuries we've been told by priests and scientists that animals are not much more than unfeeling, unthinking, unselfconscious automata. They're a gift from God and their purpose is to have paracetamol rubbed into their eyes, to be turned into fancy trousers and to be stuffed and cooked on His birthday.'

Leading ethnologist, Doctor Mark Berkoff, then added a view that Jo found utterly reasonable: 'Things are changing. There's a lot of new behavioural research, a lot of new neuroscience research that demonstrates that animals are far more complex than was thought. We're not inserting into animals things they don't have. Simply, if our brains have developed the capacity for a rich, emotional inner-life over the millions of years they've been evolving, then why not theirs? If you believe in biological continuity then, if we have emotions, they have emotions. If we have a heart, they have a heart.'

It was then back to Doctor Gay Bradshaw who concluded we shouldn't be asking why animals are turning on us but why they aren't attacking us more.

'Animals have the same capacity that we do, in terms of emotions and what we consider to be high mindedness and moral integrity. In fact, I'd argue that they have more because they haven't done to us what we have done to them. That's a sobering thought. It's amazing that all animals are as benign as they are. It's amazing their restraint. Why aren't they picking up guns?'

Jo knew nothing about Gay Bradshaw and had never heard of the author, Will Storr, but she wanted to give them both the biggest kiss of their lives. She took her mobile from her pocket and googled Will Storr and found him to be a well-regarded feature writer and photographer.

"Mum, you didn't see me score that goal!" A red-faced, cross and disappointed Danny stood inches from Jo's face.

"Oh Danny, there were so many of you down there I couldn't see who was who." She hated her little lie but it was less hurtful than agreeing with him. "Look, jump in, we're going to go home, have a cup of hot chocolate and you're going to tell me about all the bits I missed."

It didn't totally mollify Danny but went a long way towards it.

Chapter Twenty Two

A prickle of excitement was ever-present as Jo made cocoa and she and Danny sat together in the kitchen sipping slowly, chatting together about unfair tackles, a useless referee who wasn't strict enough, a stupid team mate who took the ball from him when he was about to score, a string of near misses and superb, goal-saving slide tackles. She loved it all and was acutely conscious that these moments of uninhibited chatter and intimacy were time-limited and in just a couple of years or so, he would begin to practice self-consciousness in preparation for the confusion and taciturnity of puberty and teenage. She hated the thought but accepted its inevitability.

Jo then contented herself with the reminder that she had been enthralled with each new stage of his development, always believing that the current one was the best, most rewarding. As communication replaced cuteness, so she was better able to know and understand her son and reason began to take the place of bribery and threat.

She was almost loathe to admit it but there was also a value judgment at play, a weighing of the evidence and a verdict of 'job well done!' She was utterly bemused by absent fathers such as Stephen and those who sent their little children away to boarding prep school and then public school, as though the finished product was all that mattered and that the road which led there was so unimportant that it could be sub-contacted out. There had not been any argument with Stephen that Danny would follow this course because Jo had made her feelings clear and Stephen had agreed – probably reluctantly but he had agreed and never subsequently broached the subject.

Despite her enjoyment of Danny's company, when his friend Harry arrived, Danny instantly wrenched the plug of intimacy from its socket and she was abandoned as they dashed upstairs to fire up the XBox and battle with their friends online. Jo did not mind because she had been waiting eagerly to pursue further the conclusions of Bradshaw and Storr and so immediately made her way into the study and began searching the web.

The first thing she came up with was an article in the Guardian which covered almost identical territory to the Sunday Telegraph. Either they had both been fed the same raw data or the one had lifted it from the other. She changed her search criteria, restricting her enquiries to the UK and tried to confine results to the last few years. She also refined the search to farmed animals to avoid the inevitable rash of reports about rabid Rottweilers in Rotherham and deadly Dobermans in Doncaster – important as they might turn out to be, they were always with us and the quantity might be overwhelming – but she would return to them.

Attacks from farmed animals, she reasoned, even if greatly increased in percentage terms would be significantly fewer in actual number and therefore more manageable. They would, she suspected, be more newsworthy and likely to garner greater publicity and therefore be an easier starting point.

One by one they came up – far, far more than she had anticipated. There was a chicken farmer, pecked to death by a flock of birds inside one of his broiler sheds; a dairy farmer gored and killed by a mother cow; an arable farmer killed by seagulls; and the most bizarre of all, a worker on a fish farm held under water until he had drowned by a mass of salmon acting what appeared to be co-operatively. Surely that one was a product of journalistic hype, she thought. But they kept coming, one after another.

Jo flitted around the country, looking at the archives of randomly-chosen local newspapers and then changing tack, checking with the farmer owners' body, the NFU, the National Union of Agricultural Workers, the Health & Safety Executive, Defra and everywhere she looked she found results. She scribbled each discovery on a pad beside her, turning over page after page as the list extended.

She realised the process had a long way to go and might take weeks but it felt important, a voyage of discovery, as revealing as any scientific research and she paused temporarily, wondering how best to display her findings so she could see at a glance any trends or anomalies. The old Daily Telegraph map of Great Britain pinned upon Danny's wall, and at which he rarely looked, was the answer, she decided, and dashed upstairs with an enthusiasm that almost thrilled her.

"Sorry chaps," Jo said as she burst into their concentrated war against the zombies and quickly removed the map. She paused by Danny's pin-up board and picked up a box of pins with different coloured plastic heads. There was no finesse about the relocation of the map to the study wall – strips of adhesive tape at each corner and the finished product wasn't even straight. Pad in hand Jo checked the first entry and placed a pin in the name of the village where death had occurred – except that it wouldn't penetrate the plaster behind the map.

"Shit, shit, shit," she shouted out loud and then clamped a hand over her mouth as she remembered Danny and Harry upstairs. She wasn't so concerned about Danny for he had heard far worse on many an occasion and was matter-of-factly unmoved by his mother's profanities. It was Harry she was concerned about. She didn't want him reporting back to his parents, who would then probably brand her 'that foul-mouthed woman who should know better considering her position', as though public prominence carried with it a natural neutering of all that was morally dubious or rude.

It reminded her of a poster outside a church in the oddly-named Zinzan Street in Reading where she attended one of Stephen's events. 'Swearing is the crutch of conversational cripples' it proclaimed. "Bollocks," she had said when she read it.

"Think logically," Jo told herself. A cardboard box of old files in the corner of the study grabbed her attention and no sooner had she spotted it than its contents were unceremoniously emptied into a pile on the floor and the box opened out flat. It withheld co-operation and seemed determined to arch up in places, to resist and object, making life as difficult as possible but Jo was not to be beaten by cardboard.

Strips of adhesive tape were administered as ruthlessly as manacles on a drunkard, to control its deviancy and disorderliness, until eventually the worst excesses of its resistance were overcome and she had a wobbly, undulating oblong that would suffice for her purposes. The map was placed on top and similarly restrained with tape but was smaller than the cardboard, leaving a wide border of manila-coloured brown on all sides, the top proclaiming in black print, Product of China, whilst one side carried the instruction Use No Hooks.

The final act was to attach it to the wall, also with sticky tape, ignoring the ravages it would impose on the emulsion paint when removed – had already done so.

Having finished, Jo stood back and admired her still-crooked improvisation. She had to admit, it looked appalling – worse than any primary school effort and attempting to straighten it would contribute little towards improving its appearance but she was satisfied. From the box of pins she selected three colours – yellow, green and blue. Yellow to represent farmed animals, green wild animals, and blue domesticated pets, which she would eventually get around to. She then went back to her notebook and for each entry inserted a pin in the appropriate place on the map. Jo could think of no reason why she would ever require such detail but felt a need to be as thorough as possible and against each pin wrote a reference number which was duplicated against the relevant entry in her list.

For the first time since Danny had been injured she felt as though there was finally some understanding illuminating her confusion, that she was at last finally taking charge of both the situation and her life. She didn't care a jot whether what she was doing was an exercise in the ludicrous or a serious exercise in enquiry, it was a genuine attempt to understand something more fully, a phenomenon that had exercised professional scientists and she was now a part of that same team of inquiry.

Excitement blinded her to the mundanities of life as she stuck in pin after pin, annotating both map and note book so they could be cross-referenced and the thought leaped out of nowhere that had she gone to university, should could, possibly, have been a good student, maybe an excellent student if she had chosen the right subject – one that truly grabbed her interest. How stupid she was, she now believed, to have accepted her's and everyone else's belief that serious study was beyond her and she would struggle in an academic environment.

It was a belief quietly, smilingly, reassuringly offered by her mother 'in her best interests' and undoubtedly she believed it. Or was it simply another, gently manipulative way of keeping the pea in the pod, ensuring that she would not flit the nest and leave the very desirable Stephen behind, tying up with god knows who in Manchester or Bristol or wherever.

Stupidly, Jo could feel just a trace of anger beginning to quietly pulse through her. Being a parent had to include more than loving your offspring, surely it had to incorporate encouragement, motivation, understanding and an instilling of aspiration – not the aspiration to be someone's wife but to explore one's potential and how to fulfil it. While the thoughts bounced around in her mind, Jo kept pinning and writing and quickly abandoned the idea that she had been the unwitting participant in a marriage as surely arranged as that of any Indian or Pakistani teenage girl.

She pushed the whole idea to one side for, whatever the reasons that led to her marriage with Stephen, they were her reasons, not least that she was besotted by him. But then there was a different argument to be made – that had her parents encouraged her, believed in her, saw her as an individual and not as an adjunct to someone else, would she have seen Stephen in the same light? It was all utterly academic and there was nobody to blame for anything. She had made her own choice, no one forced her and just as millions of other marriages had soured so had hers and if there was blame to be apportioned, no doubt she was as guilty as Stephen (although she didn't fully believe that).

There was a finality to her thoughts that brought closure to the subject and Jo's excitement returned as she pinned and wrote and looked and pinned some more. Eventually she had done all the pinning there was to do and went back to the computer to uncover more cases, which she was convinced would be there. And she was correct – astounded at just how many there were. Already the thought was forming that perhaps she was being too restrictive in searching solely for UK examples and maybe she should be looking globally. She chuckled out loud when she thought what the addition of other national maps might do to Stephen's prized study and the apoplexy it would undoubtedly produce in him.

Jo tore herself away from her chart to prepare tea for the gaming boys and chatted happily with them whilst they all ate, her only minimally because in one afternoon, her amateur investigation had produced an astounding, incontrovertible result and this filled her mind, quenched her appetite and elbowed all other thoughts aside.

What she had already observed appeared to have in-built faults in either her search criteria or methodology – something – because the little coloured pins showed that almost all the attacks and deaths had taken place within a few miles of the coast. From Scotland to Cornwall, the Wirral to the Wash, bar just three cases, every single pin was no more than eight or ten miles from the coast. The interior of Britain was almost entirely pin-free.

The last number she had entered in her notebook was forty-nine and forty-nine corresponding pins looked back at her from the map a little sparsely but there was no mistaking where they were positioned. Clearly, the sample was far too small and she needed to do much more work.

Jo started as the phone trilled loudly, shattering her thoughts and making her jump.

"I'm not going to have time to come home first so can you meet me there?" Stephen asked.

"Meet you where?" Jo replied, uncomprehendingly.

"Weybridge Hall, of course." There was silence from Jo. "Good god, Jo, don't tell me you've forgotten?"

"Don't be stupid Stephen, of course I haven't," she lied, as panic welled up in her. Not only had she forgotten that Stephen's first public talk as party leader was to be to his own constituents, tonight, but she had also forgotten in her moment of contrition that she had agreed to attend – and even worse, she had failed to make any baby-sitting arrangements.

"What time do you want me there?" she asked, trying very hard to sound as nonchalant as she could.

"About seven fifteen. The intro is at seven thirty and you need to be on the stage with me for that but there are couple of things I want to run past you beforehand. Okay?"

"Of course, no problem. See you there."

"Please be available, please be available," she said out loud as she dialled John Steen's number hoping that Marta would be there, willing her to be in and agreeable to baby-sit. Marta answered the phone but she was not available.

"I am supposed to be seeing a friend tonight, Jo," she said in her softly accented voice. "But it's not until eight thirty so if it is early I can do it."

"Marta, if you can do it until nine thirty I'll double your money – no, I'll quadruple it."

"What? I do not understand what you mean."

"I mean I'll pay you four times as much as I usually do – seriously, I mean it." Jo heard the incredulity in Marta's voice.

"Wow. You are serious, Jo?"

"I am totally, utterly serious, Marta but you need to be here by seven sharp."

"Okay," then she added confidentially, "he is not that good a friend anyway."

"Yes," yelled Jo as she hung up and dashed upstairs trying to decide what was appropriate to wear.

Chapter Twenty Three

Stephen ushered Jo on to the stage with his hand planted firmly in the small of her back like some prized livestock exhibit, she thought, and then dismissed it as ungracious as this was an important meeting for Stephen – the newly elected party leader, the young hopeful, the idol of the right wing and possibly premier.

Jo had always hated public appearances and increasingly so as she found herself at odds with the sentiments and policies being expressed by the entire party but particularly the right wing, her husband's coterie. How differently would she feel towards Stephen, she wondered, if he stood in front of his audiences and addressed them with passion and belief rather than the practiced, polished, perfection of a party performer.

What would it be like to hear him outline a vision of a fairer, more equitable world; for him to express genuine concern for the disadvantaged; to see him unashamedly wear his heart on his sleeve and reveal some traces of his inner vulnerability; to confess to the doubts that beset him; to reveal those things that worried his sleep; to share his feelings of fear and, yes, even inadequacy and to set these failings in front of his audience with disarming honesty.

How she would so love to see and hear all this and not tainted with apology but brandished proudly like a banner, proclaiming that these imperfections were what made him human, made us all human, and it was knowing and understanding these imperfections that provided the compass for a leadership that would eschew dogma and cant and bravely face the realities of an imperfect and often barbaric world, adapting, learning and changing as circumstances change but always working towards a better world.

An outburst of applause and cheering accompanied Jo and Stephen to their seats, she smiling embarrassedly while trying to avoid eye contact, him beaming broadly, waving to the faithful whilst holding his head aloft like some victor ludorum, the conquering hero.

Jo did not have to ponder over the core of his address for she knew it intimately. It took many different forms but the underlying message was as unchanging as time itself – let the rich prosper and the poor will be carried along on their coat tails. The flaw in this ill-formed theory was, of course, that one of the essential elements in the process of becoming rich entailed screwing the poor for all they were worth and destroying all the protection they had built over the years to defend themselves from the rapaciousness of those who wished to be rich.

Of course Stephen's beliefs had an impact on her relationship with him, Jo knew that with certainty and could trace the genesis of her disaffection with him to her questioning of his policies. They were not beliefs he had discovered through enquiry, subjected to intellectual analysis, they had simply been handed to him and like a runner in a relay race he had grabbed eagerly at this baton of belief as though it was truth itself.

At first she had raised her doubts with him in genuine enquiry but his explanations were such empty, shallow, rhetorical phantoms that she had soon stopped asking, trusting far more in her own analyses than Stephen's rote-learnt explanations, which more frequently sounded like excuses or justifications.

Stephen stood in front of the faithful and with arms gesticulating like the conductor of an orchestra began his address.

"I am honoured and humbled by the enormous responsibility that has been handed to me, a responsibility that I intend to discharge without favour in the interests of everyone…"

"Piggy power." A big, strong, hard voice bellowed out from the back of the hall and there was a momentary hiccup in Stephen's delivery. Jo felt her cheeks flush because she knew she had provided the ammunition to the man she could now identify in his military parka, standing at the back of the hall. However, she felt no guilt.

"...whether they supported me or not and whatever party they subscribe to – or no party at all. If I am elected, mine will be a unity government where everyone counts..."

"Piggy power," again the voice bellowed forth, even louder, filling the hall.

This time Stephen didn't try to hide his irritation and glared towards the source of the interruption. The shouter waved at him, an infectious smile on his face, as though they were old friends. Jo could see several of the stewards signalling to each other, pointing out where the man was standing.

"As we all know, these are difficult times and strong, determined leadership is essential if we are to handle what is no longer a little local difficulty but a global crisis. When – sorry, if – I take power..."

"Piggy power."

Jo had to fight hard to curb the laughter that was desperate to be let out and could see that Stephen was rattled as he addressed the heckler directly:

"It's all too easy to stand aside from the crowd and shout inane comments but I can promise you this – that is exactly what my government will not do. We will be engaged, at the heart of the crisis, shaping the agenda, taking difficult decisions to make the world a better place – and yes, even for piggies."

The audience laughed but not loud enough to drown the man's final comment as the stewards closed in around him.

"Not if you keep eating them, you won't."

He went without resistance but the stewards could not resist puffing themselves up with middle-aged, macho posturing, pushing, pulling, pretending they were in control when there was nothing to control. Jo wanted to shout out something, anything, to declare her solidarity with the lone protester, to salute his courage, to honour his conscience but lacked the bravery, knowing that the aftermath she faced from Stephen was going to be bloody enough as it was.

And so the speech wound its interminable way towards an end, buoyed on a cloud of rhetoric, punctuated with theatrical passion and lubricated with geysers of political oil but from start to finish not a shred of sincerity managed to weave itself into the fabric of Stephen's delivery. Surely to god, thought Jo, I cannot be the only person in this crowded hall who can see the vacuity of this self-important, pompous arse.

She then felt ashamedly guilty for failing to support the solitary objector or for not at least tossing a crumb of comfort to him to say I understand your concern, I appreciate your caring. She decided that cowardice did not suit her and vowed she would never again be so craven.

When it came to questions, Jo was surprised that clearly not everyone in the hall shared her husband's belief in his trite solutions to global governance. Some were strongly hostile, others measuredly critical and they fed into her guilt. Was she the only one whose courage had evaporated? Without thought, she filled the short silence between the answering of one question and the asking of another and, despite her trepidation, felt absolute assurance as she spoke, knowing it was precisely the right thing to do.

"I don't know if this is appropriate but we're all pretending we can't see the elephant in the room and that's me and the publicity surrounding my visit to a pig factory farm."

Jo was surprised, almost shocked, by the strong applause that filled the hall and which continued far longer than was necessary for a mere gesture. She nodded in acknowledgment and raised her hand for quiet, hoping passionately that the clapping was for her and her actions and not a signal of the audience's solidarity with Stephen, a reassurance that they would not stop loving him for something his silly wife had done. But it was for her, she could tell.

"Clearly, it was my actions which prompted the heckling earlier. Whatever your views on it, he had a point and I would like to expand on it by asking Stephen a question," she turned towards him and could see his struggle to control the thunder that was banging and crashing inside him, "if that's alright?"

"Of course darling, of course!"

"The conditions inside factory intensive farms are appalling and I have to confess that when I saw them for myself I felt ashamed at what we, as a society, are doing to animals. But it's much wider than that. We can thank the edible products of these places for many of our most deadly diseases and there's now no doubt that animal farming poses the single greatest threat to the environment on all the most urgent issues."

Jo knew that she had to be very careful how she phrased the next bit in order not to lose credibility. "And incredible as it might sound, both the Daily Telegraph and the Guardian are reporting from scientists who believe that the animals are now fighting back – attacking and killing humans in increasing numbers. Put simply, they've had enough. How will your government approach these really disturbing issues, Stephen?"

Even as she said it, Jo wished to god she had omitted the last part of the question because by verbalising it she realised how flaky it sounded even though she had been careful to quote the sources. She watched Stephen as he prepared to answer and she knew him well enough to know that he was cringing with embarrassment beneath the anger that cloaked his face like a cowl. And then he was on his feet, a huge smile painted on where seconds before had been fury.

"A very good question, Jo." He then turned to the audience. "And I can promise you that this was not prepared and the question is as new to me as it is you. What I do know is that I'm going to be very polite to our cat when I go home this evening."

The audience laughed, almost with relief, it seemed. He was doing what she had suspected he would do, using humour to belittle the importance of the question and by the same token, to belittle her, also.

"Of course, when we were last in power we introduced a whole series of improvements in animal welfare which allows the current government to correctly claim that this country has the best animal welfare standards in the world. It has and it was thanks to us."

"No it wasn't, Mister Aldous."

Jo recognised the Manchester vowels instantly and searched the hall for their source. She found it towards the back of the hall where Wendy Carter had risen from her seat.

"The few improvements that were introduced were fiercely

fought for by the animal rights movement and every demand was bitterly opposed by both your party and the farming lobby working in unison. It was only our constant highlight of the appalling suffering that farmed animals endured that caused a public outcry demanding change and you only listened because you thought votes might be at risk. But even then you delayed, watered down and obfuscated and to see your commitment to ending animal suffering we have only to look at your party's manifesto – not a word, not a mention, nothing!"

Again Jo could see that beneath Stephen's studied calm demeanour he was quaking with rage. He did not address Wendy but the hall at large.

"I'm terribly sorry – I thought this was question time, not speech time." He then adopted one of his usual strategies for difficult situations – outraged dignity.

"If you are concerned about animal welfare, may I suggest you travel to Europe and compare the standards there with our own. I suggest you visit Thailand or India or Brazil and witness first-hand how they treat their animals. And I hope you take great pleasure in the knowledge that your actions against our farmers are driving them out of business, ensuring that we import ever more products from these very same countries who care not a jot for animals." He paused to allow his words to sink in and Wendy filled the vacuum.

"It is like listening to someone extolling the virtues of Belsen over Auschwitz."

The chairman was immediately on his feet.

"I think on that insulting note it is probably time we brought this evening's proceedings to a close. I would sincerely like to thank…"

Stephen leant across to Jo, ensuring his face was turned away from the audience. "How fucking dare you…?" It was the first time she had ever heard him use that word.

Jo got up and made her way from the stage to the reception room behind it, ignoring Stephen. After he had taken his bow he joined her but he was surrounded by well-wishers and it was impossible for him to say what he so desperately wanted to. Before he could say anything, she thrust eighty pounds into his hand and said brightly: "Give that to Marta will you Stephen – it's what I promised her for baby-sitting. I have to go on to another appointment. I'll see you tomorrow."

It all sounded as normal as could be and she ran the gamut of handshakes and cheek kisses and tried to curb her desperation to be elsewhere. She knew she was not running away but simply making a strategic withdrawal in order to pick the ground upon which to have the inevitable confrontation with Stephen – the final confrontation – for this was a situation that could not endure for another day. Further procrastination was not an option.

Having got out of the place she dashed around to the front of the hall, hoping to catch Wendy before she disappeared home. As it was, she was waiting by the entrance. Jo linked arms with her and steered her up the High Street.

"I need some urgent support."

"I bet you do," Wendy replied.

Chapter Twenty Four

It was on the Sunday, two days after their joint public meeting, that Jo finally met face to face with Stephen. She had stayed at the Ship Hotel that night with Wendy in an atmosphere that Jo thought might compare with that experienced by air force pilots in the second world war – one dreadful confrontation over, another one to come, so live for today.

They had laughed and laughed and drank and laughed again and determined that they would fix a time to go out as a group – she and Danny, Wendy and Maisie. And they laughed at the prospect of the two kids becoming boyfriend and girlfriend. Despite the next day being a Sunday, Jo knew that Stephen had to leave the house at 8.30 am and texted him to drop Danny off at her mother's on his way to London so she could pick him up later. The text she received in reply began, 'If I have to' and she read no further down the screed of almost certain abuse.

The two days interregnum had turned Jo's foreboding into anger as she decided that, whatever his position, he had no right to try and control her in the way he did, as though everything should first be run past him for his approval. You have chosen the wrong person she thought. When they finally met, it was in the hallway of their house – she had essentially ambushed him, having heard his car drive up and had gone forth to do battle, allowing him no time to take the initiative and choose the timing of the injured tirade she knew would follow.

"Don't ever speak to me like that again in public, do you hear me?"

He was immediately on the defensive. "No one heard me!"

"I bloody heard you and I saw the ludicrous fury written all over your face like some bloody potentate who the servants have dared to answer back. I asked you a legitimate question, Stephen, and did you hear the response from the audience, did you? You could have had them eating out of your hand and you blew it."

'No, your gang of unsavoury acolytes blew it – how could you do that, how could you co-ordinate an attack on my first public speech as leader, trying to humiliate me? And you're supposed to be my wife!"

"You stupid arse. I had no idea who the heckler was and I had no idea that Wendy Carter was in the audience either…"

"Maybe not but it was your actions of going into a pig farm that provided them with the ammunition…"

"For Christ's sake, you don't really believe you'd have been given a free ride if I hadn't done that? A large section of the population of Britain might think you're their salvation but there's an even bigger section that thinks you're an arsehole – and they're going to tell you so, so you'd better bloody get used to it."

"And what's all this nonsense about the animals talking to you, you feeling their pain and them fighting back – they're going to take over the world, I suppose?"

"I was simply reporting what I'd read – studies by legitimate scientists, concerned scientists… Just a minute, what do you mean, animals talking to me and me feeling their pain? I've never said any of that to you. Where did you get it from?"

Stephen turned away from her. "It's common knowledge." From the tone of his voice, the slouch of his shoulders and the fact that he could not look her in the eye, she knew he was lying.

"Who told you, Stephen? Who bloody told you?"

He turned and thrust his face towards hers. "I don't remember, okay?" And again she knew he was lying but she also knew that he was very aware he had inadvertently strayed into a minefield and that he could not now possibly answer her honestly. If she battered and threatened him all day long he would never tell her.

The revelation that someone had betrayed her defused Jo's anger but replaced it with despair and she turned away from the confrontation, fighting back the need to cry. Who could have done this to her – who could have gone to Stephen and revealed this most personal of secrets, the one thing that touched her so deeply that it amounted to an emotional assault of overwhelming proportions and made her feel utterly vulnerable, despairing. It was a betrayal of such enormity that it felt as though the guilty person had entered her very soul and vandalised it, caring not a jot what havoc was wreaked and what pain would ensue. It was clearly someone who identified with Stephen and his interests and who had contempt for hers.

Jo went to her room and allowed the tears to flow as if they could wash away the traitor's stain. She did not want to confront the question of who it might be but knew she had no option. She had told only two people, Wendy and Reece. It could not, must not, would not be either of them – but what if it was? If so, it must surely have been an act of omission rather than one of commission – words that had accidentally been let slip. It could not be Wendy as she had had no contact with Stephen unless, of course, she had purposely picked up the phone and told him, wresting from him some quid pro quo for her insider's knowledge.

And Reece? Had Stephen been to see him and had Reece unburdened himself, betraying her confidence – 'I'm very worried about Jo, she's having what I think are hallucinations.' No, he would never have done that and in any case he didn't believe that. Jo shook herself and detested the person responsible, not because Stephen now knew intimate details about her which she did not want him to know but because of the awful, spiteful, corrosive, destructive process she was now engaged in, doubting the people she considered close and trustworthy friends, eroding that trust which had helped to sustain her over the past few weeks. Whoever it was she would not allow them to succeed and thrust any thought from her mind that these two people would have cavalierly betrayed her.

In desperation, Jo constructed a scenario in which Reece had told Beth of his concerns but had failed to caution her that Stephen knew nothing of them. In turn, Beth had bumped into Stephen and enquired about Jo's condition. Stephen would then have bled her dry of information without betraying his lack of knowledge because it was the kind of thing he was good at, thrived on as part and parcel of the political dark arts.

Jo polished and honed this scenario, making it distinctly possible – believable – and even as she rounded off the few remaining sharp edges knew it was complete bollocks. This was not how her friends behaved.

She lay on her bed and as nearly as she could, allowed her mind to empty itself of these destructive thoughts. She propped herself up on the pillows so she could see out of the windows into her beloved garden, winter bleak and numbingly cold but extraordinarily beautiful nevertheless. Little birds flitted back and forth from bush to branch to lawn in their desperate search for food that would provide sufficient body warmth to enable them to survive the night – or not! She felt guilty as she had forgotten to top up the bird feeders for the last two days and promised herself she would do it in just a minute, as soon as the turmoil that was abating had finally exhausted itself. Compared to her, these little creatures had real problems, life or death problems.

There was one thought, however, that Jo could not dispel and it kept recurring, just as it had from the very beginning, from the moment Stephen had revealed his knowledge of her dreams. The guilty person was female. In whatever direction Jo's mind travelled, whatever explanations she sought, they were punctuated with 'her' and 'she,' never 'him' or 'he.' That was why the Reece scenario had fallen at the first fence. It was a she, of that she was certain although she had no idea why.

The realisation, when it came, did so with utter certainty, appearing from nowhere and beyond questioning. Once revealed, Jo had no reason to revisit it. The guilty person was Hillie. Jo's admission to her had been so brief and Hillie's interest so ephemeral that Jo had completely forgotten about it. Hillie, her sister, had betrayed her confidences to Stephen and Jo felt a huge flood of relief wash over her. It was only her! You could expect little else.

The where's and why's and when's surrounding her and Stephen's exchanges of such intimacies were of no interest to

Jo at all – she simply didn't care. It was not one of her friends and that was all that mattered and she had been right to maintain her trust in them. Hillie would have passed on Jo's intimate details without artifice or venom, like pulling the plug out of a basin, whatever information was in her would spill out until every last drop was drained and it would be called gossip, silly cow that she was.

The relief that Jo felt was almost life affirming and she knew she could now get on with the rest of her day, doing the things she had to do but had avoided for so long – but first the bird feeder.

She stepped out into the garden armed with peanuts, seeds and suet balls and felt the scything bitter chill of the still northerly wind as it swept between the Scots pines and demanded the leafless shrubs bend to its will, which they did compliantly. She was buoyant, determined, eager to bring her tortuous marriage to an end, or at least to give it formal closure for the end itself had long since come and gone.

The chill bit through her thin clothing and she hurried to be done and return to the warmth indoors and then she spotted them, tossing their heads to and fro beneath bushes that, now leafless, offered no shelter – the first little white snowdrops of the winter, timeless, triumphant and undaunted by the penetrating cold. Sublimely beautiful in their own right they were also heralds of better times to come, presaging the arrival of other blooms that would follow in their stead, one after another, each a different hue, form and texture, ticking down the time like a floral advent calendar until Spring once again burst forth in all its glory and the garden was awash with colour and perfume.

She had lovingly planted almost every one of them, planning carefully how each season of the year would produce its own display of beauty, whose arrival she would welcome but whose leaving she would never mourn for it was only ever au revoir until their eventual return another year.

Jo felt emotion born of loss clutching at her, saddening her, for this time it was goodbye. She would never again see these particular, perfect little blossoms nor their colourful cousins who were even now preparing themselves below ground, readying themselves to burst forth, each at their allotted time.

She had never anticipated magnanimity from Stephen and had always believed that he would insist on retaining the house, not for its garden or wildlife but because it had appreciated enormously in value since they had bought it. Jo had never contemplated battling over retention of her house and had accepted that the simplest, most effective way of bringing closure was to get up and walk out, avoiding the spite and acrimony that would inevitably follow in the wake of a battle over possession. He would provide for them of that there was no doubt – he had no option in his position.

But amidst the sadness that enveloped Jo were other, more dominant emotions, not least a determination to avoid a scene and a mellow certainty that there was no going back – a calmness that would hopefully help smooth what was to come. She dashed back in doors but not before pausing for a moment by the kitchen door to see if the birds had spotted her gifts. They had and she felt happy.

An afternoon with a friend had purposely been arranged for Danny so that it was just Stephen and her in the house and for some reason she could not fully explain, she had cooked a roast lamb lunch, a free-range offering which, following several meat-free days, filled her with guilt. Why she had done it she didn't really know. Perhaps it was a gesture of compromise, a meeting with Stephen on his own territory; a reassurance that she was prepared to cede ground – although she could not immediately identify any other ground that she felt like ceding. In truth, she hoped that a civilised setting would set the tone for adult debate about a situation that could no longer be avoided and had to be resolved.

She busied around cooking pre-prepared vegetables and for once in her life seemed to have got the timing of the lunch right and with any luck, all its component parts would be cooked and ready at the same time. After years of always getting it wrong, why perfection now?

"Lunch in ten minutes, Stephen," she shouted from the kitchen to the house in general and then added: "We need to talk."

As she said the words Jo could feel her heart begin to race. It was as though a starting gun had been fired and there was now no return. Oh fuck, she admitted to herself, I feel nervous. Nervousness had not been in her plans even as a contingency, only calmness and determination. She busied and prepared and when all was ready shouted again at the top of her voice, "lunch", as if the louder she said it, the more it would dissipate her foreboding.

She had just started to carve the leg joint when Stephen appeared in the dining-room doorway.

"What the bloody hell is that monstrosity on my study wall?"

"Our study wall, Stephen. It's a map. It's my map." Oh please god let me be less confrontational, she intoned to herself. "Actually, it's some research I'm doing and it's only temporary. As soon as I can get to the shops I'll replace it with something a bit more St George's Hill."

"It's absolutely hideous – ruins the whole study."

"Like I said, it's very temporary. The shops are open tomorrow and I'll make it my first job to get a nice, neat, new map and a proper pin board that doesn't want to mimic Saharan sand dunes."

"I don't want a damn big map in the study – and what research? You've never researched anything in your life."

"Well it's time I did, don't you think?" Please let me remain calm, Jo pleaded with herself. "It may be nothing, it's too early to tell yet. As soon as there is something worth telling, I'll let you know. In the meantime, let me have my little secret."

"And you've already ripped off strips of emulsion – it looks appalling."

"There's some of the same paint in the shed, I've checked, and when I put the new board up I won't use sticky tape and I'll paint over the bare bits. Okay your majesty?" No matter how hard she tried, Jo found it impossible to strip her words free of all barbs – it had simply become too ingrained.

"You could have discussed it," Stephen harrumphed as he took his seat and Jo transferred her attention back to carving the meat.

"I hope you like it pink," she offered, "because it is pink. Very pink."

TONY WARDLE

She removed a couple of slices and as she worked the carving knife backwards and forwards, she noticed a blood vessel close to the bone and with each downwards pressure on the knife, thickened blood bellied from its severed end. When she raised the knife and removed the pressure, it was drawn back inside the blood vessel like a child snorting back snot.

"Oh, fucking hell, I can't do this," she spat out and the carving knife and fork clattered on to the carving dish as she dropped them. "If you want meat, carve it yourself, Stephen!"

"Do you have to use that language?"

"No I don't but I choose to because I'm not anally retentive like you." No, no, no, she told herself, stay calm, be cool. "Sorry Stephen, I didn't mean that but this is the last piece of meat I will ever touch."

"What? What do you mean?"

"I mean I'm giving up eating meat."

"For the day?" There was hope in Stephen's question and a trace of desperation.

"No, not just for the day – permanently, forever."

"Oh, for god's sake, Jo! How can I possibly tell every dinner host, every function organiser that my wife is a veggie. They'll think we've gone mad."

"Well, in that case, I wonder what they'll think when you also tell them that I don't eat dairy or drink milk – and while we're at it you can add eggs and fish to the list as well."

Stephen stopped his carving and stood there, towering over the dining table, a carving knife in one hand, a fork in the other and a look on his face that was little short of horror.

"For god's sake you stupid woman, please tell me this is a joke – a wind up. You're not serious are you?" Even as he said it he was mortified to read in Jo's expression that, yes, she did mean it. "You're just doing this to spite me, aren't you? I honestly believe there's something seriously wrong with you, Josephine, and I'm extremely worried. What the hell do you think people are going to think. Are they going to vote for a prime minister who's so damned weak that he allows his wife to eat nothing but lettuce leaves and lentils and tolerates her open hostility towards him in public? They'll view me as a

307

complete failure, a hen-pecked failure and you don't put a failure in charge of a country."

Jo was about to respond with barbs about personal choice, her right to do what she wished and that there was no question of him 'allowing' her to do or not do anything but instead, she went silent and pushed the vegetables around on her plate absent mindedly, staring at them as though her thoughts were entirely elsewhere but they weren't, they were focused on the present as she searched for the least antagonistic way to advance the conversation to its ultimate conclusion. When she eventually spoke it was quietly, intimately.

"It's all academic, Stephen, as I'm not going to be your wife much longer, I want a divorce." Oh dear god, it was not how she had intended to deliver the news; boing, springing up from nowhere like a jack-in-the box – surprise, surprise!

Stephen did not respond immediately but remained standing, clutching the carving knife and fork and Jo was unnerved to see that he was grasping them so tightly that the skin on his knuckles was stretched thinly white.

"I beg your pardon?"

The question was rhetorical for Jo knew he had heard her clearly and understood precisely the import of her words. She knew because his face told her so – a face that she had never before seen in the twenty years she had known him, a dark, ominous, threatening face where the eyes bulged, the jaw hung slackly, the colour was gone and his countenance lowered, murderously. Jo knew that the sad, shameful truth was that his shock did not spring from the losing of love, the impending departure of his soul mate or the end of a marriage nor even the pain of rejection; it was solely the danger it posed to his plans. Could this potential scandal end his dream just as he was preparing for it to become a reality? Jo could see him trembling and was suddenly, genuinely frightened and began talking quickly to make clear her intentions, to outline what she proposed, to explain but above all to mollify and in trying to do them all at once, she garbled.

"I'm not talking like now, today, or even next week. I know how important the elections are and I do want you to win and

I don't intend to do anything before then. I'm just saying that we haven't had a marriage for years but I will support you as best I can until it's all over and you've got what you want. Three months, I thought. Once you've been in office for three months I'll quietly disappear and no one will probably know the difference." She laughed falsely, nervously. "I imagine they'd all be bloody relieved. I know they like a prime minister to have a wife but Ted Heath didn't and once you're elected there's not much they can do anyway, is there? You'll have the power and they'll just have to lump it and by the next time you stand for election again everyone will have got used to it except, of course, you'll probably have met someone new by then, someone who likes being in the public eye and can support you properly – someone who eats meat. No one will know until after you've been elected and I will attend meetings with you when you think it necessary and I will try my hardest to keep my mouth shut and support you…"

Finally, Jo ran out of steam and finished her explanation calmly and slowly, almost imploringly: "I don't want conflict, Stephen, I just want you to be you and me to be me – to do the things that I want to do and for you to have someone who can truly support you instead of me carping on at you all the time." Her final words echoed with quiet desperation: "It's over Stephen, you know it's over."

Stephen had remained silent throughout her outpourings. Jo hoped he was not aware that she meant little of what she was saying and that each offering was being proffered for the here and now, in order to defuse, reassure, placate – each sentence another slosh of oil to smooth and smother the troubled waters which she could see frothing and fomenting before her eyes. For Jo, truth now ran a distant second to the need to control the fear that was welling up in her, shocking her, numbing her, terrifying her as she looked at this big man, whose stature appeared to have doubled in size, looming between her and the door, threatening, intimidating, overwhelming.

When he did speak, Jo froze as she watched the spittle flying from his thinly stretched lips, finding its way between his almost clenched teeth. She now knew why she had delayed ending her marriage for so long. She was certain that, deep down inside, she had known that this is how he would react and had not been able to face it. Now she had no choice but to weather it as she was in the eye of the storm and the only haven would have to be of her own making, constructed from her own guile.

Stephen inclined his body towards her, stuck his face out aggressively, domineeringly: "You fucking cow. You stupid, selfish, spiteful, insane fucking bitch. Do you know what you are? You're a piece of shit on the sole of my shoe that I should have scraped off years ago. You're a frigid, fucking, sour lesbian who deserves none of the things I've given you. You deserve nothing, nothing do you hear me and nothing's what you're going to get. Look at me you tight-arsed whore. Look at me!"

He screamed the words so loudly that it made Jo start like a terrified animal. It was, she knew, the outpouring of years of frustration, of rejection, of the contempt she had shown towards him; it was fear and loathing, it was spite and emasculation which had been building beneath his apparently calm surface. It was crude, unbridled mysogyny. But it was something else, too, something which had never occurred to her, even fleetingly in all the years she had known him. It was jealousy. He, the supremely arrogant leader, poised on the edge of greatness, was jealous of her. He was jealous of her self-containment, her search for understanding and yes, he was jealous of her confidence as she had grown from an adoring teenager into a strong, self-possessed woman trying to find a way in life without the comforting straightjacket of ideology. She was all the things he wasn't. But it wasn't over yet.

"You walk out of this house with your shrivelled fucking cunt and you'll never see Danny again – ever. Do you understand that? Do you? I will take your precious fucking son away from you. You will not poison him. I won't allow you to infect him with your madness. Do you hear me you crazy cow? Do you?"

The final, ultimate attempt at control. Jo stared back at him, incapable of speech, incapable of moving, incapable even of blinking. He raised the carving knife above his head and thrust it down into the table with all the force he could muster and it penetrated its surface deeply with an echoing 'thunk' where it quivered rapidly backwards and forwards, the noise of its vibrations amplified by the sounding board of the wooden table top. Stephen turned and moved quickly to the door, throwing it open with such venom that it crashed against the wall with a startling bang, its momentum forcing it back again to close behind him.

Before Jo could relax a muscle, ease the faintest of breaths into her frozen lungs, the door flew open again with equal force and Stephen lurched back into the room, his head forward, his teeth clenched, his eyes staring and in his left hand he still grasped the carving fork.

Jo's hand shot out, seemingly of its own volition, without precognition, and grasped at the first thing to hand on the table in an innate, electrifying, lighting reaction of self-preservation. She flung the object with all her might directly at Stephen's face and it was then that the world momentarily appeared to switch into slow motion. She saw the small jar of redcurrant jelly leave her hand and rotate over and over as it travelled silently across the room, through the intervening space between her and Stephen, and there was no doubt that her aim was true. It struck just below his right eye with a hollow, echoing, sickening thud like someone banging on an empty barrel. Stephen collapsed to the floor whimpering, both hands clasped to his face and Jo saw the blood slowly penetrating the gaps between his fingers.

She remained motionless, unsure what to do, assessing how she could reach the door without stepping within his reach. And then she moved, fast and fleet, inadvertently banging into the wall in her determination to keep as far away from him as possible but it cannoned her towards him and she had to jump over his legs. Then she was out of the room into the hallway and the front door and safety stood before her. She did not exit through it but paused and waited and listened, afraid of what she might have done.

The whimpering continued but it was not the distressed sounds of the ogre who had only a minute before terrified her; it was much more the despair of a child who had been thrown from his bicycle and had not yet learned stoicism or self-control and was broadcasting the pain of his grazes, hoping that someone would magically caress them away. And then she could just detect words, crying their way through the whimpering.

"Jo, Jo, help me – please help me. Jo…" The last called name was extended imploringly.

She stood before the front door but still hesitated, not sure if the threat had evaporated or whether it was a ruse to bring her back into the room and within his grasp. Something told her that the danger had been defused and his only interest now was in being cosseted and comforted, for mummy to make the pain go away and tell him that everything would be alright.

"I'm calling an ambulance," Jo shouted, amazed that her voice sounded quite matter-of-fact, calm. As she lifted the phone, she became aware that she was anything but calm as her fingers were trembling so violently she could barely punch out the first nine of the emergency number. Having done so, she slammed the receiver back down as the instincts of a politician's wife took over. If Stephen was admitted to hospital, some orderly or nurse would immediately phone the tabloids and the place would be beset by paparazzi and reporters, all looking for a diagnosis, a prognosis but most of all an explanation of what had happened and if failing to receive one, would concoct one of their own.

She dialled again but this time it was Reece's number and a wave of relief surged through her when he answered almost immediately.

She spoke very calmly, all the fear and urgency stripped from her voice, reflecting how she was beginning to feel: "Reece, Stephen's had an accident."

"Nothing trivial I hope."

Jo had to fight back a giggle of relief that suddenly the world was almost normal again.

"No, I think it might be quite serious, not life threatening but pretty nasty. Could you come quickly, please." She didn't add that the request for speed was for her benefit, not Stephen's.

"Okay, I'm on my way."

Those simple words were like manna to Jo and all the remaining fear drained from her with barely a sigh. It was replaced with anger. She headed back to the dining room and the words were tumbling out of her mouth before she had passed through the door: "If you behave like that ever again I'll have you fucking committed, you bastard. You had a bloody big fork in your hand. What were you going to do with it, stab me like you stabbed the table?"

She looked at the huddled frame of her husband, curled up on the floor in a foetal position, and it appeared to have shrivelled to a husk. She saw the blood stains across his hands and on his shirt but they were nowhere near as prolific as she feared they might be.

"How can you say that, Jo. I didn't even know I had the damned thing in my hand, I would never have done that – ever, ever. Honestly Jo, I was angry, out of order, incensed but you can't believe I would ever have harmed you." His voice was thin and pleading, almost pathetic.

"If the awful insults you threw at me are anything to go by, you intended to carve me into little pieces and feed me to the crows."

"How is a man expected to act when his wife suddenly pops into the lunchtime conversation that she intends to divorce him?"

"Not like that, Stephen, not fucking like that. Okay, I handled it badly but…" Her voice trailed off because there was nothing really to add. "Take your hands away, let me have a look at your eye."

He did so, slowly, gingerly, as though he expected his eyeball to come away with them. Again Jo was relieved to see that he had been struck just below his cheek bone, well away from the eye and the cut was not extensive. In fact the jar was on the floor beside him, unbroken, so it was merely the weight of the jar and its impact that had broken the skin, not jagged glass. She felt relieved that she had not called an ambulance. The flesh was swelling almost as she looked at it and there was no doubt there would be a huge bruise and a shiner of all shiners, but that was a small price to pay. She dipped a napkin from the table in the water jug and handed it to him.

"Dab the blood away with that. We'll see what Reece has to say when he gets here."

For some reason Jo did believe that it was not his intention to stab her but with uncontrolled fury driving him, whatever he had in mind would not have been pleasant. She felt no remorse, no guilt and no sympathy for him and there was no longer even a trace of fear in her. The only emotion that occupied her was that of overwhelming pity. He was a future prime minister, a man who would control destinies but who could not handle his emotions, was an overpowering bully, was devoid of normal humanity, who had built an edifice of power and intrigue around him in order to disguise his failings. And like most bullies, had collapsed when confronted.

She looked at him, still on the floor, but now with his back propped against the sideboard, dabbing at his eye ineffectually and all she could see was a child – a big, pathetic, overgrown, weak, nasty, spiteful child and she hated herself for having indulged him for so many years. Never again in her life would she be so weak. And she fought back an urge to yell at him: "Get on your feet and stop snivelling – act like a man." But she didn't because there had been enough yelling.

The sound of the doorbell heralded Reece's arrival.

Chapter Twenty Five

"How did it happen?"

Reece looked at Jo from beneath lowered eyelids as he examined Stephen's face, perched as he now was on a dining chair.

They both remained silent, Stephen clearly struggling to find a convincing explanation – any explanation – Jo not interested in helping him. Eventually he spoke.

"I ran into something."

"What, at a hundred miles an hour?" Reece winked at Jo out of Stephen's vision.

"I'm not sure, I think I may have passed out, I can't quite remember."

"Could you have fainted, fallen and hit your face on the corner of the table there, huuumm? What do you think? That could account for all this." He indicated the injuries and was blatantly throwing Stephen a lifeline while at the same time finding an uncontroversial entry for his medical records.

"Possibly – yes I think that might have been what happened." Stephen grasped at it gratefully.

From the oppressive atmosphere, Jo's silence and Stephen's ludicrous fumblings to find an explanation, Reece had clearly guessed he was attending a 'domestic'.

"Well, it's not very nice and it's going to be very painful but the good news is, the eye is absolutely fine. You may have fractured the cheekbone but only an X-ray will show that and as there's not much you can do about it anyway, I wouldn't bother." There was not a trace of sympathy in his voice. "The cut is only small and it's clean now and I don't think it requires

315

a dressing – it's the bruising that's really the problem. If I were you, I'd stick an eye patch over the whole lot – it'll do wonders for your image. Didn't do Moisha Dayan any harm, did it?"

Both faces looked back at him blankly.

"Oh dear god, I am getting old! Right here's some pain killers, some anti-inflamatories and half a dozen sleeping pills to be used judiciously. Can't have you losing your beauty sleep, Stephen, can we?"

Jo looked at the closing eye, the swollen face and livid bruising and turned away to control her laughter.

She conducted Reece to the door and walked out with him to his car. He turned towards her and for the first time there was concern in his voice.

"Are you alright, Jo? Do I have any reason to be worried about you?"

"No, not now, not any longer."

"I'm on the phone for the rest of the day if you need me but then I'm not going to be around for a while. Do you want me to check back later?"

"Not necessary, Reece, but thank you so much for asking. As soon as the pain killers start working he's leaving."

"Good!" He held Jo's face in his hands and kissed her gently on the forehead. "I take it we can now invite you to dinner without you being accompanied by Lord of the Rings."

"Fuck off Reece," Jo laughed, pushing him away, "and yes you can!"

She watched his car disappear down the drive to the scrunching accompaniment of tyres on gravel but remained motionless, shivering in the chill afternoon air, long after it had disappeared from view behind a bank of rhododendrons. She did not want to go back inside, she did not want to look upon his face – not now, not ever. But then a sense of euphoria enveloped her as she realised what had happened, what she had done. She had told him. She was free and all the rest was now merely padding. More than that, his bullying, threatening, frightening behaviour had placed her in the ascendant and she felt amazingly, unassailably strong. He would not, could not, argue with the detail because his insults and actions were irredeemable – he had placed himself beyond the pale and he knew it.

Jo turned on her heel, silently saying to herself, 'Come on girl, work to be done'. When she stepped back into the hall, Stephen was at the foot of the stairs.

"I really don't feel too well. I'm just going to lie down for a little while."

Her response was immediate: "Not you're not, Stephen, you're going to take your pills, you're going to sit down and you're going to listen to me because I'm going to finish what I've started. You're not fit to drive so when I've finished, you're going to call your official car and spend the night in your Westminster flat. In fact, you're going to spend every night in Westminster because you will never again stay in this house while I'm in it."

"Jo, come on," Stephen moaned.

She picked up the pills and read the instructions. "Now, take these, go and sit down in the drawing-room and I'll fetch some water. After that I'll make a cup of tea because – well, what else do you do in a situation like this?" She was starting to enjoy herself.

When she returned with the tea there was less pathos enveloping Stephen. Does the fight back start here? she wondered.

"This is all getting out of proportion, Jo. I'm sorry, I'm really, truly, genuinely sorry for what I did, the way I behaved. It was unforgivable but I'm under such huge pressure, surely you can see that."

"I'm not interested, Stephen. It's over, it was over long before your inexcusable behaviour earlier. Until the election, you are going to live at your flat in London or wherever else you choose. After the election, if you win, you will have more fucking houses than you know what to do with – Downing Street, Chequers, your flat and I've no doubt there are lots of others hanging around somewhere…"

"And if I don't win the election?"

"You're not a poor man, Stephen, and you'll still have your flat. And anyway, if you don't win you'll probably be sacked and earn a fortune in the City so you can buy any house you want." Jo suddenly wished she had not added this last little nugget as it reminded Stephen of what she was putting at risk. But it was now too late and so she continued.

"This is the family home and the family now consists of Danny and me and we're staying in this house, make no mistake about that. I'll ensure you can see Danny regularly..." She wanted to add, 'providing he wants to see you', but that would have been spiteful and so instead said, "If you can find the time, that is. If you want to fight it, you're welcome but I think the party might have something to say about the public embarrassment that would create! What I will do is discuss it with you when Danny is eighteen or when he's finished with full-time education. If appropriate, we'll then sell it and split the proceeds."

"Jo, can't you see I'm in pain...?"

"Not as much pain as I've endured over the past few years. It's also important you understand that I'm playing no further part in your fucking election. Truth is, Stephen, I don't think you deserve to be elected – in fact I don't think any of your lot deserve to be elected and for that reason I won't do anything to stand in your way because if it's not you, it'll just be someone else with the same stamp of arrogance and the same failed policies. But by the same token, I won't do anything to help you, either. You can make whatever excuse you like for me but I'm out."

Jo watched his face intently throughout her diatribe and saw despair, disbelief but most of all fear. She could almost hear his brain whirring as he concocted excuses for the party, anticipated their objections and desperately tried to assess his odds of retaining the nomination and how he could best influence those odds.

"It doesn't have to be like this..." he wheedled.

"Oh yes it does – and make the most of this conversation because once you walk out that door all communication between us will be through solicitors." Again she saw near desperation in his eyes. "And don't worry, I don't intend initiating anything until you've had your feet under number ten's table for three months or so."

While her reason for offering this olive branch was originally to assist Stephen, that was no longer the case. A public split so close to an election would bring the full wrath of the elders down around her ears and they were capable of terrible things, the least of which would be to unleash the spite and vindictiveness of their tame news rags on her. They would trawl through every second of her life and pay anyone who would take their shilling to bear false witness against her. All the disgusting insults Stephen had thrown at her earlier would be made real by their low-life hacks. She could not allow that to happen for Danny's sake.

"I want you to be gone before Danny gets home – I don't want him seeing you like that. I'm picking him up at five so when you've finished your tea, get any things you need and call your car…"

"Jo, Jo, Jo… please."

"For Christ's sake Stephen, just do it."

"Do me one favour, Jo – just do me one favour, please and I promise I won't ask for anything else. It's next Wednesday, there's the traditional pre-election meeting in the House between the party leader and his wife and female members – potential ministers. The leader's wife always attends – it's in her honour. It will be ludicrous if you're not there"

"You're not listening to me Stephen. Fuck your meeting, fuck your party members. I wouldn't pee on them if they were on fire. Now go – just go."

She turned and hurried up to her room. What she really wanted to do was climb in her car and drive somewhere, anywhere away from the house but she would not move from it until the final chapter had been written and he had gone. And when he had, the first call she would make would be to an emergency locksmith. She heard Stephen's voice weakly following her up the stairs:

"Going to phone your animal rights nutters are you? To tell them you've done what they wanted!"

She did not intend to reply but the words came out anyway, imploringly. "Please show some dignity, Stephen, please!"

In fact Jo did not phone a locksmith, at least not immediately.

She watched Stephen's car arrive from a landing window and almost held her breath as he fiddled around, twice returning to the house to collect something or other he'd forgotten and each time he did so, her heart stood still. Eventually, the driver opened the rear door for Stephen to enter but before doing so he paused and looked around him. His eyes scanned the house from one end to the other and from top to bottom – or rather his eye did, his one good eye, as the right side of his face was now a swollen lump and just a thin slit marked where there had once been an eye.

He was, she hoped, absorbing the horrible reality of what had happened to them but, in truth, suspected he was bidding farewell to something that had been the solid, tangible totem to his achievements – the mark of a successful man – a beautiful, expensive house on St George's Hill, an accomplishment that had enormous resonance both locally and in the wider world. He was saying goodbye to the house, not her.

Jo felt emotional but it wasn't born of pity or remorse or even concern – it was something much more complex. It was the final death pangs of expectation. She had not entered marriage believing she would one day stand furtively peeking out from behind a curtain whilst her husband scurried away from her and her son, severing all the certainties with which her life had been defined; she did not offer her vows believing they were temporary. She had expected security and even complacency, mutual caring and concern to carry her through the years and to offer insulation from all that was threatening and nasty. But it hadn't. It was over, it was all over and whatever sadness she felt it was swamped by the excitement of a new age – her age, hers alone.

Jo slipped into a thick, warm coat, scooped up the untouched leg of lamb and went back out into her garden, depositing the lamb under the pines for the foxes to find and then she sauntered aimlessly around, looking, checking, reassuring herself that all was as it should be. For the first time in years there was no sadness and no regret in her wanderings because she was not leaving. Silly as it sounded, she wanted to communicate this fact to everything that made up this glorious space, every plant, every bush, every tree. She felt they would somehow read her mood and know and perhaps, as the year progressed, they might celebrate even more flamboyantly with her. At this moment, it was all the celebration she needed.

She did phone the locksmith but it was not her first call, that was to Wendy. Their conversation was brief but reminded Jo that she was not entirely alone. She would tell her parents but not yet and she would say nothing to Danny for the time being as he would notice no immediate difference. The decision was not cowardice – and she hoped never again to be guilty of that – it was that she wanted to be calm and controlled, without descending into tears when she explained the situation.

Monday brought mundanity back to life: "Not porridge again?" "You said you wanted porridge." "Do I have to go to after school club?" "Yes, you always go on a Monday and just because you've fallen out with Sam doesn't make any difference. You'll be mates again by the end of the week."

As soon as Danny was safely off to school, Jo was back in the study, back on the computer, searching, annotating and pinning on her lumpy, ugly, undulating map. She rather liked it now and offered it a reprieve – substance over form, she told herself. She ran checks on the scientists mentioned in the article and obtained the phone numbers of their institutions and, after allowing for time differences, worked out when she could decently ring them.

By Tuesday, she had contacted them all and was amazed at how welcoming they had been and how much additional information they had provided, e-mailing through lists of case studies. Most were not immediately appropriate as the majority were from countries other than Britain but nevertheless Jo looked them up in a global atlas to determine their exact location.

At the end of her second full day, she sat and reviewed her map and the atlas, almost with disbelief. Although each new case had registered with her as she had discovered and marked it, it was not until she sat and reviewed her findings overall that their true import struck home – and sent a shiver through her body. Oh boy, was she on to something – a huge increase in animal attacks on humans and most of them sited in coastal areas. A distinct border of colourful pins now defined the coastline of Great Britain, stretching inland for just a few miles, and she was certain that a similar phenomenon affected the rest of the world.

The phone rang and Jo checked the display to see if it was Stephen before answering. It wasn't, it was Aggie, of Phil and Aggie Warrener, reminding her she was coming around to a simple supper on Wednesday to talk about some resident's association conflict for which sides were forming and they were recruiting her support. Something else she had forgotten but this time Jo admitted it. She could hear the disapproval in Aggie's voice and was tempted to say, sorry I've been rather busy splitting up with my husband, just to shock her. Oh dear god, she didn't want to go but... keep everything normal!

"Sorry, Aggie, I've left it a bit late to get a baby sitter but if I can, I will." Jo determined that she would not scurry around trying but would ask only Marta and if she couldn't, that would be that.

John Steen answered the phone and Jo asked if Marta was in.

"Yes she is but I'm afraid she can't baby sit, Jo."

The words were normal enough but not the way John delivered them. They were tight, sharp almost hostile and hurried out before Jo had even made her request.

"In fact, we've been thinking for a while now that sharing Marta isn't really working out. We seem to need her more and more and she simply doesn't have time to do both. Sorry, Jo, but I'm sure you'll find someone else."

There was silence whilst Jo absorbed what he had said and whilst she struggled to comprehend why John was lying to her – because he was lying, of that she was sure. It was not a considered explanation – he was fending her off.

"I see..." There was another long pause as Jo carefully chose her words. "Now tell me the real reason, John. It's me, Jo, you're talking to." Even as she spoke, she could feel alarm rising in her, a flicker of anger surfacing and a dread suspicion.

"No, that is the reason, Jo, it's just not working out – as simple as that. Nothing to concern yourself about!"

"Who said I was concerned? I'm coming round to talk to you right now, John."

Before he could reply, she slammed the phone down and went to find Danny. "I'll be back in ten minutes, I'm just popping round to the Steens. I'm on my mobile and don't answer the door to anyone and don't answer the phone, okay?" With that she was gone, driving the few hundred yards to the Steen's house with anger surging just below the surface.

As she pulled into the drive and climbed out of her car, John opened the door to her with a smile on his face but it was a nervous, uncomfortable, forced smile.

"You didn't need to come round Jo."

"Yes I did." They stood in silence with John seemingly rooted, immobile. "Are you going to invite me in?"

"Sorry, of course. Come in." He led the way into their large, traditional drawing room where Marjorie Steen was seated alongside Marta on a large sofa, both of them looking as uncomfortable as John. "You've got tea to prepare, haven't you Marta," John asked and she went to rise. Jo extended a hand:

"Please stay, Marta, because this obviously involves you. I'm going to save you all embarrassment by asking just one question and all you have to do is answer yes or no. Has this got anything to do with Stephen?"

There was no answer but eyes flashed one to the other and embarrassment settled over them like a thick fog.

"Thank you," Jo continued, "that's all I wanted to know. Now, just to make life easier for you, I think I should tell you that I kicked the bastard out two days ago and I'm divorcing him. He will never set foot in my house again. Please, Marta, I need to know the details from you – all of them. Whatever he's done, he cannot be allowed to get away with it."

Marta glanced nervously from Marjorie to John, seeking permission to answer and Jo could see that there was nervousness at not wanting to do or say the wrong thing but there was no fear in her face, in fact her eyes looked hard, determined and Jo was glad of that. John nodded to her almost imperceptibly.

"Everything, Marta, every little detail – please!" Jo encouraged.

Marta looked down at the carpet and then directly at Jo and Jo could see there was a determination about her and that Stephen was not going to be spared.

"On Saturday, Stephen came back and as it was not too late, I thought I would still go out. But he talked and he talked and said how pretty I was and what a nice figure I had and it made me feel very uncomfortable." She looked directly into Jo's eyes. "He always makes me feel uncomfortable. I thought I would leave the money until I saw you and just go but I needed it to go out with. I asked him if he had it to give to me and he took it out of his pocket. He was smiling but not nicely. He counted it very slowly and said it was a lot of money for such a short time." Marta looked away and Jo could see it was not upset that was troubling her but anger.

"He said that I had not really earned it and maybe I should do something else to make it worthwhile, something for him. He came round behind me and touched me, took hold of me, here." She indicated her breasts. "I got up and called him a shit (she pronounced the word 'sheet') but I did not want to say it loudly because I did not want Danny to hear. Because I said it quietly maybe he thought I was not serious and he took hold of me again – he moved very quickly and held me with one hand and put his other hand between my legs…" Marta tailed off. "It was not nice…"

Had Marta told her story just a few days ago, before Sunday's outburst, Jo knew she would have been mortified, distraught and in tears but now she felt nothing but an overriding sympathy for Marta and a cold, hard hatred for the man who had been her husband. She fought off the guilt that she had caused this revolting sexual assault by placing Marta in a position of risk but… she could not have known.

"What happened then, Marta?"

"He fought with me and he was strong… he was trying to… with his fingers… I said I would tell about him and he said who would believe a silly little Lithuanian girl. So I hit him, I hit him very hard, I punched him – I punched him here." For the first time she showed embarrassment as she indicated her groin region. "He fell down and cried out so I took the money and ran."

Marta clearly felt it was necessary to expand on her coolness in thinking about the money. "I took the money because you had promised it to me – it was mine. I have not always had an easy life and I have met other men who think I am just there for them, who try to use me. I will not let them win, Jo, never, not Stephen, not no one."

Jo's heart went out to the powerful, beautiful, extremely tough little young woman in front of her and quickly stepped across the room to sit beside her, putting an arm around her shoulders as she did so, sensing momentary resistance before Marta's weight leant back against her, aware that Jo was not the enemy. John and Marjorie Steen were silent throughout, utterly shocked, Jo suspected, at having accidentally alighted in a world of such overweening nastiness – a world that was beyond their experience.

"I don't even know where to begin apologising, Marta, I am just so, so sorry. He cannot be allowed to get away with it. Will you help me to nail the bastard?" The vacant look on Marta's face made Jo realise that she had not yet mastered all colloquialisms. "Help me make him suffer for it, Marta, disgrace him, make a complaint against him."

Marta shook her head firmly: "No, Jo, I won't. I beat him. That's all that matters – I beat him. If I make a big fuss and point fingers at him in front of everybody, I will lose. He will not win but I will lose."

There was a knowledge in her young face that filled Jo with wonder and she knew instinctively that Marta was speaking the truth – a truth born from experience, presumably bitter, hard-learned experience and she also knew better than to push her request.

"What can I do, Marta?"

"You say Stephen will not be at the house again?"

"No, never, ever, ever, believe me."

"Then you can ask me to baby sit again – I like Danny, he's fun." Her face lit up like a lantern and so did everyone else's.

"Is tomorrow too soon? I have something very important to do."

Chapter Twenty Six

It was to be a theatrical performance, Jo had decided. She guided Stephen's personal car up the Kingston by-pass, wanting to get rid of it from her house and return it to him as soon as possible, removing at least one excuse for him to come home. It was dark and rainy and the windscreen wipers swished and swooshed backwards and forwards and whilst the rush hour was supposedly over, there was still heavy traffic heading in both directions. She hated driving in the dark and rain and found it did nothing to release the tension that had been building inside her since midday. She would rather not have to do what she was going to do but nothing would persuade her to abandon her mission now. Never again would she surrender to cowardice!

She had applied her make-up carefully, had chosen the dark red dress that made her feel her best, in which she was comfortable but above all, in which she knew she looked good. Her hair was taken back in its usual crocodile clip but more neatly and the ear rings were long and glittery, the eye liner a little darker than normal, the mascara just a little thicker. If this was to be a women's gathering then she would attend as an obvious, sexual woman.

Past Wimbledon, around the Wandsworth one-way system and then through Battersea, glimpses of river on her left and past the Old Father Thames pub on her right, which held some very pleasant memories. Jo indulged herself in them because they reminded her of normality and took her attention away from Westminster and what she had planned. She felt the tension building the closer she got to her destination but it dented her resolution not a scintilla. It was not what she intended to do that was unnerving her but the manner in which she proposed to do it.

And suddenly there it was, Westminster bridge and beyond it, at its northerly end, the House, still brightly illuminated at this early evening hour, the cold terraces deserted but lit, the dining rooms busy as members entertained and networked, indulged their power and impressed the impressionable. The tall finger of its clock tower stood iconically upright amidst its floodlights whilst tiny flashes of tourist's cameras tried to capture images to take home to Idaho and Tokyo, Shanghai and Sheffield. Others awaited the clanging of the majestic, booming base bells as they rang out the chimes that had inspired a million nondescript little clocks across the world. The edifice itself was prettily unchanging whilst within its walls was true drama, always and ever-changing, with just a few people privy to much of it. Jo was about to become one of those few.

She found herself swallowing nervously as the car crossed the bridge, over the dark water of the Thames as it sparkled a twinkling kaleidoscope of reflected light on its sombre, ruffled surface and then she was there, gliding silkily to a halt before the members' gate.

She was known by the duty police and all the parking credentials were in order so there were no further hindrances as she quietly steered down the ramp and found Stephen's allotted space in the underground car park. She had no idea in which dining room he was entertaining his 'ladies' but no doubt the porters would know.

Jo swallowed again, momentarily daunted, as she emerged from the car park into the House proper, obtained directions and then consciously changed into character, her legs extending with each stride of her highish heels along the corridor of this ornate, historic building, her hips swivelling and gyrating in Jo's imitation of a femme fatale. She diverted into a cloakroom and sought the comfort of a loo before checking her appearance for the final time. Having satisfied herself that she looked pretty good, she exited and, suddenly there it was.

She could see through the room's open entrance, groups of

eager women standing talking to each other, drinking, laughing, being loud, ostensibly enjoying themselves as though there was no other purpose to the evening than being jolly. In truth, their eyes spun as though on gimbles, constantly flitting to their master, the prime minister in waiting, wanting to be seen, wanting to be heard, wanting to be listened to, wanting to be wanted. For this big man, with a large dressing taped over his right eye, held in his grasp the ability to offer preferment. He could make or break their careers.

Jo knew that what she was about to do was almost certainly the wrong thing and would probably unleash a storm of fury but she felt she wanted to do it – for her, for Marta, for simple, gut-pleasing revenge. Her role was to puncture pride, to deflate ego, to prick pomposity; she was an avenging angel, although she wasn't too sure about the angel bit. She wanted to see Stephen crumble in front of his disciples in such a way that she could hold on to the image of it for eternity, take it out and comfort herself with it when necessary, stroke and cosset it, hold it close to her and feel its warmth and remind herself when necessary, when she doubted herself: this was my doing.

She had decided that, having done what she had to do, if all went pear shaped, as it almost certainly would, she'd take Danny out of school and they would quickly disappear to the Canary Islands, to Fuerteventura, where they would stroll along the little town beach together and paddle in the crystal-clear waters of the Atlantic as it washed over their feet in gentle waves; and they would throw coins into to the hats of sand sculptors in admiration of their beautifully crafted dragons and skulls and embracing couples; they would swim in the sea, eat at the harbour cafes, watch the Lanazarote ferries come and go and take a glass-bottomed boat to the volcanic Isla del Lobos, peering down at the shoals of little fish as they darted to and fro, oblivious to the eyes that watched them from above and the excited, pointing fingers.

The storm could rage and they would ignore it for as long as possible. But truthfully, she knew they would come for her even there and shred her reputation, skewer her to a cross of self-righteousness with nails of spite and feigned bitterness. And they would continue relentlessly and remorselessly as though it was she who had wallowed in the pit of unconscionable self-gratification – as if it was she who was the nonce.

She headed straight for Stephen, taking a glass of wine from a passing waiter as she did so, and smiled broadly. He had spotted her immediately but the smile was not reciprocated as he stared unbelievingly, his jaw in free fall, horror painted on his immobile face.

"Sorry I'm late, darling, but better late than never. Your keys!" She pushed them into his hand. "I've brought your car up, it's in the car park. Couldn't possibly have you driving with that eye, you might crash and kill yourself and you know how I hate wearing black." Stephen stared at her unblinking, his fearful dark eyes – eye – clouded with incomprehension and fear. Had she forgiven him and was attending as he had requested or was there some other reason, something unpleasant yet to come? He remained silent, hoping it was the former, pleading silently for it to be the former.

"Well, I'd better mingle, darling – after all, that's why I'm here."

Jo turned and headed for the group of women closest to her who she knew would immediately cease their chatter as she joined them, eager to welcome Stephen's wife into their number, hoping she would provide the avenue through which they could reach Stephen. Hellos and greetings and smiles and anticipation all bellied around until Jo turned to one of their number, an overweight, superior-looking acolyte who seemed to peer at the world down her stubby nose.

"What are you hoping for – after the election – what position?" Jo enquired.

She could feel Stephen's eyes boring into her back, could taste the concern that emanated from him but he was unaware of her conversation with Marta and so his fear was not as acute as it should have been.

"Well, of course that's entirely up to Stephen but... I would be very keen to work in the treasury – I think I'm reasonably well qualified and could offer..."

Jo raised her hand, cutting her short, and ran her eyes up and down the portly figure, blatantly appraising it: "No, no, no, afraid not. Lose two stone and get a boob job or he won't even consider you."

And she moved on to the next group, barely registering the woman's open-mouthed horror but knowing that her performance was time limited and that pandemonium was but minutes away.

"How's Danny?" asked one of the number, brightly, knowing well that the way to a woman's attention is through her children.

"He's fine, lovely, although a bit lonely. I would have liked lots of brothers and sisters for him but it's not going to happen. Stephen's only interested in anal sex – so what can you do? He blames it on his public school. It could be worse…" Jo extended her free hand, pointed the index finger towards the floor and wiggled it: "Wee Willie Winky," she laughed.

And she was on the move again, leaving disbelief in her wake, picking up a fork from someone's abandoned plate before joining another, eager, welcoming party of young hopefuls, very conscious of gathering storm clouds. She positioned herself so Stephen could see her every move.

"Hello," she offered. "Which of you stands the best chance of a junior ministerial post, do you think?" Silence followed the outrageous mentioning of the unmentionable, even though it was in the forefront of all their minds. Eventually, a young, eager, studious-looking woman, fresh out of university Jo suspected, could no longer resist the opportunity to advance her cause.

"Well I'm sure we all have an equal chance but I do think my MBA from Oxford could be very useful…"

Jo leant forward conspiratorially, motioning the others into the circle, before whispering: "But do you give good head?"

The woman looked at her blankly. "I'm not sure I know what you mean." But Jo could tell she knew precisely what she meant, at least in theory, but could not believe it had been said.

"Head," Jo repeated, "you know… head!" She held her extended fingers together, placed the simulated phallus in front of her open mouth and crudely moved it backwards and forwards, watching Stephen all the while. "It'll get you a bloody sight further with Stephen than any Oxford MBA."

Stephen saw everything, stopping dead in the middle of his conversation. It was what Jo had been waiting for – the look of sheer, unadulterated, terror that froze his face. What he had feared most had come to pass and hers was not a benign visit after all. He hesitated for just a moment and then started towards her, horror on his face.

Jo knew her time was up and so raised her glass of wine in one hand and tinkled the fork against it with the other:

"Ladies, could I please have your attention – just bear with me for one minute, please."

The hubbub died down almost instantly and Jo raised her voice so it could be heard in every corner of the large, splendid room.

"In a few weeks, there will be an important election and when it's over, Stephen will be prime minister." A huge round of applause followed and Stephen stopped his advance, now just feet away from Jo, dread anticipation on his face. "He will go into the record books as one of the youngest prime ministers in British history." Again a burst of applause rang out and all eyes turned to Stephen, who managed a wan smile and a feeble acknowledgment with one hand.

Jo continued: "He will also go into the record books for another reason – he will be the first British prime minister to have the distinction of being a paedophile."

The silence was terrifying. There, I've done it, thought Jo. The nuclear ballistic missile has been ignited and is roaring its way into people's consciousness but the explosion is yet to come. There is now no avoidance of the consequences. I have declared war with a pre-emptive strike and its import will travel around the world and be recorded in history books.

She had sat on the information for at least two years, not wanting to believe it, not daring to believe it, offering excuses for him because to face the reality was just too horrendous. She had extended every doubt she could in his favour, had grasped at every reason to believe herself wrong, contorted her intellect to sanitise the reality, to diminish it, to deny it and yet all the time she knew, deep inside her, what he was. The accusation had formed in her mind so many times but she had never verbalised it.

The discovery had sprung from the search for a computer memory stick. She had looked through her own computer desk, sifted through Danny's but to no avail and in frustration, ignored Stephen's instructions never to touch that which was his and searched his desk, but again failed to find what she wanted until, at the back of the bottom-most drawer of the small chest that stood beside his computer, she found a white, unsealed envelope with the words Wadeson Enquiry scrawled on it. Inside was what she wanted but realised that this was not a spare and was going to put it back but she remembered that Wadeson was an all-party investigation into child pornography and curiosity, nothing more than curiosity, prompted her to plug it in to her computer and view its content. Stephen had never mentioned that he was involved and she wondered why not.

What Jo expected to find was the report itself or comment on it or an outlining of the party's position but none of that was there. There were, however, images – lots of images. No small children were depicted, no boys and there appeared to be no physical coercion, just image after image of very young, pubescent girls engaging in a variety of sexual acts. She estimated their age at between twelve and thirteen. Their physical development was fairly advanced but their faces were child-like; they thought themselves to be women but were still children; they were at that delicate stage of development where they believed they knew everything but in fact knew little, they were vulnerable, impressionable, gullible, malleable, fragile, exploitable. They were still at an age that, when threatened, they should be able to run home to mum, crying, seeking safety and reassurance not have to accommodate the perverted instructions of a conscienceless pornographer. Whoever was responsible for these images had stripped these children of their childhood – and she had found them by her husband's computer.

Was it the same kind of people who had hardened and calloused Marta, who had probably corruptly exploited her beauty for their own gratification, not caring that the outcome of their lust would be the erasing of her innocence, turning her into a toughened woman way beyond her years? But she had not known Marta when she made her discovery. What she had known was that the imagery, secreted away on a memory stick in an unused drawer, perfectly aligned with the alcohol-induced fantasies that Stephen from time to time whispered hoarsely in her ear when the need for sex surged through him – never quite daring to provide the detail but hinting, wheedling Jo to step down that path with him, hoping she would take the hint, the bait, give him permission to continue and adopt the persona that he wanted. She never did and so he always diverted the orchestration into something else much more benign and acceptable without ever having committed himself; without laying himself open to allegations of impropriety. But Jo instinctively knew where he was heading and did not want to go there, but allayed her fears with the assurance that fantasy was not fact and that most people's sexual imaginings were constructs that might cause jaws to drop and eyes to pop, but rarely were they translated into reality. She had suspected then, and knew now, that Stephen was different.

She also knew exactly how he would react when challenged with her find. She could rehearse his replies: 'Good god, what are you accusing me of.' 'Of course I was involved in Wadeson and I wouldn't have dreamed of discussing something so distressing with you, what do you think I am?' 'The whole thing was segmented into different areas of the problem and rated according to severity. I seem to remember that what's on that particular memory stick was considered amongst the least extreme.' 'It was some time ago and I obviously forgot about it.' And so on, and so on until he battered her into submission with reasonableness and resentful indignity. And then would have followed a diatribe of outrage at having dared to invade his important, party, parliamentary space – and it would have gone on relentlessly. So Jo merely put the stick back in its envelope and replaced it in the drawer... but not without first raising a hand of acknowledgment to the doubt that was gnawing at her – and copied it. This had been here greatest ever capitulation to cowardice, she believed. But she still had the copy!

All his excuses were laughable, mere bluff and posturing, for she had found out that he had never had anything to do with Wadeson. The images were his own, she was sure, with which he would not dare infect his hard drive, the envelope merely a cover. She was gambling on it and if it came to confrontation, investigation or litigation she would call his bluff. There would be plenty of people who would know the truth, including Lord Wadeson himself, who was not a party member and hopefully incorruptible.

Jo stood looking at the grotesque, disbelieving, silent faces which stared back at her, each frozen in mid action of whatever it was they had been doing, a busy, jolly, dynamic gathering of people turned to stone – their bizarre faces like a modern Breugel painting.

She raised her glass again. "And so I give you Stephen Aldous. And believe me, you are fucking welcome to him."

She threw its contents into his disbelieving face and saw the other eye close amidst a deluge of lukewarm, poor-quality Sauvignon Blanc. She moved quickly to the exit with what she hoped was dignity but once through the doors and into the corridor, Jo slipped her high heels off and ran down its length, her quiet footfalls echoing faintly back from the hallowed stonework and dark portraits of past premiers. Asquith and Peel, Gladstone and Disraeli, Attlee, Wilson, Thatcher and Blair. They and all the others had used this House to make momentous statements but she felt that few were as important as the statement she had just made.

It was winter, she had left her coat in Stephen's car, she had only what she stood up in but it was as nothing because she was no longer a coward. She phoned Wendy: "Got any wine in the fridge, girl? Good! Can I come over?"

Chapter Twenty Seven

"Houston, we have a problem, " Sean Murphy exploded as he burst into the committee room, followed by a panting Julie Samuels, her high heels and pencil skirt limiting the scope of her stout legs to penguin-like steps. The long, panelled room, with windows the length of one wall providing a magnificent view over the ever-moving Thames, was already beginning to fill up with MPs and advisers and the atmosphere was as sombre as a state funeral. Not a soul noticed the slowly passing river nor the barges being chugged up and down stream.

"And it's a fuckin' big problem that's not going to be solved by a few sums on the back of an old envelope," Sean added as he swirled around the long table and threw himself into a chair near the end, pushing it back on to its two rear legs, looking in turn at the drawn faces of Charlie Whiston, Harry Cunningham, Peter Macintosh and Edward Smith who were sitting alongside him. Julie remained standing, hovering behind him.

"Gentlemen, it is game, set and fuckin' match unless we come up with something as magnificently inventive as the virgin birth. She's stuffed us good and proper."

There was a natural gravitation of those standing nearby towards their press secretary and a halo of people formed around him, all with concerned faces. Elsewhere around the room, people were gathering in small groups as they engaged in deep conversation that was intimate and muted as though an omnipotent hand had turned the volume down across the entire room. There was a commonality about their gesticulations and stances, their facial expressions and the looks in their eyes. Shoulders were being shrugged and hands held out palm upwards, heads were being shaken and brows raised.

The atmosphere was mournful but there was something else, something beyond sorrow and regret – dread apprehension stalked silently around the room, passing its potentially deadly infection from one to another; each group hoping that some other group might have picked up a little morsel of hope on the grapevine, a straw that no matter how insubstantial would provide something for them all to cling to for if someone didn't do something, the ship of state would remorselessly settle by the stern ready to disappear beneath the waves in a turbulent sea of public opinion. All they got, in fact, was a reconfirmation of what they already knew, that the iceberg still lay directly ahead only a short distance away and no one had a key to the wheelhouse. The course could not be altered nor the engines slammed astern and therefore disaster awaited them, unconcealed, immovable, unavoidable.

The contrast with the last meeting to be held in this same room was stark when self-satisfied bonhomie, laughter and back-slapping confidence excited everyone as the countdown to victory progressed according to plan and each person contemplated the position they might be allotted on the resumption of power.

"It's not gone public, has it?" Paul Malins, the party treasurer, asked nervously as he stepped forward from the group that had coalesced around Sean.

"Not public, public, but if you put your ear to the ground you can hear the overjoyed rumble of malicious gossip from Southampton to Stornoway as clearly as a tube train rattling by. There were too many witnesses for it not to have got out and the press will be looking for confirmation like it was the holy fuckin' grail."

"Well. There's no option, is there? He's got to go – now, today, kill it before it mushrooms into a national scandal," he offered eagerly. "If we instantly distance ourselves the shit might not stick so badly."

"Two problems, Paul," Sean offered. "If he stands down, it immediately becomes a national scandal – the act of his resigning will guarantee it. It's an admission that he is a paedo but worse than that, he's a Tory paedo. He's our favourite son, the chosen one, our blue-eyed boy! What does it say about our judgment, eh? Not a fuckin' lot does it? Despite all the bollocks that goes into checking out a leadership candidate, all the biometric testing and other shit – trawling through the seams of his underwear, checking his granny's inside leg measurement – know what the judgment will be, do you? What people will say? We couldn't organise a piss up in a fuckin' brewery, that's what they'll say. And worse than that, it'll confirm what most people think anyway – that the best way to fuck someone up for life is to send them to public school. And that does for more than fifty per cent of you lot."

For those with an ear for detail, Sean was distancing himself from the party's privileged sons and daughters and was making a virtue of his comprehensive school education.

"Well, I don't think we can blame his actions on that…" Paul answered defensively in solid Harrovian tones and then paused before plaintively asking: "What the hell are we going to do, Sean?"

"I know what I'd like to do – take the bastard out into Parliament Square, slice his bollocks off and stuff one up each fuckin' nostril."

Sean's tabloid past was only ever sheltering shallowly beneath the surface. He then went silent, distant, and the hope was that he had started the process of crisis management and any minute he would leap to his feet and begin pacing.

"You said there were two problems," one of the group contributed. Sean came back from where he'd gone.

"Oh yeah. If he stands down and the nomination goes to Whittington, we're in the same position. You all know the polls as well as I do and he's not going to make it."

Julie tried surreptitiously to prod Sean in the back as Andrew Whittington joined the group that was discussing him, Sean turned irritatedly: "What?" but ignored the stilted inclining of her head, the jerking of her eyes to the left. "The latest poll to rate the chances of the 'also rans' reckons that if Whittington was in the frame we'd immediately drop six points behind Labour – six points – and that's confirmed by our own doorstep polls and focus groups. He's got about as much charisma as a sweaty armpit..."

"Nice one, Sean, very literate," Julie mumbled from the corner of her mouth. This time Sean did hear her but also caught sight of Andrew Whittington but clearly felt no need to offer an apology.

"I'm a journalist, Julie, not fucking Graham Greene." He made no attempt to lower his voice but threw a sop to Andrew Whittington: "A figure of speech, Andy," was the best he could muster and then immediately returned to addressing those around him.

"On top of the disastrous Whittington effect – no offence Andy – history tells us that in the last couple of weeks of any general election campaign the polls invariably move in favour of the ruling party. There's already been some narrowing – not dramatic and not terminal – but it might well continue..."

"But the campaign proper hasn't even started yet," someone else contributed.

"Even fuckin' worse," Sean snapped at him. "As I said, history shows that there's always a narrowing but all the predictions are that we're still going to win – and comfortably at that but it won't be the majority we all originally thought it would be.

"Drop Aldous and go for Andrew here," he pointed to the man in question with his fore finger, "and you guys are not going to see power for another five years at least. Not sure you'll see it even then because the stench from this affair will stick to you like shit to a blanket. So if we don't find some way of totally neutralising Nutty Norah you might as well put your head between your legs and kiss your arses good bye."

Anger was engraved into Andrew Whittington's face as starkly as the grotesque features of the gargoyles on Westminster Abbey. He tried unsuccessfully to control it as he spoke.

"As you know, Murphy, all the pre-election publicity and photo ops are concentrated on the leader and the 'also rans', as you describe us, get very little of the limelight. I'm sure if I had had the coverage that Aldous has, I would be where he is in the polls. You're not comparing like with like."

"No you wouldn't!"

There was not even the slightest concession in Sean's delivery. It was hard, brutal and totally dismissive. Julie looked at him, unconsciously and almost imperceptibly shaking her head. He never ceased to amaze her. There were things she hated about her boss but his utter directness, his refusal to be cowed even the slightest by title, position, wealth or influence still amazed her. He was so ensconced in his own world, his own ability; so permeated with self-confidence; so driven by an overpowering determination to be correct that he used honesty like a broadsword. She had lost count of the egos that he had slashed asunder, the heads that had rolled because of him and the legs of an argument he had chopped off with one swipe. She had seen people's aspirations extinguished with a few, brutally-delivered thrusts.

Julie knew that she tried to emulate her mentor and bring a similar directness and honesty into her own professional life and managed it to some extent. But she was still a poor imitation of the master because she had a conscience and he didn't. His commitment to honesty had no moral basis whereas hers did. If circumstances demanded, he would be equally as brutal in his undermining of other people's veracity and, if necessary, transform principle into its opposite, unjustly rendering opponents fools or pariahs as the need dictated. She had no desire to absorb these traits from Sean Murphy.

He continued with barely a glance at Andrew Whittington.

"You've got a brain the size of a barn, Andrew, and an ambition to match but you're... well, you're fuckin' boring. You don't connect with the public. You're one of life's natural number twos. You ain't a leader my old son and you know it, that's why you did the deal you did with Aldous.

"If you took over the reins now – much as you might think your heavenly herald is blowing his celestial bugle for you – you'd still have to overcome the handicap of being boring and not very likeable. More than that, you'd need the persuasive powers of the Saatchis combined with the miraculous ability of dear lord Jesus in order to turn the smell of shit into the scent of roses. No, the answer has to lie with Aldous and his gob-shite wife."

Sean glanced across at Charlie Whiston who had remained silent throughout Sean's risk assessment, his eyes hard and somewhere distant, his face immobile, the knuckles of one hand rapping metronomically on the table top as he held a tight-lipped conversation with Peter, Harry and George. Sean leant over and gently pushed his shoulder to attract his attention.

"Charlie!"

Whiston swiveled his face towards Sean but the focus of his eyes appeared to remain where they had previously been residing – somewhere distant.

"Don't reckon you'll last the course, judging by your face, mate. I've seen cheerier corpses." Sean laughed whilst slapping him on the back, his gallows humour designed to alleviate the sense of despair, if only peremptorily. Charlie made no response but his demeanour communicated annoyance and irritation. Sean read it and followed up with a serious question.

"Where's Aldous? Keeping a low profile or is he going to bless us with his presence and an explanation?"

"He's busy making some rather essential phone calls," Charlie responded through barely-moving lips.

"Beat's being stoned to death," Sean added before turning away and resuming his address to the semi-circle of people around him, talking to no one in particular.

"If we don't get control of this I'm going to have a fuckin' big black mark on my CV and that will not make me happy."

Even as he said it, Sean was aware that he was again adding to the wall of separation between him and the party members around him. Failure for them meant the political wilderness, another delay in the preferment of their friends, a further stalling of their political project, public humiliation and another five years of powerless, inflated, impotent rhetoric on the back benches. For him? As he had said, merely a black mark on his CV, annoyance at not finishing up on the winning side but little else. No one would impugn his abilities when the bombshell that had been dropped was almost nuclear in its intensity and fallout. The best press secretary, strategist or media adviser in the world could not mitigate the scorched earth that would certainly result – and he did include himself in that number.

On the other hand, if he could somehow – anyhow – resurrect Aldous's chances and still guide the party to victory, what extraordinary accolades would be heaped upon him, what kudos would be attributed to him! His name would be entered into the book of all-time great opinion formers and whatever people thought of him personally, they would nevertheless speak his name with reverence. And he could, of course, if he moved on elsewhere, name his own price. On the other hand, if he decided to stay, Aldous would owe him such an enormous debt of gratitude that he could engineer it so he was effectively the second most powerful man in the government. Very, very tempting!

But then Sean dismissed the latter because no one liked being beholden and particularly someone who disliked him as much as Stephen Aldous did. Give it twelve months or so and gratitude would transmute into resentment and Aldous would engineer a confrontation that would rapidly become a 'him' or 'me' situation and Sean would be out. No, he would leave after the election on a high. But first he had to engineer that high and at the moment it seemed about as likely as Whittington ever talking to him again.

"We could call her bluff," Peter Malins offered apologetically. "She hasn't offered any proof."

"Peter, to go into the House of Commons and publicly accuse a party leader – your husband at that – of being a paedo, you've got to be pretty convinced. She might be a fruit cake but she's been around politics long enough to know how things work. She knows we'll come after her and I'll bet you a pound to a pinch of shit she's got something that Stephen fuckin' Aldous won't want anyone to see.

"Even without that, you can hear the voices now, twittering like a dawn fuckin' chorus – there's no smoke without fire; no one knows a man like his wife! Be honest, half the population of Great Britain want it to be true! Personally, I don't think she has to do a single thing more, just stay quiet, stay out of the way and the poison will spread like a bloody virus. It's a bit like a fart at a party – you drop one then stand by and watch the effect.

"Anyway, if we do challenge her and she produces some god-awful stuff that proves it, I'm emigrating because this whole fuckin' place will be besieged by tattooed, shaven-headed Neanderthals with protruding foreheads and knuckles dragging along the ground, shouting 'kill the paedo, kill the paedo' and the fuckin' Sun will be oganising coaches for them.

"I don't know if we do have any options but what I do know is this," Sean pushed his seat back and made as if to begin pacing in the limited confines of the committee room. "Nothing short of a complete retraction by the barmy bitch is likely to have any effect and in all honesty, gentlemen, I don't think even that will do it because everyone will think she's just been leant on." He was still speaking to no one in particular as he slowly strode the eight paces from the window to the opposing wall and back again. It was not the energised pacing that everyone was hoping for.

Julie Samuel raised a hand and all faces swung towards her on the extremely rare occasion of her wanting to speak. No one offered her the floor but the silence which ensued was a clear invitation.

"Am I missing something here? The party leader has been accused of being a paedophile and you're slagging off his wife. Shouldn't we be trying to find out if he is one and if he is, dropping him like a ton of bricks?"

"Oh for fuck's sake Julie, this is about survival. It's none of my concern what kind of weirdo he is in his private life, it's his public life we're concerned with and how we can rescue the stupid bastard."

"Oh," she said hesitantly, "I thought morality might pop it's ugly head up somewhere."

Sean came to halt in front of her and when he spoke, the tone was patronising, verging on exasperated.

"Julie, if we were moral people we wouldn't be in fuckin' politics!"

There was a long silence before she replied.

"You mean that, don't you Sean?"

Sean clearly failed to hear the incredulity in her voice or comprehend the censorship it implied and he began pacing properly, ignoring her eyes, which followed him backwards and forwards, to and fro across the oak-panelled room, just as he was oblivious to the sounds of muffled conversation which emanated from every corner. There was, however, a sudden sense of anticipation in the room as the hopes of an entire party rested on the inspiration of a foul-mouthed, disliked, unkempt, working class, brilliant tabloid hack. At this moment they would have bequeathed him the keys to the kingdom if he could only provide the answer they were all seeking.

What they didn't know was that this time his pacing was an artifice. Normally, it was an unthinking, spontaneous reaction to a mind that was so active, so imaginative, so creative, so busy with processing a plethora of confusing information into a logical framework, that would then dictate a course of action, so energized and charged, that his physical body had no option but to mirror his brain's over activity. He saw nothing, was aware of nothing during these perambulations, his thoughts assuming almost physical proportions as though set out on pieces of paper which would be rejected, retrieved or spiked without him consciously willing the action. When they had coalesced into a plan, he stopped pacing and as far as he was aware he had gone nowhere except inside his mind. He may well have remained ignorant of his physical actions if people had not constantly commented on it.

On this occasion, however, the process was different. He was consciously pacing, hoping it would fire into action the neurones that were conspicuous by their inaction. The thoughts were not emerging from his subconscious to tumble tantalisingly across his conscious mind, waiting to be marshalled into a comprehensible pattern. He was having to haul the information out of its hiding places but his mind could do nothing with it – it was blank.

There were two issues to grasp, Sean thought. There was the behaviour of Aldous's wife but that was the simplest aspect of the problem confronting them. He could go through her actions one by one, ticking each of them off and placing them in a timeline, exaggerating, distorting, misrepresenting wherever possible, implying false motivation, excluding all mitigating factors until he had incontrovertible evidence of a mental degeneration into a dangerous no-man's land, but when it was done and he had her nailed to a cross by every extremity, where did it get him, what then? The accusation against her husband would still dominate the skyline like a setting sun.

He didn't know the answer but what he did know was that doing nothing was unacceptable. Maybe something would happen if he went through all the known information he had regarding Josephine Aldous.

She had a long-standing reputation for sometimes drinking a bit too much at party functions – okay, she was a lush, an alcoholic. She had reacted badly to her son's accident – lost her mind, had a nervous breakdown. She had started to hear voices – obviously schizoid, once chronic, now acute. She imagined that she was feeling the suffering of others. Now that one was bloody weird and needed to be handled carefully, didn't want people viewing her as some latter-day heroine – a martyr, an English Joan of Arc.

Trespassing on a perfectly legal pig farm in the dead of night – that was not normal; bonkers for the wife of a senior politician. But... a bit dodgy that one because of the gloss he had put on it for the media, but nevertheless... what could be done could just as easily be undone. Speaking against her husband at an important public meeting? Even more weird, more troubled, confused, out of touch with reality – even if he was a twat! Believing that the animals were attacking us, fighting back against exploitation – a collapsing mind, whatever pseudo-scientific drivel some newspaper might have published to spark her delusion. Christ, she better than anyone should know what shit they publish. But the vicious attack on her husband, almost blinding him...?

Sean chuckled to himself. It was the only one of her actions for which he felt great sympathy and was prepared to excuse without even hearing her defence. But! Her son was now at risk of this violent, schizophrenic mother and that was very fertile territory! An allegation of her husband being a paedo – that had to be the end game, surely there wasn't anywhere more damaging she could go from there? Was there? Or did she have some more tinder-dry facts to toss onto the blazing funeral pyre?

Sure, he could put together some truly shitty, in-depth stories that would destroy her reputation for the rest of her life. They would be tearful with regret, dripping with concern, laced with anguish – but they would nevertheless screw her for all eternity. But how public did the party want to go with all this stuff because once it was in the public domain it would develop an existence entirely of its own and may possibly rebound on them. But… and it was a huge but… would it be enough to destroy her paedo claim about Aldous? He doubted it and certainly not in its entirety. Like the pain of an amputated limb, it would return again and again to remind a wearisome electorate of the degenerate nature of one who would be king.

And then, of course, there was the second issue. Did she have anything on Aldous – anything physical she could hold aloft in her hand; anything she could point to; anything that had his fingerprints on it, metaphorical or otherwise? He would bet his bank balance she did and it was this that was numbing his brain. She'd got them all by the bollocks unless he could not only destroy her veracity but also prevent corroboration whilst at the same time slamming shut the little locker of revelations into which she might delve again!

"What do you think, Sean?" An anonymous voice from nowhere brought him back into the orbit of the room's despair.

"What do I think? What do I fuckin' think? I think we should take a contract out on the barmy bitch." He was only half joking as it was the sole solution that ticked all necessary boxes.

"Sean, anteroom three, now please!" Charlie Whiston got up from his seat purposefully and the speed with which he moved indicated to Sean that something was afoot. He half suspected it might be an admonishment for having been so dismissive of Andrew Whittington if he was now their chosen replacement but Charlie wouldn't dare call him to account over that, like a naughty schoolboy. Peter Macintosh, Harry Cunningham, Edward Churchill Smith and George Fiennes followed behind Charlie like a sombre delegation, all imbued with the same sense of purpose. Sean tagged on behind and Julie brought up the rear.

As they reached the door of the ante room, Charlie turned and raised a hand like an elderly, well-dressed policeman on point duty.

"No Sean, not Julie. This is a need to know only meeting."

"Charlie, if I need to know then Julie needs to know, that's how it works."

"Sean..."

"No mate, it's not up for discussion. If you trust me then you trust Julie!"

Charlie hesitated as the other two elders made their way into the small chamber.

"Very well, but I'm not happy."

"None of us is exactly fuckin' delirious, Charlie."

They followed the others into the small, neat room with its leather upholstered library chairs and book-lined walls but no one sat down and they stood facing each other in two lines, the party men facing Sean and Julie. Sean could see by their stance and body posture that this was Charlie's show and whatever they had discussed together it was Charlie who was going to communicate it.

"Sean, we want you to catalogue the incidents of Josephine Aldous's rather unusual behaviour of the past few months. I'm sure you'll be able to chart the serious decline of a woman under pressure, a woman who is struggling to cope... if you understand my meaning...!"

"Like crystal, Charlie. I've just been doing precisely that. And...?"

"We need some well-placed stories which, whilst deeply sympathetic, won't shirk from reporting these uncomfortable truths."

Sean smiled. "I was there before you but it's very risky..."

Again Charlie held his hand up to stop Sean's flow.

"Let me finish. I don't want them placed until I say so but my guess is it will be two, maybe three day's time. Now, I have called a private meeting for this afternoon – a very private meeting – at which we will all be present along with Stephen and Professor Anton Kadynski."

They were clearly all mandated as there was nothing in

Charlie's tone that would brook any excuse, any absence for a prior engagement. Without him having to spell it out, the importance of what he was demanding hung heavily in the air. A slow, incredulous little smile began to tweak Sean's face into a tableaux of disbelieving admiration.

"Oh Charlie, Charlie – if you're going where I think you're going with this, then I am in awe of you. You've out-schemed me, that's for sure."

Charlie ignored Sean's contribution and continued as though he had not spoken.

"We are arranging a meeting with Josephine at her house hopefully tomorrow..."

"She won't agree," Sean interrupted.

"Protecting the health and safety of her child in these dangerous, terrorist-riven times, when both are obvious targets... I think she will." There was absolute assurance in Charlie's words which Sean did not doubt.

"Stephen will have to agree to what you've got in mind and he won't do that, he's her husband..." Sean paused and thought about what was at stake, reminded himself of Stephen's single-minded obsession with the top job, considered the ignominy of the alternative and the polarised options that faced him. It was either him or his wife... humiliation or glory. "Will he?" It was the question mark that hovered over the end of his question that gave Sean an immediate answer. "Yes he fuckin' will, won't he?"

Chapter Twenty Eight

Josephine Aldous was angry. She was both the cause and the target of an anger that had her moving blindly from one room to another, ostensibly with a purpose but each journey proving fruitless, the objective obliterated by a mind so seething with disbelief at her own complicity that it erased all else. She picked objects up and banged them down again for no apparent reason; she switched the radio on and off again as though it had offended her and she swore – not single words but strings of profanities: "Shit, shit, shit, shit, shit, bloody shit..."

She had finished with Stephen, placed him in the stocks and hurled such ordure at him that he would be lucky ever to erase its stench. It was justice, retribution, just desserts, karma and any other expression of fairness she could unearth but his presence still smothered her like a stultifying blanket. She did not want anyone from his party, none of his self-interested or sycophantic acolytes invading her territory, excusing their scheming with manufactured concerns for her son's safety.

She and Danny should have done what she had flirted with doing, taken her escape route and immediately climbed aboard a plane to the Canary Islands. But she hadn't and she had agreed to see Kadynski because of his warnings, in the quiet hushed tones of someone who pretended to care, of his expressed concern for their wellbeing, expounding the unknown dangers that might stalk her and Danny in a violent, uncertain world filled with bigots and jihadists; and it was essential that the preparedness of the emergency services was at its very best with the right blood on hand, skin tissue, compatible donated organs and a host of other safeguards which they could have standing by if only they had all the information they needed.

And there was, unspoken but heavily hinted at in apocalyptic tones, specific dangers from conscienceless organisations who might already have Danny and her in their cross hairs, might already have sown the seeds of some dreadful biological disease that only instant diagnosis and action could nullify.

"Far, far better to check now so that we start with a clean bill of health!"

She didn't believe him, she didn't believe anything he had to say because he was trying too hard, trowelling the sincerity on like icing on a cheap wedding cake; he was too insistent, too desperate, too ingratiating and her instincts were to say something rude and bang the phone down. But… but, but? What if there was some small nugget of truth in what he said, just a glimmering of fact amidst the self-serving, over-conciliatory rhetoric? And if she dismissed him and his warning came to pass and Danny fell victim, what would she do then? It would be unbearable, unliveable with.

And so she succumbed to the wheedling but only for this one occasion – and she already regretted her decision, profoundly regretted it but it was not too late: she could walk out of the door and go somewhere distant, anywhere to avoid him but he, or someone like him, would return later that day, tomorrow, the day after and the day after that – even this visit, if she stayed and confronted it, would not be the last. It would merely be the beginning of a process of attempted brow beating and threat, of oppressive persuasion, ridicule and insinuation. It would be followed by credit cards that didn't work, frozen back accounts, dark and ominous telephone calls in the middle of the night, cars that would no longer start, spiteful rumours launched on the wings of manufactured gossip and god knows what else.

She would be transformed into the bitch from hell and her life would be unbearable until she crawled over their red-hot coals, forced herself through the gauntlet of vicious flaying by their angered knives and prostrated herself in front of them and retracted every word, implored them to forgive her, begged for their absolution. And then, her penance would be to humiliate herself even further before the world's media, cowed, defeated, beaten; a croaking, bowed, tearful shell of an eviscerated wanton, simpering her apologies in monotone, blaming a mind that had disintegrated.

It would be the demons within her who had traduced her loyal husband not her, and Stephen, of course, would be standing beside her with concern etched into his every feature; love, understanding and forgiveness reflected in his sad eyes, a man who had been to hell and back but was eagerly prepared to excuse all so long as his darling wife, the mother of his child, was back from the dark places she had so recently retreated to.

He could go screw himself, they all could! But refusing to see Kadynski would not make it go away so she would use this opportunity to set out her position in great clarity and would not retreat from it. There would be no apology, no retraction and no accommodation. The sooner the process was started, the sooner it would hopefully be ended.

But Jo knew it would continue until after the election, until Stephen was firmly ensconced in the seat of power – or not! And that was her greatest hope. Once they realised that she was not for turning, she prayed that they would dump Stephen and with him gone, some of the desperation would be erased from the equation but not all of it because her accusation reflected on the entire party. But she also knew that they would be desperate to discover if she had any evidence to back up her allegation and, just as desperately, they would also want to know if there were other, as yet unspoken, skeletons rattling around in the dark and private corridors of their chosen leader's life.

She would keep them guessing for whilst they feared her there might be some possibility of controlling the onslaught that was to come. On the other hand, it could make her extremely vulnerable.

When the full import of what she was thinking filtered through into her consciousness, she found her breath deserting her and her hands beginning to tremble. This was utterly ridiculous, she told herself, but her mind refused to listen and the corrosive fear that it generated began to erode her self-belief. They wouldn't kill her, surely they wouldn't kill her, the idea was simply ludicrous. The truly terrifying thing was that no matter how hard she tried to dismiss the prospect, it clung like a cheap perfume because she felt that now they were threatened, they were capable of almost anything.

Unaware that she was doing so, she snorted briefly, dismissively. Such doubts were merely a product of the stress she was enduring, she tried to tell herself, but still a residual doubt hung on perniciously, refusing to entirely relinquish its grip. Was she out of her depth? Probably because she was not a creature of politics or intrigue, despite having been exposed to both for so long. And there was no one to whom she could begin to articulate her fears. The only people she knew who were politically aware enough to advise her were on the wrong side of the divide. Even those who hated Stephen would offer advice that promoted their interests and not hers. Reece was too honest to have any understanding of it all and Wendy operated in an entirely different world.

She suddenly felt a desperate need to talk to Wendy, share her fears with her, sound out her opinion but in reality, she simply wanted to hear the voice of someone without artifice, a friend. Even that was not the real reason, she admitted to herself. She was afraid and wanted someone to hold her hand, someone she could trust and whose presence would diminish Jo's concerns to mere wraiths. Together they could make light of whatever was to come and when they had defeated it together, they could high-five each other in celebration.

But here she was, little Josephine from St Bride's, who had never had to confront anything of substance throughout her entire life, had never even made prefect or games captain or even form captain, taking on the entire establishment in a full-frontal onslaught entirely on her own, the impact of which may already have reverberated around the world, causing a ripple of lurid headlines in every democracy – if they had not managed to keep a lid on it. Even if they had so far exercised control, it was only a matter of time before the explosion shook their institution to its roots.

She had avoided all news sources and so had no idea whether

the story had broken or not. If it had and the whole thing was public then they would have to proceed with caution but if it hadn't then she was probably more vulnerable. She had arranged for Danny to be taken to and brought back from school so had no idea if the press hyenas were preparing to dine on her. Whatever the situation, her instincts had told her to agree to the meeting and so she had.

What she wanted now was to have it over with and then, this evening, after school, she would root herself firmly back in the real world by taking Danny to the pictures and for a Chinese meal and he could even have a coke. They would laugh and he would practice with chopsticks until he became bored with them and they would share a toffee banana and the monsters would retreat back into the shadows from whence they came.

But she knew that even that was dependent upon whether the story had broken or not. If it had and she set a foot outside the protected acres of St George's Hill, she would be overwhelmed by a predatory pack of hacks and paparazzi.

Anger had now drained itself out of Jo's emotions but had been replaced by apprehension. She found herself yawning constantly and the instinct to fight was being subverted by a desire for flight. She had forgotten this leaden feeling, one that had dogged her every visit to the dentist when a child. The reverie, however, was short lived as she heard the sound of tyres on the drive outside and saw from the kitchen window a large, shiny car swing around the turning circle so that it was facing back whence it came.

She knew Anton Kadynski vaguely from party meetings and was reminded of his appearance as he climbed out of the driver's side, neat, be-suited, middle aged, bow-tied – something she hated on men as emasculating. He was tall and healthily built, good looking and oozed confident affluence but not accidentally, she suspected. It was a statement of position and authority, a construct of how he saw himself – successful, authoritative and someone to be respected, even revered. But that was not unusual amongst consultants of any discipline, she thought.

From the passenger's side emerged a very different person with a much less distinguished persona. Although much

younger than Kadynski he was in every sense a grey man – grey
clothes, grey skin, grey hair but not really grey, rather a lifeless
pale black that failed to reflect so much as a glimmer of light
from its lank and unwashed strands. He stooped slightly as he
moved forwards as though his tenure on life was reluctant,
bothered, burdened. He was of medium height – in fact
everything about him appeared medium as though not daring
to compete with the flamboyance of his master, for there was
no doubt as to who was the master. He was the dowdy hen to
Kadynski's resplendent cock.

Jo made her way to the front door to greet them,
apprehension swelling inside her until it challenged the limits
of her stomach and she gave a theatrical shudder to remind her
body that what she wanted, needed, was battle-readiness not
the emasculating effects of fear and doubt.

"Josephine, it's been a long time," Kadynski said as he
extended a hand, enfolding hers with his other hand when she
grasped it. They stepped into the hallway, Kadynski smilingly
relaxed, offering no indication of the visit's import. "This is my
houseman, doctor James Dawson." Hands were again shaken
but Jo replied not a word to either of their pleasantries but led
them through to the drawing room. Now that battle was about
to commence, confidence once again coursed through her veins
for these were but men and she knew that she had their measure.

"I don't want this to take long, Professor Kadynski. It is you
who asked to see me so I would like you to state your reasons
clearly and without embellishments as we both know the real
reason why you're here – because the party is convulsing itself
as a result of my…" There was a pause as Jo searched for the
correct word, one that had inherent gravity and would not
diminish her actions, but it wouldn't come. "…revelation." She
eventually offered.

"Quite, quite," Kadynski replied as he tried to ignore the
embarrassment that swirled around the room like a spectre.

Jo realised they were all still standing and silently indicated
for them to sit.

"These are very stressful times for everyone," Kadynski
offered in a tone that seemed to drip world-weariness from

every syllable, "and for you in particular, if I might say, what with your son's accident and so on."

Jo was not seduced by his laconic manner and was sharply aware that it was the 'and so on' that really interested him. "What I'm not clear about, Professor Kadynski, is why an eminent psychiatrist should concern himself with me and my son's physical safety. Or perhaps it's not my body that concerns you, but rather my mind?" The question was issued as a challenge.

"It's the whole person, Josephine, the whole person that concerns me because the one influences the other, but then of course, you know that. We will be taking some samples, as I think my office indicated, and checking various physiological aspects but I also wanted to run over a few..." he dramatised the pause by tilting his head back and casting his eyes upwards, as though this was the first time he had considered the proposition, "...a few of the reports that are circulating concerning you."

Having manipulated the conversation to where he wanted it, he then proceeded at a pace as though urgency would camouflage its content.

"I never believe in gossip and it is my golden rule always to return as close as possible to the source to check accuracy, background, intent. Some of these allegations are concerning, in fact quite damaging, so now is the opportunity to lay them to rest."

A prickle of concern concentrated Jo's mind.

"If you're going to delve into anyone's psyche, Professor Kadynski, then I suggest you start with my husband. I called him a paedophile because that's what he is. Either we concentrate on the perceived threats to me and my son or I end this now."

"As far as your son is concerned, perhaps you are one of the perceived threats..." he delivered the bombshell and again paused before adding in mitigation "...if the gossip is to be believed. And that's why I think we should tackle this head on, defuse it, refute it, if it deserves to refuted. Not talking about it can only exacerbate the situation."

Jo felt her heart thumping with adrenaline and anger bellied up inside her but she was determined to control it. Do not react, she told herself, as she remained motionless, breathing deep breaths. Do not assume anything until you have a clear picture of his thinking, his intent, she told herself. What is his real purpose in being here? Remain calm, do not react, lead him on until you know precisely what it is you're facing.

It took Jo long seconds before she responded and all of them were devoted to quelling the upsurge of anger. Eventually she spoke and struggled to keep her voice flat and unemotional.

"Perhaps you had better explain yourself." Jo was happy with her efforts and could see that this was not the reaction that Kadynski had expected. Momentarily, he looked flustered.

"Well, where shall we start?" He was like a salesman deploying the age old response of 'I'm glad you asked me that question', while he searched for the answer to it. She had seen her husband deploy similar tactics a thousand times. "Please understand Josephine that there is nothing pejorative about anything I say – I am entirely neutral – but unless I put to you those things that seem, on the face of it, to offer cause for concern...

"Concern to whom, Professor Kadynski? I have left my husband – permanently – I intend to play no further part in anything the party does, I will never attend another meeting of any kind. I'm out, as they say, so who's concerned?"

"It isn't that easy, I'm afraid. The ripples of your actions will continue for a long time yet. And it is incumbent upon me, as an interlocutor so to speak, to chart a path through this... mess... to ensure that everyone's interests are protected." It seemed that any pretence at protecting her and Danny's physical safety had been abandoned and Jo now understood why she had been told that it wasn't necessary for Danny to attend this first meeting – preferable that he didn't.

"You're a self-appointed interlocutor. I didn't ask for you to intercede."

Kadynski smiled and turned his hands palm upwards as though to say, 'don't be so naïve,' and then continued: "I think we have to look at issues – issues concerning you, experiences you have had – as a whole. For example, drinking too much isn't a huge problem in itself…

"How come you're pretending concern about me when half your MPs drink far more than I do but that, of course, is okay isn't it, boys being boys? How much I drink, when and where is no one's business but mine. Are we clear about that? Perhaps you should try living with Stephen before you sit in judgment on me."

Kadynski shook his head, smilingly.

"Like I say, it isn't a problem, Josephine… on its own. However, in the context of hearing voices, having visions, believing you're a receptacle for pain – animals' pain – and having the delusion that animals are attacking humankind in a global display of compulsive retribution… well, it takes on a slightly different dimension, don't you think?"

Jo did not reply, could not reply, as anger was charging around inside her like a demented blue bottle, desperately seeking an escape route through which to vent itself. If she opened her mouth to speak it would fly free and Kadnynski would be dismembered in an onslaught of foul-mouthed abuse. She merely held the man in her unblinking gaze, her eyes hard and hate-filled, her mouth set, one hand clenching the other until her knuckles showed white. Kadynski appeared to be oblivious to her barely-concealed anger and continued in his level, moderate, intimate, reasonable, infuriating tone.

"When all this is combined with displays of serious, uncontrolled violence then, much as it grieves me to have to say this, I think there is cause for concern, great concern, particularly when a child is involved. But, of course, I'm sure we can improve that situation quite simply these days. Really, all it requires is some acknowledgment from you that there are problems and you are willing to confront them and then we can swing a whole range of support behind you. The alternatives could be very difficult, not to say distressing for you."

So this was it! Jo now knew precisely where they were headed. This highly-qualified, arrogant, avaricious wealth seeker was prostituting his profession to save the party that had offered him preferment. God knows what additional inducements were on offer should he succeed in salvaging their electoral prospects. But the threat, although unspoken, was crystal clear. Either she prostrated herself and appealed for forgiveness and help, admitted her allegations were baseless, beat her breast with a tearful acknowledgment of mea culpa, or Stephen would try to take Danny away from her – with the support of an eminent psychiatrist – one Anton Kadynski – branding her an unfit, dangerous mother.

She was vaguely conscious of a large white vehicle scrunching outside and which came to a halt in the periphery of her vision and she was relieved, delighted at the timing of this delivery, whatever it was. Such normality would strip away this oppressive, offensive, threatening atmosphere that had been created. Kadynski nodded to Dawson with a barely discernible movement of his head and the grey doctor rose from his seat and headed towards the hall.

"I'll get it!" Jo snapped at him but he ignored her. However, before she followed him out she wanted to deal with Kadynski. It was a threat that he offered, nothing more, a threat she was prepared to face and was confident she could defeat. They wouldn't dare take it to court – would they? Patience had exhausted itself.

"Kadynski – fuck off!" The words were spat out with bitterness and Kadynski lowered his head, which he was shaking gently in a soft, regretful 'no'. When he raised it again he was still moving it from side to side and the rueful smile on his lips was patronising, like a father about to admonish his child, wishing he didn't have to but knowing it was necessary.

Jo was aware of movement behind her and turned to see Dawson re-entering the room carrying a doctors' bag and accompanied by two large women in nurses' uniforms, one was black, one white. Their faces were set with a wearied boredom and they seemed entirely disinterested in the surroundings or Jo. They came to halt on either side of her a few feet away whilst Dawson hovered as though unsure what precisely he should do.

"What the hell is going on?" she demanded.

"Josephine," the psychiatrist breathed as part of a deep sigh.

"For your own safety, that of your son and the public at large, I have no option but to section you under the Mental Health Act, 2010. It will be a section four, thirty-day observation and treatment order…"

The words washed over Jo without her comprehending them. There was a threat, a real threat, she was acutely aware of that but she could not grasp precisely what it was, what it meant, what he was saying, what they were intending to do. It was as though she had stepped into a play half-way through and understood neither the plot nor the dialogue.

"…I can promise you we will take very good care of you and I have every hope of a full recovery but it will require your full co-operation…"

Little by little, the import of what Kadynski was saying began to slowly filter through the unreality of the situation and her mind flushed out the incomprehension that had taken it hostage:

"Get out of my house," she said quietly. She repeated it a second time but louder, more aggressively: "Get out of my house!" And then again but this time she screamed it over and over again, spittle flying from her lips, her body arched forwards towards Kadynski, one arm gesticulating towards the door: "Get out of my fucking house you bastard, get out, get out, get out…"

She saw Kadynski nod and felt powerful hands grasping her arms and she struggled to shake them off but they held tight as though moulded from concrete. She threw herself from side to side but there was no yielding in the powerful determination of the practiced hands that held her. "Get off, get off, get off me…" The screams were unreal, ear-piercing, uncontrolled, frightened – they were the kind of screams that had disturbed her sleep in the dark of night for some time past.

Dawson had been fumbling in his bag and his hand appeared from within its Gladstonian leather holding a syringe and reality burned itself into Jo's consciousness. She had been branded as mad and was about to be taken away to somewhere she did not know, did not want to know. She was the sacrificial lamb.

Her protests turned into uncontrolled screams and she kicked at Dawson as he approached her but the futility was reinforced by the two women effortlessly forcing her to the ground, onto her back, one grasping her arms, the other sitting on her legs, nullifying any further dissent other than the screams which continued, unabated, a jumble of mal-formed, partly formed words struggling to take shape in a shrieking, screeching, wailing, outpouring that tore at the flesh of her throat as it exited her mouth. She felt the needle's sharp hurt as it penetrated her skin but still she continued with her futile struggle until the effort became too great, too exhausting as the weight of her limbs began pressing her to the ground without the assistance of those who held her. The screaming was transmuted into guttural, base, almost muted grunts like those of an animal as her tongue refused to respond to her demands and her muscles and mind slipped remorselessly beneath a tide of heavy, viscous, smothering impotence that rendered everything but breathing almost impossible.

Arms pulled her upright and impelled her towards the waiting ambulance, half carrying, half dragging her and she could offer no resistance whilst her mumbling finally took on a just-comprehensible form, like that of an old drunk collapsed by the side of an alleyway. "Danny... Danny... my son... my son."

Chapter Twenty Nine

The tap at Sean Murphy's office door was followed by its sudden opening, the door flung wide, and Charlie Whiston's energetic entry into the room.

"It's done," he offered in an entirely neutral voice. "She's on her way!" It was the first time he had spoken to Sean since the meeting with Kadynski and Stephen the previous day at which Sean's assessment of Stephen Aldous's likely compliance had been proved correct.

Sean beckoned to him to be seated but it was superfluous as he was already in the process of fetching a chair to place in front of Sean's extremely untidy desk. They were the only occupants of the room.

"I need those articles placed for tomorrow," Charlie continued. "The whole Stephen thing is still running as rumour, diary pieces, no confirmed sources, that type of thing. She has to be so thoroughly discredited that no one would believe her if she told them the time of day and wouldn't dare give this story any further credibility. With official confirmation of her having a profound illness, I think we can start to put this campaign back on course."

"No probs. It's all set up. A few phone calls and we're away. Where is she?"

"Well, Stephen was all for checking her into the Priory but I had to explain that with a general election just a month away it might look a little elitist, a little out of touch with ordinary people, to check her into probably the most expensive private clinic in London. Far better a state-of-the-art NHS facility – more sensitive."

Sean chuckled.

"And Kadynski isn't in charge of the Priory! I presume she's at his place out at Egham?"

"Yes, but don't include those details in the articles – no names just the very best NHS care available, that sort of thing... taken into temporary protective care for her own good..."

"Charlie! Granny and eggs and all that... Surely to Christ she didn't go voluntarily, did she? I can't believe that."

"No, of course not. She was sectioned. A thirty day order."

Sean did a quick calculation: "Bloody wonderful, old chum, she gets out the day before the election. Brilliant timing."

"Don't be silly – we'll get it extended. Kadynski's got a lot riding on us winning. There's a whole big research grant waiting for him amongst other things."

"That was the quid pro quo, was it?" Sean asked with a trace of accusation and Charlie inclined his head meaninglessly, which neither confirmed nor denied the question. "Anyway, it's a relief and you're right, we might, just might, be back in business but I still have an uneasy feeling that this thing could come back and bite us on the arse."

"I think we're probably alright – we managed to find her evidence about Aldous!"

"So the bloody perv was at it. Where was it?"

"On her pc. Got some of our IT boys in there after Kadynski had finished, found it almost immediately. It could have been worse but it would have been enough to bring our campaign to a full stop. Young tarts who would probably have been married if they'd been born amongst our Arab friends. They've taken the machine away and are trawling though it now to see if there's anything else that might discomfit our erstwhile leader." The last words were said with weariness.

"That's a fuckin' relief – so she wasn't making it up, then? What a way to stuff your old man. Funnily enough, on the few occasions I met her, I quite liked the woman, despite all that's happened. I always had a bit of respect for her but I think it was more to do with her refusal to hide her contempt for her old man. Cost her dear in the end, though!"

"Collateral damage, Sean, a casualty of war," Charlie said almost triumphantly.

"More like a victim of friendly fire," Sean replied with a chuckle, which sounded more contrived than spontaneous. Uncomfortable as it was, he now had to reassess his opinion of this fading old remnant of the ancient regime because he had revealed, without anguish, a ruthlessness which had almost shocked even Sean. Worse than that, he had thought of the solution and Sean hadn't – he had been usurped and upstaged and that was an uncomfortable feeling for someone who had built his reputation in the party on inventiveness and infallibility. Both had deserted him on this occasion, which was corrosive to his image.

His consolation was that no one involved would talk about what had happened as they would want it to evaporate quietly, unremarked. But Sean wasn't so sanguine. They might have got the mad woman incarcerated in the West tower but he was prepared for weird banging noises and nocturnal screams that would chill the blood. What was a short-term solution could yet turn into a long-term debacle. Please god not until after the election when he would be out of here.

He focused his thoughts back on the present.

"She had to go though, Charlie. Had to go! All that bollocks about the animals fighting back against human domination. If that's not barking I don't know what is."

Charlie smiled enigmatically.

"Actually, Sean, she's quite right about that, at least."

"What?"

"I don't know if it's human domination they're fighting against but they're certainly fighting and we humans are the target!"

"No, no, no! I'm not in the mood!"

"Sorry, but it's true."

"No, You've been on the old Bollinger haven't you. Tell me you're joking Charlie. You're taking the piss, aren't you?"

"Unfortunately, I'm not Sean. We've been tracking this phenomenon for some time now and it really is happening – it's serious, and getting more so by the day."

The one thing Sean could tell for certain was that the old boy was deadly serious and he was not someone given to self-delusion: "Where, how, why?"

"It's all around the coast, stretching inland about nine or ten miles but that zone is expanding, slowly admittedly, but it is expanding all the time. Getting treatment for Josephine..."

"You mean getting her out of the way and saving the party's bacon..." Sean knew that Charlie was quietly settling himself into justification mode, engaging in a role play of pretence that what they had done was justified, necessary, in Jo Aldous's best interests and the more he kept up this pretence, the sooner he would wrap himself entirely in it, almost believing it. Sean Murphy felt absolutely no need to sanitise his role in what was a pretty scandalous abuse of power but he could justify it and that was sufficient. He could not stand even a whiff of sanctimoniousness.

"Speak, Charlie, tell me more."

"As I was saying, getting treatment for Josephine was only part of the problem; we also needed to put a lid on this phenomenon until we can decide what best to do about it. She was in danger of making it public."

"Just a minute, Charlie, just a minute. Before you get yourself all wrapped up in the justification of it all – what the fuck is happening – in simple terms please – remember it's me you're talking to."

"Farmed animals – all animals for that matter – in this very defined area are... well, they're attacking people, not just attacking them but they're killing them, and in increasing numbers."

Sean could sense that Charlie was embarrassed by what he was saying as though he expected not to be believed, that what he was saying was, quite simply, unbelievable. "I know, I know, it sounds odd, not to say bizarre, but I'm afraid it's true."

"Why? What the fuck's going on Charlie? I mean, are you sure?"

"Unfortunately, Sean, there's no doubt about it. As to why, we don't know."

"You must have some fuckin' idea." Sean was still not sure whether to take Charlie seriously but his instincts dictated that the man did believe what he saying and had to be given credence. Such a ludicrous wind-up was simply not in his character. Was the old bugger trying to manipulate him in some way? Considering the joint enterprise they had just been involved in and which would undoubtedly hang over them forever like the sword of Damocles, and which depended entirely upon mutual trust to remain out of sight, Sean somehow doubted it. But did the fact that Charlie believed it make it kosher? Sean wasn't sure.

"I know you don't involve yourself in anything which isn't strict party politics, Sean," Charlie replied, "so you're probably unaware that we, as a nation that is, we've been pouring pollution into the oceans for decades – domestic, industrial and military. Although we in Europe have theoretically stopped actual dumping now, many countries haven't – and in any case, it's still pouring out of factory chimneys and incinerators, ours included to some degree. The upshot is that every marine creature that exists in every ocean in the world is contaminated with trace elements of all kinds of rather unpleasant chemicals – PCBs, dioxins, flame retardants – in fact, some three hundred have been identified so far and on top of that there's mercury and a whole array of heavy metals. At the moment the levels are low but at higher concentrations their impact on health can be pretty profound – cancer, infertility, birth defects, disruption of the central nervous system and a host of other nasties.

"Our boffins originally thought this rather noxious cocktail might be the cause but they've been unable to identify any vector that would explain its spread from ocean to land. Few of the creatures involved actually eat fish. It's also complicated by the fact that dioxins, PCBs and the like are distributed over land as well as the sea and infect crops, grass in particular simply because there's so much of it.

"Of course, grazing animals such as cows and sheep consume vast amounts of grass and, with it, the toxins that then accumulate in their bodies – mostly the fat. It follows that if this was the sole cause, the attacks would be happening inland as well as around the coast. They are trying to assess if levels in animals away from the coast are lower than those near the sea and so haven't yet reached the tipping point which triggers this aggressive reaction. There so far doesn't seem much evidence to support the idea."

Sean could tell that Charlie had memorised phrases he had read in briefing documents and was regurgitating them but rather than making him sound knowledgeable, erudite, it gave the impression of a not particularly bright sixth-former cramming for his A levels.

"Fuck me, Charlie, I didn't have you down as an environmentalist. You're going to have to grow your hair and buy an anorak," Sean chuckled.

"It doesn't come naturally to me, I'll give you that, but needs must. This information has been piling up and in the end it was decided that someone really ought to have a look at it, privately, quietly as it were, before it went to any shadow minister and developed a life of its own. Didn't want to start a hare running unnecessarily. Got me to take charge of it because they know my cynicism about most things environmental. If I was convinced by it they would know it was serious."

"You mean they punted it into the long grass? Isn't the government doing anything? Christ's sake, it's their watch!"

"We're not sure if they've even identified it yet but we feel they probably have. We assume they're terrified it might rebound on them; lay them open to accusations that they've put industry before the environment when they've been boasting endlessly of their green credentials. Truth is, with death rates climbing, it may be they just want to get through to the election without it biting them on the bally backside. They expect to lose and can then simply walk away and wash their hands of it, leaving us to take the difficult decisions.

"If by any chance they do win, they've got five years to try and swing opinion behind the very difficult policies they will have to introduce. To be honest, they're not putting a great deal of energy into this campaign and it may be that they don't particularly want to win because of this. I don't think we would if we didn't have better networks for hiding things, dissembling, the kind of thing that requires very good contacts and a generous measure of self-interest."

"Well what are you waiting for Charlie, nail the fuckers with it." Sean was becoming animated because the subject had suddenly taken on a party political dimension and he knew precisely what to do with that.

"Not that easy, I only wish it was."

"If you don't get it out into the public domain right now, from what you've said, we'll have to pick up the fuckin' tab for it. Come on, Charlie, we need to nail the bastards with anything we can lay our hands on."

"Let me finish Sean and you might appreciate the complications…"

"…Hang on a minute. What did you mean – every sea creature has been contaminated. Are you speaking figuratively?"

"No, that's a simple statement of fact. I'm not a scientist, Sean, but it seems that when these substances get into sea water they settle in the mud and sand and are consumed by worms and…" he clearly couldn't think of anything other than worms "…whatever creatures there are on the bottom; or they float around in the water and are absorbed by the simple plants and creatures of the oceans – phytoplankton and zooplankton."

From Charlie's smugness, Sean divined that the old man had assumed that his working class press officer would be ignorant of the terms he had used – a little twist designed to reinforce the difference in their backgrounds, but Sean didn't give a toss. He never played games and if he didn't know something he would say so.

"Okay, Charlie, what the fuck are they?"

Charlie continued with smug self-satisfaction.

"They are, Sean, the minute plant and animal growths, embryos, eggs, minuscule creatures that form the basis of the food chain. They get eaten by slightly bigger creatures along with the worms, and so on and so on up the food chain until you get to the big sea creatures, the big predators at the top. As you move up the chain, the chemical poisons become more and more concentrated and although you've probably never thought about it, we are right at the top of the food chain, Sean.

"You know in Japan they eat dolphins? Well some carcasses are so contaminated that they're toxic and have been withdrawn from sale. They wouldn't have had to wait for any accumulative effect, eating one meal would have the power to render them very ill indeed."

"I didn't know that, Charlie, so thank you," Sean replied with heavy sarcasm. "Thank Christ we don't eat little Flipper in this country."

"Maybe not, but there are plenty of contaminated fish and fish oils we do eat…"

"Don't give me a list, Charlie, whatever you do. Look, where are we going with this? You already told me that you don't think this is the cause so can we cut through the shit and get to the real reasons."

"We haven't dismissed it but we don't have anything scientifically supportable – for this or anything else, for that matter. I wish I could give you a definitive answer, old boy, I really wish I could."

"Okay then, let's start with why you can't go public and pile the shit on Labour's doorstep."

"Just for a minute, Sean, use your imagination. Humankind could not have developed without animals – for transport, clothing, food, companionship…"

"For fuck's sake forget the National Geographic and stick to politics. Why can't we use the information!" Sean was running out of patience.

"The largest industry in Britain – all over the Western world for that matter – is animals. Meat and dairy animals. Livestock! They are hugely important to our economy. When you add in all the other industries that are dependent upon meat and dairy, you're talking interrelationships of gargantuan proportions – the massive pharmaceutical companies whose drugs are central to controlling diseases in modern farming, equipment manufacturers, transport, food processing, retailing, advertising… it goes on and on…"

"This isn't the Open University, Charlie, can we get to the point?"

"Patience, Sean, be patient!" Charlie Whiston was now irritated by Sean's constant interruptions. "If I don't give you the background, you can't understand – and you need to understand, we all do because this has the potential to be the biggest crisis of this century, of the last century, of any century.

"What are we promising when we're elected? What's the magical cure for unemployment, improving standards of living, welfare funding, more police on the streets, better pensions, repaying deficits – any bally thing you can think of? And most of all, how do we fulfil our commitment to reducing taxes. Well, what is it? What is central to our whole political project, and always has been, for that matter. What lies at the core of our ethos?"

"Free markets… growth, I suppose," Sean offered reluctantly.

"Exactly, growth! How can we achieve growth if the biggest industry of all fails to perform, fails to grow sufficiently or, even worse, collapses?" The pause was short. "We can't, is the short answer. We will be thrown into a recession the like of which we have never seen before if that happens.

"We've known for twenty or thirty years of the diseases meat and dairy cause but have mounted a great defence by producing phony science, denigrating any science that threatens us, emasculating those who want to champion change, gagging public health advisory bodies – after all, you've got to die of something so it might as well be something which makes us prosperous! Why on earth do you think we still subsidise it with billions of Euros? We have become utterly dependent upon livestock as an engine of growth. What's happening around our coast is a direct challenge to that – it's a direct challenge to our very way of life."

"Your way of life, Charlie! You're an absentee farmer aren't you? You own half of fuckin' Gloucestershire!"

Charlie Whiston's eyes flashed and his face coloured.

"Coming from your background this may prove difficult to understand but if you try, I'm sure you can manage it. Look at the bigger picture. If we don't prosper, if I don't prosper, neither do the hoi polloi…"

"Sorry, Charlie old son, couldn't resist it. Bloody hell, you're taking this very seriously. Just stick the little buggers in cages. In fact, I thought we already did that with most of 'em anyway."

"Can you imagine the additional costs of having to keep every cow, every sheep or pig or chicken, not just in cages, as you put it, but separate from each other? Because there's strong evidence that they're acting together, in unison, almost as if they're planning how best to get us. They still have to be transported and slaughtered and all kinds of procedures carried out on them. Ensuring they're always immobile, incapable of turning on their handlers, is hugely problematical, not to say expensive; and pushing prices up is a sure way to reduce consumption.

"But that's not the worst part of it. People don't really want to know what goes on in the murkier parts of our lives because it discomfits them. So, when we tell them that animals are happy and content and that slaughter is humane and painless, most believe it. They believe it because they want to believe it and because the alternative presents them with a difficulty – they have to make a conscious decision whether to accept that what they eat is a product of cruelty and carry on eating it, or they change their diet. Most don't want to change their diet."

"Personally, I don't give a shit so long as the steak tastes the same – all this anthropomorphic bollocks has never impressed me," Sean threw into the conversation.

"I agree with you, Sean, but for different reasons. God gave us dominion over the animals, put them here for our use and all this febrile nonsense that people like our Ms Carter manage to stir up in the press is profoundly anti-Christian – I would go further and call it blasphemous – and damaging to the industry. She is already having a considerable impact with her so-called undercover exposes by playing the cruelty card – and playing it very effectively. Both meat and dairy consumption are falling – not a great deal but precisely at a time when what we need above all else is growth. By the way, have you given up on her? Didn't quite work out the way you promised, did it?"

Sean felt his face colouring. Charlie Whiston had not used the word 'promised' accidentally. It was an unsubtle reminder that Sean had failed and therefore was not omnipotent. It was a general of the old guard putting a mere corporal of the new guard firmly in his place.

"They didn't do what they were supposed to do, alright?" Sean made no attempt to hide his aggression. "If you or any one of the other so-called leaders of this fuckin' party had taken control of the situation when I warned you, we wouldn't be in this situation now, so don't wag your fuckin' finger at me Charlie..." Sean's voice tailed off because anger was taking control and he didn't want that. "Right – you were telling me how the four horseman of the fuckin' apocalypse were riding over the horizon to wipe out the stock exchange..."

Charlie paused before continuing, also angry but at the fact that this slippery, obnoxious little man dared to speak to him in such tones but... For the moment they were wedded together in a common cause. He breathed deeply.

"Very well, Sean, I would like you to imagine the field day this woman would have if it becomes common knowledge that animals are resisting being farmed, are fighting against being confined and really don't want to be slaughtered. Just imagine the scenes that would fill our television screens, with Ms Carter leading the charge towards a new, animal-free utopia. God, it doesn't bear thinking about! We have to keep a bally lid on this until we can find a way of dealing with it because if we don't, it will destroy the industry and our economy with it."

"You really think it's that serious?"

"I know it is but even that's not the end of it. It's not just farmed animals which are involved and if this thing continues to spread, we're looking at a world where no one dare go into the sea for fear of being bitten or even devoured; where you couldn't ride a horse without being kicked into oblivion; where your own pets want to take a chunk out of you or claw your eyes out and even garden birds suddenly become a threat to your health or even your life...! There have been two recent cases of starlings, huge flocks of them, actually attacking aircraft. They brought one down and the other made an emergency landing. They were labelled as 'bird strike' but it wasn't, it was 'bird attack'. If that were to become commonplace..." Charlie's voice tailed off.

"Shoot the bastards, shoot all of 'em, get rid of 'em, who needs the little sods anyway?" Sean's muscular response was spat out like some male, omnipotent Queen of Hearts.

"Sadly, our old communist chummie, Chairman Mao, tried that. Got all the peasants, whole families of them, to stand outside banging gongs and drums and so on to keep the sparrows and suchlike airborne until they collapsed to the ground with exhaustion and then they finished them off. They'd been eating too much grain, the old tyrant said, and the annihilation was hugely successful. Problem was, the next lot of crops was destroyed by pests of all kinds and disaster followed – and that's why we can't shoot the little blighters, Sean."

"I get the picture, Charlie, but this isn't China and we're a bit short on peasants anyway."

On the one hand, Sean Murphy was imbibing the old boy's seriousness, on the other, the nature of what he was saying was simply unbelievable. He began to wonder if they'd banged the wrong person up. He could, however, tell that the old man was deadly serious and had either to be believed or at least humoured. But Sean had to admit that it was interesting.

"You can't go off half-cocked, Charlie. You don't stand a snowball's chance of stopping it or even controlling it if you don't know why it's happening. Jesus Christ, we're always telling everyone we've got the brightest brains in the country on our side, surely they must have some idea – a theory, even an educated fuckin' guess would be better than nothing. If this does go public, we have to be able to manage it and I for one am not prepared to stand in front of a load of testosterone-ridden press guys and say: 'Sorry, fellas, there's no good asking me any questions because I don't have a fuckin' clue!'"

"Well, the theory they're currently following might offer an explanation but politically it would raise as many problems as it would cure. I'm not sure anyone would want to go public with it but we might have to," Charlie offered resignedly. "It's only just made its way into the mix and is still a theory but they're working overtime on it to see if it has any validity."

"Out with it, Charlie, out with it!"

Charlie paused and seemed to gather his thoughts before continuing.

"It's a depressing reminder for me but you probably weren't even born when all this was at its height – the space race, that is. In truth, it was much more of an arms race than a space race and the manned space missions were merely a sop to the public to excite them and avert any rebellion over the vast amounts of money that were being spent on it.

"You have no idea how many satellites the military were popping up into space over that period – thousands of the bally things. Some were launched with a public fanfare but many more were launched secretly, from both sides. Of course, each side could detect the when and where of each launch but had no idea what the payload might be."

Sean examined his finger nails minutely but no longer tried to hurry Charlie along, partly because he knew it would be futile but also because he could feel his interest continuing to grow.

"You cannot imagine what cargos some of those things were carrying – typhus, cholera, bubonic plague, anthrax and god knows what else. Rightly or wrongly, the perception was that Russia posed a real threat and it was all a matter of life and death and so anything went. Boffins everywhere were trying to come up with novel biological strains that, if they ever had to be used, were so complicated in their structure that dealing with them, neutralising them, would be very difficult indeed for the other side. Problem with biological weapons, of course, is that they have no ideological commitment and can spread rapidly and kill both sides, but that little caution appears to have been put on one side, at least at the start of this frenetic period. They may, of course, have developed antidotes at the same time but if they did, these have disappeared into the mists of time and there's no trace of them.

"Of course, they may have also developed organisms or chemicals or whatever, that could be targeted solely at the enemy. I know that in South Africa, for instance, under the apartheid regime, they were trying to develop a deadly bacterium that would attack only people with black skins. I don't think they achieved it but that kind of thinking was everywhere!"

"A vodka bug," Sean chuckled but he was now paying full attention because the subject had developed a convincing ring. He knew instinctively that this was precisely how governments would have acted so perhaps the old fellow wasn't away with the fairies.

"Most of these satellites are still spinning around above us and god knows what has happened to their payloads – they may have long since degraded and ceased to be active – or they may not. We have no way of knowing. Most of the other types of satellite, for communication, spying, radio jamming and the like, would eventually burn up on re-entry but these little beauties needed to be able to deliver their loads and so they had to be able to survive re-entry. Eventually, they're all going to come home to roost like so many deadly chickens and we're reliant on fail-safe mechanisms developed by people forty or fifty years ago, most of whom are now dead. Just as worrying, no one on our side has a list that is anything like complete of how many satellites there are, what they contain and when they might return to Earth."

Concentration had silenced Sean Murphy and as he followed Charlie Whiston's reasoning, his interest had blossomed because this was something solid, explicable, understandable and entirely probable that he could get his teeth into. If true – and there was solid reasoning behind it to suggest it might be – it could generate a political backlash of enormous proportions. It could tear the whole political system apart as any party that had held power since the 1960s was culpable. If ever there had been a residual inclination to continue in his role after the forthcoming election, it had now evaporated because, if true, this was a situation that only a masochist would want to try and manage.

"The worst case scenario we're working on," Charlie continued, "is that one of these satellites armed with a biological weapon has splashed down in the North Sea or some other ocean and has released its load, which was viable and has survived. Whatever it might be it is now spreading ashore. We don't think that animals have suddenly developed a hatred of human kind; it's far more likely that some biological or chemical agent is disrupting their brains, driving them out of control. They're experiencing a mass nervous breakdown, as it were."

Sean was now thinking hard, fully engaged in the problem.

"Yeah, but if that was the case, Charlie, humans would be doing something similar; turning on each other everywhere, like a pissed up Friday night in Sunderland?"

"As it happens, the number of people being diagnosed with depression has skyrocketed, as has the suicide rate."

"And in the same areas as the animals – there is an equivalence?"

"Mostly, but it is happening further inland, too."

"Well, it could just be coincidence then," Sean said dismissively.

"After fifty years in public life, Sean, I have ceased to believe in coincidences. At the moment there is nothing to support this theory – no traces of anything chemical or biological in any of the animals we've dissected nor the human cadavers we've managed to examine. But then, whatever it is may have been designed to be undetectable and in a way, it could be that we are being hoist by our own petard. It might also be that human brains are reacting slightly differently to animal brains, hence the different responses.

"At least we and the Americans have some surviving records which we're trying to search through but the Russians, it seems, have almost nothing – not surprising considering what happened there after the collapse of Communism. Each department working for the military on satellite warfare, whether in Russia or the US, was utterly paranoid of the enemy and even of other departments within their own organisation. The outcome was that many of the developments were so secretive that only those directly involved knew about them – and possibly some remote director who almost certainly died of old age many years ago.

"All this makes going back to the drawing board, as it were, to try and establish the original blueprint, impossible. And if that can't be done, finding a way of identifying it or hopefully neutralising this thing – whatever it might be – becomes extremely difficult. The best hope at the moment is that it burns itself out."

Sean's eyes were bright with interest.

"So, you've got two scenarios on the go. It's either a result of chemical pollution caused by us; or by agents of biological warfare, also caused by us and one or the other has poisoned just about everything?" Charlie nodded. "I think if I was an animal, Charlie, I'd want to tear someone's fuckin' throat out," Sean offered with an ironic little laugh.

Chapter Thirty

Josephine Aldous was no longer capable of disbelief nor fear nor anger. She was capable of very little, in fact, as her whole being, both physical and emotional, seemed to have been immersed in a cloying, highly viscous, syrup-like substance. Nothing would move or function without a monumental effort that ultimately failed. It wasn't just that she could not sustain a line of thought, nor that her arms and legs would not respond properly to her bidding, but that those thoughts she could generate slowly dissolved before they had even properly materialised.

When she tried to recall what it was she had thought, what she had wanted to think, what she had been prompted into thinking, there was not a trace left and so the whole process had to begin over again. It was like a dog chasing his tail in slow motion, the end game always just out of reach, tantalisingly close but constantly moving away, always unattainable. No matter how great the effort to grasp hold of her thoughts it always failed and she was left abandoned somewhere deep within herself where she had never been before. Somehow, Jo knew that it was only a question of time before exhaustion defeated her and she would curl into a ball and surrender entirely.

She knew that something horribly chemical had been introduced into her bloodstream and she was still capable of remembering who was responsible but she could not rage against him, could not plan retribution, did not have the energy to fulminate against the gross injustice for which he was responsible because those same chemicals had stripped her bare of her humanity, her emotions – even revenge.

But one remained. Just one overpowering sensation filled the void that had been vacated by the evisceration of her personality. She did not need to articulate it, had no need to wait for it to coalesce into coherent thought because it came from somewhere far deeper than any antipsychotic could ever reach and it was clear and sharp and overwhelming. It was the desperation of a mother forcibly separated from her child and who knew that he too would be terrifyingly fearful, uncomprehendingly isolated.

That desperation was articulated by mumbled groans and grunts separated out into incomprehensible syllables. The effort of forming them caused saliva to issue from the corners of Josephine Aldous's mouth, run down her chin and on to her white cotton top, forming dark stains.

She had been hauled from an ambulance, impelled through large Victorian entrance doors, travelled up in a lift and now stood in some kind of hospital ward reception setting, still supported on either side by the same two towering nurses who had evicted her from her house like some choreographed, Saturday night pas de deux for bouncer and binge drinker.

Jo suddenly felt a desperate need for the lavatory but the sensation became a reality before it had fully registered.

"Oh Christ, dearie, did you have to?"

The two large women moved her to a lavatory cubicle, the black woman remaining outside, the white woman entering with Jo, standing her with her back to the pan whilst Jo tried to make her hands do her bidding, of reaching beneath her long skirt in search of her knickers but they flapped around uselessly. The nurse issued a grunt of exasperation, turned Jo partially around and pushed her back unceremoniously against the wall of the cubicle so she could balance and then Jo felt the woman's big, rough, man-like hands beneath her skirt searching for the waistband of her knickers, which she found and having done so, pulled them down in one sudden movement devoid of any sensitivity. She then held Jo's skirt aloft with one hand and dropped her forcefully onto the lavatory seat with the other.

Now seated, Jo leant forward with her elbows on her knees, her head low, and looked down uncomprehendingly at the flimsy, expensive confection of purple lace and embroidery that stretched between both ankles, its designer elegance marred by the brown deposit that stained its gusset. She used one arm to try and gesticulate to the woman to leave the cubicle but it was in vain.

"I've seen it all before, dearie, so don't worry about that. You're on suicide watch so you'd better get used to it."

Jo had no further resistance and her bowels opened, filling the small cubicle with the cloying smell of her excreta and even in that she was denied privacy. From somewhere deep inside her, despair clawed its way out through the fog of incomprehension and settled snugly around her shoulders. The crying started with little, innocuous hiccup-like coughs but rapidly became great, all-encompassing, body-wracking sobs that then merged together into a cacophony of wailing anguish, interrupted only by rasping intakes of breath to fuel its continuance.

Chapter Thirty One

During the days that immediately followed, Josephine's nightmares became real. She was no longer an observer of suffering, not a voyeur who lived the misery second hand and she had no need to struggle in order to understand its source and causation for all this and worse was all around her in an entirely new world that consumed her. Each time she emerged from the deep, dark, dead smog of sleep, in which all time temporarily ceased and from which all dreams were banished, the horror of where she was and her utter impotence to escape it or alter it overwhelmed her.

As the level of medication was reduced, incomprehension gradually lifted but the understanding which replaced it was almost as debilitating. A cognition that had been chemically bludgeoned and coshed into subservience at least had the advantage of fuzziness, blurred edges, which helped to obscure her reality. But now she had no choice other than to stare reality in the face and this was even more discomforting as it unleashed a barrage of concerns which had shape and form and meaning, and raised an endless string of questions that demanded answers but to which no one paid heed let alone responded.

"You'll see the consultant very soon and he'll explain everything. Don't worry, dearie, you'll be fine."

Her lips no longer dribbled, her bodily functions were back under control and her tongue moved within her mouth without sticking to roof or palate but still the eyes blinked slowly and words emerged in a near monotone, expressionless. The only part of Jo that worked efficiently were her eyes, which issued tears in recurring bouts as her situation clarified, and contained within that clarity was an awareness of how hopeless was her situation.

She told herself that whatever shock and fear Danny had faced when he returned home from school on that day, it was now over and her family would have offered him reassurance, love and security – and so the desperation had diminished somewhat. But she so wanted to hear his voice, to speak to him, to assure him she had not willingly deserted him and that whatever happened she would be home soon.

She wanted to tell him that she loved him and that his love for her would provide the strength to overcome anything that she might have to confront before her nightmare was defeated and they could both return to normality. In truth, she feared it would be a new reality as their lives could never be the same again. She knew she would not be able to tell him why she had been taken away and who was responsible because, gratifying as it might be to her, it would throw Danny into a turmoil that could damage him permanently.

The comprehension that Stephen had been complicit in her incarceration was almost mind numbing, not least that he had been prepared so cavalierly to ignore the impact it might have on his son. Jo knew that the idea itself would not have sprung from Stephen as he did not have the imagination but he would have had had to agree to it. Other darker, more vicious, more sinister people would have devised the proposal as the only one that could rescue their fortunes and her husband would have lent his name to it and then justified his decision to himself as being in her best interests. There was almost something more honourable in being an out-and-out bastard than a weak, vainglorious cypher to whom ambition had become a totem and who was utterly malleable in pursuit of that goal.

Jo sat immobile and watched the people who shared the ward with her as they went about their extraordinarily limited and circumscribed morning without enthusiasm or purpose. The constantly burbling television was almost the only source of distinct sound and the sudden outbursts of laughter it emitted seemed to mock their situation. Almost no one spoke, other than the occasional muted sentence as they passed each other, either on their way somewhere to do nothing or returning from somewhere else having done nothing.

Some were dishevelled, some mumbled soundlessly to themselves, many had eyes that were distant, troubled but none looked particularly mad. Perhaps madness did not always display itself like a bad toupee. All had one thing in common, however, and it was their extraordinary ability to ignore her – not just to ignore by omitting to speak but to ignore by failing to acknowledge even her presence. Perhaps they had learnt from experience that most people newly admitted into this strangely-muted place had no wish to share the confusion that preoccupied them, perhaps could not even articulate it and hence questions were not wanted and therefore were never asked.

The only time the atmosphere changed was when a small, pretty, nurse came through the room, tossing her blonde ponytail from side to side, issuing an instruction, a direction, a request, and then the change was sudden and dramatic, like a colour sergeant walking onto the parade ground and shouting 'Attention'. Those who were engaged in boring activities suddenly applied themselves as though whatever it was they were doing was all-consuming. Those who were doing nothing did it with straighter backs, communicating intent. Those seated and dreaming or drowsing appeared to close their eyes more tightly to keep her presence excluded. And when the busying little form had departed there was, Jo could swear, a communal release of breath, a joint relaxation of tension.

The only other person who was different and who appeared not to be afflicted by a preoccupation with the nothingness that smothered the place, was an interesting-looking, maybe good looking, man with curly dark hair who, even when Jo was in the deepest recesses of sedation, would exhibit concern by pausing to offer a word or two of comfort.

"Welcome to Anderson ward... It doesn't last, it will get better. You've just got to hang on in there." Or, more intimately: "Don't let the bastards beat you. Play it cool and you will get out, you will go home." It didn't matter that he did not know her, had no knowledge of what it might be that did or did not afflict her, he still spoke reassuring words that, during the first day, Jo was incapable of acknowledging but which extended the only lifeline she had down there, in the pit into which she had descended – had been deposited.

On the second day, he pulled up a chair and sat opposite her, positioned so that he could see her eyes and she could see his. It was clearly his way of establishing a connection that might have been impossible through speech alone. When he spoke and she struggled to respond she concentrated on his eyes and could feel them encouraging her, reassuring her, inviting her to communicate. And again he spoke to her as though he had no doubt that she could comprehend him and was not lost in some hinterland of madness.

"You have to smother your emotions because anything you do in this place that isn't calm and unresponsive will be seen as being over-emotional. Don't laugh too loud, don't be rude to anyone, don't swear, don't be angry, don't be too sad, don't be fucking human." The last two words were spat out with venom. "If you want to show any emotion, go to the john and do it in private and then come out smiling like you're a Stepford wife." There was no concession to her sedated condition and he spoke as though she was fully aware and could understand him perfectly.

He would return from time to time during the day with simple words that Jo found overwhelmingly reassuring and began to look forward to his visits. "How ya doin' babe? Looks like you've returned from the land of the living dead." She was even able to raise a distorted, lop-sided smile at that. "Hey, that's better. We'll pop out for a beer later!"

It was on the morning of the third day when Jo, still on medication, albeit considerably reduced but which she did not have the strength to refuse – "to even out your moods sweetie" – found herself capable of speech and proper movement. She had eaten, showered and changed into her own, clean clothes which had appeared from nowhere and she felt herself returning, if not to normality then at least to something that approximated it.

Whoever had brought the clothes from her house had not identified themselves to her and she found that confusing, troubling. Concerns about Danny and her incarceration were all-consuming but enough spirit had returned for her to challenge someone, anyone, and she was about to get out of her chair and do so when the curly-haired man arrived and sat next to her.

"I know what you probably want to do, Josephine, but don't!"

It was seconds before it sank in that he had used her name.

"You know who I am, then?"

"Sure do. You're famous – or to be more accurate, infamous. Pegged you out to dry, didn't they?"

"Did it work?" The question was almost a Pavlovian reaction from another life.

"Let's say your old man has started polishing the knocker on the door of number ten. Rumour has it, he's been nominated for an Oscar for his grieving husband role."

Jo was back in the present with a jolt and the words tumbled out, one on the heels of the other.

"Have they talked about my son – Danny – have they said anything about him, where he is, how he is, have they mentioned him…?"

Al Dwight leant forward and put his hand on Jo's arm. "They have, but only in passing. He's staying with someone from your family, your sister I think, but as he's not in the news I guess he's alright. If he wasn't, they'd pin that on you, too so I reckon you can relax."

"I need to speak to him. I was just going to ask to use a phone."

"I guessed that's what you were going to do – you're just about compos mentis enough by now to want answers to all this." He gestured with one arm in a sweeping movement as though proudly indicating something dear to him. "But they won't let you use the phone and I reckon you might have hit the ceiling when they told you that – and then Protz would have had a needle in you before you could call her a psychopathic little shit. You've not been seen by Shrink Almighty yet and nothing happens until he's performed his benediction over you. You might call the press – but I wouldn't advise that because apart from a couple of titles they've pretty solidly lined up behind your old man. Do you have your sister's number?"

"Danny's got a mobile."

Al looked over his shoulder. "You know it? I mean can you remember it through all the shit that's in you?"

Jo nodded and then added: "What day is it?"

"Sunday," Al replied and Jo's face brightened. "I get it, he won't be at school! Wait here."

He returned a couple of minutes later and instructed Jo to follow him to the quiet room and once there, he pulled a mobile from his pocket but held it back out of reach of Jo's outstretched hand.

"Look, I don't want to lecture you but prepare yourself. You've gotta stay calm for both your sakes. Your boy needs you to be okay – not just for you to say you're okay but for him to hear you're okay. Freak out and you'll freak him out – and if Protz hears you freak out she's just as likely to use the liquid cosh on you again. Do you understand what I'm saying?" Jo's face was tight with concentration, anticipation and nodded her head vigorously. "Okay, then, sit down." She did and Al handed her the phone but her hands were trembling so violently that she found it impossible to hit the correct keys. He smiled. "Give it to me – and shout out the number."

When the phone was answered Al handed it to Jo with the caution: "Calm, remember!"

"Danny? Oh Danny, Danny, it's mum."

Al Dwight sat close to Jo so she could see his face, so he could scowl a reminder if it was necessary but once the first few words had been spoken he could see that no intervention from him would be required. Tears returned to Jo Aldous's face and rolled down it but they were cheerful tears on a face that was riven with a broad smile. She nodded as she said 'yes' in response to Danny's questions, shook it when she said 'no' and her face was glowing with satisfaction, her eyes bright and alive. She offered her son quiet, intimate reassurance and whilst her voice was heavy with emotion there was nothing about it that could disturb her son so Al moved away across the room and turned his back to her – it was simply a mother pouring out her love and concern for her son and absorbing it in return.

Jo finished the call with the words: "Always keep your phone with you, darling, and I'll ring you whenever I can," and rounded it off with more I love yous than Al could count.

Jo got up and rushed across the room, her arms outstretched, flinging them around Al's neck.

"I will love you forever for that Mister American," she sobbed into his neck and Al could feel the wetness of her tears on his skin. There was an intimacy in her closeness, in her aroma, the pressure of her breast against his chest, the warmth of her breath that triggered a rush of pleasant memories long confined to oblivion and Al hated himself for it, even though the all-enveloping pleasure it produced was entirely spontaneous.

He was not taking advantage of the woman's vulnerability, he wasn't being an insensitive asshole, he was not trying to capitalise on her desperation, he had no control over his feelings. He did allow his arms to enfold her but resisted the urge to pull her just a little tighter to him.

It was at that precise moment that the door swung silently open and nurse Protz breezed into the room on busy business. She stopped dead at the scene which confronted her and absorbed the words that Jo was saying. Al was facing her and watched the emotions flicker across her face like the staccato movements of a silent movie – surprise, shock, disbelief, anger and, unless he was very much mistaken, hatred.

"Whose phone is that?" She snapped.

"Mine," replied Al, wearily.

"Have you been letting Mrs Aldous use it – have you, have you Alexander?" Her voice was rising and nurse Protz was not attempting to disguise her fury.

"I needed to speak to my son, to let him know I was alright, to hear he was okay – that was all. For god's sake it was just a simple phone call," Jo said as she handed the phone back to Al and separated from him. She could feel the old her beginning to find its way back into her veins.

Nurse Protz stepped forwards, her hand held out.

"Did you get that from the phone store? Did you?" she demanded but did not wait for an answer. "You've been here long enough to know the rules. You ask to use your phone and when you've finished your call you hand it back. You do not

keep it in your possession. You certainly do not allow another
patient to use it, particularly one as vulnerable, confused and
damaged as Mrs Aldous. How did you get it?"

Al could hear bitterness slicing through her anger and replied
as laconically as he could as if to counterbalance it.

"It's my spare, Protz, my spare."

"You're not supposed to have a spare. Phones get stolen and
then we have the disruption of allegation and denial that always
gets out of hand. Please give it to me – now!"

Al knew that her outrage had nothing to do with the phone
but rather than confront her with Josephine Aldous present, he
felt obliged to practice what he had been trying to preach.

"Sorry, Protz, not the end of the universe is it. Here, take it if
it makes you happy."

She snapped the phone out of Al's hand, turned and exited the
room but he knew this was not the end and that the ramifications
of his simple misdemeanour, that would not have even creased
the brow of any other nurse, would rumble on for days with
shows of petulant discontent and perhaps spiteful retribution.

Nurse Protz exited with the phone and Jo turned to Al with
disbelief in her face.

"It was just a phone call."

"Sure – but she is not just a nurse. She is a damaged,
dangerous, son of a bitch."

"She can't be a son of a bitch," Jo chuckled.

"Okay, she's a bitch of a bitch but that sounds stupid."

Jo laughed again.

"What have poor little bitches done to deserve such abuse?
What is this place, anyway, a prison?"

"You got it in one, doll. It's a co-ed prison for screwballs."

"I don't care," Jo leant forward and kissed him on the cheek,
"I meant what I said – I will love you forever for that
wonderfully kind gesture. I have never needed anything as
desperately as I needed that – never, ever, in my entire life."

Again the door swung silently open, again Al and Jo were
close together, Jo's hands cupping either side of his face and
again nurse Protz appeared in the doorway. Once more her
countenance collapsed into dark, unspoken fury.

"Mrs Aldous, you will see the Consultant at 2.30. Report to the nurse's station ten minutes before that." Nurse Protz turned on her heel and Jo's voice stopped her progress.:

"What's the name of the consultant?"

Nurse Protz took several seconds to answer and looked at Jo as though she had no right to speak let alone demand an answer to a question.

"Professor Kadynski," she replied and then flounced out before anything else could be said, leaving behind an atmosphere as depressing as it had been joyful just a minute earlier.

"Bloody wonderful," Jo threw after her.

"Jo?" Al said her name as a question to which he was unsure what the answer would be, "Will you take a bit of advice from an old hand? It's advice that might help you to get through this..." he could not find the word that adequately described their situation, "...this – shit?"

"Of course I will."

"Kadynski's the guy who banged you away, right?"

"Yes."

"Then please listen to me, Jo. All your instincts are to go in there and scream and shout at him, to call him every kind of bastard that ever existed, to accuse him of everything from kidnap to death of the first born, right?" Jo didn't answer because a response wasn't called for. "You're wasting your breath! It will have no effect; in fact the opposite. It will play right into Kadynski's hands by you appearing to be hysterical and out of control. You know what he's done, he knows what he's done and some very powerful people in government know what he's done, including your old man. You're not going to change their minds or affect anything because reason isn't part of this scenario. It's all about control. Kadynski knows you shouldn't be here so how can you convince him to let you go? You can't! You can't change anything, either with reason or outrage. You're a prisoner of war and just remember that.

"It's a battle, Jo, and if you go flying over the top you'll be sliced down. They have the power, you have no power, none at all. If you want to get out of this place you've gotta be disciplined, you've gotta plan, you've gotta take back what control you can. You gotta go in there and say 'yes sir', 'no sir', 'three bags full sir'. You don't have to kiss his ass but you do have to control your emotions. Don't try and score points. Say the very minimum you can get away with and your favourite word has to be 'fine'. How are you feeling? 'Fine.' How are you being treated? 'Fine.'

"Grab yourself a shield – some words, a phrase, a description, a goal – something like, 'I'm going to get out of this place' or 'you won't beat me' and keep it in mind all the time. Whatever he asks you, first think 'you will not beat me' or whatever you decide before answering. Kadynski doesn't waste time on anyone because in practice it's Protz and Dealey who make the assessments and he'll have their notes, meaningless as they are. The longest you're likely to be in there is five minutes max. My last appearance was two minutes – two fucking minutes to supposedly sort out someone's mind. He'll be as keen as you are to get it over with."

Jo was silent throughout Al's advice as he delivered his words with a bruising intensity that did not encourage interruption. His cautions brought with them the realisation that he too was suffering but had had many weeks in which to learn how to hide it.

Jo knew he was right in everything he said and was determined to act on his advice. But now having had a little glimpse into the other Al, she felt guilty that all his concern had been concentrated on her when he, too, was almost certainly crying out for support.

She did not know if there were rules of conduct for such places, whether it was not the done thing to ask patients why they were here, in a locked security ward, presumably because they were deemed too dangerous to be let loose on the public. Perhaps it would be too disturbing, too frightening to actually know what Al had done or what mental confusion assailed him. But she had a need to know before she allowed him any closer as the years of political indoctrination had engrained caution in her too deeply even for antipsychotic drugs to erase.

"Do you want to talk about whatever it was that led you here?" Jo spoke the words as gently as she could so they did not sound probing or demand an answer; gentle enough for Al to swat them away if he so chose.

It was several seconds before he responded, during which time a half smile spread across his face.

"It's okay, Jo, I'm not a mass murderer or a crazed axe man," he then laughed out loud, "although, to be honest, an axe did come into it!

"I was an out-of-control asshole who shat on anyone who came close to me. I became a wheeler dealer who thought money was all and it cost me everything – friends, love, self-respect and eventually freedom."

He had responded almost eagerly and communicated no sense of being offended or not wanting talk. Jo felt a little bolder.

"They didn't section you for that, though, did they?"

"No they didn't but they should have because it was far more destructive than the offence that got me here."

"Which was?"

Al lowered his head and shook it with the same half smile creasing his face.

"I tried to break someone's fingers with the back of an axe. Not nice but the little shit deserved it – fleeced me out of over six grand when debtors were queuing at the door. Trouble was, the prosecution wanted to present it as attempted murder – which it wasn't. My very flexible brief did some behind the scenes dealing and then put in such a plea of mitigation that even the judge looked like he might cry: failed businessman, failed husband, failed accountant even a failed fucking failure in psychological torment. Six months in this place to help me cope instead of several year's porridge."

"Failed accountant," Jo asked incredulously.

Al adopted a theatrical façade of anger and wagged his finger at her.

"You can tell anyone you like that I'm a nut case but if you ever breathe a word about me having been an accountant I'll get my axe out again!" They both laughed.

"Are you serious – an accountant ?" Jo sniggered.

"Yes, okay and what's so funny about being an accountant, lady?"

"No, there's nothing funny about it. What's funny is that you are an accountant."

"Were, were – past tense, please." There was a pause whilst Al pretended to preen himself. "As a matter of fact, I was good, very good, successful. Problem was, it drove me screwy. Have you any idea what it's like to be an accountant? Have you?" Jo didn't want to interrupt and merely shook her head. "I'll tell you," Al continued.

"It's like being locked in a tiny room with a little barred window and a metronome. Through that window you can see a beautiful view, a view that constantly changes. One day it's a glorious woodland that rapidly goes through the seasons and you watch as leaves and green shoots appear, you see them mature and gradually they turn to gold and are then stripped away by snow and rain and wind. And all the time little animals scamper about their business and play and mate, lovingly produce their young and sometimes they fall by the wayside and die but they don't fret and worry and become so afraid of dying that they are terrified of living. And the aromas of these different worlds drift through the open bars and tantalise you but you rarely have time to step outside your little room into that picture, to absorb those aromas, to feel the wind and rain and sunshine, and all the while your metronome keeps ticking away – tick, tick, ticking away. Where are those figures? There's that report to finish! Don't forget that analysis!

"And the view changes, maybe to crested waves pounding on a sandy shore and umbrella pines stretching down to the high water mark. In the water you can see the fins of dolphins carving a wake and suddenly they hurl themselves into the air in sheer joy and exuberance but the metronome keeps tick, tick, ticking away. Hurry with that audit! Contact the revenue! Bring the ledger up to date!

"And then the scene is bitter winter, or it's summer meadows and a cacophony of birdsong, or a shaded rainforest or a family celebrating Christmas together. And because you have some money you can now take a little time off and step out into the picture more frequently but you are only ever a visitor, never a part of it. You borrow from those whose picture it is and say 'I must do this more often' before the whistle blows and you scamper back into your little room with its barred windows and the metronome continuing its relentless, urging, compelling tick, tick, ticking once more. And you accept it because you're a coward and lack the courage to shout 'stick the metronome up your ass', I want to live.

"Well I did do that and I did start to live but because I thought moderation and control was for sissies I ended up simply swapping one prison for another; I went from a closed prison to an open prison but it was still a prison." Al went silent for several seconds. "But boy, it was fun at the start!"

"And the failed marriage? Jo asked.

"Oh yes, there was a failed marriage because in my rush to a new life I forgot the only good thing about the old life and the result was I got what I deserved."

"Did you love her?"

Again Al went silent, distant, to explore his memories and when he'd retrieved them he looked directly into Jo's eyes and she could see his passion.

"Oh yes, I really loved her, I probably still love her but it's a different love now, not agonisingly painful merely regretful. I am capable of love you know," he said defensively but Jo knew he was talking to himself rather than her. She could see the pain in Al's eyes.

"I don't doubt that for one second, Al. I just wish I could say the same but it's been so long I don't think I know how to love any longer."

They talked and they talked and divulged little secrets to each other, passing the morning content in each other's company. And then the time came for Jo to attend her appointment with Kadynski and so she reported to nurse Protz at the nurse's station, who asked a few pointless questions before saying that Professor Kadynski was running a little late. Without thought, Jo responded:

"Oh, that's a pity, I've got such a full diary today." It had slipped out without warning and Jo knew that in future she would have to rein in her natural sarcasm.

It wasn't anything she said, it wasn't anything she did, it was the way the woman looked at her that made Jo feel desperately uncomfortable. Nurse Protz, it seemed, had a chilling ability to render her face immobile – not a twitch of the mouth, not a crinkle around the eyes, not a blink of an eyelid and not even the slightest communication from the eyes themselves – blank, reserved, unreadable. It was as though the head of a tailor's dummy, a wax work, had been superimposed on the body of this young woman.

Jo felt compelled to discover more about her and was sure there was something to be divined by penetrating the implacable outward image and she tried to achieve it by looking beyond the eyes, peering through them to what lay behind. The two women stood facing each other, locked eye to eye but there was no embarrassment for Jo as there would be if she was simply trying to stare the woman out for she was barely conscious of whose eyes she was staring into; she was probing for answers from a woman who had a disproportionate influence on her life and who was not prepared to provide those answers.

What she saw through those cold, hard, compassionless windows had a profound effect on Jo. It wasn't shock or fear that engulfed her but a deep sense of sadness, almost pity. What she saw through nurse Protz's eyes was loneliness, emptiness, unhappiness. What did disturb Jo profoundly, however, was the notion that this damaged woman must have spent her life manipulating others as a distraction from the terrifying void where her spirit should have resided. Equally as frightening was Jo's certainty that Protz had the ability to penetrate, expose, to effortlessly strip bare, to scorch through any defence constructed on pretence, lies or artifice with the efficiency of a laser. A person's reaction to Protz had, by necessity, to be real and heartfelt or she would see right through it.

Protz broke off the eye-to-eye encounter and Jo felt some small satisfaction in that but knew she had succeeded only because she wasn't interested in succeeding. But a shiver ran through her with the thought that this was not a good woman to make an enemy of; it was amplified by the realisation that Protz had already decided Jo was her enemy and Jo knew precisely the reason why.

With Protz's departure, Jo was able to sit and concentrate on how she would handle her meeting with Kadynski. The thought kept forcing its way into her mind that his was the man responsible for her being where she was and for all the anguish and turmoil which swirled around her. And each time Jo thrust it away as though it was poison, not wanting it near her at this vital time and so she substituted it with her chosen slogan, which she visualised as being typed in a large font before her eyes. 'You will not defeat me!'

When the call came and she entered his office she was surprised to find him alone and not surrounded by other doctors and nurses as she had been told was likely. It took little thought to decipher the reason. Had she chosen to rant and rail against him and make allegations, it would have provided an excuse for him to control her more effectively with drugs but... and it was a distinct possibility... doubts may, just may, have been raised in the minds of those who were not party to the sectioning. He clearly was not prepared to take the risk and that put him on the defensive. Correspondingly, it placed Jo exactly where she wanted to be – to some degree in charge. And she thanked Al for that.

She sat in front of the desk that acted as a barrier between the two antagonists – both physical and psychological and not accidentally, Jo thought. She consciously breathed deeply but her defensive slogan was promptly abandoned as superfluous when her eyes lighted upon his bow tie. This became the symbol that would provide all the reassurance she needed and the anchor that would hold her emotions firmly in place. It became the focal point for her eyes, which were unwavering and saw nothing else in the room but his stupid, bloody, pretentious, emasculating bow tie. That he should want – feel the need – to take a silly fragment of brightly coloured fabric and tie it into a bow to place around his neck was pathetic ostentation.

Her vision just encompassed the lower half of Kadynski's face and the upper part of his crisp, white, smoothly-ironed, shirt front, down to where it began its slight outward swell to accommodate the thickening waistline of his approaching middle age. Not once did she allow her gaze to rise high enough to encompass his eyes nor low enough to give her the appearance of subservience.

"Yes," she said emotionlessly to some futile question he had asked in his oily, privileged, patronising voice.

Despite the qualifications that adorned his stationery letterhead and despite the deference afforded him by those reliant upon him for preferment, he was a man for all that and Jo could cope with this type of man; a man she was methodically dismembering with scathing observations, each one eroding just a little more of his potency.

The bow tie was the symbol of his arrogance and desire to be different, to be remarked upon; an artificial building block, a component of a structure that he hoped would camouflage his inherently weak character. It was a studied statement of 'I am different to you', a visual shout of 'Look at me' when those who were naturally different and to whom your eyes were spontaneously drawn, had no need of fancy dress.

"No," replied Jo to another question, another pointless pretence that she had an illness and Kadynski could mitigate it through enquiry and investigation, diagnosis and treatment.

The full, rounded, well-fed jowls and neatly trimmed hair screamed affluence and privilege, the faint aroma of after shave or cologne and the drooping silk handkerchief cascading from his breast pocket, with its hand-rolled edges, were statements of status and position and as easily read as the badges of military rank.

"Fine," replied Jo to a question she had barely bothered to listen to.

And so it went on – pointless questions producing pointless answers in a synthetic pas de deux, both sides conscious of its pantomimic nature but neither able to admit it. With each exchange, Jo forensically chiselled away one little piece after another from the artificial construct that was Professor Kadynski, her hatred of him slowly transmuting into contempt and that in itself was almost liberating. He was a Stephen with qualifications and like Stephen, his shallowness was disguised with overpowering confidence and impenetrable insensitivity.

And so the session came to an end and Jo rose and had almost exited through the door when she halted. There was something wrong, something missing and it left a hollow pit of dissatisfaction gnawing at her. She knew the reason instantly – she could not leave Kadynski without providing him with something to think about, without sowing just a little fear that might come back to haunt him in the quiet of his nights.

She turned back into the room, closing the door behind her and for the first time looked Kadynski directly in the eyes. Before she had even spoken she saw a little shadow flicker across them, like a tiny cloud blown in front of a summer sun to dim its brilliance. When she did speak it was with perfect control, the words stripped of all anger:

"What you have done to me, Kadynski, is evil. That evil will come back to destroy you and your career and it will be me who makes it happen." He remained seated, his face and body immobile as though petrified and he made no response as Jo turned and left the room.

Chapter Thirty Two

With Al acting as intermediary, Peter Dealey agreed to Jo using Al's 'spare' phone until she could arrange for one of her own. They had specifically waited for Protz to disappear on her break as Jo instinctively knew that she would raise an objection and Dealey would defer to her. Having got the phone, Jo immediately called one of the few numbers she could remember.

Hillie answered and there was nothing, it seemed, that could dent her veneer of boundless optimism; shallowness is what Jo really thought.

"Good god Jo, what a to do – but you'll be out of there in two ticks I've absolutely no doubt. Some stupid hitch or other I suspect." And then the subject was changed abruptly: "Danny's absolutely fine, really okay and happy – I promise you so don't worry about that."

"I know, I spoke to him this morning. Hille, I've got no idea where my phone is so please buy me one and bring it with you when you come – if fact buy me two, a good one with email and internet and a cheap one just for calls. And Hillie, don't wave them around; give me them surreptitiously so no one else sees. Oh and my address book, which is probably on top of the desk in the study. I've changed the lock so you'll need to borrow the spare from the Steens."

"Mum and dad are coming to see you tomorrow, I'll give everything to them to bring."

"Aren't you coming?" Jo asked with incredulity.

"Not for a couple of days. Darling, I've got so much on – and you know how I detest hospitals and places like that. Anyway, you'll be out by the time I can get myself into gear." And again the subject was changed: "Danny's made you a card – a lovely, lovely card and I'll give that to the folks as well."

"Hillie, did you bring my clothes and toiletries in?"

"Yes darling, couldn't have you in hospital jimjams."

"I changed the locks – how did you get in?"

"Stephen broke in for me."

The statement hit Jo like a punch. He had no right to be anywhere near her house. She decided to allow her anger to pass but not successfully.

"Why didn't you come and see me?" Jo's temper was swirling into place ready to be deployed. "I'm stuck in a nut house, drugged up to the eyeballs and you don't even bother to see me!"

"Jojo, darling, I asked and they said you were sleeping, out of it, so of course I couldn't see you." It did nothing to placate Jo's feelings.

"Of course, how stupid of me. You couldn't possibly stroke my forehead, whisper a few words of comfort into my ear in the hope it might just register, show a little concern or maybe just look at me to check I was okay. And of course you're still not able to come in for a 'few days' because you're naturally too busy." Jo almost shouted the words down the phone. "Too busy doing what, Hilary, having your bloody nails painted, taking a facial?" Jo could hear her voice rising and feel a stultifying sense of frustration.

"Danny, of course, looking after Danny, what else?"

"He goes to school during the day, you dosey cow... Well, you can kill two birds with one stone because I'm desperate to see him so bring him with you."

There was a long, profound silence during which she could not hear Hillie even breathing.

"It's a bit difficult Jojo..." Hillie eventually replied in a quiet voice.

"What do you mean it's a bit difficult?"

Again there was a pregnant silence. "Well. I'm not Danny's next of kin, am I..."

"Quite right, you're not – and there was me thinking you were stupid. What the hell are you on about?"

"Well, with you away, Stephen's in charge of Danny, so to

speak, he is his father after all and Danny's only with me because Stephen is obviously not able to look after him at the moment..."

"Hillie, Stephen couldn't look after him at any moment – not now, not next week, next month, next year..."

Hillie ignored her. "He's asked me – in fact, to be honest Jo, he's told me – not to bring Danny to see you." There was almost panic in Hilllie's tone as she garbled: "He's frightened it might upset him considering your condition and he doesn't want that."

Jo felt her anger surging to a peak.

"Listen to me, you stupid woman. I don't have a condition! That bastard is the reason I'm in here. He had me sectioned to save his pathetic skin and you're asking me to accept what he wants, what he demands. Get your priorities right, Hillie, I'm your sister, your loyalties are to me, now more than ever before in your life. You bring Danny to see me tomorrow or I'll never speak to you again, ever!" Incredulity and fury joined hands in Jo's outrage: "Do you hear me? Do you hear me?" She separated each word out and shouted them down the phone, syllable by syllable.

"Give me the phone please – now!" Nurse Protz had appeared from behind Jo, her hand outstretched, her face set, her words threatening. "You are obviously not yet ready for such intimate contact. Give me the phone please."

Jo looked directly into the woman's eyes, which were still hard and unyielding but flitting across them was an unmistakeable vapour trail of pleasure, or at least self-satisfaction. She didn't mean to say it but in that powerless, oppressive world it was the only weapon she had. "Go screw yourself." The words came out quietly through clenched teeth but Protz could barely hide her delight.

"Assistance," she cried loudly and the large white nurse who had been at Jo's house came running.

Jo read the situation immediately and knew she had only seconds to subvert the inevitable and so thrust the phone into nurse Protz's hand and hauled self-composure from somewhere deep, even managing to paint an artificial smile on her face.

"I'm terribly sorry, nurse Protz, I didn't realise what you meant. Of course you can have the phone. Sisters! I ask you! What can you do with them?"

It was sufficient to sow confusion and the large nurse came to a halt beside them with a look of confusion on her face. Did she need to intervene or didn't she? Her countenance implied that she would have been only too happy to pinion Jo again – to pinion anyone for that matter. But the situation appeared calm and intervention unnecessary.

Nurse Protz took the phone, spun on her heel in such a manner that would have made any ballerina feel proud and busied off with a voice raised loud enough for all to hear: "This kind of outburst is simply not acceptable Josephine. We will need to reconsider your medication."

Jo walked away and threw herself into a sticky plastic-covered armchair, angry inside, scolding herself that she was allowing her feelings towards nurse Protz to run haywire. She was attributing powers to her that were verging on the supernatural when in reality, she was confronted by a sad, controlling woman who was building a tiny empire with the minds of damaged and defective people who had no power to resist her.

Al had heard it all and as Jo sat there, tight-lipped and angry and not attempting to conceal it, he lowered himself down beside her.

"Fated, that phone!"

Jo didn't look at him but kept her gaze straight ahead.

"Don't say anything! Not a bloody word, do you hear me? I know I screwed up so I don't need any advice, okay?"

"I said nothing," Al replied with a nervous smile.

"No, but you were going to."

He laughed. "Watching you respond to Brunhilde is like watching an auto crash in slow motion. If it wasn't so one-sided it would be hilarious."

"There, see, you're doing it! Slipping in a little reminder that I'm on a hiding to nothing..." but by now, a little, reluctant smile was starting to dance across Jo's face.

"Do you know what this reminds me of?" Al asked in an

intimate, pleasant tone but didn't wait for a response. "At a party I once went to long ago, before I was an official head case, I was standing in the kitchen next to a gas stove. In the middle of the burners was a little metal hood over the pilot light and stamped into it was the word 'HOT': people came and went but everyone who stood by that cooker eventually read the word 'hot' and then gingerly stretched out their finger and touched it. Do you know what happened then?" There was barely a pause in his delivery. "They yelled and pulled their hand away. Do you know why? Because it was hot and they'd burnt themselves. That's you and Obersturmbhanfuhrer Protz. And guess which one has hot stamped on them and which one gets burned?"

Al suddenly became very serious.

"You've got to learn to handle her, Jo, or she'll destroy you."

"She's only a bloody nurse but she seems to run this place. Why Al? How can that be?"

"She's efficient, dedicated, committed and all the women are shit scared of her. All the men, on the other hand, fancy the pants off her," he hesitated, "and are even more scared of her than the women because they fear rejection. It's a powerful combination for a psychopath." He then changed the subject entirely. "When you get a phone, Jo, keep hold of it and keep it secret!"

"Well, it seems I'm now blacklisted from phones so please, please Al," she leant towards him, took his arm and adopted an artificial, pleading tone, "will you do me a really big favour? If I give you her number will you please phone a friend of mine called Wendy, tell her where I am and ask her to get here a.s.a.p? Oh, and ask her to bring a mobile for me because I don't trust Hillie to remember."

Having made her request and Al having gone off to carry it out, a huge sense of satisfaction and pleasure filled Jo for she instinctively knew that Wendy would respond instantly, whatever her schedule, and do what was asked of her. And she would do it not out of obligation or guilt but because she wanted to.

The anticipation of seeing her friend almost spilled over into excitement but flushing away some of that pleasure was a sense of disbelief, a deep sadness that someone who should be the one person in the entire world who would immediately act in her best interests, without question, without being pushed, chivvied or cajoled, was her sister, one of her own family. Hillie had failed her and equally as depressing was the realisation that Jo wasn't surprised.

The old saying 'you choose your friends but you can't choose your family' came whirling into her mind from nowhere and she hated its presence, wanted to dismiss it, to spit it out like a bitter pip, but couldn't. Jo had always kidded herself that if ever Hillie was put to the test and her support was truly, genuinely needed, she would be there, dependable and reliable. Her preoccupation with vogue and style, her ability to embrace trivia as though it were a truth and her refusal to allow substance to cast shadows over a life of inconsequence merely camouflaged deeper feelings that would surface when the need arose, Jo had believed.

No, if she was honest, she hadn't believed it, she had merely hoped it and now she knew that Hillie's preoccupation with the unimportant and valueless was not the veneer Jo had always hoped it was but the very substance of her being. The realisation depressed Jo and she felt a very similar sadness for her sister as she did for a nurse she barely knew, but for different reasons. And both were failing her in their own, different ways but for much the same reason – a preoccupation with self.

Jo lay on the minimalist bed in the minimalist room with its minimalist furniture and whilst she felt no ownership over the sad, little, institutional box she inhabited, she was nevertheless grateful for the not so small mercy of having her own room. Some patients did and others did not and those who didn't had to live in small dormitories which accommodated four people.

It was utterly incomprehensible that strangers should be so intimately lumped together; to put four 'insane' people who did not know each other in one room was itself insanity. Stop any four people randomly in the street, she thought, and tell them:

"I'm going to put you all together in the same room to sleep for an indeterminate length of time, what do you think of that?" The response would be a whole mélange of emotions from anger to despair, from fear to utter dread. Not a single person would leap into the air with glee and congratulate themselves on their luck.

Were people with mental health problems purposely to be punished for their disability or was it assumed that having such problems would naturally eliminate their desire for choice and privacy? Whichever, someone, or some committee, probably a finance committee, had made just this choice on their behalf, enforced it and removed the right of objection and made this horrifying imposition an integral part of a regime for making troubled people untroubled.

Perhaps it was just one of the control mechanisms – behave yourself and we give you a room of your own, misbehave and you're back to communal sleeping!

Jo had already witnessed many crazy incidents in this place of craziness but they were little, individual exhibitions of confusion from individual people. This, however, was institutional confusion on an industrial scale or, more likely, corporate contempt that had the power to negatively impact so many vulnerable people. It was incomprehensible.

Jo would have found it utterly unbearable. It was bad enough when she had shared a room with Hilary until her rebellion separated them. "I thought it would be nicer for you two girls to be together," her mother had said for the tenth time, with her usual woolly-headed inability to read any situation until the reality of it was thrust up her nose.

The annoyance of sharing with Hillie was as nothing compared to the prospect of sharing a room in this place of damaged minds.

Jo surveyed her surroundings with a fear that had to be constantly suppressed, like the desire to shout 'shit' when she was in the presence of the priest as a teenager. If fear gained the ascendancy she was convinced her strength would ebb away like water through gravel and she would be at the mercy of the institution, its agents and even its patients.

She appraised her sad little refuge with its pale, grey-green walls that looked almost dusty such was the age of the paint – advanced maturity teetering on the edge of decay; smears of Blu-tack that had spread themselves thinly, clinging tenaciously to the gritty surface, refusing to surrender their hold despite shiny marks of innumerable attempts with scraper and knife to dislodge them; the faded patches of paintwork that had once framed pictures or posters which must have offered comfort and consolation to someone or other whose mind had deserted them by escaping to secret, unknown places or which had buckled under the weight of demands placed upon it.

Perhaps they, too, had sat on this same bed contemplating their future; perhaps a whole string of sad and lonely people, a continuum of damaged minds, had sat on this bed and had drawn some reassurance from whatever it was they had chosen to adorn the walls.

The fact that the room had been vacated and those previous occupants, whoever they were, had now gone, moved on and perhaps returned home and left their demons behind, or at least, perhaps, learnt how to contain them, gave Jo some consolation. But she determined that she would adorn these walls with not so much as a postcard, not a poster nor a single photograph for to do so would be to accept an element of permanence, the first step in genuflecting to her incarceration.

Then there was the cheap furniture; a chipboard bedside table, wardrobe and small chest of drawers all sporting printed paper veneers of oak or teak pretence but neither one matched the other – artificiality in a world that was itself so artificial that Jo was terrified of being sucked down into it and never again properly identifying what passed for normality.

The only object that was not muted or boring or artificial was the bed spread, a thin, tightly-woven, multi-coloured extravaganza of stripy cheerfulness that screamed IKEA from every florid inch, and it lay there demanding attention like a Technicolor tongue protruding from the mouth of a grey and lifeless cadaver.

'Don't worry, everything is really terribly jolly,' it seemed to shout in a futile diversionary tactic, drawing attention away from the dead and depressing surroundings and the locked doors which lay beyond.

Jo had rushed through breakfast and returned to her room for she needed to be alone to think, perhaps to plan, away from the sad reminders of where she was and who she now was – one of them!

Some of the patients appeared normal, depressed but normal, whilst for others, normality was an invention entirely of their own devising. There was Trevor the Hat with his artistic obsessions, particularly with nudity, who paranoically seemed to want to misunderstand anything that might be said to him so he could unleash his knowledge like a superior, verbose and contemptuous weapon.

Baby Doll was old, stooped and permed grey, moving restlessly around the ward like an energetic wind-up toy, scampering hither and thither but always clutching a naked doll to her breast and speaking to no one but men – and new men in particular. She would hover around the entrance door when she thought there might be visitors, waiting for a man and when he appeared she would trot along beside him as he made his way into the ward: "Will you be my boyfriend?" she would ask imploringly but constant rejection never seemed to discomfort or deter her.

The woman who had tried to slice off her husband's sexual organs with a kitchen knife to defend her long-departed virginity had been dubbed Lizzie after Lizzie Borden, the historic young American woman who had chopped up her mother and father. The new Lizzie seemed perfectly normal if constantly embarrassed. Her husband came to visit her and seemed loving and concerned but Jo couldn't help wondering if he wore a cricket box beneath his trousers – just in case.

And there was Tosser who, at any given opportunity, would disappear into the hallway and, facing the wall half crouching, would masturbate behind a particular, old fashioned column radiator as though it cast an invisibility around him.

The all-pervasive power of sex underlined the conditions of most of those in Professor Kadynski's emporium of damaged minds and that realization came to Jo almost as a shock.

POD

Official dining at the Guildhall or Downing Street, the fawning and pampering, the entertaining of foreign dignitaries and minor royals, the beaming obeisances from party loyalists was a planet apart, a juxtaposition that Jo kept at arm's length because the contrast was too disturbing. She concentrated entirely on the here and now and how to escape it but all these people from her past, with their polished accents and privilege, their status and superiority, had a common bond with her fellow inmates and she could not avoid thinking about that. They too were victims of the all-pervasive power of sex.

They were Trevor and Baby Doll and Tosser but had learned how to channel their urges – some of the time. And that realisation was equally shocking. Where she came in this Freudian examination she wasn't sure but the word 'frustration' sprang to mind.

Jo no longer had any doubt that the teaching of her school and others were only secondarily about honouring god and teaching his ways, their primary purpose was to deny, control, subvert, distort and misrepresent the driving force of all humankind, of every creature that walked, crawled, swam or flew and every plant that sprouted for that matter. Only by doing this could they sustain the pretence that we were separate and apart from every other living organism, soul-bearing chosen ones in a sea of soulless, mechanistic products of someone's omnipotent drawing board.

For us to acknowledge and surrender to the same primal force that brought us all to where we are was wrong, sinful, wicked. Why was sex presented as something shameful, a pastime of the weak and perverted, the morally reprehensible, unless practiced in precisely the manner prescribed? Like a foul-tasting medicine it was necessary but you could not expect to enjoy it.

One of the Sisters who taught Jo had been a boarder at a school run by the Sisters of Mercy in Hampstead when she was a child where, when the girls bathed, they were expected to wear a shift to cover their bodies and apply soap and water beneath it, all so they need never gaze upon their own flesh and be corrupted by it. Jo had never experienced anything so extreme but a more dilute terror of things sexual had run through so

404

much of her schooling that if she was not fucked up after twelve years of such indoctrination, then she should be.

Whilst Jo felt she had some superficial understanding of the people around her and which fuelled her sympathy, she could not help smiling at their antics. But as they were all in this locked ward because they had at some time supposedly been violent, she kept her amusement to herself. She was, however, incapable of offering them support because the profundity of their problems was far beyond her but more than that, the paralysing truth was that she did not even know how to help herself.

Jo was aware that her dreams – experiences she now called them – which had been diminishing in both frequency and intensity for some time, had disappeared entirely since she had been in this place. Was it the different geographical location? Was it the drugs that had possibly interfered with the receptivity of her mind? Or – and it was this that was at the heart of Jo's concerns – had the antipsychotic drugs eliminated them because she was psychotic? She could not afford to dwell on the thought because to allow it even a foothold in her consciousness would erode every vestige of resistance.

Instead, she sought pleasure from anticipating Wendy's visit, which was scheduled for later that morning but that pleasure had been pruned and pared by the realization that no matter how concerned and supportive Wendy might be, when the visit was over she would walk away, back into the real world of buses and taxis, cafes and commitments, hustle and bustle and Jo would be left behind in this world of profound confusion. She was very afraid that once Wendy, and all the reassurances she would surely bring with her, disappeared whence they came and the doors were locked behind her, it would be a more powerful reminder of Jo's impotence than anything she had experienced so far.

She avoided any further speculation by immersing herself in a Danish detective story called The Snowman, in which a whole string of people died horrendous deaths by being dismembered. The fiction seemed quite cheery when juxtaposed with her reality.

When a nursing assistant popped her head around the door to tell her of Wendy's arrival, Jo almost ran along the corridor to meet her friend, desperate to be in the company of someone she knew.

They hugged and kissed and Wendy stroked her face and kept repeating: "What have they done to you... what have they done to you?" Jo had been determined not to cry but she was only partially successful in containing her tears and as they gently flowed, Wendy responded in a similar vein and the two women stood holding each other, neither fully able to comprehend how they came to be where they were.

"Jesus Christ, Wendy, I've spent that last three or four days crying – I don't want to cry any more, I don't want to have reason to cry any more."

"We have to get you of here... We will get you out of here, do you hear me?" There was a pause before she added: "I presume Stephen was responsible?"

Jo nodded vigorously and realized, of course, that Wendy would know only what she had read in the papers or seen on TV and, of course, it was unlikely that any finger of suspicion would have been overtly aimed in Stephen's direction.

"What happened, Jo. How...? What excuse did they give?"

"They just came and got me at home, injected me so I was incapable and I finished up here. Told me I was a schizo, a danger to Danny and they just came and took me away..." Jo briefly went through the details of what had happened and even as she repeated them it all sounded fantastical. "It was a done deal but I didn't see it coming, I'm so stupid, I'm so bloody stupid, I almost invited it, I accommodated them."

"No you didn't, you did nothing wrong. Whatever you did, whatever you said, wherever you went, they would have come and got you because you're a threat to them." Wendy looked around the secure ward that now contained her friend and although she said nothing, a thought ripped through her mind that left fear in its wake – if they were prepared to do something as corrupt and as obscene as this, what else might they have done if this option had not been available? She knew the answer and it frightened her.

"Please Wendy, can you try and help me? My family is bloody useless and will fanny around from now to eternity without actually doing anything."

Wendy guessed she was about to step into territory of which she had no comprehension. She was dangerously out of her depth – they both were. But that could not, would not deter her. What was being asked of her, what she was determined to do, had some uncanny similarities with her day job – confronting authority with the cruelty it sanctioned but refused to acknowledge – and there was some comfort in that.

"Of course, of course, of course I'll help you, I've just got to work out where to start," Wendy replied, as she looked at the pleading face of her friend, knowing that any such action would likely provoke a whirlwind of reaction.

Jo signalled to Al who was heading for the snooker room to come and join them, which he did and she introduced the two strangers.

"Al, this is my friend on the outside, Wendy, and, Wendy, this is my friend on the inside, Al." She turned to Wendy. "He thinks he knows everything and, much as I hate to say it, he probably does. Wendy's going to rescue me," she said to Al with a smile, brushing away the last vestiges of her tears. "You're never short of advice, Mr Dwight, what do you recommend?"

Al struck the theatrical posture of a sage, stroking his chin and they laughed.

"Social media is always a good starting point," he offered. "Get a good old-fashioned protest going on Facebook and Twitter – 'Free Josephine Aldous', you know the kind of thing. Coming from mostly nameless individuals, you can put your old man well and truly in the frame – name names, make allegations, just needs a bit of managing to get it going. And the bigger it gets, the safer you are…"

"It's a bit late for that, they've already done their worst unless… Christ, you don't think there's more to come, do you?" Jo replied with a laugh. Wendy and Al exchanged unexpected glances and each knew that they had a similar vision of what could lie ahead. "But I get what you mean. Great idea!" Jo concluded.

Wendy made her contribution.

"I guess another way is to draw together as many high profile people as we can to make a public statement, to question the diagnosis and the decision to... commit you or whatever, because they're not going to listen to me and certainly not to you two," and then sheepishly added, "sorry but it's true. And we'll keep harrying them relentlessly, trying to use the media that haven't committed to Stephen Aldous, make a bloody nuisance of ourselves. It's not going to be instant, though."

"I'm only here for thirty days – I'll be out before that works," Jo replied.

Al shook his head ruefully.

"Jo, my beautiful, you ain't going to see the outside of this place until long after the election – you'll be too much of a threat even then..."

The thought had not occurred to Jo and she did not know why because it was so blindingly obvious. "Do you really think so?" she asked but the words were wrapped in so much pathos that neither Al nor Wendy could bring themselves to reply.

Al smiled gently.

"You really need to know who signed the section because there might be some avenue that could form an appeal to a Mental Health Tribunal. Listen Jo, you do not have a mental health problem and three people have lied in writing – there has to be some percentage there." The women looked at him uncomprehendingly. "I've got no idea how long it might take but if we can get some strong opinions in defence of you, and particularly a medical opinion, we can shame the bastards who prostituted themselves and you'll get a tribunal. Whether they can cook the tribunal or not is the next question but I suspect they won't find it that easy. Or am I being naïve?"

Al stopped and looked quizzically at the two women.

"You haven't got a clue what I'm talking about, have you? Didn't Kadynski explain it to you, Jo, your rights and all that?"

Jo looked embarrassed but smiled.

"I was concentrating on his stupid bloody bow tie."

Al continued: "I forget – I've been here so long and have acted as advocate for so many patients that I couldn't help picking up a bit of savvy. Okay, well, a section has to be signed by three people – two doctors and a social worker. Kadynski is obviously one of the doctors and the second was probably your GP..."

"No, no, no…" Jo almost shouted. "Reece wouldn't have signed it in a thousand years. He's my friend, one of the few true friends I've got."

"Look, Jo, anyone who can do this to you can be very persuasive, very persuasive indeed. Fear or inducement, or both together, can buy almost anyone's loyalty…"

"No, not Reece," Jo was almost shouting, "he wouldn't betray me. Reece would never betray me, he's not that kind of man." Desperation was starting to infect her voice. "I won't let you make me doubt him – he's a true friend. And anyway, I can't string together a whole load of high-profile people. It's a pathetic thing to have to say but I don't really know any. The whole political thing just washed over me and I never pursued friendships – with any of them and if there had been any, they probably wouldn't want to go near me now – I'm a pariah in their eyes. All the other people I know are just nobodies – nice but nobodies. If I can't trust Reece, there's no one else, there really is no one and that thought is about as bloody depressing as you can get."

"I hope you're sure, Jo, I really hope you're sure. To me it's inconceivable they would have dared do this without the say so of your GP. Be cautious Jo," Al said quietly. "Be very cautious."

"No! I've had all the betrayal I can take – no more, I can't countenance any more. If I can't trust Reece then I can't trust anyone. I'm entirely on my own apart from Wendy." Wendy offered her a wan little smile and a gentle hold of her arm. With her voice back to normal Jo added, almost pleadingly: "You don't know him, Al, you've never met him."

Al's face did not change and he spoke matter-of-factly.

"What other doctor interviewed you?"

"None. Kadynski didn't even interview me, he just told me what was wrong with me and what he was going to do. The drippy houseman who was with him didn't speak at all, just stuck a bloody needle in me."

"If he's the other doctor they'll just back each other up and say they did an exhaustive assessment. But the guy's hardly independent if he's Kadynski's houseman and that has to be seen as suspect…" There was a long pause before Al added quietly, "...and that's why I have doubts about your friend Reece. Okay, who was the social worker?"

"There wasn't one. I don't think I've ever met a social worker in my entire life."

"In that case they must have gone for a relative, which is allowed as an alternative, and that would obviously have been Stephen."

"Bloody marvellous," Jo spat out. "He's spent his whole life avoiding committing himself to anything in case it came back to bite him on the arse but doesn't hesitate when it comes to getting rid of me." She paused and a thought occurred to her and when she spoke it was with determination: "Did you bring a phone, Wendy?"

Wendy nodded and looked around before surreptitiously removing the mobile from her bag and slipping it to Jo.

"The number's on the Post-it."

Jo handed it on to Al. "Would you mind, just for the moment, I've got nowhere to conceal it." She looked around her. "Do you mind using yours just in case the nurse from hell comes along. See if you can get hold of Reece," she requested. "I can't remember his home number and he's probably ex-directory but get the practice number from directory – it's the Queens Road practice, Weybridge."

"Hold on a minute." There was urgency in Al's voice. "I think you can demand a copy of your section so talk to Dealey, get that and check it before you call – then you'll know for sure."

"Ring directory please, Wendy." Jo spoke with dismissive authority: "It's the Queens Road practice."

Al said nothing but cast his eyes upwards and Wendy picked out directory enquiries on her phone, got Reece's number and then dialled. There was a long, long wait with each set of eyes avoiding the other, their focus entirely on the mobile held by Wendy as though it held the key to eternal salvation. Wendy suddenly thrust it towards Jo as though it had become electrified.

"Can I speak to Reece, please?... Jo Aldous... I see... When will he be back?... That's fine, thank you," Jo pressed the end call button with an unmistakable air of dejection, her spirit deflated. "He's away, back in a few days."

"Convenient," was all that Al said and silence momentarily settled over the trio. As if by common consent, Reece Evans and the section were not referred to again and soon after, Al left Jo and Wendy to their own company. The two women managed a smile or two and a few laughs as they temporarily pushed to one side the gravity of Jo's situation. Wendy then confided that she had continued what Jo had started and had been tracking current animal on human attacks and would provide the results to Jo as soon as she got out.

"So you don't think I'm deluded then?" Jo asked half seriously.

"Jo!" Wendy admonished. "It's a problem, I know it's a problem and it's getting bigger. It seems to be remorselessly spreading further and further inland – slowly but it's happening."

"And the government, the opposition? Anything from them?"

"Not a word – nothing. They must surely know about it and you'd have thought they'd have made some comment. Maybe they know something we don't. And by the way, I never want to hear you ever again allude to yourself as being deluded, or bonkers or nutty or anything like that. There is absolutely nothing wrong with you and if you start to doubt yourself you're on a slippery slope. Do you hear me?"

Jo smiled, reached out and took Wendy by the hand without embarrassment.

"You're a clever woman."

"Why?"

"Because that's exactly what I wanted to hear – needed to hear."

One of the junior nurses approached them and in a professionally kind voice told Jo that her mother had rung and would be visiting shortly.

Wendy made to leave but paused in silence for a while before speaking.

"I obviously don't know about your doctor friend but you do need to obtain a copy of the document that authorised your being detained, the section or whatever it is, because, quite honestly, it's all we've got and is a kind of route map of who, what, where and when. If it contains bad news you have to deal with it, Jo. You can't allow it to defeat you. You have to keep fighting. You are my priority now and I will do everything

411

possible to bring this to an end. There are people I can go to for advice but it's not going to be instant and neither is the social media thing, but I think you knew that. You say they're woolly but we do need to get your parents on board."

"God, don't I know it. I just wish I had more faith in them – they get so easily overwhelmed. It's like they've lived their lives being loyal to authority and I just know they're going to find it difficult to go to war against it. Their attitude will be that someone's made a mistake and if we all just ignore it, ask nicely and be polite, everything will be put right before too long. Maybe I've got them wrong – I hope so.

"I'll text you my mum and dad's number and any others I can think of that might be useful. By the way, you'll need a nurse to let you out – all of us in here are so dangerous that we have to be kept locked in!"

Wendy initially looked incredulous but made her way to find a nurse and then paused, looked back at Jo with a smile on her face and said: "By the way, Al seems very nice – bit dishy really. Is he…" she raised one eyebrow, "…alright… not…?"

Jo laughed. "Yes, I think he is alright – nothing that a good woman couldn't sort out, I suspect," and much to her embarrassment found herself blushing. Wendy disappeared through the entrance doors with a wave and a big smile on her face.

Far from being deflated or depressed with Wendy's departure, Jo felt enervated, positive, ready for the fight and as the tentacles of contact began to snake out one by one to make more people aware of her position, she felt her isolation was diminished. She was no longer alone.

She determined to ring Reece again and leave a message with him as to what had happened and where she was and to contact her with urgency on his return from wherever he had gone. She would stress their friendship to the receptionist and urge the woman to communicate the message to him wherever he was. If Hilary or her mum ever brought her phone or her address book she would ring him immediately on his mobile. But one way or another she had to speak to him.

Like picking at a scab, she almost taunted herself with the

thought that he might have signed her section but it simply did not work. She had been through this process once before and it had not worked then either – it was literally incredible and if Reece had done it, for whatever reason, she wasn't sure she would want to continue the fight so eagerly for the landscape she had known would have fundamentally changed to become an uninviting wasteland. She felt utterly disloyal in even contemplating his betrayal.

Jo went back to her novel and more dismembered bodies until she was told her mother had arrived then went out to greet her, with some trepidation.

Her mother was standing motionless in the middle of the ward, fear in her face, acute fear, her eyes darting from one patient to another, with even a glance over her shoulder to remind herself where the exit was situated. Relief washed over her and her eyes filled with tears when she saw Jo but she remained stationary, her arms held out open wide and Jo walked into them.

They hugged and hugged and Jo wasn't sure who hugged the hardest and wasn't absolutely sure whether her mother's unusually overt expression of emotion was pleasure at seeing her daughter or relief that she was no longer alone in a psychiatric ward amongst strange patients, each one of which was probably a latter day Jack the Ripper, in her mind.

"Is Danny with you?" Jo asked eagerly.

"He's downstairs with Dad."

"Oh brilliant. No Hillie?"

"No, darling, not today. But I'm sure she'll come soon." Jo could tell there was no confidence in her mother's words and ushered her towards the quiet room and was pleased to find it devoid of people.

Even before they had sat down her mother was twittering and chirping away like a newly-arrived swallow, as though mundanity would hold at bay all thoughts of this disturbing place.

"Now, Hilary has given me your address book to give to you and I suspect the food here isn't terribly good so I've put together a few tasty things I know you like... and you didn't say if you wanted any books or magazines so I've put a little selection in this carrier bag and your address book is in there as well... and if you want anything else, it isn't very far from Weybridge to Egham – but how silly of me, you know that anyway, remember, you used to have a friend who lived here... I can't for the life of me recall her name but I'm sure you remember her, she went to Sir William Perkins school in Chertsey..."

"Mum, mum, mum, it's alright, I'm alright, I'm not ill, I'm not crazy," Jo gently impelled her mother into a chair and sat facing her holding both her hands. "I'm really okay, Mum, I need to explain things to you and you have to listen – you have to believe me. There is nothing wrong with me, mum, nothing."

Her mother looked back steadily into her eyes, her gaze remaining in contact with Jo's and those eyes contained a clarity and understanding that Jo had never seen before. She could not remember how many years it had been since she had really looked at her mother, looked deeply into her eyes to see what was there. Perhaps she had perceived her mother as empty simply because she had not bothered to look for anything, because she had not expected anything to be there. She felt the feeble fluttering of her mother's fingers beginning to still before they gripped Jo's own fingers firmly, with intent.

"I think you underestimate me, Jo. You always have. I know you're not ill and I didn't believe any of those things they printed in the paper. You are still my little Jojo, my first-born child and I know you better than anyone. I also know Stephen is a cad – I've thought so for some time – and I have no doubt that he is behind this."

Once more Jo surrendered to tears but now they were racking sobs and she leant forward and clasped her mother to her, their arms intertwined, their cheeks resting one against another, their tears intermingling as years of Jo's misunderstanding were washed away. Only now did she realize how profound that misunderstanding had been and the ache it had left inside her – a desperation to be truly loved and understood but one she had tried to deny because she thought it unattainable, had buried the desire deep beneath pretence and supposed indifference. How could she have been so wrong about her mother and it had taken something as profound as this for her to realise it?

"I'm not very strong Josephine and I'm not very brave but there is nothing I will not do to get you out of this place and to set the record straight." It was almost worth having endured all that she had simply to hear those words, Jo thought. Her use of the word Josephine indicated that this was serious and her mother was gearing up for action. "Don't be too hard on Hilary because she has always been weak and I suppose that's my fault, too. But you, Jojo, you have the strength to defeat this and we will help you."

They dried their eyes and blew their noses with no embarrassment.

"Dear, dear, dear, dearie me," her mother said, simply to fill the silence.

"Shouldn't Danny and Dad be here by now?" Jo asked.

"Oh no, dear, they're not coming up. I assumed she'd told you – I'm sorry, I should have said."

"What do you mean, they're not coming up?"

"They won't let Danny in."

"Sorry, what do you mean, they won't let him in? Who won't let him in?"

"The nurse said you weren't ready yet to see him – too emotional for you, too much of a strain, she said they couldn't risk it so Daddy took him back to the car. Absolute nonsense I know but we had no option but to agree… I'll have another word with her, see if I can persuade her to change her mind. Jo? Are you listening to me?"

Jo was not listening to her, she wasn't listening to anything as the blood drained from her face leaving behind a vengeful mask with diamond hard eyes and trembling lips.

"Which nurse?" she demanded but already knew the answer.

"The little pretty one – the one with the blonde hair and pony tail."

"Wait here, mum," Jo said quietly and left the room. She strode through the ward with frightening purpose, oblivious to everything and everybody around her, her face set rigidly, seeking out the person who had caused hatred to ignite inside her in a blinding explosion that obliterated all caution and restraint and demanded retribution. All the betrayals and injustices Jo had borne so far were as nothing compared to this wanton act of malice and spite.

When she saw nurse Protz some distance away, in the far corner of the ward, bending over to talk to a chair-bound patient, Jo shouted: "Why?" It was not her normal voice and the word issued forth like a war cry, a short, sharp bellow of angered pain that filled the large room like a rifle shot, echoing back from its faded walls, inducing instant silence and causing every head to snap towards its source and nurse Protz to spring upright, all in one lightening, seemingly choreographed movement.

Jo continued towards the nurse and again the word "Why?" exploded from her lips but by now Jo was close enough to see just a trace of fear in the woman's face that caused her eyes to open wide and her jaw to sag, but it lasted just an instant and was replaced by studied calmness and in that transition Jo could see that Protz was not only back in charge of her emotions but had anticipated Jo's anger and was fully prepared. It was only the suddenness of Jo's shout that had momentarily shocked her. Jo could see that her own fury was counterbalanced by Protz's anticipation and smug self-satisfaction.

"You sick cow," Jo screamed at her and in response, the word 'assistance' rang out. And then came the familiar vice-like grip of hard hands on her arms, a crashing to the floor, enforced immobility and the jagged, jabbing pain of a hastily-inserted needle – only this time Jo knew what to expect and as the fog rolled in, as her muscles withdrew their services and the treacle of near-oblivion decanted into her mind, she felt no fear, no apprehension only hatred and the silent phrase, 'You will not defeat me,' was silently deployed over and over again.

The last clear words she could decipher were her mother's, harsh and strident: "Leave her alone, leave her alone you horrible woman." She had never before heard such anger in her voice.

Chapter Thirty Three

Jo's personality gradually returned over the following two days and she had not been able to agonise over its absence as the enforced chemical gelding had removed all concerns and emotions. But once the medication was reduced a glimmer of resistance began to reassert itself.

During her darkest period, Al was once again her link with the real world or, more accurately, was the orchestrator of an existential phenomenon that attempted to link one unreal world with another, the real world itself existing beyond their reach. But this time he expressed his concerns more intimately.

He sat with her and from time to time held her hands in his and quietly stroked them with his thumbs. He ran the tips of his fingers down her face as reassurance, gently, caressingly. He dampened tissues and wiped her lips and eyes and found warm, wet flannels with which to refresh her face. But it all had to be done with discretion as they were both the focus of nurse Protz's attention and she reacted instantly if Al's ministrations went on too long or if she perceived his actions as 'inappropriate'. It wasn't really inappropriateness that concerned Protz but intimacy.

The pretence that Jo was a seriously disturbed woman suffering from psychoses was kept very much alive by Protz even though all three of the participants in the lop-sided drama knew it to be false. If heavy looks, serious tutting and diversionary tactics failed to disrupt Al's attention to Jo, Protz would employ her default position: "Alexander, I think you should leave Josephine to rest now!"

Al talked endlessly, sometimes quietly and reflectively, other times he was cheery and buoyant and some of the time he apologized, often profusely. He had assumed blame for her situation.

"I was in the washroom, Jo, I didn't see what was happening. I am so, so sorry – I could have stopped you, would have stopped you. You would have had to claw your way through me to get to her! I'm supposed to be your friend and I failed you, I let them do this to you!"

As the effects of the medication gradually diminished and Jo could start to marshal her thoughts into some kind of comprehensible order, she was extremely relieved that Al had not been present because she suspected that he, too, would have been embroiled and might well have also been chemically subdued. Had he used any physical force on Protz or any of the other staff, the outcome could have been disastrous and he may well have found himself, even now, en route to one or other depository for the criminally insane, Broadmoor or Rampton. But he had escaped that and now he was comforting her, the only person who could as all visits had been suspended because of her 'condition'.

Al painted verbal pictures for her that remained in her consciousness for long afterwards and at times, particularly when alone, she would unroll them and relive their warmth and normality and ride away from her incarceration on their backs.

"When we get out of here we're going down to Brighton and we'll stroll around with no intent, just looking, observing. We'll get blown by the wind on the pier and watch all our troubles take wing as gusts carry them off towards Saltdean and Rottingdean. We'll eat chips from a packet and try to stop the gulls from grabbing them but then we'll take pity on the birds and toss chips high into the air which they can swoop down and grab in their beaks.

"And you'll have your fortune told by Gypsy Petulengro who'll tell you that all your suffering is over and you will have a beautiful rest of your life and we will believe her, not because she is a clairvoyant but because we know it to be true.

"Later, we will tire ourselves out by walking to the marina to see the boats and I can show you the one that used to be mine

– a lovely, dark blue ketch built from mahogany, with tan-coloured sails that can impel her over the waves like a bird. And we'll say hello, have a nice day, to everyone we meet, because it is a nice day – a lovely day. Then we'll ride back on the little electric railway and watch clear, green waves curling onto the pebbled beach as we rattle along.

"And we'll get back to the pier just in time to stroll up to East Street for our table at Terre a Terre – don't worry, it's a veggie restaurant and the best in town – and we'll order extraordinary sounding dishes from incomprehensible descriptions on the menu and when they arrive they will be beautiful to taste and a feast for the eyes. We will choose the wine carefully to complement them and we won't care about cost and it will be perfection and explode with flavour and we will drink just a little too much of it.

"When we want to eat no more and cannot face another glass of wine, we will walk slowly to the Grand Hotel in the warm dark of the evening and I will hold your hand because you're just a little bit tipsy and your feet won't do exactly what you tell them. We will stay in rooms overlooking the sea and in the morning we'll have breakfast on the terrace, watching the comings and goings along Kings Road and the glinting of the waves as they move relentlessly shorewards. And the only decision confronting us will be what to do with the rest of the day."

When he paused, Jo looked at him with a warmth she had not felt for longer than she could remember. She knew that if she strung together every heartfelt, gentle, intimate phrase that Stephen had ever addressed to her in all their years together they would have barely amounted to the length of Al's first paragraph. She looked at him with her heavy, drooping eyes and with a small smile asked: "Rooms?" It was a while before he replied.

"Uhmmm, well, that's up for negotiation," but he looked seriously flustered as he sat there for long seconds, silently looking at her, unable to prevent his own little smile from spontaneously responding, surreptitiously creeping in to brighten his eyes. And then he leant forward and kissed Jo gently on her forehead. All that marred the magic of the moment was that he first felt obliged to cast his eyes around the ward to see if nurse Protz was within view.

As strength surged back into her body and mind, Jo got Al to phone Danny and again she drew contentment from her son but this time he was more demanding, wanting to know precisely why he was staying with his aunt and when she would be coming home.

"I've had enough of this now, mum. I want to go back home – with you. Aunty Hillie and dad are always whispering when he comes here so I can't hear and I know something's going on, that something's wrong but no one will tell me. What is it mum? Please tell me, it's not fair. Is it something I've done?"

"No, no, no, Danny, you've done nothing wrong – I promise you, nothing wrong at all." The temptation to tell Danny the truth welled up in her and she had to fight against it just as she had with her knowledge of Stephen's predilections.

"All they'll tell me is that you're not well but they won't tell me what's wrong with you... Mum?" Jo could hear the tears in his voice.

"Yes darling?"

"Mum? You're not... dying are you?"

"Danny, oh Danny, I promise you with all my heart that I'm not dying. There's nothing wrong with me Danny, nothing wrong with me at all..."

"Has it got to do with the fights you have with Dad? Have you gone away?"

The temptation to tell the truth was again overpowering but Jo fought against it.

"Listen my gorgeous. Things have gone wrong and I've been told I have to have a rest. I don't need a rest but I've got to convince the doctors of that and make them see that I need to go home – to you."

"Dad's pretty important isn't he – can't he tell them?"

"Trouble is, Danny, he's not a doctor." Jo could feel the straightjacket of not being able to be honest with her son beginning to choke her and she wanted to scream and cry and tell him the truth but it would have been through a jumble of tears and anger and frustration and hatred. She remained silent, her head in one hand, the phone in the other. Al gently turned her face towards him and mimed talking into the phone and then said:

"Introduce me."

"Danny, a very, very good friend of mine wants to talk to you," and she handed the phone to Al.

"Hi Danny, I'm Al. Funny, I don't know what you look like but I know a heck of a lot about you because your mom never stops telling me the things you've done. I'm not going to embarrass you by repeating them, okay?" He said it with a laugh. "Your secrets are safe with me, Danny!" Jo could not hear the response. "I just wanted to say that everything your mom says is true. She's fine, really fine, and that's a promise. And it's really important you believe that. What they're scared of is that she might have something infectious and she has to keep out of everyone's way, particularly kids, until they know for sure. I'm helping to look after her while she's here and we're going to get this mess sorted out and I promise she'll be home soon. It may take a few days or even a week or two but she's coming home, okay?"

Al went silent while Danny replied.

"Yeah, it is shit, you're right, but hang on in there buddy because your mom needs you. We're both going to help her and if it's okay with you I'll call you from time to time and we can talk about things, I can give you an update." Al had in mind the possibility of further lost days due to yet more sedation and did not want his calls to cause concern. "Is that okay, Danny? Great, see you soon."

He handed the phone back to Jo and she and Danny said their goodbyes and as Jo pressed the off button Al held his arms open and she leant into them. When she had finished sobbing and had wiped her eyes she asked:

"Why didn't I think of that excuse?"

"It just came to me. Seems deceit is ingrained in me."

Jo squeezed his hand: "Rubbish!... Why didn't you have children, Al?"

"It was always going to be tomorrow – and then my tomorrows disappeared."

A tiny smile found its way into Jo's face: "And by the way, you should have told him off for saying shit."

"That's his mom's job – he can say anything he likes to me. Those are the rules now," and Jo detected just a hint of genuine pleasure in a face that had been almost permanently careworn.

By the third day Jo felt as normal as she ever expected to feel so long as she was a participant in the twice daily routine of being medicated. She was normal enough to seek out Peter Dealey in his office and demand to see a copy of her section. He flustered and blustered and said he didn't have it but that it was kept by Professor Kadynski.

The oppressive weight of her situation needed to be counterbalanced by something positive and so she was determined to deploy the only weapon she had – honesty in the hope of bringing to an end the ludicrous charade of stepping lightly around the damaged psyche of a troubled nurse. That had run its course.

"This is an official demand, Dealey, I want to see it, I want to know who the bastards are who have lied to put me in here, to keep me out of the way – and don't look at me like that because you can drop the pretence; we both know there's nothing wrong with me. You may not have actually commissioned my sectioning or even known about it but you know now that I shouldn't be here. And while we're at it, that psychotic cow you call a nurse is going to kill someone one day and when she does it will be your weakness that's responsible."

Dealey's face was set with just the right proportions of professional concern, world weariness and practiced patience but beneath it Jo could detect the unmistakable flicker of concern that clearly signalled she was troubling him, touching something sensitive somewhere, excavating a truth that he had wilfully ignored and did not want to surface.

"I would like you to calm down, Josephine," he said, his own practiced calmness belying the tension that filled the room. Jo ignored him.

"God almighty, this is supposed to be a psychiatric hospital, you're supposed to be a trained psychiatric nurse, you're supposed to be capable of recognising and treating mental health problems and yet one of your number is a mad woman and you do nothing about it. It's all going to explode one day and you fucking know it Dealey! When the shit hits the fan – and it will – you'll have so much explaining to do."

"Josephine, your behaviour is unacceptable. You're not doing yourself any favours. I would like you to calm down and go to the quiet room."

"Don't call me Josephine. You call me Jo or Mrs Aldous but not fucking Josephine. Have you got that?"

As though a boil had been lanced, Jo felt the anger and frustration draining away whilst determination flooded in to fill the void vacated by them. She remained silent, maintaining eye contact with the charge nurse until he looked away, casting his eyes downwards to his desk, moving papers around aimlessly. When Jo spoke again it was quietly, without passion or anger.

"I am calm, Dealey, I've said most of what I want to say so look at me." Dealey kept his eyes averted. "Look at me, mister Dealey!" Jo spoke the words with cold, hard intensity and Dealey raised his eyes to make contact with hers but discomfort made them flicker and dart as though seeking a refuge somewhere, anywhere, like the opposite poles of a magnet brought together, incapable of remaining static.

"You know that everything I've said is true and one day I will get out of here and when I do I will expose this incestuous, perverted, immoral little empire of sad misfits for what it is!" Dealey made no response but Jo read fear in his face for a fraction of a moment. It was, however, his silence, his lack of defence, that signalled his capitulation.

"Oh, and just one more thing, you will never again prevent me from seeing my son, turn him away from the doors of this ward with the obscene pretence that I pose some kind of threat to him. Do you understand that?"

Jo watched Peter Dealey's face slump fractionally and incomprehension flush his cheeks. "Oh yes, Dealey, that's why your girlfriend sedated me, because she refused to let me see my son and I objected to her spiteful vendetta against me. You backed her actions and you didn't even know the reasons for them."

POD

Contempt dripped acidly from every word but even as she watched them strike home like tracer bullets and observed the impact they had on the man – the discomfort that he could not quite hide – the realisation came to Jo that this was not how she should leave him, it was essential to toss the floundering man a wisp of a lifeline.

"I'm sure you're not a bad man, Dealey, not a nasty man, not a vindictive man, in fact you're probably quite nice outside this place. But every decision you fail to take, every action you rubber stamp, every time you avert your gaze and walk away, it impacts on someone's life, lives that are miserable enough already without you adding to it. You have to take back control while you still can. Please think about it – seriously!"

As Jo turned and moved towards the door Dealey responded: "Oh, I forgot to say, there's a letter here for you." His words were spoken with extraordinary normality, as though they had just been having a conversation about the weather. She turned and took the pale-yellow envelope from him but his brief flirtation with attempting eye contact had come to an end and he failed to look at her.

Jo had identified immediately the portcullis logo on the back of the envelope and knew it to be from the House of Commons, although she could think of no reason why she would receive an official communication. As she walked across the ward Jo slid her finger along the top of the envelope to open it, removed the letter and on unfolding it, immediately recognised Stephen's signature beneath just nine typed lines. Even her name was typed.

Dear Josephine

I have to inform you that because of your ill health and absence in hospital, our son Daniel requires more structure in his life than he is currently experiencing. Because of the demands on my time at this important juncture, I am unable to provide that structure on a regular basis and as a consequence I have registered him at Hillside Preparatory Boarding School (www.hillsideprepschool.ed) at Box Hill, Surrey. He will attend at the end of February as a full-time

*boarder and whilst it is my intention that he should spend
some weekends with me, I cannot at this time give any
undertakings on this. I will keep you informed of his
progress.*

   Sincerely

   Stephen.

Jo stood in the middle of the ward, the letter hanging loosely
from her extended arm. She breathed deeply in silence and her
head slowly titled back until her eyes were staring at the ceiling.
When it came, it came like an eruption, a volcanic mountain
blowing its top, an explosion of enormous magnitude that was
frightening – an outward, audible expression of the far greater
turbulence that lay out of sight and hearing.

"You b-a-s-t-a-r-d." Part scream, part shout, part bellow, that
one word, in the manner of its delivery, contained anger,
despair, pain and disbelief suffused with a promise of
vengeance. The ward became silent instantly with inhalations
and exhalations of breath suspended in mid execution as if
afraid to complete their function; conversations abandoned in
mid word; scrabble letters held motionless in suspended
animation and all heads turned towards the source of the
outburst. The silence was absolute until a voice chivvied:
"Come on, I have to hurry you."

"You bastard," rang out again but this time the volume had
decreased and the voice seemed to be imploding on itself,
hatred surrendering to disbelief and despair. "You bloody,
fucking bastard – how could you, how could you?"

Other sounds began to compete with Jo's wail of anguish
and footsteps came echoing down the ward, running towards
its source.

"Control yourself, Josephine, control yourself," nurse Protz
instructed with matter-of-fact brusqueness. "You are disturbing
the other patients."

"What about me, you stupid, stupid woman? Ask me what's
wrong with me, why don't you?"

"We're getting very tired of these emotional outbursts, Josphine," nurse Protz said as she moved towards Jo with an arm extended. Jo shot out her hand to ward the woman off but mistimed it and the heel of her hand caught nurse Protz just beneath her nose and she reeled backward, clutching her face.

Almost instantly the cry went up once more: "Assistance, assistance," but there was no delay in response this time as those summoned were already standing around Jo in a semi-circle, almost within touching distance and she was immediately grasped by eager hands. Despite her blinding anger, Jo kept telling herself not to struggle, not to resist – commands which she obeyed but which did little to reduce the violence she was subjected to as she was thrust down onto the floor.

Jo was suddenly aware of a commotion other than the one generated by her actions and into her vision came Al, his face contorted with both fury and determination as he dragged Peter Dealey into the melee by his shirt front, Dealey's face fearful and uncomprehending.

Al spun him towards nurse Protz, grabbing the hair on the back of his head so he had no option but to look directly into her face just inches from him.

"Call her off, Dealey, call off your Rottweiler. This is not the way to treat anyone."

Once more the ward lapsed into absolute silence as Dealey and nurse Protz confronted each other. The delay in Dealey's answer seemed interminable and the silence intensified as the pre-recorded burble of the aimless TV quiz show continued without remission. It came from another world, another place, but its surreal jollity hung in the air without detracting from the tension; it was as though it was itself an element of that silence, one of its constituent parts, helping to escalate the electrifying suspense to unbearable heights. Protz regarded Dealey with smug certainty.

"Peter?"

Dealey's mouth moved but no words came out of a countenance seemingly riven with misery. Al relaxed his hold on Dealey's hair, allowing him to raise his head and extend the space between him and Protz.

"I need you to back me, Peter." Protz issued her words icily, not as a request but as a demand, as though instructing a recalcitrant child and every pair of eyes in the ward were focused on Peter Dealey's face, awaiting his response. It was a long time coming and when it did it was preceded by a cough before he averted his face away from Protz.

"Well, the crisis seems to have passed and so I think that any further control measures would be inappropriate. Nurse Protz, I would like you to go to my office – right now – and Alexander, you will never display that kind of behaviour again no matter what the emergency – do you understand me?"

There had been a transformation in the man as he appeared to shake off his fear and impotence and take decisive control of the situation. As he did so he seemed to grow in stature and confidence.

"What was that all about Josephine – Jo – I could hear your profanities from my office."

Jo had remained on the floor although she had raised herself to a sitting position, the letter still clutched in her hand. She offered it to Dealey wordlessly and he read it carefully before responding:

"I take it you're not in agreement with this?"

"It breaks a pledge never to send Danny to boarding school." There was so much she wanted to say but with the first flush of anger now passed she knew that she needed to meet Dealey half way and control her reactions so as not to compromise the decision he had just taken – a decision in her favour.

"Would you like me to arrange a meeting with your husband so you can discuss this in private?"

A tight-lipped, cynical smile took control of her mouth and she shook her head from side to side vigorously.

"Very well, perhaps under the circumstances it would be appropriate to have an extended visit from your son. If you don't mind being accompanied I think we can allow you to have a walk around the grounds."

"Not Protz!" Jo spat the words out as though they were on fire.

"She's much too senior for that," Dealey replied but in his smile was both acknowledgement and recognition. "By the way, Jo, you can get up now," he said, his smile broadening. She felt very silly and climbed to her feet with Al's help.

As Dealey walked away to his meeting with Protz, Jo called after him: "Peter." He turned. "Thanks." He simply nodded in response.

As the door to his office closed behind him and distant, raised, muffled voices forced their way out through the woodwork, Jo turned to Al, threw her arms around his neck and said: "You are my knight in shining armour – who needs a shave," and kissed him – an enthusiastic, long, lingering, mouth to mouth, eyes closed embrace to the accompaniment of whoops and wolf whistles from other patients.

Baby Doll scurried up and tugged at Al's sleeve. "Will you be my boyfriend?"

Chapter Thirty Four

Jo lay on her bed, an unread book in her hand, and felt some satisfaction that the meeting with Danny had been quickly arranged but anger still surged through her and right there, right then, she would have killed Stephen without agonizing over it.

The feeling of impotence that had dogged her since being admitted to the place swelled in its proportions until almost every other emotion was squeezed out of her consciousness. She had to do something, something positive, anything that would give her a sense of resisting and immediately her thoughts went back to Reece and she pulled her spare phone out of its hiding place, checked his mobile number and dialled. The recorded apology it triggered produced a grunt of frustration from between clenched teeth before she left a brief message of where she was and why. She then tried his home number, which produced a similar result.

A quick, efficient tap, tap on the door was followed by its opening without any pause for an invitation to enter and nurse Protz took two paces into the room, but not before Jo has slid the phone beneath the bedspread.

"Josephine, I think we need to talk."

"I have nothing I want to say to you," Jo replied, making no attempt to disguise the venom in her voice.

"That's as may be," nurse Protz replied as she allowed the door to swing shut but moved no closer towards Jo, "but this is not a social visit..."

"And there was me thinking you'd popped in to see how I was, to have a little girly chat about this and that," Jo replied as she sat upright, swinging her feet from the bed and on to the floor.

Nurse Protz smiled but it was a smile without warmth – a thin, stretched, forced smile like that of someone trying to pass a very resistant bowel movement and which operated independently of her eyes, which were hard, focused, unblinking.

"You're clearly unaware of the dynamics of how this ward functions and what you and Alexander did earlier is very concerning. It risks disrupting the smooth functioning that's so essential when people are disturbed and trying to come to terms with their condition."

"That a nurse can use her position and power to assault someone at any opportunity is also very concerning. It's bloody disgusting, Protz. No, it's worse than that, it's crazy. Do you understand me, Protz, it's crazy!" Jo leant her body forward so her face came close to nurse Protz and she spat the words out so that there could be no doubt that it was not just the actions she thought were crazy. Nurse Protz ignored her.

"Mental health issues often spring out of people not having clearly set boundaries and I have spent a great deal of time setting those boundaries in this ward so that patients know exactly what is acceptable and what isn't and what's expected of them. Part of this includes being utterly consistent in what I say and how I say it. I never double bind a patient, I always do what I say I will do – they know that my word is absolute, there are no moments of weakness that will lead to me varying a command or a request."

Nurse Protz paused as she appraised Jo and the same strained smile was forced back on to her face.

"You've rather destroyed that, haven't you Josephine?... And I can't allow that!"

"I did nothing! You were over-ruled by your superior. And you don't set boundaries, you terrify people – but, of course, you know that don't you."

Protz issued a brief, brittle, crackling laugh that had all the warmth of shattering glass.

"My superior...?" And she repeated the laugh.

"Stop it Protz, stop it!" Jo was almost surprised by the sound of her own voice which was now level and calm and stripped of animosity. "We both know what this is about. You fancy Al Dwight and you're bitterly jealous of the attention he pays me. He prefers me to you and you really hate that. I've come into your closed little world and changed the dynamics and you can't cope with it. I don't know what's happened in your life but you are psychologically incapable of handling rejection – of any kind. You've got problems, Protz, big, big problems."

For the first time nurse Protz allowed emotion to infect her words. "Don't be so stupid. It's just another of your delusions, Josephine." Despite the protestation Jo knew from the passion in the woman's voice that she was right – but then, she had known it almost from the beginning.

Nurse Protz turned as if to go and opened the door but immediately closed it again and faced Jo again.

"If it makes you happy to believe that then do so." All pretence of professional impartiality had been jettisoned and her face was hard, her eyes penetrating, unblinking. "But you will pay for everything you've said and done today, make no mistake. You.. will.. pay." The three words were delivered individually, each one given its own bitter prominence. And with that she was gone.

Despite her outward calm, the import of nurse Protz's words disturbed Jo because she knew that this was one person in the world who would never issue an idle threat. 'You will pay' meant precisely that and Jo knew that the price demanded by her would be utterly disproportionate to her alleged misdemeanour. She also knew that if she allowed it to, fear would gradually permeate her every thought and that could be crippling. She had to do something to circumvent the inevitable and it needed to be done quickly. She could appeal to Peter Dealey but knew that would be futile. So what?

Jo went in search of Al, not just to seek a solution but also to be in the company of someone she could talk to about the threat, whose trust was a given and who might just come up with some bright idea. She headed for the door but before exiting, turned back and faced the bed, screaming her fear and frustration at an inanimate, hidden mobile phone: "Ring me Reece, please, please ring me for Christ's sake." It was a futile gesture but one that illustrated the growing panic Jo could feel taking root.

After she had repeated nurse Protz's words to Al, they sat in silence on the plastic-covered armchairs whilst Angela Rippon's high-pitched, annoying voice patronised the participants in Cash in the Attic who wanted to sell some of their possessions at auction in order to pay for some tanning sessions.

"Oh, Jo, you shouldn't have said a word, not a word," Al cautioned and Jo could hear the concern in which his words were thickly wrapped, and that worried her. Far better he made light of it, even if only as a pretence.

"It wouldn't have made any difference. She came into my room to tell me I had crossed her and retribution was essential in order to re-establish her omnipotence. All the words did was force her to drop the psycho-babble and come out in the open. She really hates me, sees me as a threat, but then we knew that anyway."

"You've got to take this seriously, Jo, go into purdah, so to speak. I know it will be difficult but you've got to become like the three wise monkeys – say nothing, see nothing, hear nothing. And I'll keep away from you so as not to antagonise her. What about I start being nice to her?"

"I think it'll take more than that, Al, but it might help. Actually, on thinking about it, it wouldn't do any harm, would it? But I don't know how long I could keep it up – this place will be unbearable without you to talk to."

"Day at a time, Jo, day at a time. You're seeing Danny and your mom tomorrow so that's something to look forward to. Nothing must get in the way of that. And that's another day gone, another day closer to getting out of here, because you will, you know! Protz has no idea that things have started to move and she won't be looking for instant gratification. Believe me, she is prepared to bide her time."

Jo welcomed the reassurance. "Al?"

"Yes?"

"Have you ever had sex with Protz?"

The laugh was forced as Al shook his head in apparent disbelief.

"No I have not!"

"But there's something that makes her feel proprietorial towards you – something's happened between the two of you, hasn't it?"

He shook his head again: "No it hasn't... well, not exactly. She had a falling out with Dealey and came on to me big style. I couldn't believe it and like you say, she can't hack rejection so I didn't want to slap her down. So, maybe I allowed her to think that, maybe, I might be interested... if the circumstances were different – that's all, that's it, finito!"

"Me thinks he doth protest too much! There was a bit more wasn't there? It's alright, I'm not sitting in judgment on you, Al."

Al looked distinctly uncomfortable and shuffled his legs as he averted his gaze. "No, that was it... except... oh for god's sake, Jo, I'm only human. I hadn't been near a woman for a year or more and she was being charming and warm and funny – something I've never seen in her before – and for a moment, just for a moment, I might have thought that I fancied her – and that was it, nothing more, I promise. I stamped on it immediately."

"That would have been enough, Al, she would have spotted it instantly and that, to her, would have been a declaration of intent, a commitment. And then I've come along and you've betrayed her trust... she's blindingly jealous. It's alright, Al, it's not your fault, she's not normal."

"Doesn't get us any further, though, does it?" Al's voice was contrite and no matter how calmly Jo dismissed his culpability, he couldn't do the same and felt horribly guilty. "Like I say, I'll be nice to her and just keep out of your way, reduce the likelihood of her having a reason to be jealous... To be honest, Jo, I thought I'd come to terms with this god awful place until you arrived but like you, I can't bear the thought of being in here and not being... well, not being your... friend."

Jo leant forward and kissed Al on the cheek.

"It's okay mister Dwight, I feel exactly the same." They both lapsed into silence until Jo chidingly said: "There's no choice, Al, you're just going to have to have sex with her and make me your bit on the side." She watched Al's eyes open in horror. "Joke, Al, just a joke," and she laughingly pushed him. "What

we need is a trump card, something to blackmail her with."
Again they lapsed into silence. "Is there a Mrs Dealey?"

"Yeah, I think there is but I'm not sure Protz is still seeing him. But even if she is, I can see two problems. First, we can't prove they're having an affair and, secondly, Dealey is Protz's line manager and if anyone was to get the chop it would be Dealey. Protz would almost certainly be portrayed as the victim of sexual harassment at work – and she would play that hand brilliantly. The official power balance is all wrong to nail her with any complicity."

Jo ummed and ahhed.

"Power balance – let's try it in the other direction, then. Has she got up the nose of any junior staff, got them to do stuff they shouldn't, made them cross professional boundaries? Is there anyone who is hacked off enough to bear witness against her?"

"I honestly don't know of anything – there's never been so much as a whisper. You've felt the wrath of the two Valkeries – they seem to walk in her shadow."

Again Jo lapsed into thought.

"Patients – has she ever come on to any of the other patients?"

"Again it's a no – but then why would she with me here?"

Jo's laughter was polite rather than spontaneous as her mind worked overtime on finding a solution and desperation began to pluck at her.

"We need something physical – a recording, an audio recording, a video tape."

Jo suddenly jumped up with excitement.

"Al, Al, Al – I think I might have it, I really think I might have it! I know that Wendy uses all kinds of cameras when they want to expose a place they think is abusing animals. She's got remote ones that you hide somewhere and collect later; she's got cameras that are no bigger than a button and are linked by wires to a little transmitter the size of a match box that can send the picture a hundred yards or more to a separate recorder; and she's got buttonhole cameras that are minute and you carry on you, with the recorder hidden in your pocket or under a shirt behind your back. We must be able to do something with one of them, surely?"

Al knew the eagerness in Jo's voice was fuelled by fear but had to concede that she might have a solution – possibly. Certainly she had access to useful technology but the big imponderable was – what to film? He didn't want to dampen her enthusiasm but at the same time it would be cruel to extend false hope.

"Excellent, Jo," he said encouragingly, "that has to be a good starting point. Got any ideas of what we could film that would implicate Protz to such an extent that we would have power over her – sufficient to get her moved or disciplined or sacked?"

"I don't know yet, I've only just thought of the idea," she replied, testily, "but I'm sure we could think of something. Like earlier, I could get her into my room and push her until she said something that gave her away. I could provoke her, taunt her, something."

"Let's think this through, Jo, please," Al said as the role of doubter began to settle over him and which he hated but he knew that every proposal had to be subjected to the acid test of logic and that enthusiasm on its own was insufficient. "Think of all the encounters you've had with Protz and then imagine you'd recorded them. What in that footage would contain a killer blow that you could present as evidence, either to the hospital authorities or to Protz herself to scare her."

"Oh, for god's sake Al, we've got a wonderful opportunity here… Don't let's start nit picking."

"Listen to me, Jo, this is too important to piss around with!" His voice was sharp, insistent, demanding. "Do what I say because we have to see if this has legs. What has Protz done to you or said to you that is powerful enough to condemn her?"

"Well, in my room just now, she let herself really slip, showed just what a cow she is."

"Sorry, Jo, but she didn't. She gave you a psychiatric explanation as to why you had disrupted the ward. We know it was bollocks but she could defend it, particularly in front of bosses who will bend over backwards not to find against one of their staff. You introduced the whole concept of jealousy and revenge – which she denied. If what you've told me is accurate, she then accused you of being delusional – which, according to your records you are. The only thing she said that could be construed as being out of order was the threat that you would pay for your actions. Imagine Protz explaining her reasons for saying that – she would tie the management in knots."

"Whose bloody side are you on Al? What about her sedating me?"

"All you would have got on tape, on both occasions, was you shouting at Protz and her calling for assistance. Nothing else, Jo, nothing else. There is not a single thing there that she could not defend. I'm on your side and that's why I won't let you do anything that won't work because it will make things worse. Protz is too clever to be trapped in that way, has spent too many years cloaking her psychoses in phony professional concern. We have to be more creative, think out of the box – be clever. Play on any weaknesses she has…"

In truth, Jo knew Al was right and she also knew her anger was fuelled by disappointment but right then and there she felt Al was failing to support her and it hurt.

"Well, it seems the only fucking weakness she's got is you so why don't you shag her and I'll film it. How about that for a solution mister Dwight?"

She knew it was spiteful, cruel, a betrayal of the confidence he had revealed and as soon as the words were out of her mouth Jo's anger evaporated and regret overwhelmed her.

"Al, I'm sorry, I'm so sorry, please forgive me, I didn't mean a word of it but… I'm frightened, Al, I'm really frightened. I've been trying to pretend I'm not but I am. She is the scariest person I've ever met. Please forget what I said."

Before she had finished talking, Al moved towards her, taking her in his arms and stroking the back of her head.

"It's okay, I understand, it's no big deal."

They remained like that for a considerable time in silence, neither knowing quite where to go from where they were – confronted by a seemingly insurmountable problem to which they had only half an answer.

"Funnily enough, it would do it!" Al eventually muttered.

"Would do what?" Jo responded.

"Your suggestion – it would do for Protz and that's for sure."

Jo pulled herself away from Al and held him at arm's length, incredulity in her face. "I wasn't seriously suggesting it, Al, it was just frustration talking."

"Of course I know that. I'm just saying it would work, it would destroy her career. That's all I'm saying. You can't be intimate with a patient under any circumstances, particularly not a nut job. That would really crash the scales as far as power ratios go. I'm not saying I should do it, of course I'm not – anyway, it takes two to tango and she may not be that easily fooled or she may not want to."

Even as he was framing his denial, the pros and cons of the bizarre idea were tumbling around in his mind. The biggest stumbling block was whether he could actually do it, rise to the occasion, so to speak, and he doubted it. Al's thoughts were immediately followed by a sense of disbelief that he had actually contemplated such a decadent solution, no matter how intractable the problem might seem.

"Oh, she wants to, make no mistake about that and it's not just your fatal attraction, mister Dwight. She wants to break me and in her mind nothing would be more effective than to have such power over my only friend in here. Betrayal is a potent weapon." Jo went silent before lifting her face close to Al's. "She really would have one up on me then, wouldn't she...?"

The manner in which Jo asked the question, the quietness of her voice, the long, steady gaze with which she held his eyes, left Al in no doubt that there was more behind her words than simple gamesmanship and he felt his breath falter and a tingle that began somewhere low in his abdomen then spread swiftly throughout his entire body. At that moment he knew he would do anything for Josephine Aldous.

Al pulled Jo to him, kissed her cheek and whispered in her ear.

"If that's what it takes, Jo, I'll do it."

Jo pulled away, laughing.

"God almighty, Al, we're sensible, adult, middle-class people who are talking like fourth rate gangsters – entrapment, pretence, lies, passionless, functional, calculated, horrible soulless sex. It's like the plot for a bad movie. I don't think I could live with myself." Jo suddenly became serious: "It's this bloody awful place, it's stripping away our principles, allowing us to contemplate the unconscionable. What's happening to us, Al, what is happening to us?"

"Circumstances, Jo, that's all, circumstances." Even as he said the words, he was aware that Jo's use of the word 'contemplate' confirmed what he already suspected, that the seed had been sown and no matter how distasteful she found it she was considering the proposition. He was relieved because he could think of nothing else that would protect her from the spite of the psychopathic nurse Protz. He knew he now had to manage the situation – carefully – not least by hiding the fact that he, too, was scared.

"We're only talking, Jo, idle chit chat so don't get your morals in a twist. The secret camera is a great idea anyway so let's contact Wendy and get hold of one because nothing can happen without it. Back to plan one, then. We have to separate – you keep a very low profile and under no circumstances react to anything from Protz or anyone else. I will start by being nice to her to draw her sting and we'll both rack our brains to think of something the camera could be used for."

He had no intention of wasting his thought processes on trying to devise other schemes for as far as he was concerned, the one that currently occupied him ticked every necessary box.

Chapter Thirty Five

It had been a beautiful walk around the gardens with Danny, and the appointed minder had been sensitive enough to lag far behind. Jo's mother and father had accompanied them part of the way and Jo had had to borrow a car coat from her mother as she had no top coat. Quickly, her parents withdrew, leaving Jo and Danny together. It was no surprise when, later, her mother produced sandwiches and a flask, for this was her penicillin – tea and sandwiches, the antidote to any ailment of the heart or spirit – which they shared, seated on a wooden memorial bench whilst aircraft from Heathrow roared upwards through the broken cloud overhead to unknown destinations.

They were not the most attractive gardens in the world, in fact just a large stretch of grass hemmed in between a motorway and a railway line on two sides and the back of the barren-looking, Victorian institutional building and houses on the other two, but the air was fresh, the sun shone intermittently and barren branches on the handful of small trees that were dotted around, swayed their vestigial buds in a gentle breeze that was warm for the time of year.

It had reminded Jo of the other world she had not seen for what felt like a lifetime but was in fact less than two weeks and she had suddenly found herself worrying about her own garden and its birds and animals but had to immediately push these thoughts to one side – they were too painful, a too stark reminder of her other life, a life that had been denied her by treachery and duplicity. The day was for normality, for her son, for reassurance nd for calm, not recrimination.

A flock of squawking, darting, green, ring-necked parakeets

materialised as if from nowhere and hurtled overhead in an enthusiastic display of what seemed like joyous togetherness, far removed from their native homeland but now colourful residents in a foreign, semi-urban environment. It had somehow reminded Jo that life changes and adapts, overcomes adversity and continues and would do so for these birds and for her. Despite the constant calls to have these 'foreign invaders' killed – the word was, of course, sanitised and filleted by being transmuted into 'culled' – they would survive, she just knew it. And so would she!

Danny had appeared to be totally reassured by his mother as they joked and laughed and planned for the future, when Jo was back home – 'soon Danny, very soon'. She had broached the subject of prep school which lay in wait only days away and was horrified to find that Stephen had not yet told him he was to leave home to become a boarder. It had the potential to destroy the day as she saw the apprehension in Danny's face when she told him what was planned – and this time she did not spare Stephen, telling Danny that it was his father's idea and not hers and that she bitterly opposed it. She had then tried her hardest to turn it into an adventure and it had been successful.

"It will only be for a few days, maybe a week or two, but this is our secret, Danny, and I don't want you to tell anyone – not aunty Hillie, not dad and certainly, definitely, no one at the school. I am going to come and rescue you – it might be in the dark of night or the middle of the day, I don't know yet but I'm coming." She had spoken to her son in intimate, hushed, theatrical whispers but with urgency, allowing him to decide how much of it was make believe and how much reality.

"The real reason I'm here, Danny, is because I have some…" she paused and looked furtively around her "…secrets which they don't want me to reveal but I am going to escape any day now and when I do I will come and get you – straight away. That's a promise, my darling, that's a cross my heart and hope to die promise. I want you to be strong, to go to that school, not to worry but to wait for me. We're in this together and we're both going to escape together and the man you spoke to on the phone, Al, he is one of us and he's going to help us."

And so it had gone on, the weaving of a seemingly fictional story that was constructed more from fact than fantasy. Jo had been confident that Danny was capable of peering through the warp and weft of her creation to determine which hard promises he could rely on. She desperately wanted to introduced him to Al but that was impossible. Al was not allowed out and on this very special day, she did not want to take Danny inside and subject him to the sadness of Baby Doll, the pretentious aggression of Trevor the Hat nor the detached depression of Lizzie Borden.

Parting had been painful but she had kept it together and her mother had been brilliant – jolly, distracting, positive and funny as she swiftly marshalled their departure. There were no lingering good byes and suddenly it was over, but not before Jo's mother had said confidentially that she was very happy to have Danny stay with her and she was going to tell Stephen so and give him a piece of her mind. Jo knew it would have no effect but she loved her profoundly for caring, for trying.

Wendy had responded to her call for a camera instantly and arrived with it the same evening. As no one knew quite what type of filming would be undertaken, she had brought what she believed to be the most flexible system. The camera itself was tiny, smaller in diameter than a ballpoint cap and connected by a short lead to a transmitter the size of car key fob. The recorder was also small, little bigger than a cigarette packet with a hinged monitor that folded flat against its body.

If the equipment was to be secreted in someone's clothing and used on the move, the transmitter could be dispensed with and the camera wired directly to the recorder, which would easily fit into a pocket, a bum-bag or even be taped into the small of someone's back beneath their clothing. The camera itself came with a small selection of lapel badges into the centre of which the camera could be inserted or it could replace a shirt button.

If it was to be used remotely in a static position, say in a room, the camera could be placed on a shelf, between books, in the spine of a horizontal book or countless other locations whilst the transmitter could be placed in, on or behind anything up to six inches away – the length of its connecting lead – to obscure it. The radio signal would carry the picture up to one hundred metres to the recorder, which could be switched on and off by a little hand-held remote controller which would operate up to fifty metres distant from the recorder.

The advantage of using it this way was that should the camera be detected, any footage that had been obtained would be safe some distance away. It was a very cheap, simple, adaptable system: "...and no great financial loss if you get collared!" Wendy had joked.

Jo and Al sat together over their dinner of pasta and tomato sauce, which tasted more like tomato ketchup. Despite the number of patients who shared the tables around them, conversation was quiet and sparse. The only time they now met was when Protz was not on duty and for the first time Jo had started to look forward to her evening meal simply to be with Al. It was not always possible, however, as Protz seemed to work longer hours than any other nurse, as though this depressing place of confinement was her life, was what defined her.

During the day, when Protz was in charge, Jo felt safer in the main ward with other people around and where she spent her time reading or desperately trying to think of scenarios for which the camera could be used. Nothing came to her. It had the disadvantage that she was witness to Al's plan A, to divert Protz's attention away from her.

She watched Protz tossing her pony tail with increasing frequency when Al talked to her, a totem of her sexuality, Jo thought, and a blatant advertisement of her availability. She laughed more frequently, swung her hips more provocatively when she walked, batted her eyelids almost embarrassingly, when she wasn't peering up provocatively from beneath them and, and... Jo searched for a word which described the transformation in her... she smouldered.

"You're doing a bloody good job of chatting up Protz, Al, I must say." Jo tried unsuccessfully to hide the jealousy that had started to work its corrosive effect on her. "Looks like you're quite enjoying it."

"Has she bothered you over the last three days? No she hasn't and you can thank your's truly for that," Al replied with a laugh. "And as for enjoying it, getting close to her is like taking a walk down a dark alley with Jack the Ripper, like sticking your head in a lion's mouth." He leant across the table and laid his hand on Jo's arm, all humour gone. "I hate it as much as you do but stick with it, babe. We're not exactly over-burdened with options here, are we? Had any ideas, any brain waves?"

He knew what the answer would be before Jo shook her head because there was a dearth of possibilities and he was aware of it even as their enthusiasm had spurred them on to obtain a secret camera.

"Wouldn't the simplest thing be to steal one of the staff's keys and leg it?" Jo asked and he could almost hear the desperation in her voice.

"It's only the nursing staff who have keys, all the auxiliaries and assistants have to buzz to be let in so we're very limited. We'd need to take the whole bunch because the lift is key operated, too. And if you hadn't noticed, they all have their keys on chains attached to them. I really don't think it's a goer."

Because of that lack of options Al had, in fact, ceased wasting mental effort on trying to find an alternative one. There was just one plan that might work and he was already well advanced in bringing it to fruition but he had no intention of telling Jo.

"Fine covert agents we are, aren't we? We've got a secret camera and we don't even know if it works – let's at least put it through its paces to see if does what it says it'll do, that the remote will switch it on, that it does transmit and that the recorder actually records. Pretty fundamental stuff, don't you think? We'll test it between our two rooms – this evening, when it's quiet. Whaddaya say?"

Jo ignored him.

"I've lied to Danny, Al. I got carried away with enthusiasm, told him I'd come and rescue him, that I was going to escape and come for him and it wouldn't be long. I weaved such a yarn that if I don't do it, he's also going to think I'm a bullshitter. He'll never trust me again. There's no prospect of me getting out of here in the foreseeable future, is there? No bloody prospect at all. What the hell was I thinking of?"

Al could see she was fighting back tears born of impotence and desperately wanted to offer her reassurance. "Look at me, look at me, Jo. We're going to get out of here, I promise." His plan to compromise nurse Protz was momentarily side-lined in his mind as it would not provide an avenue for escape and, even if successful, would merely remove the woman from the equation and make incarceration more bearable, less fragile and threatening but incarceration it would still be.

The surprise of having Jo arrive on the ward and the overwhelming satisfaction of feeling a powerful friendship blossom and grow: the resurrection of long-departed emotions and hopes, for which she was responsible; and the subsequent deep sense of gratitude these feelings had spawned, had pushed entirely from his mind the weak and loosened iron bars that blocked one small window in a lavatory cubicle not more than a dozen or so metres distant. That would be their escape!

He looked at Jo and the flush of euphoria that had engulfed him began to evaporate almost as quickly. This was a hair-brained scheme devised by a man whose hair-brained life had landed him in this place. It was, if it had any merit at all, a construct of Boy's Own fictional derring-do devised for a single male – a Beau Geste, a James Bond or, more probably, Rowan Atkinson's Johnny English.

Al faced the sudden and sobering realisation that its true value had lay in its planning, the scheming to put in place all the necessary components, the taking on of authority and beating it. It was what had helped to keep him sane. He looked at the very middle class woman next to him and shook his head. It could never happen. "Think positively," he thought angrily and it was only when Jo replied: "God, I'm trying, Al, I'm really trying," that he realised he had spoken it out loud.

That evening, Jo took the camera equipment from beneath her bed, where she had secured it to the underside of the springs with elastic bands borrowed from the craft table, and they put it to the test, surreptitiously when the ward and its dormitories were quiet.

Al seemed hyped up, stressed, as they first placed the recorder beneath the bed cover in Jo's room before taking the camera and transmitter and placing them between the books on top of Al's chest of drawers and Jo felt a momentary stab of excitement, of naughtiness, as they switched the system on with the remote then dashed back to Jo's room to see if it was working.

They opened out the monitor and there was Al's bed neatly framed, from headboard to footboard. He then returned hurriedly to his room and posed and looned around in front of the camera whilst Jo watched his antics on the monitor in her room some twenty metres away. She put her hand to her mouth to stifle her laughter and although she still had no idea what they would do with the camera, the whole experiment made her giggle and changed her mood dramatically.

Al appeared in the doorway.

"Did you see me, did you see me?" He was like a child who had just unwrapped the Christmas present for which he had been waiting all year. "Go on, you do it – go on, go on!"

She had no option but go to Al's room and perform in front of the camera for him but she became a vamp, sitting on the bed, moving seductively, exaggeratedly leaning forward until she guessed her face was full frame and then pouted, puckered her lips and blew kisses from beneath hooded eyes.

Al reappeared in the room.

"Okay, I guess that's it, it works," but his mood had changed beyond recognition. "I'm whacked, Jo, I'm going to turn in. Don't forget to put the recorder back out of sight before you go to bed – don't want anyone accidentally stumbling across it."

The hurt Jo felt was horribly sharp. She had been looking forward to sitting and talking to him, felt a powerful desire to push their relationship forward, to risk the words of endearment that she had been feeling and had wanted to say for days because, despite their intimacy, she had never even kissed him – not really, not properly, not how she wanted to kiss him. But his tone and his body language communicated finality and she would not demean herself by pleading. If he was incapable of reading her mood, did not feel that same desire for closeness and sharing that she did – that had been so transparently hanging in the air – then perhaps he was not the sensitive and caring person she had believed him to be, perhaps he was just another arsehole – one of many she had known. Jo got up and made no attempt to hide her anger.

"Give me those bits – the camera and the other bloody thing!"

"No, it's okay, might as well leave 'em there. Just as well to split the equipment up. Good night, Jo, see you in the morning." Again his words were final, dismissive, a direct instruction that the evening was at an end and Jo stormed out of the room in a state of incomprehension.

It was impossible to sleep immediately and after again securing the recorder beneath the springs, Jo tried to rationalise Al's behaviour but in the end decided that everyone was allowed one shitty mood per month – and she should know. In the hope that its calming effect might induce sleep, Jo read the Horse Whisperer because she had been told it combined two things which gave her great pleasure – horses and a realistic, tender love story.

She read for a long time and finally could feel sleep making its demands and closed the book, climbed off her bed and went over to switch the light off at the door – the only light, the only switch. As the room was plunged into almost total darkness, Jo took the few steps back to her bed, her hand held out feeling for it when something indeterminate happened inside the room. She couldn't immediately identify what it was but there was a sudden and almost imperceptible change in the level of illumination; the darkness was not so absolute and she was sure she could detect the smallest rosy glow.

As she stooped to get into bed she could see that the source was, in fact, beneath it and she bent down to look. On the small recorder in its secured position beneath the springs, a tiny red record light was illuminated. She freed the recorder with little more than mild interest, wondering if it was a malfunction and held it in her hand, turning it over as if the answer would present itself. She knew absolutely nothing about video recorders but in an instinctive action, opened the little hinged monitor and it burst into vision, glowing brightly, colourfully, in the dark room, accompanied by the sound of voices.

Jo's breathing almost stopped yet her heart raced as she

looked at a small but crystal clear image of Al and Protz sitting on his bed each holding a glass. Protz reached for what looked like a half bottle of brandy or Scotch on top of the chest of drawers, about half of which had been consumed.

"Top up, Alexander?" she asked, over emphasising his name and then smiling.

"You're very naughty, nurse Protz, a very naughty nurse indeed." Jo found it a little odd as he only ever referred to her by her surname and never used the prefix, nurse. "So which category of medication does this come under?" he asked laughingly, raising his glass. Jo couldn't make out the reply but then Al asked: "You sure you locked the door? I don't want Lizzie inviting herself..." They both laughed at the joke.

"Oh shit," she said, "actually, I forgot" and she leaped up to disappear out of vision and Jo could hear the sound of keys and a lock turning. When she returned Protz remained standing and mostly out of vision but Jo could hear her voice and see her hands:

"Right, Al, enough's enough," Articles of clothing looped through the air on to the end of the bed and when she returned to sit next to Al she was naked and posed without embarrassment. She was leaning back with her arms positioned behind her for support, her back arched inwards, her breasts pushed upwards and her chin raised. It was pure page three. "I've seen you looking, Al, so here you are! It's your birthday!" As Jo looked at the woman's almost perfect body, pert and rounded, smooth and firm, visions of her own tell-tale little stretch marks and darkened nipples came to mind and she felt ugly, inadequate.

Jo wasn't sure if she was even breathing as she looked at the tiny portal that gave her access to a world even more disturbing than the one she hoped to escape from. She was only partially aware of her shallow little sobs that continued without end and the tears that tumbled down her face in huge droplets. The emotional pain was so unbearable that it almost eclipsed all the other forms of emotional suffering she had endured since being dragged into this house of horrors. She silently repeated the words "he's doing it for me, he's doing it for me," but she didn't believe it for she felt certain that Al would have told her what he intended but still she tried to cling on to that belief simply because she had nothing else to console her, nothing to soften this act of betrayal.

And yet she could not tear her eyes away from the little screen and the shocking act of intimacy it revealed.

"Are you waiting for a written invitation?" Protz asked and without replying Al leant towards the woman, enfolded her in his arms and they kissed and Jo sobbed out loud but still she continued to watch, soaking up every detail, unable to avert her eyes.

Protz was making small guttural noises in the back of her throat which sounded more animal than human and she almost attacked Al's mouth with her own, wide open one moment closed the next, twisting, turning, licking, sucking, head angled first one way then then the other her hands clutching at his hair.

"Shit," Al cried as he pulled away from her and shot his hand to his mouth. "You bit me!"

"Strong, Al, you've got to be strong," and she started trying to undress him almost frenetically, pulling and tugging at the belt of his jeans but in the end he had to assist her. The jeans were only half way down when she thrust him backwards so he was prone on the bed on his back. The guttural noises she had been making became louder as she swiftly moved on top of Al and knelt over his head with her back to the camera.

Jo watched as the woman spread her knees on either side of him and lowered herself on to his face and began to move her lower body rhythmically backwards and forwards as the sexual noises which emanated from her grew even more animal like. Jo stopped breathing as she saw Al's erection beginning to swell in response and she slammed the monitor shut, threw the recorder under her bed and climbed beneath the sheets, pulling the pillow over her head, clamping her hands over her ears. She chanted a mantra through her tears: "No, no, no, no, no, no, no, no..." like a little girl drowning out talk of the bogeyman.

Al had not known what to expect if his deceit ever got this far but it had and it was too late to ponder now – he was in it, a

448

player in a drama in which he felt almost superfluous. The reality was far more demanding, confusing, disturbing, than he could ever have imagined. The visual stimulation of a very pretty woman whose body was almost stunningly perfect was the only positive element in a torrid encounter that was outside his experience.

He was a liar, a male whore who had proffered sex for his own purposes. She was a sad, sad woman who was also using sex for purposes of her own and which also had little to do with desire. Somewhere far distant in time she had been so profoundly damaged that her psyche had been stripped bare of all normal responses; warmth and tenderness had been hacked away. As things progressed, Al realised that this supposedly intimate act was nothing more than an extension of Protz's normal calculating, compassionless need to control.

From her squatting position, she pushed her depilated vulva in to his face and moved backwards and forwards in a rocking motion, leaning forward, so she could grind her most sensitive area down on to the promontories of his nose and chin, seeking stimulation but failing to find it as the folded wrinkles of her labia remained dry and closed. Almost by instinct, Al raised his hands and encircled her breasts but it was prompted by memories of what he would normally do rather than any desire to indulge in a mutual sharing of pleasure.

If he was to complete what he had set out to do, Al knew he had to perform and tried to expunge all thoughts other than desire and pleasant imagery and could feel the tingling response he needed. It seemed Protz was aware of it too for as soon as Al began to harden she forced herself down on him even more firmly, spreading her legs as wide as possible but still nothing moistened his face.

The grunting and groaning emanating from her grew deeper and louder and Al could tell that the sounds were issuing through her clenched teeth and he could sense her desperation as the pressure on him increased.

Any pleasure he had managed to conjure from masturbatory imagery was gone and he now felt he was undergoing an ordeal but one he was prepared to endure only for Jo's sake and silent prayers were offered up that Protz's increasingly abandoned acts were being recorded.

Her noise increased in volume and desperation and the weight on his face grew heavier and heavier as she forced herself down ever harder, to such a degree that he could barely breathe and was reduced to sneaking in a little air at the end of each of her gyrations. It was not enough and in desperation, he removed his hands from her breasts and quickly placed them beneath her buttocks, trying to take her weight, to raise her a little so he could fill his lungs.

It had an electrifying effect and Protz responded by grasping the underside of the bed head rail in order to give her greater purchase and used it to force herself down on Al with extraordinary force and her guttural moans turned into recognisable words, which still issued from between tightly clenched teeth: "Yes... yes... yes... yes." Al felt a trace of wetness on his skin which rapidly became free-flowing, covering his entire face and her musty, sweet smell filled his nostrils but he was only vaguely aware of both because as Protz hissed out her satisfaction he lost all ability to breathe.

It took several efforts for Al to force the woman upwards, but even in mid-air she did not cease her frantic backwards and forwards motion nor end her gloating cries of success. He thrust her against the wall and in a state of panic to escape from beneath her, sat upright and swung his feet to the floor, sitting with his head over his knees. He could not speak immediately as his lungs were void of air and he filled them with desperate gulps as he got off the bed and paced the little room, the noise of his inhalations drowning out the sound of Protz's diminishing orgasmic triumphalism. When Al eventually spoke it was hard and angry.

"That was rape, Protz, that was fucking rape!"

"What's the matter, Al, can't you hack it?" All the coquettishness of the last three days was gone.

"Sorry, Protz, that's it." His words were superfluous as they both knew it was over.

Her eyes never left his as she reached for her clothes and quickly slipped them on. Al felt so uncomfortable, so distressed, so desperate that he could not bear to look at her and stretched out his arm and switched off the light. Protz stepped forward as if it was her right and switched it on again without a word. She found her keys, unlocked the door and as she passed through it turned and faced him.

"You'll be back for more, Alexander, they always are." And she was gone but it was several minutes before he could be certain, before he could relax.

Al found the remote and pressed the off switch before sitting on the bed and wiping his face with the bedspread almost frantically. But then a tiny smile slowly appeared.

"Gotcha, Protz, I sure as hell gotcha!" Within seconds of his preening Al felt deflated and a sense of deep uncertainty appeared from nowhere and it took a little time to understand its origins. And then it revealed itself with surprising clarity – he felt profoundly sorry for Protz and a deep sense of disgust for himself.

Jo had barely slept and appeared at breakfast only to pick up a cup of watery, instant coffee. She hoped to avoid Al but he saw her and came over.

"Hello, gorgeous, how are you?" He was bubbly and buoyant and Jo could not respond because she hurt too much. He looked around to see if anyone was close. "I need to check the recorder because I think I may have solved one of our problems." He was brimming over with self-satisfaction.

"Was she a good fuck?"

There was a long, long silence before Al responded and when he did he no longer looked jolly but sheepish. "Are you guessing?"

Jo could hear the hope in his voice.

"No, Al, I'm not guessing, I had a ringside seat," she replied, before her voice became hurt and bitter. "No wonder you didn't want to stay and talk last night, no wonder you didn't want to be with me. I'm such a bloody fool!"

When Al responded his voice was low and controlled, business-like, devoid of guilt and unapologetic.

"Stop it Jo, stop it. There's nothing to be jealous about. If I have to explain my actions I'll do it later when we're alone but right now I want you to listen to me – this is too important to get wrong. Go back to your room and check whether last night's..." he was momentarily stumped for a bland enough description but Jo beat him to it:

"Shag?"

"...last night's 'events' are on tape. If they are, I want you to phone Wendy and get her to come and collect it – today, now, it's vital?"

"I think I'll spare myself that little treat, if you don't mind."

"You're doubting me and I don't like that. If you won't watch it then give it to me and I will. Jo, if that recording hasn't worked than my ass is on the line, big time. If it has..." With that he raised his eyebrows and nodded as if confidentially, got up and walked away.

It was not the response Jo had anticipated and doubt, confusion and regret immediately queued up and took it in turns to prod and pierce her mood of self-righteous outrage.

Later that morning she folded a newspaper around the recorder and handled it to Al out of sight of other people, wordlessly, and he took it without responding. A little while later he sought her out and said: "Phone Wendy, phone her now, tell her to get here as quickly as she can." Al paused and Jo could sense the excitement he was trying to control. "You and me, we're both off the hook once we've got that footage out of here. Result, Jo, result!" And once again he was gone and remained out of Jo's way for the rest of the day.

He put in a brief appearance to hand over the recorder when Wendy arrived and again his words were curt, to the point and devoid of pleasantries.

"As soon as you get it back to your offices I want you to upload it to YouTube, on restricted access for the time being, and let Jo and I know the address. Get ready to release it on YouTube, Myspace, LinkedIn, Flickr and any other goddam media you can think of but don't do it until you hear from one of us. If for any reason we go silent and you don't hear for, say, three days, then publish it everywhere. Okay? They'll probably take it down again but notify the press so they can view it before it disappears."

"Okay." Wendy replied, equally curtly, picking up on his mood.

Al disappeared with a muted 'bye' and Wendy turned to Jo. "What's wrong?"

"I don't know – either nothing or everything."

"You're both as surly as a London cabbie." She paused and thought. "Has it got anything to do with this?" She touched the recorder in her bag.

Jo did not reply for some considerable time.

"Yes. I saw some of what's on there but for real, while it was happening... by accident... on the monitor. I don't know if I'm just being jealous or whether..."

Wendy immediately became irritated.

"Listen to me, Jo, he thinks he's got enough on here to give you leverage. Go with that and forget everything else until you get out of this bloody place. Do you hear me? Do you?" She took hold of Jo's shoulders. "That's all that matters – nothing else!"

Jo and Al's paths did not cross throughout the day but they passed each other from time to time at a distance but neither proffered any acknowledgment of the other. Jo kept repeating to herself what Wendy had said and tried to put it into practice but somehow it just didn't work.

Even Protz appeared to be a player in the same drama, moving around with a face set hard, not looking to either left or right, concentrating on trivia. Jo watched her, desperate to know what thoughts were churning through her mind which, on this one particular day, appeared even more troubled than usual.

It was not until late in the evening, when Jo was seated in front of the TV with her eyes closed, at the back of the passive and silent audience, allowing the inane burble to wash over her like a sedative, that Al appeared suddenly. She felt his hand grip her arm firmly, impelling her upwards: "We need to talk!" He did not release his hold and directed her towards the quiet room, which was deserted and in darkness. He left it that way. "Why are you giving me the silent treatment?"

His voice was harder, more demanding than Jo had ever heard before. She had pondered all day over what had happened between Al and Protz and her reaction to it. Her head was telling her that it was not a betrayal but smart, clever, admirable, heroic even and was intended only to protect her – but her heart kept grasping hold of the imagery and would not let go. She wanted to thank him, to congratulate him, to end the painful division she had allowed to develop between them and return to how it was before. She oh so desperately wanted to do that… but couldn't. The imagery kept recurring as though in flash-back, taunting, goading, forcing her to relive the emotional carnage it had created.

Jo put a finger to her chin in parody.

"Oh dear, I wonder what could possibly have happened to make me do that?" Even as she spoke her words she hated herself. It was not what she wanted to say but the other, more forgiving, understanding, conciliatory words had gone into hiding and were nowhere to be found.

"You're hurt are you? Feel betrayed, hard done by, eh?" Again, there was no relenting in Al's insistent tone but it was devoid of anger: "It was painful to see me with another woman, wasn't it? If you'd seen it to the end you might not be acting like a spoilt eighth grader."

"It was the fact that you were enjoying it!" She spat out the words with bitter passion but even as she did so she was aware that, yes, she was living the emotions that Al had identified and others of her own creation, too. In reality, it was none of these that dominated her thinking because pole position was reserved for one emotion only – and that was guilt, a guilt so disabling, so persuasive, that she could not cope with it, had denied its existence and pushed it into hiding beneath a blanket of outraged indignity. But it had reappeared to shock her and she now had to muster the strength to admit her own complicity in what had happened.

As soon as she had mentioned the bizarre idea of filming Al and Protz in a compromising position she had known, without acknowledging it even to herself, that it was the only scenario that stood any chance of success. She knew that obtaining the camera had always been to facilitate it; the supposed search for alternatives was a sham; she had expected Al to execute the deed that was required, it was what she had anticipated and her silence had encouraged it. All this she had known but her delicate, middle class sensibilities had prevented her from acknowledging it – too distasteful, too base, too much of a burden to bear.

As a consequence she had allowed Al to carry the responsibility alone, without being able to share it, without support and now she was punishing him for what she had wanted him to do – defend her. She knew she could have stopped him at any point but didn't. Jo turned and tried to take Al in her arms, to begin her apologies but he brushed her aside.

"I don't doubt it was painful to watch me with Protz – and had I been in your shoes I would have been just as hurt, maybe more so. But I'm suffering too, Jo, I'm sure as hell suffering."

Jo tried to put one hand on his arm and placed her other fingers on his lips to indicate he no longer had any need to explain but again he brushed them away.

"No, let me speak, Jo! Being sent to a place like this ends all your certainties and I spent the first few weeks tearing my life to shreds, promising to discard the bits that shamed me and holding on to only those that made me feel good, satisfied me, gave me some sense of pride. I wasn't left with much, not much at all, just a few threads and patches but they were to be my template for rebuilding my life once I got out of here. I promised myself I would never lie again, I wouldn't deceive anyone, I would be more respectful of people's feelings, I wouldn't manipulate anyone ever again and a whole string of other right-on principles. And do you know what? They've all fallen at the first hurdle!

"I've spent the last few days lying, deceiving, totally disrespecting someone else's feelings, offering them something that didn't exist – offering them a person who didn't exist on the pretext that she didn't deserve consideration. I planned to have sex with someone I detested! What about that, Jo, what about that for sheer, venal, masculine insensitivity? The only consolation I have is that I did it for you but even you, despite knowing my reasons, aren't prepared to accept it because you're shocked. It was a step too far. The end does not always justify the means, does it?"

The pause was short and Al continued before Jo could interject, his voice wavering with passion.

"Do you know what hurts most, do you? Because of her spite and cruelty, I felt it was okay to manipulate that woman but her problems are profound, Jo, deep-rooted, frighteningly profound. Staff are not supposed to have sex with patients because of their vulnerability. That rule should apply in reverse, Jo, because I feel like a child abuser – that's what I feel like, a perverted nonce."

Jo reached out for him and this time refused to be dissuaded, threw her arms around his neck and kissed his face, little kisses one after another, his forehead, his cheeks, his nose, his chin, his lips. And between kisses, in staccato, disconnected words desperately tried to offer him reassurance.

"I knew... I knew... what you planned... to do... and I let you... I could... have stopped you... but didn't... because I... wanted you... to do it... you're... my hero." She then kissed him properly, fully on the lips and Al responded to her passion, their mouths open, their warm, wet tongues playing one with the other and each inhaled the others breath in age-old intimacy. Suddenly, Al broke off the embrace.

"You knew?"

"It's complicated Al but, yes, I think I knew. And I want you to listen to me, now. The fact that you're agonising over what you've done tells me that you're a wonderfully, caring, sensitive, gentle, kind... and very, very, very sexy man."

She pushed him backwards into the corner of the darkened room before once more finding his mouth with hers and with her sighs, her body, her hands, her lips, her tongue she tried desperately to communicate the passion she had felt for him almost since their first meeting.

Al responded immediately and they kissed with a passion driven by the emptiness they had both felt for so long. He spun her around so her back was against the low corner cupboard and she could feel his hands on her skin, exploring her back beneath her clothes. He ran his fingers up and down lightly, gently and then his finger nails traced their more demanding path from waist to neck and back again but never interrupting the hunger of his kissing. Jo could feel her legs trembling in response and almost as though to rescue her from collapse, Al eased her effortlessly up so she was seated on the cupboard.

And still they kissed as she felt Al's hand beneath her skirt, the flat of his palm urgently stroking her inner thighs, seeking, searching and she willingly provided the access he needed until she could feel his fingers gently sliding through her wetness. There was no fumbling, no embarrassment, her clothing seemed to know what was needed and provided no obstacles and suddenly Al's body was pressing against hers and she moved herself forward to meet him, felt him enter her, effortlessly, smoothly, insistently, hard.

And still they kissed as he slowly began to move in her. As his motion grew faster, more demanding, Jo could hear the sound of chessmen, draughts, tiddlywink counters and backgammon pieces in their cardboard boxes, in the cupboard that bore her weight, rattling in harmony with their movements but managed to ignore it. But neither could ignore the sudden loud noise just outside the door to the quiet room. They stopped and Al looked over his shoulder in alarm but the door did not open.

"We must be fucking crazy, Mrs Aldous!"

"We are, mister Dwight – officially crazy and we're…" Jo began to giggle and once started she could not stop until laughter took over. The muscular contractions it caused squeezed Al from her and he joined in with her laughter.

The moment had passed and so they sat on the sofa in the dark holding hands and spoke about warm, personal things, about when each had first been attracted to the other, what it was that had been responsible, when passion had first raised its head and so on and so on. They were now at ease with each other and with their smiles, and encouragements, their reassurances and intimacy, they looked for all the world like lovers.

It was not supposedly allowed but when the ward had slipped into silent sleep, Al tip toed to Jo's room but not before she had received a text from Wendy saying: 'You have nothing to be jealous about.' Her reply was simple: "I know!"

They lay on the single bed and made love, less frenetically but no less passionately. They had all the time necessary to explore each other's bodies and minds and they did so with enthusiasm until time exerted a caution. In the near dark of early morning, Al slipped from her bed to return to his own. They had not slept at all and whilst Al was dressing, Jo felt herself beginning to slip away into sleep but was suddenly conscious of Al's face next to hers as he knelt on the floor beside her bed, looking at her with a warmth that made her melt. He remained on his knees silently looking at her and in the partial light Jo could see tears rolling down his face. She said nothing but raised her hand and stroked them away with her fingers.

"I love you, Mrs Aldous!"

"I love you, mister Dwight"

Chapter Thirty Seven

Tiredness dogged Jo all morning but it was as nothing compared to the glow that warmed her as she sat at a stained dining table drinking disgusting black tea amongst strangers. It was so long since that unique hum of self-satisfaction and contentment had filled her life that she could barely remember it and yet it seemed as fresh as yesterday. Introspection that had sat side by side with her for two weeks or more, demanding her attention, had been elbowed to one side and its place taken by something else, something much more exciting.

Instead of 'me' it was now 'him and me' 'us' and all the new permutations and possibilities this unlocked flowed through her thought,s, one merging into the other as new and tantalising landscapes unfurled before her, revealing infinite possibilities. Imagination and hope now furnished her future and although still a world of pretend, she could travel down whatever avenue she chose and all the journeys were magical, all involved change and they all terminated with a sense of contentment. She was happy!

That happiness received a jolt when Jo went in search of Al. As she exited the dining room and turned left, her eye line naturally took in the nurses' station and its flanking offices, which lay on the far side of the ward. The door to Kadynski's office was open inwards and a broad-shouldered man in a sports jacket with greying, curly hair was leaning with one hand on the door frame, the other holding the door handle whilst his head was inclined forwards and she could sense that an intense conversation was taking place.

Jo paused, froze. It looked like Reece. She looked away then looked back afresh. It was Reece and her new-found confidence drained away as all the doubt and fear she had refused to countenance suddenly replaced it. Why was Reece talking to Kadynski, why hadn't he immediately come to see her, why had he been incommunicado, why hadn't he returned her calls, was this meeting a regular thing, did he and Kadynski have a common purpose, were they in this together? All these doubts about Reece's implication in her sectioning had been kept at bay because she refused to believe them but now, in this one moment, they swirled around her demanding to be let in like winged demons at the window.

She paused, her face ashen, her breathing suspended and then Reece closed the door and in that one action relief flushed away all doubts because he had closed it with force, with anger and frustration and she just knew he had not betrayed her. He was a very angry man and that was confirmed when he turned towards her and she could see a face flushed and etched with fury. He raised his head and recognition was instant and the dark pools of his eyes were suddenly illuminated, the furrows in his brow relaxed and tension eased from his tight mouth as it slowly curled upwards into a beaming smile.

"Jo, my lovely," he bellowed across the ward in a big Welsh voice and jogged towards her, swaying first one way and then the other to avoid pieces of furniture, like a rugby player evading tackles as he headed for the tri line.

Jo did not cry but clung to him as he hugged her, mouthing reassurances in a deep, comforting voice.

"I'm not going to let the bastards get away with this... I'm going to have you out of here as soon as I can... That man is a pretentious, pompous prick... Are you alright my darling woman? What have they done to you?"

Gradually, Reece's outrage mellowed and Jo felt the reassurance he always carried with him, enfold her like a mantle. He suddenly became serious.

"We need to talk, urgently. Do you have a room?"

"I do but I'm not allowed to take visitors to it. We'll try the snooker room, that's usually empty," and it was.

"Where've you been Reece?" She hadn't meant it to come out

that way but there was censure and dismay in her voice.

"I'm so sorry, Jo, I've been out of the country. Beth was researching the health services in Cuba and Costa Rica and, well... what with everything, I thought a break might do me good... and it is my subject..."

"But you didn't return my calls, reply to messages!"

"Costa Rica was our second stop, which would have coincided with your coming here, and while it might have a brilliant health service, it's telephone service is shit! It'll take too long to explain why but you can't use your mobile there and it takes six months to get a new one – hence the silence. I rang you when I got back yesterday and left a message..."

"Oh god!... We're not allowed to carry our phones with us and even though I've got a secret one I sometimes forget to check it. Actually, sometimes I'm not capable of checking it."

"The point is, Jo, I'm going to get you out of here. You're on a thirty day order which has got fourteen days to run and I intend to apply for a Mental Health Tribunal but never having dealt with anything like this before I've no idea how long it takes. I promise you I'll push it as hard and fast as I can." His voice became suddenly gentle and intimate. "What I really want to do is gather you up and carry you away from this place – to take you home where you belong. How could this happen, Jo, how could he do this to you?"

She kissed him on the cheek with intimacy, hoping he could feel her gratitude.

"I don't know, Reece, I really don't know. Do you have any idea why I'm here, what I did to warrant this?"

"The newspaper reports were spread all over my desk for me when I got back – that's why I rang."

"The real stuff, the stuff that threatens Stephen – the whole party – wasn't really covered by the press because they couldn't back it up. I went to the House of Commons and in front of his acolytes accused him of being a paedophile and that's why they won't let me out before the election and probably not for a long time after it. I'm too much of a threat, Reece! Oh, and I'm violent – a threat to him."

"Jesus – and is he – a paedophile?"

"Yes!" Jo was emphatic in her response.

"Why doesn't that surprise me? Okay, the point is, Jo, their old boy's network might allow them to bang you up in here but I seriously doubt they can rig a Tribunal. I just can't believe that's possible but like I say, I'm no expert…"

"I wouldn't be so sure, Reece, everything's at stake – Kadynski's career, Stephen's career, the reputations of people we don't even know about, they all hinge on this and then there's the whole future of the Tory party itself. It could destroy them for years."

Reece pondered for a considerable time.

"Look, I'm only a GP but we've got a mental health team at the practice and although they mainly deal with care in the community, that kind of thing, they'll certainly know more than I do. I do know that if we can't get a Tribunal before your order ends, I'm pretty sure there will have to be one before they can extend it. But that's only a fall-back position because I don't intend to leave you in here that long. I can organise a very powerful representation on your behalf." A wry smile came over Reece's face. "I can even legitimately say that you consulted me about any possible mental health problem only days before you were sectioned and I had no doubt that you were perfectly healthy… no trace of any problems."

Jo began to giggle.

"You could even tell them that despite getting totally pissed I still managed to learn the words to the Internationale so I must be sane!"

Reece chuckled.

"I think we might forget to mention that bit… But I did attend your domestic and did see that bloody great carving knife sticking out of the table – Stephen I presume?" Jo nodded. "We can destroy this plank by plank. A jar of redcurrant jelly is hardly the weapon of choice when you've got a meat cleaver at your disposal."

Reece went momentarily silent as though embarrassed to continue.

"Do you have any evidence of the… the other thing… the paedophilia?"

Jo looked at him for some considerable time as the frightening awareness dawned that battle was about to commence and she knew that her opponents were far more ruthless, more devious, more vicious than Reece could ever imagine – than he could ever be. She was afraid that, if necessary, they would destroy him, too, so how deeply did she want to involve him? She did not have any option.

"Reece, I want to introduce you to someone," and then, as a coy afterthought, added: "someone special!"

When she returned with Al, Jo made the introductions and knew she was beaming as she did so, finding huge pleasure in that simple act without really knowing why. Perhaps it was the very first step in making the transition from an old life into a new one, of merging two lives together but she didn't agonise over it and just knew that she desperately wanted them to like each other.

After filling Al in on the conversation, Jo turned to Reece.

"Al has a Masters in cynicism so if you want to know how low people can stoop in pursuit of self-interest, he's your man."

"As an observer, buddy, strictly an observer," Al laughed before becoming serious. "Whenever I'm in any situation where there's conflict I try and put myself in the other guy's shoes – I don't mean just play at it but immerse myself, seriously, lining up what I want to achieve, what I may lose, what I'm prepared to lose and how far I can allow myself to be compromised – if I were them.

"The starting point here is as clear as a boil on a stripper's ass. Jo has the potential to destroy a political party – jobs, reputation, influence, money, power – everything. Instead of tossing Stephen to the dogs as they should have done, risk not getting elected and fighting with a new guy at the head, they went for broke and chose the illegal route. They're in a hole now and they can't stop digging. The stakes are goddam monumental and they've already shown how far they're prepared to go." He inclined his heads towards Jo. "That won't be the end – cannot be the end because their only lifeline is silence. Anyone breaks that silence and they're screwed.

"If they think Jo has enough shit to nail them, she'll be

disappeared immediately." He tried not to look at Jo but as he spoke he reached out and took hold of her hand as reassurance. "They will concoct something violent that can be laid at her door and she will disappear into the system – be sent to Broadmoor or Rampton. Criminally insane! And it's a long way back from there. If for any reason they can't pull that off..." Al hesitated before adding "they'll kill her – or more likely, she'll kill herself – 'Everything became too much for her,' that sort of thing!" He felt Jo's hand tighten in his. "And if, in the meantime, they think you're likely to get anywhere with your rescue mission – they'll get you, too, Reece!"

"What, kill me?" Reece's voice shot up an octave with incredulity.

"More likely to be a patient accusing you of sexual assault, rape or some little beauty like that, or maybe incompetence, corruption – destroy your reputation, you get the picture? But if necessary, yeah, I guess they might well take you out, too."

A huge exhalation of disbelief emanated from Reece's shaking head.

"Come on, Al, what world are you in? This isn't the movies! I mean, where do you get all this stuff from, the internet?"

"History, Reece, history, it's all there. Oh, but they're subtle. Someone will call in the security services and with a nod and a whisper they'll be told what's needed – not outright, nothing too obvious but they all know the shorthand. And that person will instruct an outside agency and they will pass it on to a different agency and so on until it gets to the shitty little operators at the bottom of the heap and they'll arrange an accident – a car strike when you're crossing the road, a surreptitious push under a train at the station, or under a tube train. Two of the favourites are a mugging that supposedly goes wrong or an overdose – there's no shortage of options – and it's all arranged by word of mouth and person to person, never in front of a witness, and payment is by cash. You get the picture?"

Al could see scepticism in Reece's face, in his body language.

"Okay, look at it another way. Can they afford to let any of this come out? Bye bye election, bye bye everything."

Reece was struggling to demolish Al's reasoning. "They'll

present Jo's sectioning as a genuine medical difference of opinion – so they got it wrong for once – terribly sorry, have some compensation." He simply couldn't accept the alternatives. "Look mate, the Tories aren't even in power yet, how can they wield that kind of influence?"

Al heard a smirk from Jo that indicated she knew the answer only too well. Al continued:

"Reece, buddy, the Tories are always in power even when they're not. You don't think senior civil servants, security services, the whole freaking establishment, you don't really think they're neutral do you? They're mostly Tories from the same public schools, universities and military backgrounds – it's an ethos – and they're backed by most of the press. And so they obstruct and confuse, oppose and delay the policies of other parties if they ever get elected, unless it has their approval or it's something they can live with. And they keep that up until the rightful pretenders to the throne return to power – the natural party of government. Why do you think every Labour government since Attlee has finished up with conservative policies?"

"Bloody weakness, that's why – weak bastards they are," Reece spat out.

"Maybe there's some of that but the Tories are the civil services' natural masters and so they will do their bidding, make no mistake, particularly now when they believe that in a couple of weeks they'll be their actual masters once again."

"For an American you seem pretty knowledgeable about our system," Reece said.

"It's the same with most systems, it's just the form that's different." Al turned to Jo for the first time. "I'm sorry but it's true and I've always known what you were up against. I don't want you to do something that puts your ass on the line," there was a long pause during which his eyes never left hers. "I've got too much to lose now – much too much!"

Despite having just been told that hit men were possibly queuing up to take pot shots at her, Jo's heart almost melted.

Reece noticed the exchange but his thoughts were elsewhere.

"Then how do you think this should be handled, Al? What are our options?"

"Okay, I guess I might be overplaying things. Bit of a weakness – I storm in on the basis that bullshit baffles brains but I've got no first-hand knowledge, I've not been involved in anything like this for real, it's all from books, reports, whistle blowers, that kind of thing… I've got an interest in how societies are manipulated, how power is abused – that's all really."

"No, no, I know you're right," Reece replied with all traces of disbelief now expunged. "It's bloody obvious when you think about it – even from my limited experience – it's how the arrogant bastards operate. But that still leaves us with what to do next."

Al was enthusiastic once more.

"Okay, you've got to cover your ass, Reece. Do all the things you plan to do but put everything down in writing – all your doubts, all your fears, what you've seen, statements from Jo and her family, why you're afraid for your life – along with any evidence you can get and give it to a reliable lawyer – someone radical who spends their life bucking the system, who isn't gonna shit on you – there's a few out there, I can give you names. Everything goes to them, all the originals, and you keep certified copies. But don't leave any trace of them in your office or at home.

"Write letters by hand, not on your computer, and photocopy them. Don't put the details of anyone involved in this in your address book or on your computer, keep their letters and your copies – everything – somewhere safe because you may well be broken into and your phone may be hacked. Use your mobile only for innocuous calls and buy yourself a cheap, pay-as-you-go alternative – and think about changing it regularly. And if anything happens to you – the instructions are that it all goes public!"

"Oh, marvellous, just what I need – martyrdom and posthumous glory," Reece said with cynical laughter. "Should have stayed with the sodding chapel, at least they'd have appreciated that – made me a working class saint!"

Al returned his laughter.

"You protect yourself by letting Kadynski know precisely what you're doing and why. He will feed it back up the line and they'll know they can't get away with taking a contract out on you."

Reece looked at Al quizzically.

"Are you a patient in here?"

Al knew exactly where his thoughts were heading.

"Sure am – but this isn't paranoia, I promise you!"

Reece simply shook his head, smiling, and it broke the tension

"Jo, you didn't say if you had any evidence of Stephen's... predilections. It could be the key to all this."

"I don't know. They may have found it – I guess they would have searched. It was footage of pubescent girls having sex with grown men from his flash drive and I copied it onto my computer and tried to hide it..." She shuddered and shook her head as she said it.

"You encrypted it?" Al asked.

Jo looked embarrassed: "Not exactly, I filed it with my cookery demos – labelled it 'quick puff pastry', Do you think they would have found it?"

Reece and Al both laughed – at the incongruity and the thought that such subterfuge would secure it. Al replied: "They will have found it as sure as hell." There was an air of disappointment and finality in his voice. "Shame!"

Jo looked uncomfortable. "Well, don't have a go, I'm no computer expert and I didn't have a spare flash drive!... Actually, just before I went to the House and blew the whistle on Stephen, I remembered his copy, went to his desk and it was still there. I took his original memory stick along with the envelope which claimed it was something to do with the Wadeson Enquiry. Don't know why, but having made my own copy, I'd forgotten all about his. It was only the thought of what I was going to do that brought it back to mind."

Both men looked at her in surprised admiration. "You little beauty," Reece exclaimed.

Al became animated. "Please, please, Jo, please tell me you didn't hide it in your panty drawer!"

"Why would I do that?"

"Because women always hide secrets in their panty drawer – letters from illicit boyfriends, lovers' tokens, passionate poetry, pregnancy kits…! It's the first place they would have looked."

"Well I didn't. There's an old VCR in the TV room under piles of stuff that hasn't been used for ages – I stuffed it in the slot and shoved a video half way in after it. Looked pretty safe to me. I knew I might need the original but didn't want Danny to find it. There's no way he'd use a VCR – I don't think he'd know how."

"Excellent. We need to get a hold of it," Al said with finality.

Jo cut across him: "Reece, why were you talking to Kadynski – I presume it was him?"

"When I got back and read what had happened to you, I couldn't get hold of you so I phoned your mum. She was incensed, Jo, really incensed and told me which hospital you were at. I found out who your consultant was, phoned him and insisted on seeing him – immediately, as your GP. When I got here I demanded to see a copy of your section and he produced it – reluctantly – but he didn't have any option. When I saw it was him who'd signed it, I gave him a good Welsh mouthful…"

"Who else signed it, was it doctor Dawson?" Jo asked eagerly.

"Yes." Reece seemed somehow diffident.

"So it was those two laughing boys – and my ever-loving husband, just as we thought."

Reece fidgeted and coughed before speaking – very quietly.

"Actually, Jo, Stephen didn't sign it."

"Sorry? Who else would have?"

Reece remained silent and looked away. When he did speak, his words were heavy with regret. "It was Hilary – your sister!"

Jo's reaction had been like that of an inflating balloon – nothing much discernible at first, just a lot of huffing and puffing as she bid farewell to Reece but Al could see it gradually expanding with each exhalation and as it did so she began to move her arms and legs restlessly, in silence, ignoring Al's enquiry as to whether she was alright. Then she took to her feet and began pacing backwards and forwards within the confines of the room. Al waited, knowing what was inevitably to come as the strides became faster and the turns more violent until it happened and the balloon exploded.

"The stupid, stupid, stupid cow. I've spent the last decade or more with her hovering over me like some starving Ethiopian waif waiting to grab something from my dinner plate, living on the scraps that were left – jealous, selfish, obsessed." She turned to Al. "I wouldn't have minded her having my husband, in fact she would have been welcome to him but how could a sister – my sister – be so deceitful, such a liar, so duplicitous?

"They've been sleeping together for more than six months and when I think about it, I can tell you exactly when it started but you dismiss things like that, you don't believe them because you can't credit that anyone could be that... that... callous. Oh, don't get me wrong, I don't mean Stephen because I've always known he would shag a pretty donkey given half a chance – but Hillie, my sister...!"

The tears began to slowly flow and Jo turned to Al.

"How much betrayal is anyone supposed to take, Al? It's one step forward two steps back all the time. How can I go on like this – feeling like everyone's punch bag, like I'm constantly being punished – but I don't know what for. Am I a horrible person Al? Am I?"

He had remained silent knowing that the explosion had to subside before anything he said would even be heard let alone welcomed. He knew she hadn't finished yet and simply said: "Your Mom, Wendy, Reece, even me – you're not on your own!" He saw a flicker of comprehension in her angry face as she continued:

"Was she nurturing this jealousy all through our childhood. Is that why she wheedled around my mum the whole time, demanding her attention at my expense. Is it a life-long hatred and this is the final act?" Jo paced again in silence, head down her still-moving lips revealing an angry, silent debate that continued internally. She again turned to Al.

"She's weak, vain and stupid – just the kind of person that Stephen eats for breakfast. I told you his name wouldn't be on the section; I told you he would keep his distance so if it all went wobbly he would have a glimmer of an escape route. I can tell you exactly what he would have said to my stupid, craven sister, how signing my section was in my best interests blah de blah de blah but they both knew it was a cover for their ambition – but hers only second-hand ambition, to live vicariously in the shadow cast by Stephen. It was just all too tempting for her.

"Do you know what, Al, I can't even hate her because it's entirely in character. I've tried and tried to feel sisterly towards her even though I've always known what kind of person she is – that's what you do, isn't it, you make excuses for family, you make allowances but this... They won't beat me Al, they won't fucking beat me because I've been through too much to allow an empty-headed clothes horse and a self-obsessed moron come out on top..."

Al could sense the storm abating and threw in a few positive words to help it on its way – words he believed wholeheartedly.

"I don't think anyone could beat you – not now!"

"Jo...!" The word was spoken almost apologetically as one of the young orderlies entered the room and intruded on Jo's wrath.

"What?" she snapped back.

"There's someone to see you – her name's Julie."

"Julie? Julie who? I don't know any Julies. Ask her what her other name is." Jo's anger infected her words and the orderly responded in kind:

"I'm not your p.a. Jo, either you want to see her or you don't!"

"I'm sorry, I'm sorry – that was rude of me. I've just had some bad news."

The girl's look indicated acceptance of the apology.

"Do you want to see her or not?"

"I guess so. Would you mind asking her to come up here?" Jo turned back to Al. "Do I tell my mother? Or do I stay quiet to save her from being hurt and at the same time let Hillie off the hook?" Jo paused in thought: "Actually, I've got a sneaky feeling mum already knows or at least has a strong suspicion. I thought cad was a strange word to use about Stephen – but you can't get more caddish than what he's done, can you?... I have so underestimated my mum!"

The orderly had left the door to the room open and the view stretched back down the ward to the nurses' station and Jo looked unthinkingly along its length, her mind still trying to come to terms with the news Reece had delivered. She barely saw the figure who strode firmly towards her on stout legs, her high heels seemingly trying to beat the polished floor into submission.

Gradually, some distant sliver of recognition began to signal at Jo and she looked at the woman more closely, aware that she had seen her before but was unable to provide the context that would reveal an identity. Her stocky frame, peroxided hair and purposeful stride all looked familiar.

"Mrs Aldous," she said immediately as she arrived in the room, "can I talk to you – in private?" She turned her face questioningly towards Al and Jo nodded in response that it was okay to speak, the woman's identity still not clear. Jo tried to place her in a variety of different scenarios but recognition still didn't break cover.

"Julie Samuels, Sean Murphy's assistant. We've seen each other a few times in the House but I don't think we've ever spoken." Immediately visions of a woman invariably silent, usually on the periphery of things but never far from her Svengali, Sean Murphy, came back to Jo.

"Of course, of course," Jo replied, as much to herself as to Julie Samuel. "Sorry, I didn't recognise you out of context."

"That's okay... Look, this isn't easy for me but I've come here to apologise to you..." There was hesitation in her voice as if she did not know quite how to proceed.

Al indicated they should sit and the trio lowered themselves into three, sticky, finger-marked, faux leather-covered armchairs, trying not to speculate as to what might have caused the tackiness.

"For what?" Jo responded, her concentration now fully on her unexpected visitor.

Julie did not reply immediately and for the first time lost eye contact with Jo, who remained silent, sensing that she needed to allow the woman space. She guessed that whatever she had come to this miserable place to say, it was not trivial.

Julie was clearly marshalling her thoughts and did not seem certain how to start. In the end she almost blurted it out.

"You shouldn't be in here... and I could have prevented it."

Jo said nothing but her upper body moved forward from its reclined position and her posture became upright, almost tense, as though on a given signal she would leap from her armchair.

Again Julie took her time before continuing, discomfort painted across her face. "Mrs Aldous, I'm a woman in a man's world and I've faced sexism and seen it around me for most of my working life but nowhere more so than in the House. I took a decision a long time ago not to remain silent when I witnessed it but to speak up. And I've done that." She deployed the last few words as if in mitigation.

"Most of the time I think I'm probably dismissed as that dyke with a chip on her shoulder but I have had an effect – I know I have... But then there was you... Your sectioning was entirely concocted."

"Yes, I am aware of that." Whatever doubts or discomfort the woman was suffering, Jo did not feel inclined to help her and her words were sharp.

"It was Charlie Whiston's idea, backed by Harry Cunningham, George Fiennes and Edward Churchill Smith. Peter Macintosh might also have been involved and Sean grabbed hold of the idea with open arms – I think he wished he'd thought of it. When it was put to your husband, all tied up in quasi medical terms, as a fait accompli, he didn't hesitate. He didn't ask a single question other than whether they could get away with it – not directly, of course, but in that polite, seemingly concerned, roundabout sort of way he excels at. I couldn't believe it. There were two meetings to set it all up and I was present at both. They didn't want me there but Sean insisted.

"Me, the terror of the sexist male, the bitter one always ready to challenge, to admonish, always ready to do my bit for equality but when it came to something really important, the most important thing I've ever witnessed, I said nothing. I said nothing, Mrs Aldous, and let them put you away. How's that for cowardice? What's even worse, it was self-interested cowardice. It was you or my job and my job won! I am so, so sorry!"

There was not so much as a glimmer of sympathy on Jo's face.

"I can't give you absolution, Ms Samuels – I've been through shit."

"I don't doubt it and that's why I'm here."

"Was Kadynski there – at the meetings?"

"At the second one."

"And he was a willing party to it all? I just need to be sure"

"Completely!... I knew the gravity of what was being planned and I stored in my mind every detail and every word – they wouldn't let anyone take notes but immediately after both meetings I wrote it all down. Not contemporaneous, I know, but almost as good. Those notes are entirely at your disposal."

Jo remained silent, staring at the woman as though her words were incomprehensible. When she did speak it was quietly.

"Are you prepared to back them up, make a statement – to bear witness against your bosses?"

"Of course – whatever's necessary."

"That's your job gone!"

Julie Samuels shrugged, "I think I knew that from the moment I was privy to their scheme."

"We're a couple of weeks off an election – have you thought about what that means?" Jo felt her contempt dissolving somewhat as she reminded herself that there were others far more complicit than Julie Samuel – not least her husband.

"I'm aware it makes me very vulnerable," Julie replied.

Al gestured to Jo, requesting her approval to speak.

"Julie, it makes you more than vulnerable! Does anyone know that you're prepared to speak out – that you were coming here to tell Jo about what happened? He's hardly ever there but did Kadynski see you on your way in?"

"No, I don't think so but I didn't try to be evasive. I'm very aware that those notes are dynamite so I've had a certified copy done. The originals are in my flat and the other copy I've sent to myself poste restante at... well, where exactly doesn't matter, the fewer people who know the better."

Jo's mind had gone elsewhere and then she rejoined the group.

"Didn't Stephen show any concerns, didn't he mention the effect it would have on our son... nothing... no cautions at all?" Jo asked incredulously.

Julie paused before answering. "I'm sorry, Mrs Aldous, nothing, absolutely nothing... How do you want me to proceed?"

Jo didn't answer immediately, she was struggling with confirmation of what she already suspected – that the man she had lived with for twelve years, who she had had a child with, had ignored her like he might a parking fine. Eventually she said: "Al's the detail man."

Al became serious and Jo still found it incredible that there really was reason for him to speak in near apocalyptic tones.

"If anyone finds out what you're doing, I believe your life will be on the line. Look, you know these people, I don't – am I going over the top or are we right to be scared?"

Julie Samuel thought for long moments, her head down. When she did speak it was measured and careful. "They've started down a particular path and because they can subcontract out any dirty work so they're not implicated – yes, I think you're right," She then again went silent for a moment. "Jesus, I'd not really thought of it in such detail until now but I think their choices are very simple, in their terms – if what they did to you comes to light, they're finished. If, on the other hand, they need to get rid of someone to prevent that from happening and there are few risks involved... I can assure you morality won't even enter into it."

"Okay, then", Al interjected. "Jo's doctor is organising everything and we'll give you his safe number. You need to buy a new, cheap mobile – and give false details and pay in cash. Leave no trace at all. You need to get a copy of those notes to Reece a.s.a.p. I'll also give you the number of Jo's friend, Wendy, as another means of contact. Be very cautious – circumspect – when you talk to anyone."

"Okay," Julie replied and then thought for a moment. "The really bizarre thing is, they don't think they're horrible people – psychopaths or anything like that. They've so convinced themselves that they're entitled to power, that they're the nation's saviours and can therefore justify anything, just like a general sending troops into battle – so I really don't have any doubts about what they're capable of."

Finally, Jo spoke again. "Are you strong, Julie, really strong? Are you going to see this through? Can I rely on you whatever happens?"

There was no hesitation this time. "I'm ashamed enough as it is – I couldn't add to it!"

Chapter Thirty Eight

It was hope, riding on the back of determination that had kept Jo going through her incarceration. Now that chinks of light were appearing in the darkness, she refused to celebrate and kept her hope in check, reigning it back, always remembering the ingrained experience of one step forward two steps back. Euphoria, she knew, might make her incautious because in truth, nothing had changed in her world. She was still exactly where she had been a day ago – she still had no power and the institution had an abundance of it. Anything could happen at any time, as she had already discovered.

Despite this, the atmosphere surrounding her and Al's evening was one of contentment – ready laughter, whispered endearances, touches, looks and smiles – lots and lots of smiles.

When Jo went early to sleep it was with equanimity as her bed mate. The rude awakening by fierce whispers that followed only a short time afterwards was in stark contrast.

"Jo, Jo, wake up. Wake up baby…" Al shook her shoulder insistently. "Come on baby, you've got to get up, get dressed!"

Jo struggled to wakefulness. "What the hell, Al? What are you doing?"

"Come on, Jo, get your head in gear – you've got to read this." He thrust an illuminated mobile phone display in front of her and she struggled to focus but could not and so pushed it aside.

"Read it to me if it's that important."

"Okay – now listen. 'In UCH. Hit by car on pavement near my flat. Leg badly broken. V poorly v frightened. More determined than ever but immobile. Will take some time.'"

Jo was awake. "Christ! Julie!"

"Yes, Julie! They've got to her. That means they know she's been here. What they don't know is if she's given you anything, provided you with something concrete. Listen to me, Jo, you're next! We're getting out of here. Get dressed, put a coat on but be quiet and don't take anything with you. Put a dressing gown over your clothes and pretend like you're going to the John."

"What the hell, Al, how...?"

"Just do what I say and come as quickly as you can." With that, Al left the room and Jo struggled into her clothes with fear, concern and uncertainty all crashing around in her head. For no good reason she tiptoed along the corridor by the glow from emergency night lights, dressed as instructed but with no coat as she did not have one and with her shoes clutched to her chest beneath the gown, trying to ignore the few remaining patients who were still up watching TV and the night staff in the office who were chatting and laughing together.

It was not easy to behave normally. She had made this trip at night many times but not driven by subterfuge and she felt her ulterior motive was illuminated with flashing neon lights – even though she had no idea what that ulterior motive might be.

She opened the door to find the small lavatory block illuminated, with Al beckoning to her, hissing conspiratorially from the end stall. "Here, here – come here, Jo."

The door to the stall was open inwards and Jo could see that the glass and its frame had been removed and stood against a wall whilst the bars that had reminded her of her impotence every time she used the place, were missing. She could feel the cold night air puffing through the small, gaping hole. Coiled up on top of the cistern was a mound of material that could only be sheets tied together, with one end secured around the base of the lavatory pan. Al spoke quietly, urgently but his words were suffused with pride.

"I've been planning this for weeks. Dug the bars out, nicked some sheets... Never really thought it'd work – well, not for you – but we don't have a lot of options..." A smile illuminated his face.

Jo surveyed the escape route that Al had produced like a magician's rabbit.

"Al?… You want me to climb through that little window?… And clamber forty feet down a sheet… To the ground…?"

Al's response tumbled out with enthusiasm: "No, Jo, it's only about thirty feet. And if you don't think you can make it, I'll tie the sheets around your waist and lower you down… I've worked it all out… I've made sure the sheets are long enough… and they're strong, really strong… I've tested them…"

It began as a chuckle but quickly transformed into a giggle which became uncontrollable as Jo crossed her hands over her midriff and leant against the wall of the cubicle for support and snorted with each intake of breath, the giggle turning to full-blown laughter.

"Oh, Al, Al, Al… You are a wonderful man… but what planet do you come from?… Me?… down there?… Al you're gorgeous – but barking mad!"

Al's proud face collapsed into crestfallen rejection.

"Jo, we don't have any options, this is it, the only one." Jo was still laughing and snorting when the outer door of the lavatories swung inwards as nurse Protz entered. She paused and wordlessly surveyed the scene, both her clothing and her hair looking dishevelled.

"What do you think you're doing?" she demanded.

Both Al and Jo eased out of the cubicle and into the central aisle to face her.

"I think there's been a burglary," Al said, not even trying to hide the humour in his voice and Jo began giggling once again. "Clever bloke, climbed up the sheets. Must have had an accomplice."

Before Protz could answer, the door again swung open and Peter Dealey entered, looking equally as dishevelled. Al let out a barking laugh:

"Ah ha – back in the saddle are we Pete? Destry rides again. Bet Mrs Pete's delighted."

Dealey ignored Al's gibe. "What's going on? What the hell are you doing?"

Jo became serious: "I told you the shit would hit the fan, Peter, and it's about to. We have conclusive proof that I was sectioned for political purposes… illegally. Can you work out the implications…?

"I had nothing to do with it," Dealey cut across her. He was immediately on the back foot and Jo felt emboldened.

"No, I don't suppose you did but you knew the whole thing stunk and remained silent – so if I were you, Peter, I'd start planning my justification. 'I was only following orders' won't cut it."

"I'm going to get security," Protz snapped and turned to exit but Peter Dealley grabbed her arm:

"No, just a minute, Disa."

Al raised his eyebrows and smiled: "Diesel, eh – no wonder everyone just calls you Protz!"

Dealley ignored him and turned back to Jo: "Why the Famous Five escape routine?"

"I don't have the proof in my hand yet but if I stay here, by this time tomorrow I'll be lucky if I'm still alive! If I am, I will have been disappeared. Work it out, Peter, for Christ's sake!"

Dealey went silent and Jo could sense the indecision churning through his mind, the weighing up of options, perhaps even the contemplation of what was the right thing to do.

"For god's sake, Peter, don't be so weak, don't let her manipulate you. Call for security – now! If you won't I will!" Protz's voice rose in pitch until she was almost screaming. "Do it, do it, do it, don't let her control you – do your job, do what you're paid to do. Be a man!" The last words screeched out of her ashen face, her once pretty blue eyes bulging in fury. Dealey still held on to her but Jo felt panic rising as Protz tried to wield her power over the man like a sledge hammer.

"Whoa, whoa, whoa – hold your horses, don't do anything yet." Jo was surprised to hear the calmness in Al's voice as the cynical humour with which he had started the confrontation still held sway. He seemed almost to be enjoying himself. "We're going to the movies!" he said with a smile and produced a mobile phone from his pocket. A few stabs at the screen and it burst into life with the sound of echoey, tinny voices. It was Protz and Al together. "You need to see this too, Pete," he said encouragingly.

Jo did not move to view the images, did not want to, but observed those who did. Scenes of extraordinary intimacy were watched by two frozen faces and one which glowed with self-satisfaction. Guttural, gasping sounds of sex filled the small space with its aroma of disinfectant and stale urine.

As soon as he realised what he was viewing, Peter Dealey took an instinctive look over his shoulder to ensure no one else could see and in that fleeting moment, Protz lunged at Al. She kicked out and lashed with her nails to scratch and opened her mouth with the clear intention of biting. Protz had no intention of grabbing the phone; her priority was to attack, to inflict pain. Dealey controlled her with surprising ease. "You bastard, you bastard..." she screamed at Al.

Al's voice became serious, almost regretful.

"I'm sorry, Protz, I don't take any pride in this but you are so fucked up you left me no option."

Protz had ceased trying to reach Al but stood, motionless, straining against Dealey's locked arms, her head thrust forward, eyes fixated on Al, the coarse rasping of her breath momentarily the only sound in the echoing little room.

Jo looked at the crazed woman, whose face was distorted by hatred, betrayal and impotence and tried to share Al's regret but couldn't.

"You almost destroyed me, Protz, for no other reason than you could. You're not fit to be in charge of vulnerable people – of anyone – and you'll hand your notice in tomorrow with immediate effect. If you'll take my advice, you'll also get some psychiatric help."

"Although I suggest not from Kadynsi," Al said, still with a smile in his voice.

Protz lunged her head forward and spat across the space between Al and Jo but missed, leaving traces of spittle dangling wetly from her chin.

"This footage is sitting waiting, uploaded on all the social media and whatever happens to us, it will go viral in the next couple of days, I can guarantee it," Jo added. "I can prevent it but only if you do what I say."

Jo turned and spoke directly to Peter Dealey.

"It's over, Peter, it's over. Kadynski's shitty little empire is about to fall apart and combined with this footage, the whole world will be crawling over this place, setting up enquiries and trying to find out who knew what and who did what. Do the right thing, Peter, while you've got time, walk away, leave us alone and keep her under control for the next hour."

Dealey's eyes ran over the gaping window and sheets.

"You're going out of there?" he asked incredulously. Without waiting for an answer he turned, took Protz silently with one hand beneath her upper arm and nonchalantly, it seemed, put his hand into his pocket. As they exited through the door something clattered on to the tiled floor. Al stepped forward and picked it up. Looking at Jo with a mixture of disbelief and utter joy, he dangled a large bunch of keys before her.

"Come on baby, let's get our asses out of this place."

Dealey had just reached the offices as Al and Jo confronted the ward's locked doors and could hear Protz screaming and ranting hysterically. They felt confident there would be no attention focussed on them but that confidence turned to panic as one key after another failed to fit the lock – until finally one slipped easily into the keyhole and turned. The lift was easier as Al immediately identified the correct little triangular key that looked nothing like a normal one.

Jo felt almost like an observer, disembodied, as though watching from above. Each separate action had its own entity and its completion was the only goal before them, until another task presented itself and then it, too, had to be completed, another final action. There was no sense that each represented a step along the road to an end goal because she had not allowed herself even to consider what that end goal might be. Anything other than the here and now was formless, distant, unattainable and just too, too cruel to consider if it was to be snatched away when just within reach.

"I think it's probably better to take your gown off now," Al said with a smile, as the noisy, capacious lift whirred and clunked slowly downwards. Jo felt stupid as she shed it and had just slipped into her shoes when the lift stopped with a jolt and its doors slid open to reveal a large but almost deserted reception area. Ahead of them, to the right of double glass entry doors, was a semi-circular reception desk. Jo recalled none of the detail although she recognised enough to know she had been brought into the hospital this way.

Two people sat watching a tiny TV behind the desk and Al whispered: "Talk to me in a normal voice," and then louder, "What time does your last train go – will you be okay?" Jo responded and they discussed imaginary train timetables as they passed in front of the two disinterested staff but just as they pushed the entrance doors partially open, Al stopped, allowed his door to close again, turned and walked towards the reception desk.

Jo felt her breathing cease as she watched him, her body paralysed, mouth wide open, eyes unblinking, disbelief jostling for position with fear. He deposited the keys on the counter with a clatter and in a voice entirely normal, even chatty, said:

"Make sure Peter Dealey gets these will you please – charge nurse, Anderson ward." One of the night workers raised a hand in acknowledgement but his eyes never left the TV screen. It was a display of sang froid that left Jo gasping in amazement.

They stepped through the exit doors into a dark, blustery and chilly night and Jo grabbed Al's arm as she matched his unhurried pace.

"Why? Why the hell did you do that? I nearly fainted."

Al maintained his pace. "Have you ever lost a bunch of keys? It's really annoying, really inconvenient – expensive, too."

"That's the accountant in you talking."

"No it isn't!"

"Yes it is!"

"Okay, maybe a bit of an accountant – a very little bit."

Jo laughed. "Oh my god, Al, feel that wind, taste it, smell it – not a trace of boiled cabbage, despair or incontinence," Jo said as they walked down the tree-lined gravel drive that curved between mown lawns, heading towards the entrance gate and street lights beyond. "I think Egham is the most beautiful place in the world!" She then hesitated and held Al's arm more firmly. "I keep expecting someone to shout 'halt', floodlights to switch on and sirens to sound."

"Nah," Al replied with a chuckle. "It's a common or garden psychiatric hospital not Dartmoor. To be honest, no one really gives a damn. They're not gonna get the dogs out for the failed finger breaker of Feltham and the wicked redcurrant jelly woman from Weybridge!"

Jo laughed, stopped, threw her arms around Al's neck and kissed him, his silly words having banished her fears.

"No," he replied and eventually added, "it's not these people we need to worry about…!" and her fears immediately fluttered back to resume their old positions.

Jo stopped again as they reached the gates.

"Al, where are we going? We don't have a penny between us, no credit cards, no car – I don't even have a coat."

"Wrong, Madam, I have five pounds forty pence." He looked at his watch. "It's quarter past ten and we're going to the nearest Indian restaurant because I could murder a tarka dhal and a pint of Cobra! But we need to get a move on, they might close." Jo looked at him disbelievingly. "It's okay, I phoned Wendy earlier and she's coming with all the necessary. I'll text her with the rendezvous when we find a place."

"Mr Dwight, you are without doubt the coolest man I have ever met in my life."

There was no danger of the Mughal Spice closing as the last of the late pub goers were still ordering. They had almost finished their meal by the time Wendy arrived and their greetings were like those of long lost friends rather than people who had met just two days earlier. Wendy appeared almost as disbelieving as Jo that they were once again seemingly ordinary people, doing ordinary things in an ordinary late-night restaurant.

Through the laughter and jokes, the relating of what had happened and who had said what to whom, was an outpouring of relief that demanded words and one talked over the other – silence an impossibility after two weeks of the constraining fear of Anderson ward – months in Al's case.

Jo looked around the unassuming little place and found it almost inconceivable that each evening, here at these same tables, whilst she was being sedated and threatened, perhaps the very same jolly people ordered their birianis and sag aloos oblivious to what was happening just four or five hundred metres away. While she was consumed with concern and despair, they enjoyed this warm refuge with its tantalising aromas and thought nothing of the dramas taking place out of sight in their unremarkable town.

But the other side of the coin also demanded her attention as images of the muddled, befuddled and sad inhabitants she had got to know gnawed away at her – still victims of others' ego and need to control. But perhaps, just perhaps, not for much longer.

Reality asserted itself suddenly as Wendy pushed an envelope across the table towards her. "There's two thousand quid in there – the best I could do at short notice. Plus there's a credit cards in the name of Lane, Mr James Lane, which can't be traced to either me or the organisation – as you asked, Al. It's an account we use for our activities when we want to remain incognito. It's got an eight thousand pound limit with nothing on it at the moment and the PIN is here." She handed over a slip of paper. "So what's your next move? You're welcome to stay with me for the night but I don't think that would be too wise."

"An anonymous Travelodge or Premier Inn near Heathrow will do the trick, I reckon, people coming and going all night long," Al replied. "We can hire a car in the morning, buy some clothes, whatever gear we need and then do what we have to do."

"You've got your licence?" Jo enquired with surprise.

"They didn't take my wallet away from me, just my money and passport. I don't have any credit cards."

Jo suddenly looked concerned. "Are they going to plaster our pictures in the papers, on TV?"

"I don't think there's any chance of that – it's the last thing your husband and his cronies will want. Focuses attention back on you just before the election and raises all the doubts that a lot of people originally had… and besides…" Al suddenly stopped short.

"And besides what?" Jo asked insistently. There was a long pause before Al replied.

"Nothing." He was dismissive and then, looking at Jo's determined face, added, "…Okay, and besides, it makes it more difficult to get rid of you surreptitiously should they want to!"

"Oh, is that all," Jo replied with a levity she did not feel and then dragged her mind back to what had to be done and was surprised at her clarity of thought. "I have to get Danny – that's absolute priority. Julie should have some support. I'll talk to mum later, and Reece and then I need to get hold of Stephen's shitty little porn flash drive."

"It might put Danny in danger," Al said quietly, "to be with you – with us."

"It's not up for debate," Jo replied emphatically. "I made a promise! Perhaps if we all got out of the way somewhere, went abroad until we get Julie's statement and notes. It would only be for a few days, hopefully. Actually, I think that's the only thing we can do to keep us safe." Jo read a lack of enthusiasm in Al's face. "What's wrong with that, then?"

"Look, I have no idea what resources the bad guys are going to throw at this but if they want to they can track every credit card transaction, every mobile call, every cash withdrawal but the more they do, the more people are involved and the dangers of someone talking increase. One thing I reckon they will certainly do is put us on the watch list."

"What the hell's that?" Jo asked.

"Our names given to emigration at ports and airports – stop us leaving the country."

There was a long silence whilst the trio considered the problem until Wendy interrupted it, tentatively.

"Look, I'm not certain about this but if I'm right, it may be a way round it. I travel quite a lot – we've got offices in Bristol and Poland and I usually visit them on the same trip. I go to Bristol first and then on to Warsaw and back the same way. I've noticed on the last few trips that although there are batteries of immigration officials when you arrive in Bristol and they scan your passport, stare you in the eyes and all that stuff, when you depart from there it's very different.

"If you've got only hand luggage and have checked in online, the first time you show your passport is when you go through security and all they do is check it against your boarding card – no scanning, no monitoring, nothing. The only other time you show it is when you leave the holding area outside the actual gate to board the aircraft – and then it's just an Easyjet or Ryanair employee not emigration. They do have a monitor but it looks as if all they're doing is checking your name against their passenger list. There's certainly no scanning." Wendy added with a shrug of her shoulders. "I don't know but it might be a possibility."

Al went into deep thought but eventually shook his head.

"I don't think so – API." There were looks of incomprehension from the two women. "Advanced Passenger Information – you have to provide all your passport details when you book and it would be simplicity itself for them to run this through their computer to get a match with the watch list – they probably do it automatically with every passenger."

"There has to be some bloody way," Wendy added, showing her irritation.

Again Al went silent briefly.

"Of course, of course, how stupid of me. We just go down to Brighton, I borrow my old boat – I know where the keys are kept – and we sail across to Fécamp in France. Couldn't be easier." His face showed delight – problem solved.

Jo looked unconvinced.

"Al, it's not a very big boat – to sail right across the Channel. How long will it take?"

"Depends on the winds, really, anything from fourteen to sixteen hours, but she's very sturdy, timber built!"

"Oh dear God," Jo Almost shouted. "Sixteen hours bobbing around in the English Channel in that little bloody thing, most of it in the dark, in Winter... I'd sooner spend the rest of my life on Anderson ward. Are you sure you're not a Catholic, Al, because everything you suggest involves penances."

"It's spring," Al offered but without conviction. "Well, almost."

"There has to be some other way," Jo said, ignoring Al's defence. They lapsed into silence once more until she again spoke, tentatively. "Couldn't we go over to Northern Ireland from Stranraer – to Belfast – you don't need a passport and once you're there it must be simple to slip across the border into the Republic. Everyone's always saying how porous the border is."

"Oh Jo, you know how to pick 'em," Al laughed. "That's the one route that has more security men watching it than you can count. They're still jittery about the Continuity IRA, the Real IRA and god knows who else. You might not need a passport but you sure as hell need identity."

Again they lapsed into silence until Wendy spoke.

"Okay then, I've got another suggestion. Twice I've been on holiday to Brittany and both times we've gone on a high-speed ferry – a catamaran or trimaran kind of thing – from Poole and it's all so low key. You show your passport with your tickets when you check in but that's just confirmation of your identity for the shipping company and the only other time is when you're asked to report to the passport office on the boat before landing in St Malo. There's no check on whether you actually go to the office or not and no one asks you for your ticket once you're on the boat."

Al looked as though he wanted to interrupt and Wendy waived him aside: "Now, if I hid you in the back of the people carrier we could get you onto the ferry without any difficulty because they never inspect the car – any car as far as I could see. Once aboard, you can quietly slip into the accommodation with me and act like any other passenger until we return to our cars for disembarking and then you can hide again until we're ashore in France." She paused while everyone considered the proposition. "I can't see any reason why it wouldn't work," Wendy added.

"But that would involve you," Jo said.

"Christ, don't worry about that – I've done much riskier things," Wendy replied. "Let me work out the details but I reckon we have a solution. When do you think you'll be ready to go – the boat sails in the afternoon, about one, one thirty."

Jo looked at Al as if he might have the answer but he shrugged his shoulders and so she thought out loud: "Well, we need to get some clothes and things and we can do that tomorrow daytime, evening we can pick up stuff from my house – passport, flash drive – see mum and Reece and then get down to Poole, picking Danny up on the way. Day after tomorrow I guess!" There was an air of unreality about Jo's words and silence followed while all three considered the proposition.

"We could, of course, forget all this and just go straight to the press!" Al threw in but unconvincingly.

"No!" Jo's response was emphatic. "You don't know these people the way I do. Just the slightest chink in my allegations and they'll wriggle through it like slippery eels and I'll be the one who's seen as guilty – the nut case. We have to have absolutely conclusive evidence of everything that's happened and I'm not going public until I've got it – everything! At the moment, Al, we've got nothing.

"If Reece has done what you suggested, and protected himself, I'll ask him to visit Julie with his chosen solicitor and take a statement from her, if he hasn't already planned it. It will still be dynamite even without the notes. Perhaps he could borrow her keys, go to her flat and get the notes. I think he should also contact Dealey and see if he will make a statement. The poor, downtrodden bugger seems to have finally decided which side of the fence he's now on so it might work. My mum should make a statement too – I think she might surprise us all."

"Do you want me to publish the video? We've got absolutely thousands of 'shares' on Facebook and it really will go viral. There's a huge campaign building up. 'Let Jo Go!' it's called – sorry." Wendy sounded embarrassed at the name but Jo laughed:

"No! Don't do it yet. There's something that worries me about Protz having international infamy. She's so manipulative that I'm scared she'll turn it to her advantage. What I would like you to do, Wendy, is send the link to Reece and ask him to forward it to the directors of the hospital trust – he'll know who they are. Oh, and to Kadynski too. That should start the ball rolling." Jo poured out the remainder of the Verdiccio and took a long sip."I can't tell you how civilised this feels."

"What about Danny?" Al asked, "How are you planning on getting him?"

"I thought I'd just walk in to the school, prove I'm his mother and ask to see him urgently. Say we're going for a walk and then drive off!"

"Might work," Al replied without conviction, "but just one refusal, one decision to check with Stephen and you're stuffed."

"Then we'll grab him somehow," Jo replied and then added with a smile and a gentle push: "You're the action man – you can sort that one out."

Wendy spoke almost apologetically: "Probably not the best time to raise the subject but I presume you've given up on the animal attacks – you've had a lot on your mind."

Jo took her time before answering and in that hiatus her mind whirled around retrieving all the powerful memories and certainties that had been eclipsed by the recent struggle for day to day survival. The window onto pain and suffering that had so troubled her opened once more; her belief that she understood their origins again flooded through her; and she was reminded of her determination to unearth the reasons for them. She realised instantly that the last two weeks had been little more than an interruption in a mystery that had to be solved; that matched in importance all the machinations of ensuring her survival. When she replied it was with absolute conviction: "No I haven't, Wendy, I certainly haven't! But when you think about it, it's the reason why we're all here."

Wendy, looked pleased, even relieved.

"Is now a good time?"

"Absolutely!"

"Okay then," Wendy replied enthusiastically, picking up her bag and delving into it to find a piece of folded paper. "I've had two of my campaigners working on this full-time for the last two weeks and you're quite right, something huge is happening. We've been plotting each case that we've tracked down and they're still occurring around the coasts everywhere but remorselessly moving slowly inland and it's now up to fifteen miles from the coast. The only common feature between all of them is that they're close to the sea with no other linking factors which makes it impossible to identify a possible cause. So what we've been looking for are anomalies – any one attack that's different to the others in the hope that we may be able to find the causal element." Both Al and Jo looked at her with blank faces.

"I'm not being clear, am I?" Wendy asked rhetorically and then quickly unfolded the paper with an air of triumph. "We've found one such anomaly – just one! Look at this." She smoothed out the paper – a map print-out-with ball point dots and annotated dates and brief details.

"It's San Antonio, Texas, and not only is it not on the coast, it's a hundred and sixty miles inland. There've been over ninety attacks within an approximate thirty mile radius. Thirty miles! Don't you see?" Again there was incomprehension on their faces. "Go to the centre of that thirty mile spread and you may have your answer. If you can identify something there that can also be found in the sea…"

Jo did not reply but her face was alight, her eyes focussed.

"Any indication of what that might be?"

"No, but residents of San Antonio are aware that something's happening and the debate in local media points the finger at the military – there are several bases in the town, one of them huge. They think it might be nukes or chemical weapons leaking."

Jo perused the print-out carefully and then looked smilingly at Al.

"You're going home boy, we're off to San Antonio!"

Chapter Thirty Nine

Jo lay beneath a fluffy duvet with her head on soft pillows and felt Al nested into her back, his arm across her waist, his hand cupping one of her breasts but sleep would not come. The flood of tranquillity that normally followed passionate love making had not made an appearance and apprehension played tunes inside her head, plucking first at one chord and then another.

Would the phone ring suddenly and a voice demand they present themselves to reception where police were waiting? Would there be loud, insistent knocks on the door and a call for it to be opened immediately? But there were other, less materialistic concerns that demanded her wakefulness.

She had known Al just a short time and then only under the duress of control, confinement and threat. Now they were once more back in the real world, both free to follow their own agendas, would they each reject the mutual support that had sustained them now it was no longer needed? Or even worse, would it be Al alone who did that? Had their friendship grown out of need and nothing else and was now at an end?

She heard the quiet, rhythmic breathing of the complicated but adorable man behind her and prayed that none of her fears were real. Clearly, similar doubts were not troubling him as the regular breathing of deep sleep continued reassuringly.

They had discussed Danny and whether to collect him immediately or not and the experience had been an entirely novel one for Jo. She was used to Stephen adopting a position on whatever it was they were discussing, from the simplest to the most complicated decision making, and then arguing relentlessly for that position as if winning was more important than the outcome. With Al, she had outlined her need to keep her promise, her desperation to get him away from the school and her desire to be reunited with him. He had simply presented other options and spelt out his concerns and suggested perhaps she should consider them before making a final decision. He had not proselytised for them.

He believed it would be impossible for her to arrange an amicable departure for Danny from the school as she had had no contact with them and Stephen may well have outlined her 'infirmity' – he certainly thought they would first check with Stephen before agreeing. He said if Jo simply took Danny without approval there would almost certainly be a massive police and press reaction and their steps would be dogged far more assiduously than at present. It would no longer be covert but the police and every other agency, along with press and television and the public, in a public campaign to find them. Just as importantly, she would surrender the moral high ground and be portrayed as a mad women grabbing her child to abscond with a failed axe murderer.

Al also stressed that they did not know what they faced either immediately or when they reached the States.

His final thought was that Danny had been at the school just a couple of days and another few was probably neither here nor there as the dread apprehension of anticipation – always the worst part – was over. Danny had not been answering his phone and the assumption was that he was not allowed to keep it permanently with him. Al suggested Jo contact the school and arrange a time to talk to him over the phone, to tell him she would be there in just a few days and that he would be leaving with her. That would provide sufficient hope to keep his spirits buoyant and remind him that her promise was alive and well.

Jo had listened to it all, had offered mild protest on most points but when Al had finished she sat quietly for some considerable time, thought about what he had said and eventually agreed with him. It was an uncomfortable reversal but she knew there really was no other option.

A sense of unreality had still not left Jo even as they sat in the Vegetariana Restaurant, with the Thames gliding by just feet away on the other side of the floor-to-ceiling windows, shopping bags stacked in the corner alongside them, lunch on the table before them. She guessed they looked like any other couple taking a break from shopping, lost in their own pleasures and intimacies, enjoying a retreat from Kingston's crowded streets and stores.

The slate grey of the moving river matched exactly the colour of a leaden sky which sat over them like an immoveable lid but neither constrained the colourful ducks or the black and white gulls as they busied themselves between the few moored craft seeking sustenance.

An old lady appeared on the footpath beyond the glass and delved into a plastic bag to produce slices of bread which she crumbled and threw to the gulls and ducks, transforming the scene into one of frantic activity as birds from everywhere converged on the stretch of water in front of her. Jo was pleased that they, too, were enjoying a lunch.

The hire car was across the road in a multi-storey car park, her new clothes somehow offered reconfirmation of who she really was and the reassurance of Al sitting opposite her mulling over their newly-agreed plan of action should all have combined to ensure Jo's peace of mind. But they didn't – not entirely. Perhaps it was her Catholic upbringing, which could elicit guilt at the drop of a hat; perhaps it was the insecurity of their situation; perhaps it was the thought of visiting her house just a twenty-five minute drive away and the feelings that would almost certainly resurrect; perhaps it was her decision to leave Danny where he was for the time being; but these and other thoughts had conspired together to keep apprehension fluttering around her, as insistent as the birds outside.

Perhaps the most pervasive feeling was guilt for those she had left behind in the hospital no more than a few miles away, even though her actions offered their very best prospect for change. There was, however, one emotion that was dominant enough to corral all others into manageable form and that was her feelings for Al.

With first light, her reservations had slowly evaporated and she was now happily certain of her feelings towards the man opposite her – and those feelings were powerful and positive.

She leant across the table, placed her hand on his arm and, fighting to keep her emotion under control, waited for him to look at her before quietly saying: "I love you, Al." She watched the warmth flood into his eyes and a smile illuminate his face in what appeared to be a crystalisation of pleasure and she knew she could cope with everything.

For obvious reasons, they had decided not to visit St George's Hill until late evening when it would be dark. Jo felt certain the house would be empty and that collecting a few possessions, her passport and the flash drive would be simple. She hoped that no one had already beaten her to the passport. And so they continued their shopping through the afternoon and ended the day in the cinema where they sat holding hands. On leaving it, Jo could feel her apprehension growing and was annoyed with herself – it was her home for god's sake!

She had no need to direct Al as he knew the area almost as well as she did and so they exited on the river road, crossed over the roundabout at the end of the Kingston by-pass and then continued the short distance down the A3 to Esher, where they turned off towards Hersham and Weybridge. Only as they travelled along Queens Road and past Reece's surgery did Jo direct Al into St George's Hill and along its darkened, tree-lined drives with their sparse street lights.

"It's about four hundred yards along here, on the left," Jo instructed.

"Does the road continue on past your house," Al asked in serious tone, as he slowed the car only slightly.

"Yes, why?"

"So I'm not going to run into a dead end or cul-de-sac if I keep going?"

"No, but why? This is the house, here – you're going to miss it!"

"That's why," Al replied as he maintained the car's speed through the semi-darkness between banks of mature trees. "Why do you think that car's parked there, on the road directly outside the entrance to your house, with someone sitting in it? Do you recognise it – could it be a neighbour's?"

Jo didn't immediately reply and the reason for Al's caution became obvious.

"No it's not a neighbour – but it might not be what you think. Did you see – in the driveway – two cars? One was Stephen's and the other Hillie's. It could well be his security so close to an election." Her voice was almost strangulated as the reality of the situation crawled inside her and filled her with hatred and loathing but most of all, contempt. "Fucking bastards!"

"Stay cool, baby, you've got work to do – and now, where the hell am I going?"

Jo's directions were issued through tight lips. "We'll go in the back way. Take the next left and when you get to the big white house with a summerhouse in front of it, slow down. There's a very narrow little lane on your left but go carefully, it's full of pot holes."

She went silent as Al followed her directions and swung into the lane, reducing the car's speed to less than walking pace as they bumped and bounced between high bushes, their branches occasionally squeaking along the side of the car. "There's a turning space at the end – stop there." Again Al did as instructed and Jo turned to him: "If the key is not in the garden shed or the utility room door's been bolted, I'm going to ring the front door bell and confront them."

Al's response was instant: "No you're not. You'll have security all over you and it will be game over. Take control, Jo, take control, you can do it! Don't let them beat you. Stick to the plan and when you've got what you need we'll quietly disappear out of this place and get on with what we have to do – and that includes destroying your husband. Lose control and we'll be back at Egham!"

Jo listened to Al's insistent words, hoped she was persuaded, reminded herself of what she had to lose, but wasn't entirely convinced. Retribution was a very attractive proposition.

They scrambled along a narrow path through seemingly interminable bushes before emerging into a copse of tall trees where there was little undergrowth to impede them and then finally the house appeared out of the darkness on the other side of the lawn, with faint lights in one of its upstairs rooms – Stephen's bedroom – and what Jo knew to be landing and hall lights.

Al put his arm out to stop Jo's progress and looked first one way and then the other across the lawn.

"What? What is it?" Jo whispered.

"Just thinking. They don't make council houses the way they used to!" Jo stifled a laugh and kicked him gently.

Jo found herself pointlessly tiptoeing across her own lawn, again waiting for shouts and search lights but none came. She went to the garden shed, found the key, took it to the utility room door, that was almost hidden by ivy, and inserted it into the keyhole. It turned and the door opened inwards without resistance and she quickly made her way across it and into the kitchen – her beautiful kitchen yet it felt almost alien. Al was directly behind her.

Sufficient light spilled thorough its open doorway from the hall to illuminate it clearly. Before they exited into the hall, Al looked at Jo and placed his fingers to his lips. Jo responded with a V sign.

He followed her up the stairs, listening intently all the time, and across the landing where she disappeared into her bedroom. Al positioned himself outside so he was between Jo and the bedroom which appeared to contain her husband and her sister, judging by the little sliver of light that showed from beneath the door. The sudden noises which emanated from it left him in no doubt that they did both occupy it.

"You're a very naughty girl," said a distant, muffled male voice, which was followed by what could only have been a slap and then another and another. They were loud slaps and their source was not a mystery. They were immediately followed by a female voice: "I'm sorry, Daddy, I've been very, very naughty," and yet more slaps echoed around the tasteful, neutrally-decorated walls of the expensive, highly-desirable and substantial Surrey house.

Al found himself gritting his teeth as though that would reduce the volume of the fantasy being played out just a door's width from him. "Please," he silently implored, "please get it over with, please don't let Jo hear you."

His supplication was in vain as Jo appeared from her room clutching a suitcase, her face set like a mask. Again came the voices: "You're so naughty you need my special punishment – for very naughty girls!" "Oh, yes, yes please, Daddy!"

Al watched Jo's face with horror and raised his hands in front of her to create a barrier and shook his head vigorously, mouthing the word 'no' over and over again, waving his hands backwards and forwards as tough signalling in semaphore. He could feel panic rising and then he watched with disbelief as the fury in Jo's face gradually melted away and he saw her eyes light up and a smile gradually spread across her face. Within seconds she was holding her stomach, bent over as silent giggles shook her body. She reached out with one hand for Al's support and the giggles were no longer entirely silent. He quickly took her by an arm and impelled her down the stairs, fighting back his own laughter.

He knew that they had to control it and spun Jo towards him, mouthing the words "flash drive." It worked and she sobered up, disappeared into a room and returned within seconds brandishing an envelope and a triumphant smile.

Chapter Forty

"Fasten your seat belts in preparation for landing." The day had been filled with aircraft and airports and for the second time Jo felt vibration as air brakes whirred down and an undercarriage clunked into position. Texas countryside glided past beneath as the Continental Airlines flight from Dallas/Fort Worth prepared to lower itself onto the runway at San Antonio airport and anticipation gave way to exhaustion.

After leaving Jo's house, they had arranged a hurried, late-night, roadside meeting with Reece and her mother opposite the southerly exit to St George's Hill, on the far side of the West Byfleet road, in the secluded entrance to the stables where it had all begun. The fact that the venue had been communicated in code added to the conspiratorial air and the result was almost a feeling of excitement.

She and her mother had hugged tightly and more naturally than she could ever remember. The sense of closeness had almost dissuaded her from talking about Hilary as she had not wanted to shatter the bond that was growing between them but it had to be done for her and Al's security as much as anything else. There was also a question of common justice and so she reluctantly told her the details. Afterwards, her mother had remained silent for long moments, her head down and when she did speak it was with remarkable calmness.

"I knew about Stephen – well, I was pretty certain but knowing what to do about it was something else." She had then adopted a self-deprecating tone. "It won't surprise you, Jo darling, that I did what I always do in situations I find difficult – ignored it and hoped it would go away, believing it was an infatuation and that Hilary would quickly become bored as she

498

usually does. I am so, so sorry, it was cowardly and I'm ashamed of myself."

Jo squeezed her hand and wanted to throw her a lifeline, to say she understood and that most people would have acted similarly but her mother had continued, not inviting interruption:

"That Hilary was complicit in sending you to a mental hospital is a shame I will forever find difficult to live with. What must I have done, what kind of mother have I been to produce a child so stripped of all conscience that she could betray her own sister?" The question was meant to be rhetorical but Jo took her by the shoulders and spoke firmly:

"Stop it, stop it now! You can't take responsibility for the morals of a thirty-four year old woman who's spent far more of her life with the amoral, hedonistic arseholes who make up her Weybridge set than she has with you. And anyway, you know what a vain airhead she is – I doubt she even bothered to think through what she did..."

"You're too kind to her Josephine, much too kind. She is nowhere near as ditzy as she pretends and no one can be that divorced from real life. She's selfish, self-obsessed and jealous – jealous of you and always has been – and I have to carry much of the blame. Don't get me wrong, darling, I love her and always will because she is my child, but all that's happened has forced me to be honest with myself."

Jo had hugged her mother once more but knew there was little more she could do right at that moment and so she had remained silent. She then handed the flash drive to Reece, but not before having copied it onto her newly-purchased laptop. She had hugged him, too, and although he had returned her hug he had appeared preoccupied. Finally, he had put his thoughts into words.

"I think Julie Samuels is still at great risk even though she's in hospital – particularly as she's in hospital and totally immobile. I have to do something about that with urgency – in the morning, first thing." Jo merely nodded her agreement.

They had kissed and joked and bid each other goodbye as Jo and Al climbed into their hire car and headed towards the M30 and thence down to Poole, enveloped in a cloud of unreality.

Was all the subterfuge really necessary? They had the flash drive, Reece's support as to her sanity, they could now offer some proof of the animal attacks... Were they being ridiculously over cautious? None of these would necessarily stand up without Julie's notes and her statement. She knew there was no choice and Al had voiced it perfectly.

"Are you prepared to bet your freedom against a bunch of rabid dogs backed into a corner?"

She wasn't and so the deception had to continue. They had checked into an hotel in Poole and in the morning deposited the hire car near to the Hertz office with the key on the offside front wheel. The intention was to ring them with the details once they were out of the country just in case Al's licence had been traced. The rendezvous with Wendy was not until 12.30 and so they had spent a lazy morning mooching around Poole.

She had tried ringing Danny's phone several times over the preceding couple of days but again got no response. She had wanted to ring the school and ask to speak to her son but Al had persuaded her to wait until they were in St Malo – just as a precaution.

Wendy had arrived at the rendezvous on time and with her in the people carrier was Phil, who Jo had met during her pig farm escapade.

"I did think of bringing Maisie – there's nothing like a nice little family to present a picture of normality – but then..." Wendy had said, her caution not requiring the detail.

The two rear seats had been removed from the vehicle and when then tailgate was raised they could see that Phil had constructed a simple framework of wood which effectively acted as a shelf, leaving a void below. On top of the shelf were piled back packs, personal possessions, coats and a blanket to disguise its structure and the overall impression was of a car laden for the holidays. Away from prying eyes, Jo and Al had eased themselves into the space created for them and tried to find comfort on the cushions Wendy had provided.

As the tailgate was lowered and the car began moving, they found themselves in almost complete darkness and Jo had begun to giggle and despite Al's hisses, could not stop. After several minutes and repeated bouts of schoolgirl giggling, Wendy's voice had cut into their isolation with hard authority: "Be quiet, we're approaching the check in." Jo had needed no other instruction.

A window had whirred down, there had been an exchange of greetings and presumably the showing of paperwork and passports and then the car was once more on the move. A sudden upwards incline and the rattle and clank of metal beneath the tyres, followed by hollow, echoing noises confirmed they were aboard the ferry.

There had been a long delay before the tailgate was raised and she and Al were able to slip out of their hidey hole to find themselves on a dimly-lit car deck smelling of diesel and exhaust fumes: "Sorry about the delay – just avoiding eyes," Wendy had offered and then continued, "Okay, let's go and have a cup of tea."

Jo wondered, her heart in her mouth, if she was the only one amongst them who was not inherently cool.

What followed was boredom – more than four hours of endless cups of tea and coffee, a wilted salad roll, a microwaved baked potato and, in the end, a glass of mediocre white wine as the jet-propelled craft sped at high speed across the Channel towards France.

Jo's breathing had momentarily shallowed as they pulled smoothly into St Peter Port, Jersey. Her relief when it put to sea again was short lived as the tannoy bellowed out for passengers to present themselves and their passports to the passport office on the main deck. The three legitimate travellers had done so whilst Jo and Al had remained in their reclining chairs in the main saloon. It had all gone precisely as Wendy had predicted.

They had been amongst the first on the car deck as the ferry approached St Malo and Phil had flapped a blanket around near the tailgate as if shaking it out and they had used its screening to disappear from view once more beneath the false shelf. Even Jo had been able to relax as experience over the years had shown her that French immigration never showed the slightest interest in arrivals from the UK.

Wendy had placed her immigration clearance sticker in the

windscreen and then it was all over. Within minutes, Jo and Al were able to slip out of the back on a cloudy French street and join the others in the car's interior as Wendy accelerated away once more, following signs to St Malo railway station.

There had been time for a quick meal together before the Paris train departed and the atmosphere in which it was eaten, in a small and very French restaurant, had been lighthearted, almost joyous. They had done it. They were out of Britain.

Jo had telephoned the school and battled to speak to Danny: "Yes, I realise he is doing prep but this is a family emergency and, no, you don't know me but I can promise you that Danny does." She had found it hard not to infect her words with the resentment she felt towards the school. Eventually, Danny had come to the phone and Jo maintained her secret agent fantasy to tell him, amidst declarations of love, that she was going to get him 'out of that dreadful place' and in just a few days she would come for him. He had gone back to his prep a very happy boy.

When it came to goodbyes, Jo had hugged Wendy and kissed her several times before holding her at arms length, looking at her silently. She had not even known her just a few weeks ago and yet Wendy had become one of her most trusted friends, not only putting her own safety at risk but doing it without fuss and seemingly without a demand for recognition or thank yous. It had all been delivered in the manner of a job that simply had to be done and Jo loved her for it, knowing she was now faced with a wait until morning before the two of them could return home. She kissed her several times more until Wendy laughed, either with bewilderment or embarrassment – but her blushes and her demeanour told Jo that she understood perfectly the reasons for it.

A train ride, an hotel near Charles de Gaulle airport and an Air France flight to Dallas/Fort Worth the following morning and then a connecting flight to San Antonio. The only emotion Jo now felt was tiredness. By her internal time clock it was just after midnight while on the ground below it had just passed six pm and she could not even think about how to organise the research she had come to do as her motivation was eclipsed by the need for a hot bath, something decent to eat and a lie down on a comfortable, motionless bed.

"Do you want to see the Alamo," Al asked enthusiastically as the plane taxied towards the terminal building and she smiled, not able to summon sufficient energy to answer. "It's here, this is the home of the Alamo, part of our heritage. You've gotta see it."

She loved his enthusiasm but...

"Tomorrow, my gorgeous, tomorrow. I guess we've got to start somewhere and that's as good a place as any."

As they strolled into arrivals, this time with no fear of what immigration might hold as they had cleared in Dallas/Fort Worth, Jo switched on her phone and before their bags arrived on the carousel the beep – beep beep of an incoming text sounded and Jo checked the display anxiously but it was merely the welcome message from AT&T. As they queued for a taxi, it beeped again but this time it was a delayed message from Reece: 'Julie discharged into my care. She is now in a place of safety.' Jo felt great relief.

As they left the taxi to enter the overly-opulent Hyatt hotel – their choice only because it sat directly alongside the Alamo – again the beep – beep beep demanded her attention. Also delayed, it was from her mother: 'Went to her house and challenged Hilary. She became hysterical. Stuart knows. Disappeared to her room in floods of tears and refuses to come out. Left her your new number. Made a statement to Reece's solicitor friend.'

Jo relished the three essentials which she had been eagerly anticipating – shower, dinner and rest but as she lay on the ridiculously large and comfortable bed, holding Al's hand in a room big enough to host dance classes, relaxation refused to come. Eventually she arose and tackled what had been occupying her mind by unfolding the chart of incidents Wendy had provided. Like a join-the-dots picture she connected each of the outermost marks and they formed a rough but recognizable circle after leaving out just a few stragglers that were far outside the main pattern. With a Google search, she looked up what military establishments there were in the city and marked them on the map also.

"It doesn't work, Al, it just doesn't work." He clambered off the bed and joined her, clad in his plush Wyatt white-cotton robe.

"What doesn't?"

"The military bases. There are four of them in the area and they're all pretty innocuous. There's Lackland Air Force base, which is a recruit training facility; there's Fort Sam Houston, some kind of national monument; Randolph Air Force base is for pilot and instructor training and USO San Antonio operates outreach services – none of them are active service bases and so the likelihood of having chemical or nuclear weapons isn't that strong, I would have thought."

"Come on Jo! They're hardly likely to name them 'poison gas base' or 'deadly chemical storage depot.' What they say they are and what they actually are could be entirely different."

"No, it's more than that – they're nowhere near the centre of this thing that's happening, whatever it is."

"Wind, water even a road might make the distribution irregular, carrying the stuff responsible in one direction but not another."

"Possibly, but I don't think so or the pattern on this map would be irregular, elongated, but it isn't, it's more or less round." She grabbed a complimentary pen from beside the phone and with the edge of a Gideon bible began to do some simple calculations and draw a number of radii across the irregular circle.

Beep-beep beep. She dropped the pen and reached for her phone. It was Reece again.

'Went to Julie's flat. Completely trashed computer and notes taken. Sorry. But she has made damning statement. Might be ok without notes (but much better with them). Has to collect her copy of notes from post office in person but not yet physically capable.'

It was as though the bubble of energy that had kept her awake and functioning, still eager and determined, had been punctured and all her rediscovered motivation fizzed out in a moment. She dropped the pen and switched the phone off before standing up and holding on to Al.

"I'm exhausted, Al, let's go to sleep."

But she didn't sleep and lay there sensing the same old dreams, visions, hallucinations – whatever they were – beginning to announce their presence once more but it seemed they had mellowed and almost assumed the status of old acquaintances – not friends she was happy to greet but people she would prefer to live without but if necessary, could tolerate. They had originally burst in as invaders, challenging, disrupting the entire household, causing panic with their aggression and demands for attention, their threats and fear but now they were sitting in the corner almost unobtrusively, just doing enough so their presence was felt. But a constant companion was the fear that they might kick off once more.

It added to Jo's sense of defeat for what she had originally perceived as an insight into another world was probably nothing of the sort. These apparitions were surely of her own creation, subdued and emasculated by medication perhaps and now that it had worn off, back they had come, albeit a little chastened and subdued – almost benign. But they were back. It was utterly dispiriting but sleep intervened before she could decide just how deep the feeling of depression went.

Morning, however, and the arrival of sparkling bright sunlight expunged the night-time shadows and all those doubts that lurked within them, banished the embryo of depression and replaced it with renewed enthusiasm. Whilst Al still sprawled beneath the covers, Jo was again calculating radii and applying them to her map.

Within minutes of switching on her phone, a beep-beep beep sounded and she checked it. 'Nurse Protz dismissed (or resigned – not sure which) but am assured she will never obtain reference to work with vulnerable people. Reece.'

There was not the sense of euphoria that Jo had anticipated only an immediate transportation back to the cloying, frightening atmosphere of Anderson ward that had nearly destroyed her. But then she remembered that it hadn't destroyed her and she finally allowed herself a momentary flush of satisfaction – not at Protz's undoing but her own resilience.

She turned to look at Al, who was just beginning to stir and was reminded of how he had been her rock, accepting her, never doubting her and without him she would not be in a plush hotel room following her instincts. She decided he needed to be thanked – again – for all his steadfast help and climbed back into bed with him, her hand bringing him to consciousness in a rather direct manner. The map could wait for a while.

Sometime later Jo took her by now, rather tatty map to breakfast and showed it to Al over pancakes and coffee.

"You see, the lines don't intersect neatly, not precisely, but they all cross this central point within just a few blocks of each other." She folded the map to a manageable size and pointed to an area of the city that was almost entirely obliterated by intersecting lines of smudged blue ball point.

"Very impressive Mrs Holmes but the question is, what's there, underneath your ink frenzy. Any idea?"

Jo did not respond but rose, took her map and headed for reception to see if they had their own map of the area. The smiley, perfectly-groomed receptionist handed her one supplied by a car hire company and Jo laid the two side by side on the reception desk and identified the obliterated area of her old map on the new one and with her ballpoint encircled the few blocks it encompassed. The interested receptionist watched with fascination and then, looking at Jo's new circle, asked cheerily: "Are y'all going to the sea life centre. It's a great day out."

Jo felt her heart stop as the import of the question momentarily stunned her. Here was the link she had hoped to find – in a tourist attraction in a south Texas town she had never heard of until two days ago. Sea was the link and it lay no more than a mile or two away from where she now stood. Ludicrous though it was, almost overwhelming excitement bubbled up inside her.

Beep-beep beep. Jo jumped alarmingly as her phone sounded. The text was from Hilary: 'I am so ashamed of what ive done that I cant eat or sleep. Please please please please Jo can you ever think of forgiving me. No excuse but Stephen battered me into signing it made me believe it would help you. I knew it was wrong and was why I couldnt visit you. Stuart has left me. I am so sorry Jo.'

Jo felt no sympathy for her sister, only contempt and a great deal of regret – how could she have been so stupidly self-centered. But even that was diluted by the discovery she had just made, which was so consuming she could hardly stand still as the receptionist prattled on. However, she forced herself to respond to Hilary: 'You only feel guilty because you were caught. No i cant forgive you but you can mitigate your actions by contacting reece evans and making a statement about stephens involvement – immediately.' Jo pressed 'send' with anger.

Al looked up with near amazement as Jo whirled into the dining room, grabbed him by an arm and hauled him from his seat, coffee cup still in hand.

"We're going out and we're going to find some answers. We've come to exactly the right place mister Dwight!"

"Have I got this right – we're going to see performing sea lions or some such thing – is that the idea?" Al asked as the cab trundled down town.

"I don't know." Jo pushed her newly annotated map in front of him and pointed to the circle she had drawn. "According to Miss Delectable on reception, the only thing of note here is the sea life centre – it takes up almost this entire area. I don't know what's there; I don't know what we're going to find; I don't know what we're going to do; and I have no idea what will happen but I know for certain we're in the right place – I know it, Al. Don't ask me how I know it but I do – it's in here." She touched her heart and then her head.

Al went silent and looked away, out of the window as the boring, single-storey architecture of provincial USA, with its fast food joints, shopping malls and over-blown shop fronts, slid remorselessly past. Eventually he turned to face her.

"I don't do scared, but I've got the strangest feeling in my guts that's doing a very good impression of it and it bothers me." There was another pause before he added: "I don't like it, Jo!"

507

Their anticipation and apprehension seemed in stark contrast to the crowds of jolly holiday-making families at the venue, with their baseball caps, buckets of popcorn and stiff card beakers of Coca Cola, so large that a toddler could drown in one. An obscene smell drifted from one stall that offered fried turkey legs for sale, all uniform in size, all coloured the same uninviting brown and each glimmering with an identical film of greasiness, as though the whole batch had been stamped out by some Taiwanese plastics factory.

None of these characteristics appeared to present an obstacle to sales and people walked around smilingly with their turkey legs, a napkin around the end that had once been a hock joint, gnawing from time to time on their gigantic snacks, which resembled parts of a not-so-small dinosaur. Jo looked at the extra wide backsides, which seemed commonplace, the voluminous drooping busts and hugely distended stomachs and wondered just how much coke and how many dismembered turkeys it had taken to produce them. But to observe conspicuous over-consumption was not why they had come, she reminded herself.

Beep-beep beep. Again the text was from Reece. 'Your ma has made v telling statement praising your sanity and motherhood – demolishing stephen and (sadly) implicating H. She is an angry woman. Solicitor gwen powell now working full time for us and going directly from witness to witness to take statements and speed things up. All happening v quickly now. Brilliant woman.'

Jo texted back: 'Excellent. Try the steens and their au pair marta. Stephen sexually assaulted her. Did not want to make sttmnt but might now that so many others are. I love u reece 4 all yr doing.'

The scale of the marine park was extraordinary – the largest in the world it was claimed. Two hundred and thirty acres of packaged entertainment for three-and-half million visitors a year, so the blurb said. Corporate America at its most successful.

They sat and drank ludicrously big, watery coffees in the open under sunny blue skies because they simply did not know what else to do or where to start, such was the immensity of the place. They trawled through the brightly-coloured maps and promotional literature which had been provided and tried to plan a route but Jo had lapsed into silence. When she did eventually speak it was not to make suggestions but was conclusive, decisive.

"We're going here, here and here," she said, jabbing a finger first at the dolphin pool, then the killer whale 'performance' area and finally the beluga whale 'encounter' pool. "The only common thread we have is the sea and these are sea creatures – mostly very big sea creatures – so if there's anything to discover this is where we'll find it."

"Good logic," Al offered.

"It's more than just logic." Jo replied. "I know it!" She looked unwaveringly into his eyes and he did not doubt her.

They wandered through the brash, theatrical, theme park architecture and its gushing slogans and almost wordlessly went from one big attraction to another. From the very first pool, where they watched Bottlenose dolphins leaping in unison and heard their mysterious clicks of communication, a strange atmosphere settled over them. They did not hold hands and did not talk but observed from separate, seemingly isolated worlds.

They moved on and saw a pair of killer whales burst through the surface of their confining tank together and splash back to send spray cascading over their audience, whose response was to scream with delight. There was no delight on view from either Al or Jo. They looked at huge, dome-headed beluga whales as they 'interacted' with customers and expressed their revulsion wordlessly when asked to participate by an overly-enthusiastic employee wearing a gaudy t-shirt with the identification 'Whale Experience'.

Jo found herself bitterly reacting against the endless hype that remorselessly sold artificiality, capture and imprisonment as natural and educational; that turned incarceration into profit and desperation into entertainment. Nowhere were the families of paying patrons – citizens of a country that supposedly deified family values – made cognisant of the reality that entertained them, that many of the animals they cheered and clapped had been wrested from their own families in the wild. They were now forced to live amongst others they did not know and did not love and if they were lucky enough to develop a new relationship, no mention was made that it might be ended overnight as animals were separated and transported to new prisons as a swap with other theme parks in order to boost revenues. Or it might be to participate in a breeding programme in which they exercised no choice.

But such truths were not factored into the experience for that way lay financial ruin. And the reverse of the coin was that inconvenient enquiry did not fit comfortably with a family day out and so by unspoken, mutual agreement it seemed, between provider and consumer, a tapestry of pretence obscured reality and camouflaged suffering.

By the same token, in none of the literature and on none of the happy hoardings was there an explanation that few of the creatures on display chose to indulge the most natural of all their desires and reproduce. But the few who did, and those who were coerced through artificial insemination, would have their progeny proclaimed as 'born in captivity,' a meaningless accolade pretending to some great achievement.

It was, of course, an achievement only for their captors who could then perpetuate the myth that these new arrivals, never having known the open oceans, never having swum endless distances in close company with others of their kind; never having sung their own distinct family songs of mutual recognition, would never weep for freedom and never miss it. A conspiracy of self-interested parties had conveniently, between them, erased tens of thousands of years of evolution almost overnight to suit corporate convenience and mollify critical voices.

And, of course, little would be said as these new innocents died after only months or a few frustrated years, never reaching maturity. And no attention would be focused on those adults whose desperation would cause them to attempt suicide by constantly swimming into the walls of their enclosures at speed.

Jo was aware that when she walked into the place she knew none of these things, had never viewed captive cetaceans and had never given their plight a thought and yet suddenly, she understood their desperation with extraordinary clarity, without a single person having spoken a single word to her. But there was no confusion in her mind as to how she had obtained the knowledge – she had felt it and knew exactly from whence it had come.

She turned to Al, seated alongside her in the amphitheatre, and was shocked by what she saw. His face was pale, drained of almost all colour and his jaw hung slackly; his eyes were dead, unblinking, focused rigidly on the sea creatures in front of them. She was even more shocked when she looked along the terraced banks of seats and saw several other people standing to leave, their faces like masks, exactly matching Al's, two actually holding their heads in their hands, grimacing, as though in pain.

Beep-beep beep. "Bugger," Jo said as she reached for her phone once more. 'When peter dealey started talking he wouldn't stop – has chopped the legs from under kadynski. Seeing hilary tomor. R.' Suddenly, it all seemed unimportant.

"Jesus Christ, Jo, I've got to get out of here." Without waiting for her response, Al rose and quickly headed out of the performance area and Jo could see him searching desperately for the park's exit signs and hurried to catch up with him.

"What is it, Al, what's wrong?" He did not respond but maintained his rapid pace.

"Talk to me, Al, tell me what it is."

He stopped and swung towards her.

"I can't – I don't know what it is." He began walking again, speaking as he went. "I'm scared, Jo, I'm losing control of my mind!"

Chapter Forty One

"Welcome to my world, Al." Jo spoke the words carefully to ensure they were not infected with any hint of glibness or flippancy for that was not how she felt. They lay on the bed together, curtains drawn and Jo stroked his hair gently. "Has it gone now?"

He nodded almost imperceptibly.

"Yeah… but it'll be back won't it, like with you?"

"Do you want to describe it to me – what you felt?"

It was some time before Al responded.

"Like when you start coming round out of a nightmare – you're crippled by horror and fear until you get back to full consciousness only this time I didn't come round, it just kept going…"

"Try to put it into words."

"Fear, pain, dread, anguish – just about all the shit you can imagine and… and guilt – overpowering, goddam guilt but I don't know for what…"

"And the animals – the ones we saw performing – you understood what they were feeling?"

"Oh yeah – that and so much more. How the hell have you coped with it all this time, Jo?"

She thought carefully about his question but wasn't really sure of the answer. When she spoke she was still exploring the reasons, hoping for clarity.

"I don't have any answers, Al – to anything. All I know is that I didn't just react against it but tried to understand it. I had to know how such god-awful suffering could exist in my little world of plenty, if I'd done anything to promote it and what I could do to stop it. I started to empathise and, I suppose, started to change my life because of it and it seemed the more I did that, the less accusatorial the feelings became. Again you're probably going to think I'm crazy..."

"Jo, Jo, Jo... something pretty profound happened to me today that's gonna live with me forever and nothing you could say will sound crazy..."

"Okay then, I think it might be a two-way street. Feelings of suffering are being channelled to us in some way but I think our feelings are being channelled back, are being noted and acted on by who or whatever's responsible – don't ask me how or why 'cos I don't know, I've only just thought of it. There are lots of things it doesn't explain but that's what I think. And I'm certain that those magnificent creatures we saw today are slap bang in the middle of all this. One thing I do know – I've got to find out more about them, and that's for certain."

Al raised himself into a sitting position on the bed and kissed Jo lightly on the forehead.

"Okay Madame (he pronounced it like a Frenchman), here's what I suggest. Wimp that I am, I need a little break from it all – not long but enough to remind me that I'm really just a regular dude. We started so early, it's still not even twelve-thirty so why don't we go down and have a pleasant little lunch – sit outside, even, with a glass or two of wine because it's certainly a nice day – and not discuss anything to do with this stuff. Then we'll pretend we're tourists and take a stroll around the Alamo. By that time I might have returned from the land of the mind benders so when we come back, I'll hire a laptop or a pc from the hotel and we can sit together researching whales until we're all googled out. How about that?"

"Sounds good to me," Jo said with a smile, and meant it. And that's what they did. After lunch, they strolled the short distance to the mission building with its mixture of arched and square windows, four decorative columns and arched entrance guarded by a stout wooden door. It was not particularly big nor ornate nor even impressive and its mottled stonework and simple design reflected its almost three-hundred year history in a country where there was probably nothing older from the early settler days. It looked what it was – a simple, unpretentious, religious mission building.

Al seemed to be genuinely enjoying himself.

"The country's biggest tourist attraction," he offered.

"Of course, that accounts for why those sea creatures are nearly two hundred miles from the sea – to cash in on the trade."

"Jo! No!" he said, and meant it.

They read the history of Mexican Texas and its Texians, although Al knew most of it already. The conflict between liberal immigrants moving in from the north but refusing to adapt to their host's culture, and the subsequent conflict with an autocratic Mexican government. And then, of course, there was the Roman Catholic church which had built the mission and four others to expand its influence northwards out of Mexico but also to convert the heathen Indians. Might have bloody known it! Jo thought to herself.

It was, it seemed, a time of revolution – first Mexico against Spain and then the Texians against Mexico.

"The Texians wanted freedom from Mexico and in 1823 kicked their troops out of the mission. That was fighting talk and General Santa Ana was sent with a thousand soldiers to teach 'em a lesson, with a couple of thousand more as back up." Al offered, playing the educator. "The Texians holed up here in the mission and Santa Ana launched one attack after another – more than a thousand men against two hundred or so and he didn't care how many of his men were killed. And finally, on the third assault, the Alamo fell and every person inside was bayoneted or shot as retribution, including Davy Crockett and Jim Bowie. Between four and six hundred Mexicans were casualties."

Jo looked at the unprepossessing little mission building and could not conjure up any image of its past bloodshed or feel the passion, fear and barbarity the two groups of people must have felt as they fought to the death, each believing they had right on their side and each probably deceiving themselves that god fought alongside them.

As groups of schoolchildren dashed about with happy excitement, from one clue to the next to compete their quiz sheets, it was impossible to imagine the darkness as it must have been, illuminated by flashing musket discharges and exploding cannon shells, which glinted from bayonet and sword.

"Seems to me, a bit like us Brits and Dunkirk – a great ability to turn a serious thumping into a national triumph," Jo said, trying to wind Al up.

"Yeah, but a few weeks later the revolution succeeded – and such characters," he replied, sliding into the part. "The incredible Colonel Jim Bowie and Davy Crockett..." He broke into song with the old TV theme:

"Born on a mountain top in Tennessee, Greenest state in the land of the free. Raised in the woods so's he knew every tree, Killed him a bear when he was only three. Davy, Davy Crockett, King of the Wild Frontier."

"Oh, bloody wonderful!" Jo responded with a laugh. "Two national heroes – a vicious knife fighter and a psychotic backwoodsman who abused animals as a toddler rather than admire them."

"Listen, my dear," replied Al, adopting a phoney Shakespearian tone, "we colonials are mere amateurs at slaughter compared to your royals and their philosophy of 'if it moves kill it.'"

"Yeah, but we can blame the Germans for them – just as we do for everything else."

They laughed and kissed and to any idle observer appeared carefree and they were – almost, temporarily. Jo consciously tried to push away thoughts of power struggles and despots, church and state acting in collusion with each other, men's egos and ambition, which were probably all the same everywhere and at every point throughout history.

The Alamo, she concluded, stood as a monument to one group of people who fought for their rights to attain freedom; the other group fought for their own and different rights – the right to control territory and advance the interests of their country and their church. And both sides ignored entirely the rights of those whose land it really was, who had worked it for thousands of years and who wanted nothing more than the freedom to raise their children in safety and exercise their culture. Their lives, it seemed, were valueless other than to swell the numbers of an alien church with their newly-given names which would erase their history.

She could not help wondering how different the world would have been without arrogance and power seekers. Or how different it would now be if history was not constantly air brushed and sanitized to remove the discomforting parts for how was it possible to learn from facades and fictions and skeletons stripped of flesh?

She did not want her mind to go there but it did and she thought of Stephen and his backers and how their whole adult lives had been spent scheming and conniving whilst paying lip service to the concept of rights, as probably did those who preceded them and those who would follow them. And would it all make one real, genuine, important, indelible mark on history or would time just wash over them and their supposed achievements and bleach them like the walls of the Alamo? Would it cause their names simply to fade and crumble into dust, just as it had most other politicians – even prime ministers and presidents – the majority of whom few people could even name, let alone recall their impact? It seemed only those who met an untimely death demanded immortality and then it was for the manner of their going and not their politics.

Give it twenty or thirty years and Jo felt certain her husband's name would be reduced to a question in a pub quiz: 'Which party leader had his wife sectioned in order to silence her?' What the hell was it all about?

For a reason she could not at first explain, she was suddenly standing in her garden as tableaux of past scenes flitted through her mind – of beautiful colours and perfumes so natural, so heady that they tingled as she inhaled them; of fluttering birds revealing flashes of salmon and gold, scarlet and blue, going about their business; of bright green shoots and unfolding leaves; of sharp little eyes watching from the camouflage of a thicket; of rain forming droplets on foliage whilst bumble bees hung upside down beneath to shelter from it. She felt not sad but satisfied and knew with certainty it was an emotion that would forever elude Stephen – but not Al, of that she was certain. It was from that belief, that understanding that so much of her affection for him grew. It was then she realised why she had been transported to her favourite spot on Earth.

When they returned to their hotel room, Al's requested computer was in place and so they sat, side by side, Jo with her new laptop, as though waiting for someone to say 'go.'

"Okay, babe, where do we start?" Al enquired.

"I guess intelligence – oh yes, and communication."

The first to offer information was Al. "Okay, we have the Atlantic Spotted dolphin – a mother looks after her young for five years and when they do finally separate, they keep in touch with a signature whistle. And what about this, the members of the family call each other by name. If young calves really misbehave, their mother pins them to the seabed and tells them off with loud clicks – but then she's quite happy to forgive the youngster.

"Young males form into the equivalent of teenage gangs and guess what they do? Wouldn't you know it, they chase females. All sounds a bit familiar, doesn't it? Now this is interesting, if they get into trouble with their elders, there's no physical punishment but a lot of furious clicking to put 'em in their place. My mom used to call it giving me a piece of her mind."

Jo then added her first discovery: "There's a bloke in the Bahamas who's been blowing bubble rings under the water for Bottlenose dolphins, like the ones we saw. They were cautious to begin with but their curiosity got the better of them and they just had to investigate. In no time they started experimenting with the bubbles and creating games, each dolphin inventing its own game."

Al contributed again: "Hey, those Belugas we saw, they come from the Arctic and swim under the ice sheets – so what the hell are they doing here in the heat of Texas? It says they live in extended family groups of up to twenty five or even more. Jo, how deep do you reckon their pool was – twenty, thirty feet?" Jo nodded. "Well, they can dive down a thousand feet so who's great idea was it to capture them and stick them in a tank– what's even more important, why are they allowed to?"

"Oh dear god," Jo replied. "Talking of that, can you believe this? They're an endangered species yet some bloody profit-driven organisation has applied for permission to capture sixteen in the wild to supply a string of bloody aquariums – for educational purposes. Doesn't it make you despair?"

"They're also known as sea canaries, apparently," Al added, "because of the way they sing and chatter. There's one called Noc who's been mimicking the human voice, not actual words 'cos they don't have vocal chords but with its blow hole – sounds for all the world like someone speaking."

And so it went on, each communicating their findings to the other as they tried to build a picture of whale intelligence.

"There's all sorts of studies showing how they work co-operatively to catch fish – creating visual nets from muddy silt or by blowing bubbles in a circle around fish so they think they're trapped and don't try to escape. And they understand what a mirror is and pose in front of it. Apparently there are very few animals who'll do that," Jo threw in.

"And what about this," Al responded: "In California, Grey whales congregate to give birth in huge numbers and, of course, once upon a time it attracted whalers because it was easy to slaughter them. Gave them the name 'devil fish' because they fought ferociously and would attack their boats. But whaling ended in 1972 and they don't attack boats any more, like they know, like they understand there's no longer a threat and even bring their calves alongside visitors' boats to show them off. It's not like they're new whales, born since those days, because they live so long that many of them would have been alive during the whaling days and witnessed the carnage.

"There's a story from an old-time whaler who went out to visit them recently and a whale came alongside his boat, put its head above water and looked the old guy straight in the eye and he says it made him ashamed of what he once did. He says he knows the whale was aware of his past and was forgiving him."

"Not as hippy dippy as it sounds," Jo replied. "There's a scientist here who claims whales have things called spindle cells, which are linked with awareness, empathy and compassion. Humans have them too – although god knows what we've done with them – but whales have three times as many as we do.

She's convinced there's a special connection between humans and whales and they're trying to talk to us. And to think, for decades we turned them into corset stays and soap! Concentrate on that, Al, communication."

And so they continued, one gem of information after another, revealing the extraordinary complexity of whale communication – infinitely more complex than human speech. Suddenly, Jo became extremely animated.

"This is it, I think this is what I was looking for, the kind of thing I was hoping to find. It's only a theory but the man responsible is a serious scientist, a biologist." Al stopped what he was doing while Jo continued: "Now listen to this – he's developed a theory called rhythm-based communication – RBC for short. He says that it's pointless trying to relate whale communication to human speech because they're entirely different. He maintains that a whale off the Canadian coast may well be heard by one in the Caribbean. He relates their communication more to morse code or – get this – quantum theory and says that a click or sound from a whale lasting a tenth of a second may be equivalent to an hour's conversation between humans." The words began to tumble out as Jo made no attempt to hide her excitement and then she paused. "Al, what is quantum theory?"

He took a time before answering and then coughed a couple of times before responding slowly, cautiously.

"Well – I'm trying to remember this, Jo – it's something to do with matter at a sub-atomic level, the smallest possible level, about the belief that anything which exists, in whatever state, may also exist in a different state – a kind of parallel universe…" He then ran out of words and looking at Jo's raised eyebrow added: "Okay, I don't have a clue but I know it's important. It's the basis of modern physics – along with the theory of relativity."

"Really profound stuff then, just as I expected. This is it – this is what I was hoping to find. Just listen, Al, he says we're misguided to look solely for verbal communication because they and many other species don't need to produce sounds that are audible to us because – now get this – there is nothing para about the so-called para-normal because telepathy is quite normal in nature. I knew it, I just bloody knew it!"

"I bet you that's a controversial theory," Al added.

"Of course it's controversial, he's out on his own but just look who his principle detractor is – a scientist working with captive dolphins for the bloody military, probably training these extraordinary creatures to carry bombs on their backs to blow up submarines or whatever. Now he's someone with an open mind, who cares about the animals, who wants to understand them – I don't think. God, Al, every page you turn, every click you make, unearths something that just makes you despair of humankind."

"Forget that for a minute, babe, because I think you might find this right up your street. There's a guy at Houston University – a doctor Roberto Martinez – who's doing research on communication between humans and cetaceans in the wild."

"Where's Houston?"

"Down on the Gulf coast, less than a couple of hundred miles away." Al replied.

Jo went over to Al's computer and sat with him.

"Where's Galveston? It says he operates his field work out of there."

"It's just a bit further along the coast, not far from Houston. It's on an island – a pretty small city I seem to remember but lots of marinas and cruise ships."

Jo jotted down the man's contact details and went to the phone and Al listened to her pushing hard to be put through to him and then turning on the charm as she spoke to doctor Martinez himself, asking insistently if she could accompany him on one of his field trips. She blatantly used her (once) potential position as Britain's first lady in waiting.

Al could sense a change in the man's tenor but his response still appeared to be negative until Jo suddenly offered a donation for his research and unashamedly dangled the prospect of UK government interest in his work. It began at a thousand dollars but the canny Doctor Martinez seemingly upped the sum as Al heard Jo agree to paying him fifteen hundred dollars. She then went silent as she wrote details on the hotel note pad. When she had hung up she turned to Al triumphantly.

"I'm going to meet some whales face to face in the open sea."

"Quite right, what else do first ladies do?"

Jo laughed. "You weren't meant to be listening. Well, the bastard owes me! Tomorrow, two thirty at Pelican's Rest marina – says to look for a boat called Pod 2. Doctor Martinez won't be going himself but one of his technicians will, to carry out a bit of simple work. It's about a four-hour trip, they say, and they'll have all the gear I need. What about that, then?"

Beep, beep beep. Jo looked at the phone's display almost in surprise: 'Hilary cried n sobbed her way through a statement earlier today. Think shes trying to compensate for her betrayal as she has made toast of Stephen. When are u coming back? We're almost ready. We need you. R' Jo turned to Al.

"Reece has got just about all the information he needs and I'm desperate to get Danny. After the trip tomorrow, I think it's time to go home. If there's more to discover we can always come back." Jo paused and when she spoke it was hesitantly: "Is it still your home, Al – Britain – or is your home here in the States?"

Al did not respond immediately but held Jo in his gaze for long, long seconds.

"I hope, I really hope, my home is wherever you are. If you'll have a nutty, unemployed car dealer with an aversion to accountancy." Jo made no effort to prevent her eyes from filling with tears and went to Al. They held each other tightly and kissed tenderly – it was a kiss of commitment.

Later they strolled hand in hand along the San Antonio river walk which snaked through the town and was entirely urban but with its overhanging trees and reeds and rushes felt almost rural. They dined at a pretty place overlooking the water and confirmed their plans.

"I don't think it's worth flying. It's about a four-hour drive so we need to hire a car this evening to save time and leave about nine in the morning." Al offered.

"Can we fly back from Galveston? UK flights usually leave in the evening from the US so we'll be too late for tomorrow. I guess we'd better book it for the day after." Jo felt a chill as though someone had walked over her grave as she contemplated the whirlpool they would be returning to.

"We'll have to go from Houston but it all works out quite well, it's not far away from where we're going."

Jo nodded, filled with thought, but remained silent. She had decided Al was not coming on the boat with her but she would save that news until they were at the marina.

Jo had not switched off her phone overnight and the irritating beep, beep beep awoke her shortly after seven. Again it was Reece: 'With the aid of wendys big car and a wheelchair I took Julie to Croydon post office this morning. WE HAVE HER NOTES. Its game set and match my lovely. Come home now. R'

Jo replied: 'You are a wonderful man Reece. Go public immediately don't wait for me, election too close. Jo'

Back came the reply within a minute or two: 'You need to be here. R.' and Jo replied immediately.

'No I dont. Go public tomorrow with all you've got. I'll be back day after. All it will mean is two days of headlines instead of one. Please do it tomorrow my gorgeous to have the greatest impact on the election. Jo.' Back came the single word 'Okay.'

While she and Al were having an early breakfast, Reece beeped her again. 'Press conference arranged for 2.30 pm our time tomorrow in Holborn. Gwen the hr solicitor and I doing it jointly. Contacting all media. R'

Jo was relieved she would not be there but knew it was only a stay of execution.

They began the journey to the Gulf coast through dry, scrubby-looking countryside and less than an hour had passed when Jo turned to Al.

"What the hell is that smell?" The car filled with an acrid stench that grew stronger with each passing mile.

"Crap," Al replied. "This is Texas and that means cattle. I reckon you're smelling the wonderful waste products of our biggest agricultural industry. Just as well there isn't smelly TV or Dallas would have bombed."

No sooner had he spoken than they came around a bend in the road and there they were ahead of them, countless cattle. It took Jo a while to grasp the magnitude of the phenomenon. Cattle watched them unmovingly from both sides of the road, their heads looking over the wire fence that paralleled it. "Slow down, Al, I can't believe this."

As far as they could see ahead, one pen followed another. Each was less than a hundred yards square but every one contained hundreds of cattle. One pen was divided from another only by strands of barbed wire and they filled both sides of the road, stretching as far as Jo could see in every direction, the chilling vista broken only by wide access roads that intersected the pens.

"Feed lots," Al volunteered, quietly. It was an extraordinary chequered panorama of thousands of acres cut up into squares, each one identifiable only by the disparate grouping of steers in each. There were thousands of steers, tens of thousands over many square miles, possibly even hundreds of thousands and they stood almost motionless on bare earth, shiny from constantly excreted urine and faeces, because there was no point in moving, nowhere to go, not a blade of grass on which to graze. The nearest steers were only a few yards away from the road verge.

"Stop the car, please, Al," Jo requested. She climbed out and stood as motionless as the cattle, looking at those closest to her, some brown, some white, some mostly black and some mottled. She took in their big, broad heads with tight little curls separating curved, sweeping horns. She could see caution in their huge, gentle eyes as curiosity partially overcame their fear. Something new, something unusual was happening in their world of stultifying nothingness.

Jo looked around for farm workers and all she could see, in the middle distance, were two men on horseback wearing Stetson hats as though they were prairie cowboys. It struck her that if one of these beautiful animals was ill or injured there was no chance of attention. And then she recalled the footage she had seen in Wendy's office of cattle being slaughtered and realised that a similar fate awaited each one of these individual animals in a production line of death that would be so overwhelming in its enormity that it was almost impossible for her to contemplate it, whilst for others it would be nothing more than digits on a balance sheet. And all the time the stench of excreta burnt her nostrils. She climbed back in to the car.

"I give up, Al, I just fucking give up. What happened in our evolution that produced a species so devoid of compassion – the very thing that's supposed to mark us out from other animals?"

"This is the hamburger trade, Jo, and that's how they're viewed – burgers on legs. This is efficiency- from an accountant's perspective – and I should know. According to the balance sheet, it makes much greater sense to take food to the animals rather than taking the animals to the food. And still they'll tell you that their primary concern is for the welfare of the cattle. It's bullshit elevated to an art form. This is just one feed lot operation, Jo, but up on the Texas panhandle there are hundreds of them."

"Are the animals born here?"

"No, they're ranch bred and moved to these places when they're a few months old. They're slaughtered at anything from twenty-four to thirty months so they'll spend the best part of two years in these conditions."

"You're very knowledgeable. How come?" Jo asked.

"Don't ask. I was a consultant and worked for lots of different companies in my time."

Jo was silent for a while. "You've come a long way, Al."

"Yeah, but I've still got a way to go. Let's drive on, I've had enough of this." Jo did not argue.

They arrived in Galveston in good time but with a whole plethora of marinas it took a while to find Pelican's Rest and its pretty wooden walkways and piers. When they finally clattered across the planks there was just one boat on the seaward side of the marina – a powerful-looking craft with forward superstructure and accommodation beneath whilst the rear deck was expansive and open, providing ample space for divers and their gear. Two men were making themselves busy.

Jo introduced herself from the jetty and one of the men clambered ashore and shook hands with her and Al. "Hi, I'm

Hank, the doc's technician. This here is Jesus (he pronounced it the Spanish way – Hayzoos), he's the boatman." Jesus raised a hand in acknowledgement. "I was only expecting one person!"

"Yes, that's right," Jo said, "just give me a moment." She moved Al out of earshot but she could see the concern in his face. "I'm going on my own, Al, it's something I have to do."

"Why?" The question came out hard, demanding, but she had nothing additional to add.

"I just have to do it on my own – try and understand. And anyway, only one of us can dive."

"Bullshit, Jo. What's the real reason?"

"I've given you the only reason I have. That's it, no other reason. Look, I need to get aboard. Please try to understand."

"I don't understand Jo, not a bit, not the tiniest little bit," and he turned and walked away with anger emanating from every movement. He felt rejection stabbing painfully into him, incomprehension, confusion. When he was half way back to the marina buildings he stopped suddenly as he saw with clarity Jo's reasoning. He turned and ran back towards the boat where Jesus was about to cast off.

"Hold it buddy, hold it." Without hesitation he jumped into the boat where Jo was the only person on the open deck. He took hold of her shoulders and pushed her back against the side.

"I know why you don't want me to come along – you've worked it all out haven't you?" There was no longer any trace of anger in his words. "You're afraid you might discover something pretty profound, aren't you? That whales are involved in the attacks. And if you do and they're aware of your knowledge, you'll become a threat to them. One word out of place when you come back, one whisper gets out and the world will know and governments everywhere will scour the seas for every whale and dolphin that exists and blast them into eternity. They'll wipe out every goddam cetacean on the planet to end it, won't they? And you're afraid they may not let you come back because of that and you don't want me to be there, to witness it. That's right, isn't it? That's your reason!"

"Oh, Al, don't be ridiculous, you're imagining it all – as if!"

But Jo was blustering, her face was flushed and she refused to look at him and he could tell he was right. Eventually she became still and quiet and reached up to take his face in her hands.

"I know what you're saying makes sense, Al, but come on, how likely is it? From the start of this whole thing I've been guided by my instincts – and they haven't let me down. Yes, I'm sure I'm going to discover something but I'm also sure I'm going to come back. You have to respect my decision, it's important you do."

"Okay, so why don't you want me to come? The truth please."

Jo took a long time to answer and Hank's voice cut in: "Are you going ashore or not, buddy?"

Finally Jo answered: "Just in case! That's all, just in case. Go ashore now, Al!"

He fought a battle with himself but in the end knew it was vital he respected her wishes for a hundred different reasons and simply said: "Hurry back my beautiful woman," and clambered up onto the jetty. The huge, twin, ninety-horse-power Yamahas burst into life and the boat eased away from the jetty and headed towards the sea. As soon as it was out into open waters the engines roared as Jesus opened them up to full throttle and the boat skipped across the surface leaving a huge wake behind. He watched Jo's waving arm for as long as he could see it, responding with his own waves.

Even when he could no longer discern her figure, he remained watching the craft until it was little more than a dot in the distance, linked to the land only by the ribbon of its wake. Only then did he turn to walk back along the jetty towards where their car was parked, with a dreadful feeling of emptiness gnawing away at him. It came almost as a shock to realize that in the little more than three weeks or since he had met Jo, he had hardly been out of her company. And now, plaguing him, was the awful thought that he might never see her again.

Further down the jetty, two men were fishing and one, a huge man in a vest whose body was seemingly held together by tattoos, let out a whoop, "Alright," he cried and Al stopped to watch as the tip of his rod bent over and jerked up and down as it pointed towards the sea's surface and whatever it was that struggled on the end of the line beneath it. The tattooed man then lifted clear of the water a silver fish about a foot long, flashing in the sunlight as it struggled to be free. Again he yelled "Alright" to his buddy as he took the fish in his hand, unhooked it and tossed it into a bucket alongside him. Without a second look, he re-baited the hook and cast out while the fish thrashed around in its container, suffocating in an alien environment.

Al walked past the men but not before bending down and in a continuous movement, taking the fish in his hand and dropping it gently over the edge of the jetty into the sea. Reflected sun rays flashed from its scales as it finned down through the green, milky marina water and disappeared.

"What the hell ya'll doin'?" cried the multi-coloured fisherman. "You a crazy man?"

"That's where it belongs," Al replied and walked on, still with fear and emptiness clawing at him but just a little less so. He knew Jo would be proud of him and that helped. The cry "Asshole!" echoed after him and he raised an arm in recognition as though having been paid a compliment.

Wind whipped through Jo's hair as the boat roared them out to sea but eventually she had to seek shelter by sitting down in the lea of the accommodation. Hank was preparing the materials for his session with the whales and Jo asked him how the project worked.

"There's a particular pod of Humpback whales that no longer migrate for some reason so we can see them whenever we want – they've grown to trust us. They're not able to speak as we do because they don't have a voice box and so doc Martinez is constructing – well I guess you'd say a whole new language just for whales. He's made a stack of recordings of their voices and from them takes little sections and uses them as words. We show them images and play a different sound – one of their natural sounds – for each one so they build a kind of vocabulary.

"It's not our language and it certainly ain't what the sounds really means to them but between the two we're starting to communicate. It's still pretty simple, just nouns, no verbs yet but they pick up new words straight away – no problem."

Jo felt real disappointment for she knew in her heart that showing flash cards and playing nonsensical snippets of whale song would not reveal any great truths, which is what she had hoped for.

"Do you find the whales extraordinary?" she asked Hank. He laughed.

"Not like the doc does. He treats 'em like they were his kin, he's obsessed by 'em, sometimes talks to them non-stop in American as if they can understand everything he says. I guess you could genuinely say he's crazy about them." He laughed at his own humour.

"But not for you, Hank, you're not in awe of them?"

"Ma'am, they're animals. They're sure as hell big animals and they're sure as hell smart animals but they're still animals."

Again Jo felt her heart sink and knew she would prefer to be with Roberto Martinez but this was all that was on offer. She realized that the sense of anticipation, almost fear, that had accompanied her from the moment she boarded the boat had suddenly deserted her, leaving a sense of disappointment behind. She comforted herself with the thought that she would be seeing whales in the wild, close up, even if they did only whistle to name a boat, an anchor, a person or a fish. It was better than nothing.

Hank helped her into her dry suit with its full Perspex face mask.

"We're only going down a few feet, just below the surface, so you don't need to be Jacques Cousteau. There's not the usual on-demand valve so just breathe normally. There's radio contact between us so anything you say I'll hear and the other way round. If you get into any difficulty at all or you feel you need to get out, give this valve half a turn and your buoyancy aid will inflate and up you'll go. Jesus will be right on hand to haul you out. Okay?"

Jo nodded. "Can I talk to the whales?"

Hank threw back his head and laughed.

"You sure can but they won't understand a goddam word you say. Doc made these suits so they transmit out into the water as well as with each other for that reason. Okay, when we get there, I'll hang this speaker over the side and transmit a specific Humpback song and if they're in a good mood, they'll come to us. We won't go into the water until they do."

Despite her initial disappointment, Jo felt excited as the whole adventure suddenly became real again. She was no longer a seeker after truth but a tourist – a very special, privileged tourist who was about to have a very special encounter. When Jesus throttled back the engines to a chattering idle and Hank swung the speaker over the side, Jo could feel her heart racing as she scanned the blue green waters of the Gulf of Mexico – it almost stopped when she saw a spout of spray not a hundred yards from the boat and could hear the animal's deep, resonant exhalation. She could see other jets of water behind it, some distance from the boat.

"Okay – ready?" Hank enquired and Jo gave him an affirmative with her thumb and fore finger forming a circle. She lowered herself down the ladder after him and pushed out into the waters of the Gulf with a sense almost of euphoria. Following his crackled instructions, she released just enough air from her buoyancy device so that her body hung motionless, in balance, neither rising nor descending, about ten feet below the surface. Ahead of her in the almost crystal clear waters, the huge grey shape of a whale approached, its skin gnarled and scarred and lightly pock marked with barnacles and other sea growths. Breathe normally, Hank had said, but she could barely breathe at all. Excitement and anticipation coursed through her but underlying both was again the tingle of fear.

Hank began his tuition, retrieving flash cards from a bag which had been lowered by Jesus and Jo could clearly hear the brief whale song that Hank was emitting electronically to accompany each one. He then showed cards without an identifying audio signal but back from the whale came its recognition in brief, staccato song. It was fascinating but, in truth, Jo had no interest in this guessing game, her attention being entirely on the mammoth in front of her and the other grey shapes that she could just discern a little way off, as though keeping a respectful distance.

She surreptitiously moved a little closer by finning her feet and ignored the caution Hank barked at her through her headphones. She achieved what she had wanted and could make eye contact with the whale.

"Does he or she have a name?" Jo asked and Hank responded: "He's a male and we call him Jonah. It's not a game, ma'am, you have to be careful."

She tried as best she could to keep eye contact through her Perspex shield and then felt rather stupid as she quietly said: "Hello, Jonah, I'm very pleased to meet you. Thank you for coming." She heard a guffaw from Hank in response: "You and the doc sure would get on well together."

Jo continued to look at the enormous creature with awe as he occasionally rose to the surface to breathe with a roar of expelled air. She was captivated by every aspect of him – his battle scars, his immensity, his seeming position of authority in the pod but above all his eyes. She had looked into the eyes of many animals and seen great intelligence but his were more knowing than any she had ever seen. They contained no threat but a wealth of understanding. They reflected weariness and had experienced great pain; they were enquiring and compassionate, inquisitive and cautious. She could also see a huge capacity for love and that knowledge almost reduced her to tears.

She also knew with certainty that as she was appraising him so he was appraising her but doubted he would observe even a fraction of the complexity she did.

"Why have you come here? What do you want?"

The voice came not through the water but emanated from within her. It was deep, vibrant, resonant and encompassed her entire body, almost as though it had the capacity to fill her with its richness, to smother her, to choke her. And even when it ceased it left its imprint behind as does a stone when dropped into water, its ripples continuing, its impact not entirely spent.

Jo was so overwhelmed that at first she could not reply, could not believe she had heard the words, doubted it was the whale who was responsible. But those reactions quickly evaporated as she was flooded with the realisation that this was why she had come, this is what she had hoped to experience, this, or something like it, was what she had expected. She replied tremulously.

"There are things I want to know and I suspect it's only you who has the answers."

"I doubt that, ma'am, I'm just a hired hand," Hank's voice crackled into her helmet. "You need to speak to the doc if there's anything special you want to know."

Before Jo could feel any embarrassment, the voice came again, as full and soft and warm and enfolding as it had been before.

"You have no need to speak your words, simply think them." It was then that Jo realised the nature of the communication between them. It momentarily left her speechless – thoughtless.

"Are you – or your kind – responsible for the attacks being carried out on humans by other animals?" she eventually asked.

"Why do you need to know?" echoed the response.

"I am not sitting in judgment on you but I have been through a very painful time in trying to understand why... my son was one of the victims."

"Yes, I know you have suffered. I can read all that you have felt."

"I need to know if my suppositions are correct – just for my own peace of mind."

There was a long pause before the reply came.

"Yes, but only out of necessity not vengeance."

"What had my son done that required his life to be threatened?" Jo was astounded by the way her thoughts had immediately returned to the excruciating memories of fear and dread that paralysed her after Danny's accident. And she was not asking – thinking – merely out of interest for there was accusation and anger in her question. This had never been her intention when she started her quest for answers but at the first admission of responsibility, her frustrations and fears took control and she wanted to hit out, to condemn.

"It will take time to explain but these actions can be imprecise. It is a fight for survival – not just the survival of my kind but of all things and there will be much suffering as a result. You are not alone in experiencing pain because of the plight of your child. Those who kill us with harpoons have always targeted our children even though they are too small to be of value. They do so because they know, just as you know, that a mother cannot abandon her children to pain and suffering and she will remain with them – and it is her they want. We have seen too many of our children speared with explosives, dying in agony. How sad it is that a most noble emotion essential to survival, one that is understood by all species, should be exploited to dispense painful death."

Laced throughout his words was a depth of suffering that chilled Jo. She could feel what he felt, she was sharing his history and she instantly recognized the agony as another strand in the dreams that had plagued her. She realised she had been in touch with these extraordinary creatures from the very start but that realisation felt unremarkable, it was merely like having a truth revealed that she should have already known. Her reaction was simply, 'of course!'

"Why – why are you attacking us?" The question was tentative for Jo felt certain she already knew part of the answer. While she waited for a reply she could hear Hank continuing with his vocabulary building and could hear Jonah playing his part as though everything was normal.

"I'll tell you somethin' ma'am, these guys can sure talk to each other. It ain't always Jonah who comes but when it's one of the others, they already know everything we taught him at the last session. I reckon they're teachin' each other. Now ain't that somethin'?"

Hank's tinny, two-dimensional revelations made Jo want to laugh. Perhaps this was quantum theory in action – one apparent, quantifiable, distinct state but two utterly different levels; the prosaic sitting alongside the profound and one part of the whole oblivious to the other. She again felt the deep, dark vibrato swelling inside her before it took the form of words.

"We have been very patient over the millennia as the different strands of your consciousness have developed. There have been those among you who have struggled to understand the laws which govern the physical structure of our universe and there have been others who have tried to comprehend morality, good and evil, and the laws by which life itself should be governed and to establish a template that others may follow. The word by which this noble search is known is itself noble – philosophy – the love of wisdom. We look around us now and ask what has happened to that love, what has happened to that wisdom?

"You have learned much and the depth of your knowledge is, in some ways, profound. But there is little intelligence in the application of your knowledge – so little that it challenges your claims to be an intelligent species. Who would continue with an action that is known to damage the fabric that sustains them? Who would hide behind platitudes to defend those actions for short-term advantage – and who would allow them to continue unless they were complicit in that betrayal? Who would pretend they had discovered the only viable course that humankind can navigate to guide it into the future when almost every piece of evidence screams that this is a fallacy? Knowledge and truth have become obstacles to be avoided and no species can advance on this basis.

"We could ignore you as we have in the past and allow these inherent contradictions to come to their natural conclusion, witness the collapse that will inevitably follow and hope that from it will spring a greater understanding of life and your interrelationship with other species. But we can no longer do that as the damage is too profound, the decline too rapid, the time far too limited."

Jo knew instinctively that she was not hearing actual words but that one mind was speaking to another in a manner that transcended language and she would comprehend it in precisely the same way whatever her tongue or dialect. It was, she realised, her mind that was forming the dialogue as the only way to turn Jonah's thought into structured communication. She was not even sure it was Jonah alone she was listening to or whether he was a channel for the collective wisdom of many.

"So the only solution is for us all to die? There are people who share your concerns, are doing all they can because they also know we have to change. Are they to be victims, too?"

"That is true and some are but it is not always as simple as you pretend. Many of those who protest want some change but not enough; many want others to change but not themselves;

many identify the problem but have simplified the solution to make it more palatable. Many others cling tightly to child-like images of omnipotent beings and pretend that he or she will provide deliverance if only people would believe more fervently. They offer faith as the solution when in reality it is a platitude, a soporific which removes the need for both enquiry and action.

"Your history does not encourage us to believe that change is possible. Our knowledge of you is not simply handed down through the generations for some of our kind have been alive for more than two hundred years. They have been witness to some of your greatest excesses. You went to unknown continents and discovered people and creatures who were new to you but rather than react with wonder, you enslaved the one and slaughtered the other in their millions.

"But you have never confronted your relationship with the other animals of this planet and there is not a species in existence that you have not destroyed, tortured or imprisoned for your own supposed benefit. And it is your barbarous suspension of compassion towards those with whom you are required to share this world that has finally become your undoing."

"I share your disgust at the way we treat animals and there are others who do, too. I have been shocked at the things I've seen such as the cattle…" Jo was not expecting to be interrupted.

"I know what you have seen because I can also see it – through your eyes. And yet there are those of you who wish to spread that misery across the planet, just as the range of species they want to confine and kill and consume grows ever longer."

"But you kill…" Jo could not believe she was challenging the mammoth.

"Yes, we do kill but we do it to live, we do not live to kill. Ours is part of the balance that keeps our oceans – our home – in equilibrium. You have no need to kill and that absence of killing in your predecessors was also once part of the equilibrium and your insistence on doing so now is destroying it.

"Those sad cattle you witnessed and the others you have incarcerated are some of the unwitting tools of that destruction. Their excreta and emissions do more than produce a noxious smell, they reach the sea and cause toxic growth. Here, in this very ocean, is an area the size of one of your small countries where nothing can live, which is entirely dead. And there are many more of these poisonous creations across the oceans which we know well for we have to circumvent them or die.

"Would not an intelligent species look at this devastation and say 'something is wrong with the way we live our lives, we must act to correct it?' But you do not, you continue as if it is of no concern. Just as you ignore the acid which is accumulating in these and all other waters; acid that will eventually make it difficult or impossible for shell-bearing creatures to form that which they need to live – a shell. And coursing through our veins and those of every other sea creatures are powerful toxins that you have jettisoned and are still jettisoning into this, the source of all life.

"You should care what happens to these complex, watery expanses because you are still as dependent upon them as we are. If their balance is disturbed too greatly by you, the great volumes of oxygen they produce, the very thing that sustains us all, may simply cease."

"Have we really done all this?" Jo asked but she was not sure she wanted to hear the answer.

"This and much, much more. Look across the planet, Jo, look at the forests which are still being emasculated to graze animals and grow their fodder for a food you do not need. Look at the soil which provides ample plants to sustain you but which is surrendering its fertility because of the demands you make upon it, again simply to feed the animals you eat. Look at the deserts which are reaching out their arms further every year because of grazing by the animals you devour. Look up to the skies, which are laden with destructive chemicals from your profligacy and which are now profoundly affecting the planet. Look to the icy wildernesses which are vanishing, even as we watch, through a combination of all these reasons. And look to those who have assumed custody of your world and try to find a single one who is shouting, shouting, shouting 'enough, we have to stop.'

"Our planet has experienced periods of great extinction in its long history, usually from some external intervention. It has now embarked upon another great extinction but this one is entirely of your making – of man's making – and not through ignorance but from arrogance. Unless we act with urgency, we may all be victims for there is little time left. Do you now understand why we have to do what we are doing?"

Jo was still trying to recover from the shock of being called by her name as she formulated her question. "Perhaps I do but I would also like to understand how you're doing it, why I have experienced contact with you but others haven't and why it appears to take different forms." Again the enveloping, trembling, swelling prelude to response engulfed her but this time it felt markedly different and did not immediately form words. Jo could swear that Jonah was laughing at her.

"I have just delivered to you a rationale for our..." there was a pause while he formulated the word and Jo knew she was witnessing diplomacy "...censoring of your kind. Some would find it challenging, even devastating, and yet you wish to know the mechanics of how it is being delivered. You have a very enquiring mind, Jo Aldous."

She smiled through her Perspex and nodded in acknowledgement. She felt a warm glow at having been called Jo and an even greater one at not having been called Josephine and wondered if the decision was a calculated one. She saw an almost imperceptible movement of Noah's huge grey head and had her answer. She chuckled inside her plastic bubble.

"Okay, ma'am, time to be going. Use your buoyancy device." Hank's irritating voice crackled once more in her ears and not having any idea what the sign language was for 'no', Jo wagged her hand to and fro dismissively.

The deep vibrato resumed: "Like us, no two of your kind are identical. Some are more receptive than others, more sensitive, more seeking. We lost contact with you for a while as you were out of our range. Because of our affinity we can communicate with you over greater distances than we can with the other animals and that range is expanding day by day as we learn how to exercise our ability to communicate. How you respond to that communication also varies – some find it unbearable and some, like you, seek to understand it but eventually we will contact everyone, even Hank."

Again Jo chuckled in amazement at what was unmistakeably humour, albeit gallows humour.

"And doctor Martinez?"

"He has just begun the process of understanding us and I suspect he will soon abandon this game of his." The exchange was becoming so candid that Jo could barely believe it.

"Ma'am – we have to go," Hank demanded.

"Do I have sufficient air," Jo responded into her mask.

"Yes ma'am, you have about another thirty minutes but me and Jesus have to get back."

"Just a couple of minutes, Hank, I won't be long." Her response was entirely dismissive. She just wanted him to shut up and go away.

"Jonah, you see your actions as imperative and you may well be right but don't you feel any guilt for the devastation you're beginning to wreak?" She realised after she had said it that she had used his name. "Do you mind me using that name for you?" Again she felt the enfolding bubble of tingling sensation.

"I have a name but you could not say it or even think it. It is better you call me no name at all for sadly we cannot afford familiarity and I should not have called you by your name but admiration seduced me." Jo felt a deep sadness, almost rejection, at the whale's words.

"Why should we feel guilt? Truth should never carry with it the stigma of guilt. It is not a weapon and it is all we have. The many species of other animals have evolved differently to us and for most, it is not in their nature to confront or to seek retribution but to retreat, to avoid. All we have done is to raise their eyes above their individual survival to view their species as a whole and understand its relationship with your kind. What they have chosen to do with that knowledge is their decision alone.

"Are they wrong to resist the captivity you have imposed upon them? Are they wrong to seek retribution from those who torment them? Or are they of such a lesser nature in your eyes that their survival is secondary to your own."

Jo wanted to challenge the whale but all that came out was the word, "No!" And then she added: "What about us humans, how does your truth affect us?"

"All we have done is provide the clarity you avoid. You use trite little phrases that you pass from one to another as truths and never enquire into their veracity. 'They know no better', 'they feel no pain', 'they think differently to us.' But all the time and all around you there is a profundity of suffering – of all animals, including your own kind.

"Denial has become such a part of your existence that you can close your eyes to anything which disturbs you and blame it on others, on nature, on chance, on fate, on anything but your own actions. You slide remorselessly into discontent and even unhappiness by pursuing goals you know are self-defeating but refuse to recognise the reasons for this unhappiness – either in yourselves or in others. Your answer is to allow the self-interested who persuade you that the cure for your ills is more of what caused them. And although you know it to be untrue you accept it and continue to consume the world to death. And all we are doing is allowing you to see the falsity of the myths with which you gird yourselves."

Jo's headset crackled "We really have to go, ma'am, now! Please surface."

She did not mean to do so but she shouted at Hank in frustration: "Just bloody-well shut up for a minute, will you. I won't be long." She heard the muttered reply, "What the hell?"

"There is nothing else on this planet that approximates your species," the whale continued but he seemed to have distanced himself from her, become more judgemental, "for you have become an aberration and aberrations cannot survive. You have assumed the nature of a virus to which there is little resistance. It consumes its host and its life is briefly triumphant like a short-lived explosion. Only with time does it learn that be truly successful, to be long-lasting, it must attenuate itself and allow its host to live, to develop a symbiotic relationship with it. We no longer have time for that process."

There was a finality about his words and Jo guessed that the revelations for which she had waited were now at an end and yet she felt the prelude to more words.

"I have to tell you that what you do even to the most insignificant of my brothers and sisters you do to me and so the time has come for your world to be judged and I have no doubt that those who have led the way, your rulers, will be dispensed with. But not only them because you must also be aware that what you as individuals say and what you do will also be judged, not by your own kind but against the natural laws of liberty. And make no mistake, for those who have never shown mercy, there will be no mercy; for those who have, they will triumph over this judgement."

Jo felt a cold chill throughout her body but it also seemed to flush her mind with ice as she comprehended precisely what the whale was saying. She was overwhelmed, speechless and had nothing to say in response. She wanted to be gone, needed to be gone to preserve her sanity but as she reached for the valve on her buoyancy device, the whale spoke again.

"I cannot help but use your name, Jo Aldous, for you are a brave woman, a very brave woman and I salute you. When you came here to discover our secrets, you were aware that should you be successful there may well be a price to pay – a high price, the ultimate price in order to protect my kind until our work is complete. It did not deter you so again I salute you."

Jo watched the enormous grey presence move towards her and for the first time saw his jaw open like a huge portal into another world and she no longer felt brave but small and ineffably vulnerable. She struggled with the valve on her suit for she did not want to die.

Chapter Forty Two

Al barely saw the marina and its array of handsome, tethered boats as he arrived back on the jetty to await Jo's return – his attention was entirely on the open sea. He alternately scanned the horizon and then his watch and when the boat's expected arrival time came and went and there was still no sight, he started to pace. When it was nearly thirty minutes late he began to talk to himself: "You bloody idiot, you should never have let her go." "What kind of useless shit are you?" Backwards and forwards on the decking, muttering and mumbling like a down-and-out but inside, fear and panic were competing for dominance.

When a small dot came into view from behind the headland he stopped pacing and stood motionless, watching intently. He told himself that it probably wasn't the right boat – too small, too big – whilst praying with all his heart that it was Pod 2. As it came closer, the huge plume of wake was unmistakeable and he knew it was what he had been waiting for and began to scan it intently looking for Jo. Closer and closer it came and he could make out Jesus on the wheel and Hank fiddling with something on the open deck but no Jo. It came around the protective arm outside the marina entrance and then swung into the marina itself, with Jesus throttling back so the craft glided towards the jetty, its speed just sufficient to carry it smoothly through the calm water to its mooring.

Al did not move as Hank leapt ashore with a mooring line but he was aware that both men were avoiding him, their eyes were averted. Something was wrong and he could feel his heart racing.

"Where's Jo, where's Jo?" he demanded to know at a bellow. Hank secured the bowline and then took the stern line which Jesus tossed ashore and also secured that over a bollard but still neither man looked at him.

Al took hold of Hank's shoulder and spun him around so he was face to face: "Where's Jo, what's happened to her?" The man's face was dark and sombre.

"I'll tell you what's happened to your lady, sir. She's ignored every safety rule in the goddam book, she's been disrespectful and she's kept Jesus and I out at sea for a hell of a lot longer than we should've been. We should be bowling now but we ain't and I'm pissed, man, I'm well and truly pissed."

"Where is she then?" Al asked.

"She's in the cabin." Hank answered, like it was a stupid question.

Al leapt into the boat and thrust his head through the open cabin door to see Jo curled up on one of the side bunks in a foetal position, asleep. All he could say was: "Wow, baby, are you okay?" as he gently roused her.

She turned her head to Al, her eyes bleary.

"God I'm so exhausted, Al – I can't believe how exhausted."

"You're not used to the exercise," Al quipped, relieved she was okay. "An eventful outing?" he added.

Jo answered as though she had to consider the question, to remind herself whether the day had been eventful or not.

"Yes. Yes, you could say that," she finally said, struggling through the physical and emotional weight that dragged her down. The truth was, she could not face the thought of trying to relive her experience, attempting to explain the intensity of what had happened to her with simple words when it had been so much greater than any words could describe. She was truly fearful that it would be diminished, not just in Al's understanding but in her own mind, too. She had to preserve it in its original form for a little longer, until she had absorbed, internalised its complexities, afraid that attempting to describe it would trivialise what she had discovered. "God I need to sleep, Al. I'll tell you the interesting bits afterwards. Is that okay?"

"Of course, sweetie. Come on, I'll help you down the pier."

Jo seemed distant, placid, almost detached, as they walked the short distance to the harbour-side hotel Al had booked in her absence but he knew from the extraordinarily firm grip on his arm that there was something else beneath the tranquillity, a feeling of deep tension.

"Are you sure you're okay?"

She smiled a half smile at him: "Just tired, Al, very, very tired."

"Do you want to talk about it?"

"Later, when I've had a rest."

In fact Jo didn't rest for as soon as they reached their room she walked out onto the balcony and sat quietly at the little table in one of the patio chairs facing the sea. Although the sun had almost set, there was still just enough light to make out the swell of the Gulf beyond the marina and the shifting patterns that were reflected from its surface. She did not move for a long, long time and as the temperature dropped, Al draped a dressing gown around her shoulders but did not interrupt her thoughts.

Those thoughts were bewildering. She was transfixed by the sea's apparent tranquillity but her knowledge of what it contained ensured it had no calming effect on her. She was almost desperate to see the whale again as there were a thousand questions she wanted to ask him, a lifetime of false assumptions to question and which only he could correct, mysteries he could reveal, truths he could impart but she knew that her time with him was at an end and would never be repeated – it was now for her to find the answers that would determine her future.

Eventually she called Al out and he sat at the table with her and she reached across and put a hand on his arm.

"I talked to a whale today, Al, and he spoke to me with such extraordinary wisdom that I can never again be the person I once was." She spoke with a quiet, soft intensity. "They are responsible for what's happening and because I knew their secret, I thought I would have to die – I thought I was going to die."

"But you didn't, so what saved you?"

"The animals who are fighting back against us are doing so because the whales have altered their awareness and they now comprehend what's happening to them, what's always been happening to them – they've lost their innocence. It's been a slow process hence the gradual spreading of the attacks but now the animals have the ability to pass that awareness from one to another so the whales' job is done. They'll continue to influence us humans but essentially they've passed the baton on, so to speak, and so killing me was unnecessary. There is now nothing that can stop what's happening. With us humans, they're simply making us see the truths that we avoid – truths about ourselves and are lives. They're stripping away our innocence too, in a sense."

"If you can face it, I think you need to tell me everything. Come inside, it's getting cold." Al said quietly.

They lay on the bed and Jo went through every detail of her experience, relating every word, every feeling, every emotion she could recall until she got to one of the creature's final observations, which she related with extraordinary intensity.

"He said that whatever we did to other creatures it was the same as if we did it to him. He also said that it was time for our world, I think meaning humans, to be judged and as a result our leaders would be dispensed with. And then he added that everyone would be judged against the laws of liberty and it would be without mercy."

"Sounds almost biblical," Al said matter of factly.

"I was weaned on this stuff, Al, and it is biblical. See if there's a Gideon bible in the bedside drawer." There was and he produced it and Jo spent a few minutes flicking from section to section and turning down the corner of pages to mark their places.

"Listen to this, Al. 'Truly I say to you, to the extent that you did it to one of these brothers of Mine, even the least of them, you did it to Me.' Matthew 25, verses 31 to 46. She turned to another page. "And this! 'So speak and so act as those who are to be judged under the law of liberty. For judgement is without mercy to one who has shown no mercy. Mercy triumphs over judgement.' James 2, verses 12 to 13. And then this. 'Now is the judgement of this world; now will the rulers of this world be cast out.' John verses 12 to 31. It's all from different parts of the bible but it's all about the same thing."

There was a long pause before Jo could bring herself to say the words. "It's judgement day!"

"Oh dear god, you're not serious; you're not misinterpreting are you?"

"Don't doubt me, Al."

"I'm not babe, it's just words because I don't know what else to say. What the hell does it mean?"

"I don't know, I really don't know but one thing's certain – our lives are going to change beyond recognition and all the old values, the certainties, the expectations that we've lived with our entire lives are going fly straight out of the window."

"Aren't you scared?"

Jo thought carefully and then turned to him with a smile on her face.

"Do you know what, Al, I'm not and I don't know why I'm not – it's the old instincts again. In fact I'm so un-scared that we're going to go down to the bar and you're going to buy me a very big glass of very nice, chilled wine."

The electronic alarm sounded but Jo was already awake and immediately reached for her phone. It was seven-thirty, which made it one-thirty in the UK. She phoned her mother and asked if she and her father could get down to Dorking and pick Danny up from his school later that afternoon. The response was an immediate 'yes'. She then phoned Danny's school and asked to speak to the head teacher but the authority behind her request made it sound more like an expectation that a request.

"Colonel Thomas," the clipped voice responded.

"This is Jo Aldous, Danny's mother. In an hour or so, a press conference will be held at which my husband will be accused of a string of very serious criminal offences..."

"I see," the military voice interrupted, "there has been some speculation in the press this morning but no specific detail."

"My husband is facing a serious situation that will almost certainly destroy his political career and some of the allegations are extremely disturbing. I don't want Danny to hear any of it and I don't want other boys taunting him so you need to remove him from class immediately and keep him away from all media. The one thing he desperately needs is the reassurance of his family around him but I'm in the States and can't get home until tomorrow. So, my parents will be collecting Danny later this afternoon – John and Jennifer Greene."

"I see," came the response but with an upwards inflection implying there was need for debate.

"There's no, 'I see' about it, Colonel Thomas, this is an instruction and I'll email you through my authority immediately. I suggest you tune to the BBC News Channel and listen to the gravity of what's being alleged. I now need to speak to Danny so he knows what's happening."

There was a long pause before the head teacher responded.

"This is rather difficult as your husband informed me you were having... mental health problems and I was to take instructions only from him."

"That claim was entirely bogus and is at the heart of the allegations that are going to be made against him. There is nothing wrong with me and even if you doubt that, there is certainly nothing wrong with my parents and by the time they arrive you will know all the sordid details so I now want to speak to my son."

Al listened to Jo with fascination because there was something different about her – she was more confident, more authoritative and spoke with natural gravitas, someone with whom you did not pick an argument without careful thought.

Again there was a long hesitation before the man squeezed out a reluctant, "Very well, but it's extremely irregular. I'm not at all happy about it."

Jo did not respond and waited to hear Danny's voice. His enthusiasm filled her with joy but she kept the pleasantries short.

"Danny, I can't be there until tomorrow because I'm out of the country but you're leaving school today – two of my very best special agents are coming to collect you this afternoon."

"Wow, who are they?"

"They go by the code names Grandma Jenny and Grandpa John. So get your things together ready to go."

"Cool, mum, are you serious? Is it really grandma and grandpa?"

"I'm absolutely serious."

"I knew you'd do it," he replied. After Jo had said her goodbyes the world felt right for the first time in weeks and she emailed her authority through to the school. She even got reception to scan her passport and sent a copy of that also, to prove she was who she said she was. She then brought the BBC up on her laptop whilst Al sent down for some breakfast. They sat and waited, desultorily picking at their food as the anticipation of what they believed was to come stifled conversation.

It was not until almost three-thirty UK time that the continuity announcer said they were going over to political editor Nigel Robertson in Red Lion Square, Holborn. He stood looking to camera, his overcoat on, his scarf knotted, his bald head gleaming and his horn-rimmed glasses glinting but it was the look of sheer joy on his face that commanded attention.

"I have been reporting on politics for over twenty years but in all that time I have never witnessed anything like that which took place behind me here in Conway Hall a little while ago." He indicated over his shoulder with his head to the building in the corner of the square. "Highly-respected, high-profile human rights solicitor, Gwendoline Powell, and the Aldous family's GP, Doctor Reece Evans, delivered an excoriating attack on Tory party leader Stephen Aldous and other senior members of the party.

"He accused them of a conspiracy to commit an abuse of public office, false imprisonment, forcibly administering a noxious substance, physical and mental assault and attempted murder. Those accused along with Stephen Aldous are Sean Murphy, the party's press secretary, but they also include Charles Whiston, party chairman, Harold Cunningham, the Right Honourable George Fiennes, Peter Macintosh and Edward Churchill Smith, all party grandees. Also cited is consultant psychiatrist Professor Anton Kadynski, who is chair of the party's Mental Health working group. On top of all this, two other allegations have been made against Stephen Aldous individually: that he illegally downloaded pornographic images of children and that he committed a sexual assault on a seventeen-year-old Lithuanian girl when she was babysitting at his house.

"You may remember that a little over three weeks ago, Stephen Aldous's wife, Josephine Aldous, was sectioned under the Mental Health Act and sent to Egham Hall Hospital, supposedly for her own safety and that of her young son. All the conspiracy allegations relate to this event and issues surrounding it. Dr Evans was forthright in his condemnation of what happened." The programme cut to a VT of Reece speaking inside the hall to a packed audience of journalists.

"I have known Jo Aldous for fifteen years, have been her doctor for all that time and a more rational person you could not wish to meet. She was sectioned to silence her, forcibly sedated with powerful antipsychotic drugs on two occasions because she had discovered images she believed showed her husband to be a paedophile and she had every intention of going public with that information. Again we have an insight into the incestuous nature of the relationship between a political party and the press. They ran the stories they were handed, brutally condemning Jo without conducting a single enquiry. They should be accused along with the others because they were equally complicit."

"Jo. You've done it – you've sure as hell done it. You have beaten the bastards hands down, my gorgeous!" Al's face was wreathed in smiles.

"Why don't I feel triumphant then, Al? Why can't I gloat and cheer as the tumbril rolls along? Why does it all feel just tawdry and pathetic and why do I feel sad – sad at the stupidity and arrogance that led to this, sad that my son's father jettisoned him without a thought, sad that Danny will probably have to live knowing his father is a criminal. None of it feels very joyous to me, I'm afraid."

"You had no choice, Jo. You either had to languish in that god-awful hospital, which would have destroyed you, or fight for justice – for your freedom."

"I know you're right, I just wish none of it had been necessary and after what happened yesterday it all feels just so... so pathetic, so irrelevant."

Nigel Robertson continued to speak excitedly to camera.

"What makes these allegations so damaging is the number of witness statements that back them up." He waved a sheaf of papers in front of the camera. "They include one from the nurse in charge of the ward where Josephine Aldous was held, her family doctor and even her sister, who was one of the signatories on the section that committed Mrs Aldous. She admits she was having an affair with Stephen Aldous and that he strongly pressurised her into signing the document. Lawyer Gwendoline Powell was scathing about what happened."

Again the report cut to a VT with Gwen Powell speaking softly to a silent audience, her eyes looking out from beneath a heavy fringe.

"The idea of sectioning Josephine Aldous in order to silence her and keep her out of the way was concocted by very senior party officials and implemented by a doctor who had never examined her, one who had never before met her and a sister who admits she was pressurised into doing so. This is reminiscent of the once totalitarian states of Eastern Europe where madness was used as a convenient tool to silence people. It is an unbelievable abuse of power." The picture cut back to Nigel Robertson.

"When Ms Powell refers to the idea having been concocted by senior party members she is relying on the most damaging of all the many statements, this one by Julie Samuels, assistant to press secretary Sean Murphy." Again he brandished a statement in front of the camera. "She is known to us journalists as a very efficient person, a reliable person – a safe pair of hands. She claims to have attended meetings where the decision was taken and to have made detailed notes immediately afterwards. We have been provided with a copy of those notes and they are deeply damaging.

"The allegation of attempted murder refers to an event where Ms Samuels was hit and seriously injured by a car which mounted the pavement outside her flat in central London before she had gone public with these claimed revelations. It failed to stop and drove away afterwards.

"The missing link in all this, of course, is Josephine Aldous herself. We understand she absconded from the secure hospital over a week ago and left the country because she felt her life was at risk. She is returning to Heathrow airport tomorrow morning where chaos is likely to reign because the whole world wants to talk to her. She will be conducting a press conference in the VIP arrivals lounge of terminal five at 11.00 am and we are told it will be brief.

"We are also told that all information has been handed to the Metropolitan Police by Ms Powell along with the imagery Stephen Aldous is accused of downloading as well as footage from the same ward where Mrs Aldous was kept. We haven't seen it but it purports to show one of his female nurses plying a patient with alcohol and committing a sexual assault against him. A Senior police officer has told the BBC that later today, detectives will be going to Manchester, where Stephen Aldous is scheduled to give a major campaign speech this evening, in order to interview him. What had seemed a reasonably safe election for the Conservatives has been thrown into serious doubt.

"Someone once said that a week is a long time in politics but so, it seems, is a day. This morning, Stephen Aldous was contemplating stepping over the threshold of number ten Downing Street in seven day's time. I suspect he is now contemplating the possibility of stepping over the threshold of accommodation far less inviting."

Dimmed lights and the constant hum of a large aircraft acted like a sedative on Jo Aldous as she sat holding hands with Al Dwight in the twin seats alongside the fuselage. "What do you think will happen – to Stephen and the others," he asked quietly.

"Sean Murphy, Stephen and the other professionals will deny, deny, deny and maintain a solid front – they'll concede nothing. You'd be amazed how effective that can be. Their weak spot is Doctor bloody Dawson and Kadynski. Even when he was sedating me, when they first took me in, Dawson was petrified, like the proverbial rabbit caught in the headlights. He'll crack the moment the police interview him because he'll be terrified of going to prison. They won't be able to stop him talking and he'll blame it all on Kadynski.

"Kadynski isn't much better. He's a pumped up, egotistical peacock and there's no substance inside – he's hollow and will implode. Once that happens, Sean Murphy will run for cover: 'not my decision, I just issued press statements, I'm only an employee,' anything to keep him out of prison. And he'll probably get away with it but he'll dish the dirt on the others without thinking twice. That will do for them.

"I think it'll be difficult to make the attempted murder stick and sexual assault is always a tricky one when there are no witnesses but in this climate I think it may stick."

"What's your plan now?"

"To sue everyone and get a divorce but more immediately get the bloody press conference over with... Well, that's if it takes place." Al looked at her in bemusement. "Well, all it'll take to kill it is for a royal to die or some teenage celeb to flash her knickers at the paparazzi, in which case just a man and his dog will turn up and the story will be relegated to page seventeen."

"That is so cynical... Really, are you nervous, Jo?"

Jo though carefully before answering.

"No, I'm not – not the slightest, just irritated by the necessity. I need to see Wendy because I haven't told her any details yet of what I've discovered but first I'm going to pick Danny up from my parents – that's the only thing that's really on my mind. Except, there is one other thing that's bothering me." There was a long hesitation while she waited for Al to ask what it was but he didn't and so she continued: "Al, do you think you can live with me?" She turned towards him and he could see it was a genuine, heartfelt enquiry.

"Wrong question, Jo, wrong question."

"What's the right question, then?"

"Can I live without you?"

"And what's the answer to that?"

He leant across and kissed her. "That'll be a no!"

Jo squeezed his hand tightly.

"Al, in two or three weeks, when all this has died down, I want you to take me down to Brighton and bring to life that beautiful fantasy you wove for me – I want to make it real, do all the things you said and in the same order. You'll never know how important your words were to me."

Al smiled at her: "I'll even arrange the weather… Jo?"

"Yes."

"Your encounter – it sounded as if it was all about being judged, didn't it? Well, judgment is a combination of condemnation and acquittal isn't it? It implies a weighing of evidence and verdicts of both guilt and innocence. Doesn't it? 'Mercy triumphs over judgement', he said. I hope it means what I think it means."

"Yeah?"

"Yeah! Because I want to grow old with you, Madam." Al went silent for a long time: "Jo, you're not going to mention whales are you – at the press conference?"

"No, Al, I'm not. No need to… They'll find out soon enough… They'll find out!"

POD

About the Author

Christened on the day World War Two broke out, Tony Wardle insists there was no connection between the two events. He is a journalist and writer and was a TV producer before becoming the associate director of the vegan campaign group, Viva!

He is the only British journalist ever to win a Hibakusha Travel Grant to visit Japan and research the medical, social and psychological after effects of the atomic bombings of Hiroshima and Nagasaki.

Through his TV production company, Vanson Wardle Productions (formed with producer/director Yvette Vanson), he conceived, researched, wrote and co-produced programmes for most of the main broadcast channels, winning a Royal Television Society award and an RTS nomination. The landmark Channel 4 documentary, *The Battle for Orgreave*, was chosen for screening at the Edinburgh TV Festival.

Awards for non-broadcast work include gold and bronze medals at the New York Film & TV Festival, two bronze medals at Prague Ekofest, a PR Week Public Relations Award, an IVCA Golden Reel Award and an ITVA Award of Excellence.

Book credits include:
- *Presumed Guilty* (with Michael Mansfield QC)
- *The Silent Ark*
- *Born to be Wild*
- *The Livewire Guide to Going Being and Staying Veggie* (all with Juliet Gellatley).
- *The Battle for Orgreave* (to accompany the film).
- *The Inquest* (a novel with Michael Mansfield QC)

He has a daughter, Niki, grandchildren Max and Livvy and twin sons Jazz and Finn, born in 2002. He currently lives in Chepstow and works in Bristol.

POD